DEEPWATER CREEK

MICHAEL REGINA

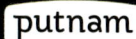

G.P. Putnam's Sons

G. P. PUTNAM'S SONS
An imprint of Penguin Random House LLC
1745 Broadway, New York, New York 10019

First published in the United States of America by G. P. Putnam's Sons,
an imprint of Penguin Random House LLC, 2025

Copyright © 2025 by Michael Regina

Penguin Random House values and supports copyright. Copyright fuels creativity, encourages diverse voices, promotes free speech, and creates a vibrant culture. Thank you for buying an authorized edition of this book and for complying with copyright laws by not reproducing, scanning, or distributing any part of it in any form without permission. You are supporting writers and allowing Penguin Random House to continue to publish books for every reader. Please note that no part of this book may be used or reproduced in any manner for the purpose of training artificial intelligence technologies or systems.

G. P. Putnam's Sons is a registered trademark of Penguin Random House LLC.
The Penguin colophon is a registered trademark of Penguin Books Limited.

Visit us online at PenguinRandomHouse.com.

Library of Congress Cataloging-in-Publication Data
Names: Regina, Michael, author.
Title: Deepwater creek / Michael Regina.
Description: New York : G.P. Putnam's Sons, 2025. | Audience term: Preteens |
Audience: Ages 8–12 years. | Summary: "A middle grade graphic horror
novel about two brothers who must uncover what terrors may be lurking in
the depths of their local creek."—Provided by publisher.
Identifiers: LCCN 2024045776 (print) | LCCN 2024045777 (ebook) |
ISBN 9780593117378 (hardcover) | ISBN 9780593117392 (paperback) |
ISBN 9780593620366 (nook edition) | ISBN 9780593117385 (kindle edition) |
ISBN 9780593620359
Subjects: CYAC: Monsters—Fiction. | Lakes—Fiction. | Friendship—Fiction.
| Horror. | LCGFT: Monster comics.
Classification: LCC PZ7.7.R4456 De 2025 (print) | LCC PZ7.7.R4456 (ebook) |
DDC 741.5/973—dc23/eng/20241107
LC record available at https://lccn.loc.gov/2024045776
LC ebook record available at https://lccn.loc.gov/2024045777

ISBN 9780593117378 (hardcover)
1 3 5 7 9 10 8 6 4 2

ISBN 9780593117392 (paperback)
1 3 5 7 9 10 8 6 4 2

Manufactured in China

TOPL

Edited by Christopher Hernandez
Design by Danielle Ceccolini
Dialogue text set in Milk Mustache BB

The artwork for this book was illustrated in Clip Studio Paint. It was painted using traditional watercolors and airbrush, with additional digital adjustments in Clip Studio Paint.

This book is a work of fiction. Any references to historical events, real people, or real places are used fictitiously. Other names, characters, places, and events are products of the author's imagination, and any resemblance to actual events or places or persons, living or dead, is entirely coincidental.

The publisher does not have any control over and does not assume any responsibility for author or third-party websites or their content.

The authorized representative in the EU for product safety and compliance is Penguin Random House Ireland, Morrison Chambers, 32 Nassau Street, Dublin D02 YH68, Ireland, https://eu-contact.penguin.ie.

Dedicated to the memory of my dear friends Bryan Mosier and Christen Blythe and my grandmother Elvira Robertson. We miss you all so much.

—MICHAEL REGINA

HAVE YOU EXPLORED THE SPRINGS FROM WHICH THE SEAS COME?
HAVE YOU EXPLORED THEIR DEPTHS? . . .
HAVE YOU SEEN THE GATES OF UTTER GLOOM?
DO YOU REALIZE THE EXTENT OF THE EARTH?

—THE BOOK OF JOB

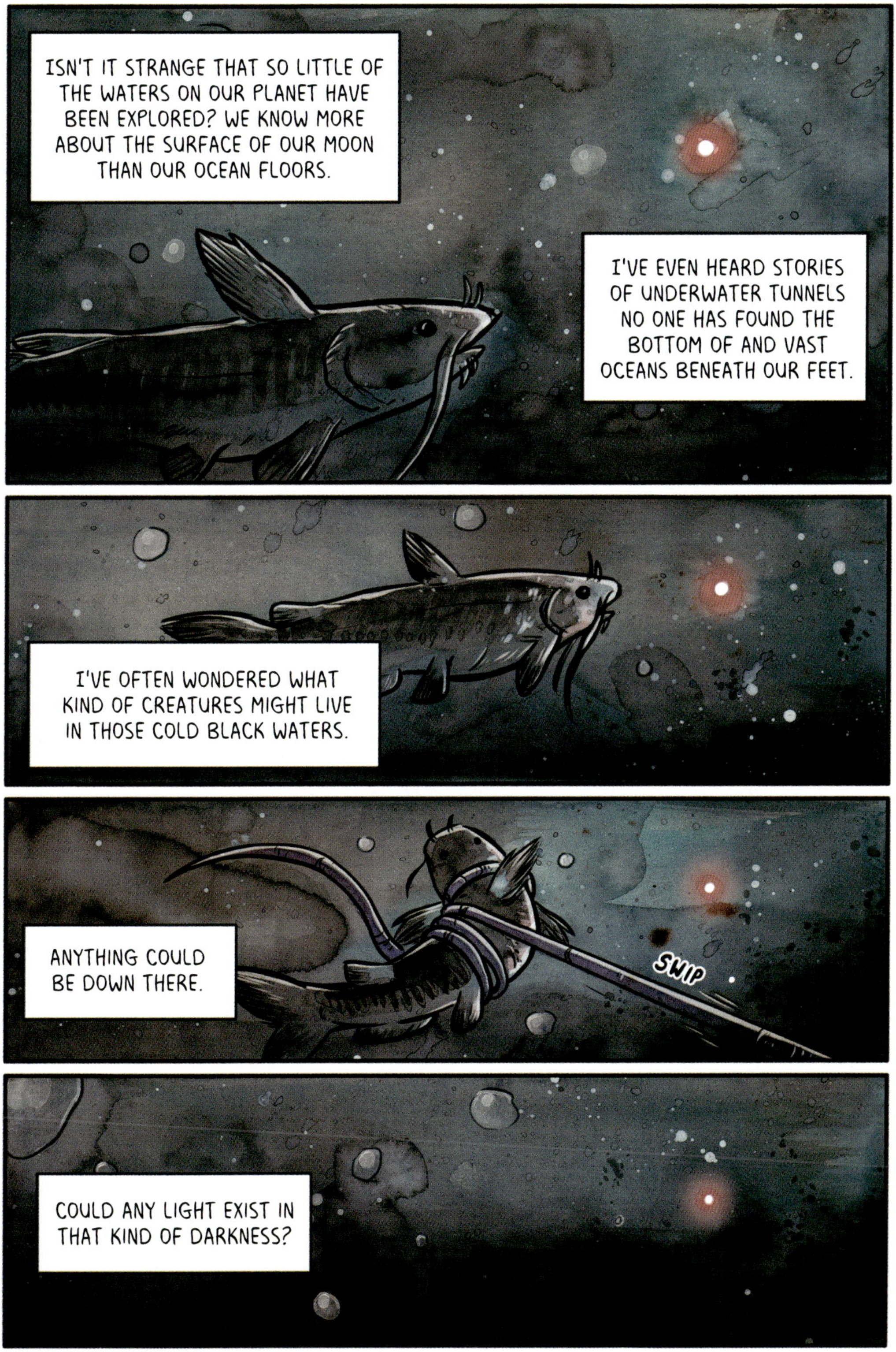
ISN'T IT STRANGE THAT SO LITTLE OF THE WATERS ON OUR PLANET HAVE BEEN EXPLORED? WE KNOW MORE ABOUT THE SURFACE OF OUR MOON THAN OUR OCEAN FLOORS.
I'VE EVEN HEARD STORIES OF UNDERWATER TUNNELS NO ONE HAS FOUND THE BOTTOM OF AND VAST OCEANS BENEATH OUR FEET.
I'VE OFTEN WONDERED WHAT KIND OF CREATURES MIGHT LIVE IN THOSE COLD BLACK WATERS.
ANYTHING COULD BE DOWN THERE.
SWIP
COULD ANY LIGHT EXIST IN THAT KIND OF DARKNESS?

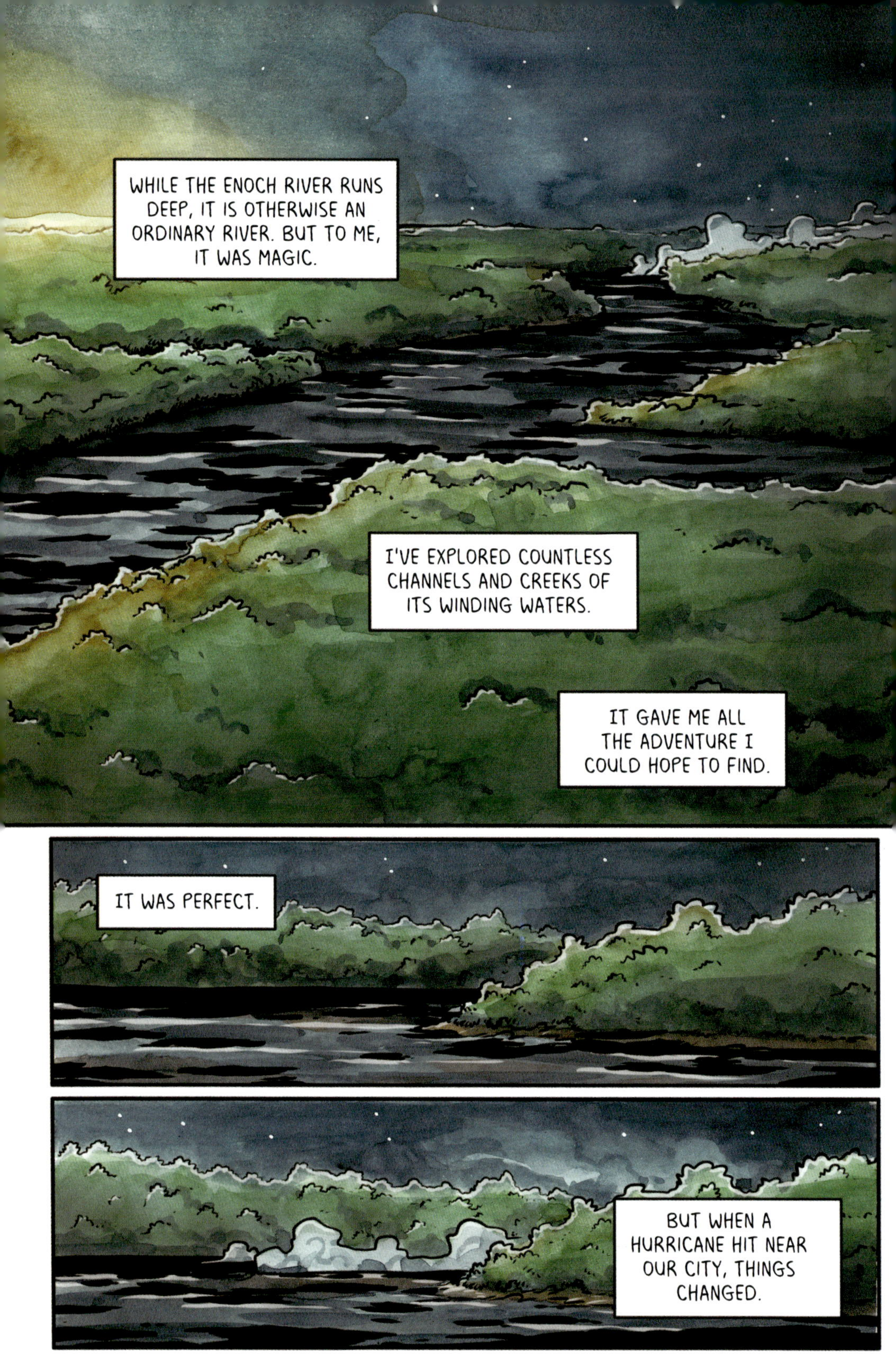
WHILE THE ENOCH RIVER RUNS DEEP, IT IS OTHERWISE AN ORDINARY RIVER. BUT TO ME, IT WAS MAGIC.
I'VE EXPLORED COUNTLESS CHANNELS AND CREEKS OF ITS WINDING WATERS.
IT GAVE ME ALL THE ADVENTURE I COULD HOPE TO FIND.
IT WAS PERFECT.
BUT WHEN A HURRICANE HIT NEAR OUR CITY, THINGS CHANGED.

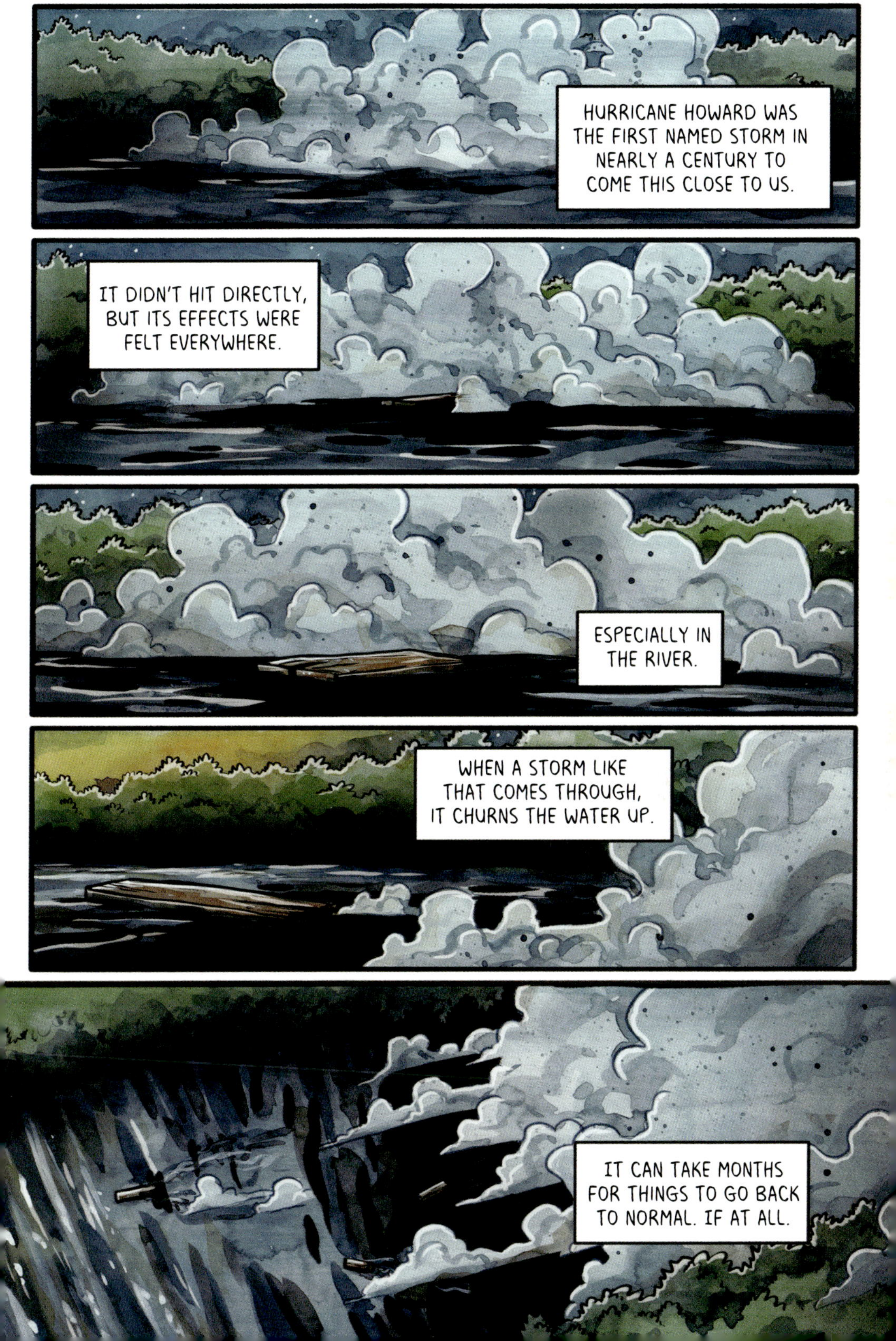
HURRICANE HOWARD WAS THE FIRST NAMED STORM IN NEARLY A CENTURY TO COME THIS CLOSE TO US.
IT DIDN'T HIT DIRECTLY, BUT ITS EFFECTS WERE FELT EVERYWHERE.
ESPECIALLY IN THE RIVER.
WHEN A STORM LIKE THAT COMES THROUGH, IT CHURNS THE WATER UP.
IT CAN TAKE MONTHS FOR THINGS TO GO BACK TO NORMAL. IF AT ALL.

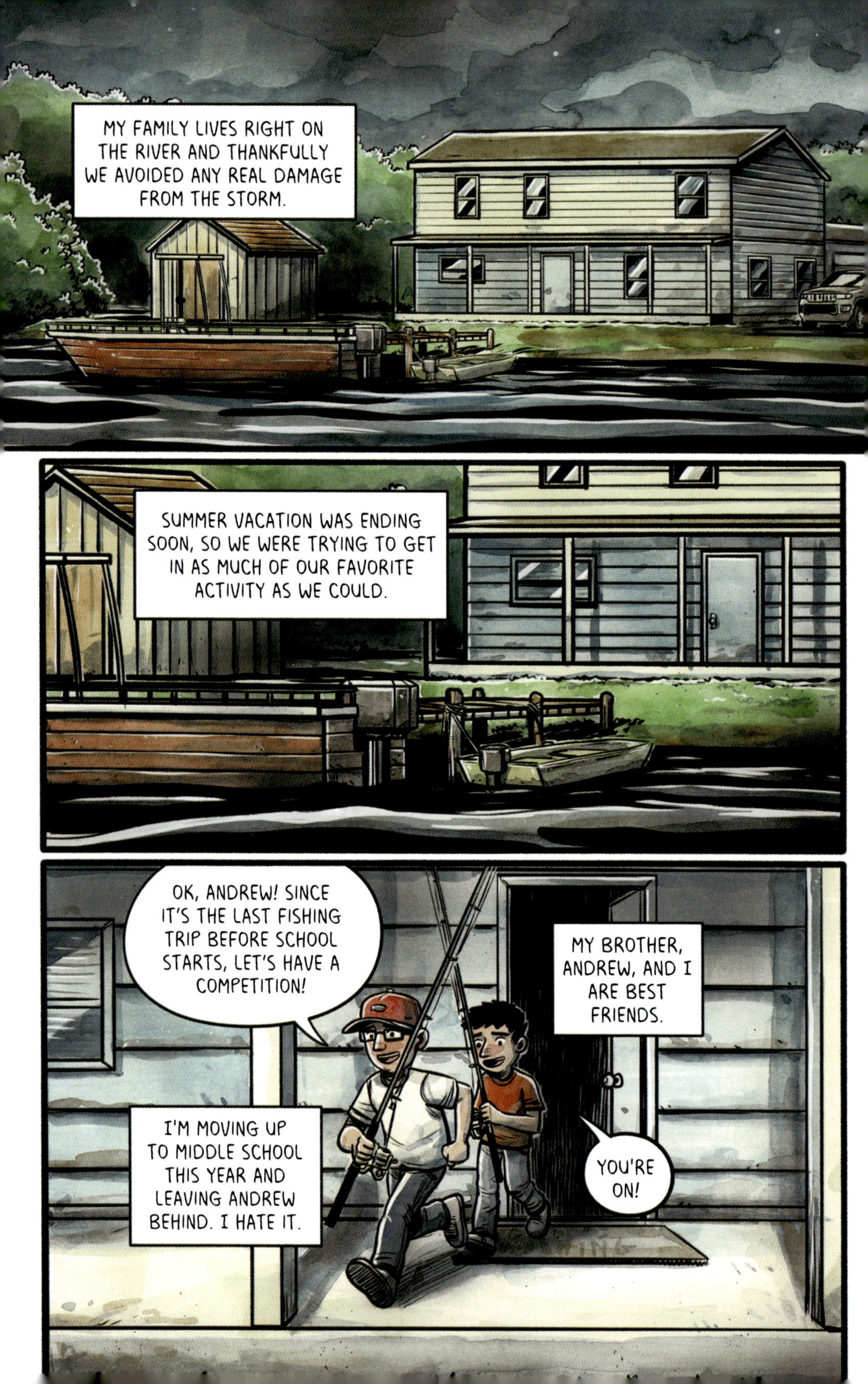
MY FAMILY LIVES RIGHT ON THE RIVER AND THANKFULLY WE AVOIDED ANY REAL DAMAGE FROM THE STORM.
SUMMER VACATION WAS ENDING SOON, SO WE WERE TRYING TO GET IN AS MUCH OF OUR FAVORITE ACTIVITY AS WE COULD.
OK, ANDREW! SINCE IT'S THE LAST FISHING TRIP BEFORE SCHOOL STARTS, LET'S HAVE A COMPETITION!
MY BROTHER, ANDREW, AND I ARE BEST FRIENDS.
I'M MOVING UP TO MIDDLE SCHOOL THIS YEAR AND LEAVING ANDREW BEHIND. I HATE IT.
YOU'RE ON!

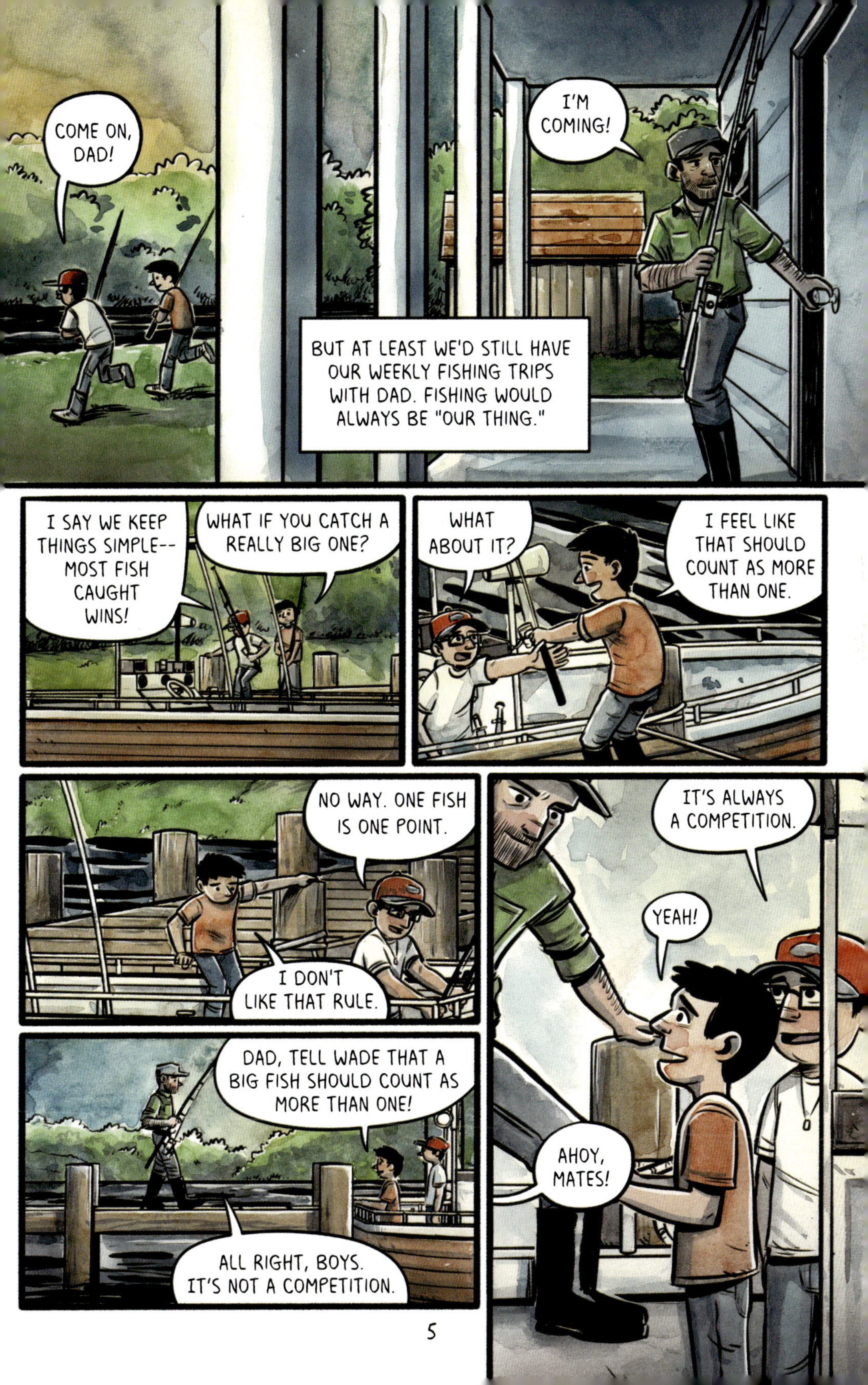
COME ON, DAD!
I'M COMING!
BUT AT LEAST WE'D STILL HAVE OUR WEEKLY FISHING TRIPS WITH DAD. FISHING WOULD ALWAYS BE "OUR THING."
I SAY WE KEEP THINGS SIMPLE-- MOST FISH CAUGHT WINS!
WHAT IF YOU CATCH A REALLY BIG ONE?
WHAT ABOUT IT?
I FEEL LIKE THAT SHOULD COUNT AS MORE THAN ONE.
NO WAY. ONE FISH IS ONE POINT.
I DON'T LIKE THAT RULE.
DAD, TELL WADE THAT A BIG FISH SHOULD COUNT AS MORE THAN ONE!
ALL RIGHT, BOYS. IT'S NOT A COMPETITION.
IT'S ALWAYS A COMPETITION.
YEAH!
AHOY, MATES!

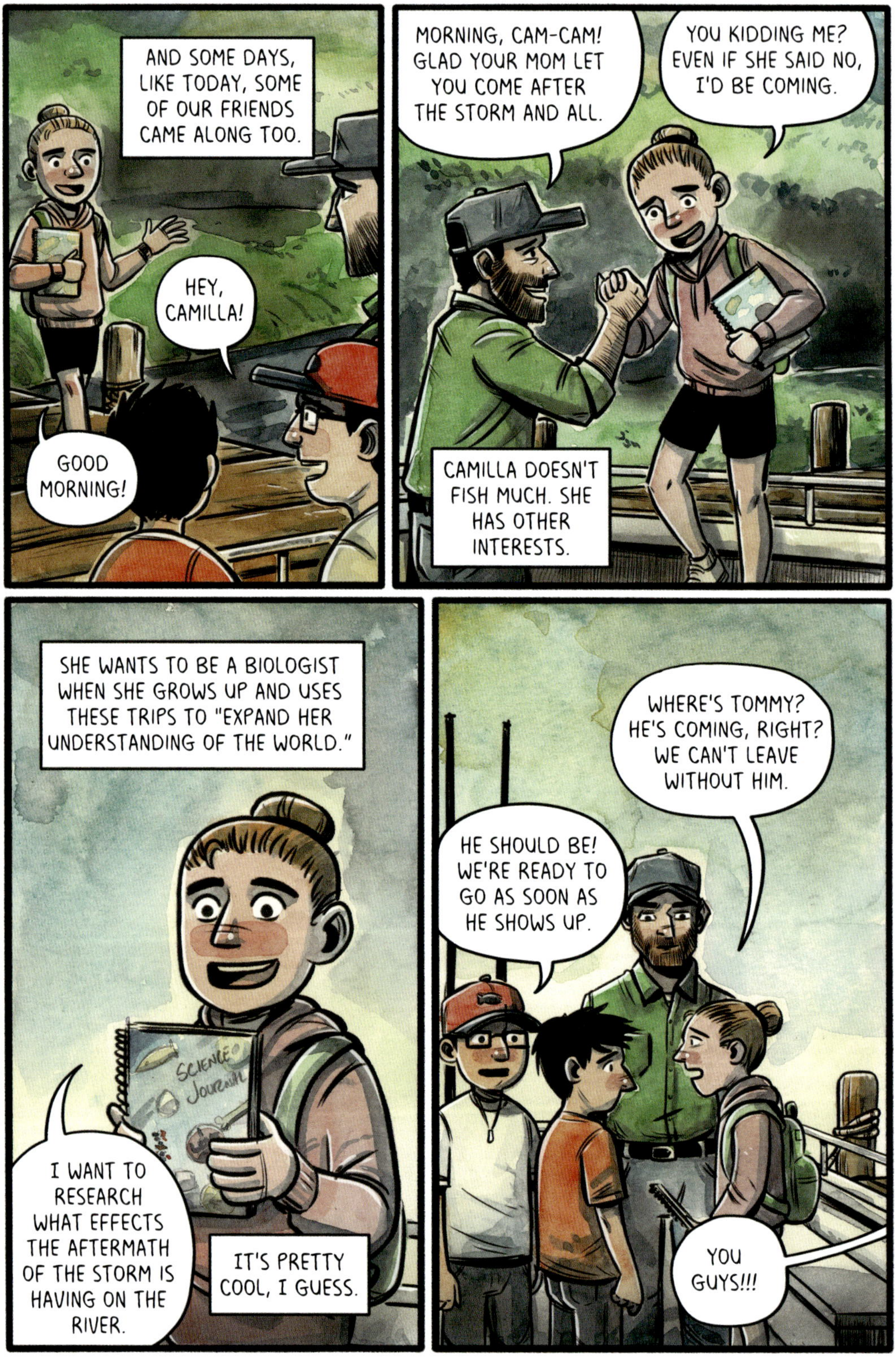
AND SOME DAYS, LIKE TODAY, SOME OF OUR FRIENDS CAME ALONG TOO.
HEY, CAMILLA!
GOOD MORNING!
MORNING, CAM-CAM! GLAD YOUR MOM LET YOU COME AFTER THE STORM AND ALL.
YOU KIDDING ME? EVEN IF SHE SAID NO, I'D BE COMING.
CAMILLA DOESN'T FISH MUCH. SHE HAS OTHER INTERESTS.
SHE WANTS TO BE A BIOLOGIST WHEN SHE GROWS UP AND USES THESE TRIPS TO "EXPAND HER UNDERSTANDING OF THE WORLD."
SCIENCE JOURNAL
I WANT TO RESEARCH WHAT EFFECTS THE AFTERMATH OF THE STORM IS HAVING ON THE RIVER.
IT'S PRETTY COOL, I GUESS.
WHERE'S TOMMY? HE'S COMING, RIGHT? WE CAN'T LEAVE WITHOUT HIM.
HE SHOULD BE! WE'RE READY TO GO AS SOON AS HE SHOWS UP.
YOU GUYS!!!

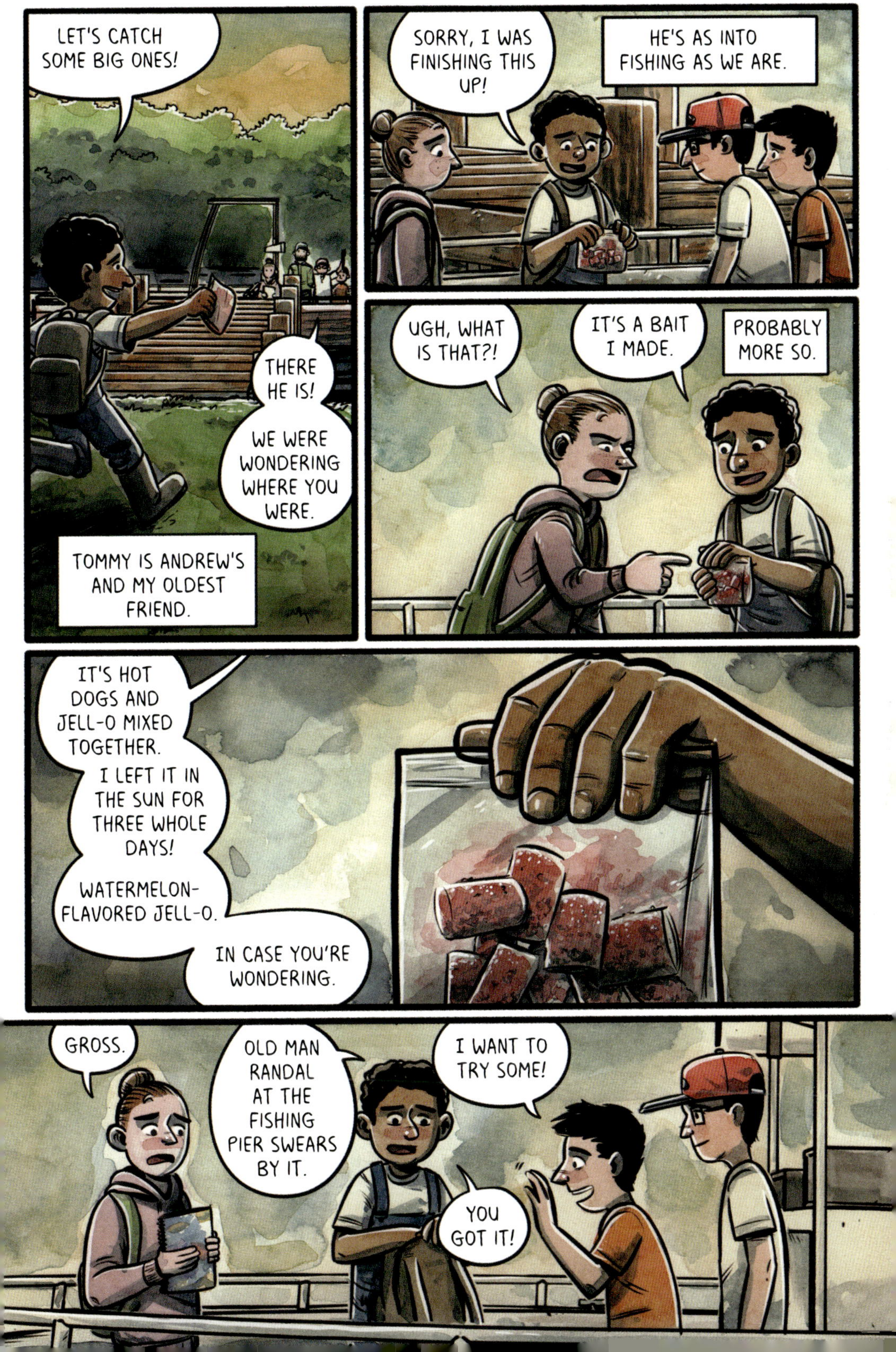
LET'S CATCH SOME BIG ONES!
THERE HE IS!
WE WERE WONDERING WHERE YOU WERE.
TOMMY IS ANDREW'S AND MY OLDEST FRIEND.
SORRY, I WAS FINISHING THIS UP!
HE'S AS INTO FISHING AS WE ARE.
UGH, WHAT IS THAT?!
IT'S A BAIT I MADE.
PROBABLY MORE SO.
IT'S HOT DOGS AND JELL-O MIXED TOGETHER.
I LEFT IT IN THE SUN FOR THREE WHOLE DAYS!
WATERMELON-FLAVORED JELL-O.
IN CASE YOU'RE WONDERING.
GROSS.
OLD MAN RANDAL AT THE FISHING PIER SWEARS BY IT.
I WANT TO TRY SOME!
YOU GOT IT!

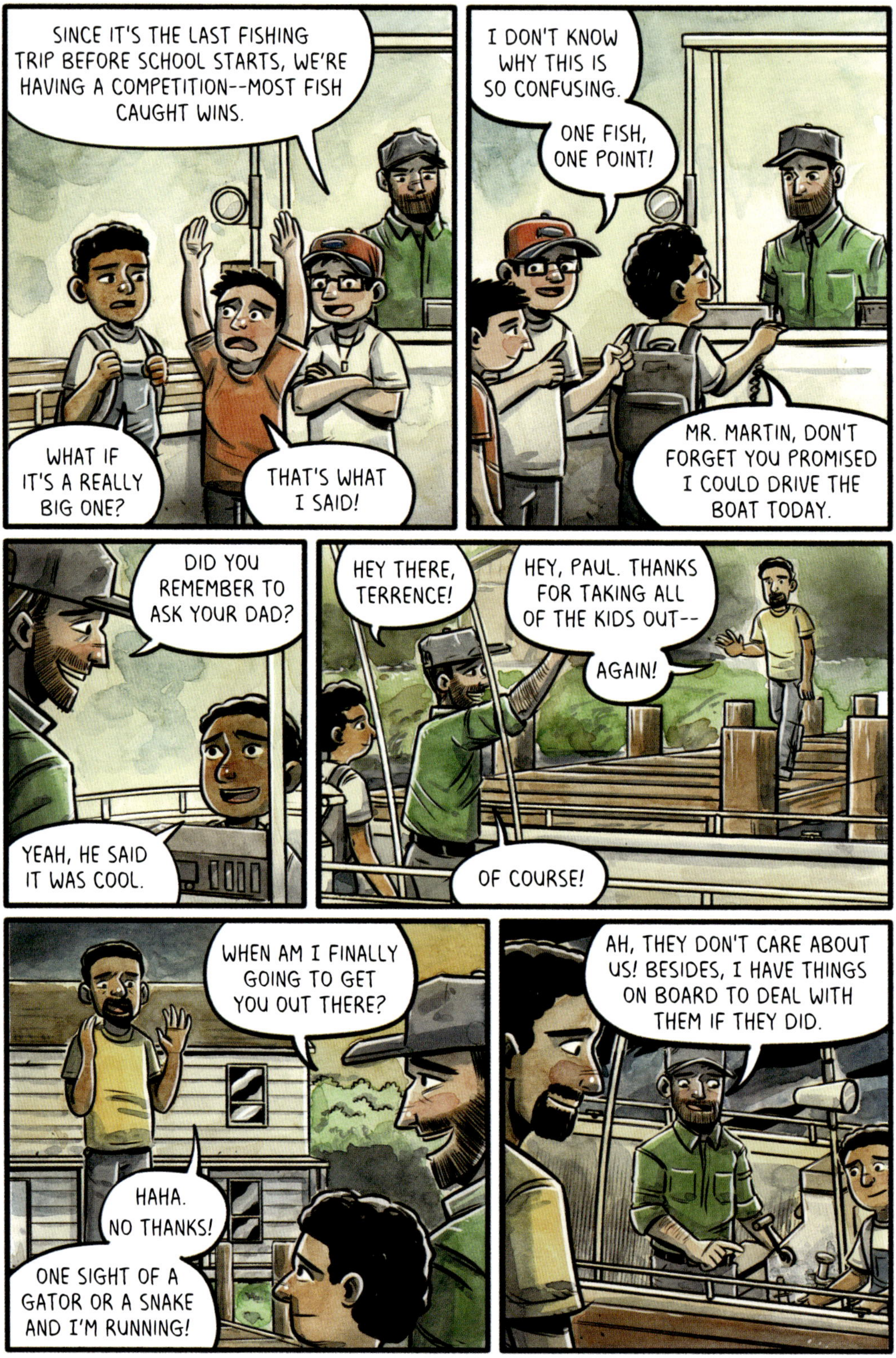
SINCE IT'S THE LAST FISHING TRIP BEFORE SCHOOL STARTS, WE'RE HAVING A COMPETITION--MOST FISH CAUGHT WINS.
WHAT IF IT'S A REALLY BIG ONE?
THAT'S WHAT I SAID!
I DON'T KNOW WHY THIS IS SO CONFUSING.
ONE FISH, ONE POINT!
MR. MARTIN, DON'T FORGET YOU PROMISED I COULD DRIVE THE BOAT TODAY.
DID YOU REMEMBER TO ASK YOUR DAD?
YEAH, HE SAID IT WAS COOL.
HEY THERE, TERRENCE!
HEY, PAUL. THANKS FOR TAKING ALL OF THE KIDS OUT--
AGAIN!
OF COURSE!
WHEN AM I FINALLY GOING TO GET YOU OUT THERE?
HAHA. NO THANKS!
ONE SIGHT OF A GATOR OR A SNAKE AND I'M RUNNING!
AH, THEY DON'T CARE ABOUT US! BESIDES, I HAVE THINGS ON BOARD TO DEAL WITH THEM IF THEY DID.

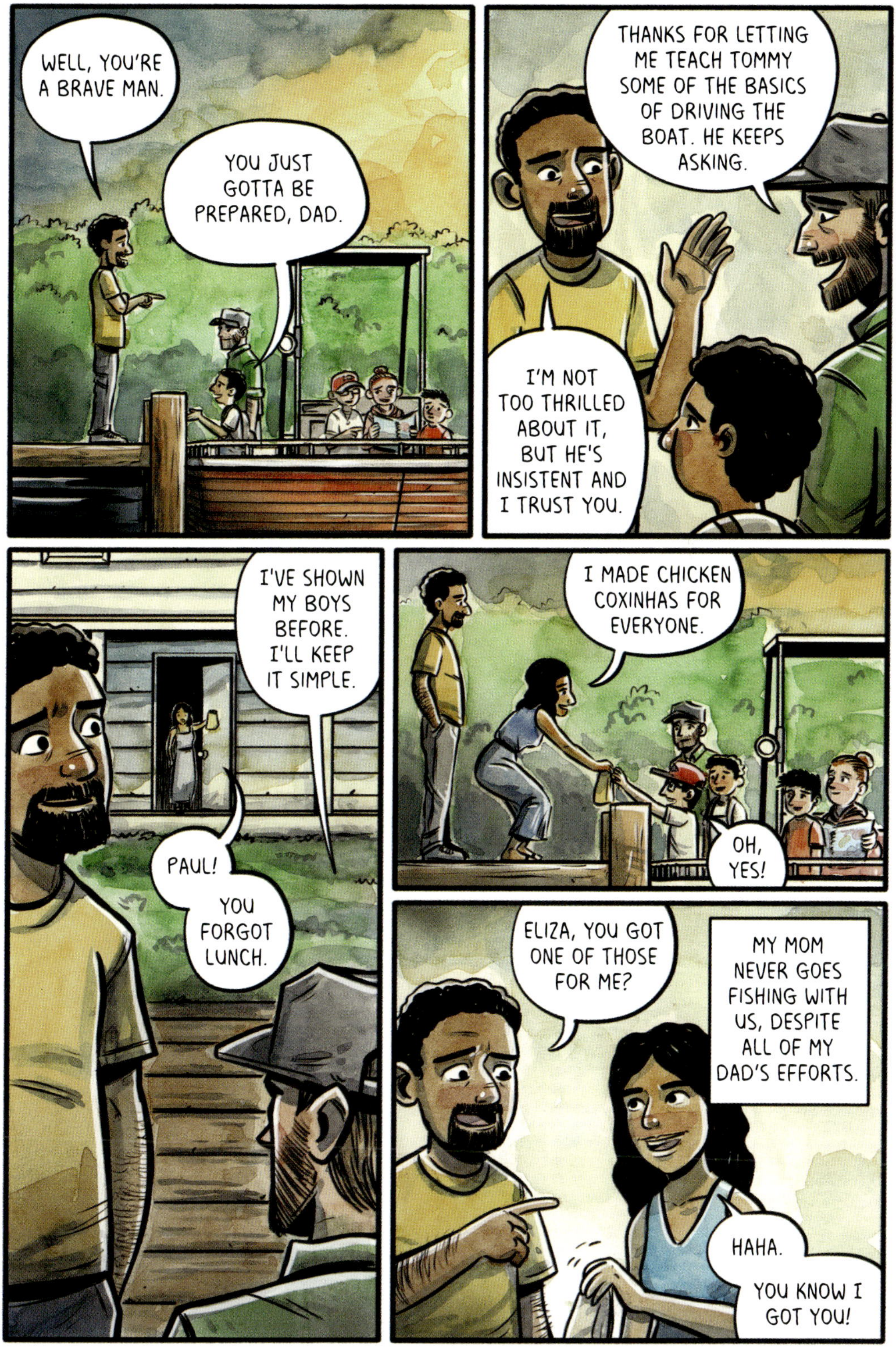
WELL, YOU'RE A BRAVE MAN.
YOU JUST GOTTA BE PREPARED, DAD.
THANKS FOR LETTING ME TEACH TOMMY SOME OF THE BASICS OF DRIVING THE BOAT. HE KEEPS ASKING.
I'M NOT TOO THRILLED ABOUT IT, BUT HE'S INSISTENT AND I TRUST YOU.
I'VE SHOWN MY BOYS BEFORE. I'LL KEEP IT SIMPLE.
PAUL!
YOU FORGOT LUNCH.
I MADE CHICKEN COXINHAS FOR EVERYONE.
OH, YES!
ELIZA, YOU GOT ONE OF THOSE FOR ME?
MY MOM NEVER GOES FISHING WITH US, DESPITE ALL OF MY DAD'S EFFORTS.
HAHA.
YOU KNOW I GOT YOU!

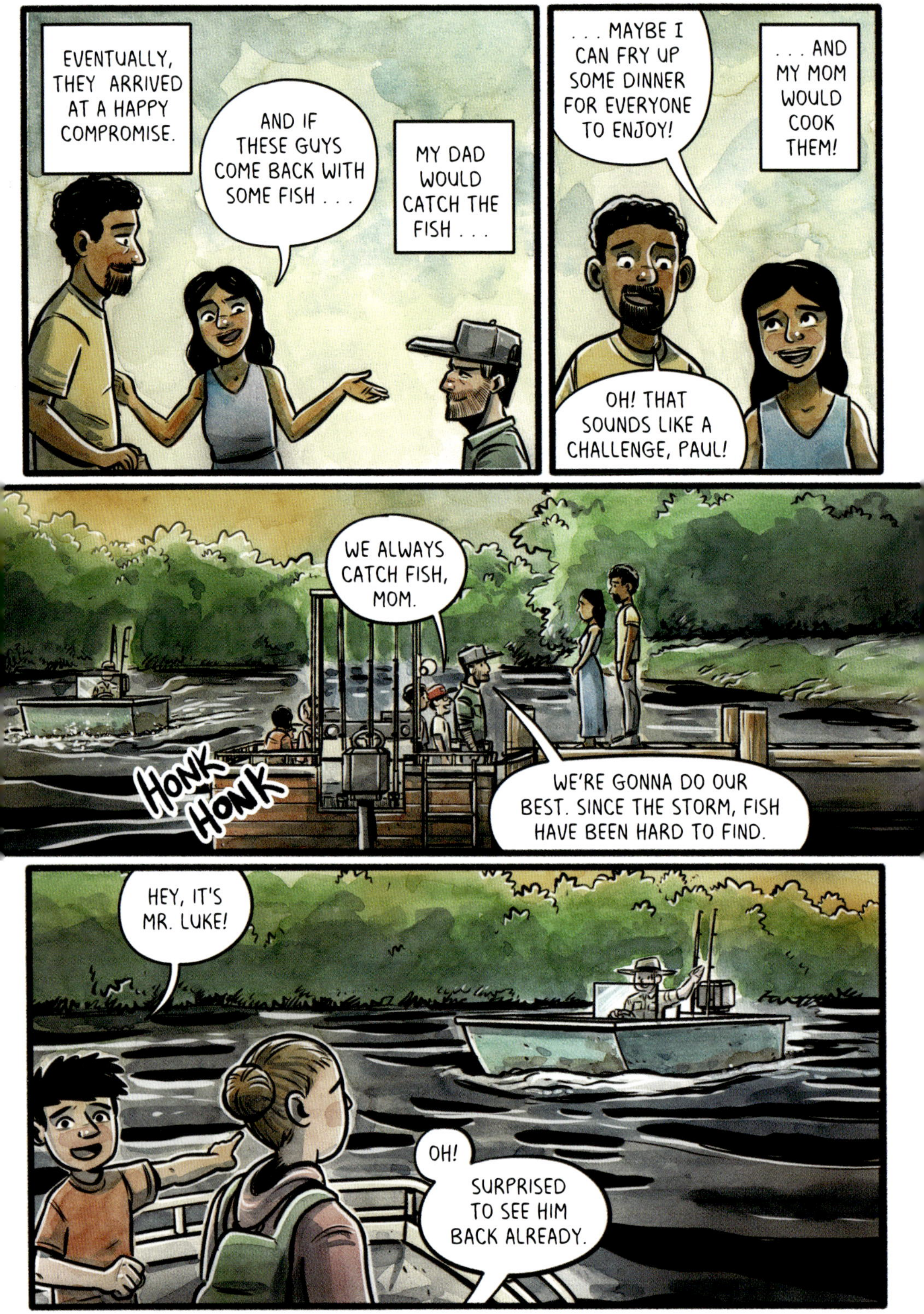
EVENTUALLY, THEY ARRIVED AT A HAPPY COMPROMISE.
AND IF THESE GUYS COME BACK WITH SOME FISH . . .
MY DAD WOULD CATCH THE FISH . . .
. . . MAYBE I CAN FRY UP SOME DINNER FOR EVERYONE TO ENJOY!
. . . AND MY MOM WOULD COOK THEM!
OH! THAT SOUNDS LIKE A CHALLENGE, PAUL!
WE ALWAYS CATCH FISH, MOM.
HONK HONK
WE'RE GONNA DO OUR BEST. SINCE THE STORM, FISH HAVE BEEN HARD TO FIND.
HEY, IT'S MR. LUKE!
OH!
SURPRISED TO SEE HIM BACK ALREADY.

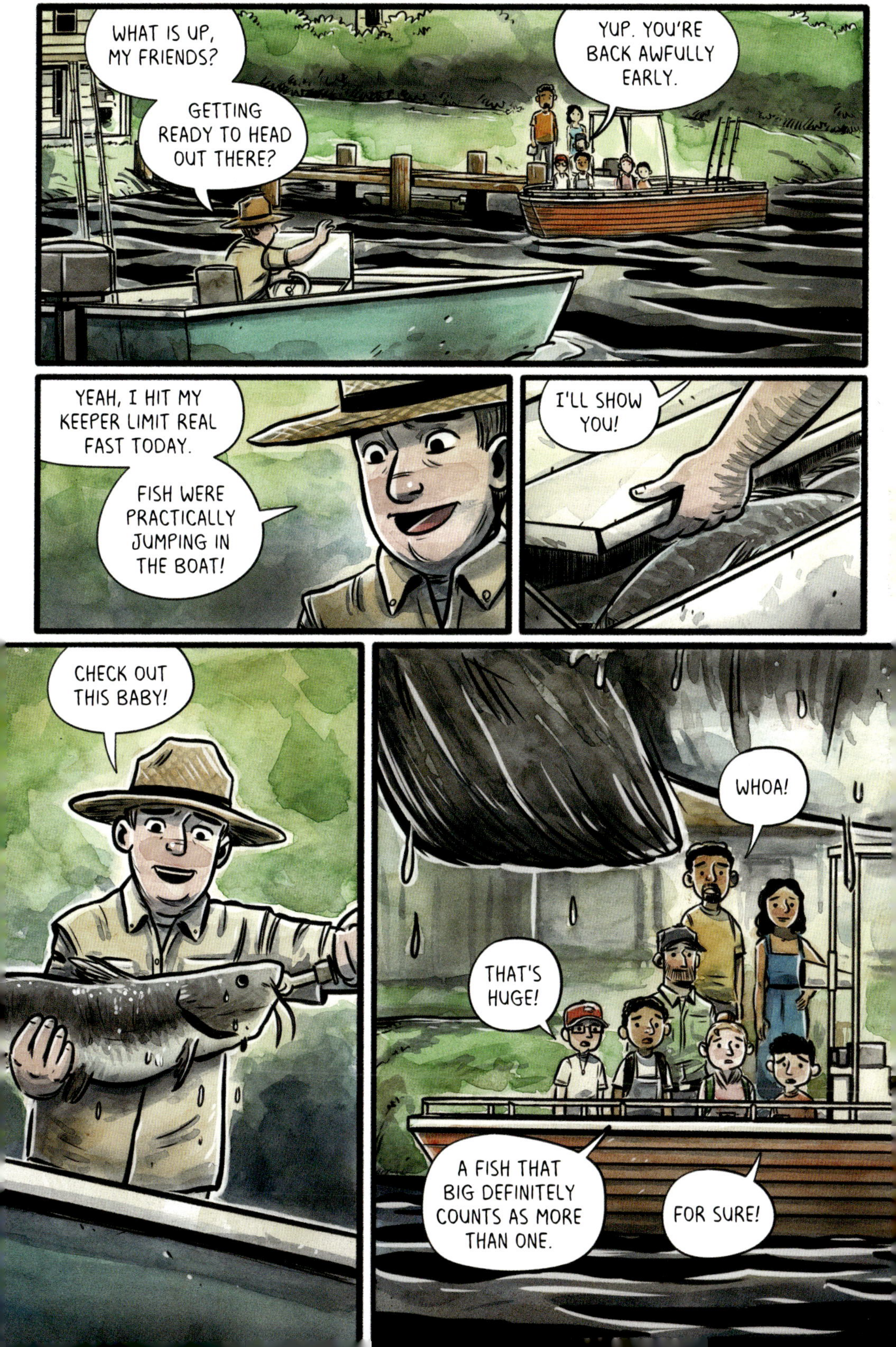
WHAT IS UP, MY FRIENDS?
GETTING READY TO HEAD OUT THERE?
YUP. YOU'RE BACK AWFULLY EARLY.
YEAH, I HIT MY KEEPER LIMIT REAL FAST TODAY.
FISH WERE PRACTICALLY JUMPING IN THE BOAT!
I'LL SHOW YOU!
CHECK OUT THIS BABY!
WHOA!
THAT'S HUGE!
A FISH THAT BIG DEFINITELY COUNTS AS MORE THAN ONE.
FOR SURE!

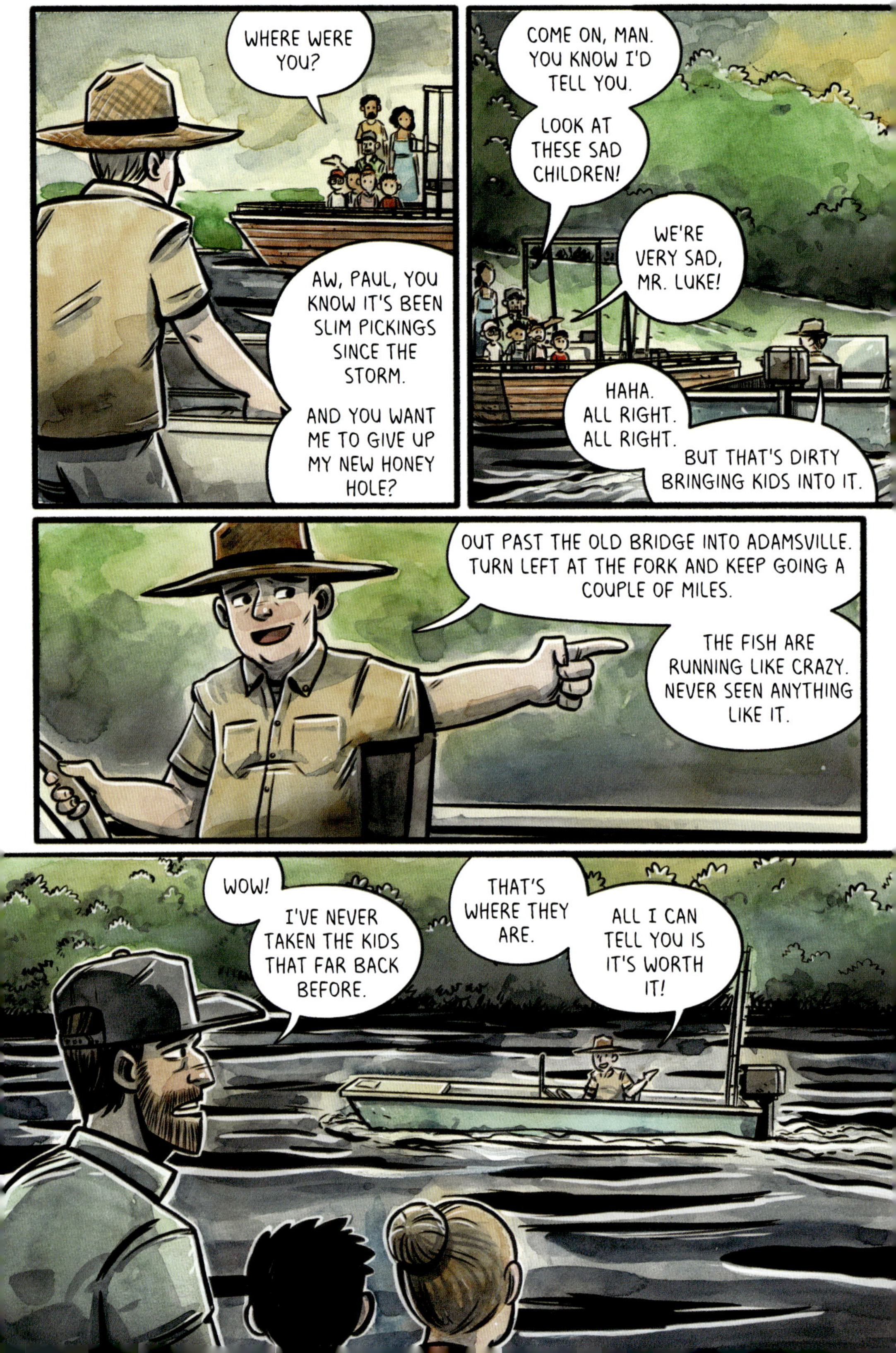
WHERE WERE YOU?
AW, PAUL, YOU KNOW IT'S BEEN SLIM PICKINGS SINCE THE STORM.
AND YOU WANT ME TO GIVE UP MY NEW HONEY HOLE?
COME ON, MAN. YOU KNOW I'D TELL YOU.
LOOK AT THESE SAD CHILDREN!
WE'RE VERY SAD, MR. LUKE!
HAHA. ALL RIGHT. ALL RIGHT.
BUT THAT'S DIRTY BRINGING KIDS INTO IT.
OUT PAST THE OLD BRIDGE INTO ADAMSVILLE. TURN LEFT AT THE FORK AND KEEP GOING A COUPLE OF MILES.
THE FISH ARE RUNNING LIKE CRAZY. NEVER SEEN ANYTHING LIKE IT.
WOW!
I'VE NEVER TAKEN THE KIDS THAT FAR BACK BEFORE.
THAT'S WHERE THEY ARE.
ALL I CAN TELL YOU IS IT'S WORTH IT!

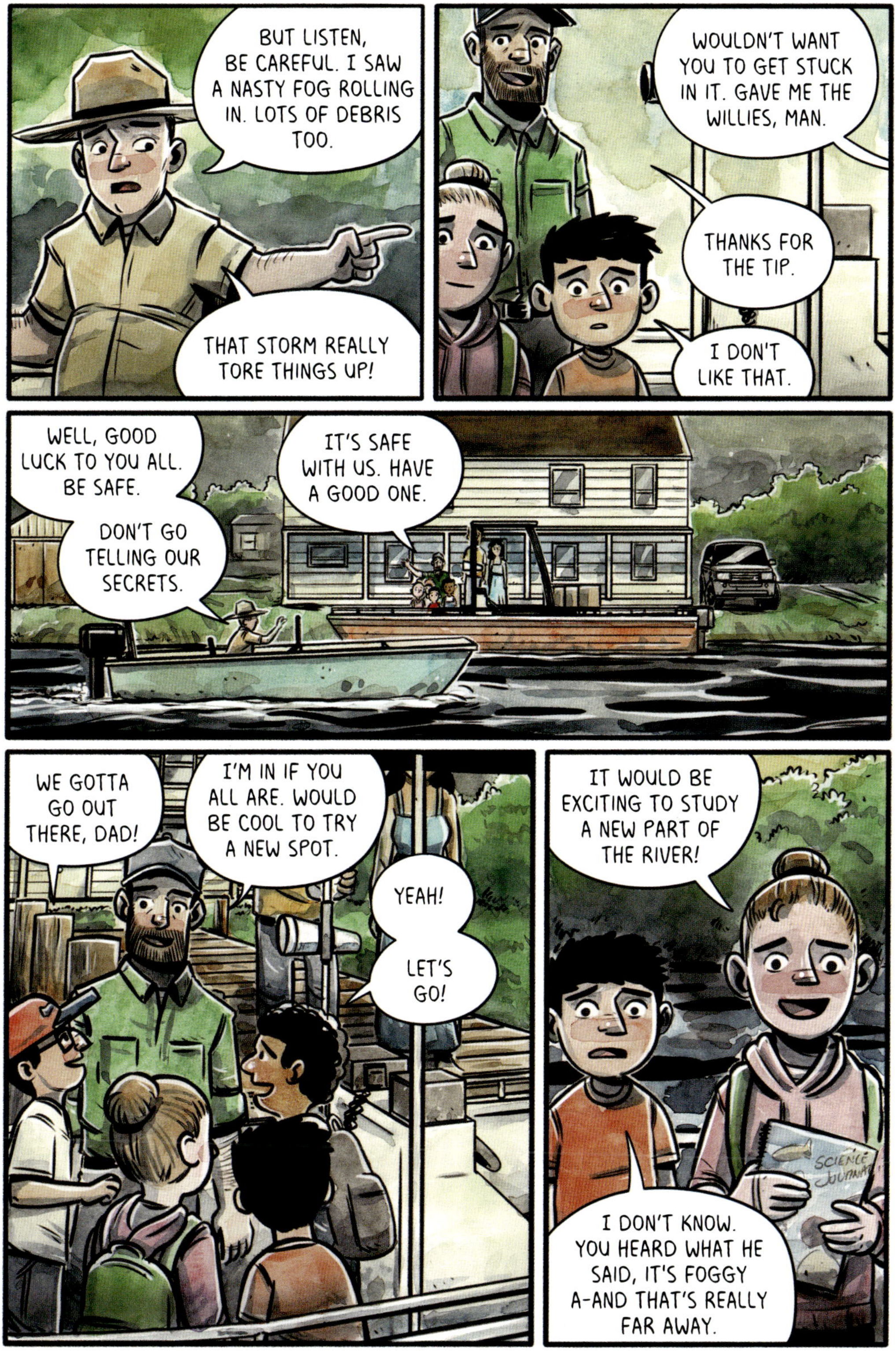
BUT LISTEN, BE CAREFUL. I SAW A NASTY FOG ROLLING IN. LOTS OF DEBRIS TOO.
THAT STORM REALLY TORE THINGS UP!
WOULDN'T WANT YOU TO GET STUCK IN IT. GAVE ME THE WILLIES, MAN.
THANKS FOR THE TIP.
I DON'T LIKE THAT.
WELL, GOOD LUCK TO YOU ALL. BE SAFE.
DON'T GO TELLING OUR SECRETS.
IT'S SAFE WITH US. HAVE A GOOD ONE.
WE GOTTA GO OUT THERE, DAD!
I'M IN IF YOU ALL ARE. WOULD BE COOL TO TRY A NEW SPOT.
YEAH!
LET'S GO!
IT WOULD BE EXCITING TO STUDY A NEW PART OF THE RIVER!
I DON'T KNOW. YOU HEARD WHAT HE SAID, IT'S FOGGY A-AND THAT'S REALLY FAR AWAY.

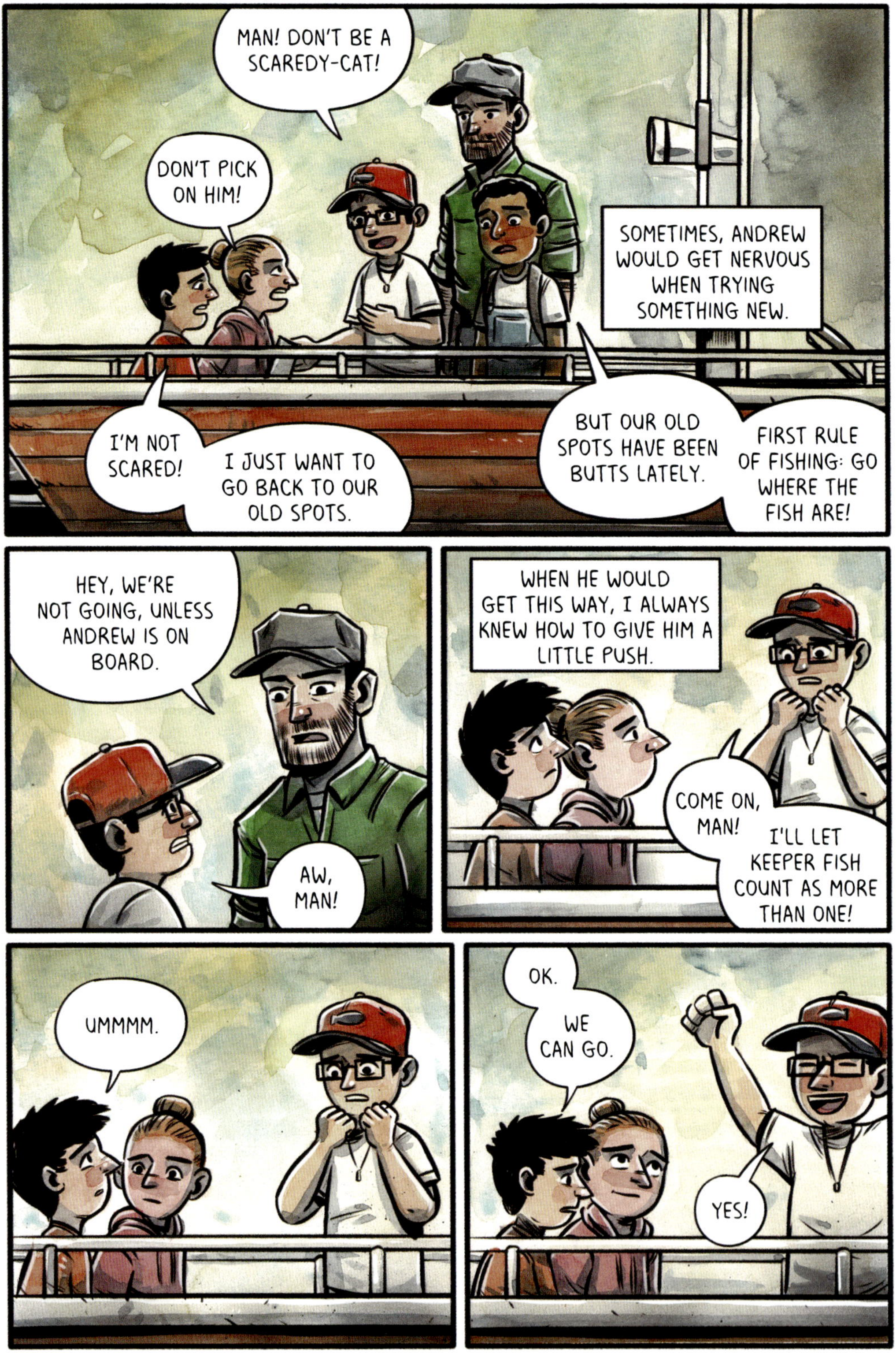
MAN! DON'T BE A SCAREDY-CAT!
DON'T PICK ON HIM!
SOMETIMES, ANDREW WOULD GET NERVOUS WHEN TRYING SOMETHING NEW.
I'M NOT SCARED!
I JUST WANT TO GO BACK TO OUR OLD SPOTS.
BUT OUR OLD SPOTS HAVE BEEN BUTTS LATELY.
FIRST RULE OF FISHING: GO WHERE THE FISH ARE!
HEY, WE'RE NOT GOING, UNLESS ANDREW IS ON BOARD.
AW, MAN!
WHEN HE WOULD GET THIS WAY, I ALWAYS KNEW HOW TO GIVE HIM A LITTLE PUSH.
COME ON, MAN!
I'LL LET KEEPER FISH COUNT AS MORE THAN ONE!
UMMMM.
OK.
WE CAN GO.
YES!

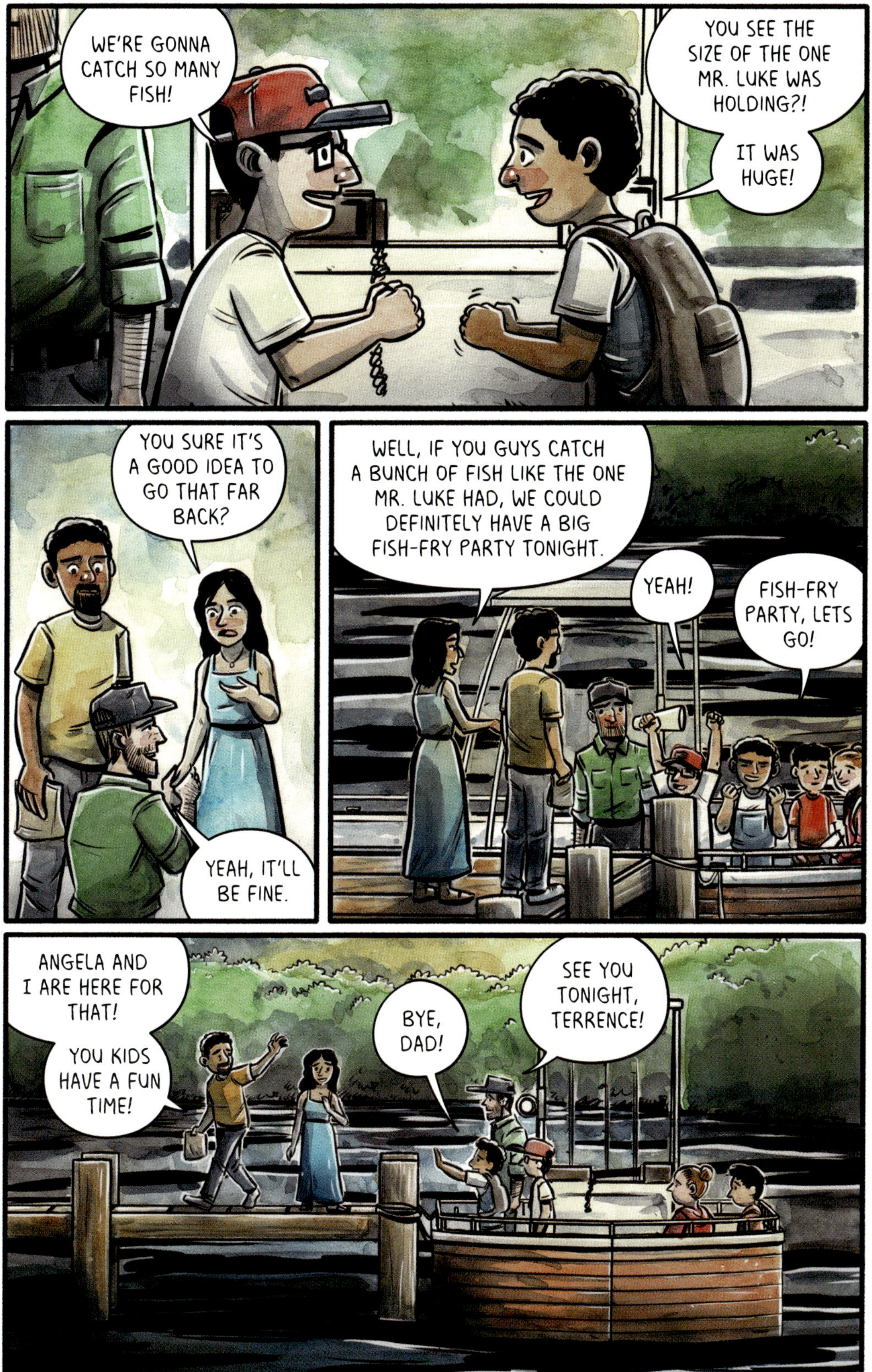
WE'RE GONNA CATCH SO MANY FISH!
YOU SEE THE SIZE OF THE ONE MR. LUKE WAS HOLDING?!
IT WAS HUGE!
YOU SURE IT'S A GOOD IDEA TO GO THAT FAR BACK?
YEAH, IT'LL BE FINE.
WELL, IF YOU GUYS CATCH A BUNCH OF FISH LIKE THE ONE MR. LUKE HAD, WE COULD DEFINITELY HAVE A BIG FISH-FRY PARTY TONIGHT.
YEAH!
FISH-FRY PARTY, LETS GO!
ANGELA AND I ARE HERE FOR THAT!
YOU KIDS HAVE A FUN TIME!
BYE, DAD!
SEE YOU TONIGHT, TERRENCE!

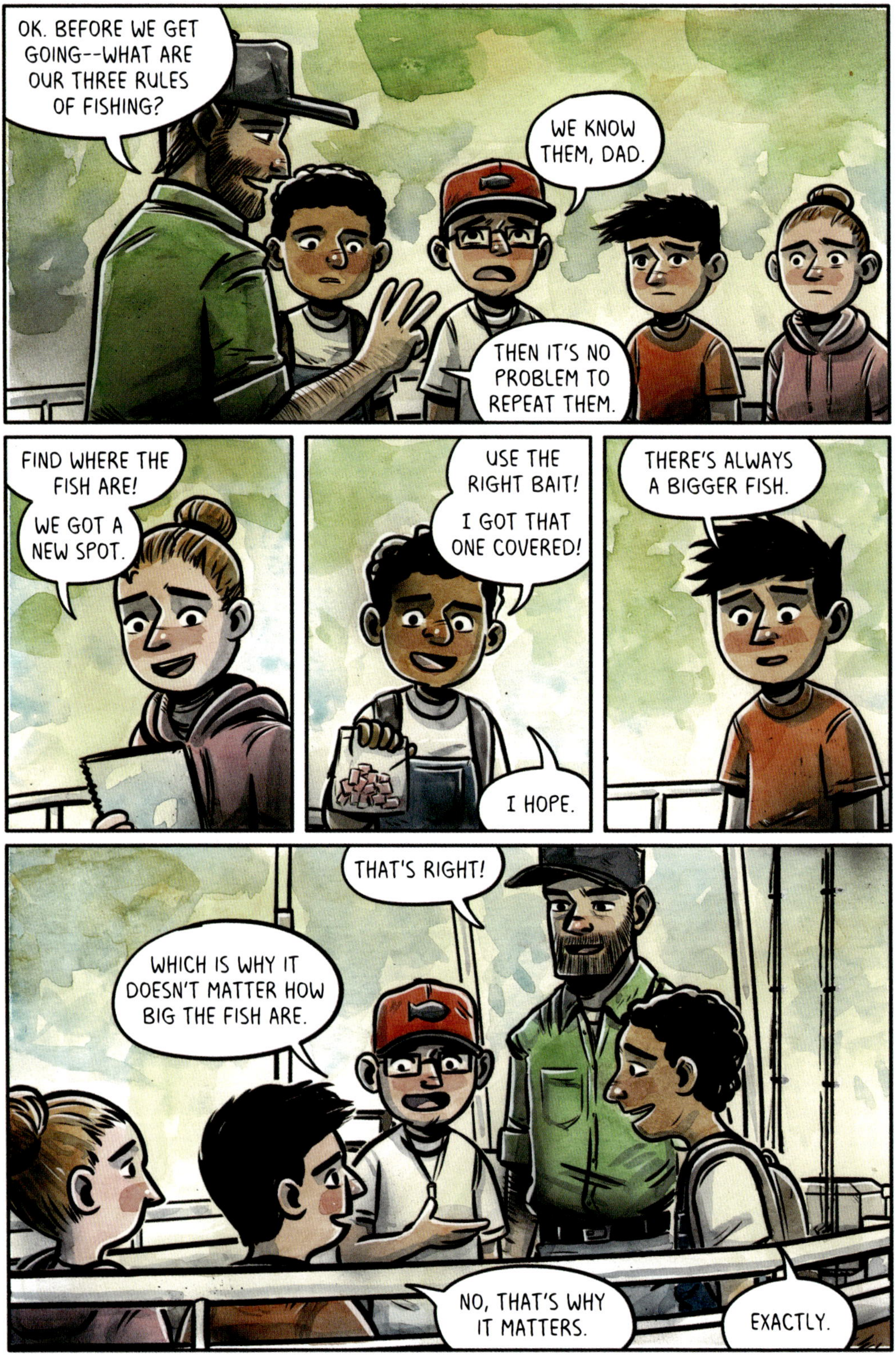
OK. BEFORE WE GET GOING--WHAT ARE OUR THREE RULES OF FISHING?
WE KNOW THEM, DAD.
THEN IT'S NO PROBLEM TO REPEAT THEM.
FIND WHERE THE FISH ARE!
WE GOT A NEW SPOT.
USE THE RIGHT BAIT!
I GOT THAT ONE COVERED!
I HOPE.
THERE'S ALWAYS A BIGGER FISH.
THAT'S RIGHT!
WHICH IS WHY IT DOESN'T MATTER HOW BIG THE FISH ARE.
NO, THAT'S WHY IT MATTERS.
EXACTLY.

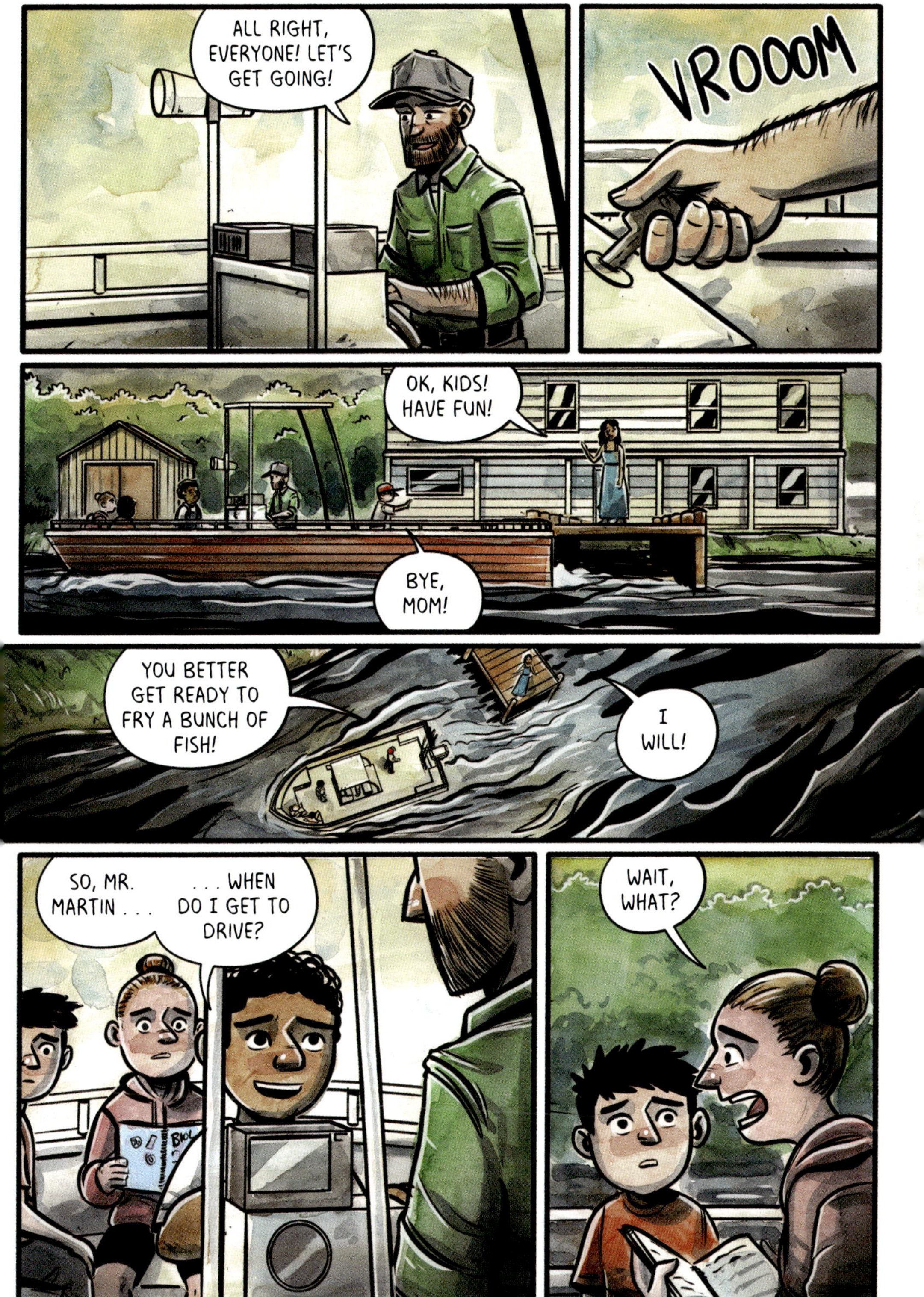
ALL RIGHT, EVERYONE! LET'S GET GOING!
VROOOM
OK, KIDS! HAVE FUN!
BYE, MOM!
YOU BETTER GET READY TO FRY A BUNCH OF FISH!
I WILL!
SO, MR. MARTIN . . .
. . . WHEN DO I GET TO DRIVE?
WAIT, WHAT?

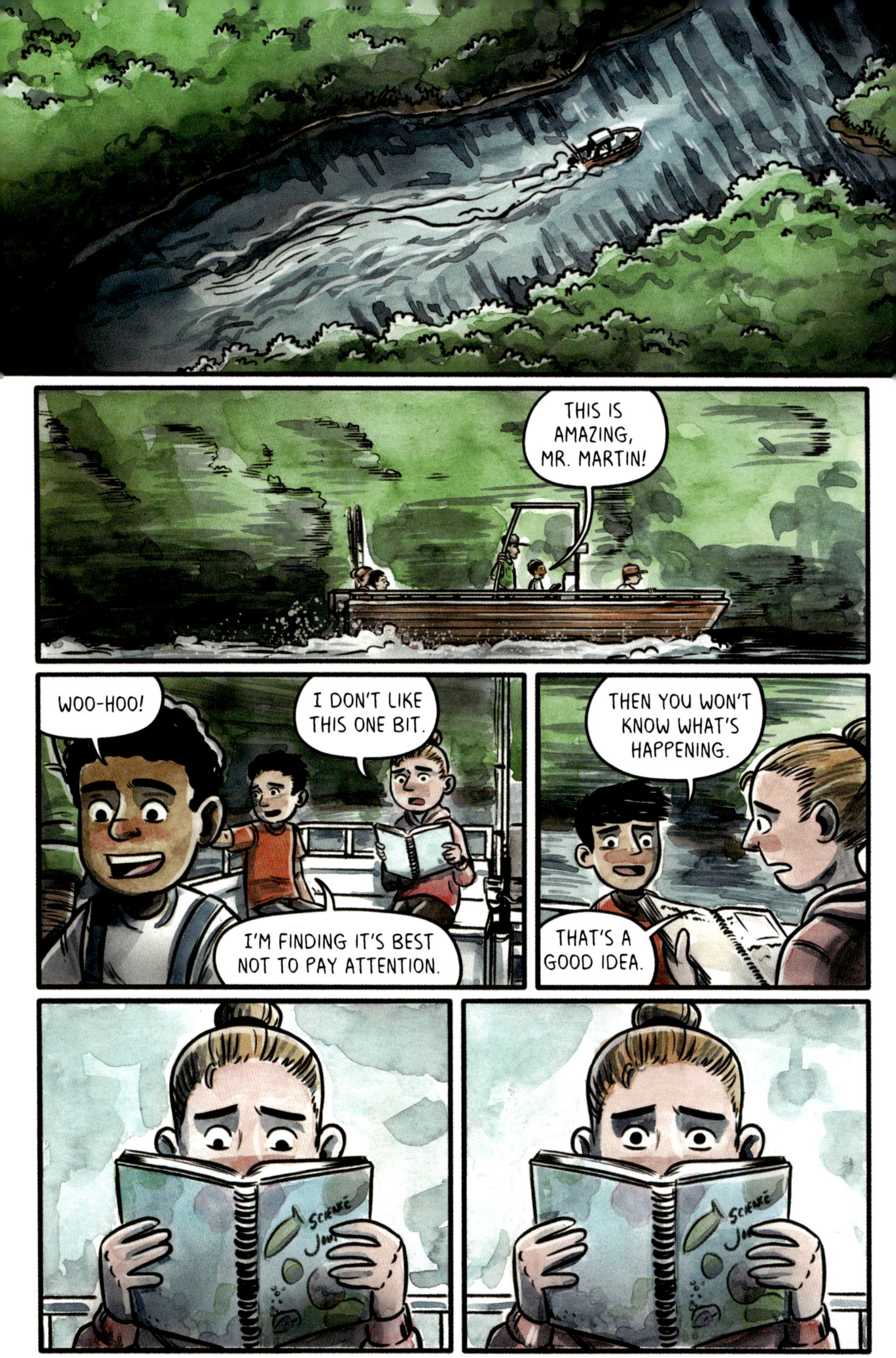
THIS IS AMAZING, MR. MARTIN!
WOO-HOO!
I DON'T LIKE THIS ONE BIT.
I'M FINDING IT'S BEST NOT TO PAY ATTENTION.
THEN YOU WON'T KNOW WHAT'S HAPPENING.
THAT'S A GOOD IDEA.

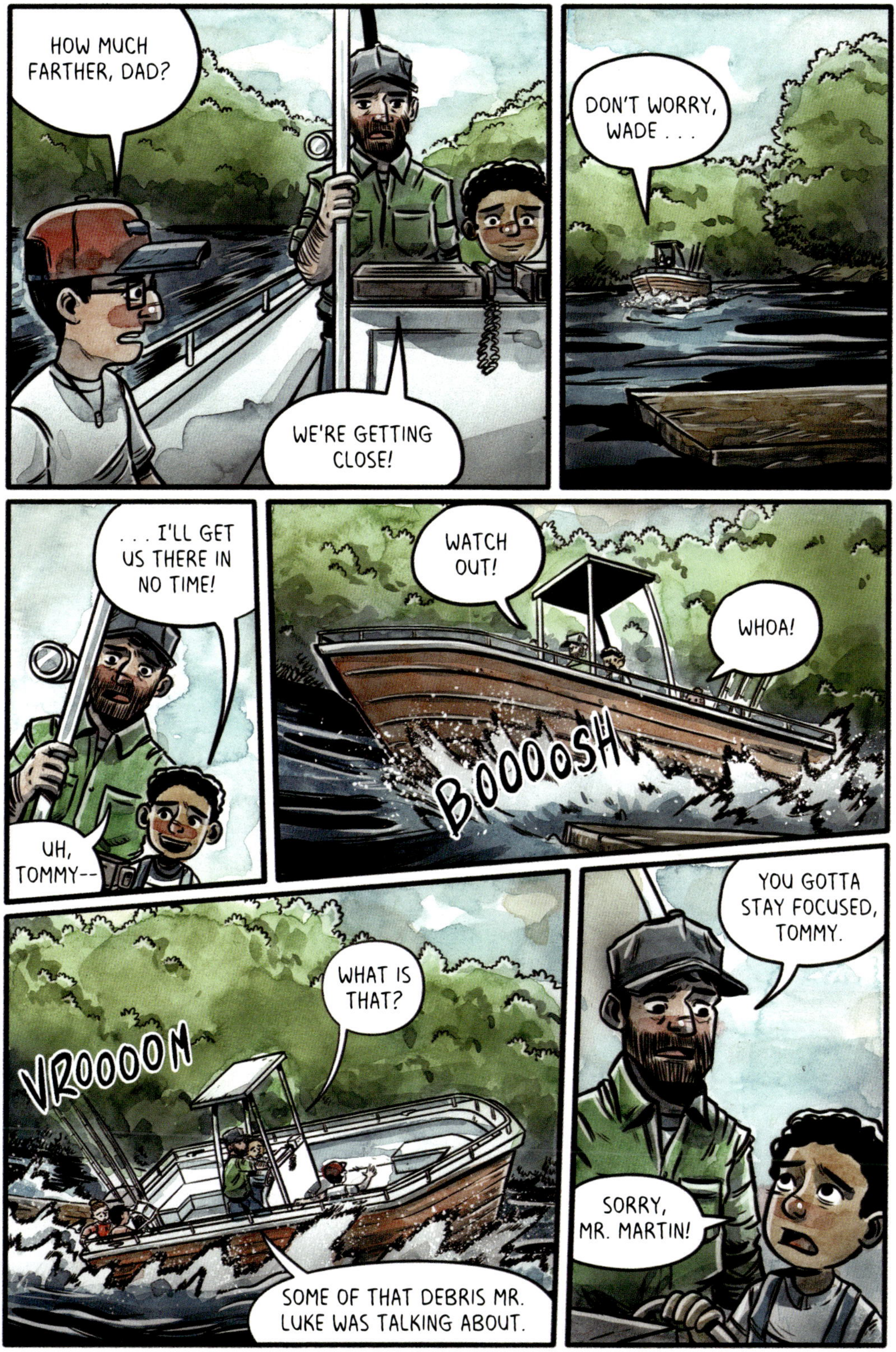
HOW MUCH FARTHER, DAD?
WE'RE GETTING CLOSE!
DON'T WORRY, WADE . . .
. . . I'LL GET US THERE IN NO TIME!
UH, TOMMY--
WATCH OUT!
WHOA!
BOOOoSH
VROOOON
WHAT IS THAT?
SOME OF THAT DEBRIS MR. LUKE WAS TALKING ABOUT.
YOU GOTTA STAY FOCUSED, TOMMY.
SORRY, MR. MARTIN!

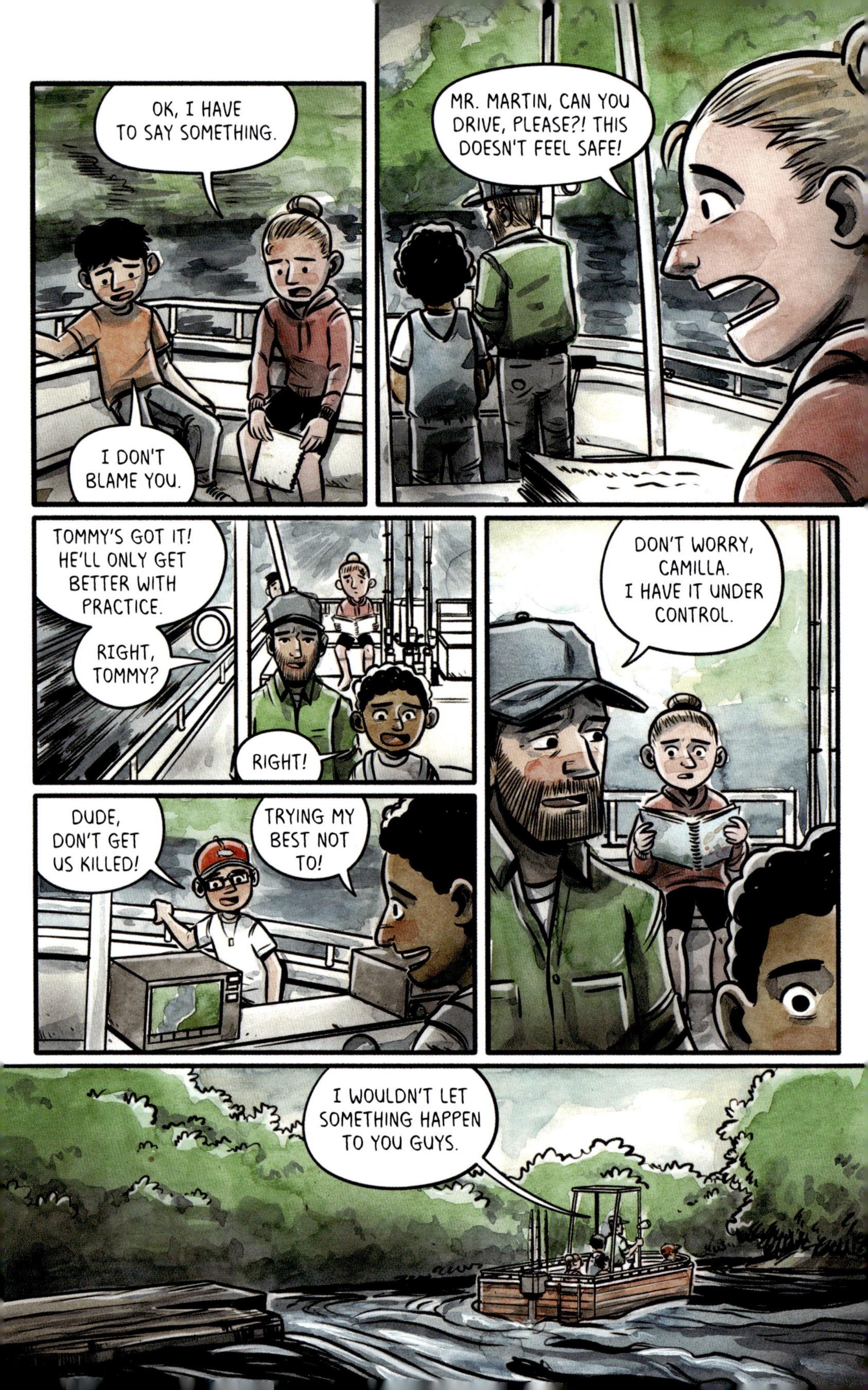
OK, I HAVE TO SAY SOMETHING.
I DON'T BLAME YOU.
MR. MARTIN, CAN YOU DRIVE, PLEASE?! THIS DOESN'T FEEL SAFE!
TOMMY'S GOT IT! HE'LL ONLY GET BETTER WITH PRACTICE.
RIGHT, TOMMY?
RIGHT!
DON'T WORRY, CAMILLA. I HAVE IT UNDER CONTROL.
DUDE, DON'T GET US KILLED!
TRYING MY BEST NOT TO!
I WOULDN'T LET SOMETHING HAPPEN TO YOU GUYS.

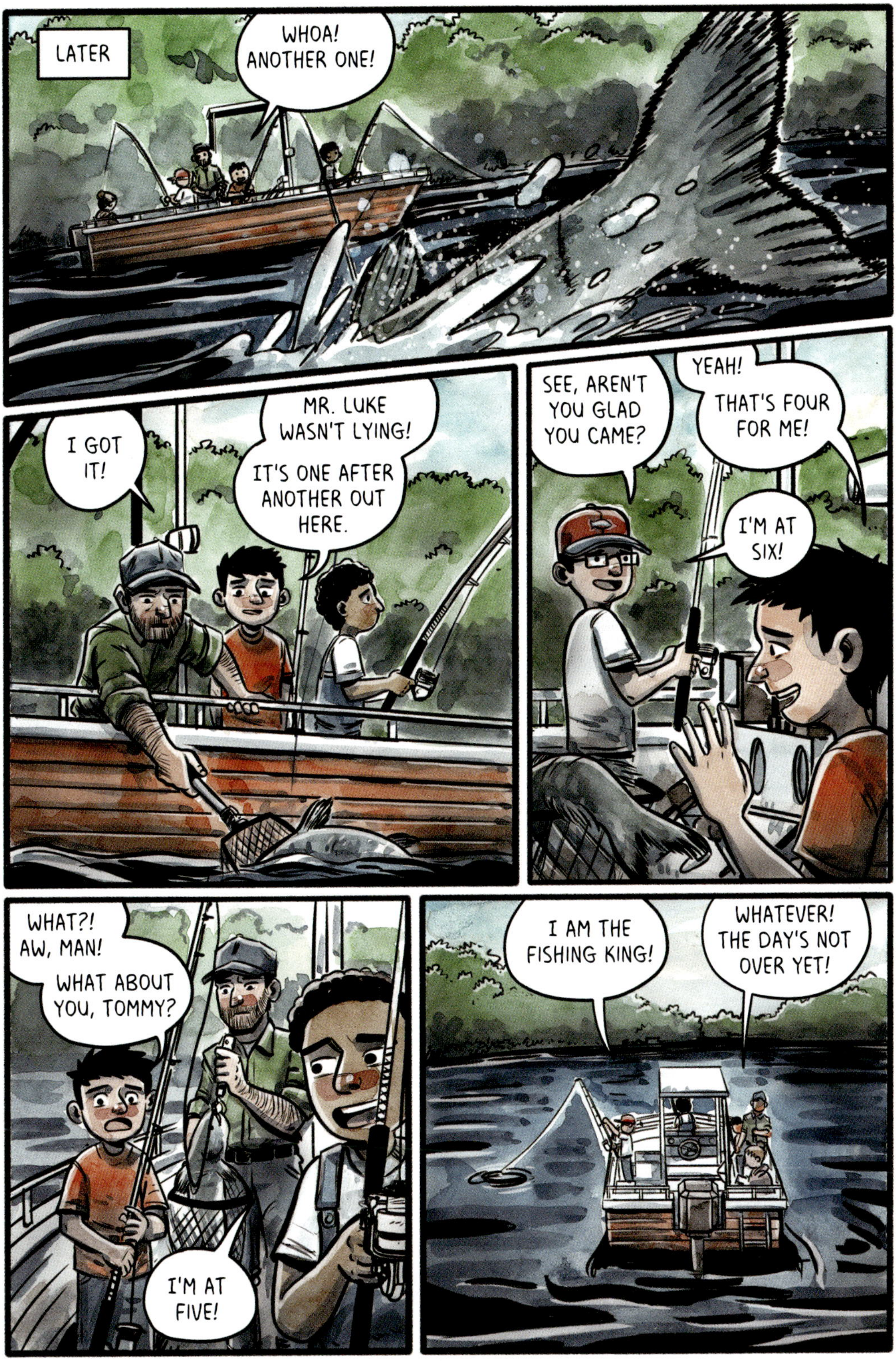
LATER
WHOA! ANOTHER ONE!
I GOT IT!
MR. LUKE WASN'T LYING!
IT'S ONE AFTER ANOTHER OUT HERE.
SEE, AREN'T YOU GLAD YOU CAME?
YEAH!
THAT'S FOUR FOR ME!
I'M AT SIX!
WHAT?! AW, MAN!
WHAT ABOUT YOU, TOMMY?
I'M AT FIVE!
I AM THE FISHING KING!
WHATEVER! THE DAY'S NOT OVER YET!

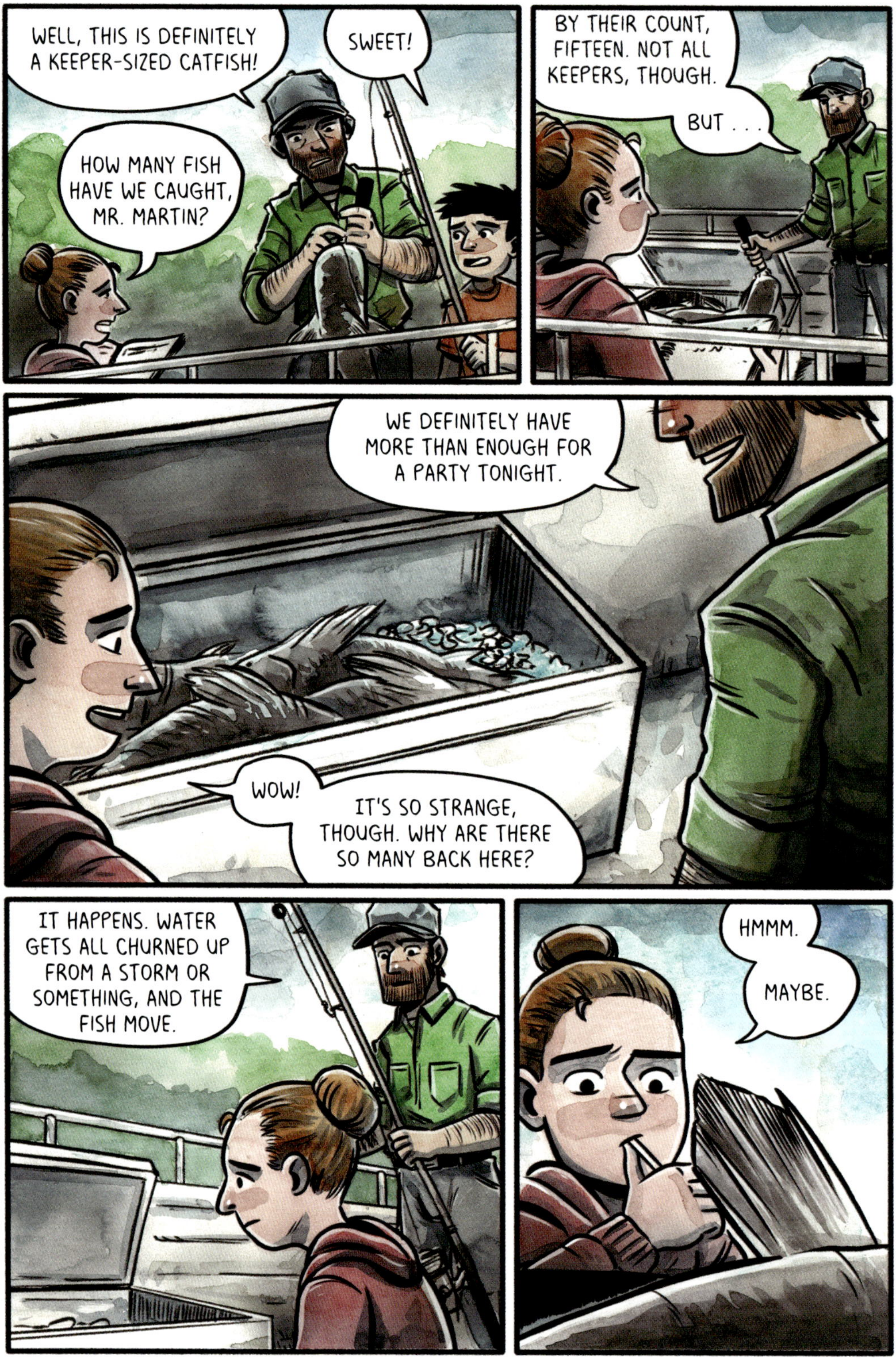
WELL, THIS IS DEFINITELY A KEEPER-SIZED CATFISH!
SWEET!
HOW MANY FISH HAVE WE CAUGHT, MR. MARTIN?
BY THEIR COUNT, FIFTEEN. NOT ALL KEEPERS, THOUGH.
BUT . . .
WE DEFINITELY HAVE MORE THAN ENOUGH FOR A PARTY TONIGHT.
WOW!
IT'S SO STRANGE, THOUGH. WHY ARE THERE SO MANY BACK HERE?
IT HAPPENS. WATER GETS ALL CHURNED UP FROM A STORM OR SOMETHING, AND THE FISH MOVE.
HMMM.
MAYBE.

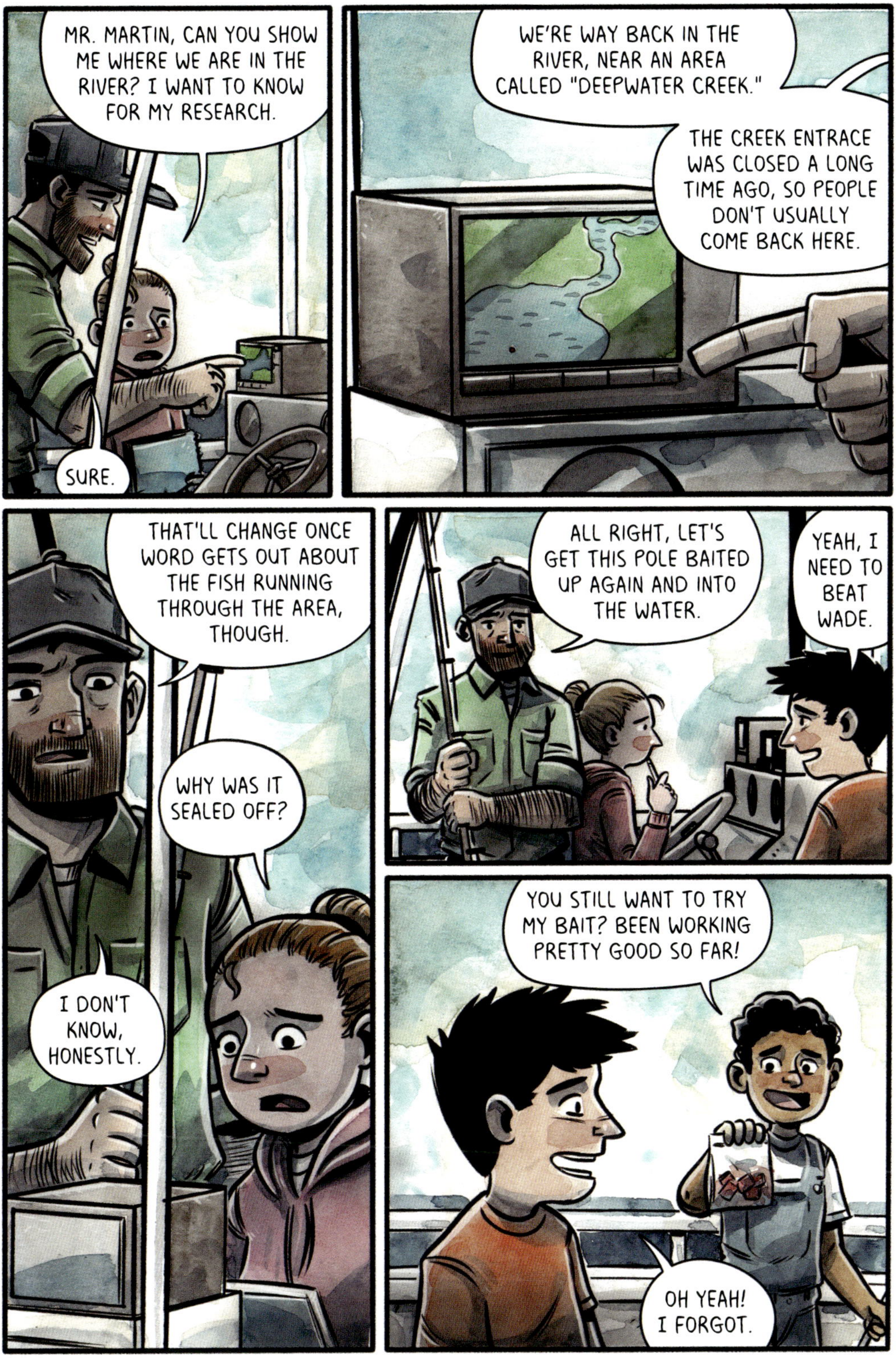
MR. MARTIN, CAN YOU SHOW ME WHERE WE ARE IN THE RIVER? I WANT TO KNOW FOR MY RESEARCH.
SURE.
WE'RE WAY BACK IN THE RIVER, NEAR AN AREA CALLED "DEEPWATER CREEK."
THE CREEK ENTRACE WAS CLOSED A LONG TIME AGO, SO PEOPLE DON'T USUALLY COME BACK HERE.
THAT'LL CHANGE ONCE WORD GETS OUT ABOUT THE FISH RUNNING THROUGH THE AREA, THOUGH.
WHY WAS IT SEALED OFF?
I DON'T KNOW, HONESTLY.
ALL RIGHT, LET'S GET THIS POLE BAITED UP AGAIN AND INTO THE WATER.
YEAH, I NEED TO BEAT WADE.
YOU STILL WANT TO TRY MY BAIT? BEEN WORKING PRETTY GOOD SO FAR!
OH YEAH! I FORGOT.

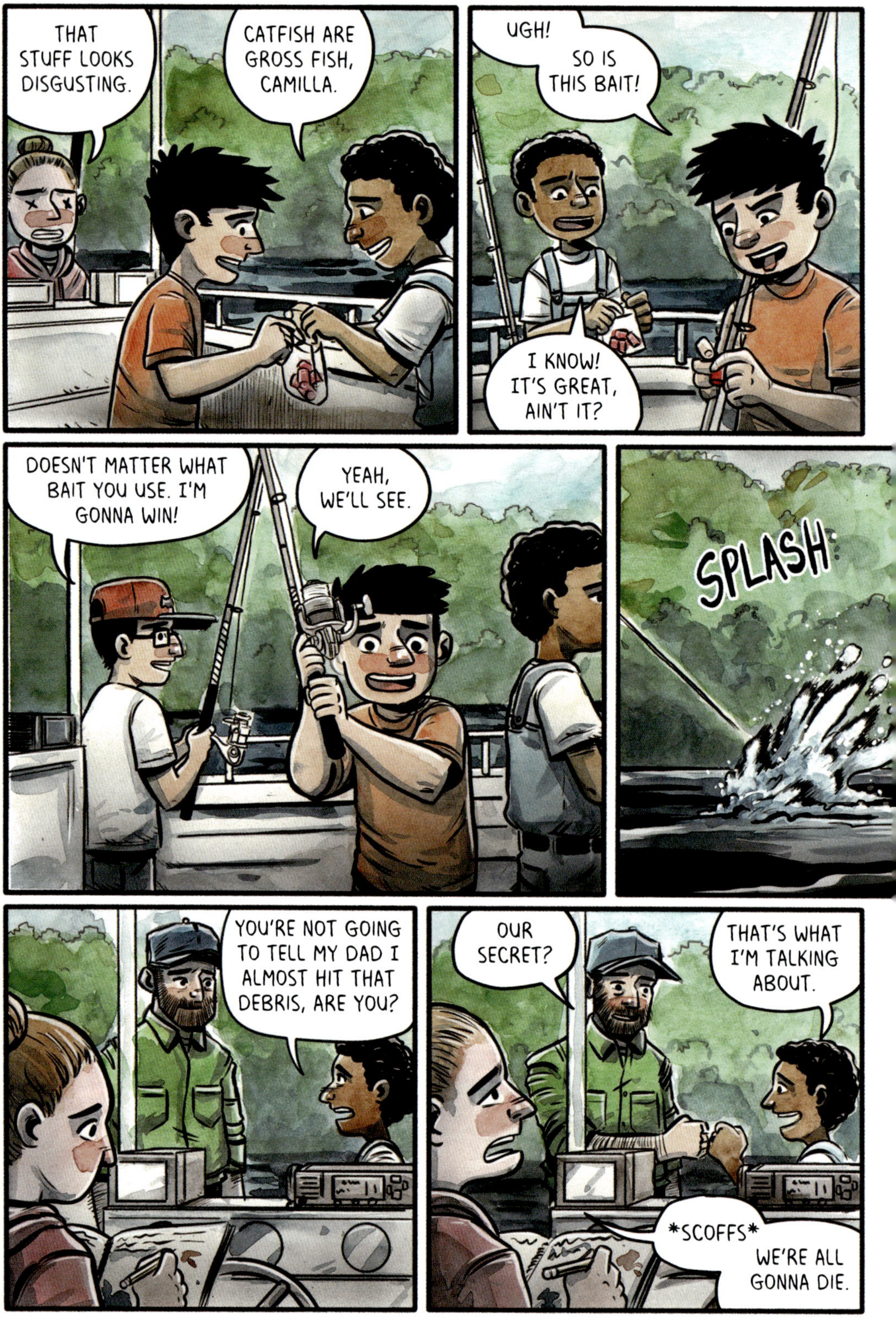
THAT STUFF LOOKS DISGUSTING.
CATFISH ARE GROSS FISH, CAMILLA.
UGH!
SO IS THIS BAIT!
I KNOW! IT'S GREAT, AIN'T IT?
DOESN'T MATTER WHAT BAIT YOU USE. I'M GONNA WIN!
YEAH, WE'LL SEE.
SPLASH
YOU'RE NOT GOING TO TELL MY DAD I ALMOST HIT THAT DEBRIS, ARE YOU?
OUR SECRET?
THAT'S WHAT I'M TALKING ABOUT.
SCOFFS WE'RE ALL GONNA DIE.

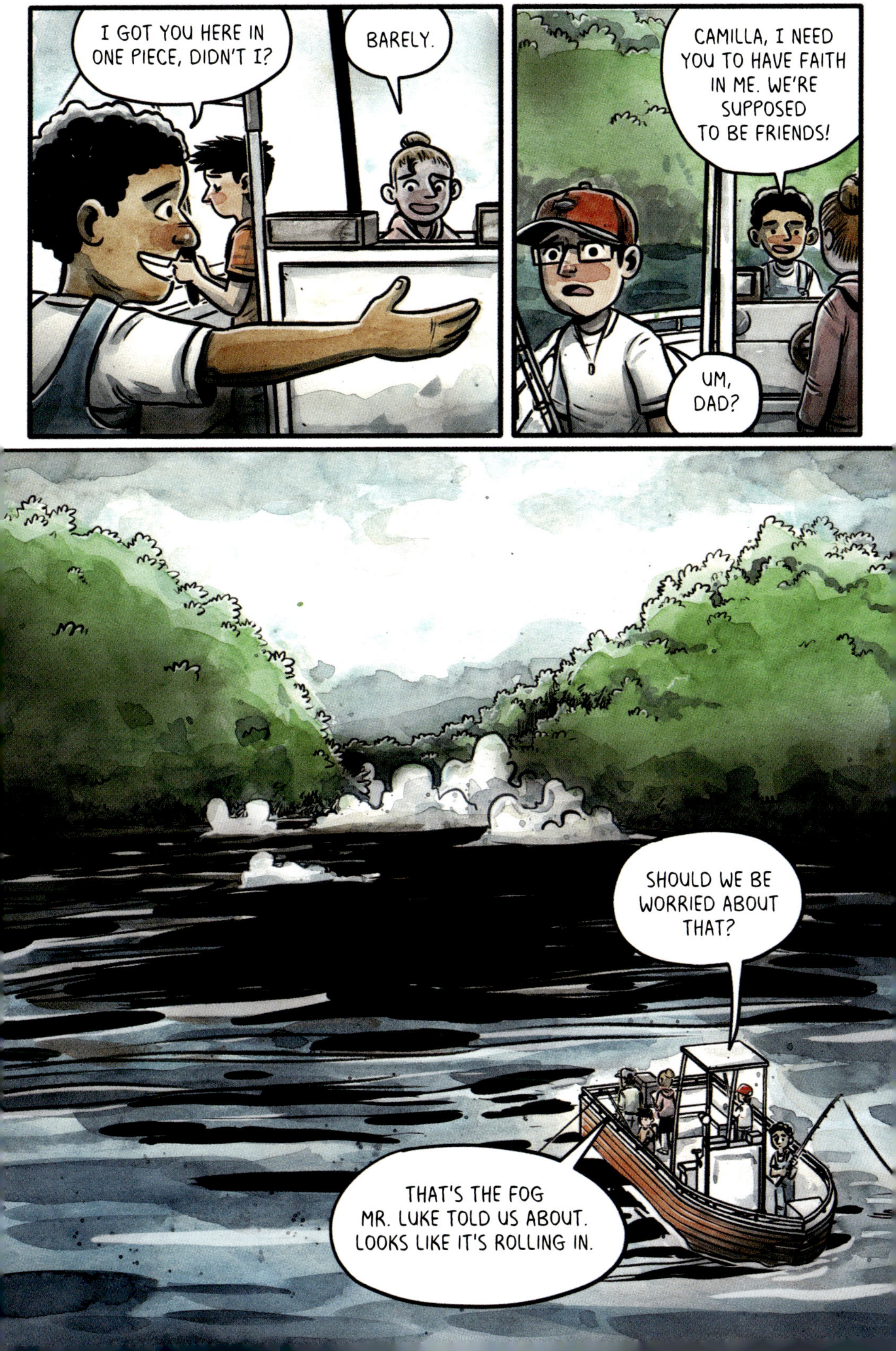
I GOT YOU HERE IN ONE PIECE, DIDN'T I?
BARELY.
CAMILLA, I NEED YOU TO HAVE FAITH IN ME. WE'RE SUPPOSED TO BE FRIENDS!
UM, DAD?
SHOULD WE BE WORRIED ABOUT THAT?
THAT'S THE FOG MR. LUKE TOLD US ABOUT. LOOKS LIKE IT'S ROLLING IN.

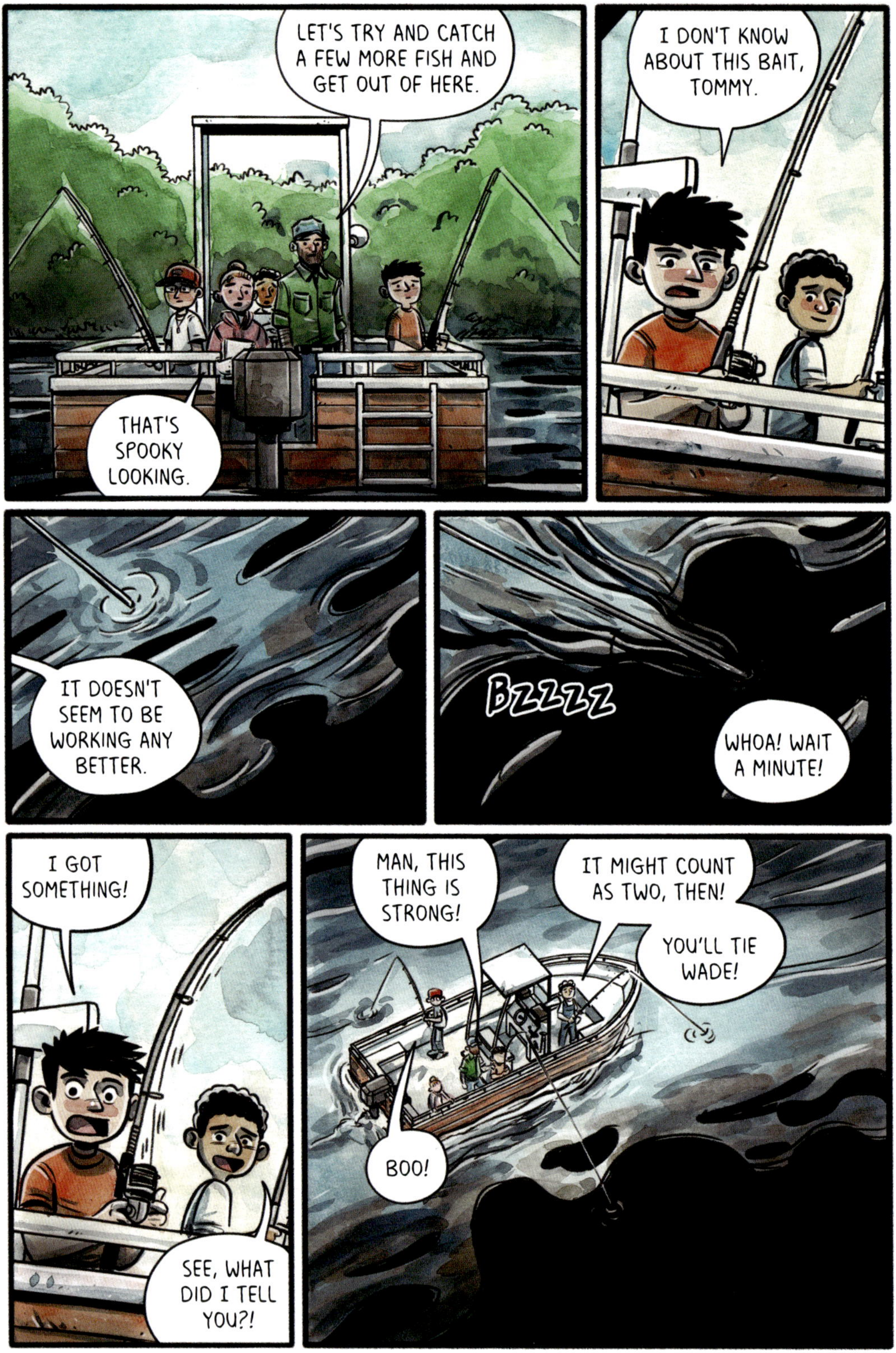
LET'S TRY AND CATCH A FEW MORE FISH AND GET OUT OF HERE.
THAT'S SPOOKY LOOKING.
I DON'T KNOW ABOUT THIS BAIT, TOMMY.
IT DOESN'T SEEM TO BE WORKING ANY BETTER.
BZZZZ
WHOA! WAIT A MINUTE!
I GOT SOMETHING!
SEE, WHAT DID I TELL YOU?!
MAN, THIS THING IS STRONG!
BOO!
IT MIGHT COUNT AS TWO, THEN!
YOU'LL TIE WADE!

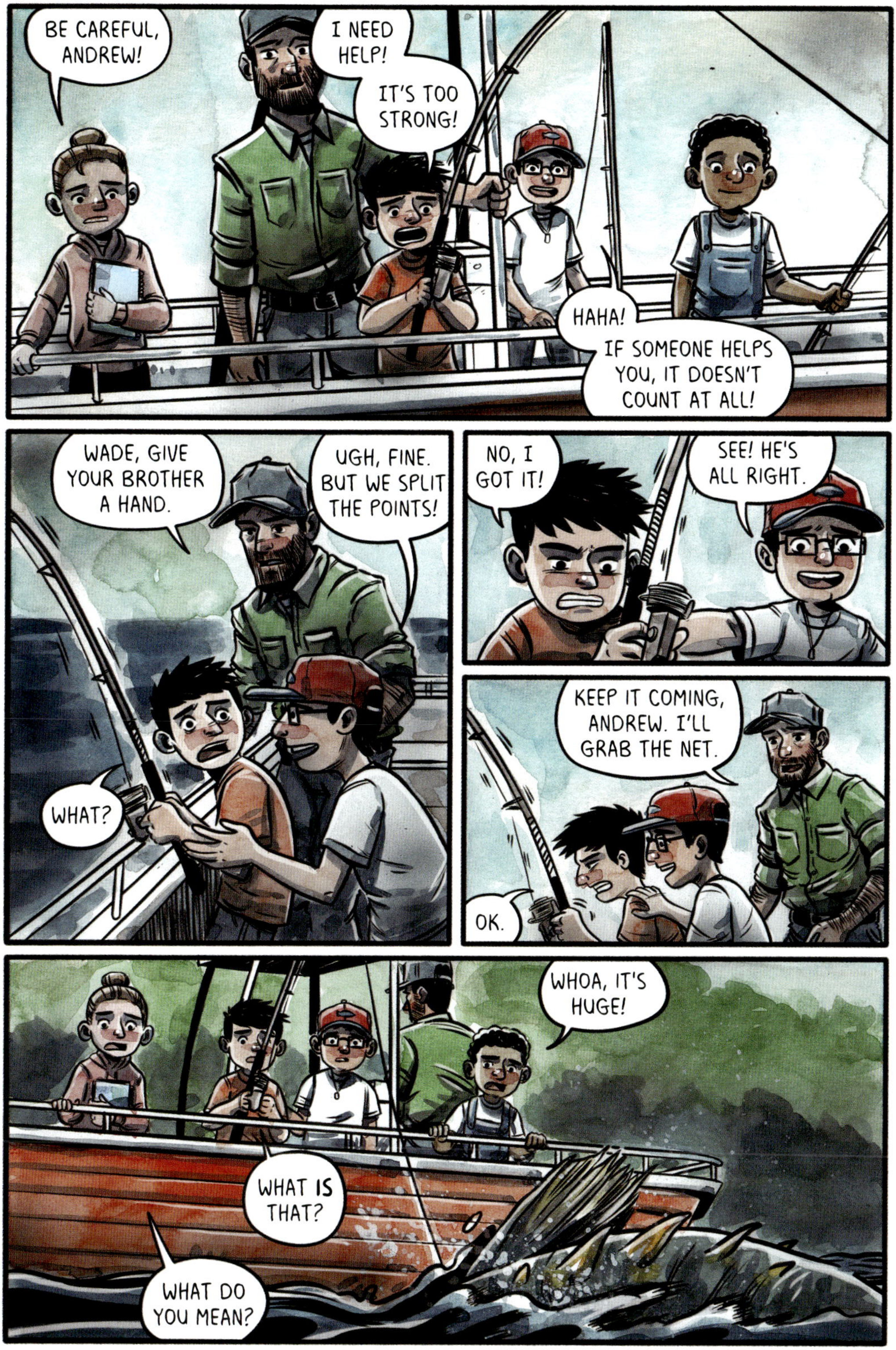
BE CAREFUL, ANDREW!
I NEED HELP!
IT'S TOO STRONG!
HAHA!
IF SOMEONE HELPS YOU, IT DOESN'T COUNT AT ALL!
WADE, GIVE YOUR BROTHER A HAND.
UGH, FINE. BUT WE SPLIT THE POINTS!
WHAT?
NO, I GOT IT!
SEE! HE'S ALL RIGHT.
KEEP IT COMING, ANDREW. I'LL GRAB THE NET.
OK.
WHOA, IT'S HUGE!
WHAT **IS** THAT?
WHAT DO YOU MEAN?

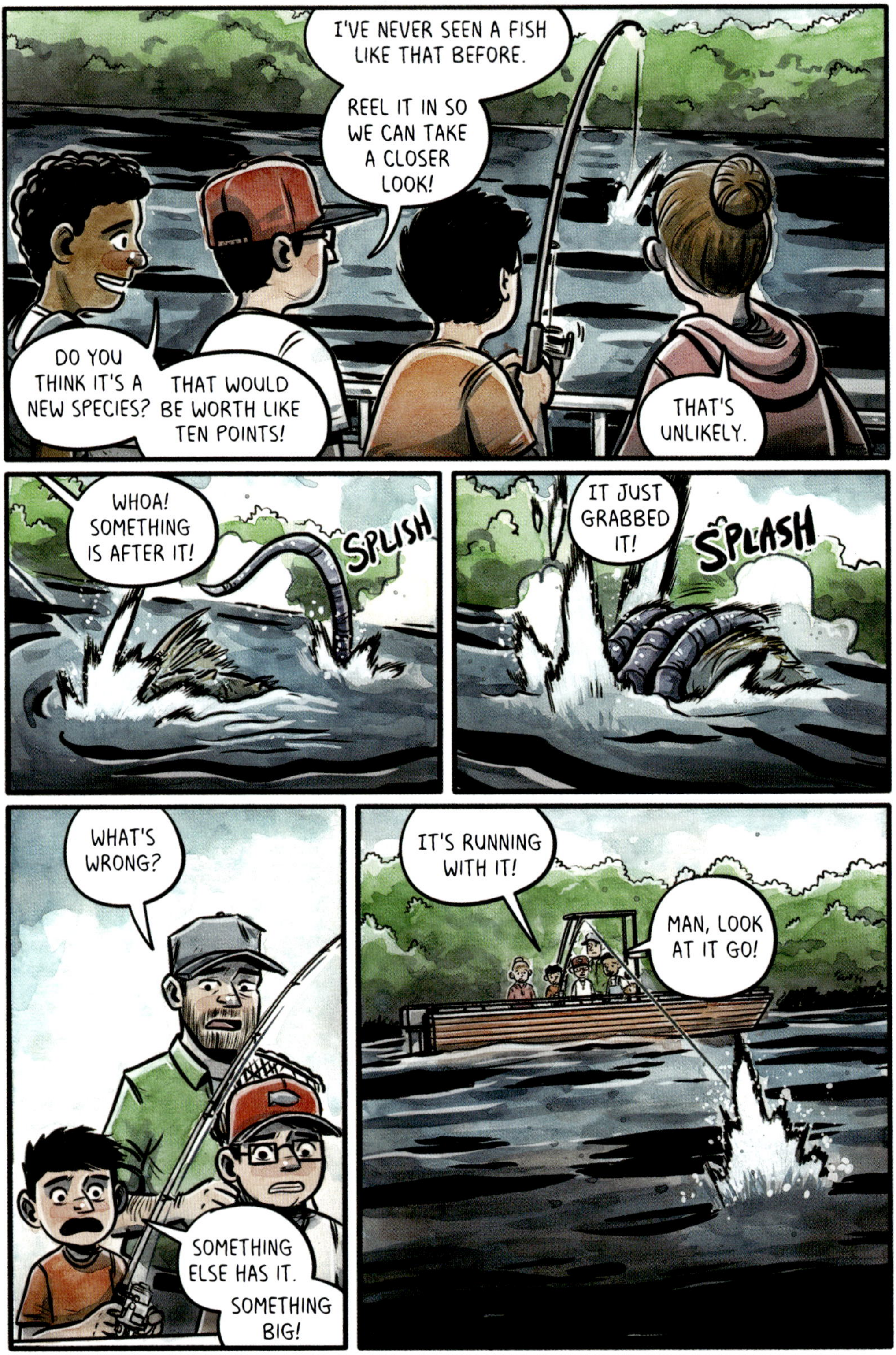
I'VE NEVER SEEN A FISH LIKE THAT BEFORE.
REEL IT IN SO WE CAN TAKE A CLOSER LOOK!
DO YOU THINK IT'S A NEW SPECIES?
THAT WOULD BE WORTH LIKE TEN POINTS!
THAT'S UNLIKELY.
WHOA! SOMETHING IS AFTER IT!
SPLISH
IT JUST GRABBED IT!
SPLASH
WHAT'S WRONG?
SOMETHING ELSE HAS IT.
SOMETHING BIG!
IT'S RUNNING WITH IT!
MAN, LOOK AT IT GO!

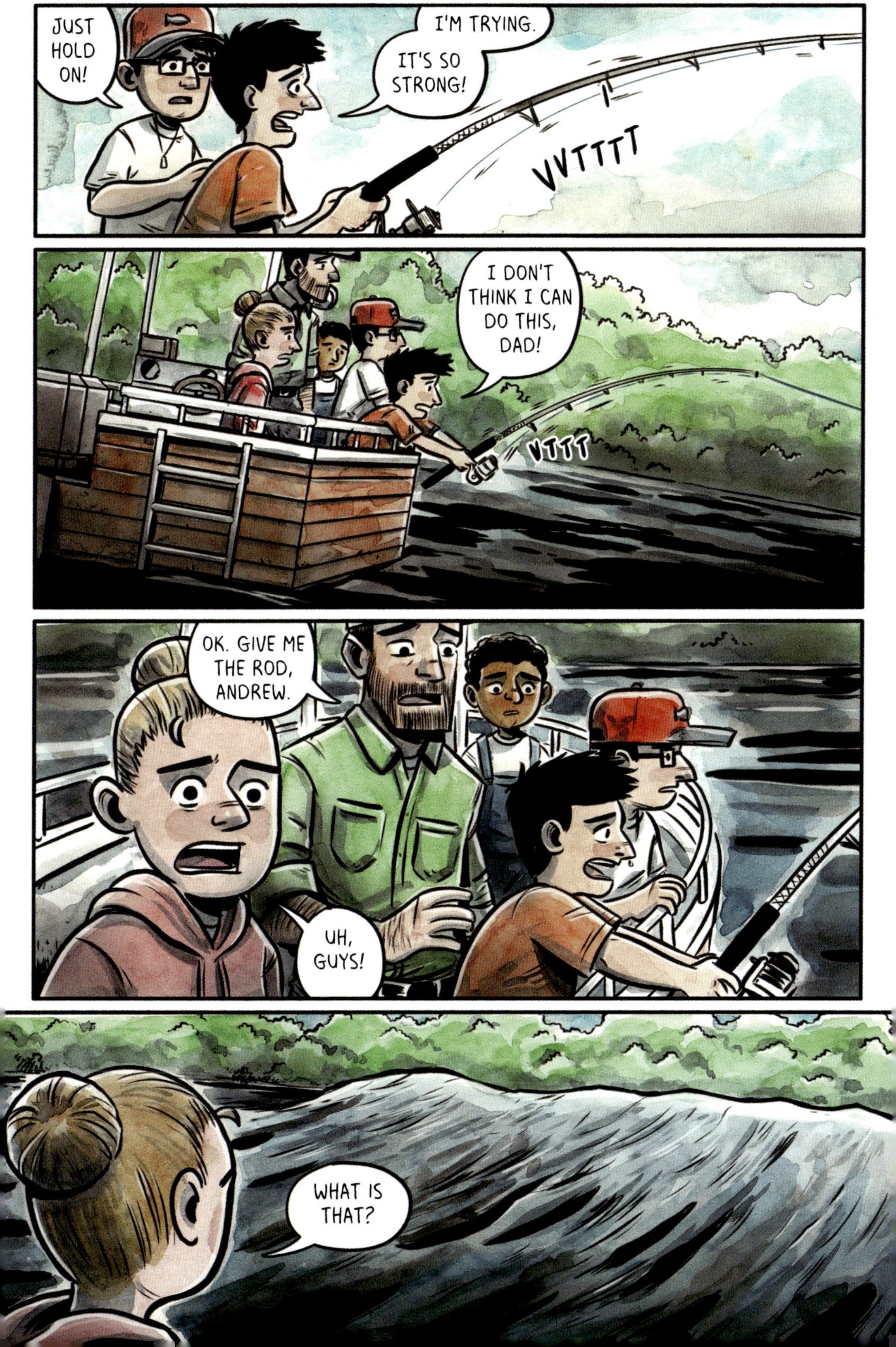
JUST HOLD ON!
I'M TRYING.
IT'S SO STRONG!
VVTTTT
I DON'T THINK I CAN DO THIS, DAD!
VTTT
OK. GIVE ME THE ROD, ANDREW.
UH, GUYS!
WHAT IS THAT?

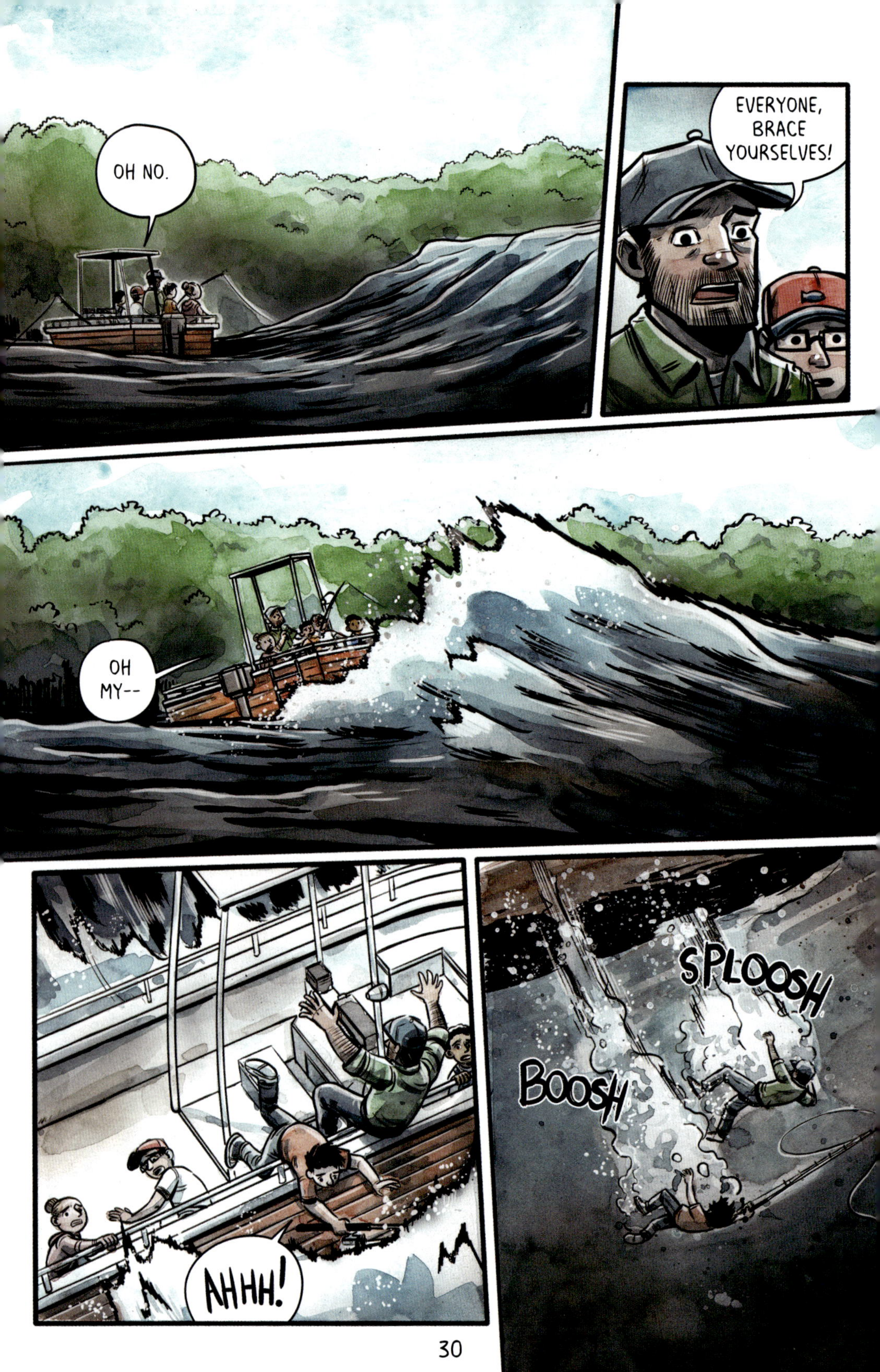
OH NO.
EVERYONE, BRACE YOURSELVES!
OH MY--
AHHH!
SPLOOSH
BOOSH

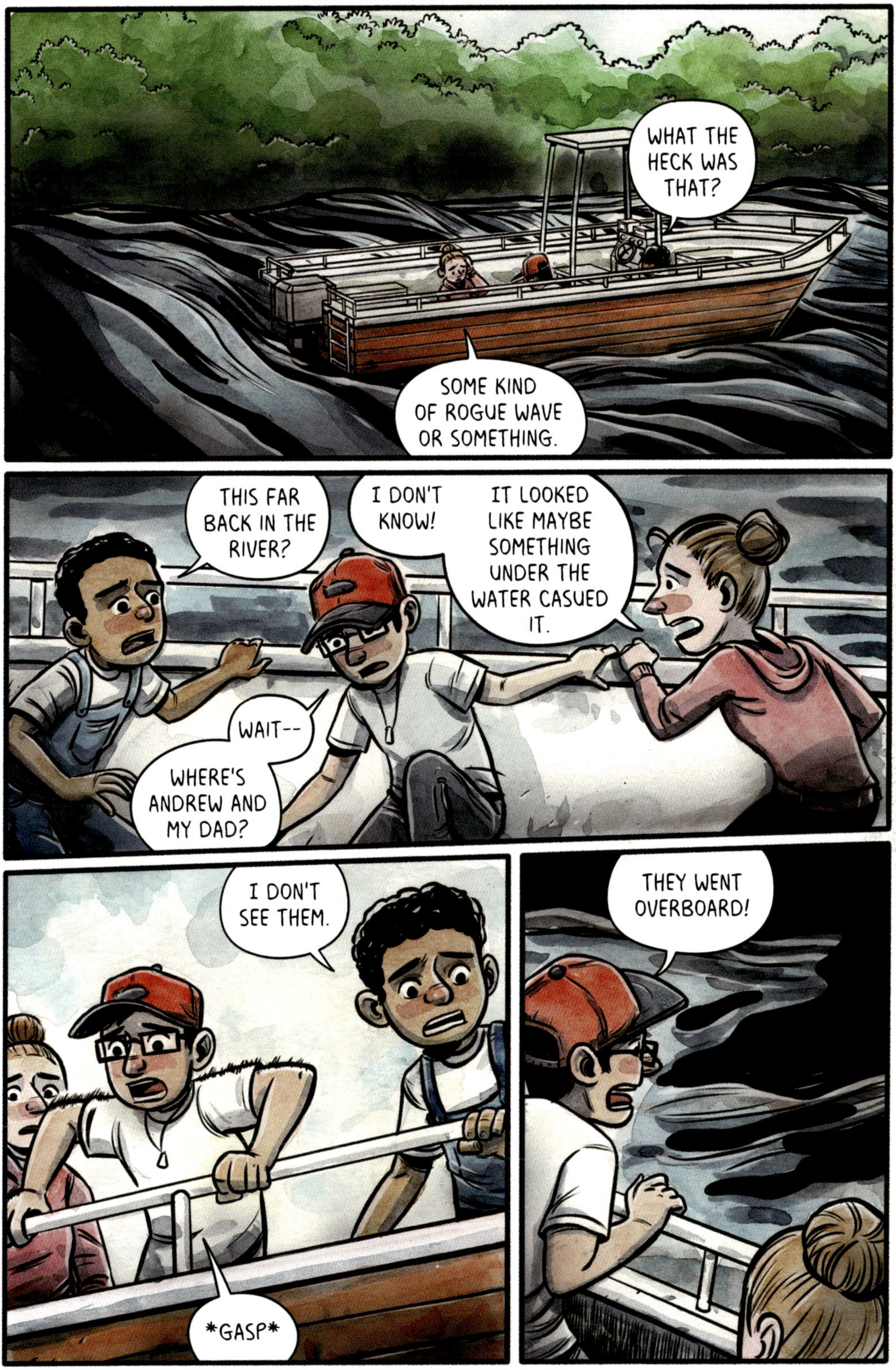
WHAT THE HECK WAS THAT?
SOME KIND OF ROGUE WAVE OR SOMETHING.
THIS FAR BACK IN THE RIVER?
I DON'T KNOW!
IT LOOKED LIKE MAYBE SOMETHING UNDER THE WATER CASUED IT.
WAIT--
WHERE'S ANDREW AND MY DAD?
I DON'T SEE THEM.
GASP
THEY WENT OVERBOARD!

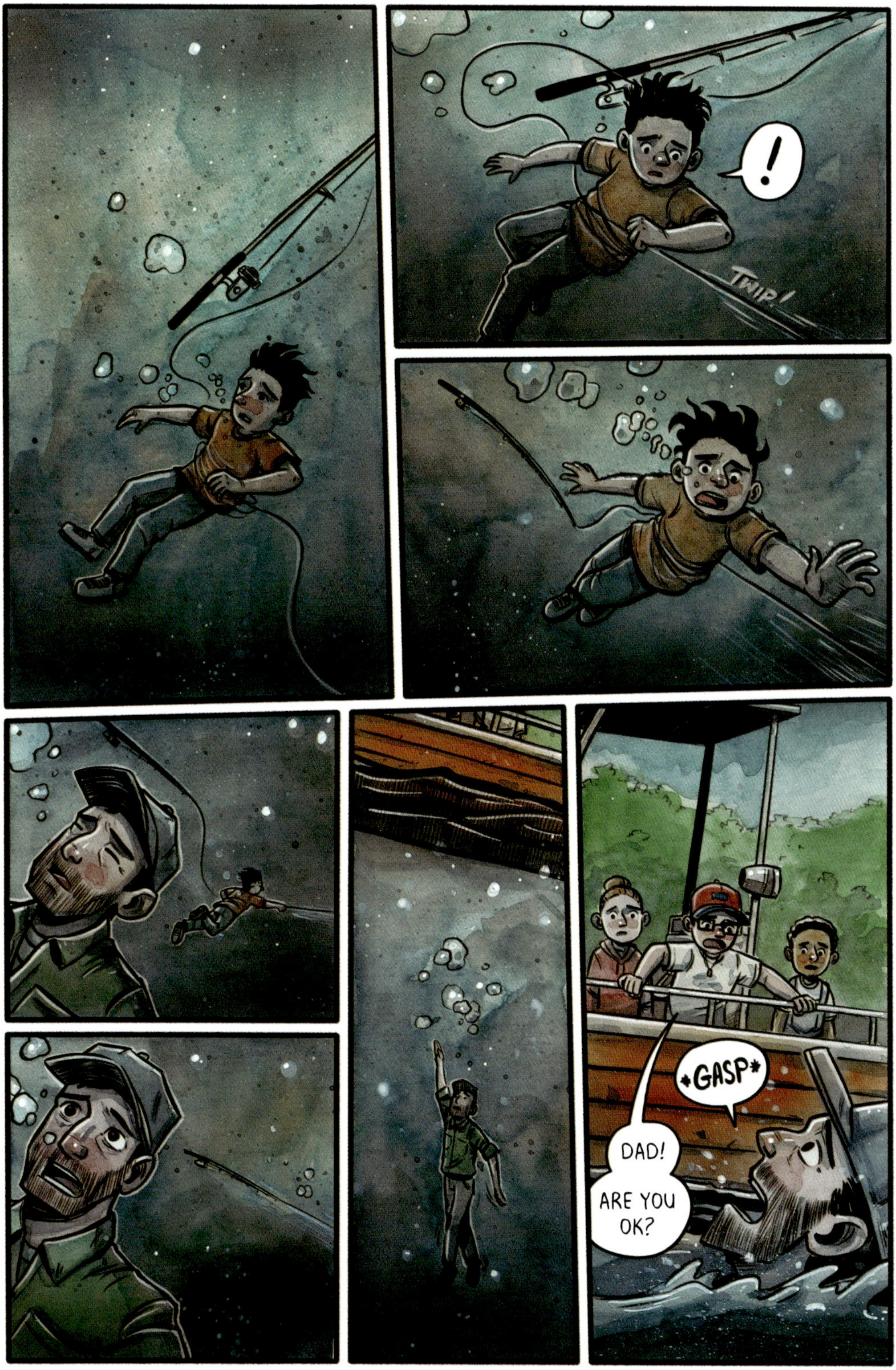
!
TWIP!
GASP
DAD!
ARE YOU OK?

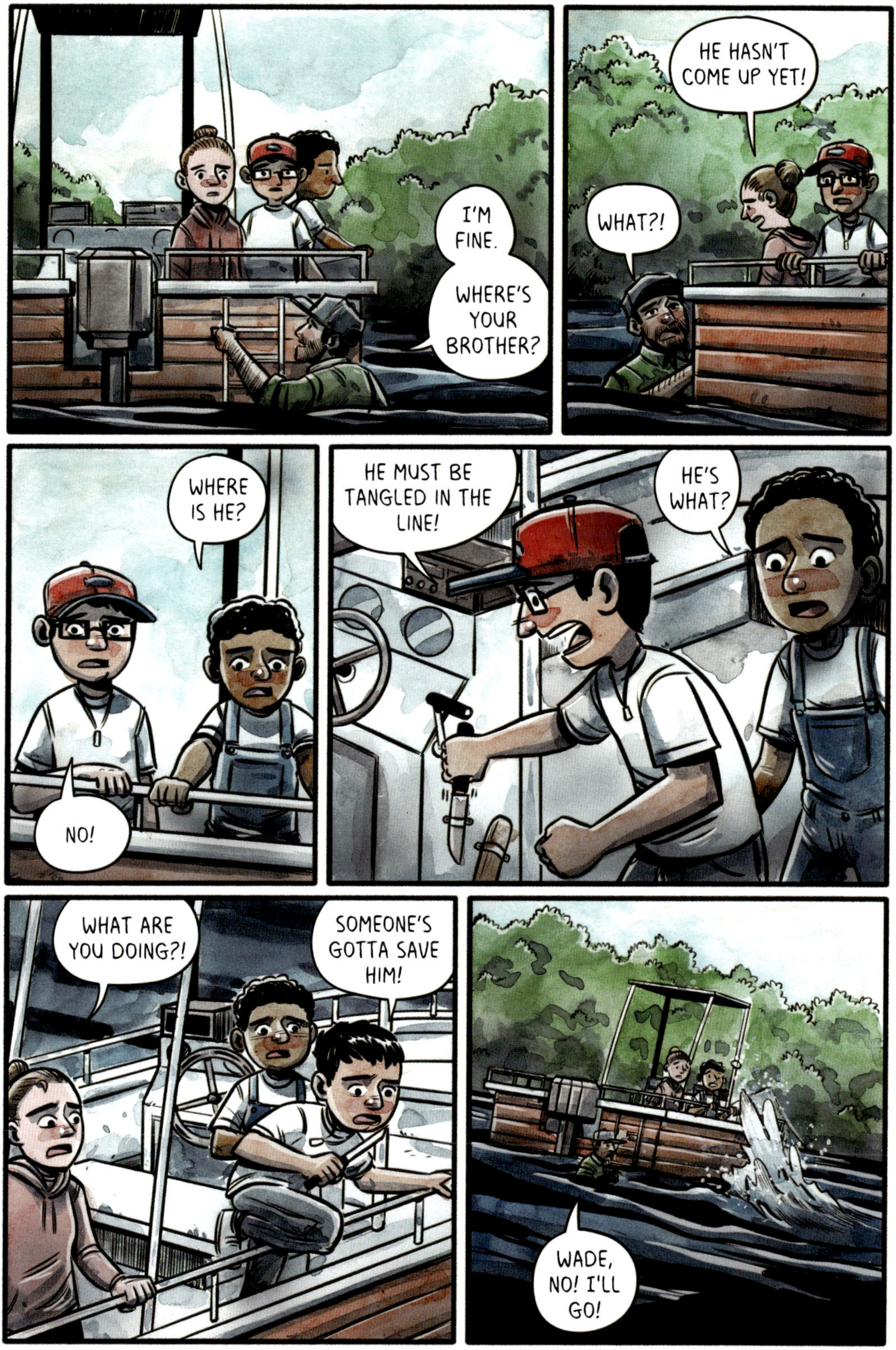
I'M FINE.
WHERE'S YOUR BROTHER?
HE HASN'T COME UP YET!
WHAT?!
WHERE IS HE?
NO!
HE MUST BE TANGLED IN THE LINE!
HE'S WHAT?
WHAT ARE YOU DOING?!
SOMEONE'S GOTTA SAVE HIM!
WADE, NO! I'LL GO!

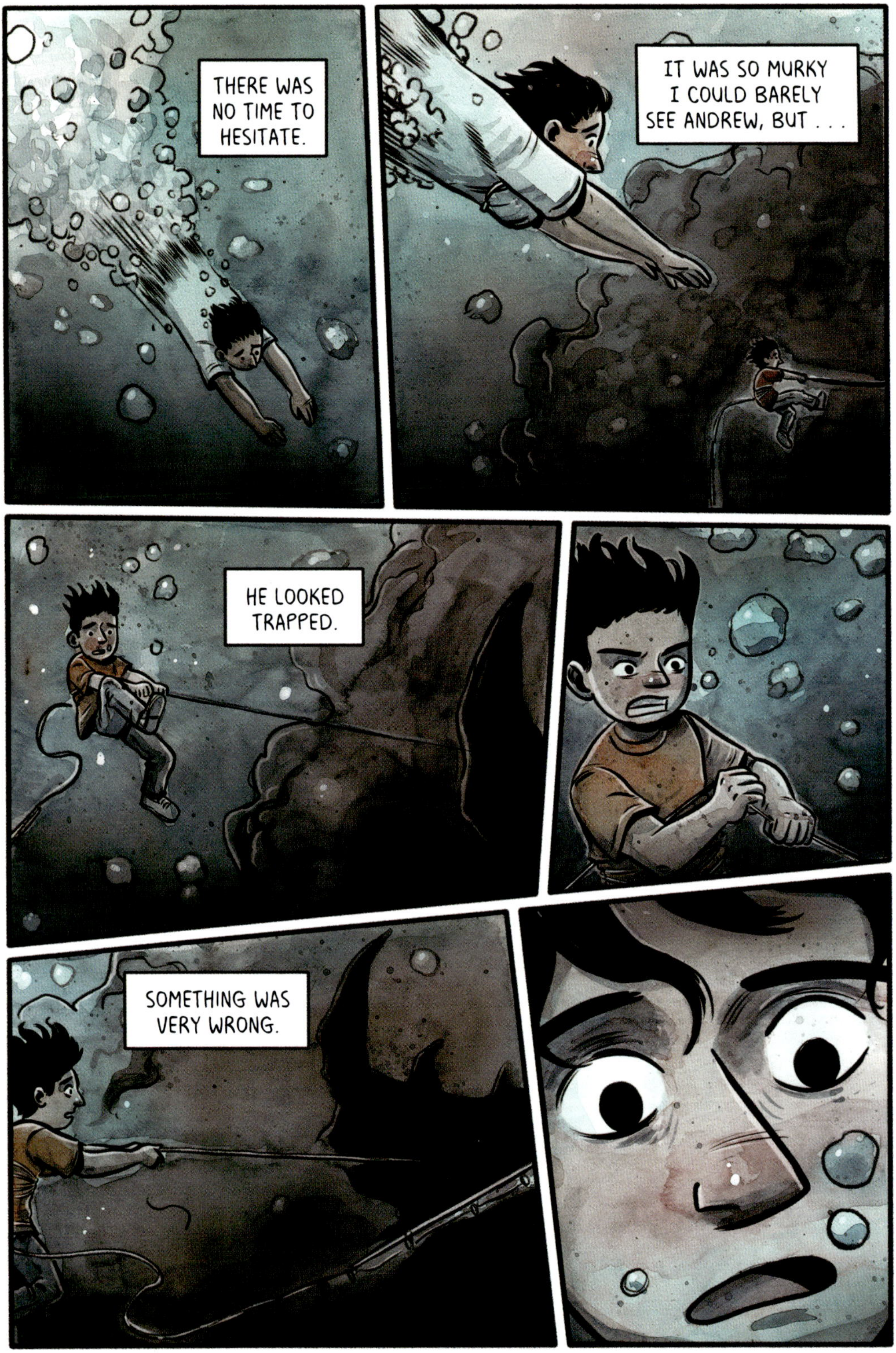
THERE WAS NO TIME TO HESITATE.
IT WAS SO MURKY I COULD BARELY SEE ANDREW, BUT . . .
HE LOOKED TRAPPED.
SOMETHING WAS VERY WRONG.

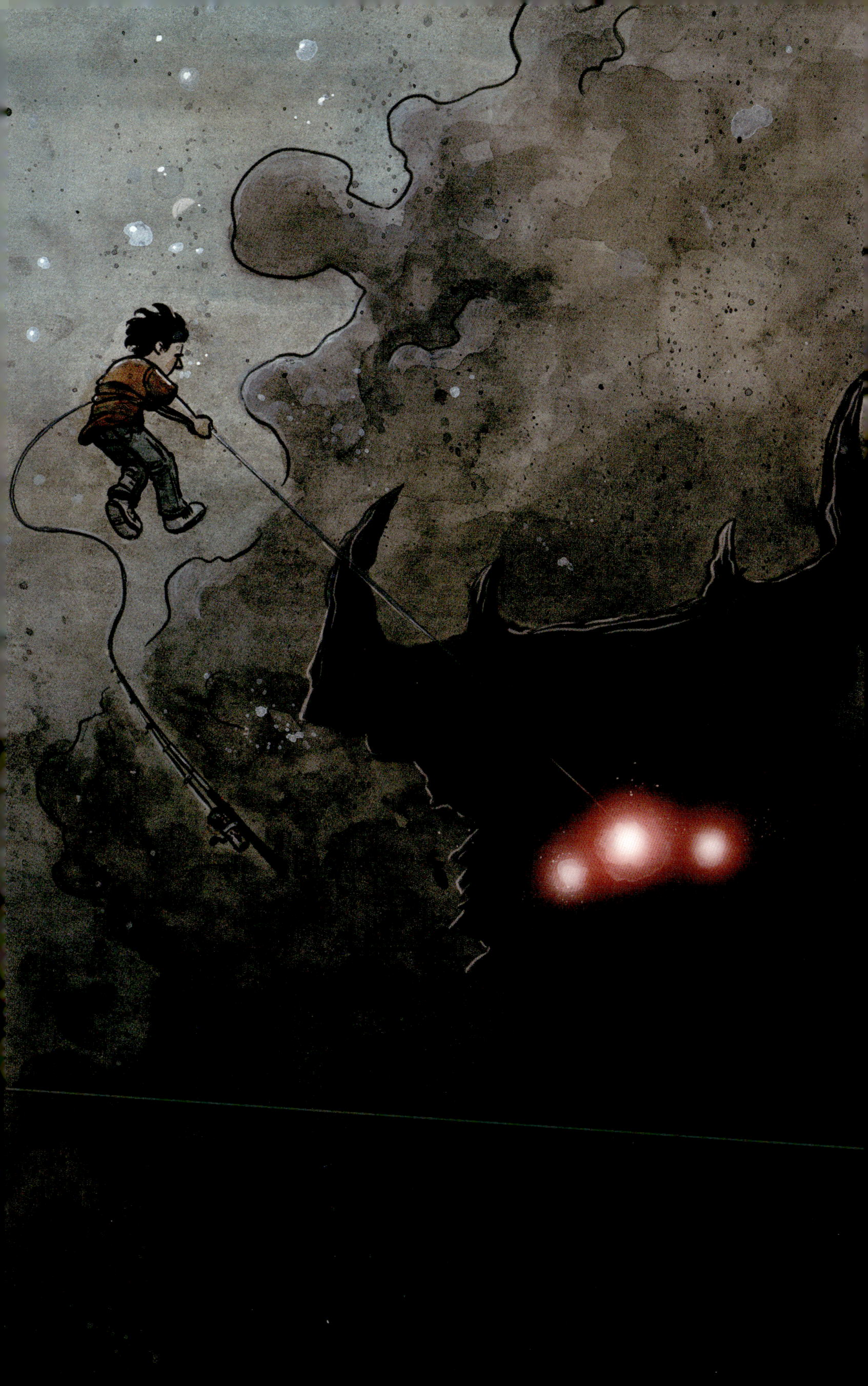

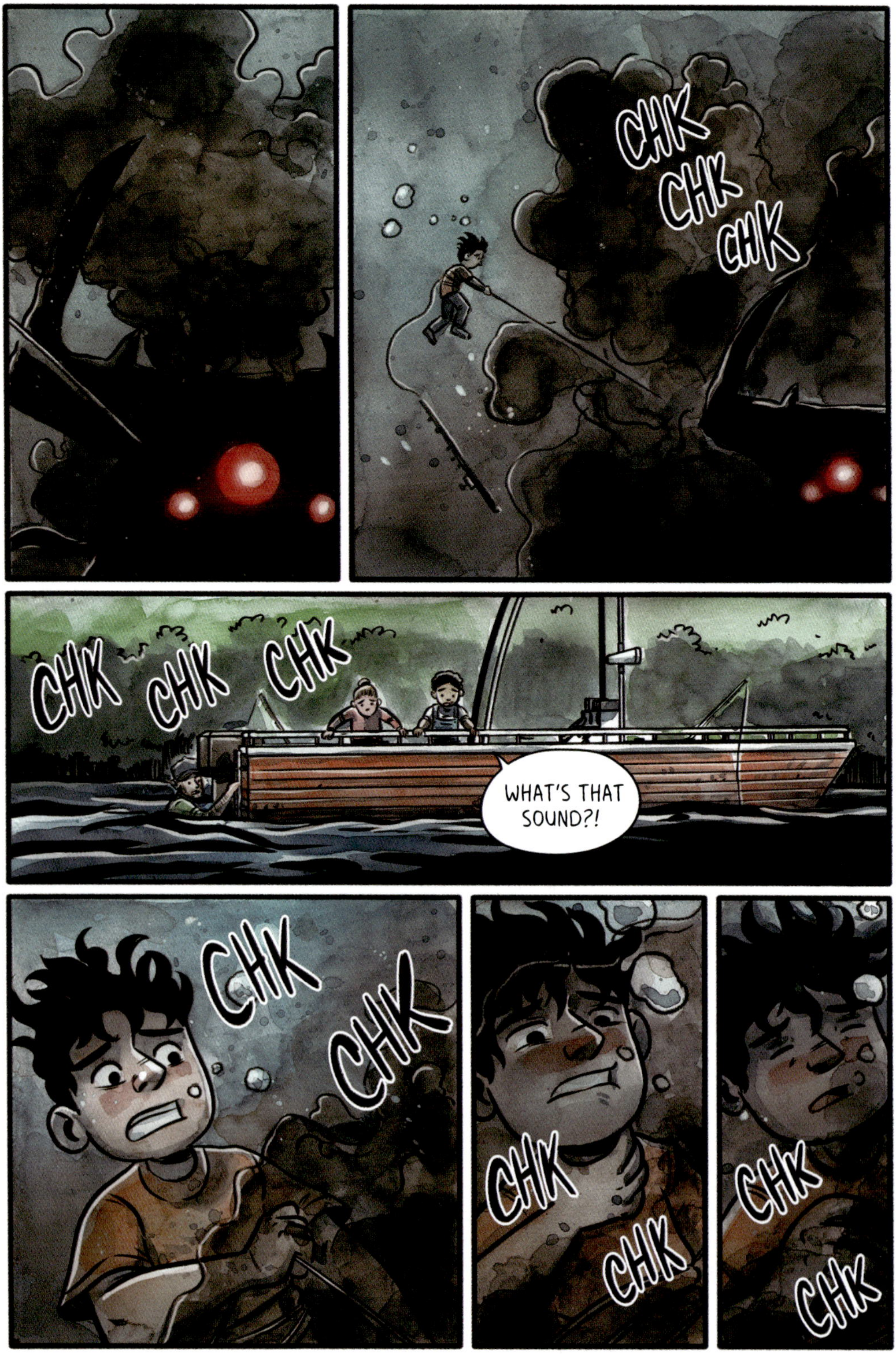
CHK
CHK
CHK
CHK
CHK
CHK
WHAT'S THAT SOUND?!
CHK
CHK
CHK
CHK
CHK
CHK

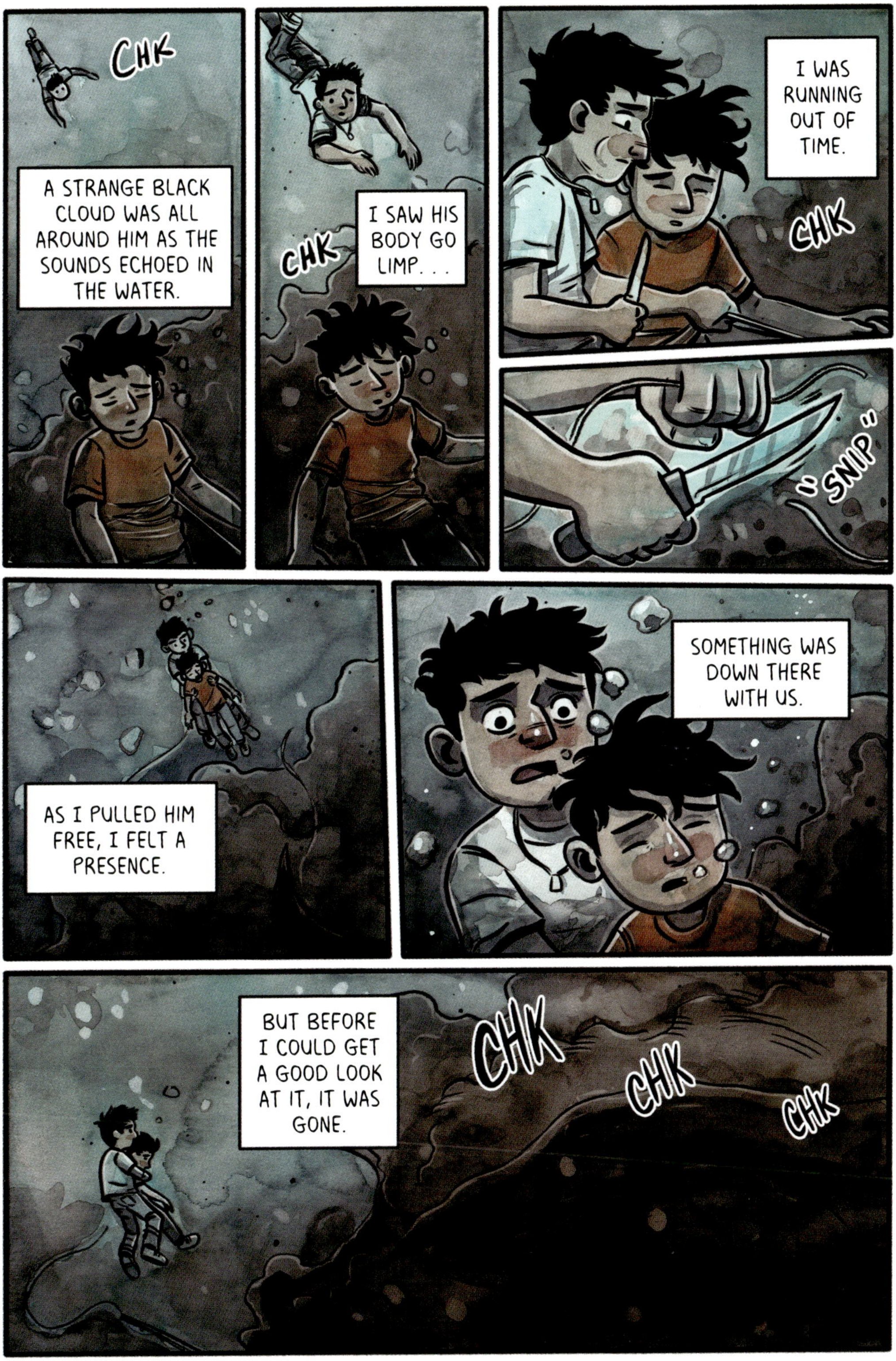
CHK
A STRANGE BLACK CLOUD WAS ALL AROUND HIM AS THE SOUNDS ECHOED IN THE WATER.
CHK
I SAW HIS BODY GO LIMP. . .
I WAS RUNNING OUT OF TIME.
CHK
"SNIP"
AS I PULLED HIM FREE, I FELT A PRESENCE.
SOMETHING WAS DOWN THERE WITH US.
BUT BEFORE I COULD GET A GOOD LOOK AT IT, IT WAS GONE.
CHK
CHK
CHK

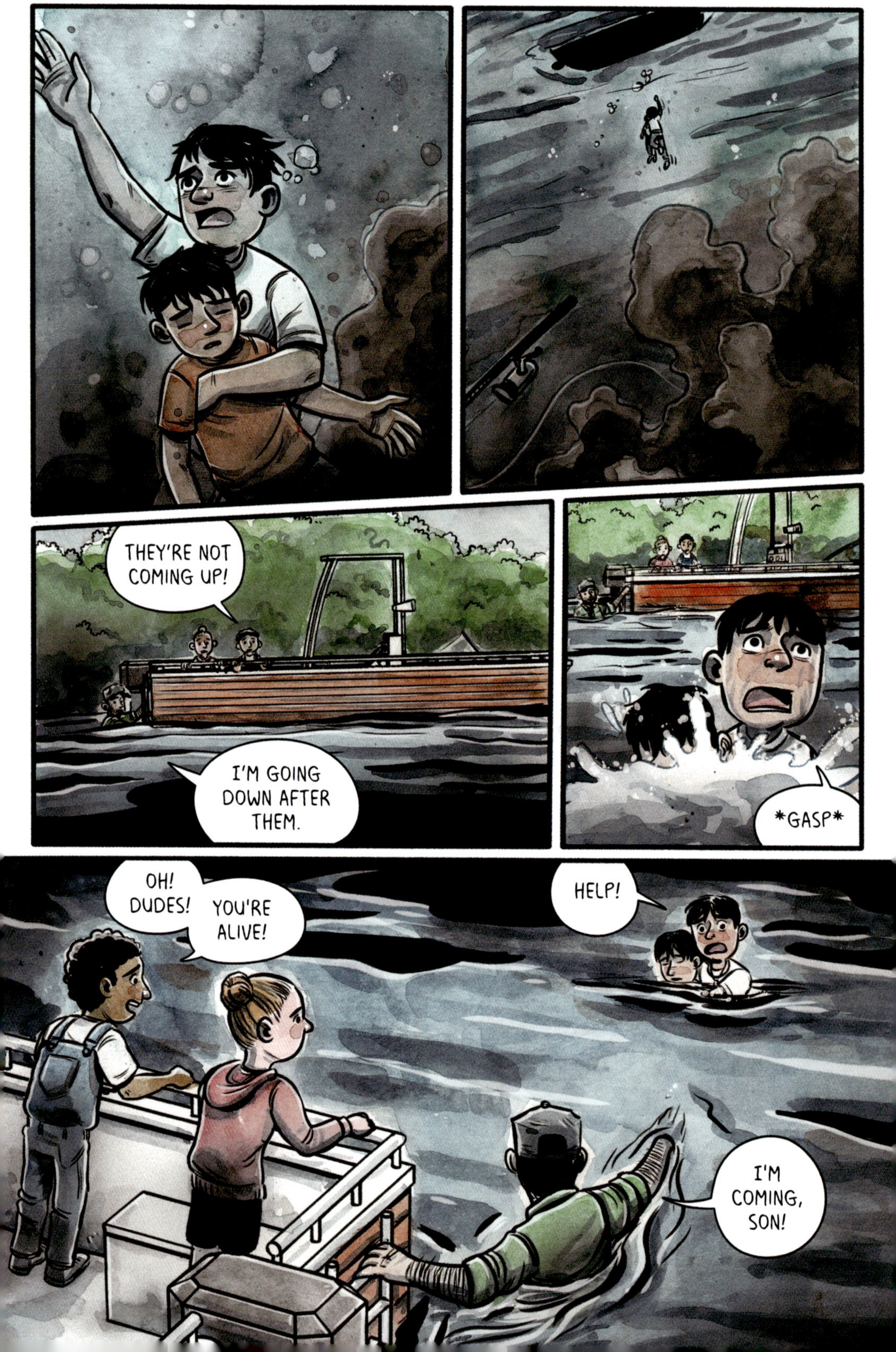
THEY'RE NOT COMING UP!
I'M GOING DOWN AFTER THEM.
GASP
OH! DUDES!
YOU'RE ALIVE!
HELP!
I'M COMING, SON!

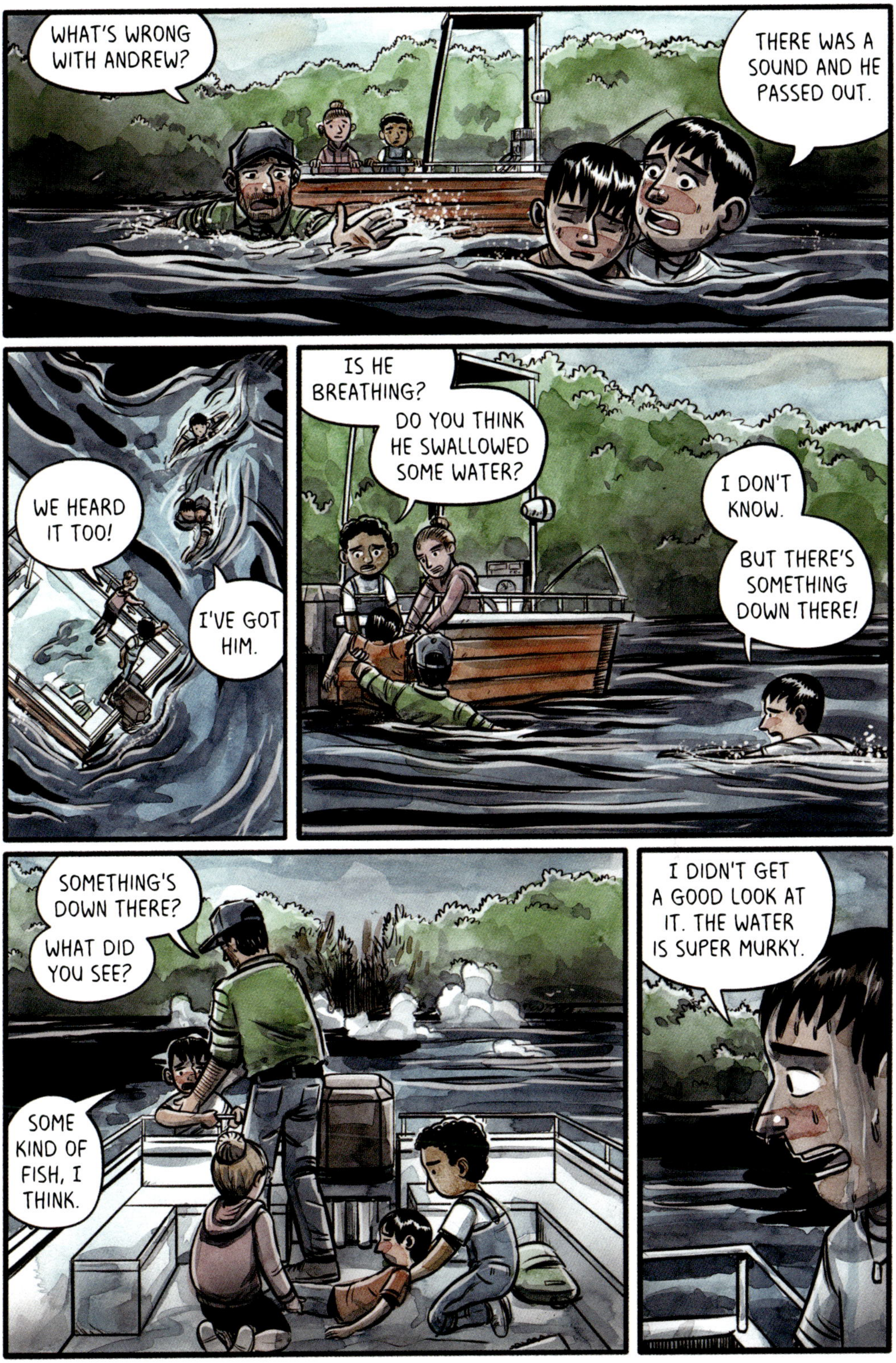
WHAT'S WRONG WITH ANDREW?
THERE WAS A SOUND AND HE PASSED OUT.
WE HEARD IT TOO!
I'VE GOT HIM.
IS HE BREATHING?
DO YOU THINK HE SWALLOWED SOME WATER?
I DON'T KNOW.
BUT THERE'S SOMETHING DOWN THERE!
SOMETHING'S DOWN THERE?
WHAT DID YOU SEE?
SOME KIND OF FISH, I THINK.
I DIDN'T GET A GOOD LOOK AT IT. THE WATER IS SUPER MURKY.

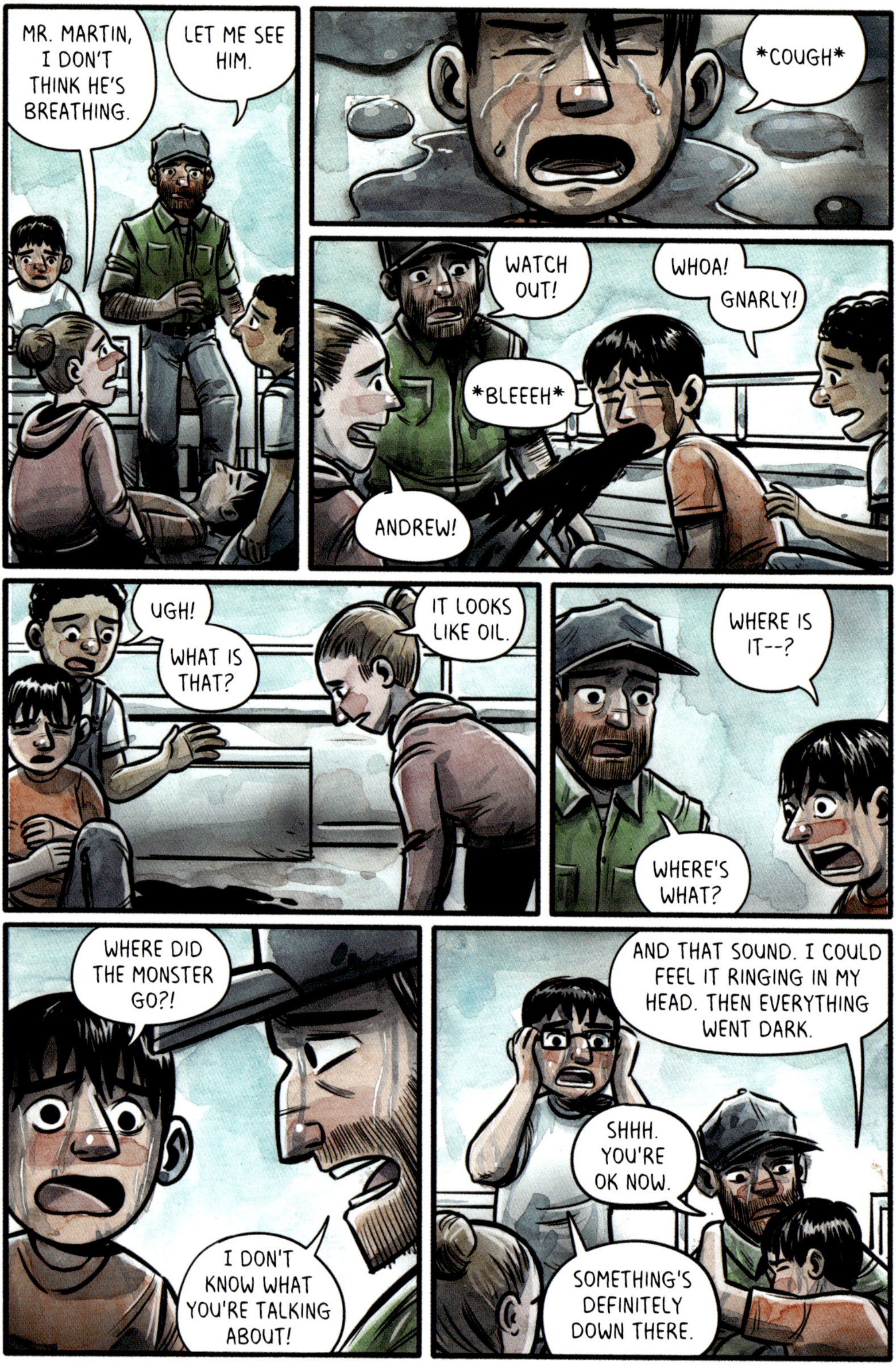
MR. MARTIN, I DON'T THINK HE'S BREATHING.
LET ME SEE HIM.
COUGH
WATCH OUT!
WHOA! GNARLY!
BLEEEH
ANDREW!
UGH!
WHAT IS THAT?
IT LOOKS LIKE OIL.
WHERE IS IT--?
WHERE'S WHAT?
WHERE DID THE MONSTER GO?!
I DON'T KNOW WHAT YOU'RE TALKING ABOUT!
AND THAT SOUND. I COULD FEEL IT RINGING IN MY HEAD. THEN EVERYTHING WENT DARK.
SHHH. YOU'RE OK NOW.
SOMETHING'S DEFINITELY DOWN THERE.

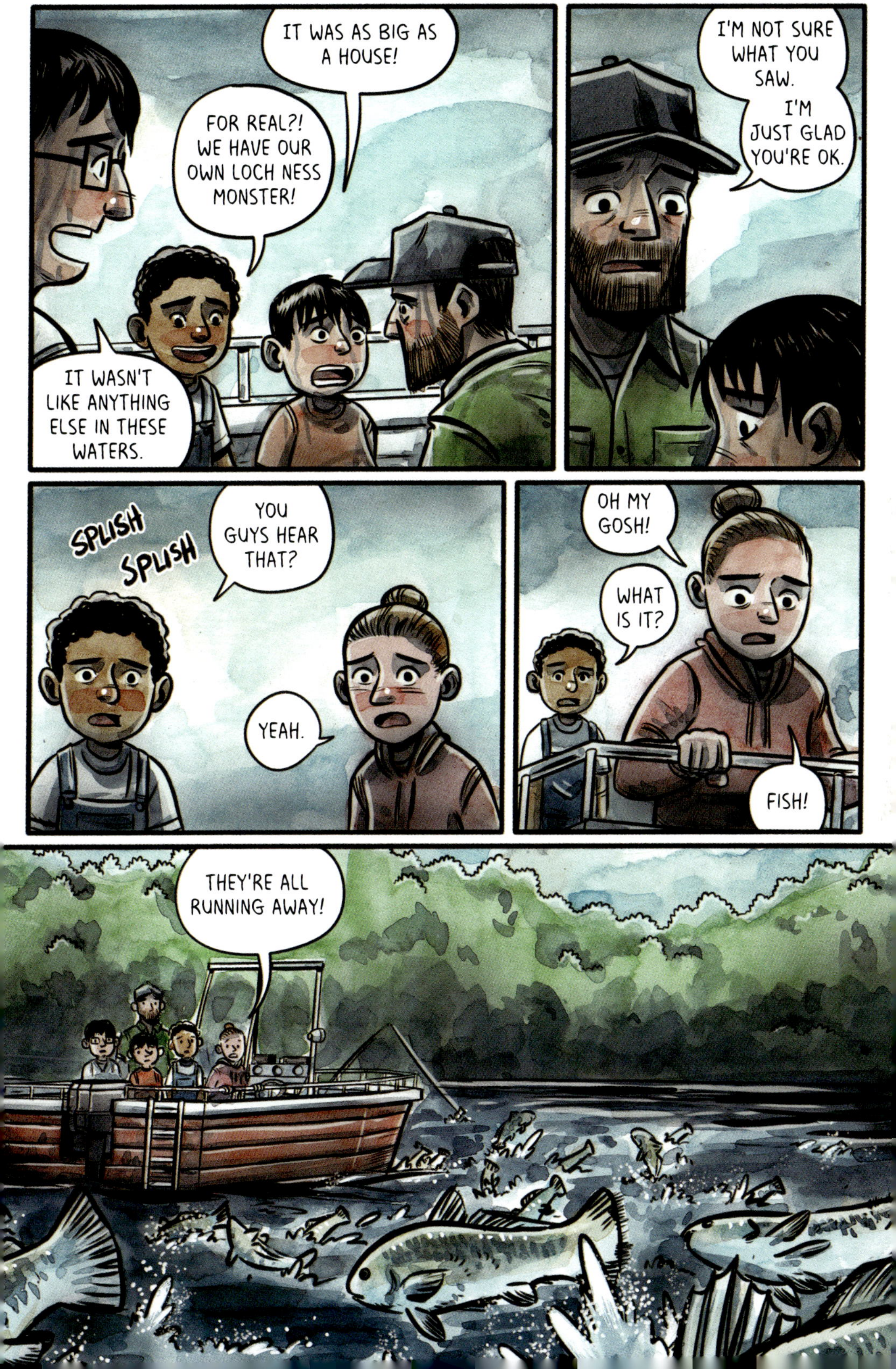
IT WAS AS BIG AS A HOUSE!
FOR REAL?! WE HAVE OUR OWN LOCH NESS MONSTER!
IT WASN'T LIKE ANYTHING ELSE IN THESE WATERS.
I'M NOT SURE WHAT YOU SAW.
I'M JUST GLAD YOU'RE OK.
SPLISH
SPLISH
YOU GUYS HEAR THAT?
YEAH.
OH MY GOSH!
WHAT IS IT?
FISH!
THEY'RE ALL RUNNING AWAY!

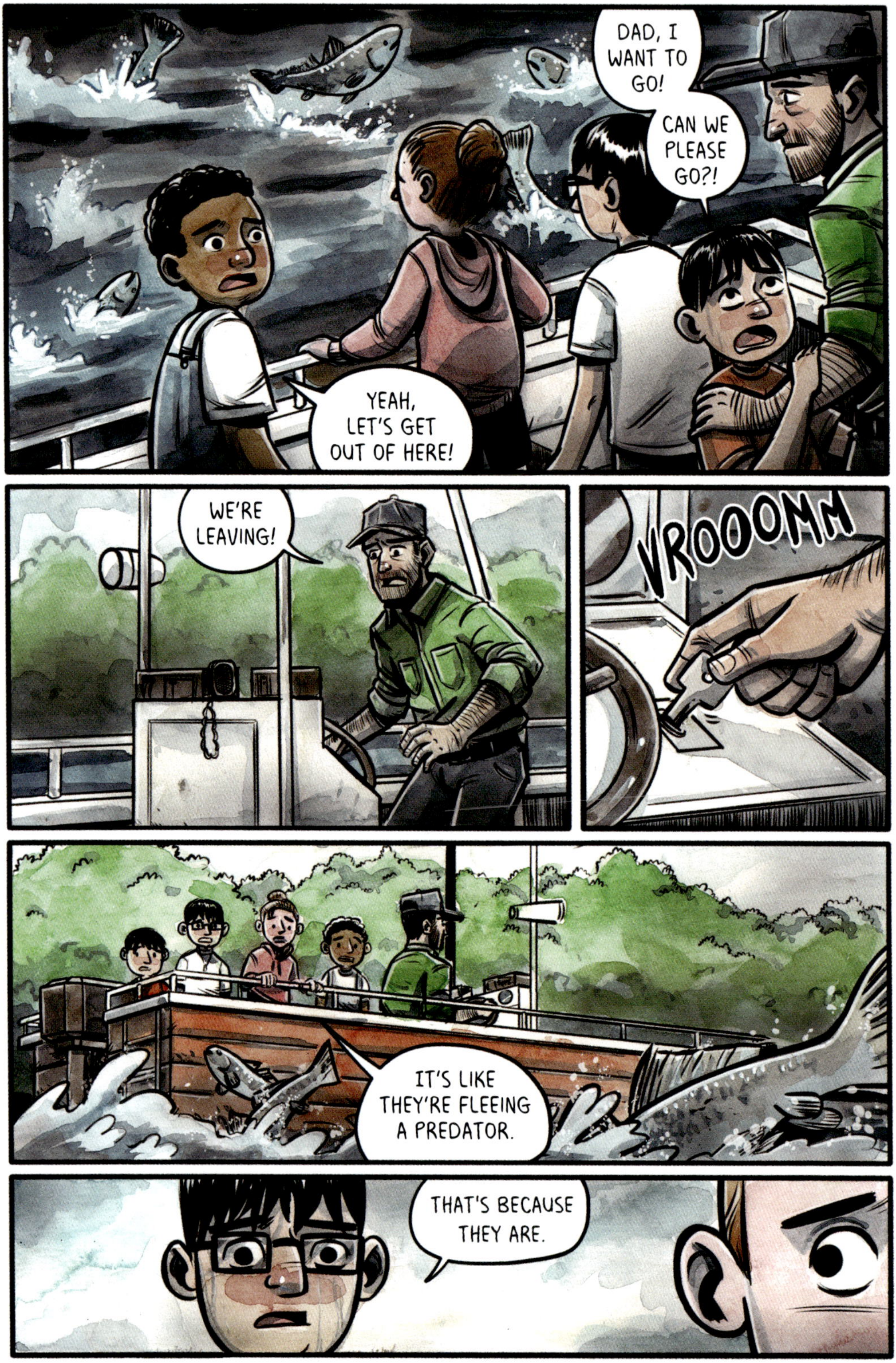
DAD, I WANT TO GO!
CAN WE PLEASE GO?!
YEAH, LET'S GET OUT OF HERE!
WE'RE LEAVING!
VROOOMM
IT'S LIKE THEY'RE FLEEING A PREDATOR.
THAT'S BECAUSE THEY ARE.

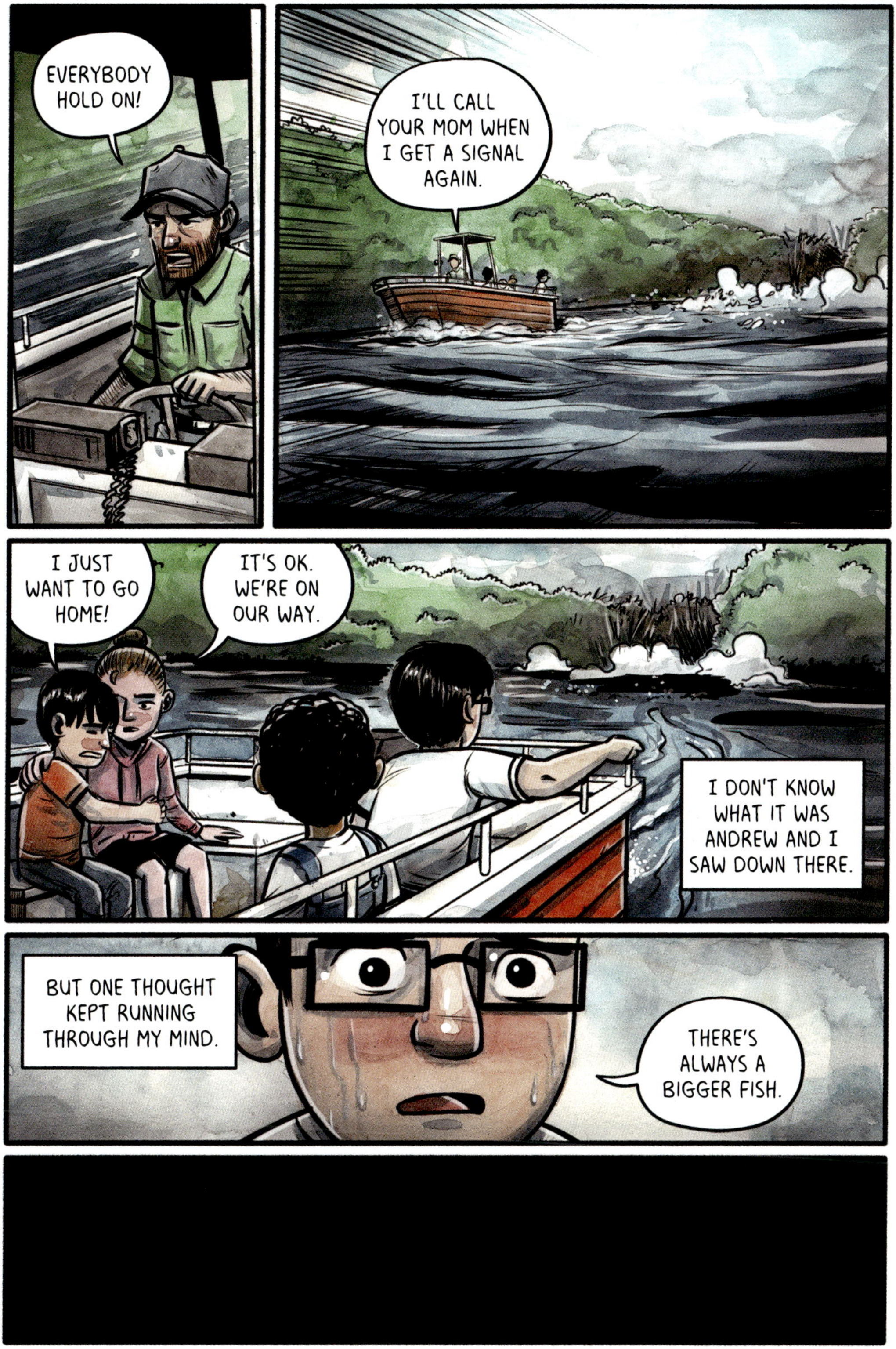
EVERYBODY HOLD ON!
I'LL CALL YOUR MOM WHEN I GET A SIGNAL AGAIN.
I JUST WANT TO GO HOME!
IT'S OK. WE'RE ON OUR WAY.
I DON'T KNOW WHAT IT WAS ANDREW AND I SAW DOWN THERE.
BUT ONE THOUGHT KEPT RUNNING THROUGH MY MIND.
THERE'S ALWAYS A BIGGER FISH.

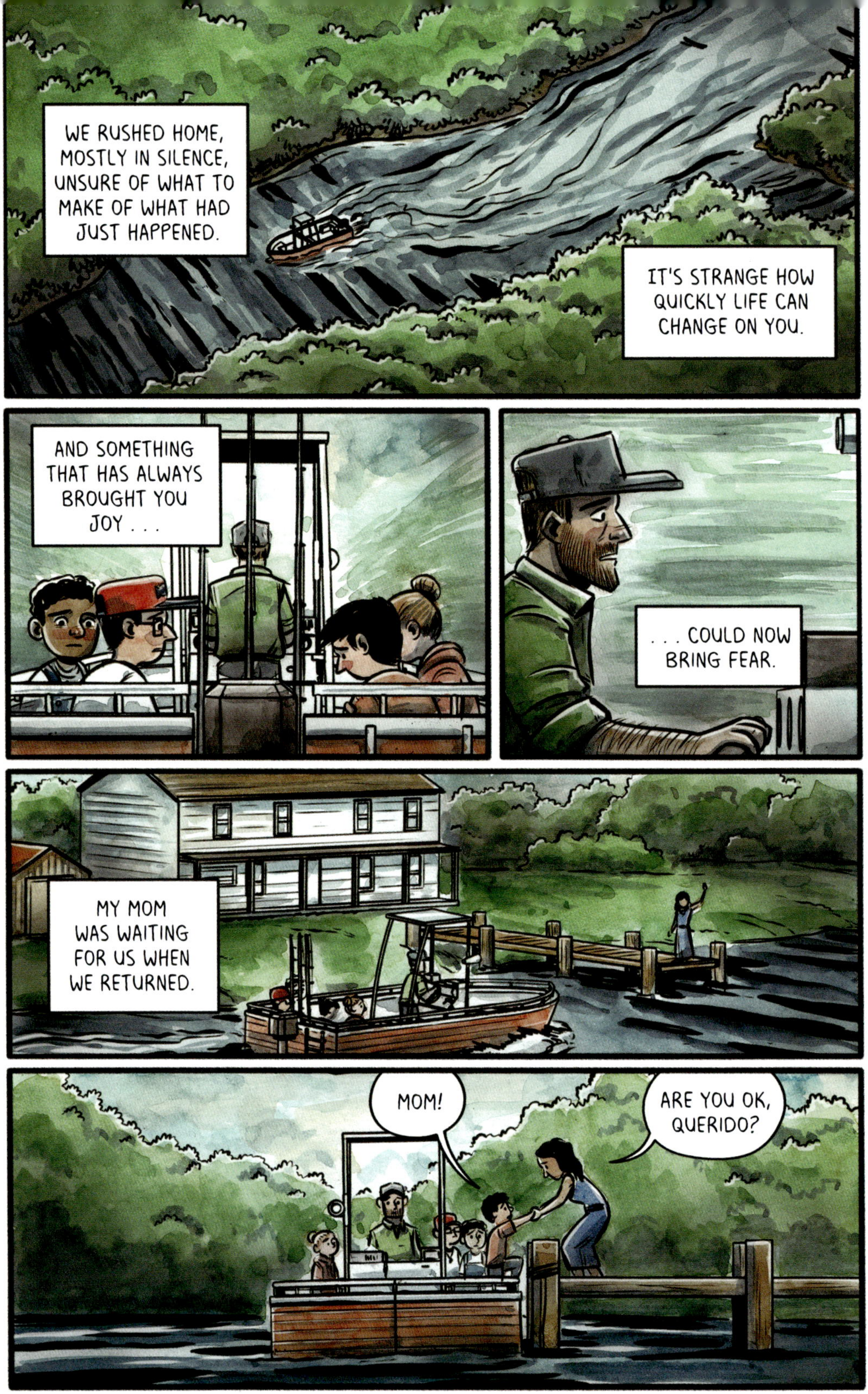
WE RUSHED HOME, MOSTLY IN SILENCE, UNSURE OF WHAT TO MAKE OF WHAT HAD JUST HAPPENED.
IT'S STRANGE HOW QUICKLY LIFE CAN CHANGE ON YOU.
AND SOMETHING THAT HAS ALWAYS BROUGHT YOU JOY . . .
. . . COULD NOW BRING FEAR.
MY MOM WAS WAITING FOR US WHEN WE RETURNED.
MOM!
ARE YOU OK, QUERIDO?

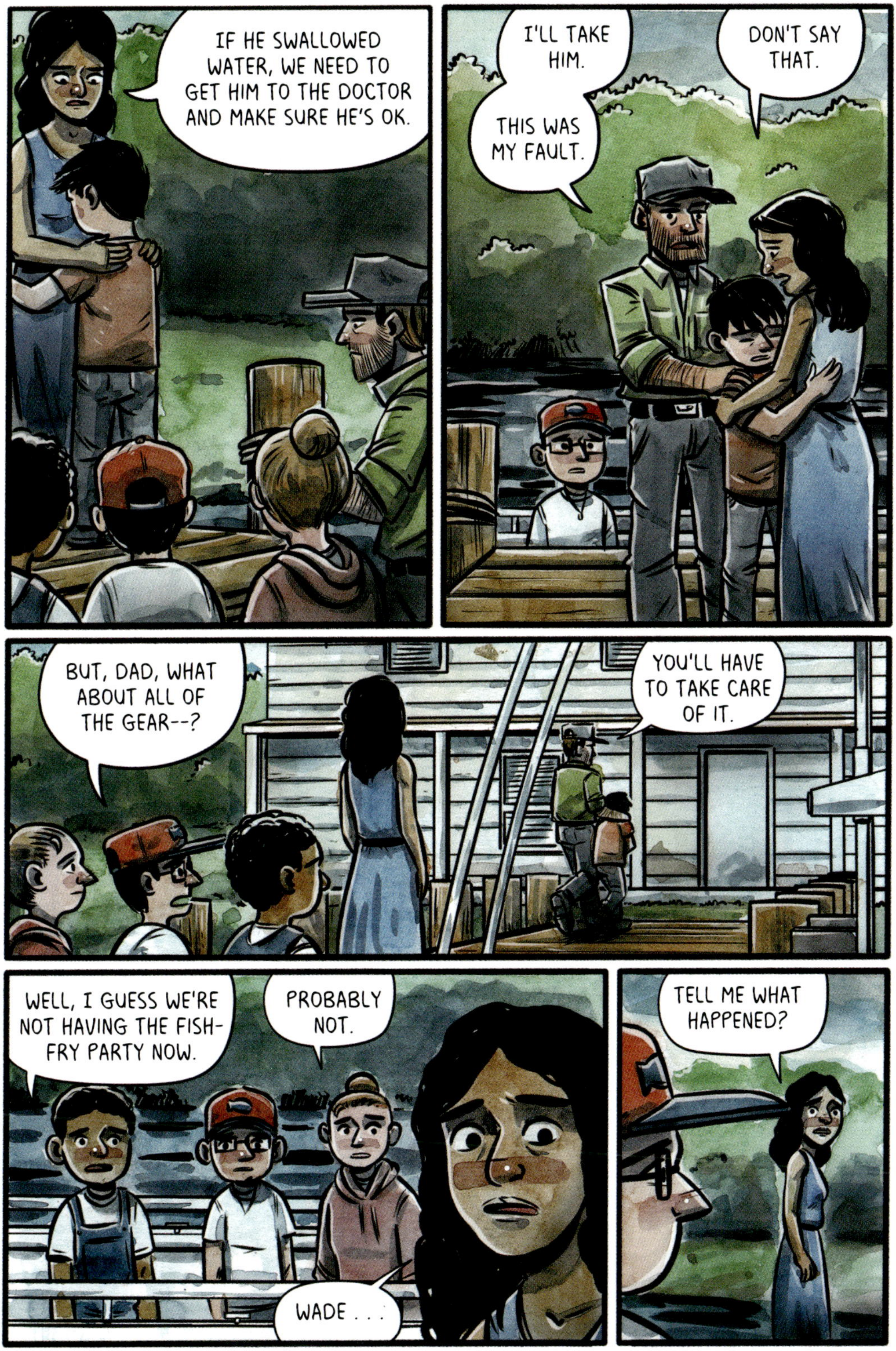
IF HE SWALLOWED WATER, WE NEED TO GET HIM TO THE DOCTOR AND MAKE SURE HE'S OK.
I'LL TAKE HIM.
THIS WAS MY FAULT.
DON'T SAY THAT.
BUT, DAD, WHAT ABOUT ALL OF THE GEAR--?
YOU'LL HAVE TO TAKE CARE OF IT.
WELL, I GUESS WE'RE NOT HAVING THE FISH-FRY PARTY NOW.
PROBABLY NOT.
WADE . . .
TELL ME WHAT HAPPENED?

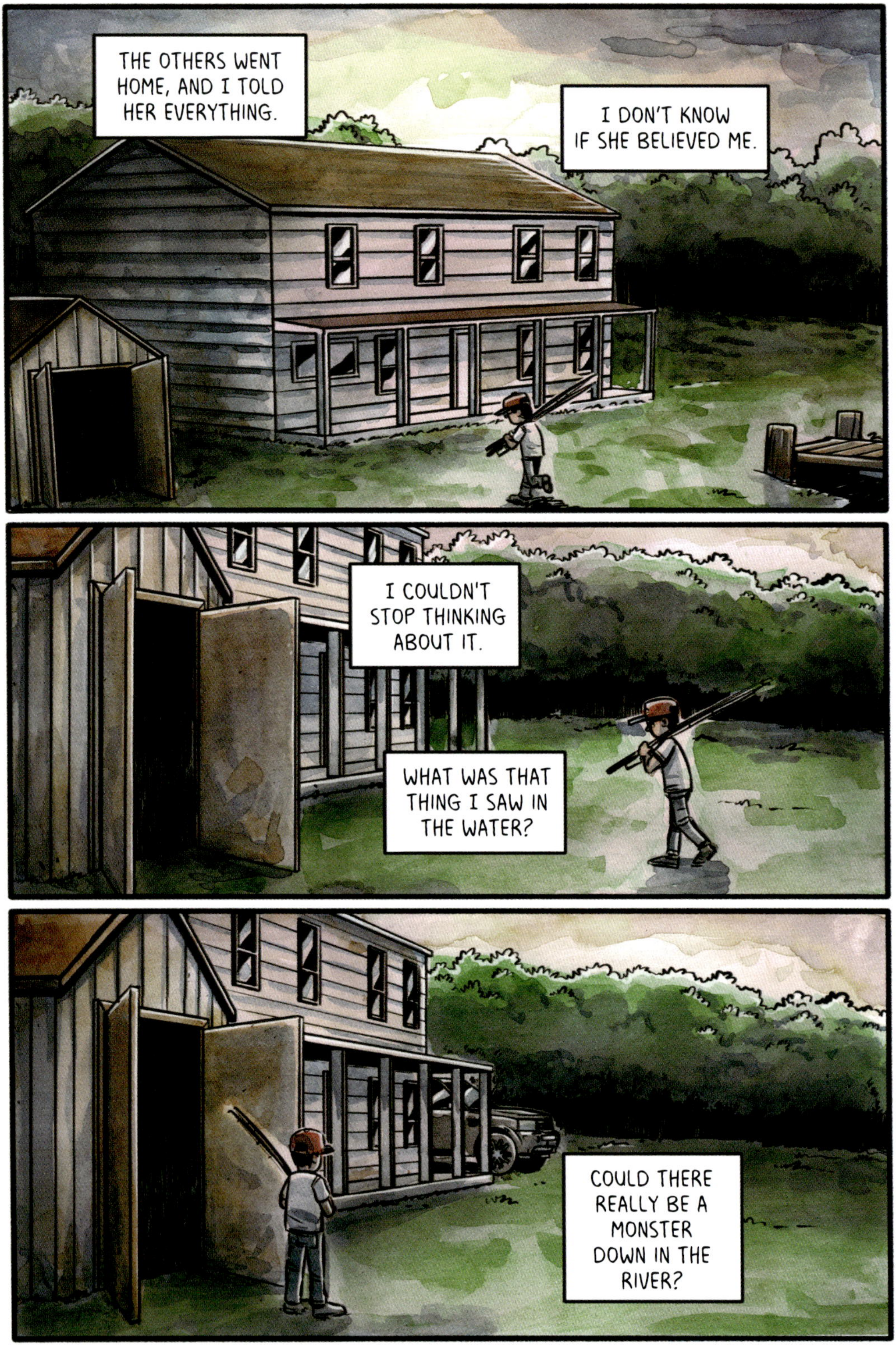
THE OTHERS WENT HOME, AND I TOLD HER EVERYTHING.
I DON'T KNOW IF SHE BELIEVED ME.
I COULDN'T STOP THINKING ABOUT IT.
WHAT WAS THAT THING I SAW IN THE WATER?
COULD THERE REALLY BE A MONSTER DOWN IN THE RIVER?

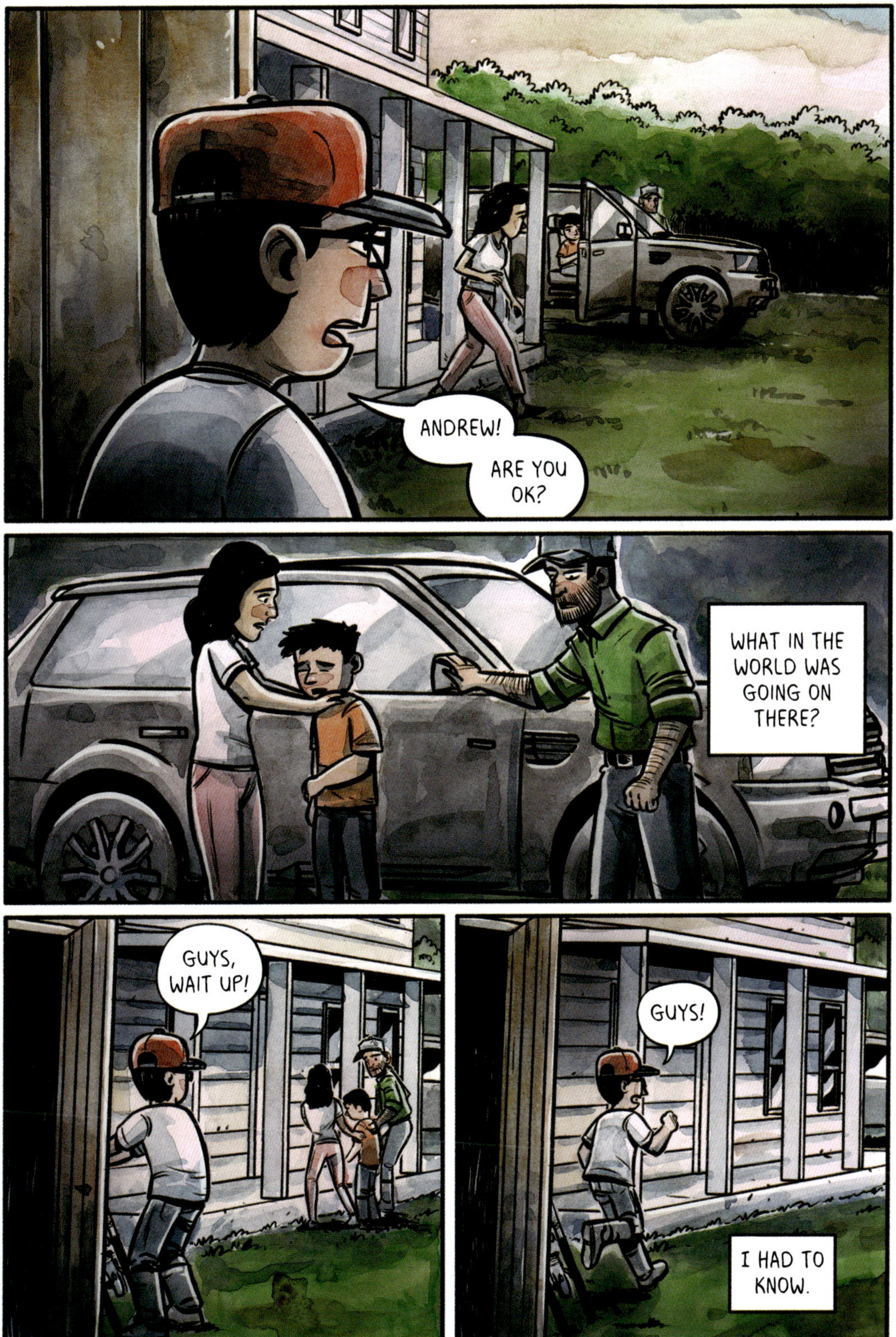
ANDREW!
ARE YOU OK?
WHAT IN THE WORLD WAS GOING ON THERE?
GUYS, WAIT UP!
GUYS!
I HAD TO KNOW.

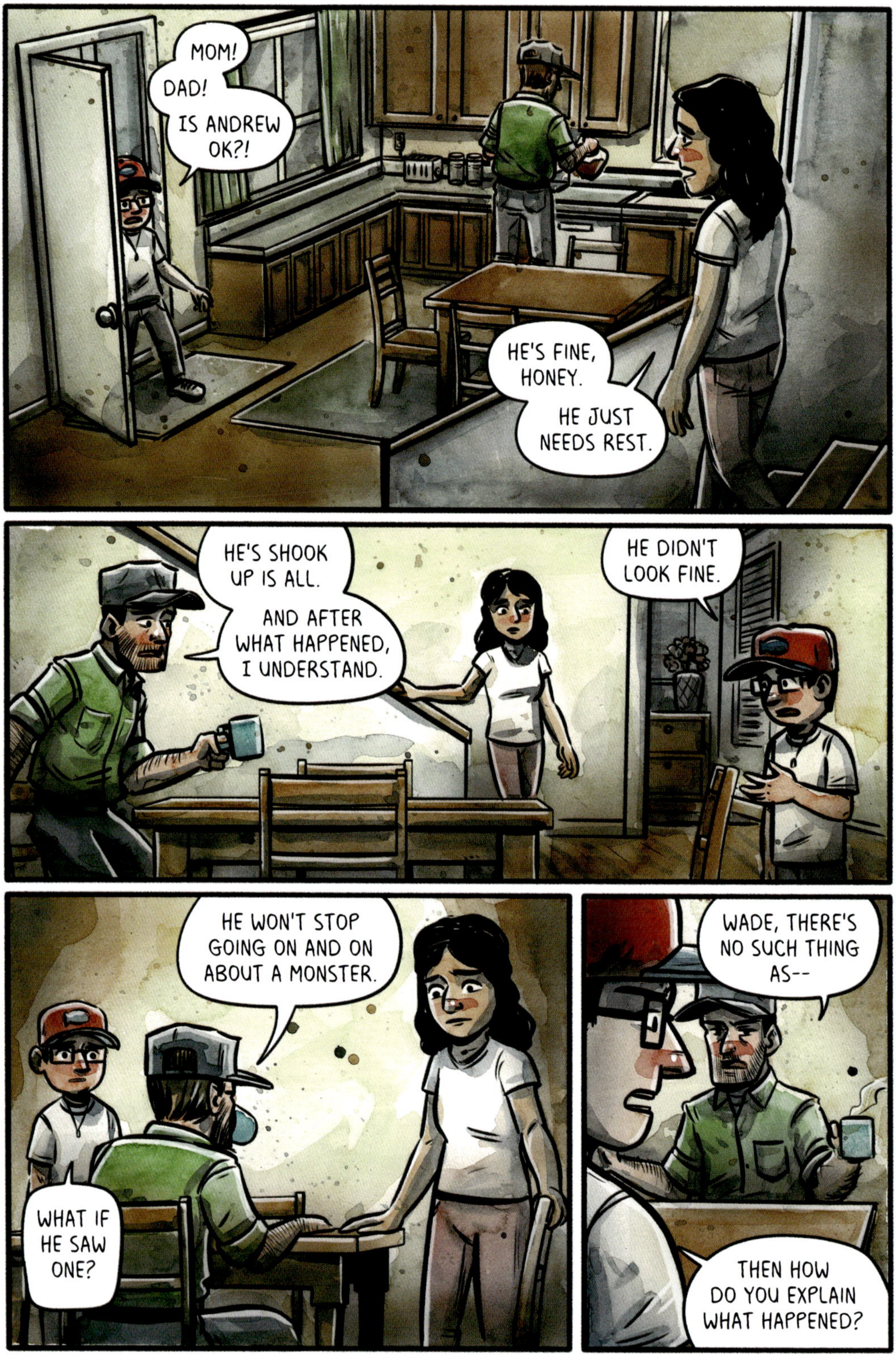
MOM!
DAD!
IS ANDREW OK?!
HE'S FINE, HONEY.
HE JUST NEEDS REST.
HE'S SHOOK UP IS ALL.
AND AFTER WHAT HAPPENED, I UNDERSTAND.
HE DIDN'T LOOK FINE.
HE WON'T STOP GOING ON AND ON ABOUT A MONSTER.
WHAT IF HE SAW ONE?
WADE, THERE'S NO SUCH THING AS--
THEN HOW DO YOU EXPLAIN WHAT HAPPENED?

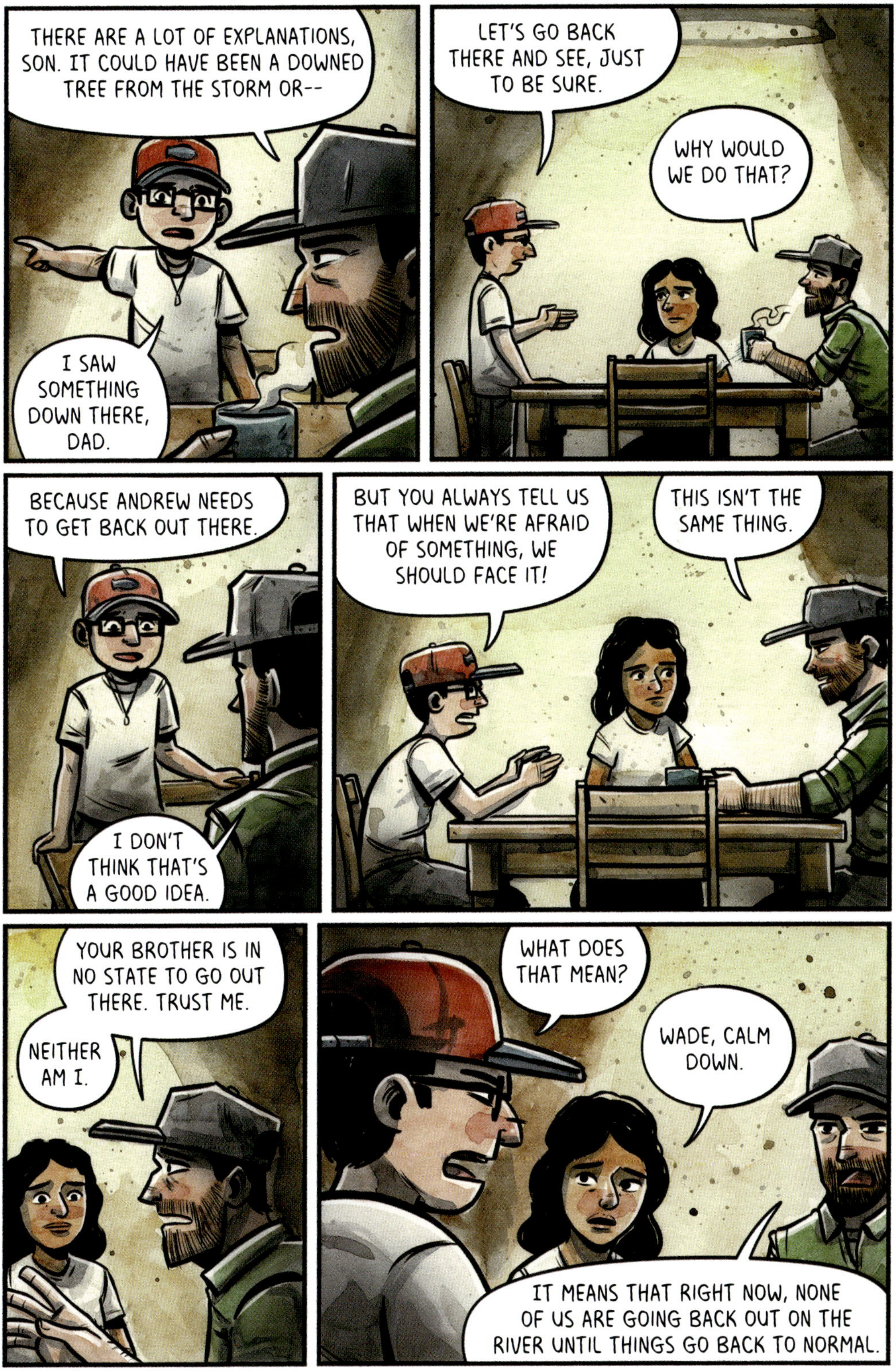
THERE ARE A LOT OF EXPLANATIONS, SON. IT COULD HAVE BEEN A DOWNED TREE FROM THE STORM OR--
I SAW SOMETHING DOWN THERE, DAD.
LET'S GO BACK THERE AND SEE, JUST TO BE SURE.
WHY WOULD WE DO THAT?
BECAUSE ANDREW NEEDS TO GET BACK OUT THERE.
I DON'T THINK THAT'S A GOOD IDEA.
BUT YOU ALWAYS TELL US THAT WHEN WE'RE AFRAID OF SOMETHING, WE SHOULD FACE IT!
THIS ISN'T THE SAME THING.
YOUR BROTHER IS IN NO STATE TO GO OUT THERE. TRUST ME.
NEITHER AM I.
WHAT DOES THAT MEAN?
WADE, CALM DOWN.
IT MEANS THAT RIGHT NOW, NONE OF US ARE GOING BACK OUT ON THE RIVER UNTIL THINGS GO BACK TO NORMAL.

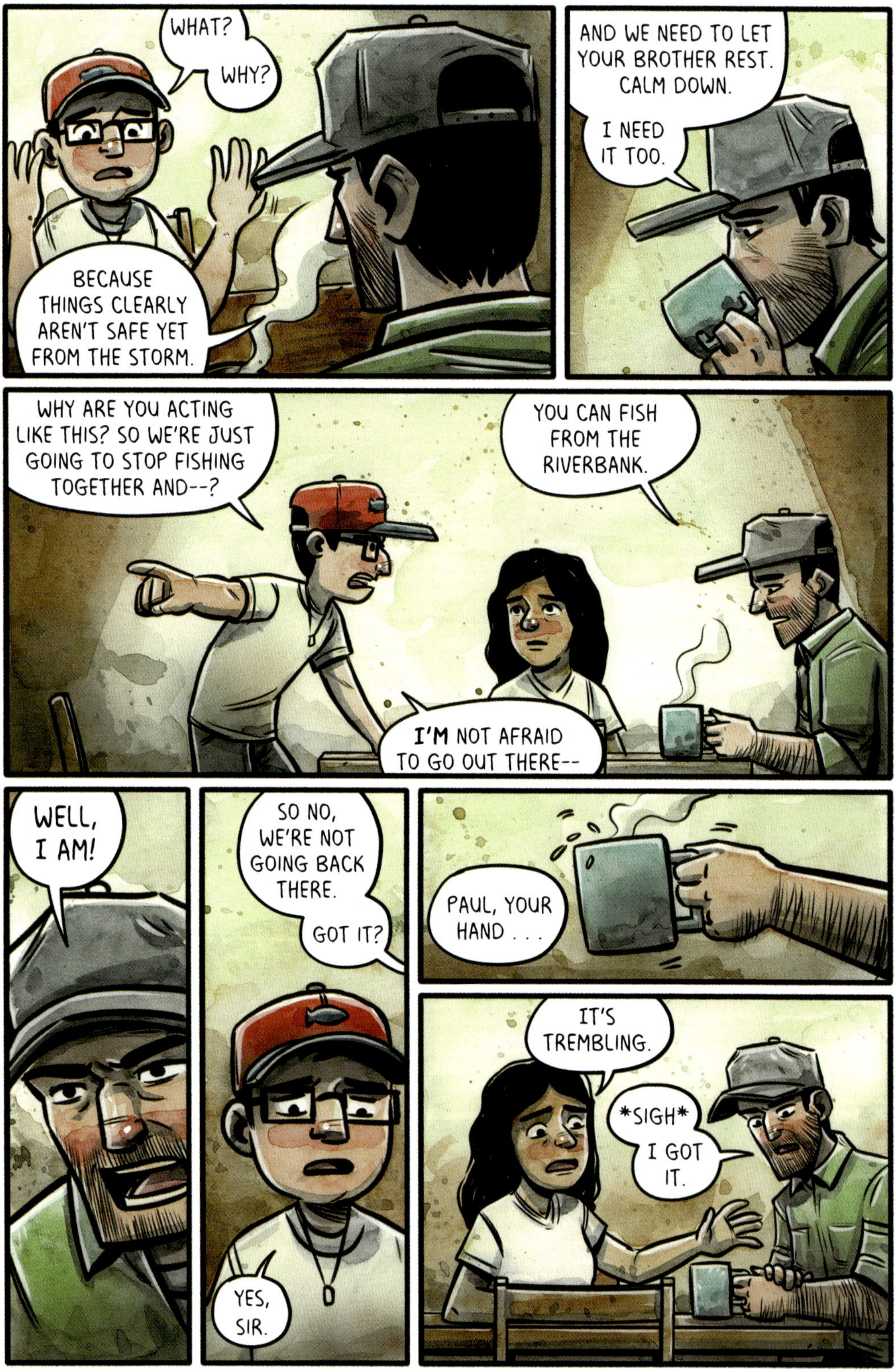
WHAT?
WHY?
BECAUSE THINGS CLEARLY AREN'T SAFE YET FROM THE STORM.
AND WE NEED TO LET YOUR BROTHER REST. CALM DOWN.
I NEED IT TOO.
WHY ARE YOU ACTING LIKE THIS? SO WE'RE JUST GOING TO STOP FISHING TOGETHER AND--?
YOU CAN FISH FROM THE RIVERBANK.
I'M NOT AFRAID TO GO OUT THERE--
WELL, I AM!
SO NO, WE'RE NOT GOING BACK THERE.
GOT IT?
YES, SIR.
PAUL, YOUR HAND . . .
IT'S TREMBLING.
SIGH
I GOT IT.

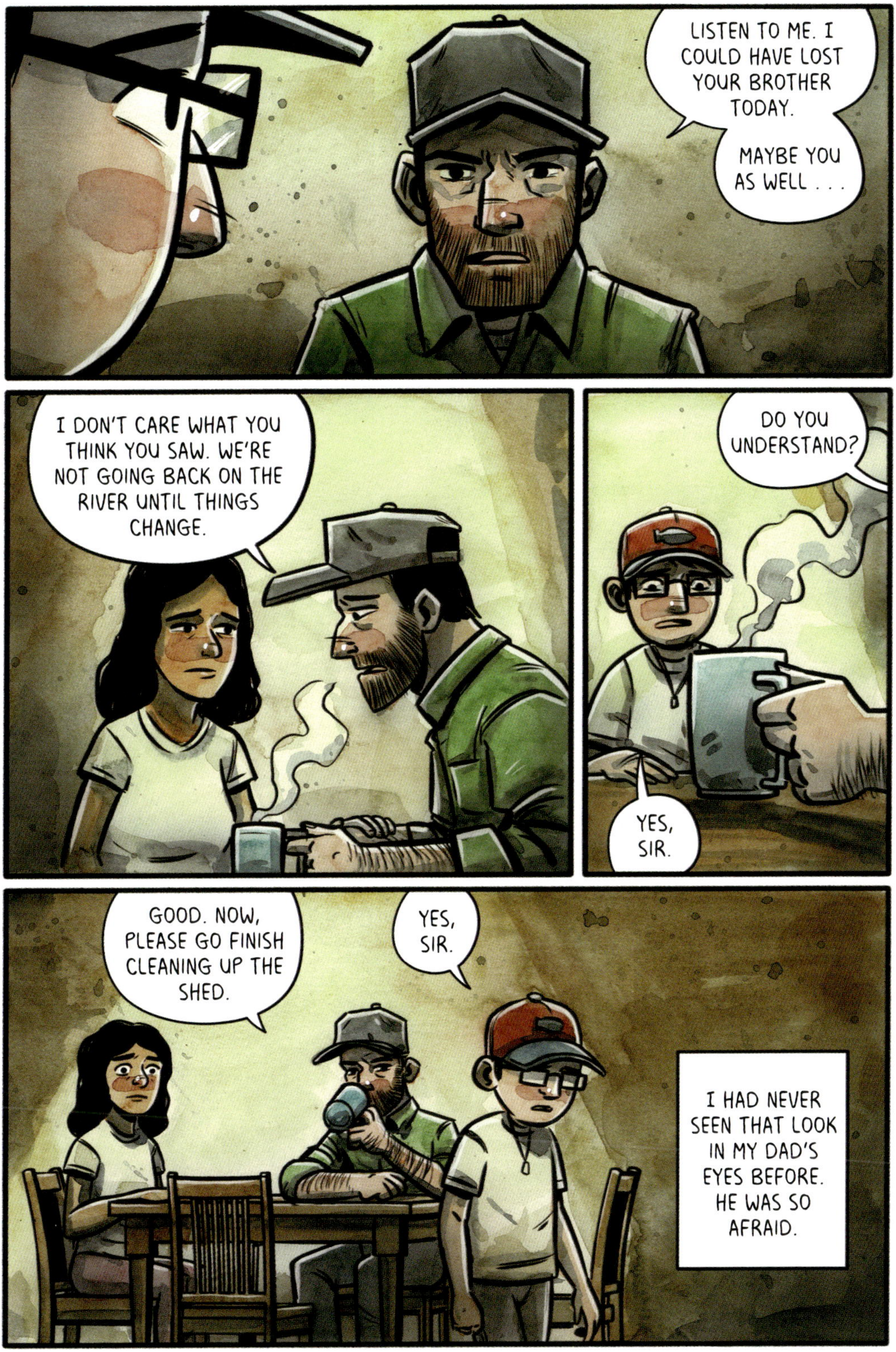
LISTEN TO ME. I COULD HAVE LOST YOUR BROTHER TODAY.
MAYBE YOU AS WELL . . .
I DON'T CARE WHAT YOU THINK YOU SAW. WE'RE NOT GOING BACK ON THE RIVER UNTIL THINGS CHANGE.
DO YOU UNDERSTAND?
YES, SIR.
GOOD. NOW, PLEASE GO FINISH CLEANING UP THE SHED.
YES, SIR.
I HAD NEVER SEEN THAT LOOK IN MY DAD'S EYES BEFORE. HE WAS SO AFRAID.

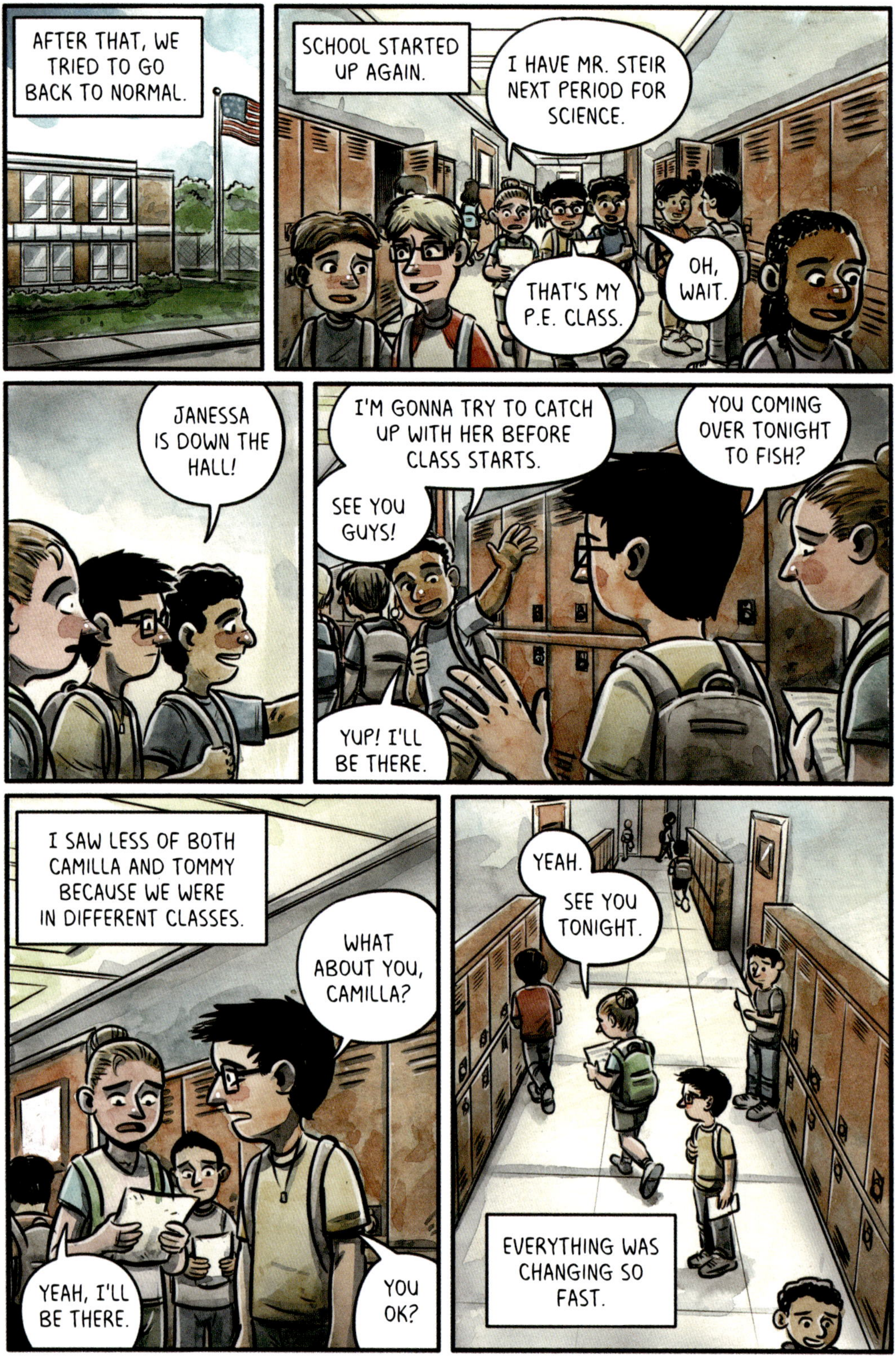
AFTER THAT, WE TRIED TO GO BACK TO NORMAL.
SCHOOL STARTED UP AGAIN.
I HAVE MR. STEIR NEXT PERIOD FOR SCIENCE.
THAT'S MY P.E. CLASS.
OH, WAIT.
JANESSA IS DOWN THE HALL!
I'M GONNA TRY TO CATCH UP WITH HER BEFORE CLASS STARTS.
SEE YOU GUYS!
YOU COMING OVER TONIGHT TO FISH?
YUP! I'LL BE THERE.
I SAW LESS OF BOTH CAMILLA AND TOMMY BECAUSE WE WERE IN DIFFERENT CLASSES.
WHAT ABOUT YOU, CAMILLA?
YEAH, I'LL BE THERE.
YOU OK?
YEAH.
SEE YOU TONIGHT.
EVERYTHING WAS CHANGING SO FAST.

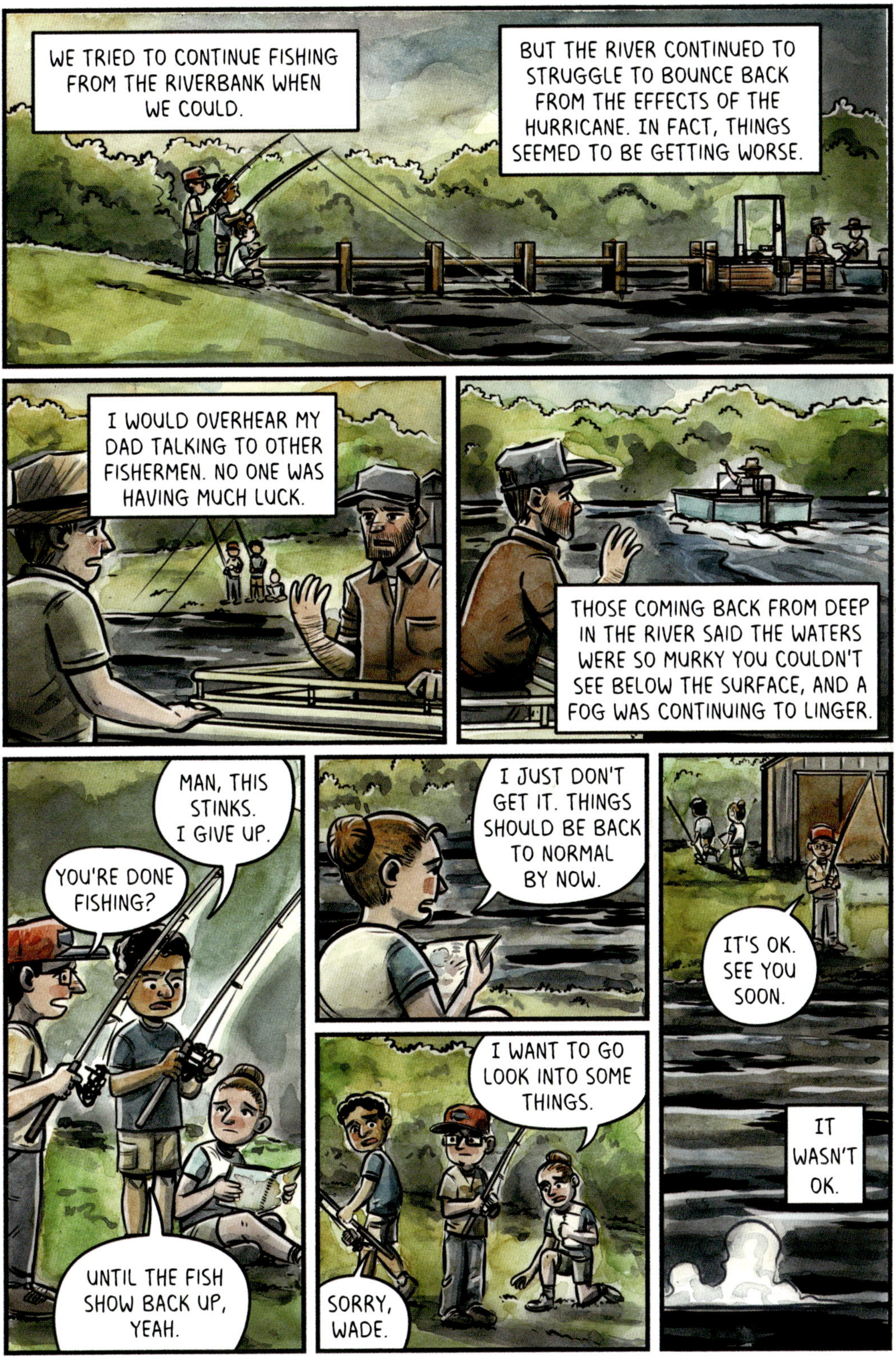
WE TRIED TO CONTINUE FISHING FROM THE RIVERBANK WHEN WE COULD.
BUT THE RIVER CONTINUED TO STRUGGLE TO BOUNCE BACK FROM THE EFFECTS OF THE HURRICANE. IN FACT, THINGS SEEMED TO BE GETTING WORSE.
I WOULD OVERHEAR MY DAD TALKING TO OTHER FISHERMEN. NO ONE WAS HAVING MUCH LUCK.
THOSE COMING BACK FROM DEEP IN THE RIVER SAID THE WATERS WERE SO MURKY YOU COULDN'T SEE BELOW THE SURFACE, AND A FOG WAS CONTINUING TO LINGER.
MAN, THIS STINKS. I GIVE UP.
YOU'RE DONE FISHING?
UNTIL THE FISH SHOW BACK UP, YEAH.
I JUST DON'T GET IT. THINGS SHOULD BE BACK TO NORMAL BY NOW.
I WANT TO GO LOOK INTO SOME THINGS.
SORRY, WADE.
IT'S OK. SEE YOU SOON.
IT WASN'T OK.

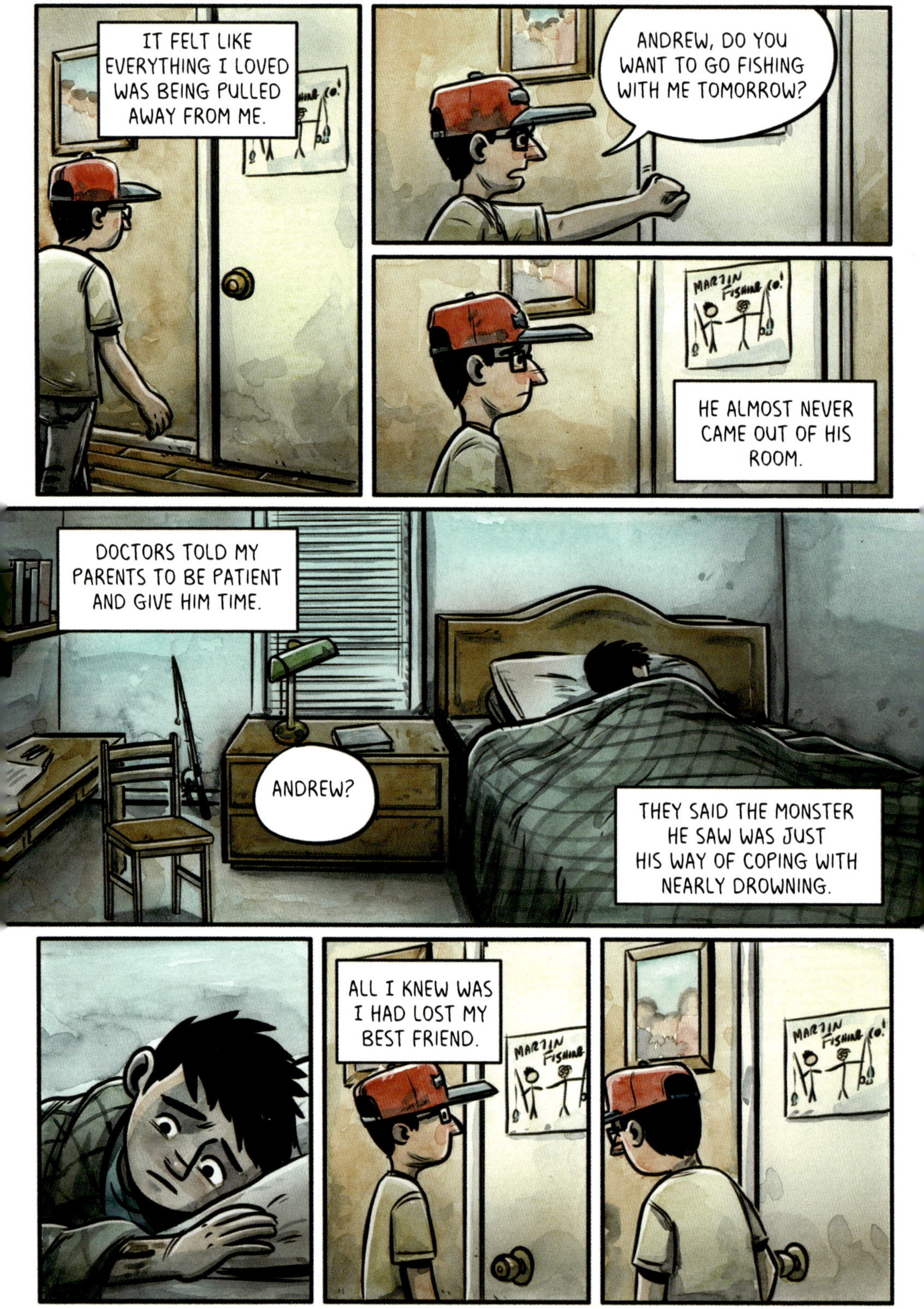
IT FELT LIKE EVERYTHING I LOVED WAS BEING PULLED AWAY FROM ME.
ANDREW, DO YOU WANT TO GO FISHING WITH ME TOMORROW?
MARTIN FISHING CO.!
HE ALMOST NEVER CAME OUT OF HIS ROOM.
DOCTORS TOLD MY PARENTS TO BE PATIENT AND GIVE HIM TIME.
ANDREW?
THEY SAID THE MONSTER HE SAW WAS JUST HIS WAY OF COPING WITH NEARLY DROWNING.
ALL I KNEW WAS I HAD LOST MY BEST FRIEND.
MARTIN FISHING
MARTIN FISHING CO.!

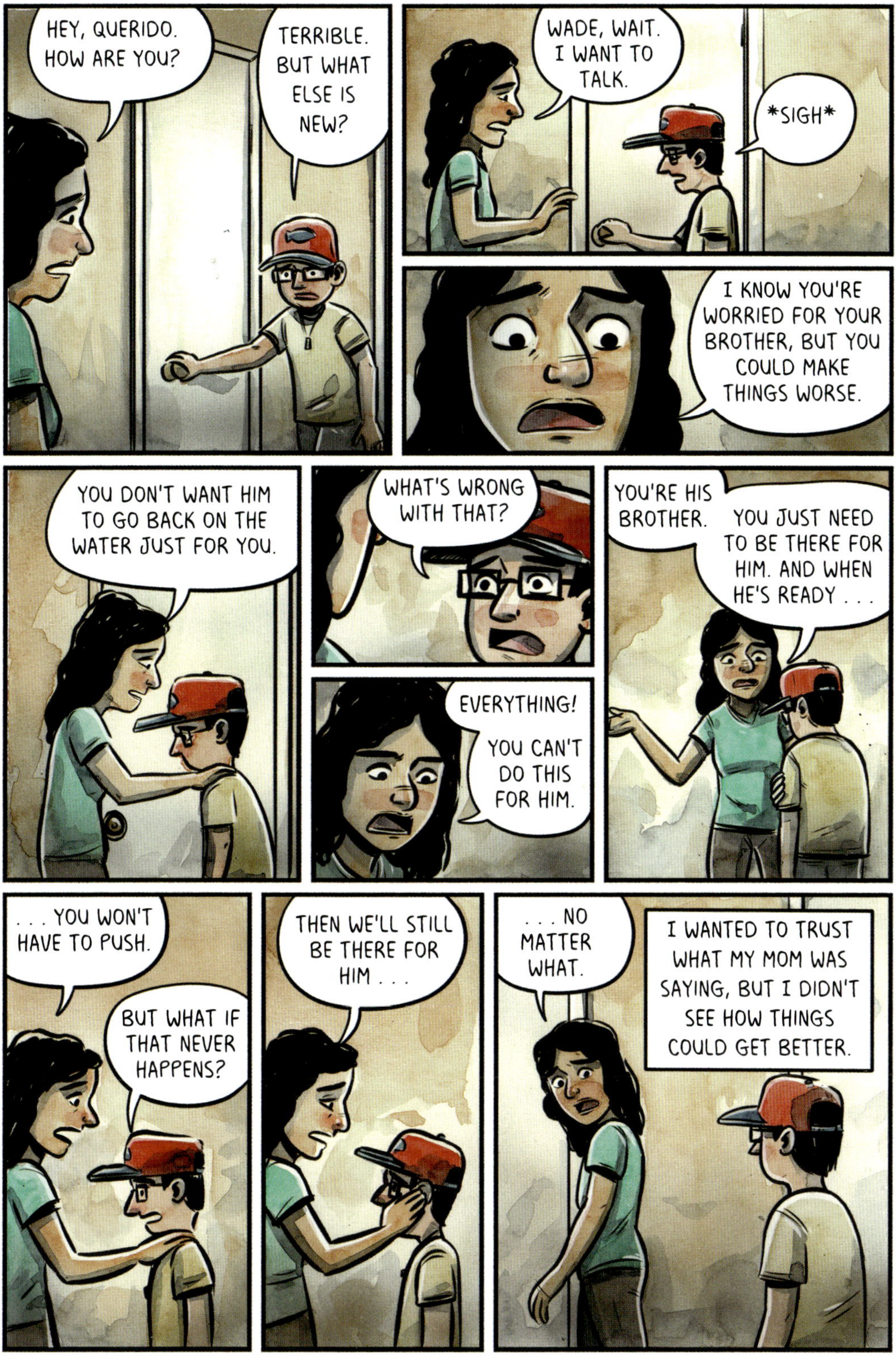
HEY, QUERIDO. HOW ARE YOU?
TERRIBLE. BUT WHAT ELSE IS NEW?
WADE, WAIT. I WANT TO TALK.
SIGH
I KNOW YOU'RE WORRIED FOR YOUR BROTHER, BUT YOU COULD MAKE THINGS WORSE.
YOU DON'T WANT HIM TO GO BACK ON THE WATER JUST FOR YOU.
WHAT'S WRONG WITH THAT?
EVERYTHING!
YOU CAN'T DO THIS FOR HIM.
YOU'RE HIS BROTHER.
YOU JUST NEED TO BE THERE FOR HIM. AND WHEN HE'S READY . . .
. . . YOU WON'T HAVE TO PUSH.
BUT WHAT IF THAT NEVER HAPPENS?
THEN WE'LL STILL BE THERE FOR HIM . . .
. . . NO MATTER WHAT.
I WANTED TO TRUST WHAT MY MOM WAS SAYING, BUT I DIDN'T SEE HOW THINGS COULD GET BETTER.

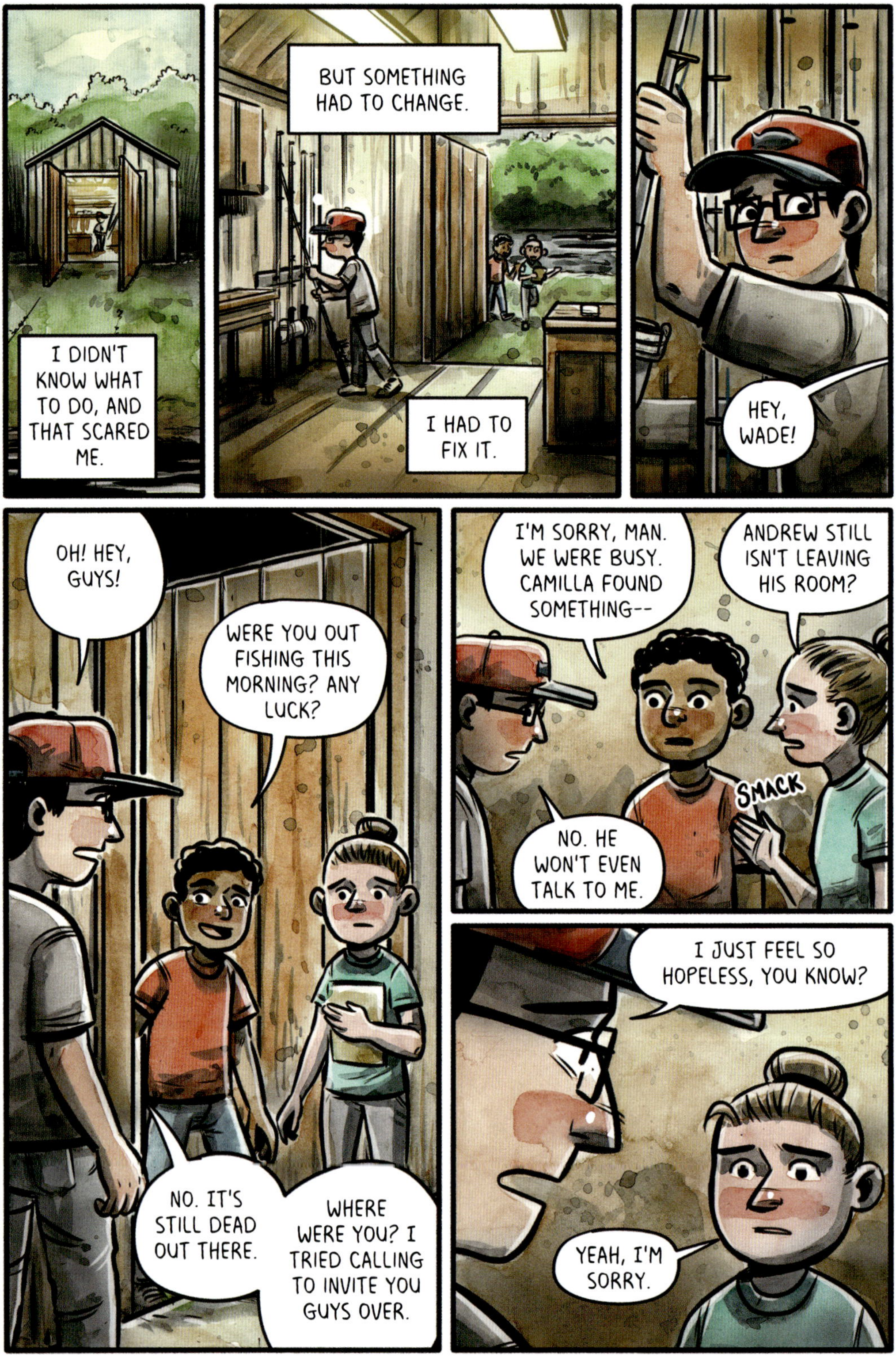
I DIDN'T KNOW WHAT TO DO, AND THAT SCARED ME.
BUT SOMETHING HAD TO CHANGE.
I HAD TO FIX IT.
HEY, WADE!
OH! HEY, GUYS!
WERE YOU OUT FISHING THIS MORNING? ANY LUCK?
NO. IT'S STILL DEAD OUT THERE.
WHERE WERE YOU? I TRIED CALLING TO INVITE YOU GUYS OVER.
I'M SORRY, MAN. WE WERE BUSY. CAMILLA FOUND SOMETHING--
ANDREW STILL ISN'T LEAVING HIS ROOM?
SMACK
NO. HE WON'T EVEN TALK TO ME.
I JUST FEEL SO HOPELESS, YOU KNOW?
YEAH, I'M SORRY.

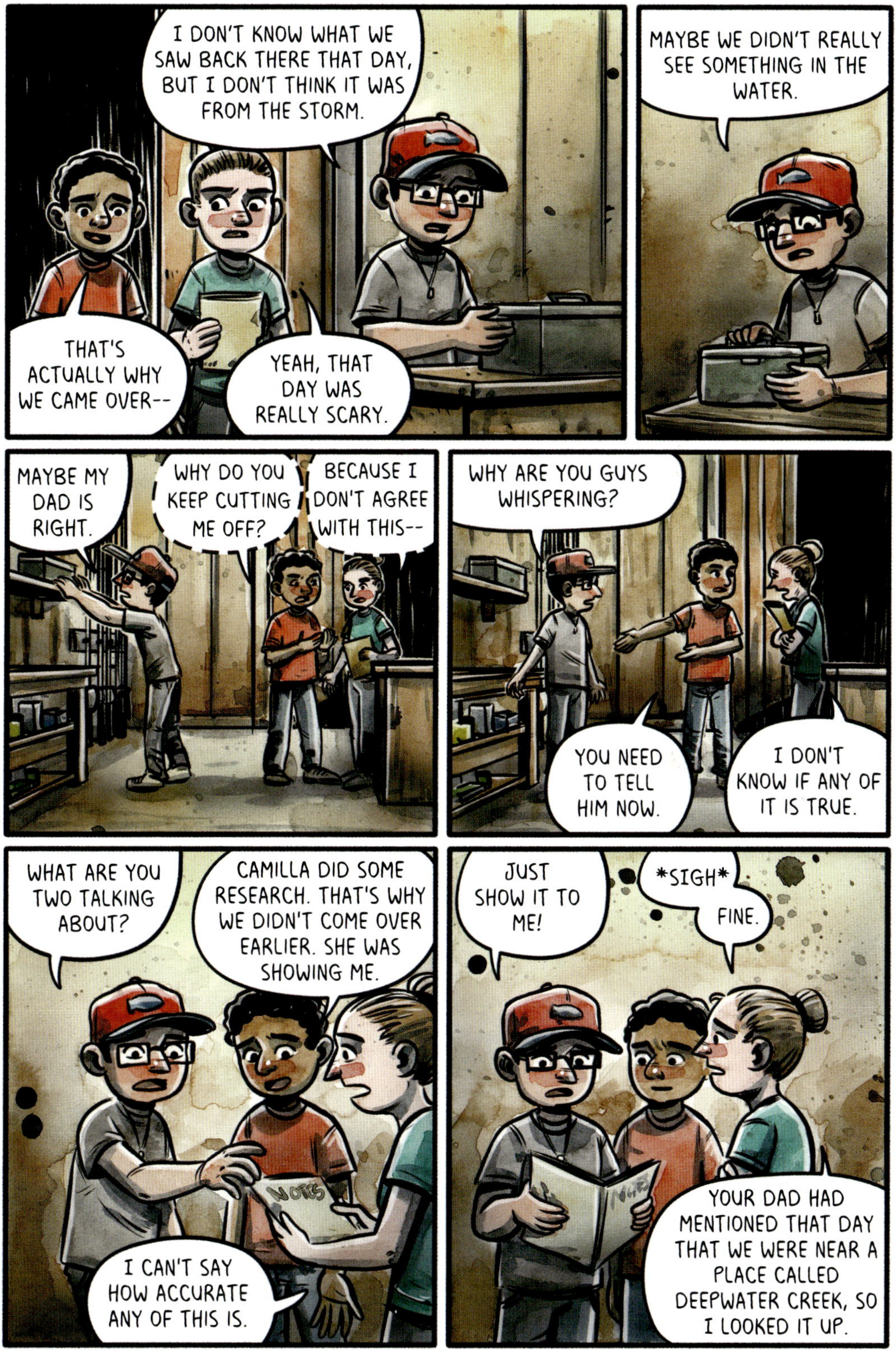
I DON'T KNOW WHAT WE SAW BACK THERE THAT DAY, BUT I DON'T THINK IT WAS FROM THE STORM.
THAT'S ACTUALLY WHY WE CAME OVER--
YEAH, THAT DAY WAS REALLY SCARY.
MAYBE WE DIDN'T REALLY SEE SOMETHING IN THE WATER.
MAYBE MY DAD IS RIGHT.
WHY DO YOU KEEP CUTTING ME OFF?
BECAUSE I DON'T AGREE WITH THIS--
WHY ARE YOU GUYS WHISPERING?
YOU NEED TO TELL HIM NOW.
I DON'T KNOW IF ANY OF IT IS TRUE.
WHAT ARE YOU TWO TALKING ABOUT?
CAMILLA DID SOME RESEARCH. THAT'S WHY WE DIDN'T COME OVER EARLIER. SHE WAS SHOWING ME.
NOTES
I CAN'T SAY HOW ACCURATE ANY OF THIS IS.
JUST SHOW IT TO ME!
SIGH
FINE.
NOTES
YOUR DAD HAD MENTIONED THAT DAY THAT WE WERE NEAR A PLACE CALLED DEEPWATER CREEK, SO I LOOKED IT UP.

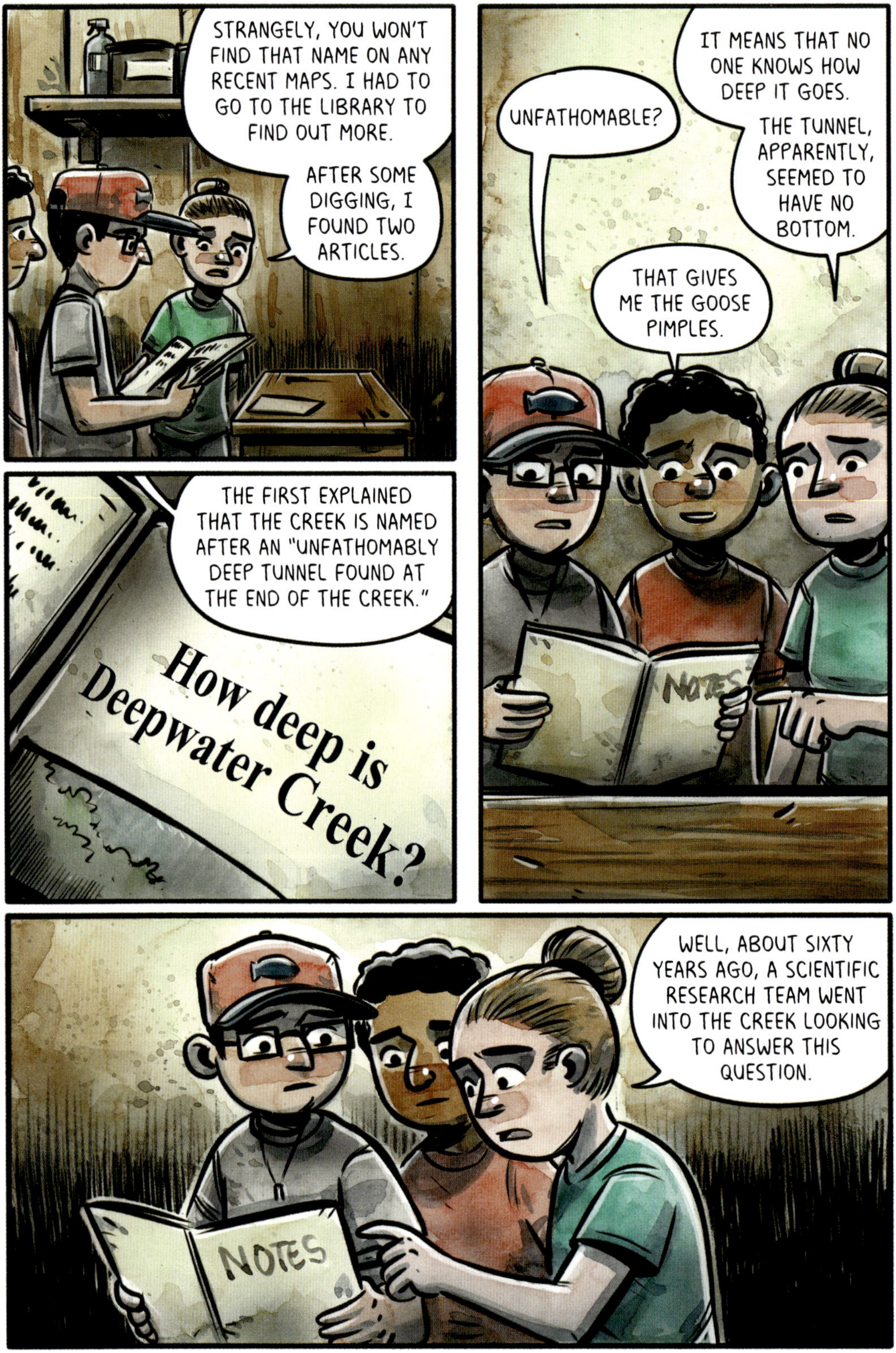

STRANGELY, YOU WON'T FIND THAT NAME ON ANY RECENT MAPS. I HAD TO GO TO THE LIBRARY TO FIND OUT MORE.
AFTER SOME DIGGING, I FOUND TWO ARTICLES.
THE FIRST EXPLAINED THAT THE CREEK IS NAMED AFTER AN "UNFATHOMABLY DEEP TUNNEL FOUND AT THE END OF THE CREEK."
How deep is Deepwater Creek?
UNFATHOMABLE?
IT MEANS THAT NO ONE KNOWS HOW DEEP IT GOES.
THE TUNNEL, APPARENTLY, SEEMED TO HAVE NO BOTTOM.
THAT GIVES ME THE GOOSE PIMPLES.
NOTES
WELL, ABOUT SIXTY YEARS AGO, A SCIENTIFIC RESEARCH TEAM WENT INTO THE CREEK LOOKING TO ANSWER THIS QUESTION.
NOTES

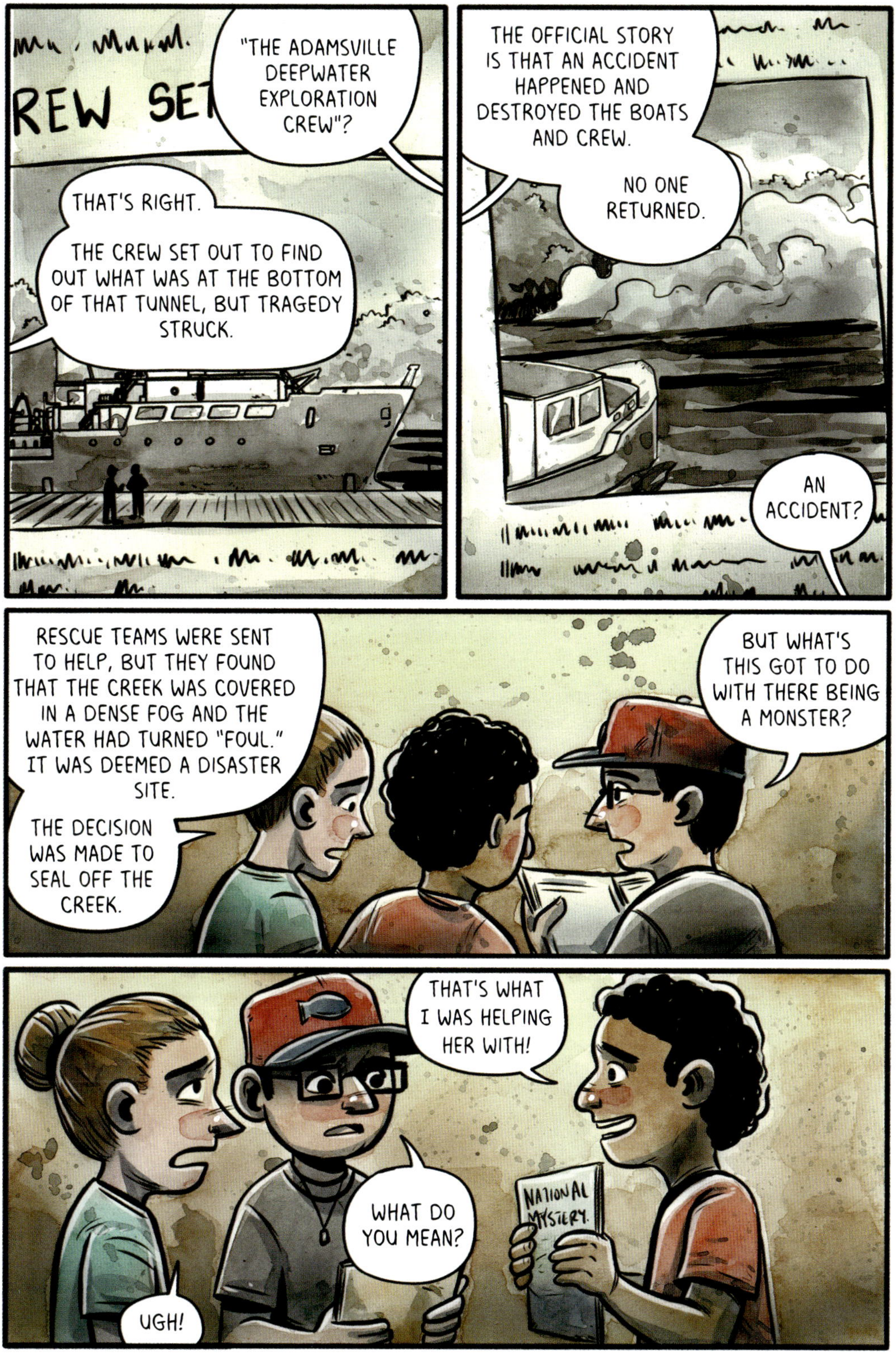
REW SET
"THE ADAMSVILLE DEEPWATER EXPLORATION CREW"?
THAT'S RIGHT.
THE CREW SET OUT TO FIND OUT WHAT WAS AT THE BOTTOM OF THAT TUNNEL, BUT TRAGEDY STRUCK.
THE OFFICIAL STORY IS THAT AN ACCIDENT HAPPENED AND DESTROYED THE BOATS AND CREW.
NO ONE RETURNED.
AN ACCIDENT?
RESCUE TEAMS WERE SENT TO HELP, BUT THEY FOUND THAT THE CREEK WAS COVERED IN A DENSE FOG AND THE WATER HAD TURNED "FOUL." IT WAS DEEMED A DISASTER SITE.
THE DECISION WAS MADE TO SEAL OFF THE CREEK.
BUT WHAT'S THIS GOT TO DO WITH THERE BEING A MONSTER?
THAT'S WHAT I WAS HELPING HER WITH!
WHAT DO YOU MEAN?
UGH!
NATIONAL MYSTERY

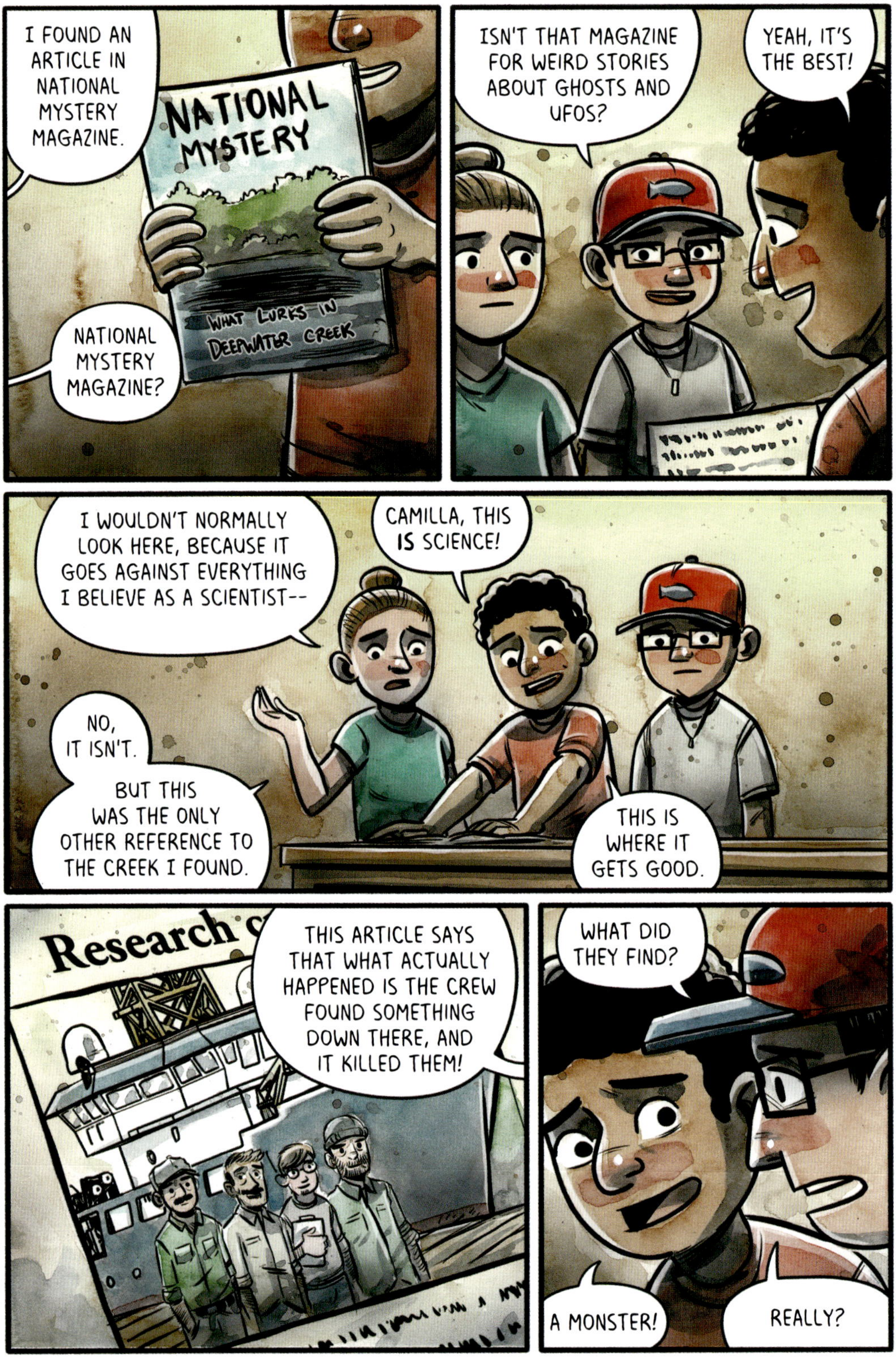
I FOUND AN ARTICLE IN NATIONAL MYSTERY MAGAZINE.
NATIONAL MYSTERY
WHAT LURKS IN DEEPWATER CREEK
NATIONAL MYSTERY MAGAZINE?
ISN'T THAT MAGAZINE FOR WEIRD STORIES ABOUT GHOSTS AND UFOS?
YEAH, IT'S THE BEST!
I WOULDN'T NORMALLY LOOK HERE, BECAUSE IT GOES AGAINST EVERYTHING I BELIEVE AS A SCIENTIST--
CAMILLA, THIS **IS** SCIENCE!
NO, IT ISN'T.
BUT THIS WAS THE ONLY OTHER REFERENCE TO THE CREEK I FOUND.
THIS IS WHERE IT GETS GOOD.
Research
THIS ARTICLE SAYS THAT WHAT ACTUALLY HAPPENED IS THE CREW FOUND SOMETHING DOWN THERE, AND IT KILLED THEM!
WHAT DID THEY FIND?
A MONSTER!
REALLY?

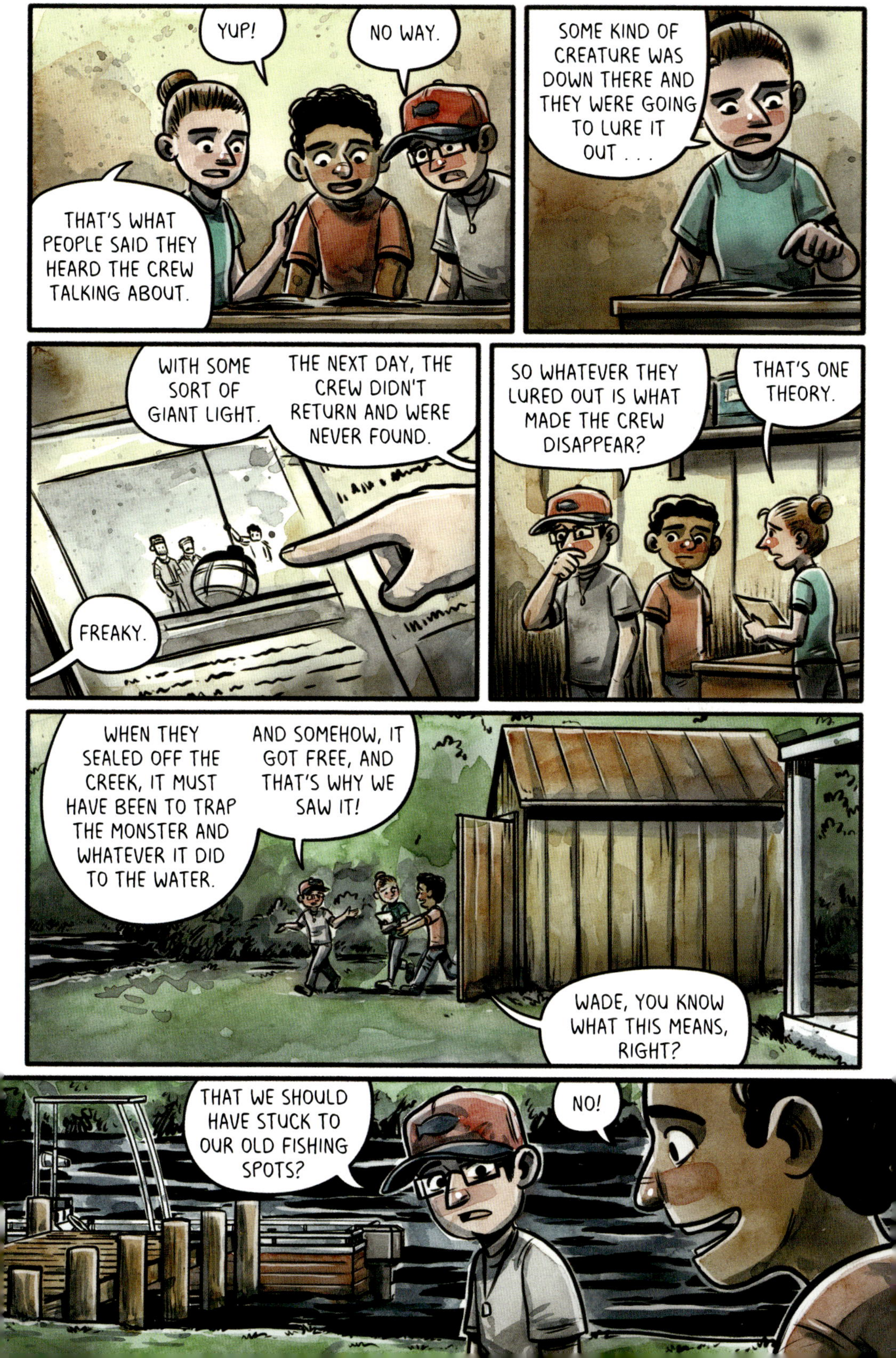
YUP!
NO WAY.
THAT'S WHAT PEOPLE SAID THEY HEARD THE CREW TALKING ABOUT.
SOME KIND OF CREATURE WAS DOWN THERE AND THEY WERE GOING TO LURE IT OUT . . .
WITH SOME SORT OF GIANT LIGHT.
THE NEXT DAY, THE CREW DIDN'T RETURN AND WERE NEVER FOUND.
FREAKY.
SO WHATEVER THEY LURED OUT IS WHAT MADE THE CREW DISAPPEAR?
THAT'S ONE THEORY.
WHEN THEY SEALED OFF THE CREEK, IT MUST HAVE BEEN TO TRAP THE MONSTER AND WHATEVER IT DID TO THE WATER.
AND SOMEHOW, IT GOT FREE, AND THAT'S WHY WE SAW IT!
WADE, YOU KNOW WHAT THIS MEANS, RIGHT?
THAT WE SHOULD HAVE STUCK TO OUR OLD FISHING SPOTS?
NO!

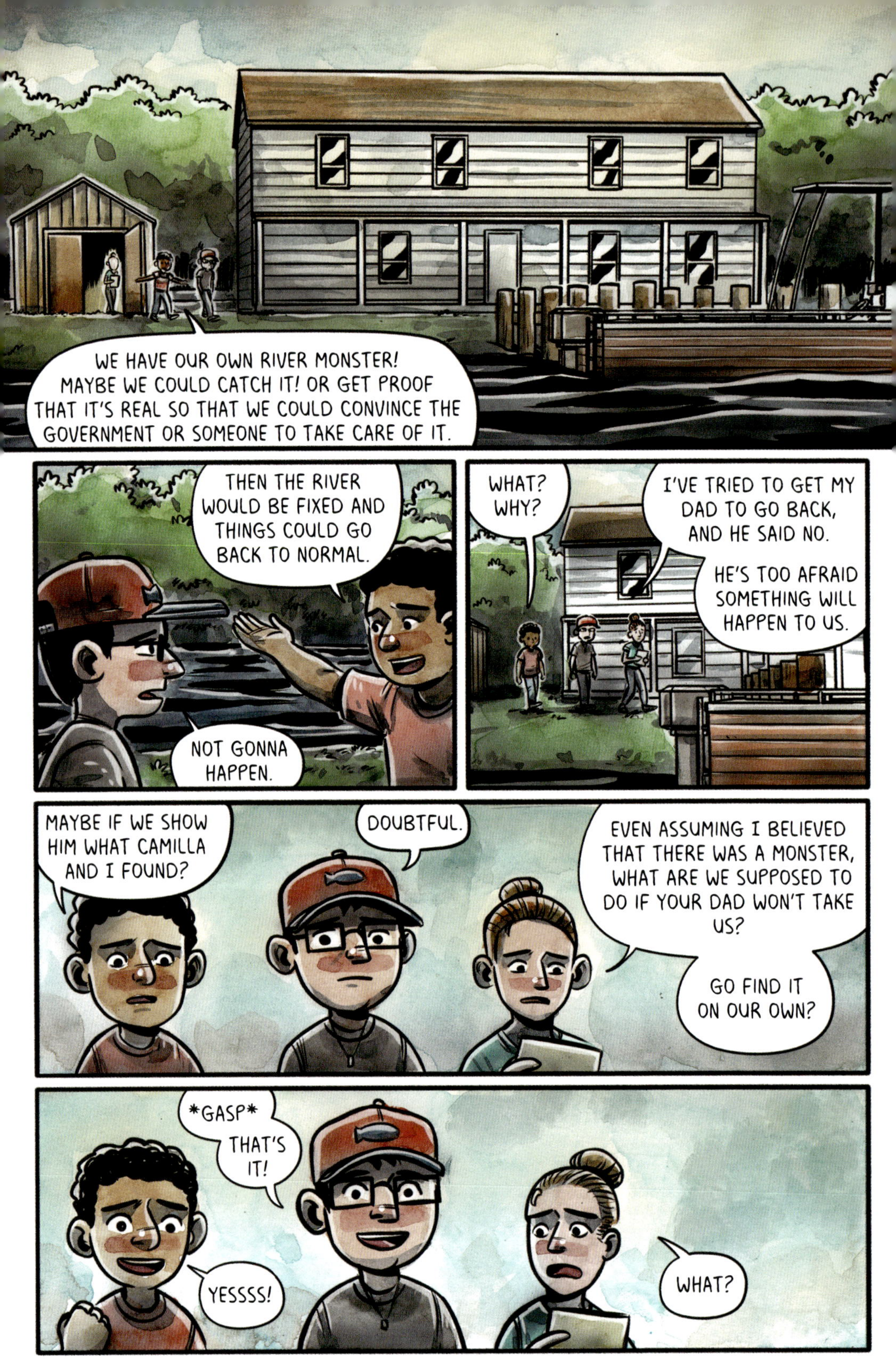
WE HAVE OUR OWN RIVER MONSTER! MAYBE WE COULD CATCH IT! OR GET PROOF THAT IT'S REAL SO THAT WE COULD CONVINCE THE GOVERNMENT OR SOMEONE TO TAKE CARE OF IT.
THEN THE RIVER WOULD BE FIXED AND THINGS COULD GO BACK TO NORMAL.
NOT GONNA HAPPEN.
WHAT? WHY?
I'VE TRIED TO GET MY DAD TO GO BACK, AND HE SAID NO.
HE'S TOO AFRAID SOMETHING WILL HAPPEN TO US.
MAYBE IF WE SHOW HIM WHAT CAMILLA AND I FOUND?
DOUBTFUL.
EVEN ASSUMING I BELIEVED THAT THERE WAS A MONSTER, WHAT ARE WE SUPPOSED TO DO IF YOUR DAD WON'T TAKE US?
GO FIND IT ON OUR OWN?
GASP
THAT'S IT!
YESSSS!
WHAT?

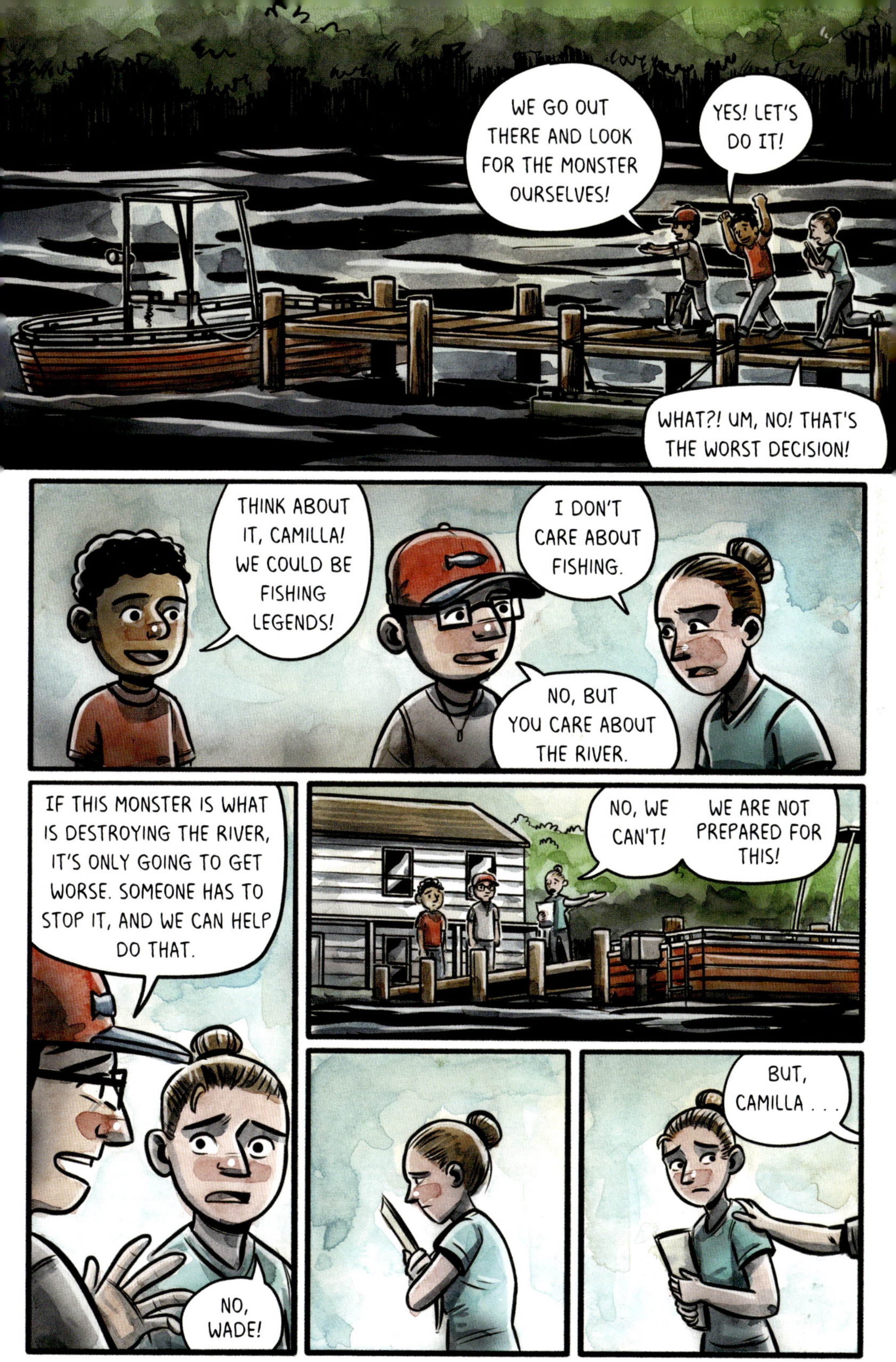
WE GO OUT THERE AND LOOK FOR THE MONSTER OURSELVES!
YES! LET'S DO IT!
WHAT?! UM, NO! THAT'S THE WORST DECISION!
THINK ABOUT IT, CAMILLA! WE COULD BE FISHING LEGENDS!
I DON'T CARE ABOUT FISHING.
NO, BUT YOU CARE ABOUT THE RIVER.
IF THIS MONSTER IS WHAT IS DESTROYING THE RIVER, IT'S ONLY GOING TO GET WORSE. SOMEONE HAS TO STOP IT, AND WE CAN HELP DO THAT.
NO, WADE!
NO, WE CAN'T!
WE ARE NOT PREPARED FOR THIS!
BUT, CAMILLA . . .

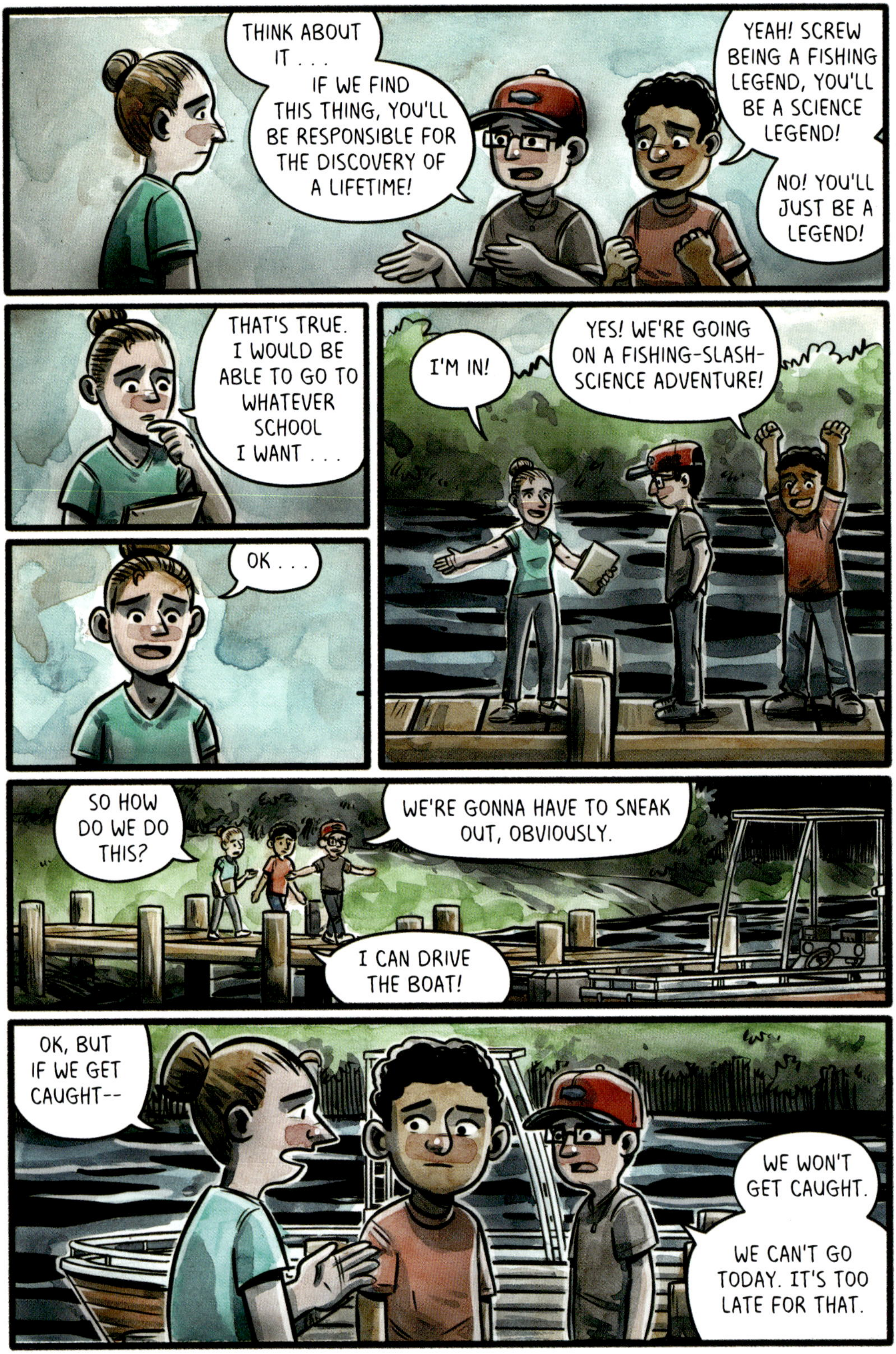
THINK ABOUT IT . . . IF WE FIND THIS THING, YOU'LL BE RESPONSIBLE FOR THE DISCOVERY OF A LIFETIME!
YEAH! SCREW BEING A FISHING LEGEND, YOU'LL BE A SCIENCE LEGEND!
NO! YOU'LL JUST BE A LEGEND!
THAT'S TRUE. I WOULD BE ABLE TO GO TO WHATEVER SCHOOL I WANT . . .
OK . . .
I'M IN!
YES! WE'RE GOING ON A FISHING-SLASH-SCIENCE ADVENTURE!
SO HOW DO WE DO THIS?
WE'RE GONNA HAVE TO SNEAK OUT, OBVIOUSLY.
I CAN DRIVE THE BOAT!
OK, BUT IF WE GET CAUGHT--
WE WON'T GET CAUGHT.
WE CAN'T GO TODAY. IT'S TOO LATE FOR THAT.

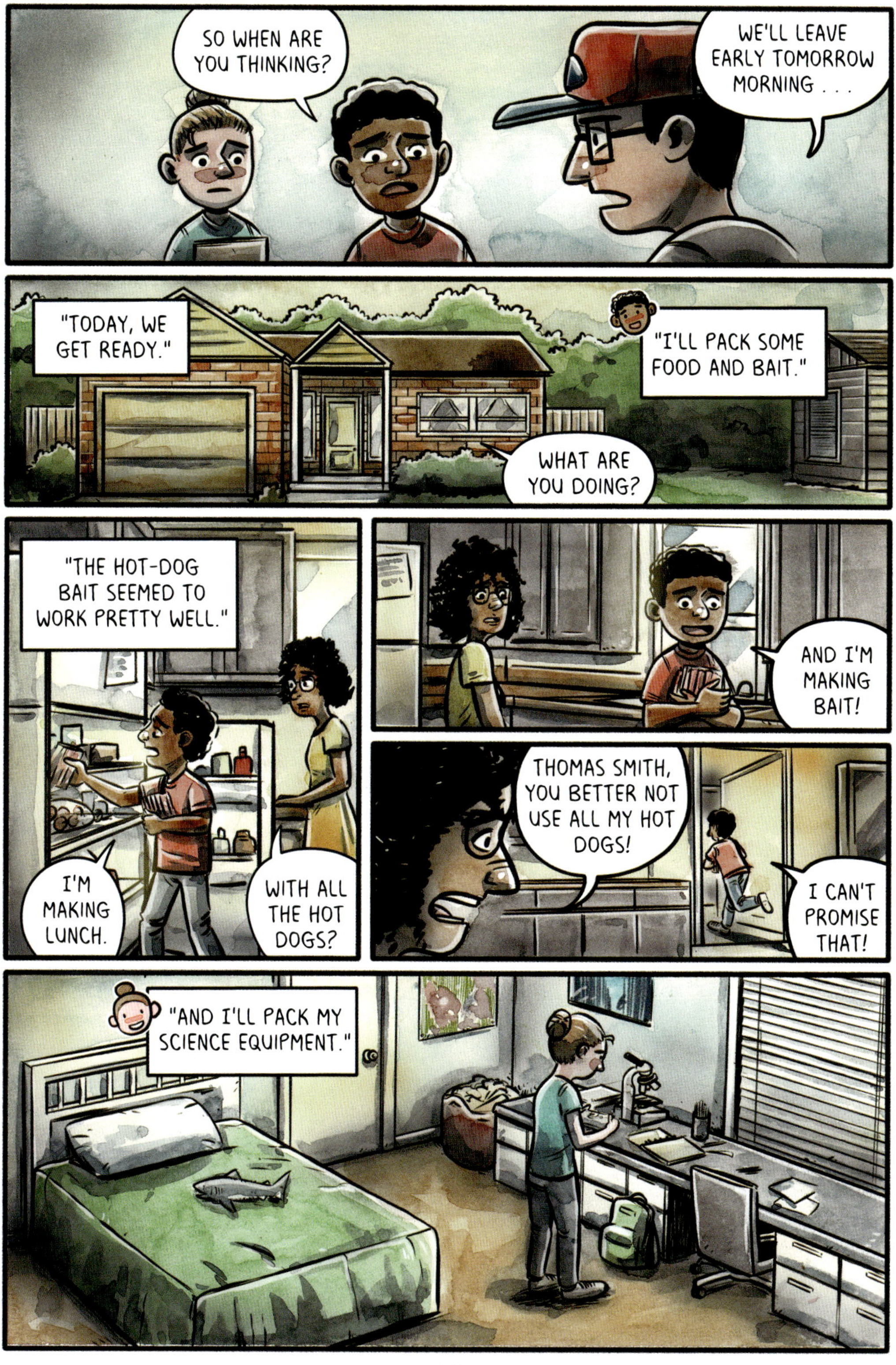
SO WHEN ARE YOU THINKING?
WE'LL LEAVE EARLY TOMORROW MORNING . . .
"TODAY, WE GET READY."
"I'LL PACK SOME FOOD AND BAIT."
WHAT ARE YOU DOING?
"THE HOT-DOG BAIT SEEMED TO WORK PRETTY WELL."
I'M MAKING LUNCH.
WITH ALL THE HOT DOGS?
AND I'M MAKING BAIT!
THOMAS SMITH, YOU BETTER NOT USE ALL MY HOT DOGS!
I CAN'T PROMISE THAT!
"AND I'LL PACK MY SCIENCE EQUIPMENT."

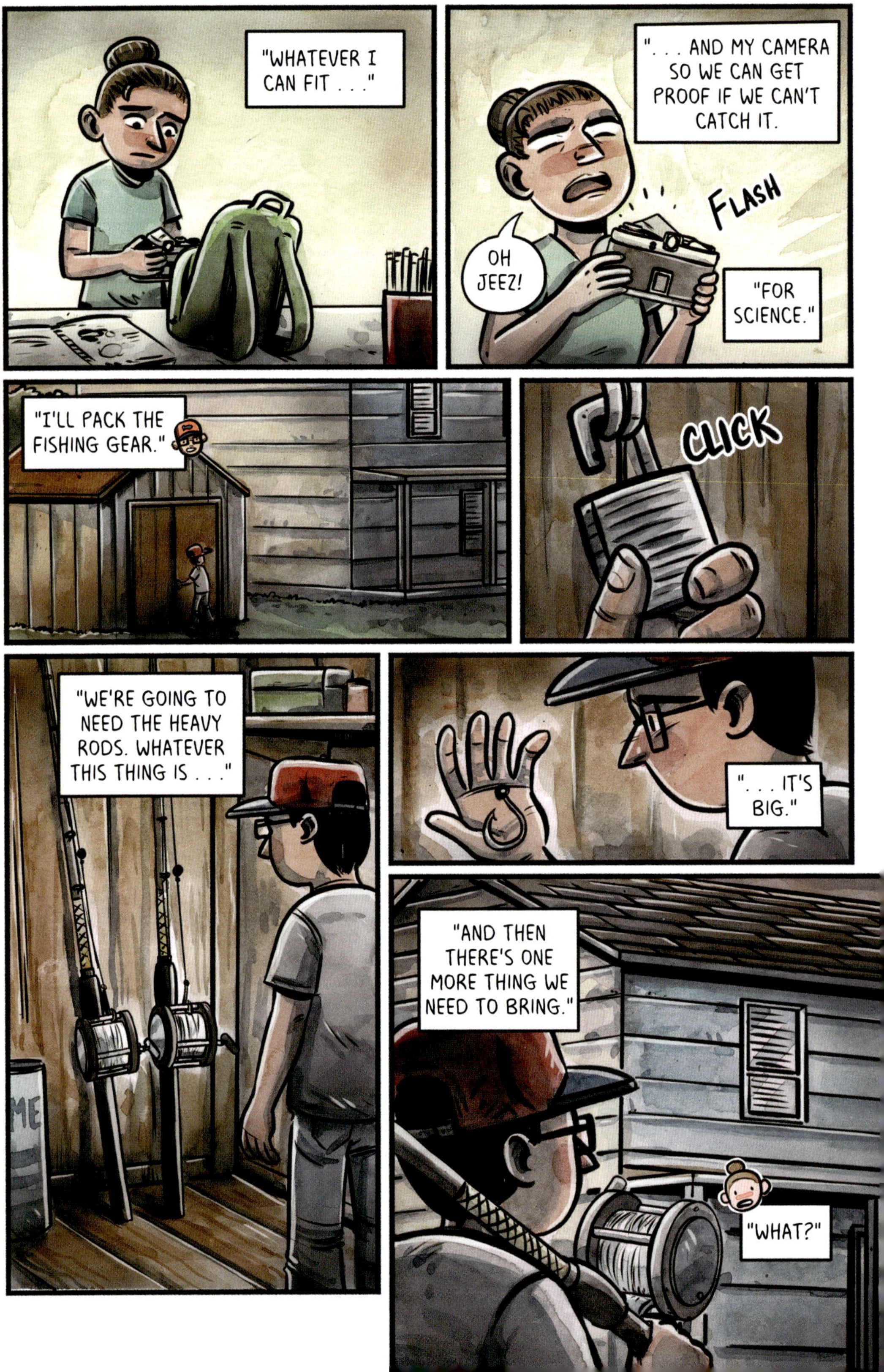
"WHATEVER I CAN FIT . . ."
". . . AND MY CAMERA SO WE CAN GET PROOF IF WE CAN'T CATCH IT.
FLASH
OH JEEZ!
"FOR SCIENCE."
"I'LL PACK THE FISHING GEAR."
CLICK
"WE'RE GOING TO NEED THE HEAVY RODS. WHATEVER THIS THING IS . . ."
". . . IT'S BIG."
"AND THEN THERE'S ONE MORE THING WE NEED TO BRING."
"WHAT?"

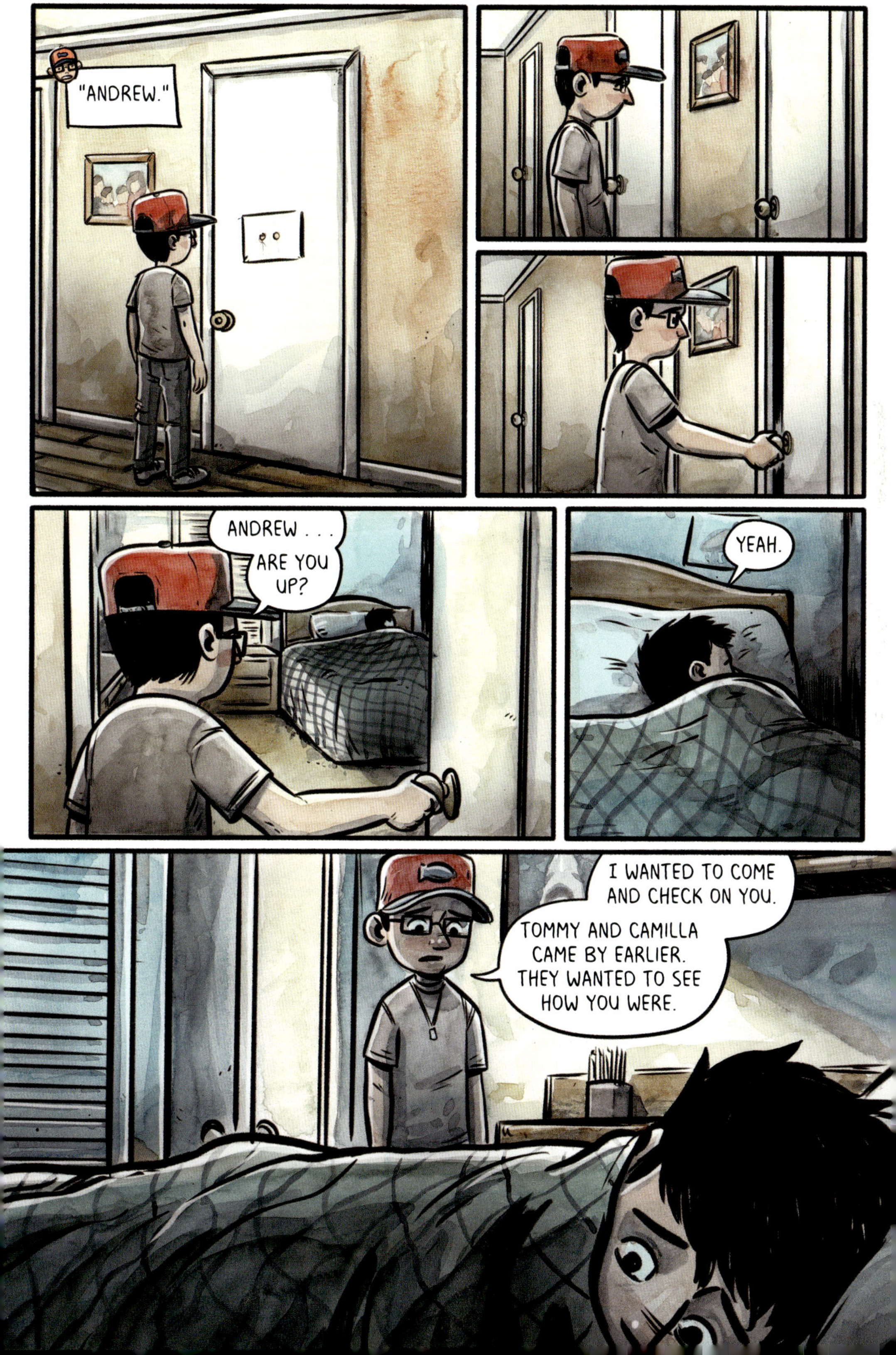
"ANDREW."
ANDREW . . .
ARE YOU UP?
YEAH.
I WANTED TO COME AND CHECK ON YOU.
TOMMY AND CAMILLA CAME BY EARLIER. THEY WANTED TO SEE HOW YOU WERE.

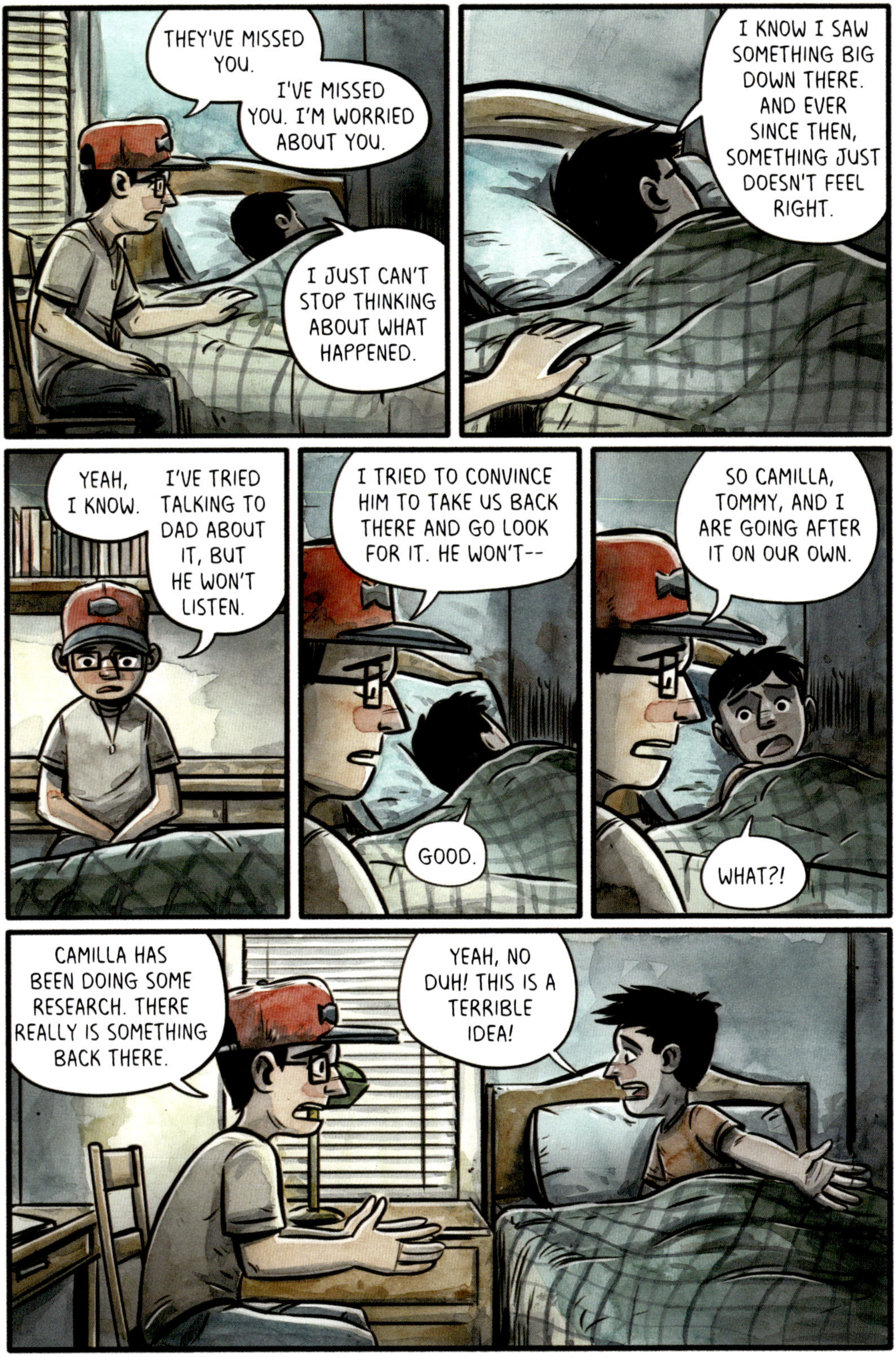
THEY'VE MISSED YOU.
I'VE MISSED YOU. I'M WORRIED ABOUT YOU.
I JUST CAN'T STOP THINKING ABOUT WHAT HAPPENED.
I KNOW I SAW SOMETHING BIG DOWN THERE. AND EVER SINCE THEN, SOMETHING JUST DOESN'T FEEL RIGHT.
YEAH, I KNOW.
I'VE TRIED TALKING TO DAD ABOUT IT, BUT HE WON'T LISTEN.
I TRIED TO CONVINCE HIM TO TAKE US BACK THERE AND GO LOOK FOR IT. HE WON'T--
GOOD.
SO CAMILLA, TOMMY, AND I ARE GOING AFTER IT ON OUR OWN.
WHAT?!
CAMILLA HAS BEEN DOING SOME RESEARCH. THERE REALLY IS SOMETHING BACK THERE.
YEAH, NO DUH! THIS IS A TERRIBLE IDEA!

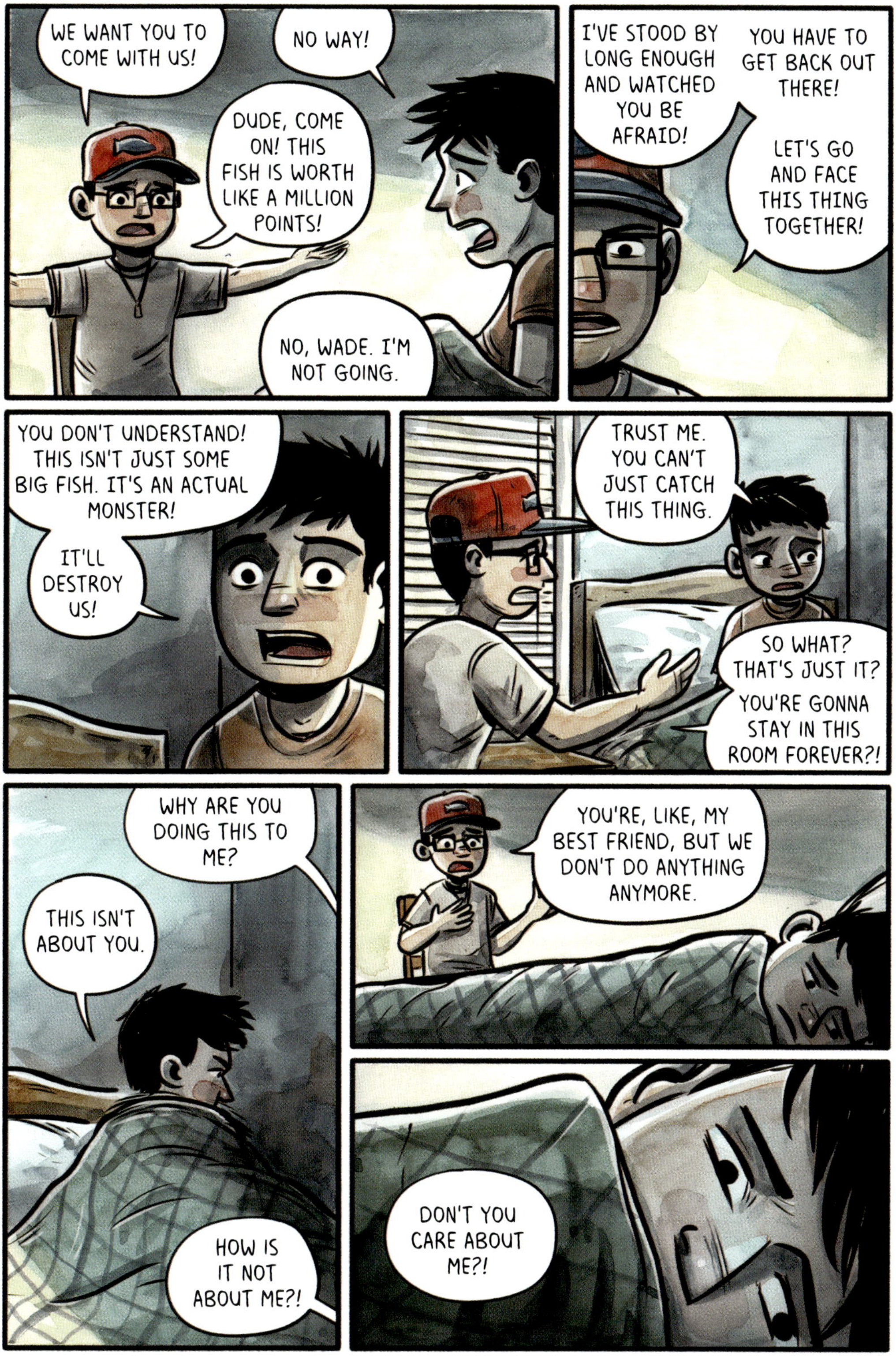
WE WANT YOU TO COME WITH US!
NO WAY!
DUDE, COME ON! THIS FISH IS WORTH LIKE A MILLION POINTS!
NO, WADE. I'M NOT GOING.
I'VE STOOD BY LONG ENOUGH AND WATCHED YOU BE AFRAID!
YOU HAVE TO GET BACK OUT THERE!
LET'S GO AND FACE THIS THING TOGETHER!
YOU DON'T UNDERSTAND! THIS ISN'T JUST SOME BIG FISH. IT'S AN ACTUAL MONSTER!
IT'LL DESTROY US!
TRUST ME. YOU CAN'T JUST CATCH THIS THING.
SO WHAT? THAT'S JUST IT?
YOU'RE GONNA STAY IN THIS ROOM FOREVER?!
WHY ARE YOU DOING THIS TO ME?
THIS ISN'T ABOUT YOU.
HOW IS IT NOT ABOUT ME?!
YOU'RE, LIKE, MY BEST FRIEND, BUT WE DON'T DO ANYTHING ANYMORE.
DON'T YOU CARE ABOUT ME?!

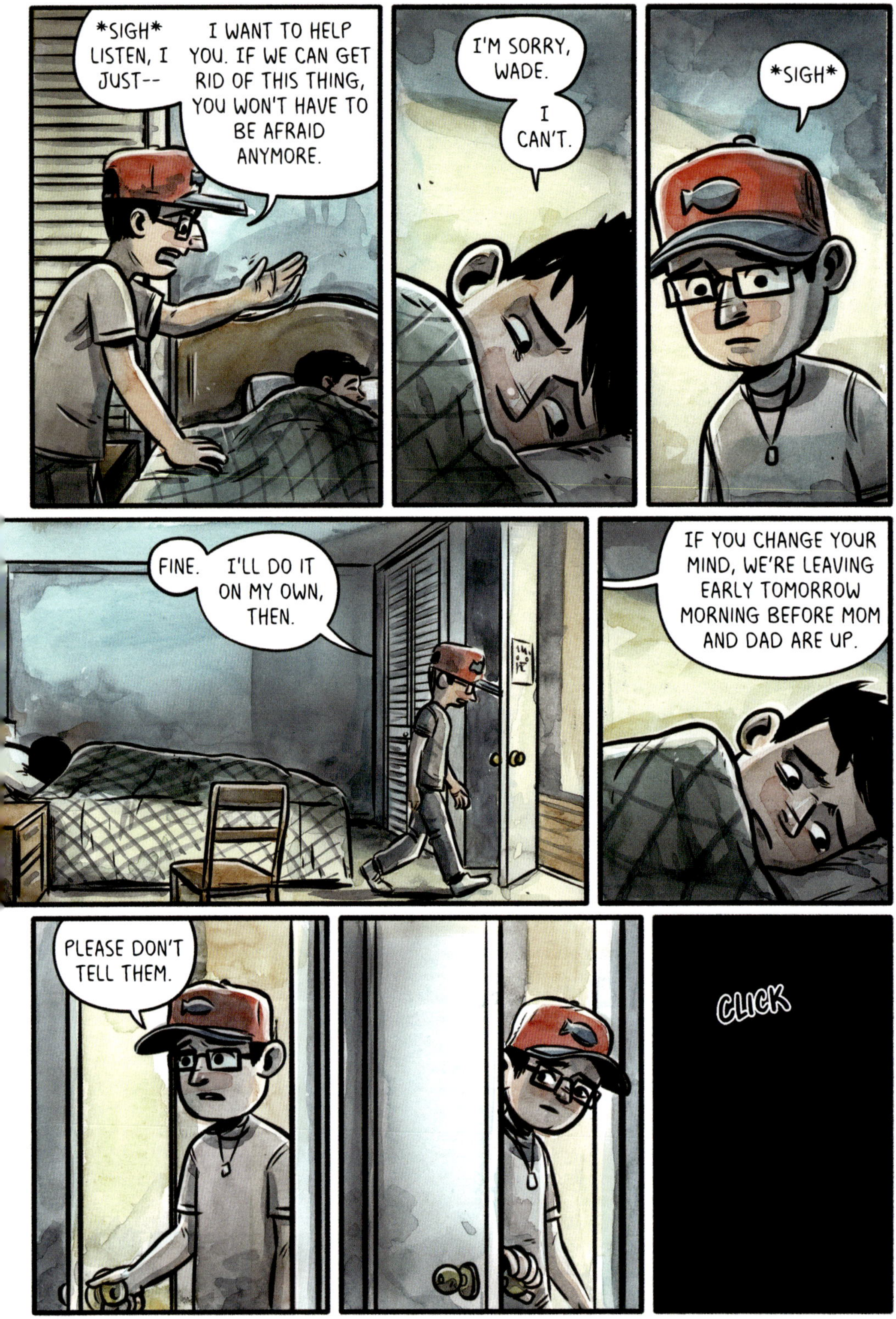
SIGH LISTEN, I JUST--
I WANT TO HELP YOU. IF WE CAN GET RID OF THIS THING, YOU WON'T HAVE TO BE AFRAID ANYMORE.
I'M SORRY, WADE.
I CAN'T.
SIGH
FINE.
I'LL DO IT ON MY OWN, THEN.
IF YOU CHANGE YOUR MIND, WE'RE LEAVING EARLY TOMORROW MORNING BEFORE MOM AND DAD ARE UP.
PLEASE DON'T TELL THEM.
CLICK

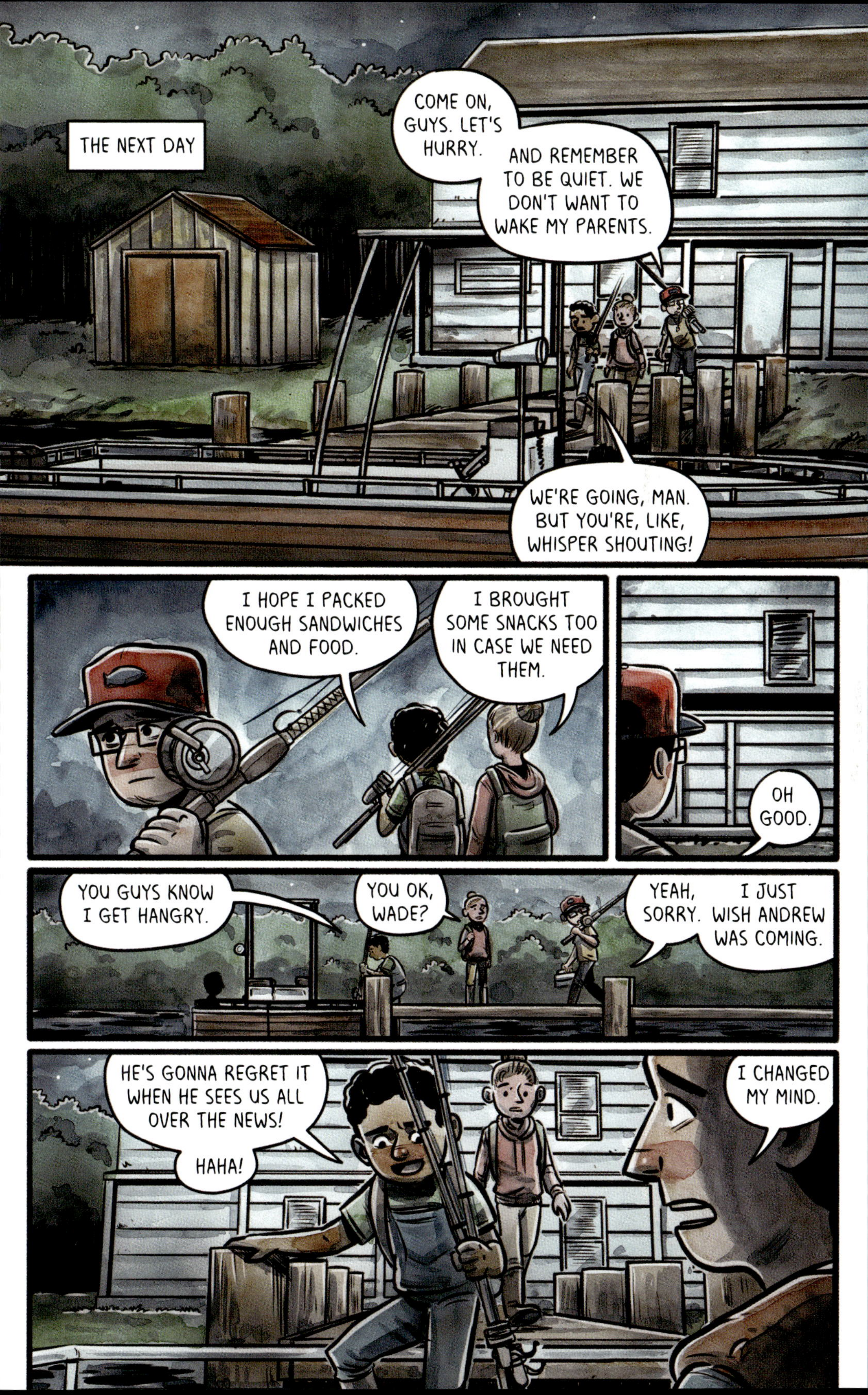

THE NEXT DAY
COME ON, GUYS. LET'S HURRY.
AND REMEMBER TO BE QUIET. WE DON'T WANT TO WAKE MY PARENTS.
WE'RE GOING, MAN. BUT YOU'RE, LIKE, WHISPER SHOUTING!
I HOPE I PACKED ENOUGH SANDWICHES AND FOOD.
I BROUGHT SOME SNACKS TOO IN CASE WE NEED THEM.
OH GOOD.
YOU GUYS KNOW I GET HANGRY.
YOU OK, WADE?
YEAH, SORRY.
I JUST WISH ANDREW WAS COMING.
HE'S GONNA REGRET IT WHEN HE SEES US ALL OVER THE NEWS!
HAHA!
I CHANGED MY MIND.

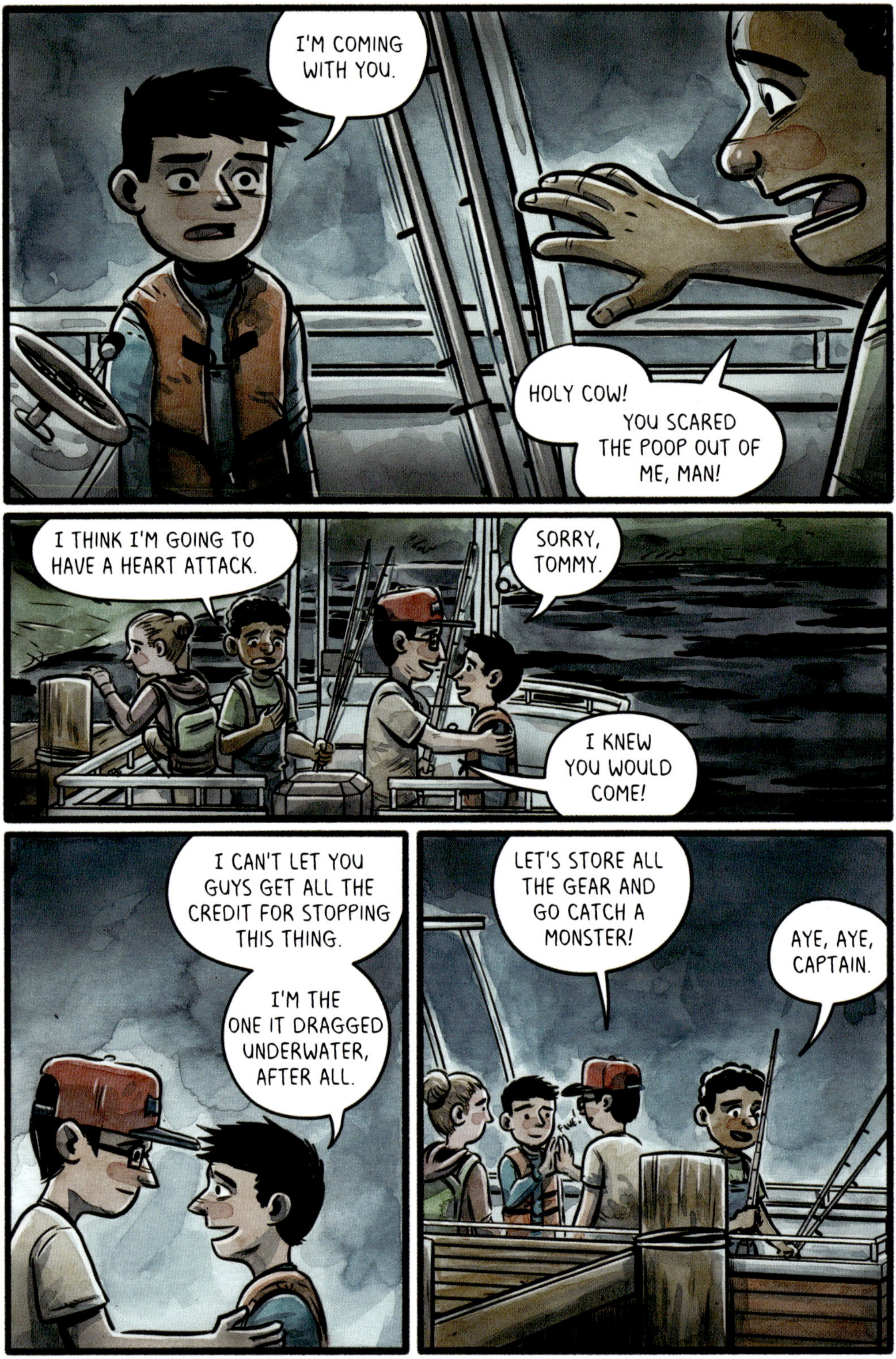
I'M COMING WITH YOU.
HOLY COW! YOU SCARED THE POOP OUT OF ME, MAN!
I THINK I'M GOING TO HAVE A HEART ATTACK.
SORRY, TOMMY.
I KNEW YOU WOULD COME!
I CAN'T LET YOU GUYS GET ALL THE CREDIT FOR STOPPING THIS THING.
I'M THE ONE IT DRAGGED UNDERWATER, AFTER ALL.
LET'S STORE ALL THE GEAR AND GO CATCH A MONSTER!
AYE, AYE, CAPTAIN.

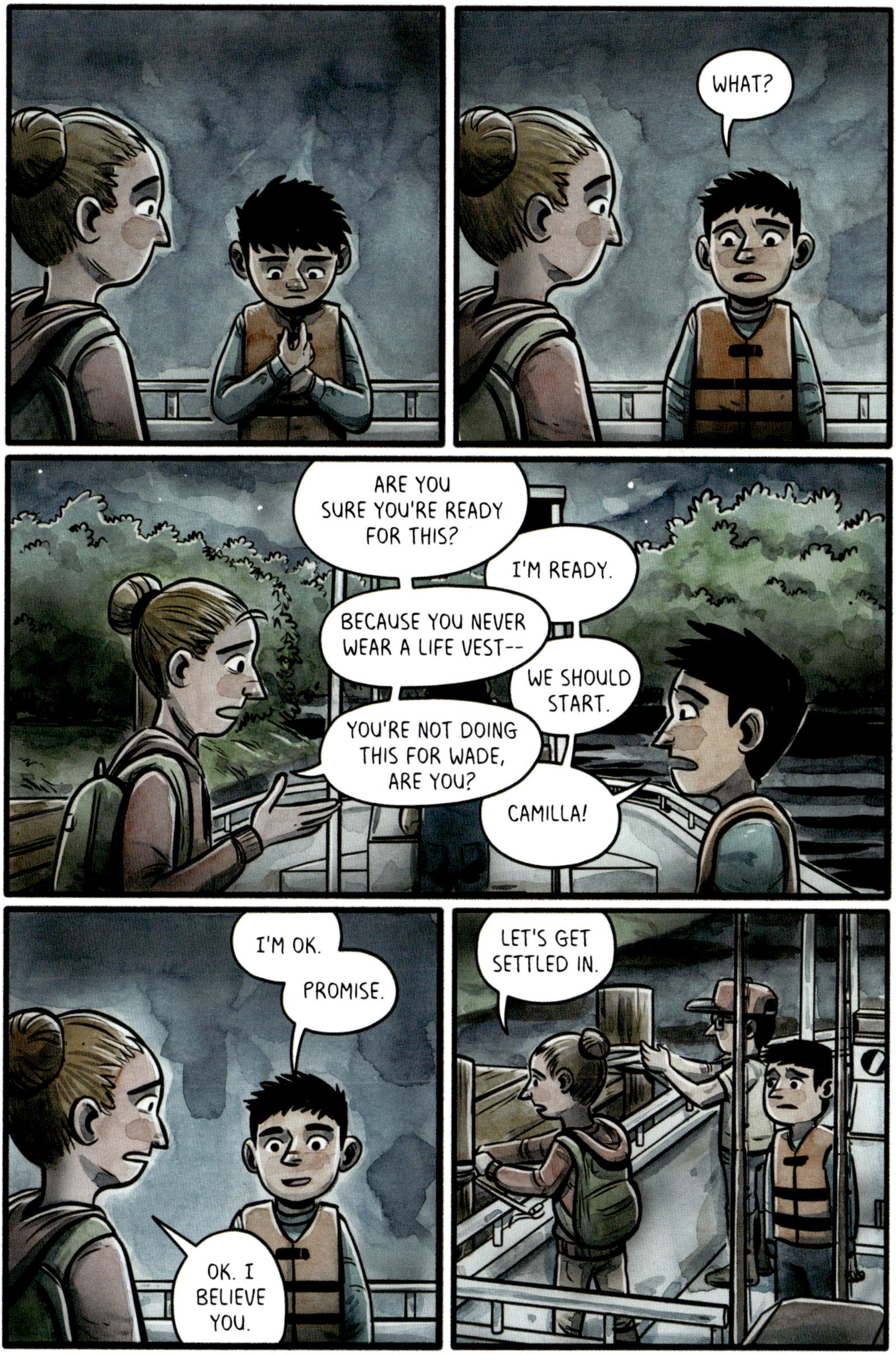
WHAT?
ARE YOU SURE YOU'RE READY FOR THIS?
I'M READY.
BECAUSE YOU NEVER WEAR A LIFE VEST--
WE SHOULD START.
YOU'RE NOT DOING THIS FOR WADE, ARE YOU?
CAMILLA!
I'M OK.
PROMISE.
OK. I BELIEVE YOU.
LET'S GET SETTLED IN.

AND WE'RE OFF.
WE NEED TO GO THE OTHER WAY.
THERE'S A LOOP UP AHEAD I CAN TAKE.

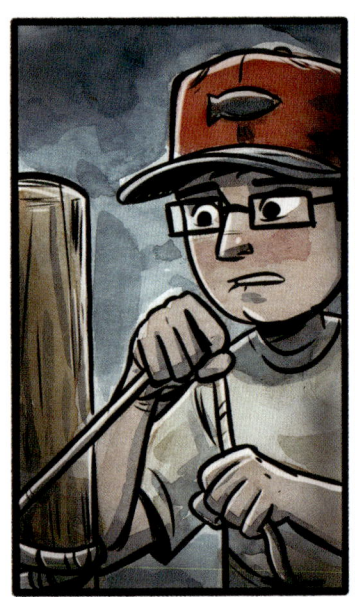

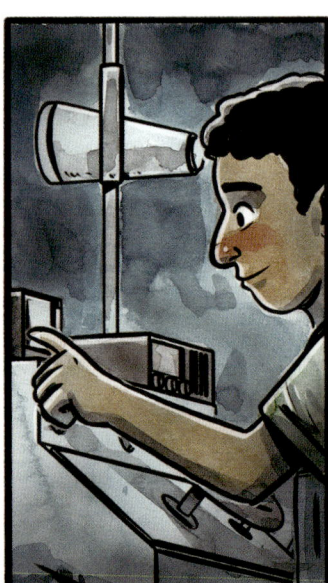

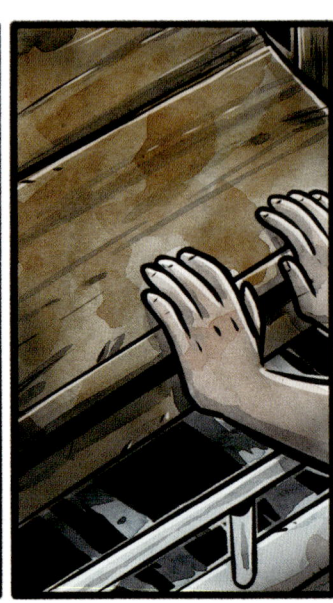

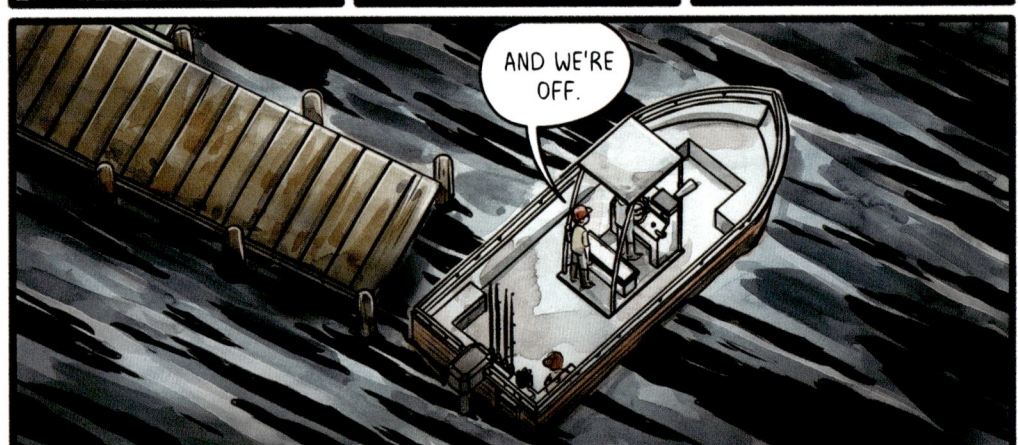

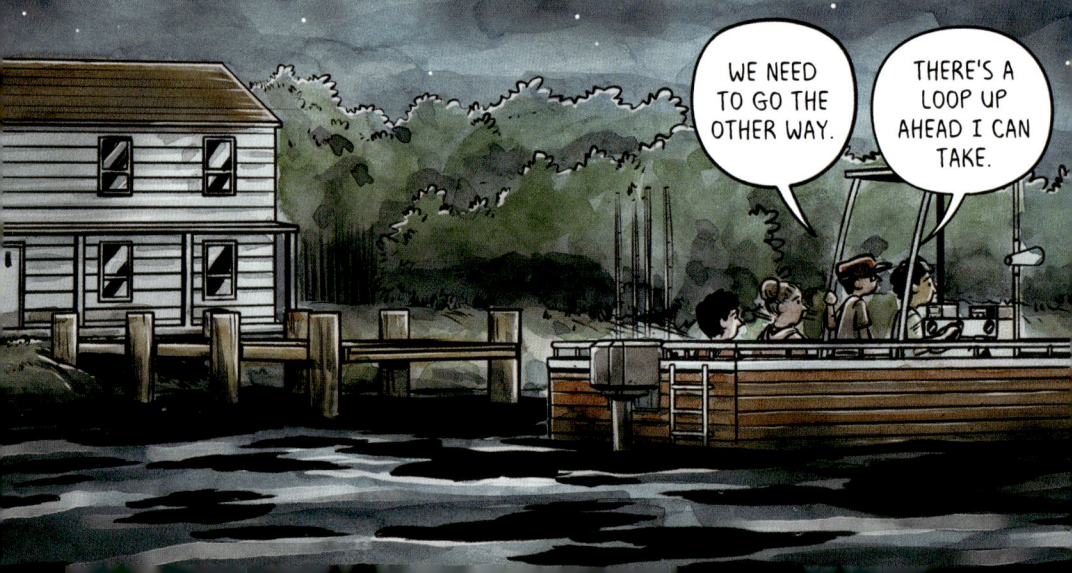

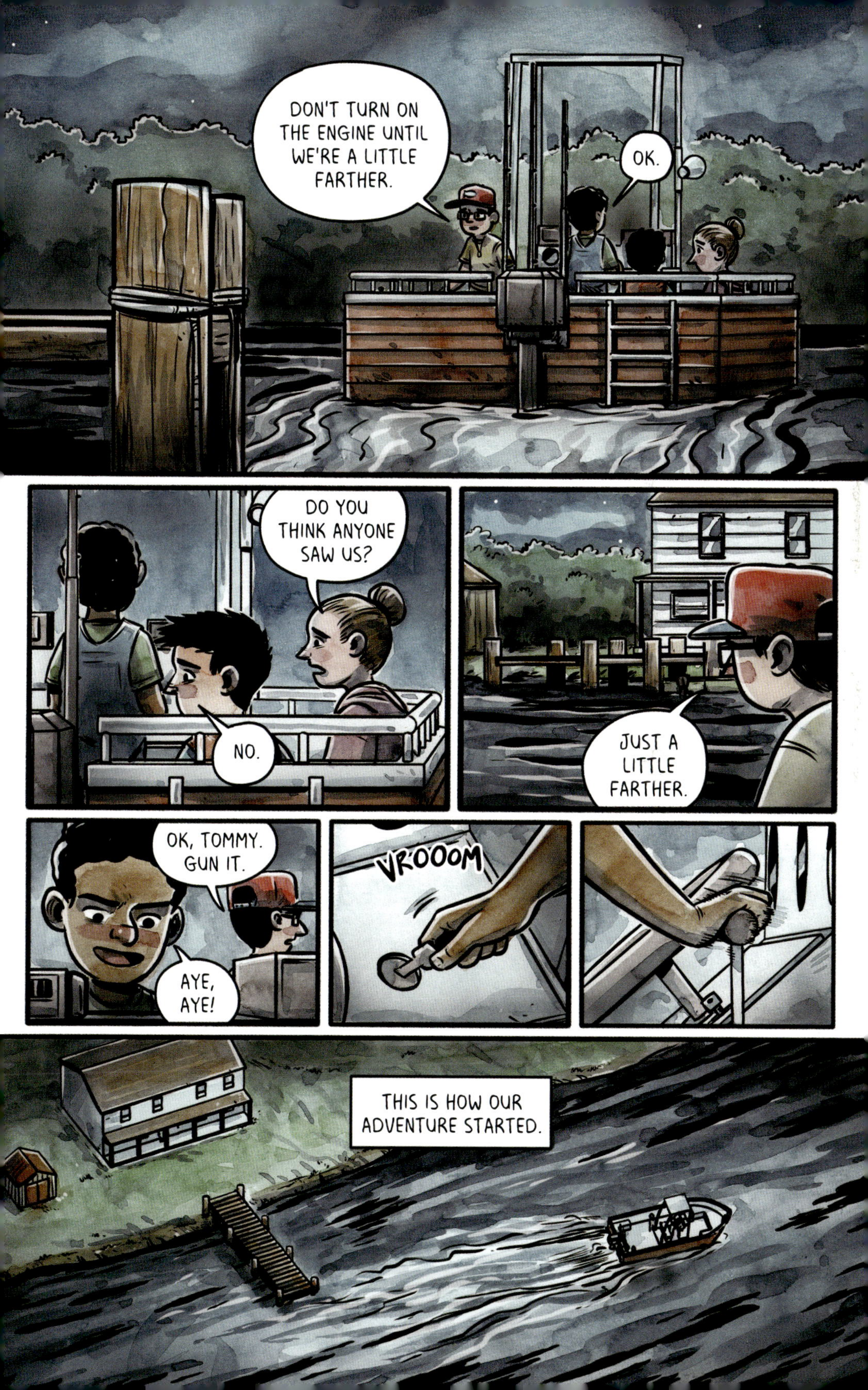
DON'T TURN ON THE ENGINE UNTIL WE'RE A LITTLE FARTHER.
OK.
DO YOU THINK ANYONE SAW US?
NO.
JUST A LITTLE FARTHER.
OK, TOMMY. GUN IT.
AYE, AYE!
VROOOM
THIS IS HOW OUR ADVENTURE STARTED.

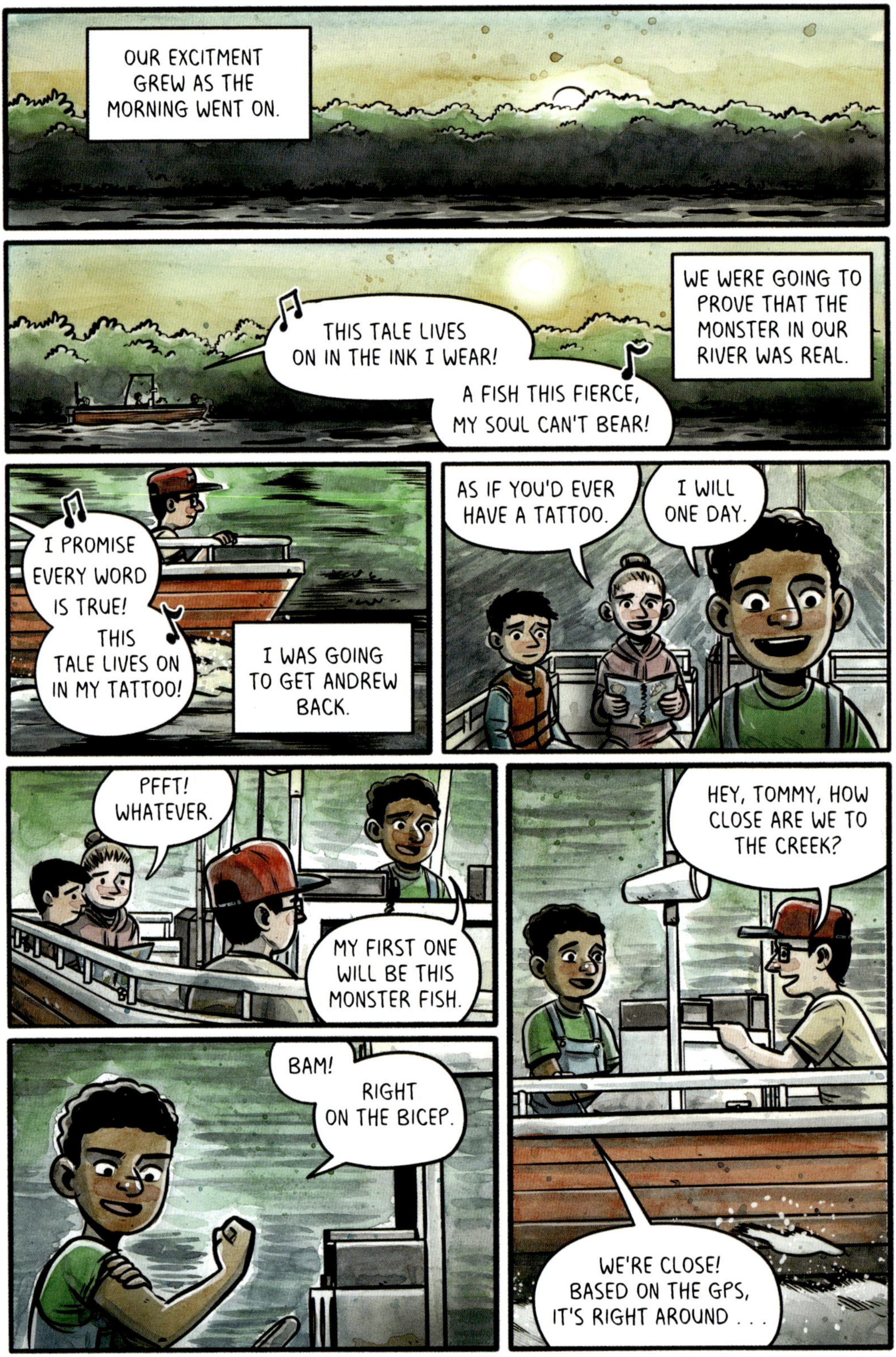
OUR EXCITMENT GREW AS THE MORNING WENT ON.
THIS TALE LIVES ON IN THE INK I WEAR!
A FISH THIS FIERCE, MY SOUL CAN'T BEAR!
WE WERE GOING TO PROVE THAT THE MONSTER IN OUR RIVER WAS REAL.
I PROMISE EVERY WORD IS TRUE!
THIS TALE LIVES ON IN MY TATTOO!
I WAS GOING TO GET ANDREW BACK.
AS IF YOU'D EVER HAVE A TATTOO.
I WILL ONE DAY.
PFFT! WHATEVER.
MY FIRST ONE WILL BE THIS MONSTER FISH.
BAM!
RIGHT ON THE BICEP.
HEY, TOMMY, HOW CLOSE ARE WE TO THE CREEK?
WE'RE CLOSE! BASED ON THE GPS, IT'S RIGHT AROUND . . .

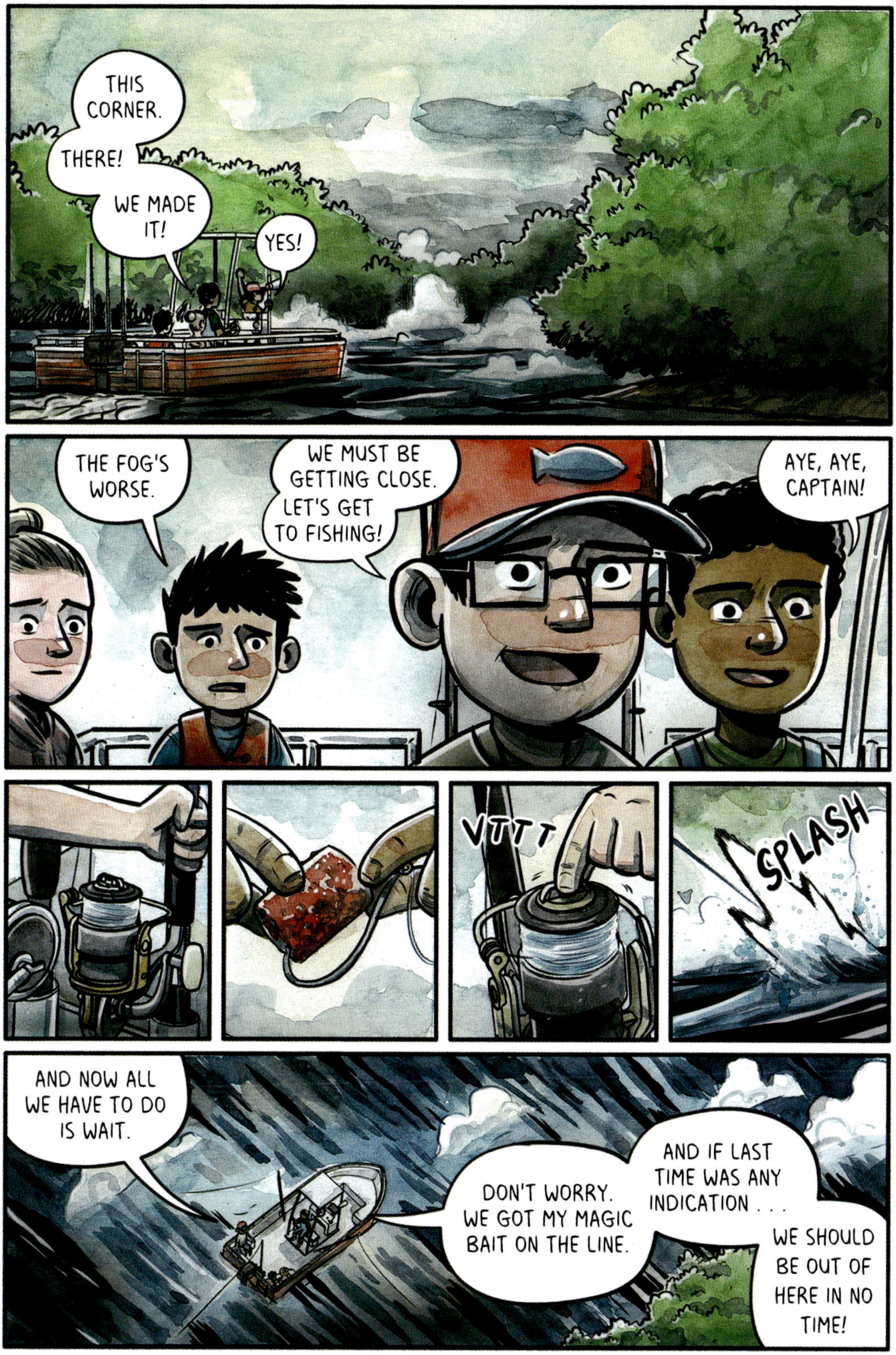
THIS CORNER.
THERE!
WE MADE IT!
YES!
THE FOG'S WORSE.
WE MUST BE GETTING CLOSE. LET'S GET TO FISHING!
AYE, AYE, CAPTAIN!
VTTT
SPLASH
AND NOW ALL WE HAVE TO DO IS WAIT.
DON'T WORRY. WE GOT MY MAGIC BAIT ON THE LINE.
AND IF LAST TIME WAS ANY INDICATION . . .
WE SHOULD BE OUT OF HERE IN NO TIME!

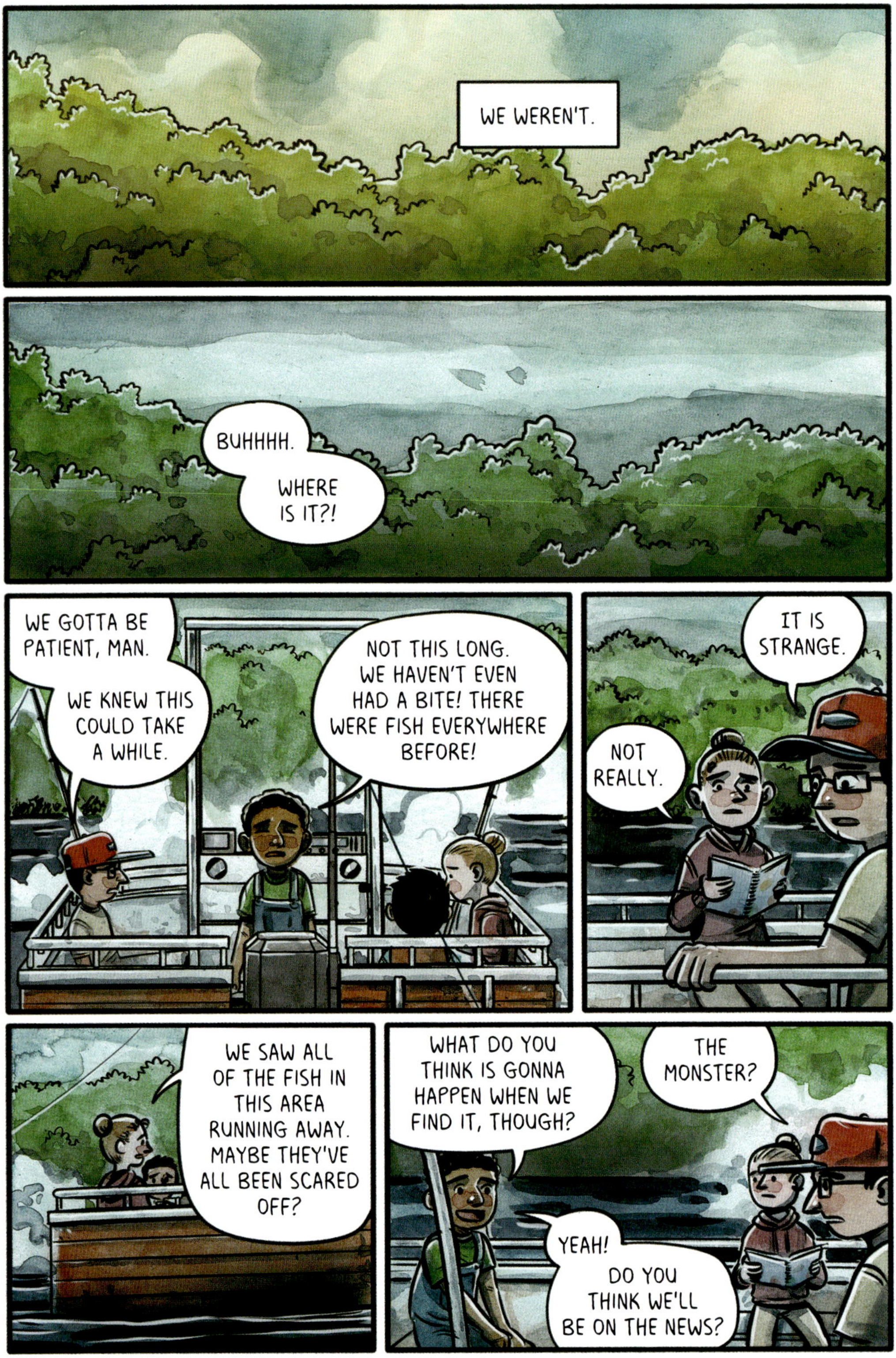
WE WEREN'T.
BUHHHH.
WHERE IS IT?!
WE GOTTA BE PATIENT, MAN.
WE KNEW THIS COULD TAKE A WHILE.
NOT THIS LONG. WE HAVEN'T EVEN HAD A BITE! THERE WERE FISH EVERYWHERE BEFORE!
IT IS STRANGE.
NOT REALLY.
WE SAW ALL OF THE FISH IN THIS AREA RUNNING AWAY. MAYBE THEY'VE ALL BEEN SCARED OFF?
WHAT DO YOU THINK IS GONNA HAPPEN WHEN WE FIND IT, THOUGH?
THE MONSTER?
YEAH!
DO YOU THINK WE'LL BE ON THE NEWS?

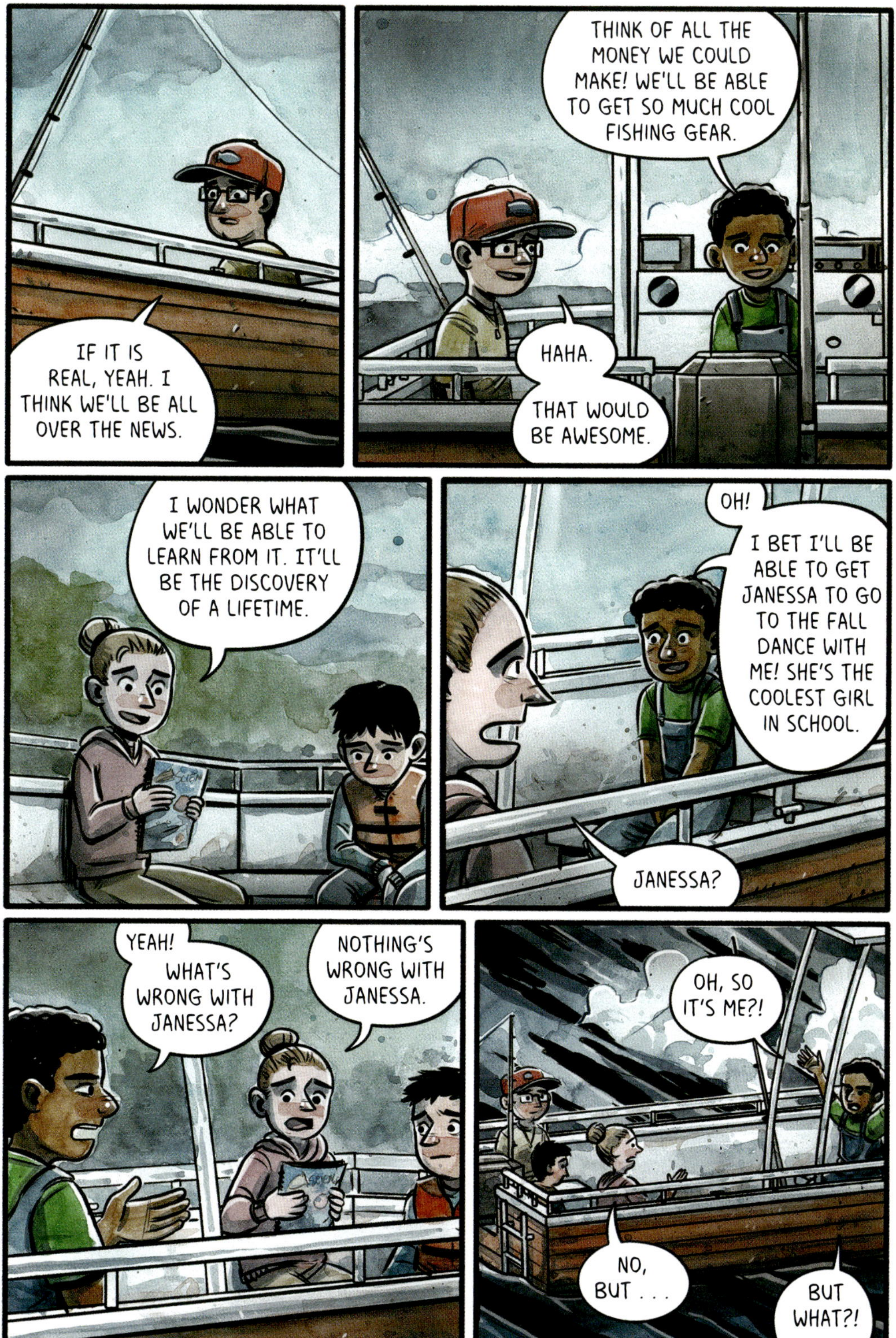
IF IT IS REAL, YEAH. I THINK WE'LL BE ALL OVER THE NEWS.
THINK OF ALL THE MONEY WE COULD MAKE! WE'LL BE ABLE TO GET SO MUCH COOL FISHING GEAR.
HAHA.
THAT WOULD BE AWESOME.
I WONDER WHAT WE'LL BE ABLE TO LEARN FROM IT. IT'LL BE THE DISCOVERY OF A LIFETIME.
OH!
I BET I'LL BE ABLE TO GET JANESSA TO GO TO THE FALL DANCE WITH ME! SHE'S THE COOLEST GIRL IN SCHOOL.
JANESSA?
YEAH!
WHAT'S WRONG WITH JANESSA?
NOTHING'S WRONG WITH JANESSA.
OH, SO IT'S ME?!
NO, BUT . . .
BUT WHAT?!

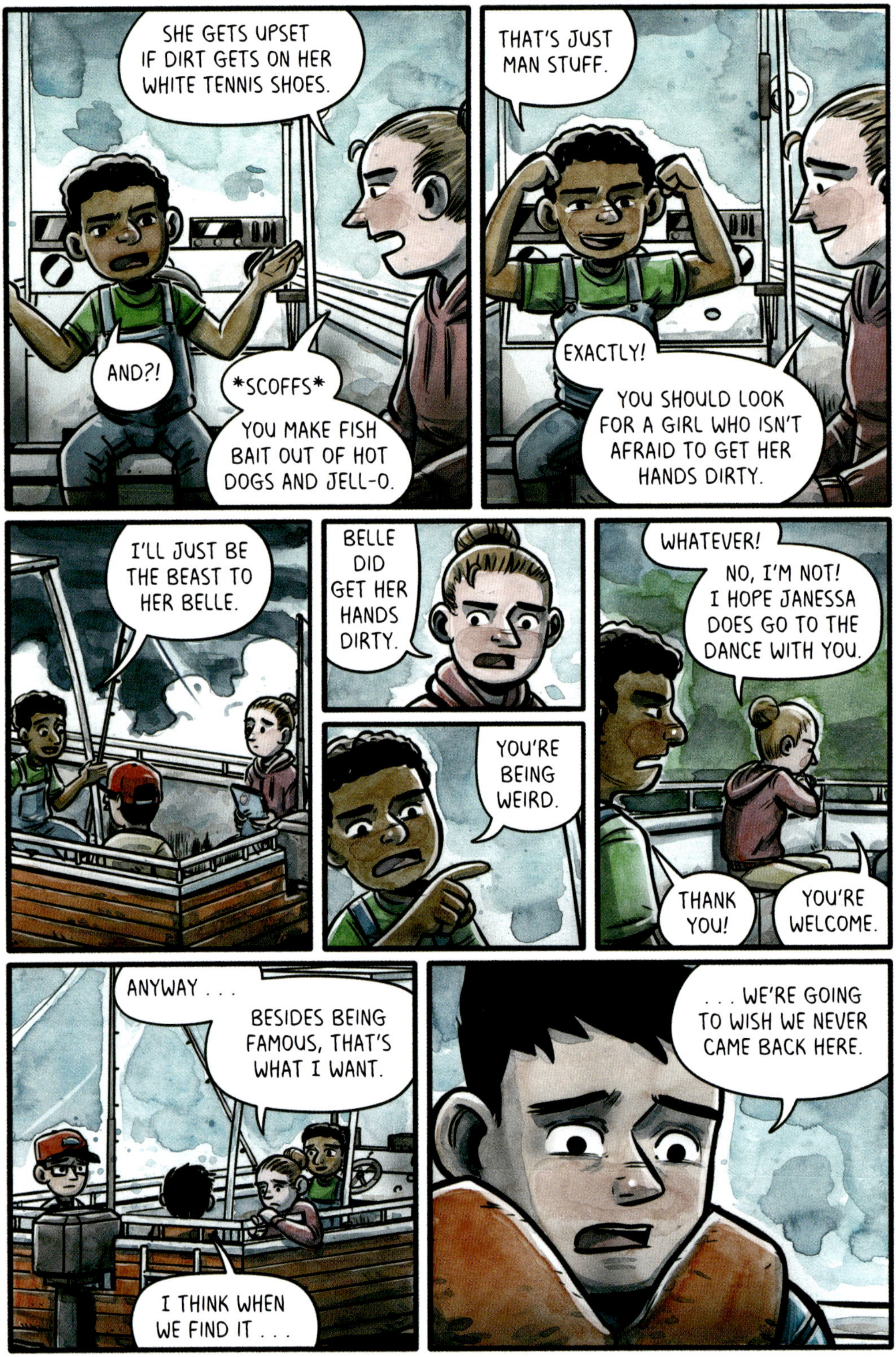
SHE GETS UPSET IF DIRT GETS ON HER WHITE TENNIS SHOES.
AND?!
SCOFFS
YOU MAKE FISH BAIT OUT OF HOT DOGS AND JELL-O.
THAT'S JUST MAN STUFF.
EXACTLY!
YOU SHOULD LOOK FOR A GIRL WHO ISN'T AFRAID TO GET HER HANDS DIRTY.
I'LL JUST BE THE BEAST TO HER BELLE.
BELLE DID GET HER HANDS DIRTY.
YOU'RE BEING WEIRD.
WHATEVER!
NO, I'M NOT! I HOPE JANESSA DOES GO TO THE DANCE WITH YOU.
THANK YOU!
YOU'RE WELCOME.
ANYWAY . . .
BESIDES BEING FAMOUS, THAT'S WHAT I WANT.
I THINK WHEN WE FIND IT . . .
. . . WE'RE GOING TO WISH WE NEVER CAME BACK HERE.

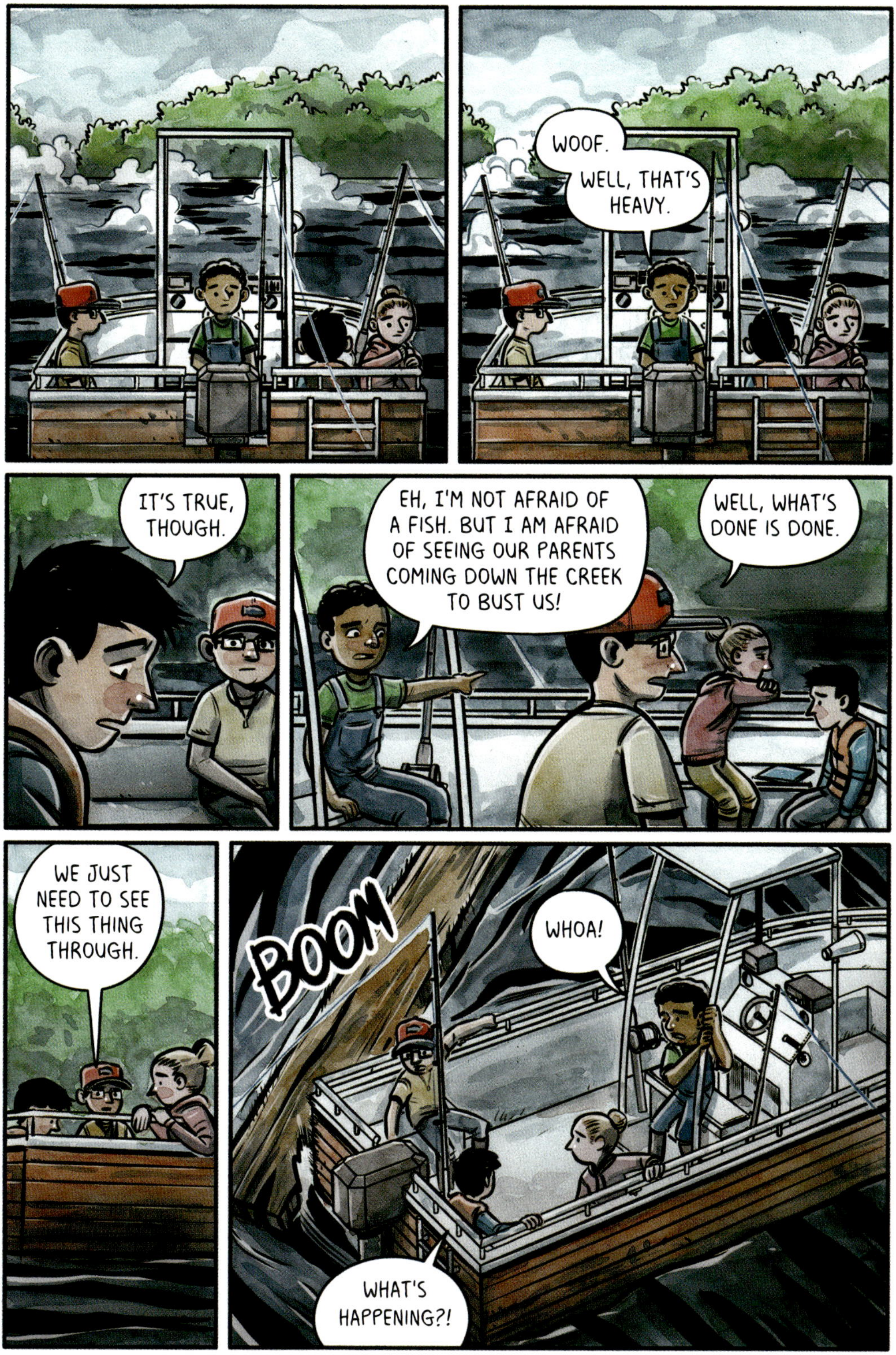
WOOF.
WELL, THAT'S HEAVY.
IT'S TRUE, THOUGH.
EH, I'M NOT AFRAID OF A FISH. BUT I AM AFRAID OF SEEING OUR PARENTS COMING DOWN THE CREEK TO BUST US!
WELL, WHAT'S DONE IS DONE.
WE JUST NEED TO SEE THIS THING THROUGH.
BOOM
WHOA!
WHAT'S HAPPENING?!

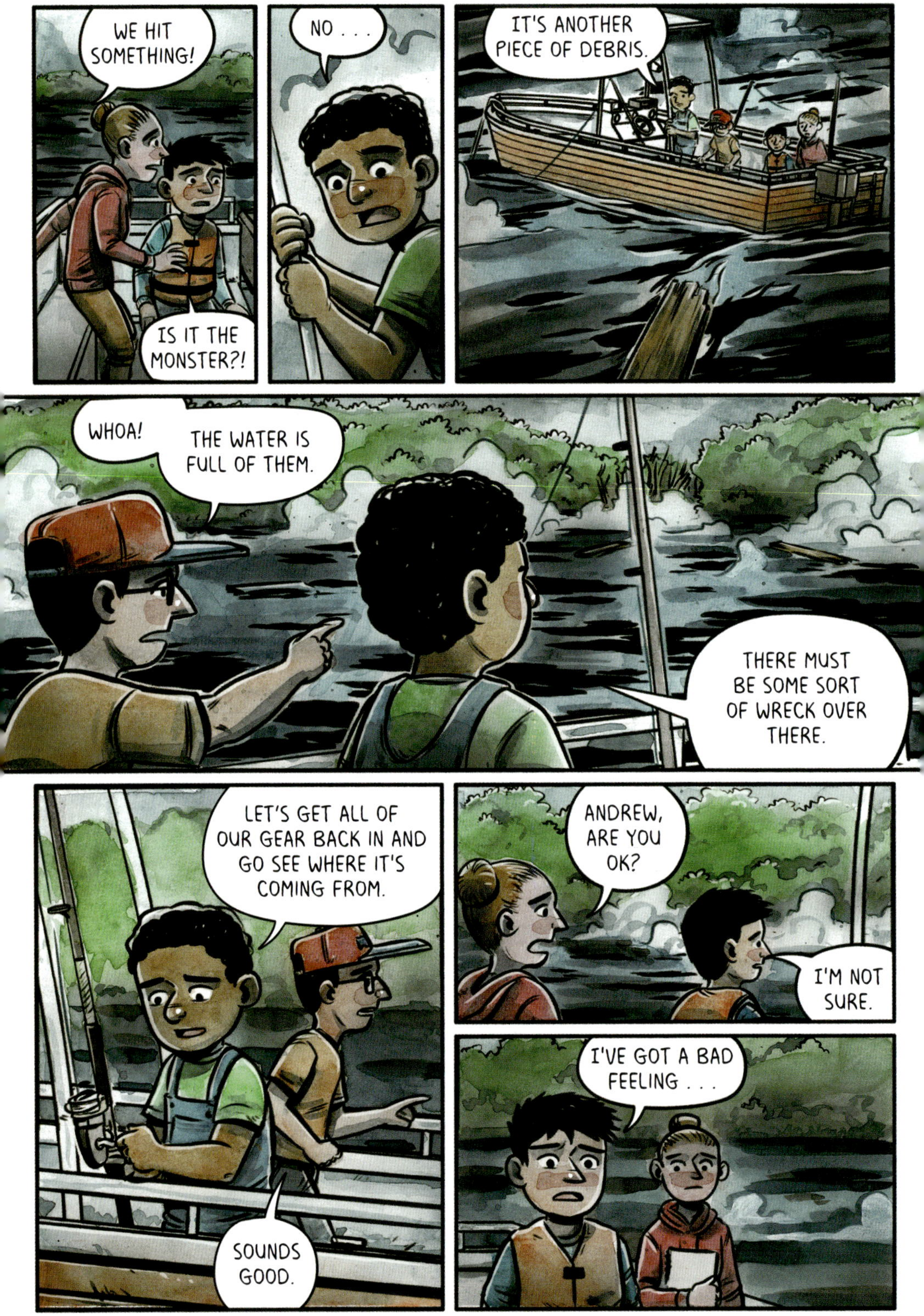
WE HIT SOMETHING!
IS IT THE MONSTER?!
NO . . .
IT'S ANOTHER PIECE OF DEBRIS.
WHOA!
THE WATER IS FULL OF THEM.
THERE MUST BE SOME SORT OF WRECK OVER THERE.
LET'S GET ALL OF OUR GEAR BACK IN AND GO SEE WHERE IT'S COMING FROM.
SOUNDS GOOD.
ANDREW, ARE YOU OK?
I'M NOT SURE.
I'VE GOT A BAD FEELING . . .

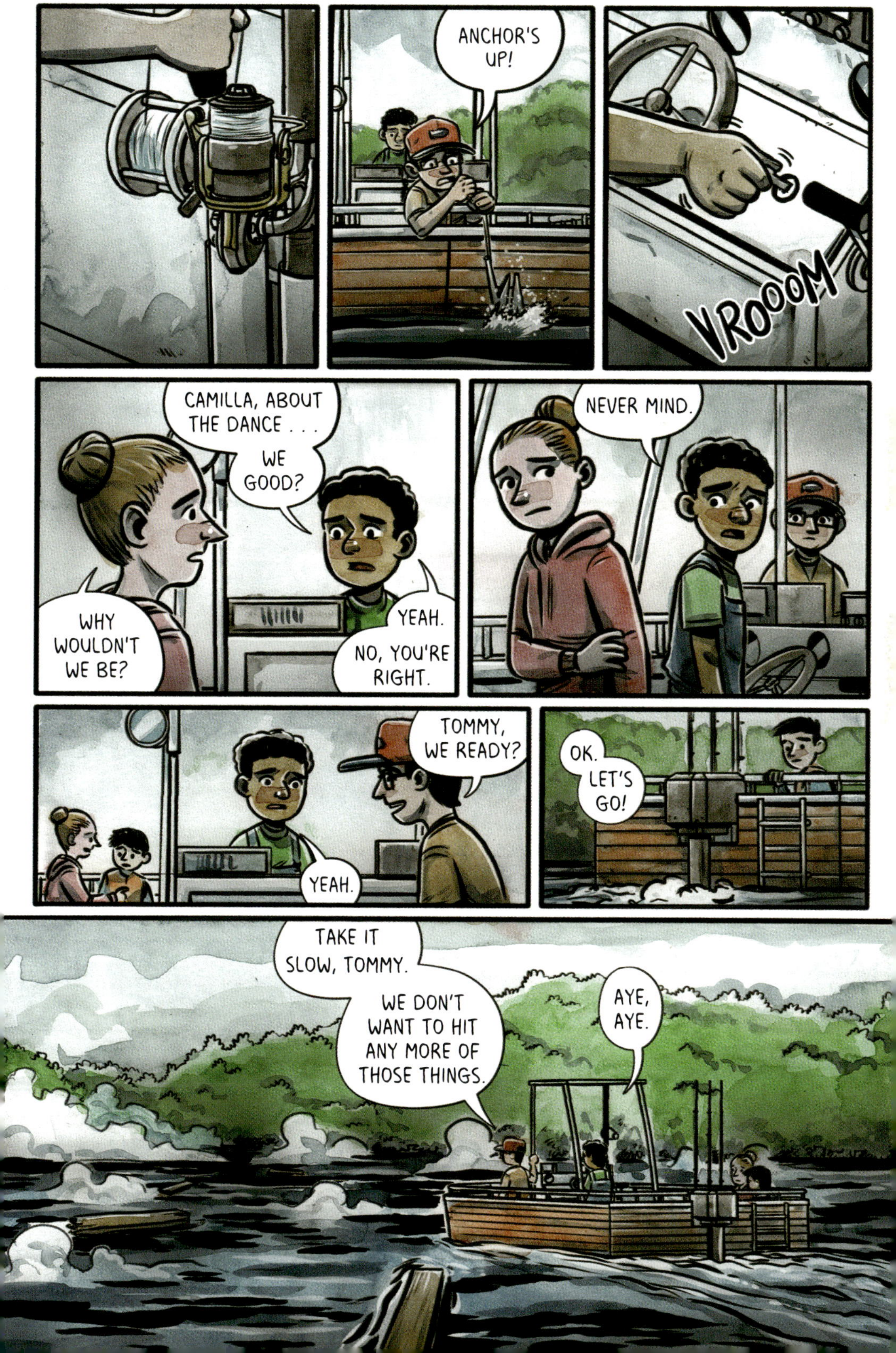
ANCHOR'S UP!
VROOOM
CAMILLA, ABOUT THE DANCE . . .
WE GOOD?
WHY WOULDN'T WE BE?
YEAH.
NO, YOU'RE RIGHT.
NEVER MIND.
TOMMY, WE READY?
YEAH.
OK.
LET'S GO!
TAKE IT SLOW, TOMMY.
WE DON'T WANT TO HIT ANY MORE OF THOSE THINGS.
AYE, AYE.

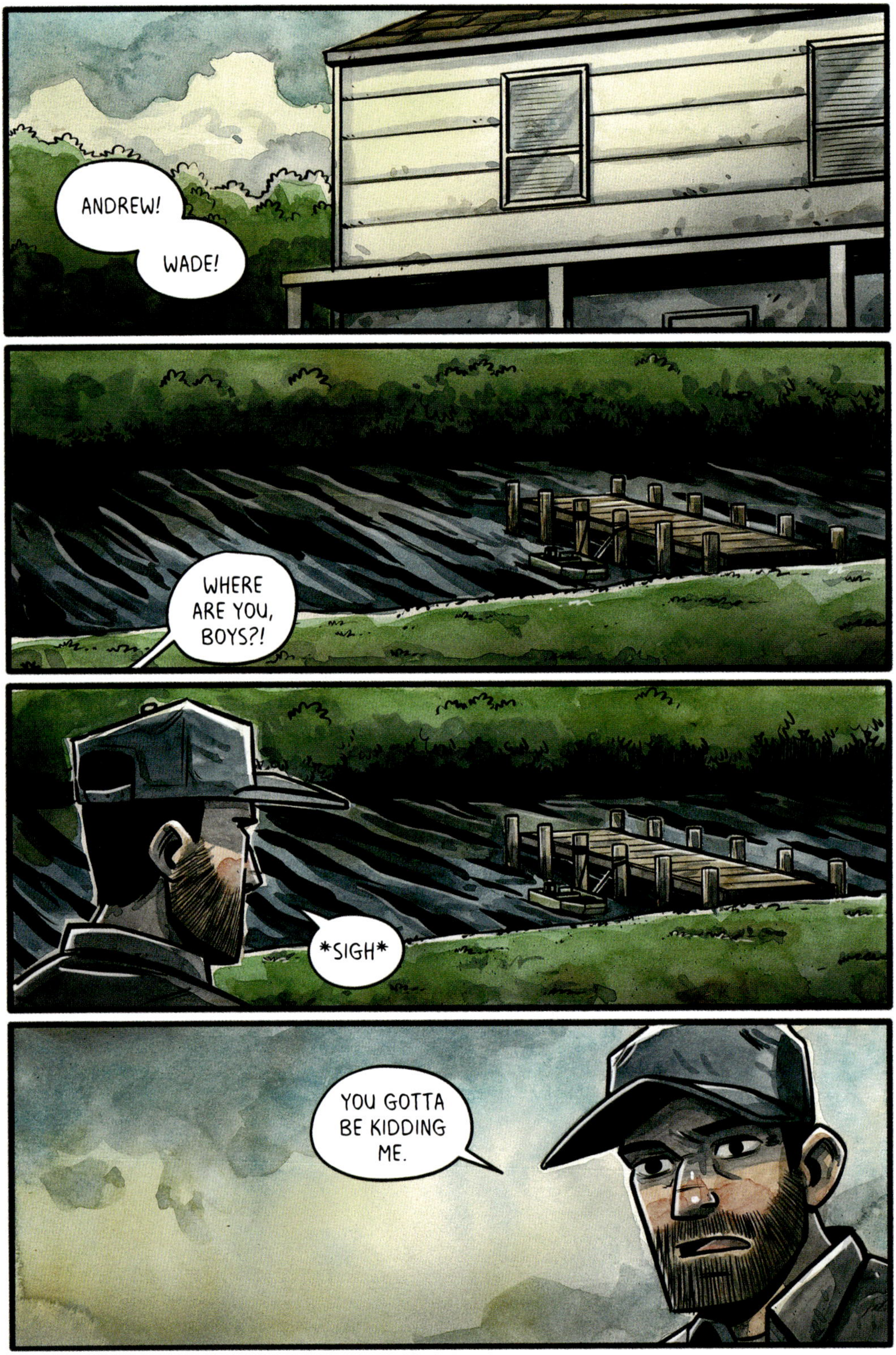
ANDREW!
WADE!
WHERE ARE YOU, BOYS?!
SIGH
YOU GOTTA BE KIDDING ME.

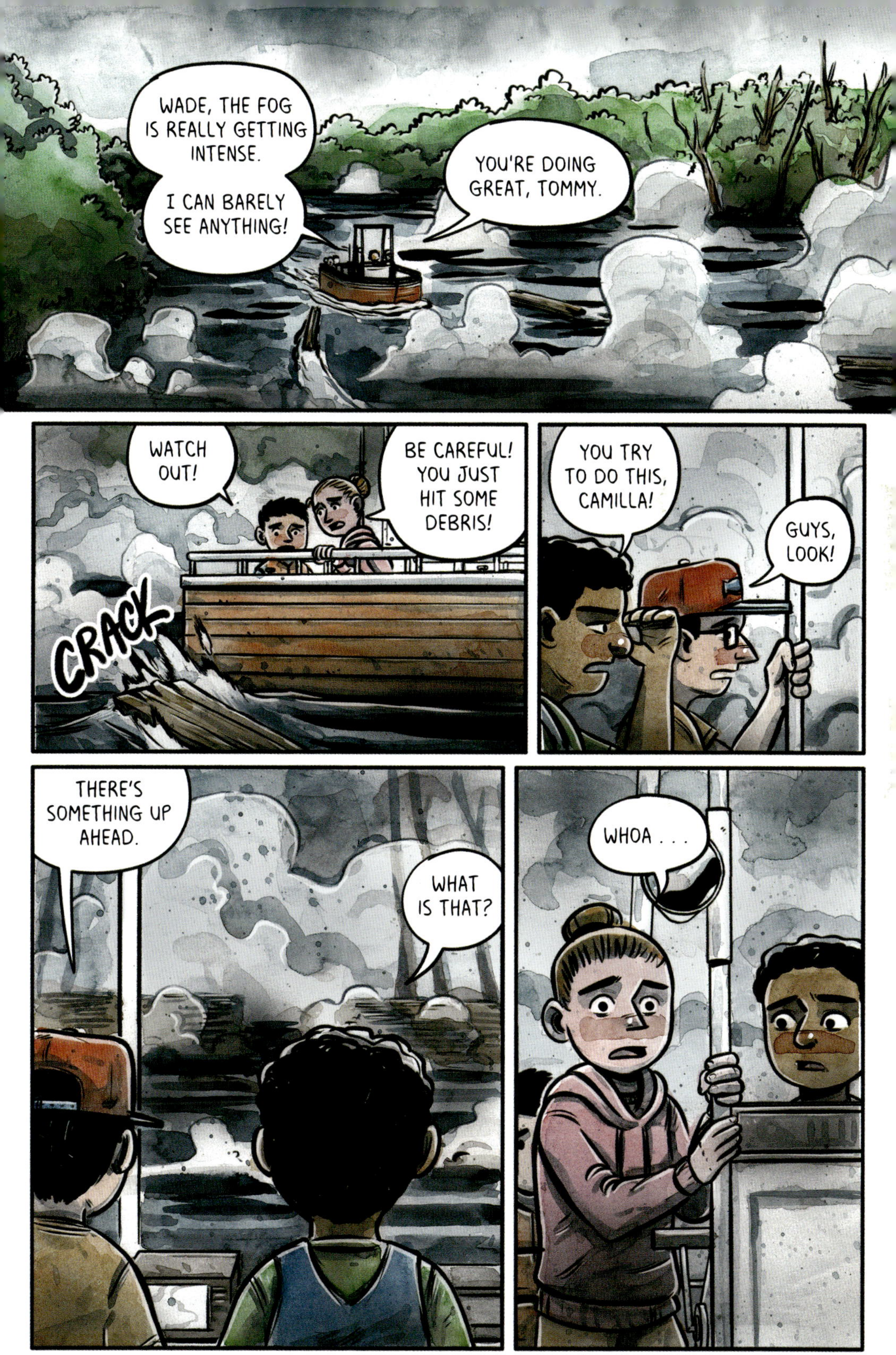
WADE, THE FOG IS REALLY GETTING INTENSE.
I CAN BARELY SEE ANYTHING!
YOU'RE DOING GREAT, TOMMY.
WATCH OUT!
BE CAREFUL! YOU JUST HIT SOME DEBRIS!
CRACK
YOU TRY TO DO THIS, CAMILLA!
GUYS, LOOK!
THERE'S SOMETHING UP AHEAD.
WHAT IS THAT?
WHOA . . .

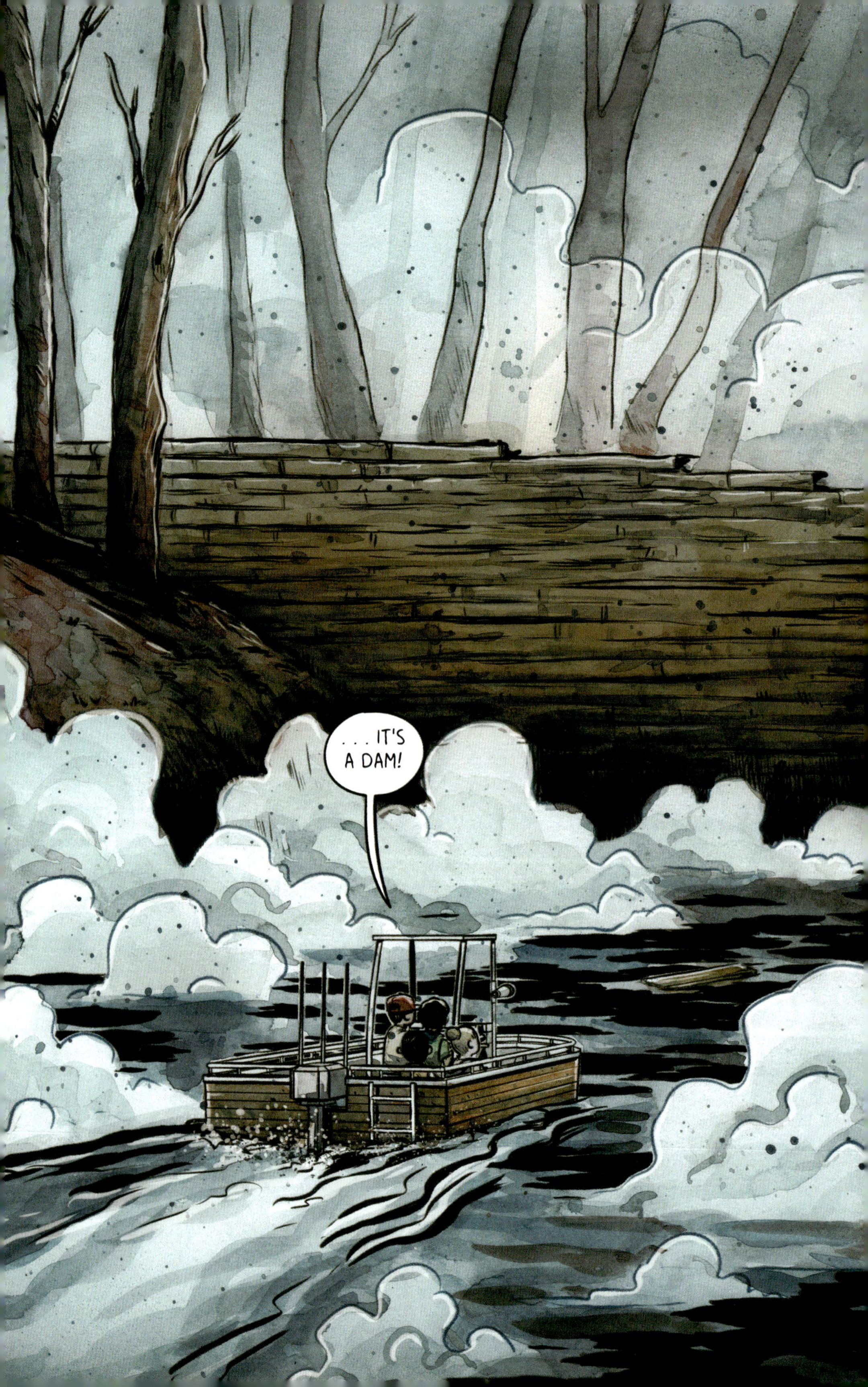
. . . IT'S A DAM!

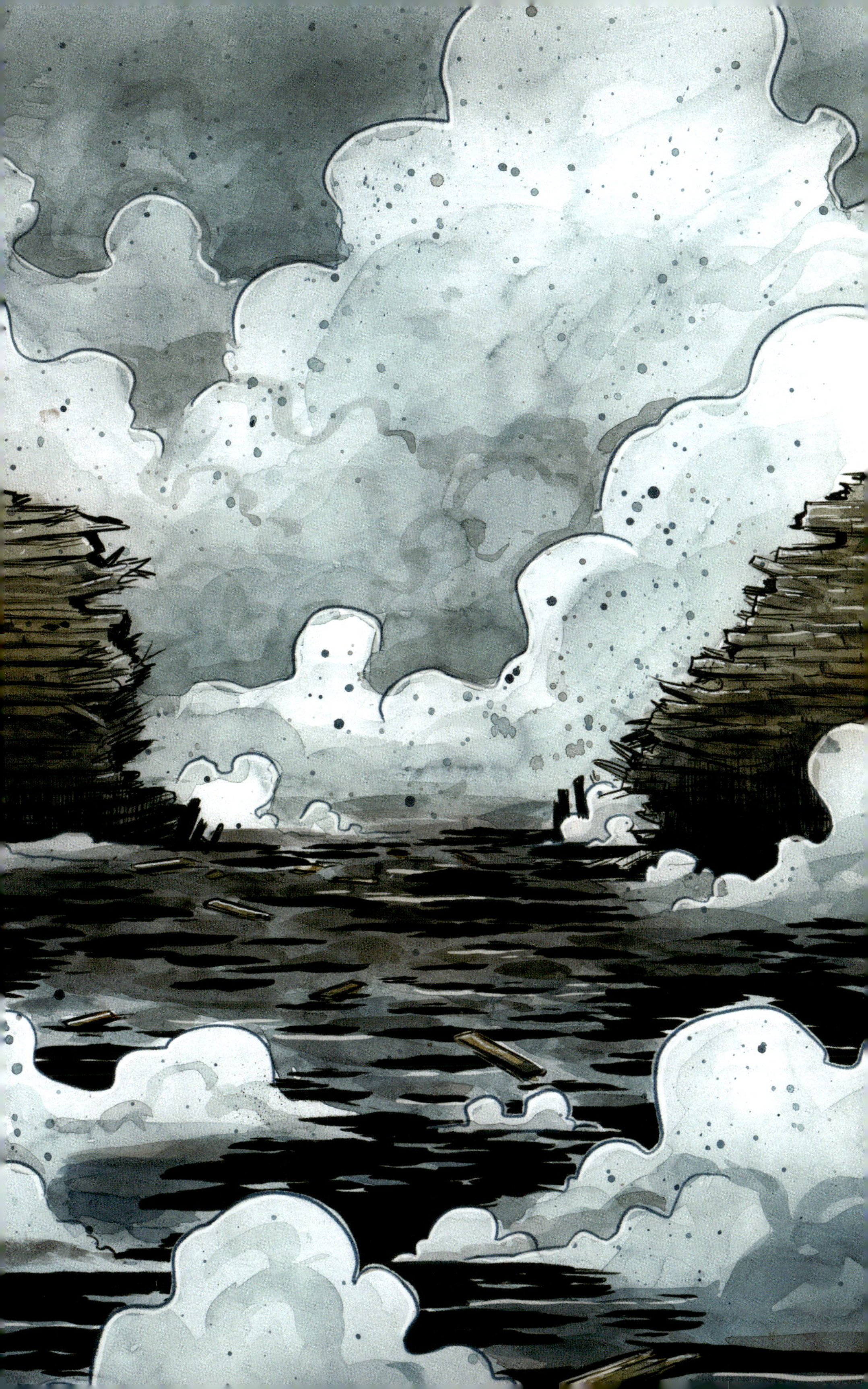

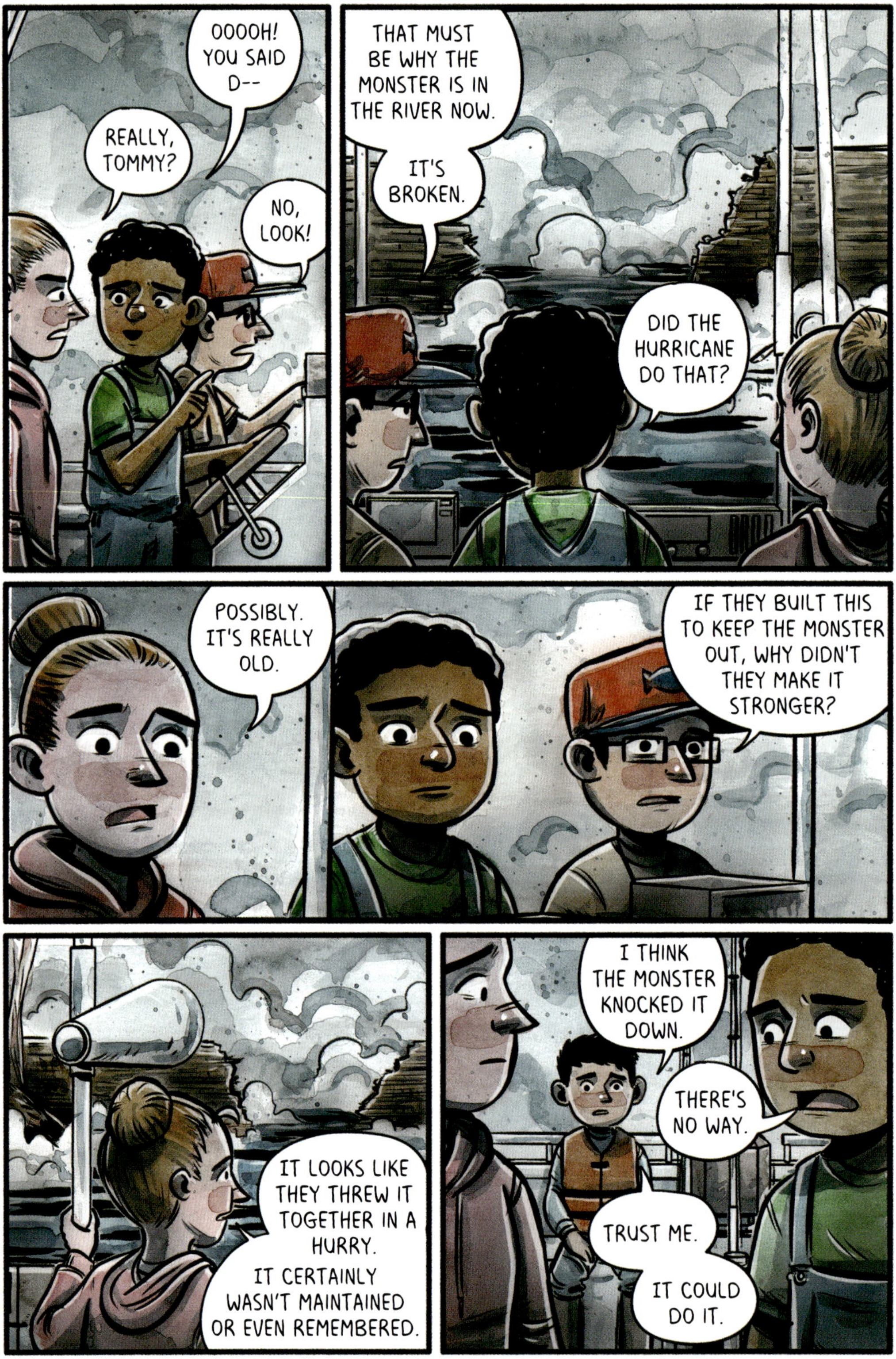
OOOOH! YOU SAID D--
REALLY, TOMMY?
NO, LOOK!
THAT MUST BE WHY THE MONSTER IS IN THE RIVER NOW.
IT'S BROKEN.
DID THE HURRICANE DO THAT?
POSSIBLY. IT'S REALLY OLD.
IF THEY BUILT THIS TO KEEP THE MONSTER OUT, WHY DIDN'T THEY MAKE IT STRONGER?
IT LOOKS LIKE THEY THREW IT TOGETHER IN A HURRY.
IT CERTAINLY WASN'T MAINTAINED OR EVEN REMEMBERED.
I THINK THE MONSTER KNOCKED IT DOWN.
THERE'S NO WAY.
TRUST ME.
IT COULD DO IT.

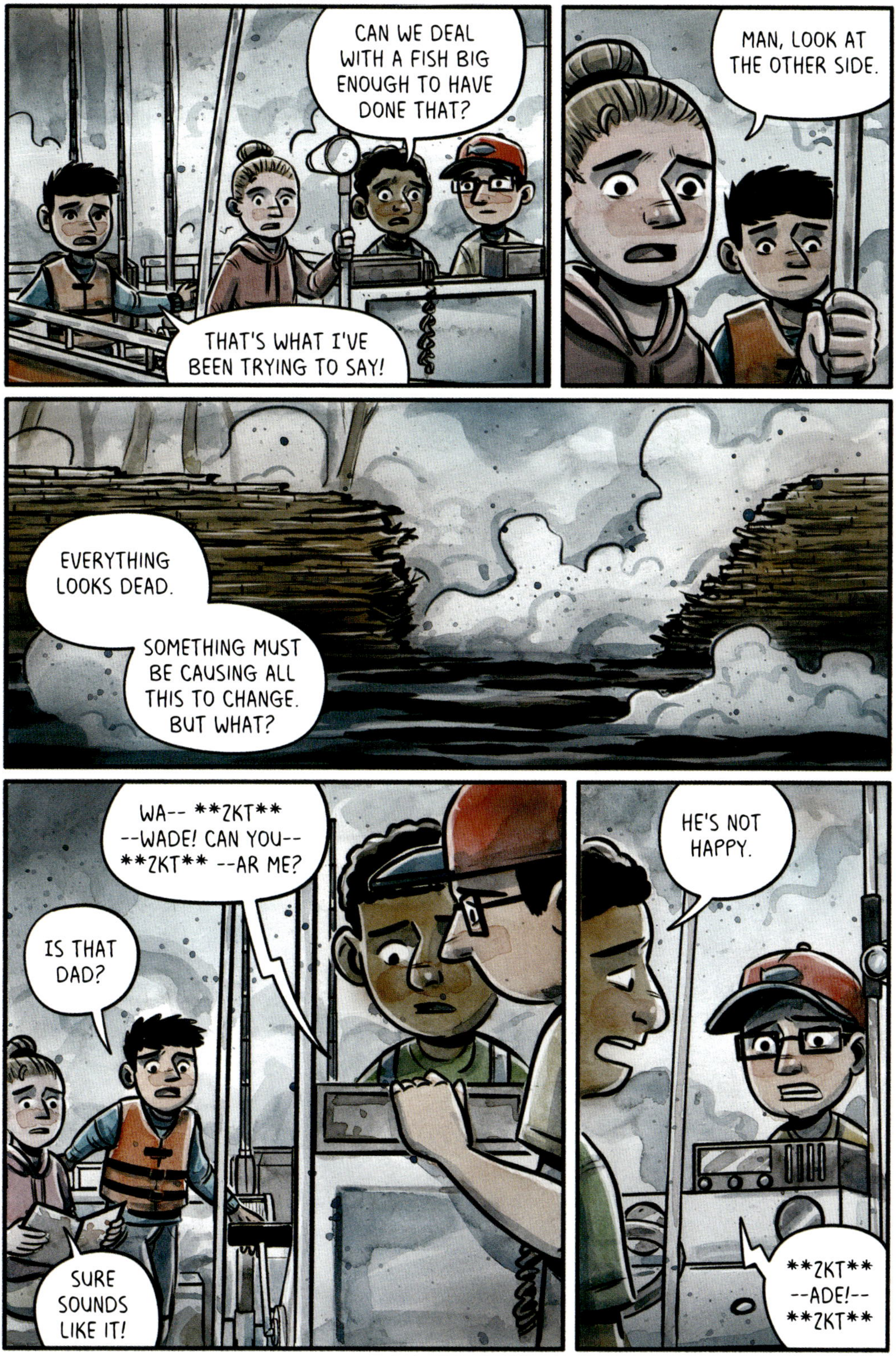
CAN WE DEAL WITH A FISH BIG ENOUGH TO HAVE DONE THAT?
THAT'S WHAT I'VE BEEN TRYING TO SAY!
MAN, LOOK AT THE OTHER SIDE.
EVERYTHING LOOKS DEAD.
SOMETHING MUST BE CAUSING ALL THIS TO CHANGE. BUT WHAT?
WA-- **ZKT** --WADE! CAN YOU-- **ZKT** --AR ME?
IS THAT DAD?
SURE SOUNDS LIKE IT!
HE'S NOT HAPPY.
ZKT --ADE!-- **ZKT**

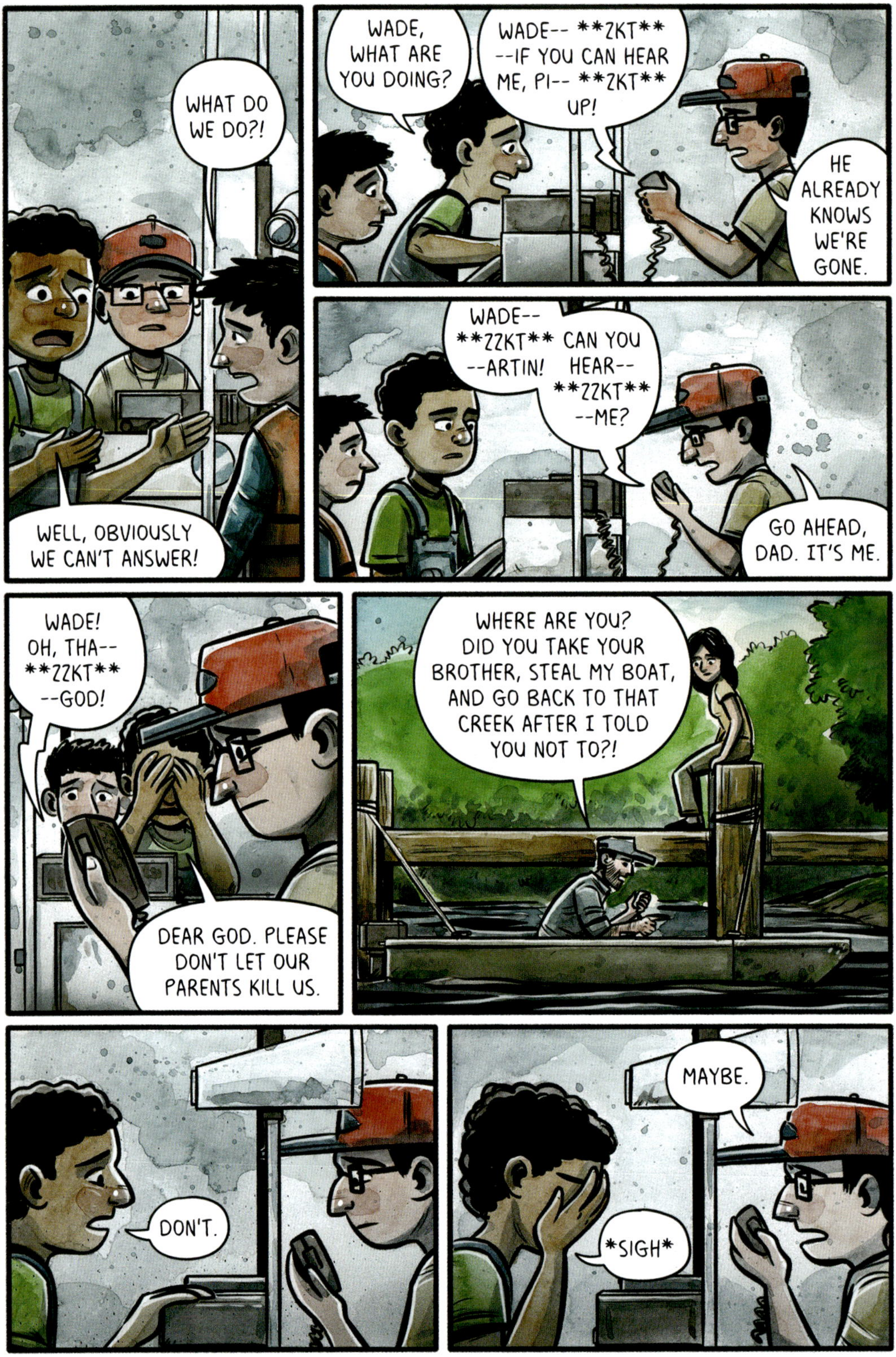
WHAT DO WE DO?!
WELL, OBVIOUSLY WE CAN'T ANSWER!
WADE, WHAT ARE YOU DOING?
WADE-- **ZKT** --IF YOU CAN HEAR ME, PI-- **ZKT** UP!
HE ALREADY KNOWS WE'RE GONE.
WADE-- **ZZKT** --ARTIN!
CAN YOU HEAR-- **ZZKT** --ME?
GO AHEAD, DAD. IT'S ME.
WADE! OH, THA-- **ZZKT** --GOD!
DEAR GOD. PLEASE DON'T LET OUR PARENTS KILL US.
WHERE ARE YOU? DID YOU TAKE YOUR BROTHER, STEAL MY BOAT, AND GO BACK TO THAT CREEK AFTER I TOLD YOU NOT TO?!
DON'T.
MAYBE.
SIGH

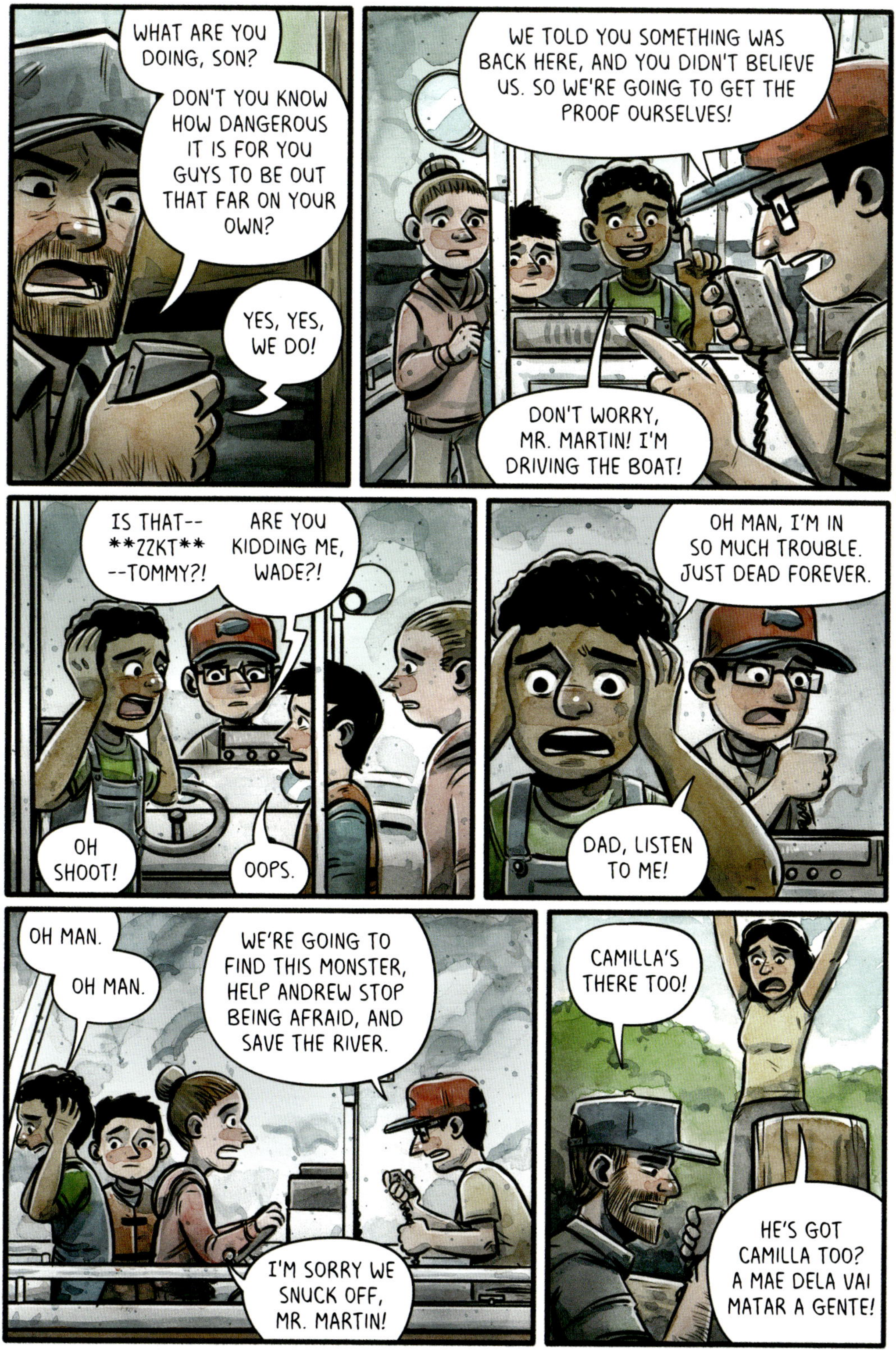
WHAT ARE YOU DOING, SON?
DON'T YOU KNOW HOW DANGEROUS IT IS FOR YOU GUYS TO BE OUT THAT FAR ON YOUR OWN?
YES, YES, WE DO!
WE TOLD YOU SOMETHING WAS BACK HERE, AND YOU DIDN'T BELIEVE US. SO WE'RE GOING TO GET THE PROOF OURSELVES!
DON'T WORRY, MR. MARTIN! I'M DRIVING THE BOAT!
IS THAT-- **ZZKT** --TOMMY?!
ARE YOU KIDDING ME, WADE?!
OH SHOOT!
OOPS.
OH MAN, I'M IN SO MUCH TROUBLE. JUST DEAD FOREVER.
DAD, LISTEN TO ME!
OH MAN.
OH MAN.
WE'RE GOING TO FIND THIS MONSTER, HELP ANDREW STOP BEING AFRAID, AND SAVE THE RIVER.
I'M SORRY WE SNUCK OFF, MR. MARTIN!
CAMILLA'S THERE TOO!
HE'S GOT CAMILLA TOO? A MAE DELA VAI MATAR A GENTE!

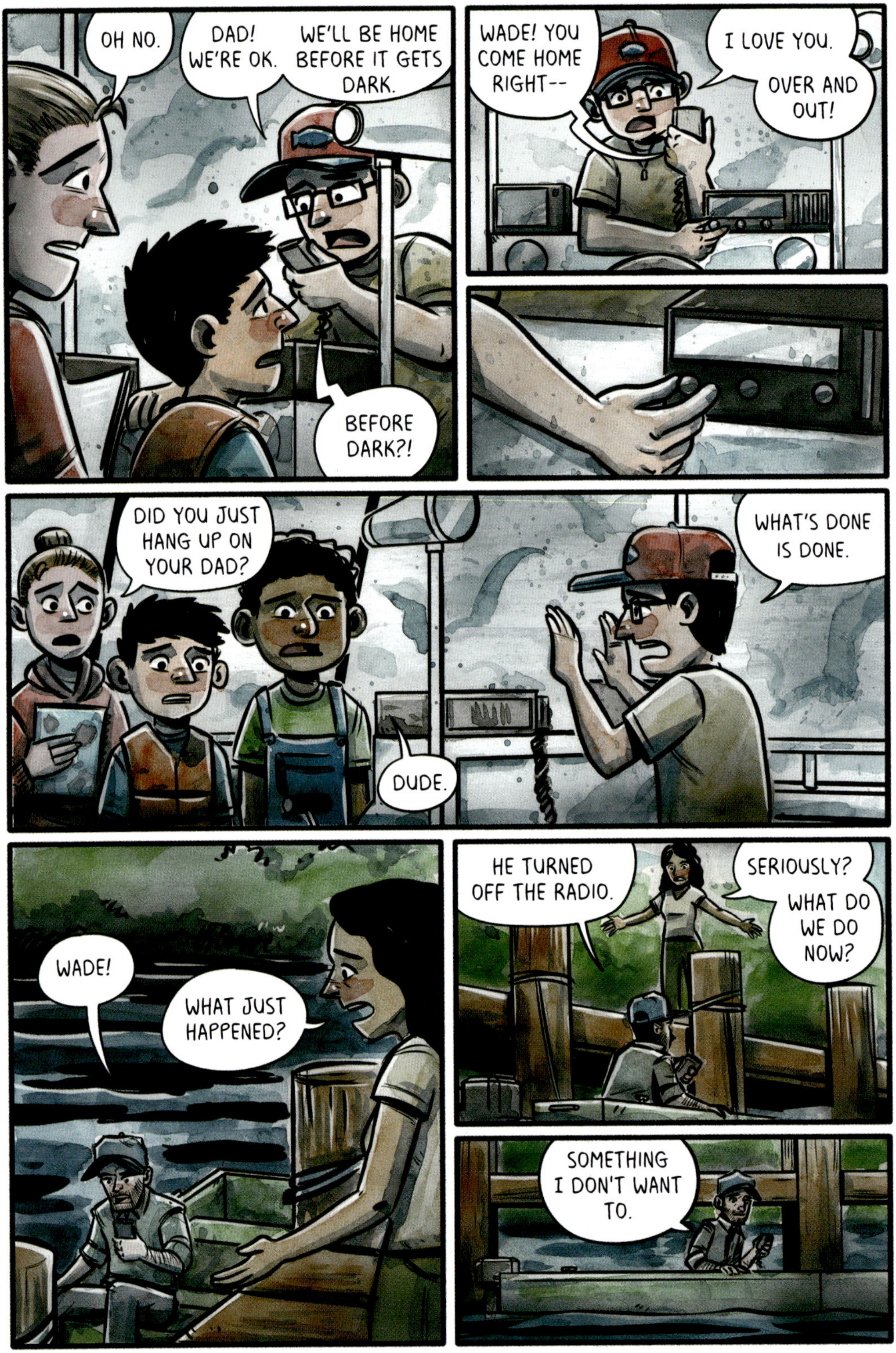
OH NO.
DAD! WE'RE OK.
WE'LL BE HOME BEFORE IT GETS DARK.
BEFORE DARK?!
WADE! YOU COME HOME RIGHT--
I LOVE YOU.
OVER AND OUT!
DID YOU JUST HANG UP ON YOUR DAD?
DUDE.
WHAT'S DONE IS DONE.
WADE!
WHAT JUST HAPPENED?
HE TURNED OFF THE RADIO.
SERIOUSLY?
WHAT DO WE DO NOW?
SOMETHING I DON'T WANT TO.

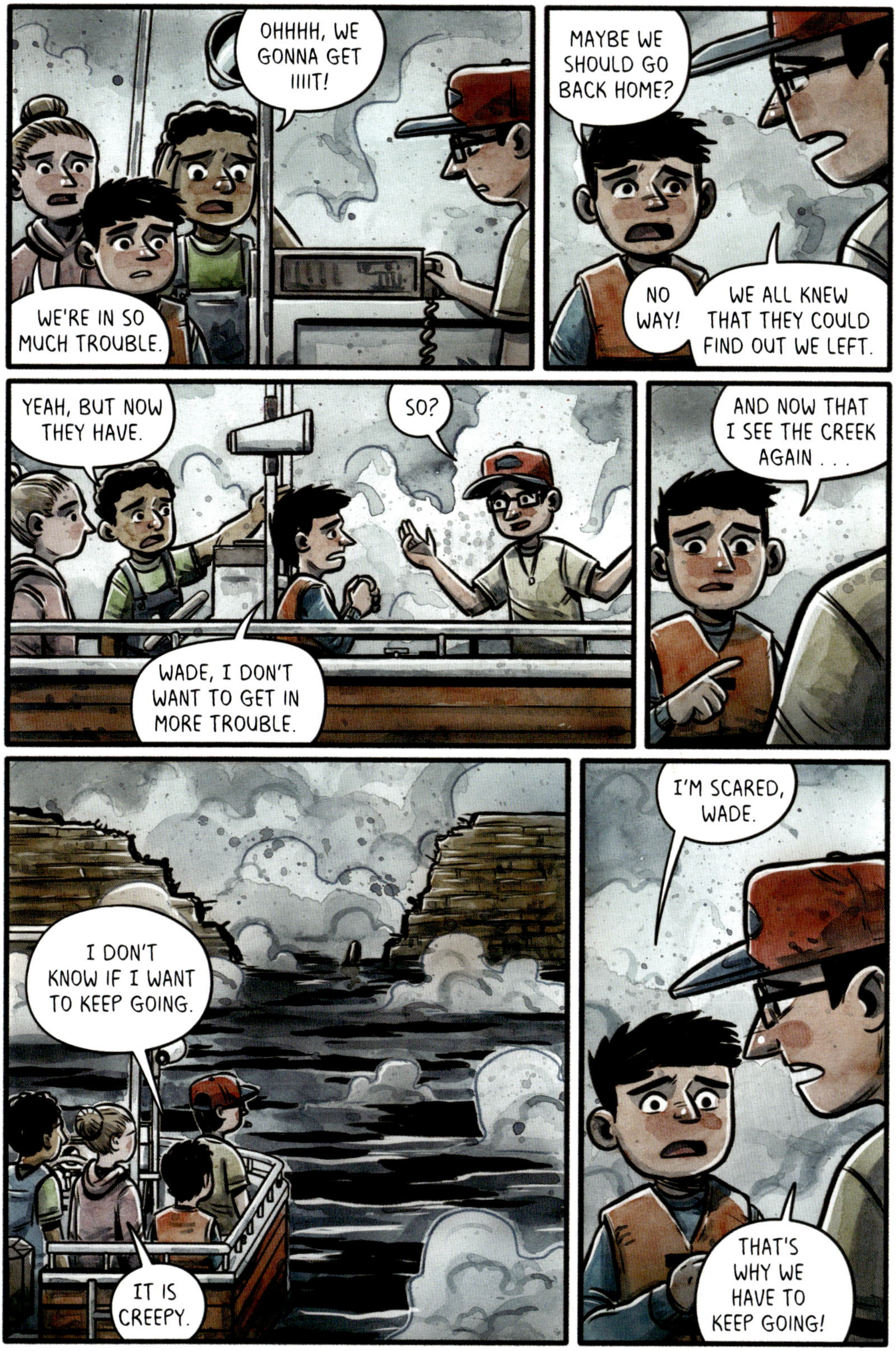
OHHHH, WE GONNA GET IIIIT!
WE'RE IN SO MUCH TROUBLE.
MAYBE WE SHOULD GO BACK HOME?
NO WAY!
WE ALL KNEW THAT THEY COULD FIND OUT WE LEFT.
YEAH, BUT NOW THEY HAVE.
SO?
WADE, I DON'T WANT TO GET IN MORE TROUBLE.
AND NOW THAT I SEE THE CREEK AGAIN . . .
I DON'T KNOW IF I WANT TO KEEP GOING.
IT IS CREEPY.
I'M SCARED, WADE.
THAT'S WHY WE HAVE TO KEEP GOING!

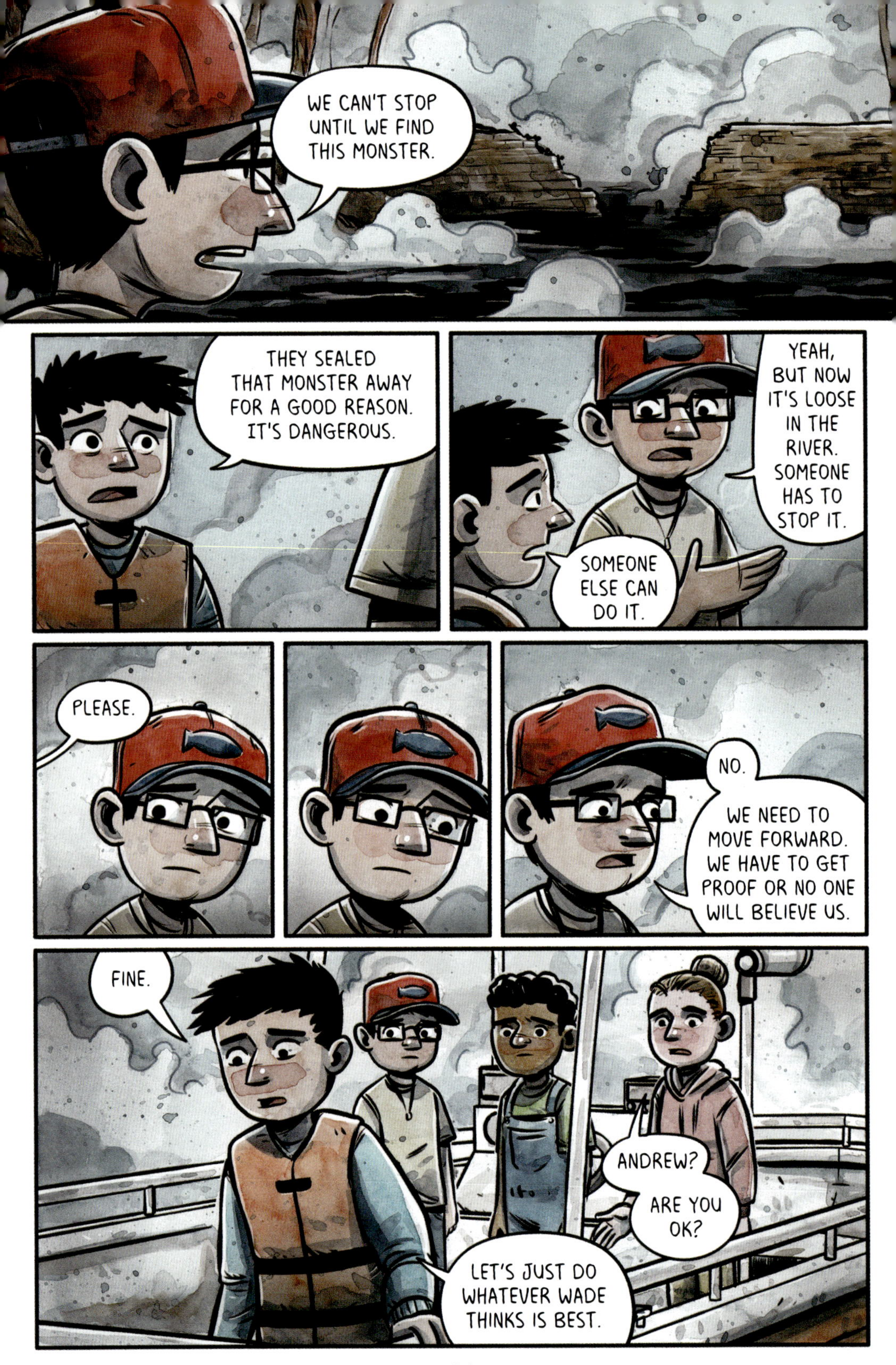
WE CAN'T STOP UNTIL WE FIND THIS MONSTER.
THEY SEALED THAT MONSTER AWAY FOR A GOOD REASON. IT'S DANGEROUS.
YEAH, BUT NOW IT'S LOOSE IN THE RIVER. SOMEONE HAS TO STOP IT.
SOMEONE ELSE CAN DO IT.
PLEASE.
NO.
WE NEED TO MOVE FORWARD. WE HAVE TO GET PROOF OR NO ONE WILL BELIEVE US.
FINE.
ANDREW?
ARE YOU OK?
LET'S JUST DO WHATEVER WADE THINKS IS BEST.

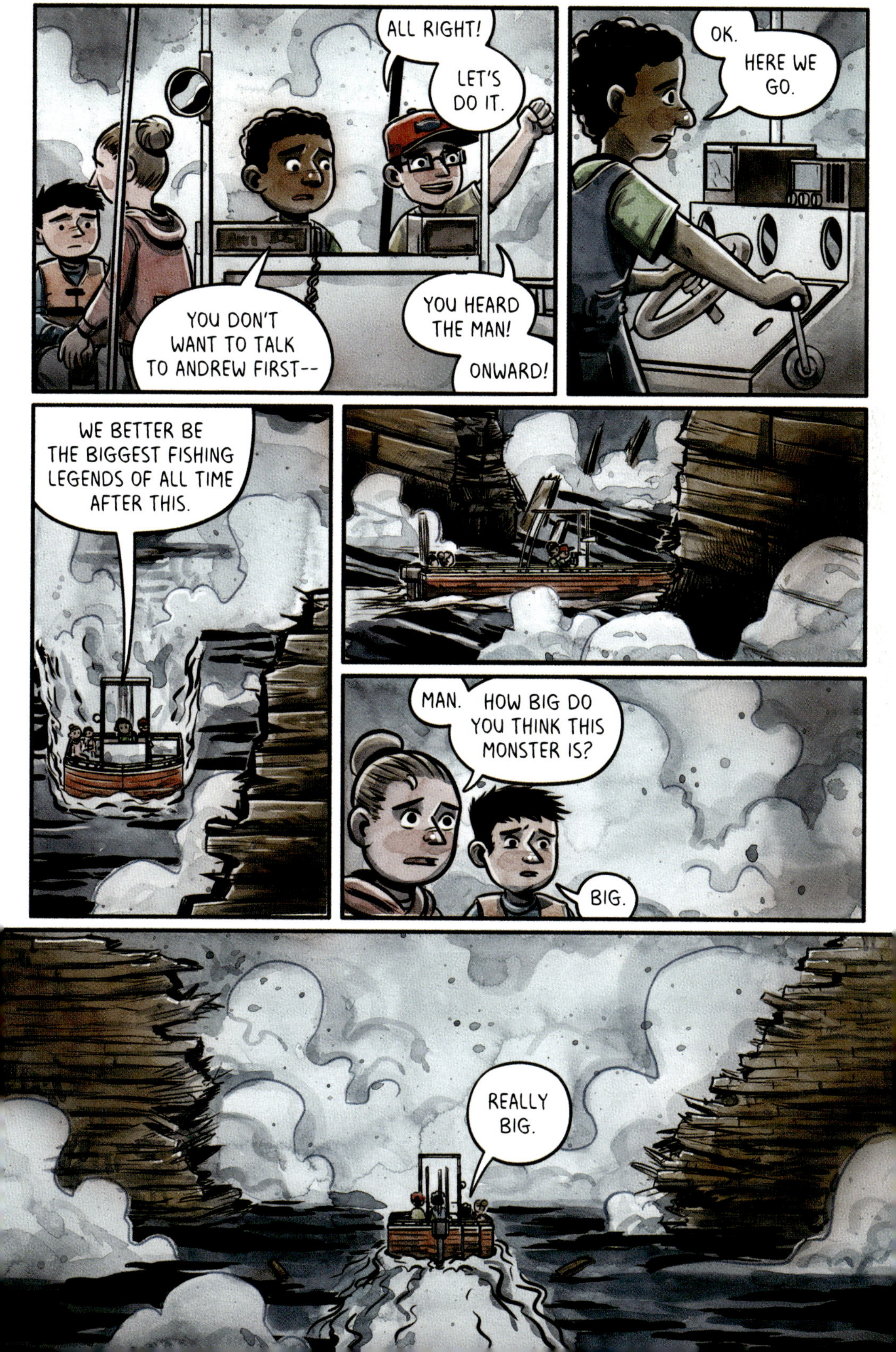
ALL RIGHT!
LET'S DO IT.
YOU DON'T WANT TO TALK TO ANDREW FIRST--
YOU HEARD THE MAN!
ONWARD!
OK.
HERE WE GO.
WE BETTER BE THE BIGGEST FISHING LEGENDS OF ALL TIME AFTER THIS.
MAN.
HOW BIG DO YOU THINK THIS MONSTER IS?
BIG.
REALLY BIG.

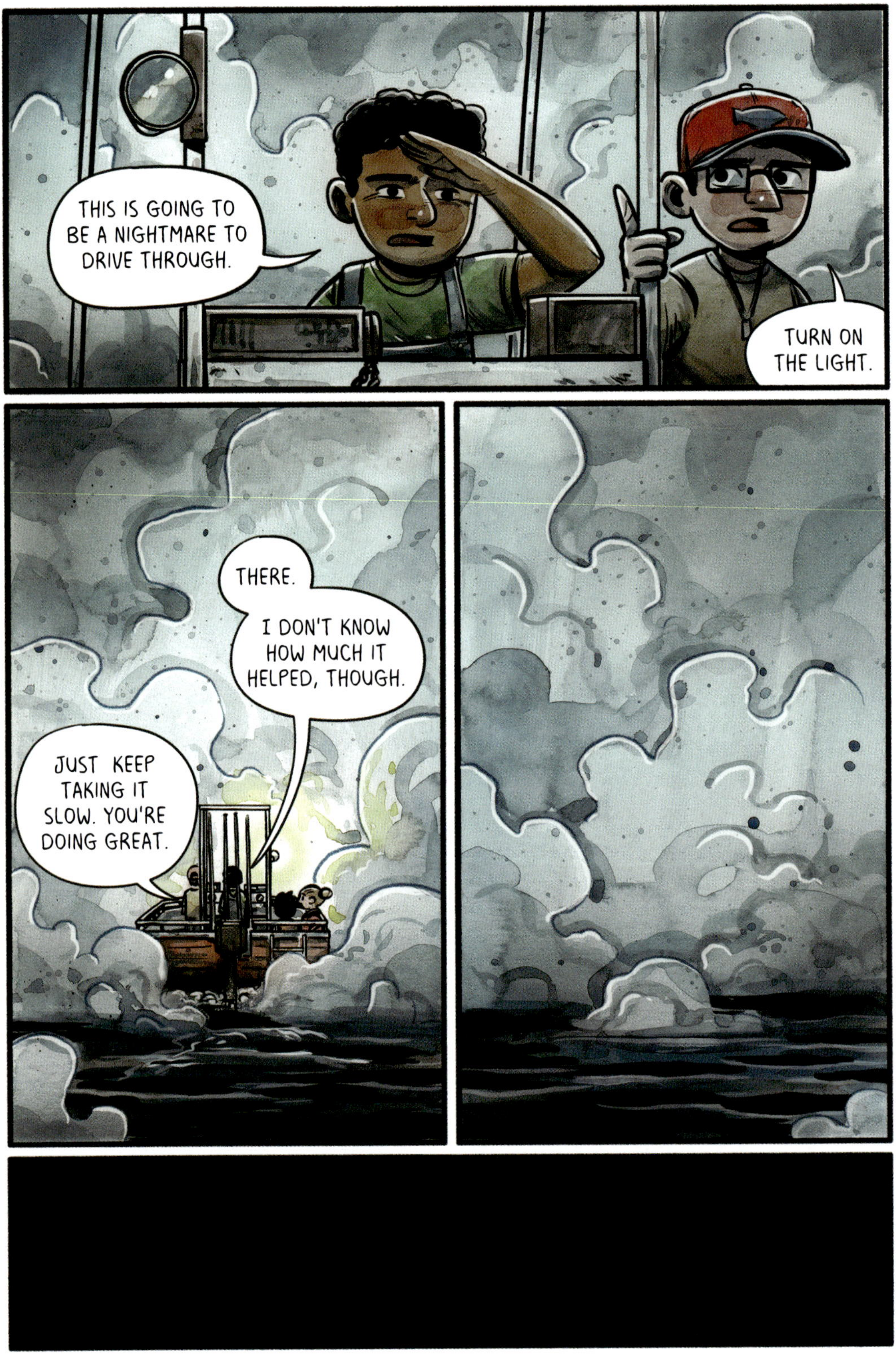
THIS IS GOING TO BE A NIGHTMARE TO DRIVE THROUGH.
TURN ON THE LIGHT.
THERE.
I DON'T KNOW HOW MUCH IT HELPED, THOUGH.
JUST KEEP TAKING IT SLOW. YOU'RE DOING GREAT.

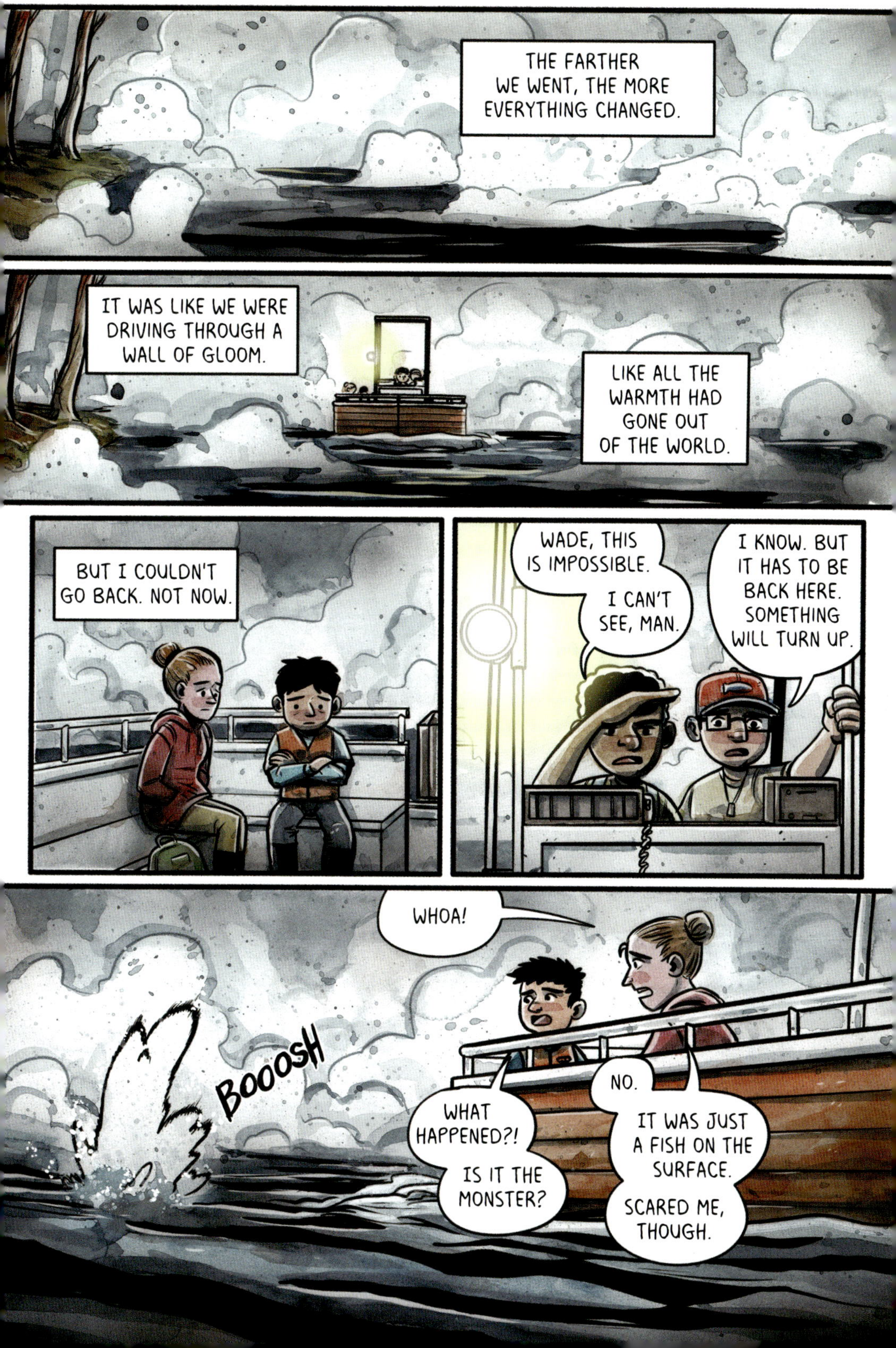

THE FARTHER WE WENT, THE MORE EVERYTHING CHANGED.
IT WAS LIKE WE WERE DRIVING THROUGH A WALL OF GLOOM.
LIKE ALL THE WARMTH HAD GONE OUT OF THE WORLD.
BUT I COULDN'T GO BACK. NOT NOW.
WADE, THIS IS IMPOSSIBLE.
I CAN'T SEE, MAN.
I KNOW. BUT IT HAS TO BE BACK HERE. SOMETHING WILL TURN UP.
WHOA!
BOOOSH
WHAT HAPPENED?!
IS IT THE MONSTER?
NO.
IT WAS JUST A FISH ON THE SURFACE.
SCARED ME, THOUGH.

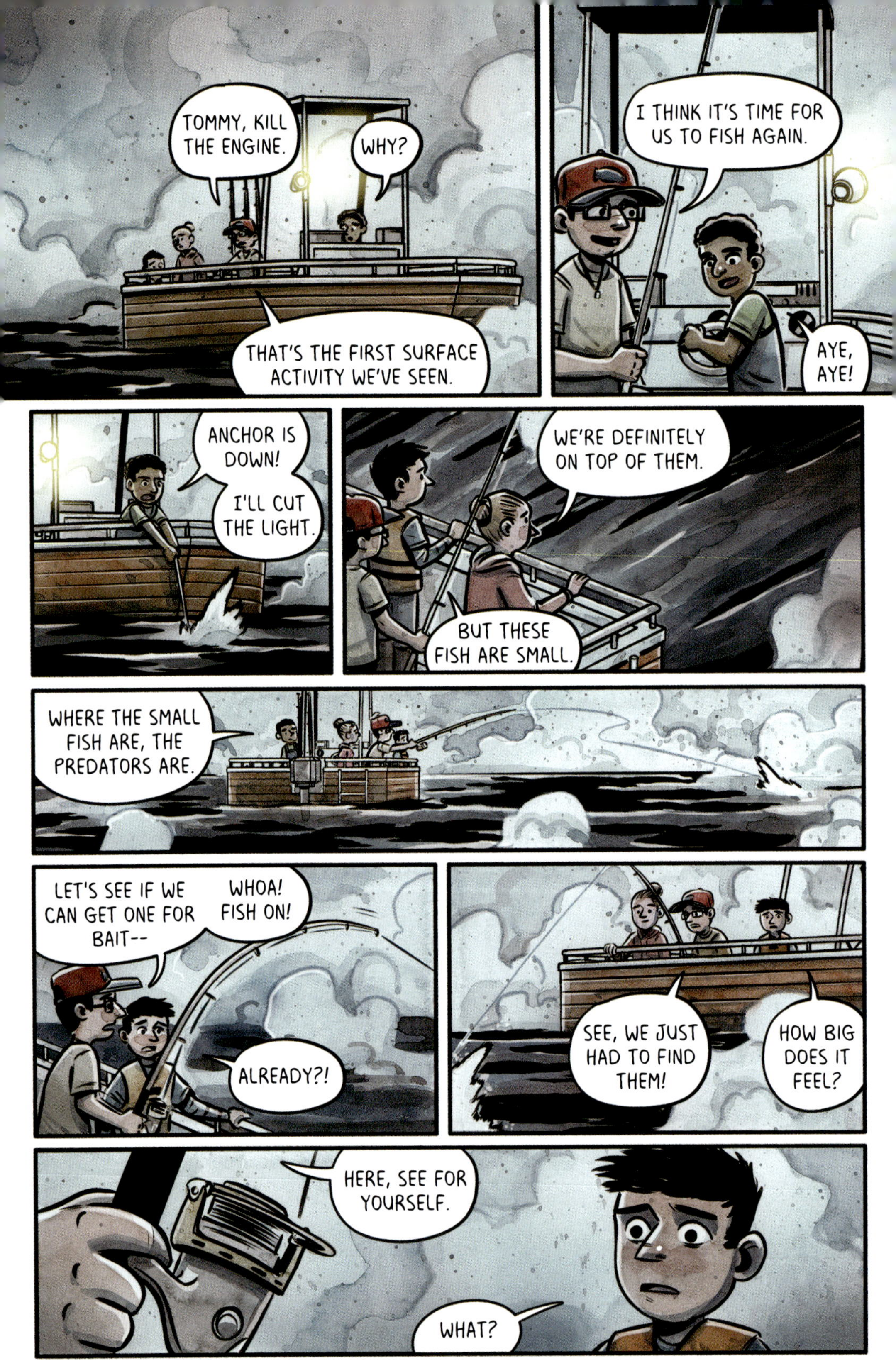
TOMMY, KILL THE ENGINE.
WHY?
THAT'S THE FIRST SURFACE ACTIVITY WE'VE SEEN.
I THINK IT'S TIME FOR US TO FISH AGAIN.
AYE, AYE!
ANCHOR IS DOWN!
I'LL CUT THE LIGHT.
WE'RE DEFINITELY ON TOP OF THEM.
BUT THESE FISH ARE SMALL.
WHERE THE SMALL FISH ARE, THE PREDATORS ARE.
LET'S SEE IF WE CAN GET ONE FOR BAIT--
WHOA! FISH ON!
ALREADY?!
SEE, WE JUST HAD TO FIND THEM!
HOW BIG DOES IT FEEL?
HERE, SEE FOR YOURSELF.
WHAT?

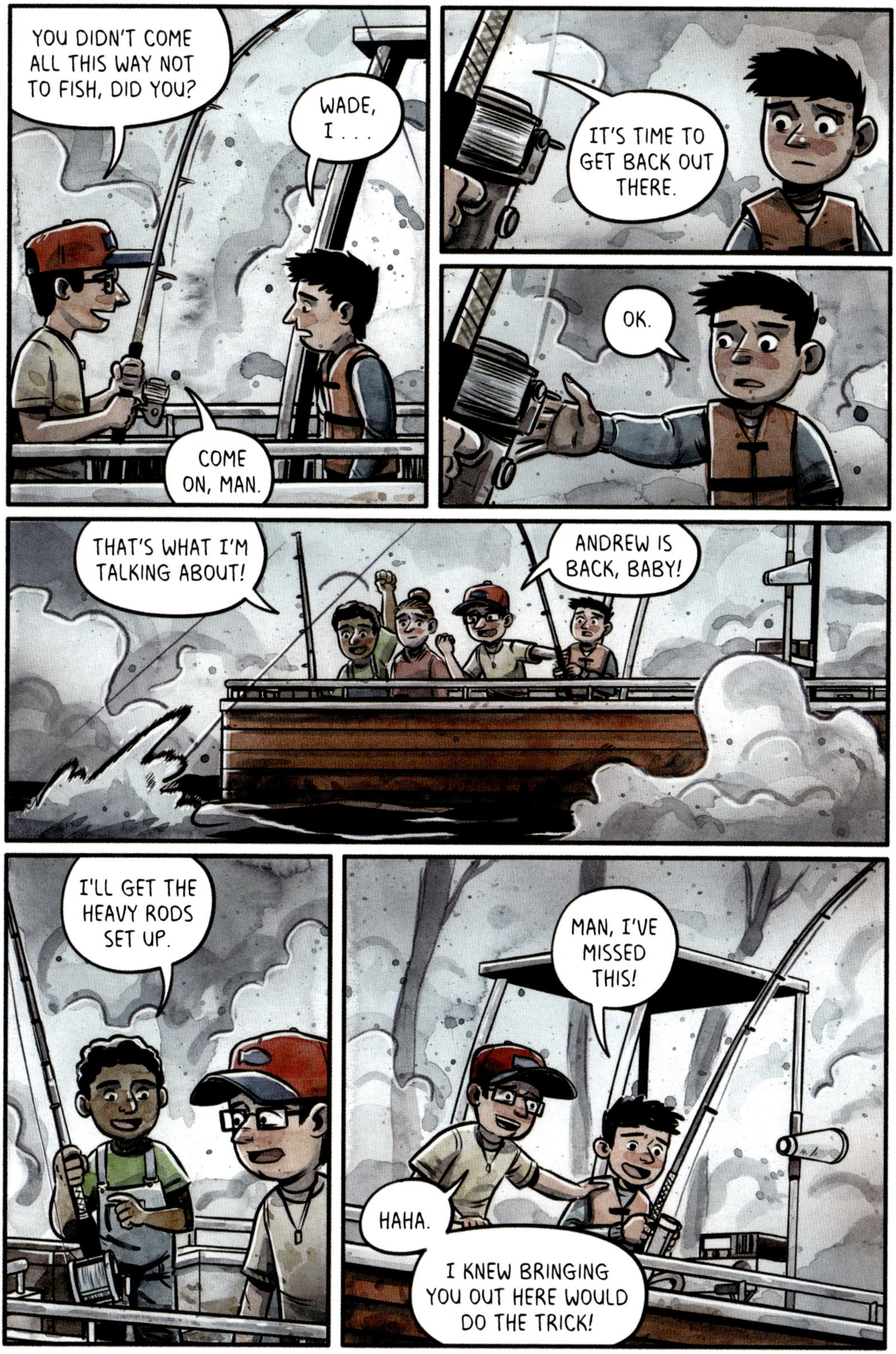
YOU DIDN'T COME ALL THIS WAY NOT TO FISH, DID YOU?
WADE, I . . .
COME ON, MAN.
IT'S TIME TO GET BACK OUT THERE.
OK.
THAT'S WHAT I'M TALKING ABOUT!
ANDREW IS BACK, BABY!
I'LL GET THE HEAVY RODS SET UP.
MAN, I'VE MISSED THIS!
HAHA.
I KNEW BRINGING YOU OUT HERE WOULD DO THE TRICK!

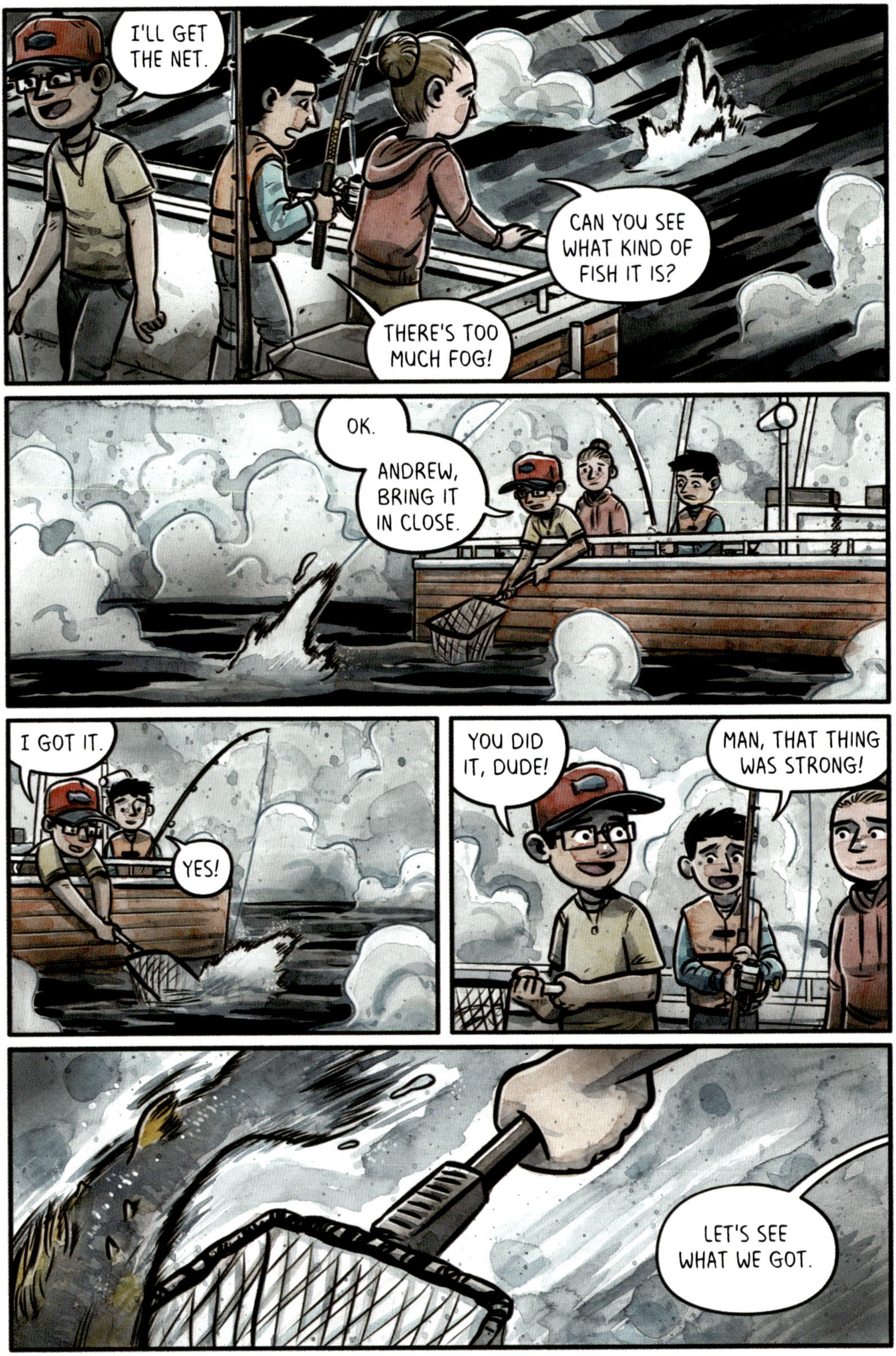
I'LL GET THE NET.
CAN YOU SEE WHAT KIND OF FISH IT IS?
THERE'S TOO MUCH FOG!
OK.
ANDREW, BRING IT IN CLOSE.
I GOT IT.
YES!
YOU DID IT, DUDE!
MAN, THAT THING WAS STRONG!
LET'S SEE WHAT WE GOT.

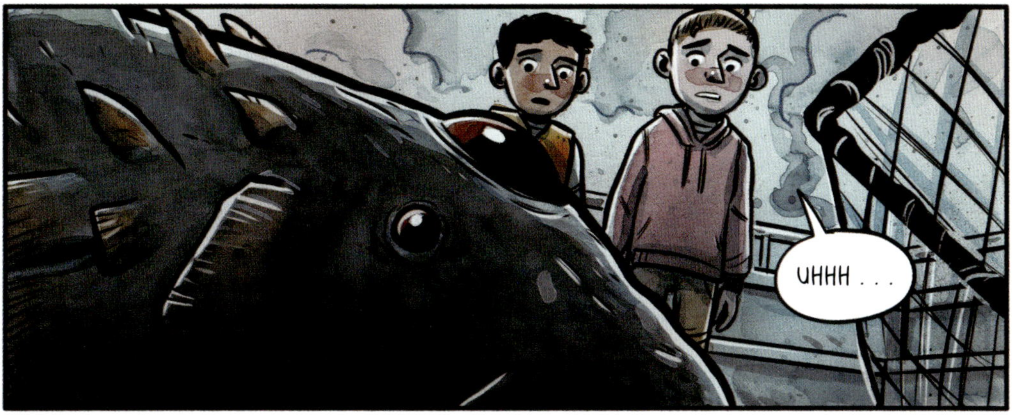
UHHH . . .

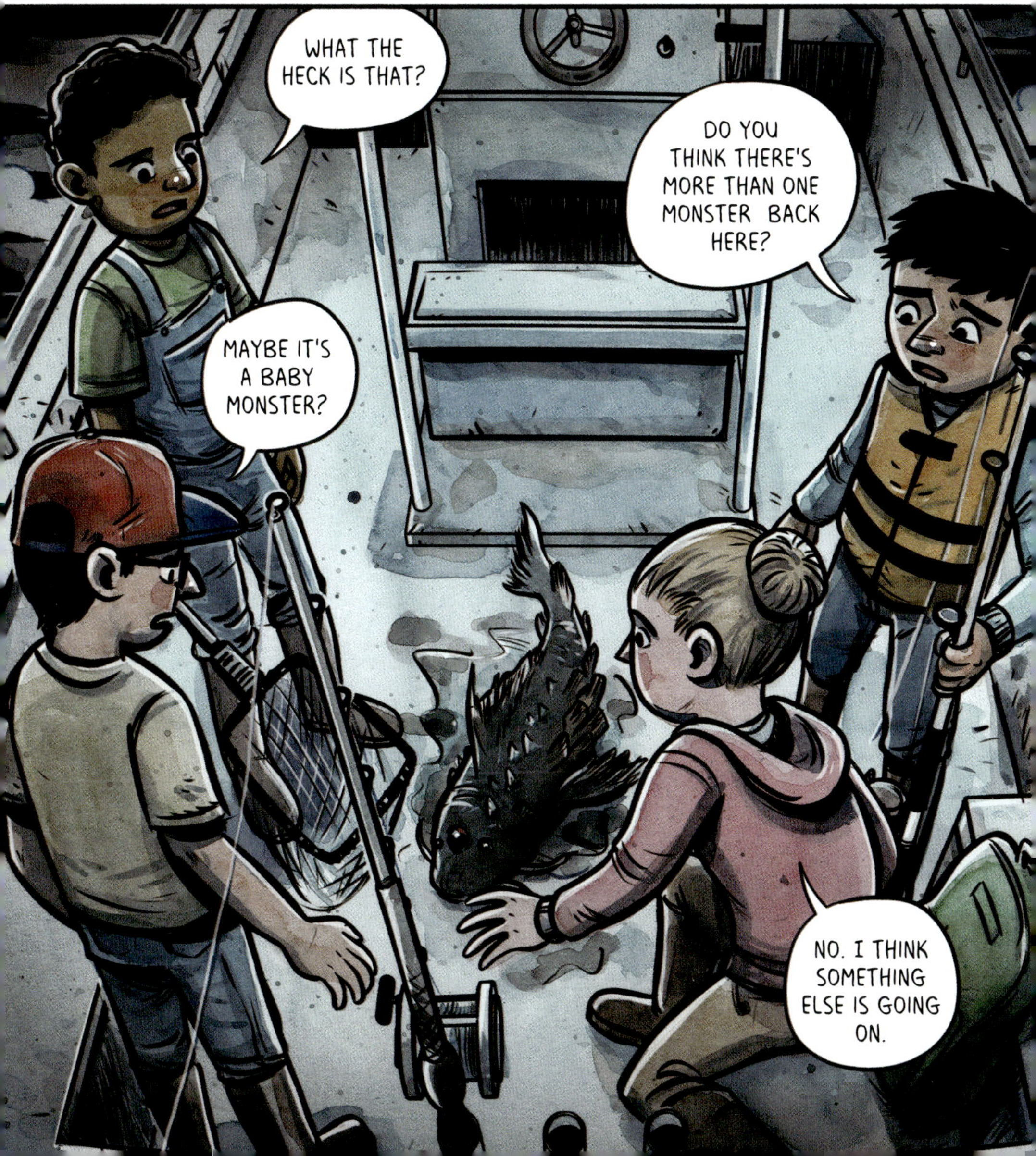
WHAT THE HECK IS THAT?
DO YOU THINK THERE'S MORE THAN ONE MONSTER BACK HERE?
MAYBE IT'S A BABY MONSTER?
NO. I THINK SOMETHING ELSE IS GOING ON.

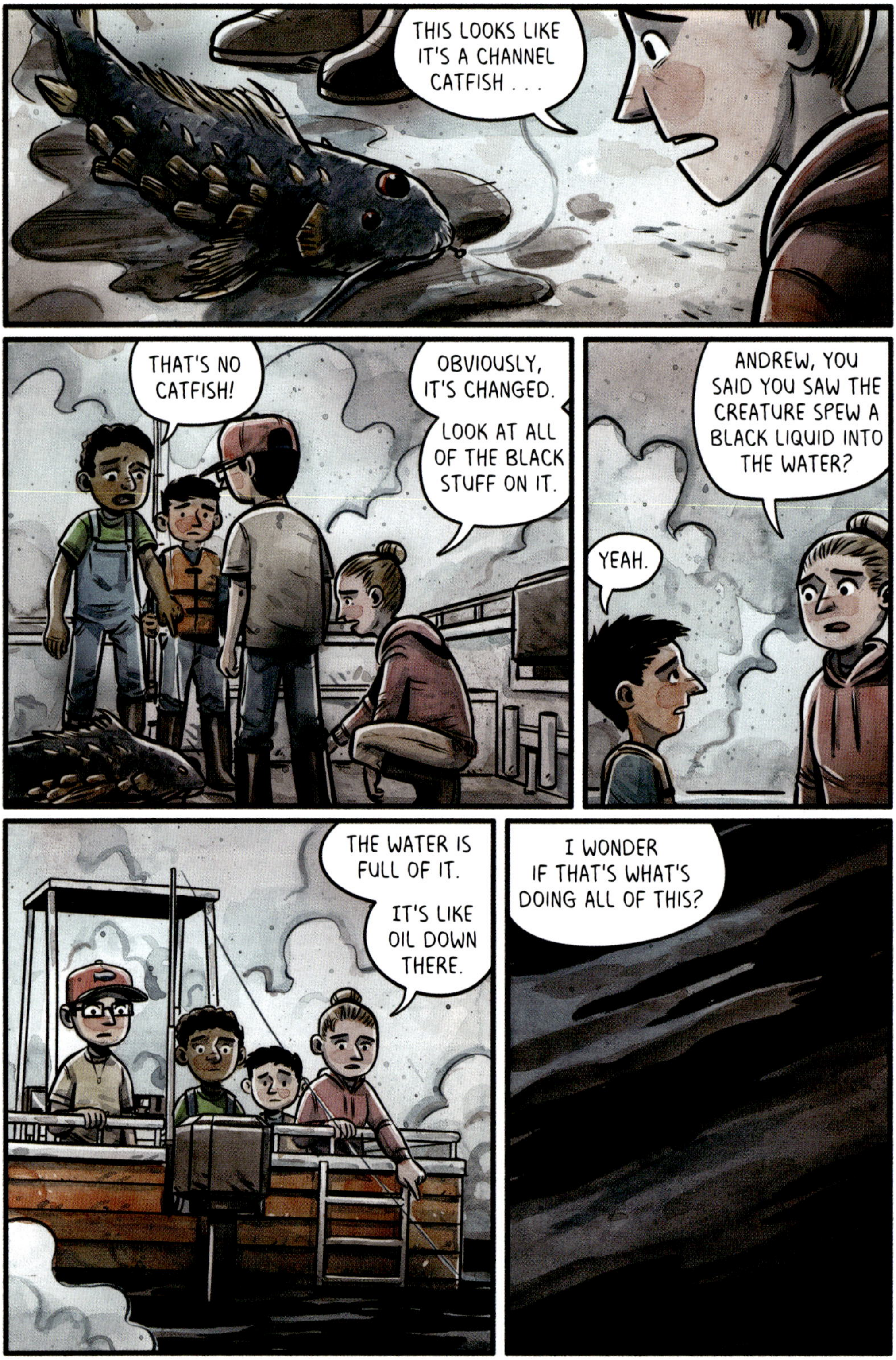
THIS LOOKS LIKE IT'S A CHANNEL CATFISH . . .
THAT'S NO CATFISH!
OBVIOUSLY, IT'S CHANGED.
LOOK AT ALL OF THE BLACK STUFF ON IT.
ANDREW, YOU SAID YOU SAW THE CREATURE SPEW A BLACK LIQUID INTO THE WATER?
YEAH.
THE WATER IS FULL OF IT.
IT'S LIKE OIL DOWN THERE.
I WONDER IF THAT'S WHAT'S DOING ALL OF THIS?

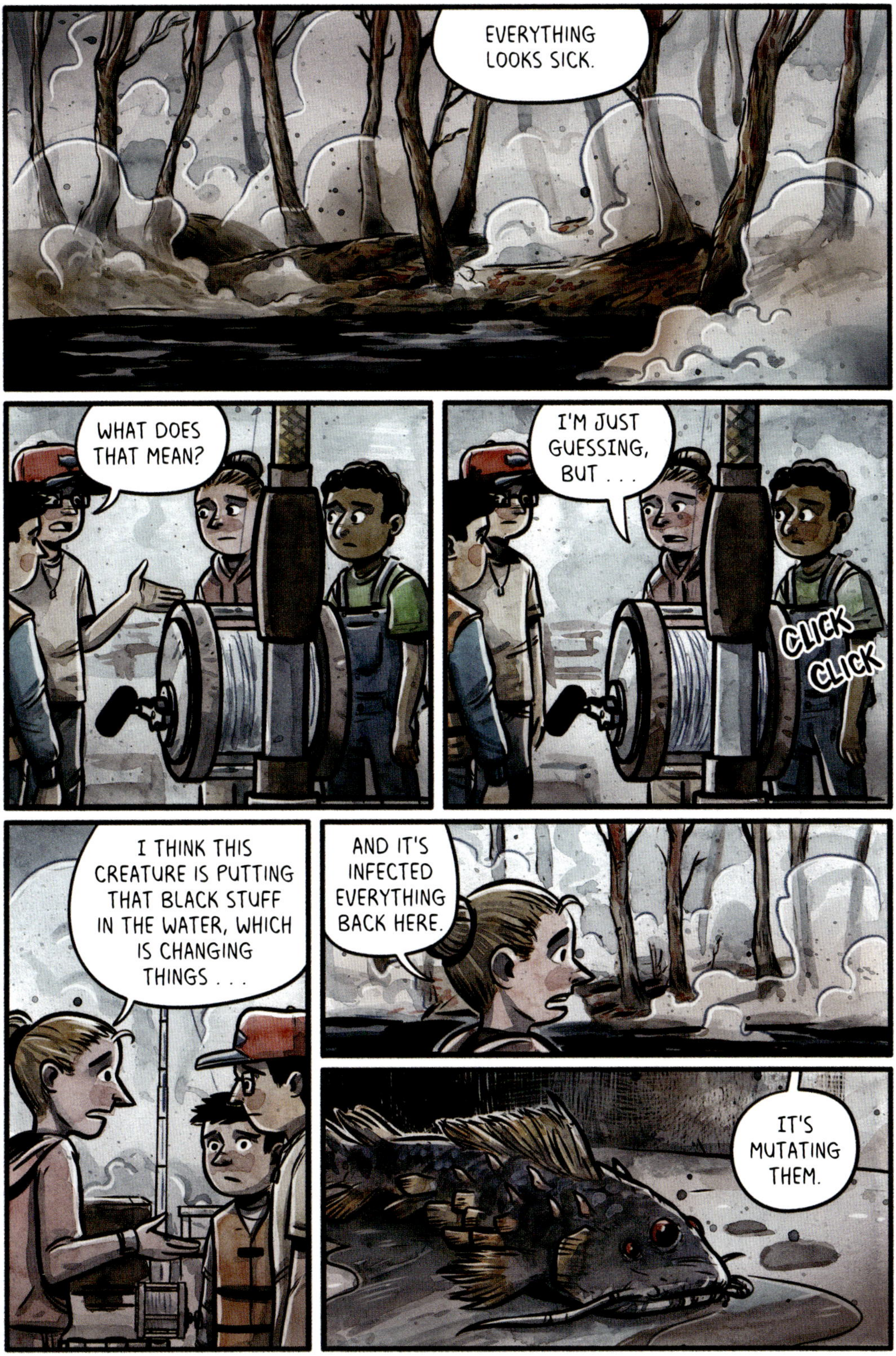
EVERYTHING LOOKS SICK.
WHAT DOES THAT MEAN?
I'M JUST GUESSING, BUT . . .
CLICK
CLICK
I THINK THIS CREATURE IS PUTTING THAT BLACK STUFF IN THE WATER, WHICH IS CHANGING THINGS . . .
AND IT'S INFECTED EVERYTHING BACK HERE.
IT'S MUTATING THEM.

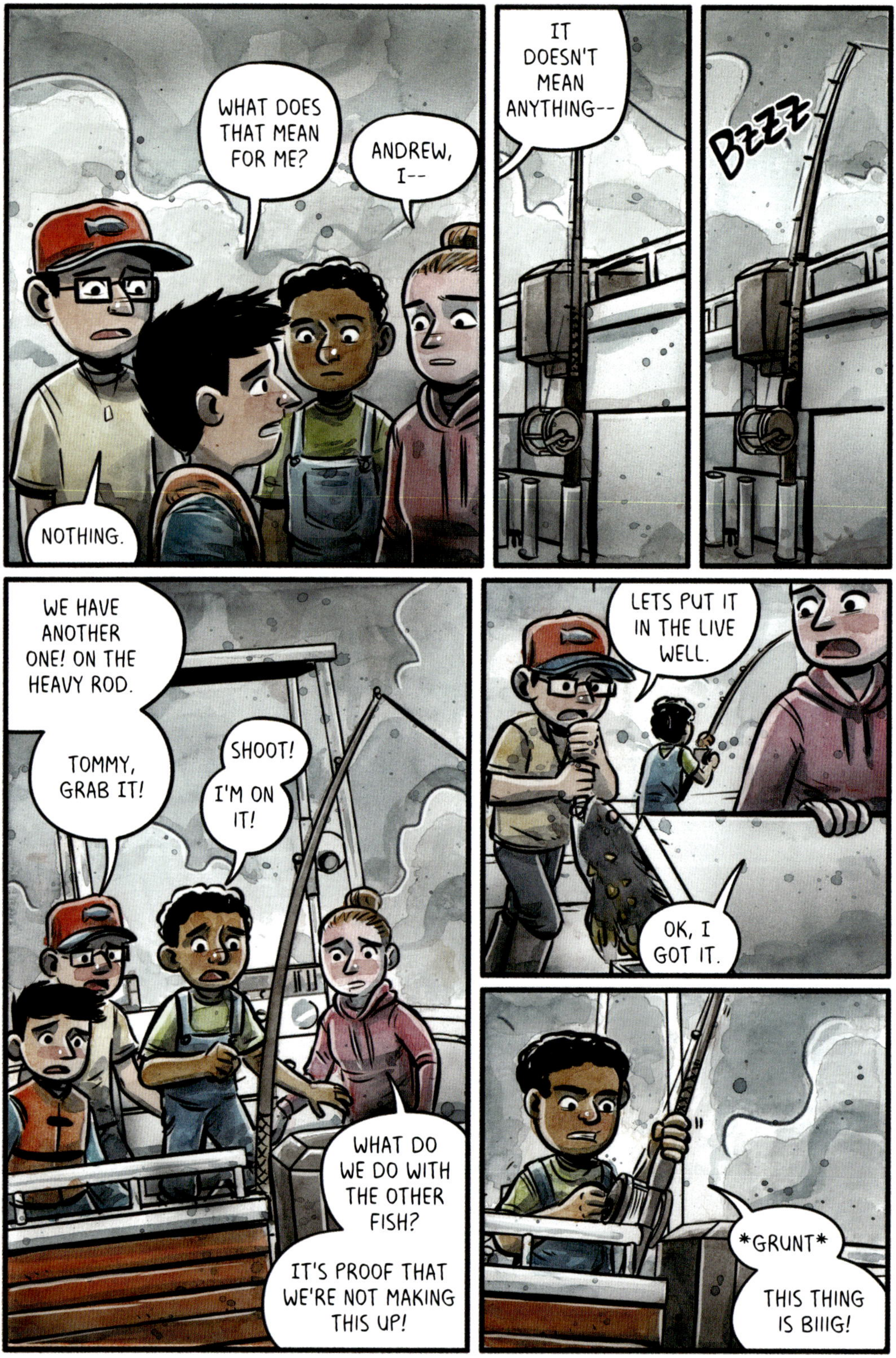
WHAT DOES THAT MEAN FOR ME?
ANDREW, I--
NOTHING.
IT DOESN'T MEAN ANYTHING--
BZZZ
WE HAVE ANOTHER ONE! ON THE HEAVY ROD.
TOMMY, GRAB IT!
SHOOT!
I'M ON IT!
WHAT DO WE DO WITH THE OTHER FISH?
IT'S PROOF THAT WE'RE NOT MAKING THIS UP!
LETS PUT IT IN THE LIVE WELL.
OK, I GOT IT.
GRUNT
THIS THING IS BIIIG!

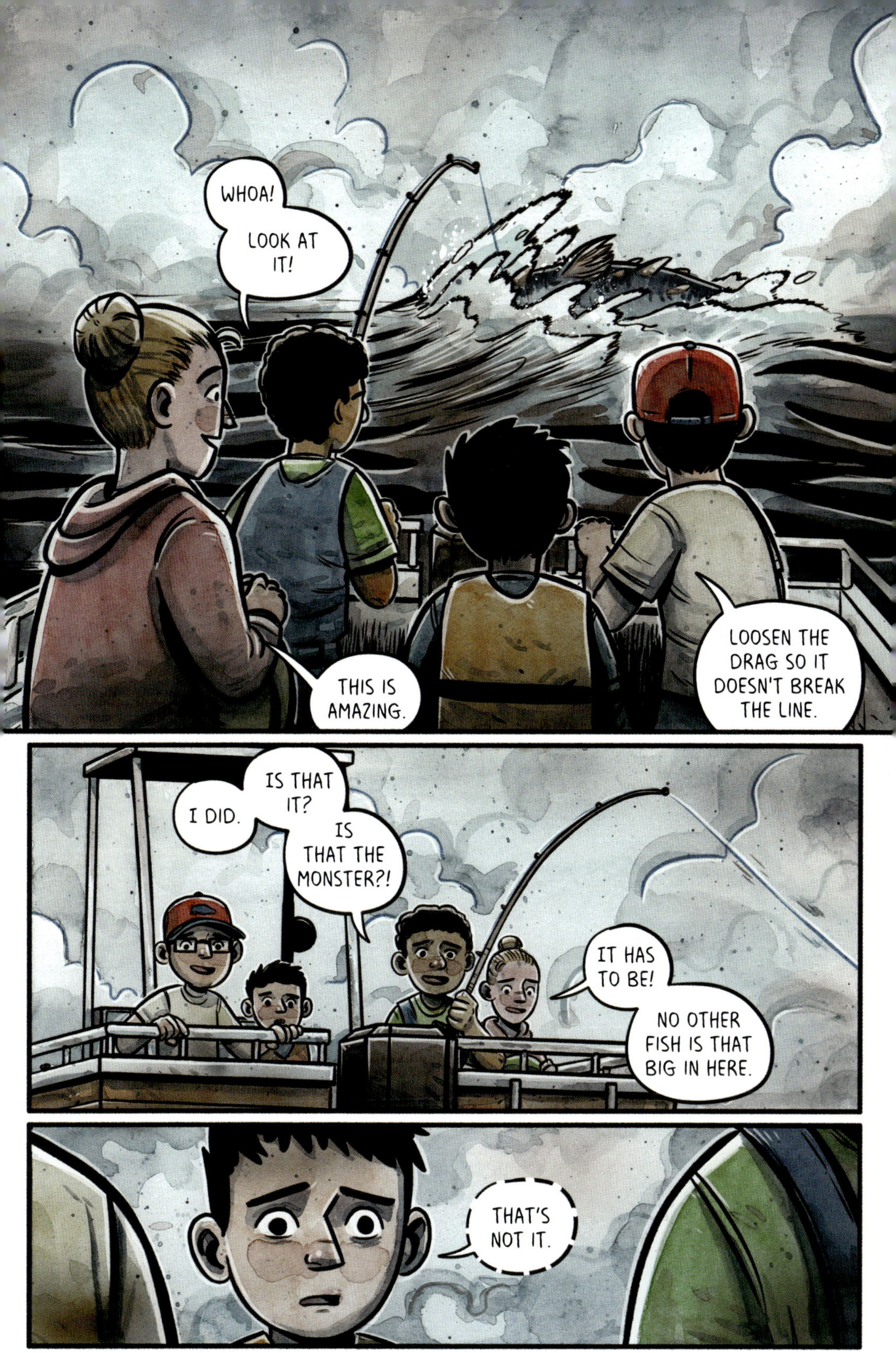
WHOA!
LOOK AT IT!
THIS IS AMAZING.
LOOSEN THE DRAG SO IT DOESN'T BREAK THE LINE.
I DID.
IS THAT IT?
IS THAT THE MONSTER?!
IT HAS TO BE!
NO OTHER FISH IS THAT BIG IN HERE.
THAT'S NOT IT.

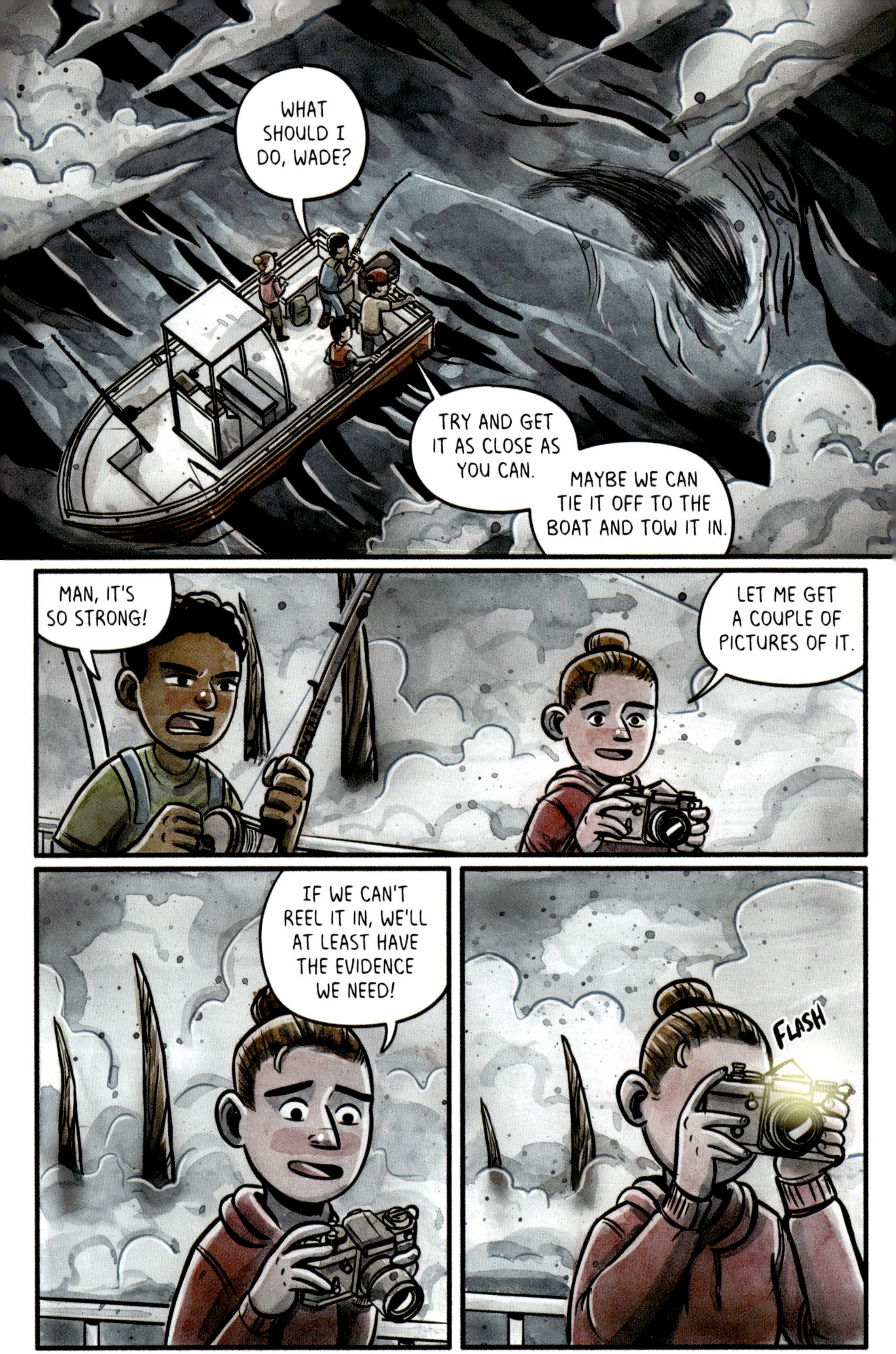
WHAT SHOULD I DO, WADE?
TRY AND GET IT AS CLOSE AS YOU CAN.
MAYBE WE CAN TIE IT OFF TO THE BOAT AND TOW IT IN.
MAN, IT'S SO STRONG!
LET ME GET A COUPLE OF PICTURES OF IT.
IF WE CAN'T REEL IT IN, WE'LL AT LEAST HAVE THE EVIDENCE WE NEED!
FLASH

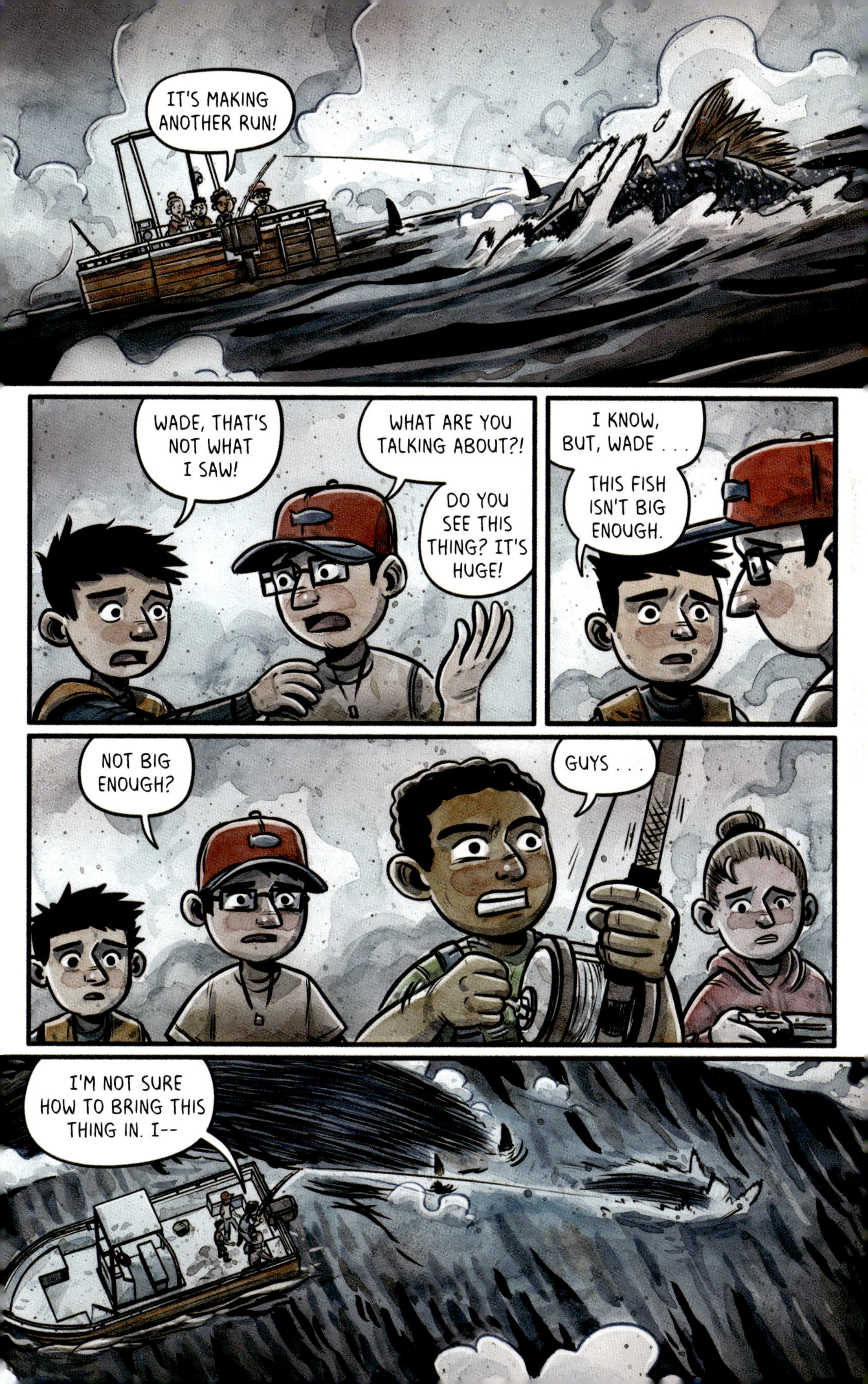
IT'S MAKING ANOTHER RUN!
WADE, THAT'S NOT WHAT I SAW!
WHAT ARE YOU TALKING ABOUT?!
DO YOU SEE THIS THING? IT'S HUGE!
I KNOW, BUT, WADE . . .
THIS FISH ISN'T BIG ENOUGH.
NOT BIG ENOUGH?
GUYS . . .
I'M NOT SURE HOW TO BRING THIS THING IN. I--

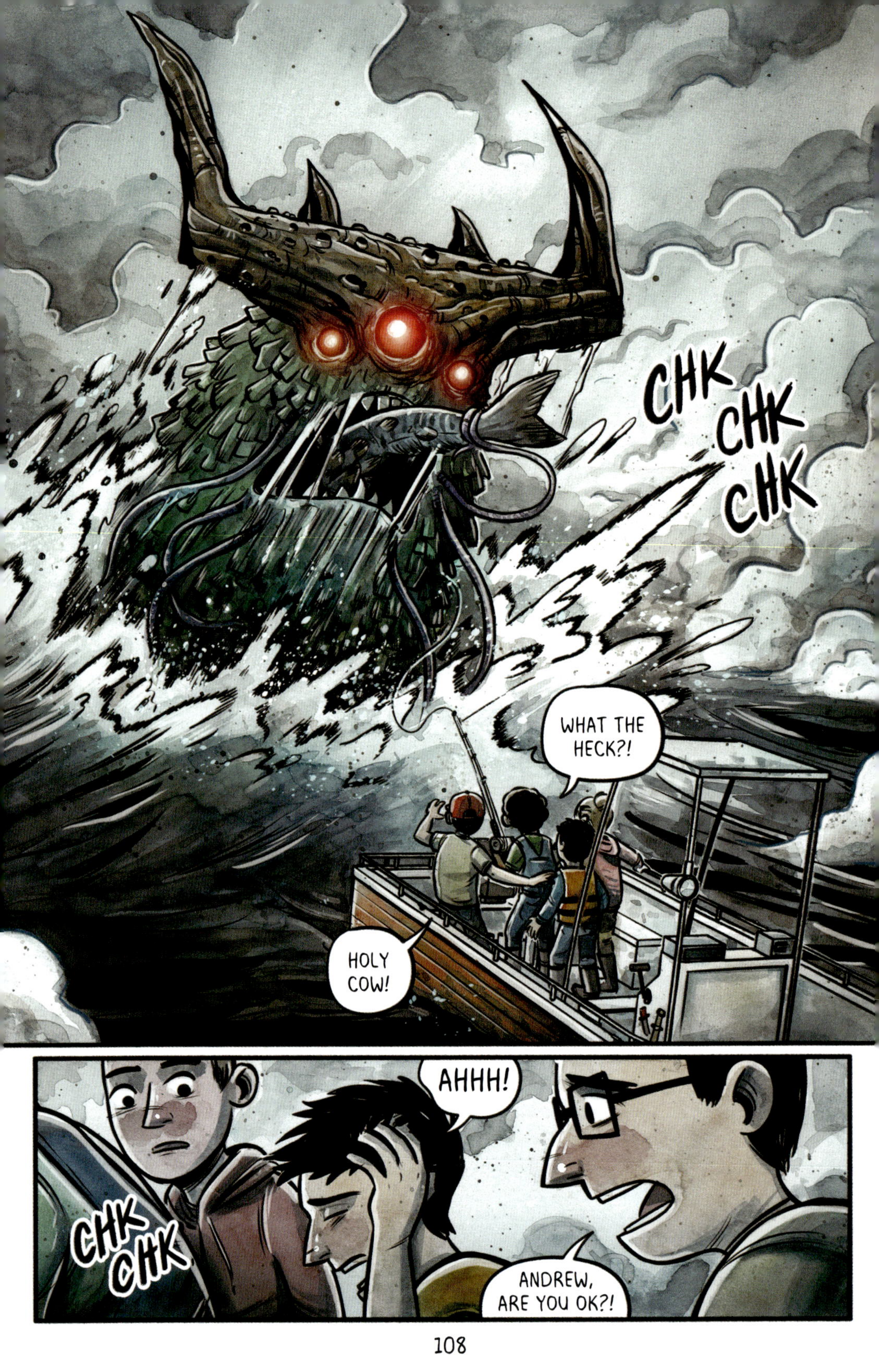
CHK
CHK
CHK
WHAT THE HECK?!
HOLY COW!
AHHH!
CHK CHK
ANDREW, ARE YOU OK?!

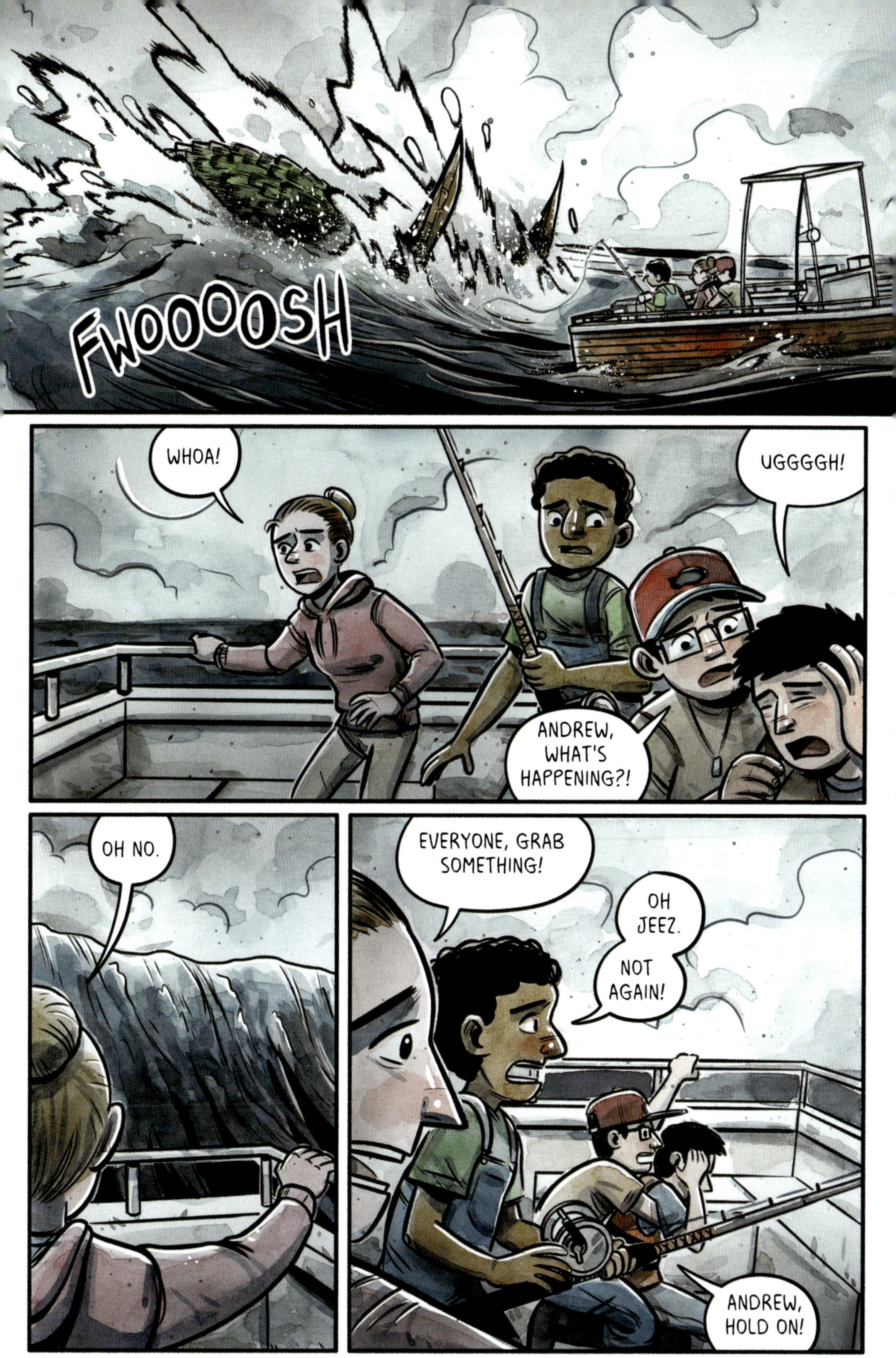
FWOOOOSH
WHOA!
UGGGGH!
ANDREW, WHAT'S HAPPENING?!
OH NO.
EVERYONE, GRAB SOMETHING!
OH JEEZ.
NOT AGAIN!
ANDREW, HOLD ON!

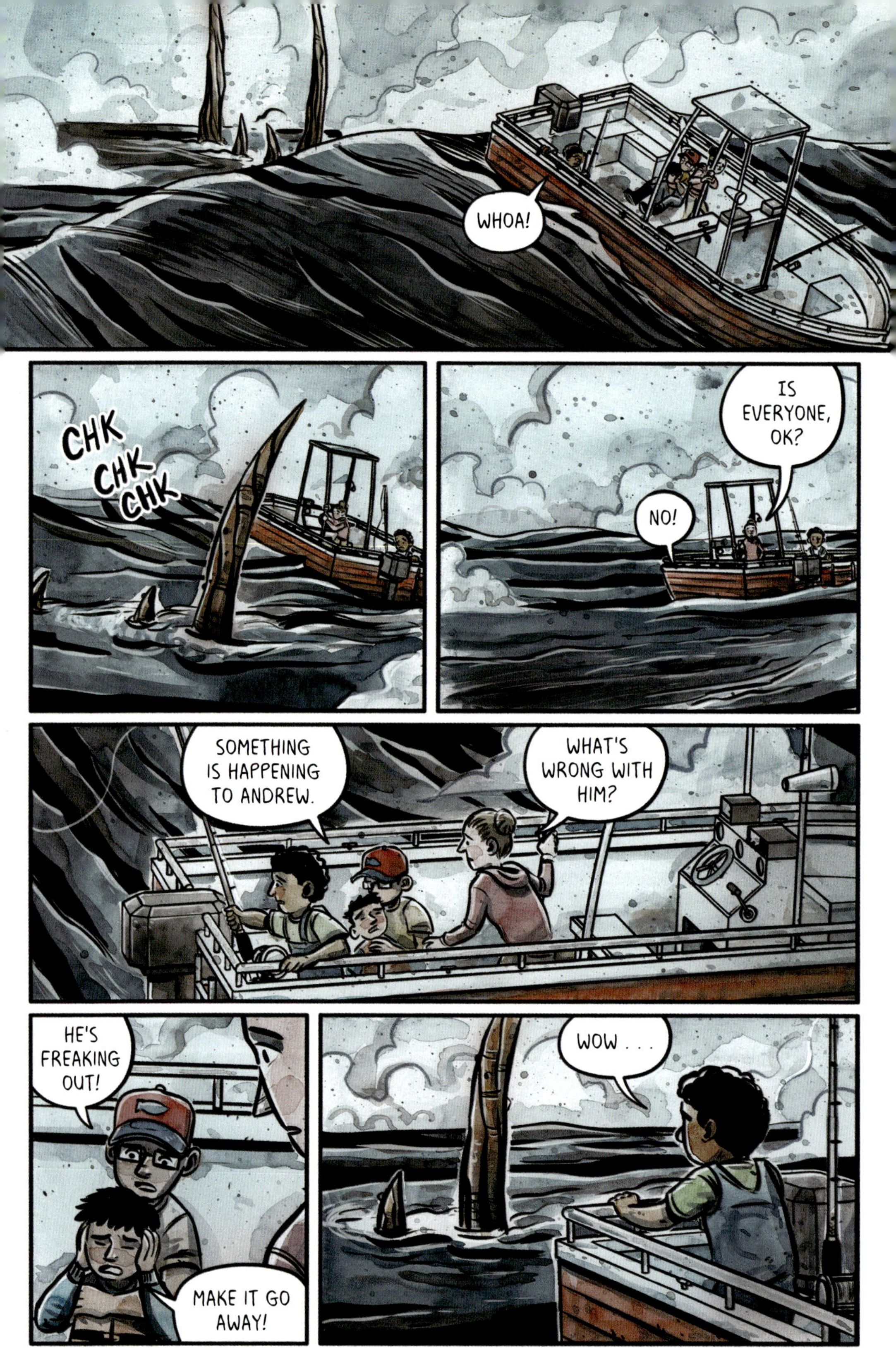
WHOA!
CHK CHK CHK
IS EVERYONE, OK?
NO!
SOMETHING IS HAPPENING TO ANDREW.
WHAT'S WRONG WITH HIM?
HE'S FREAKING OUT!
MAKE IT GO AWAY!
WOW . . .

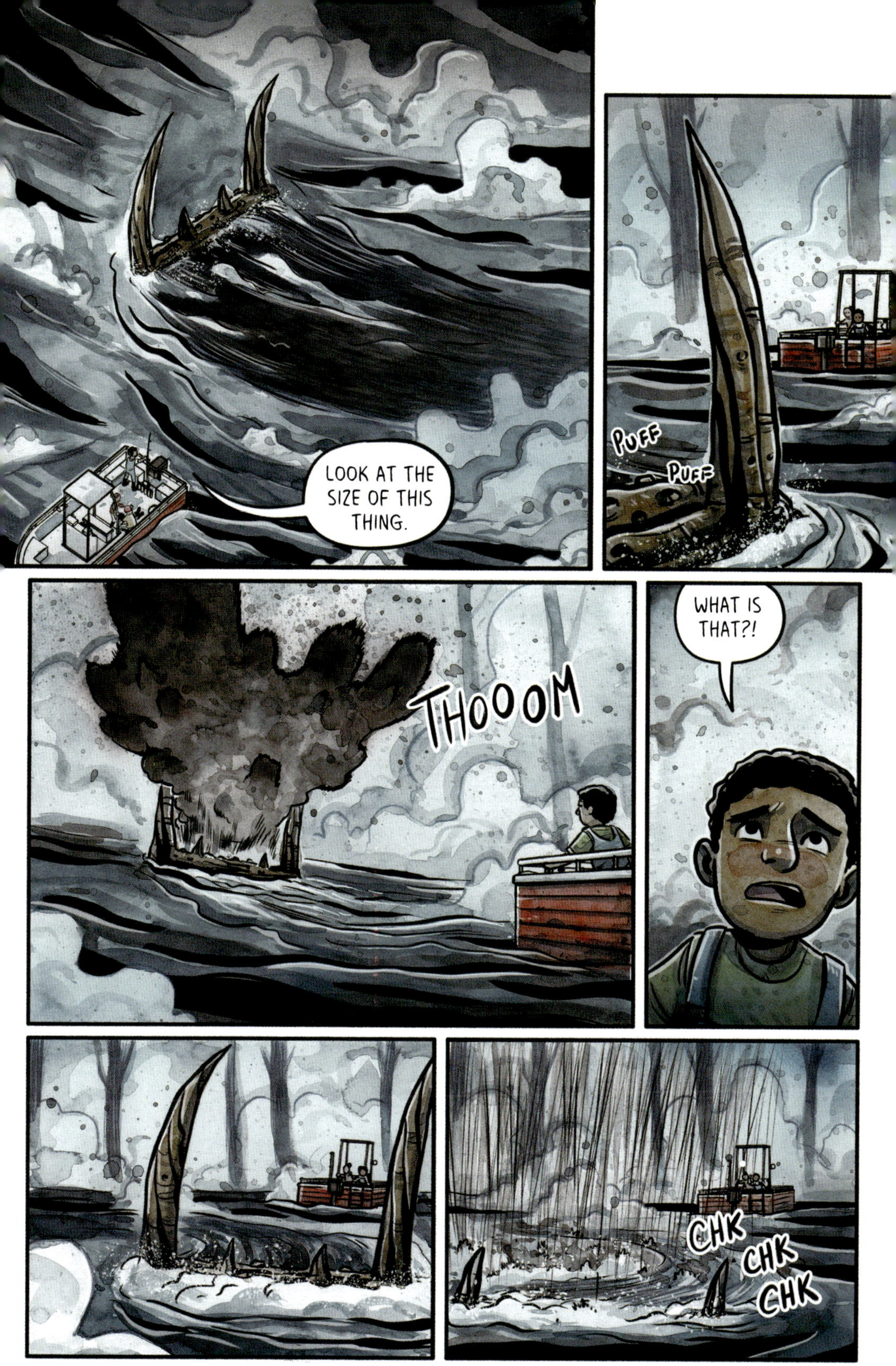
LOOK AT THE SIZE OF THIS THING.
PUFF
PUFF
THOOOM
WHAT IS THAT?!
CHK
CHK
CHK

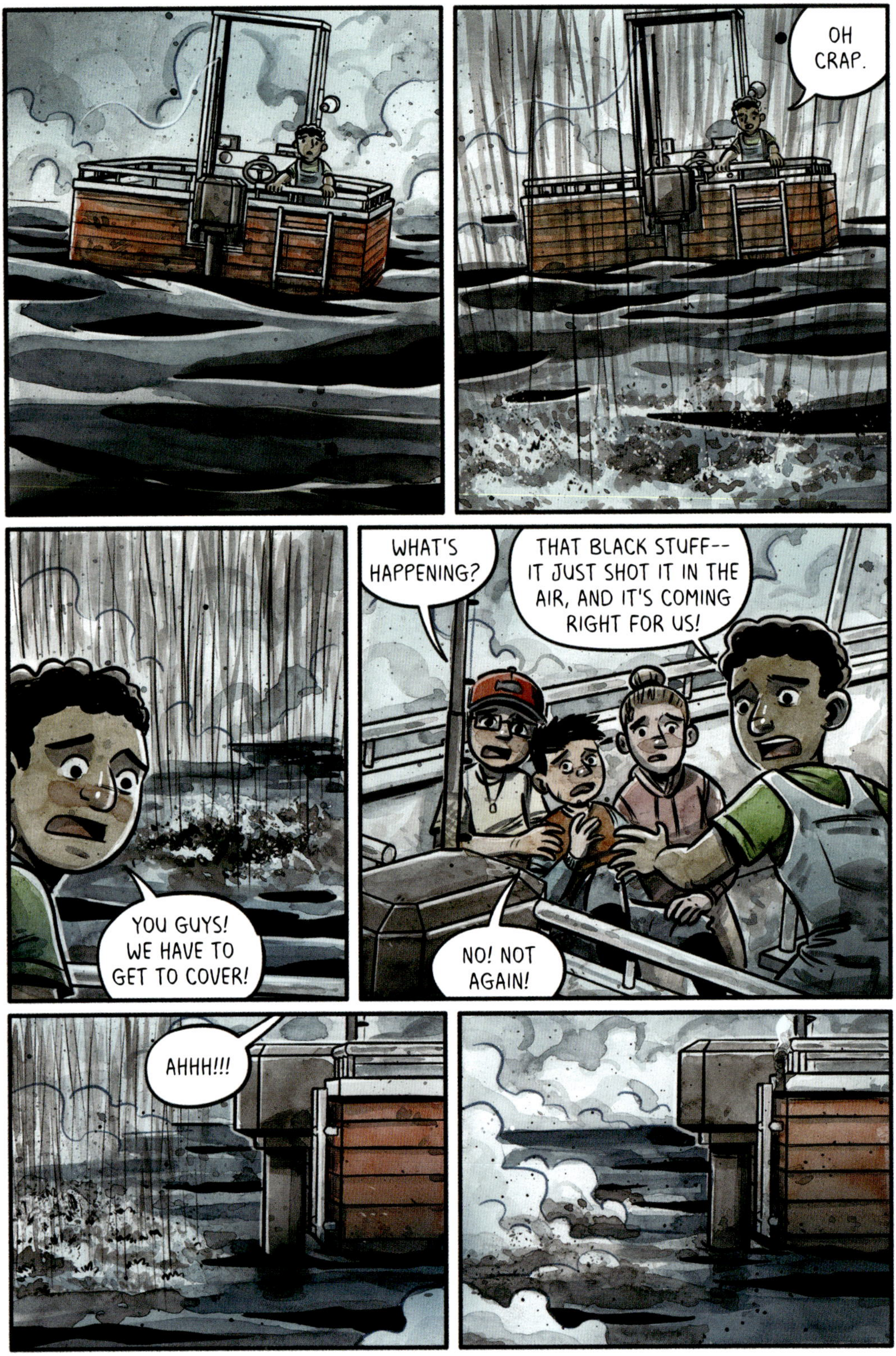
OH CRAP.
WHAT'S HAPPENING?
THAT BLACK STUFF-- IT JUST SHOT IT IN THE AIR, AND IT'S COMING RIGHT FOR US!
YOU GUYS! WE HAVE TO GET TO COVER!
NO! NOT AGAIN!
AHHH!!!

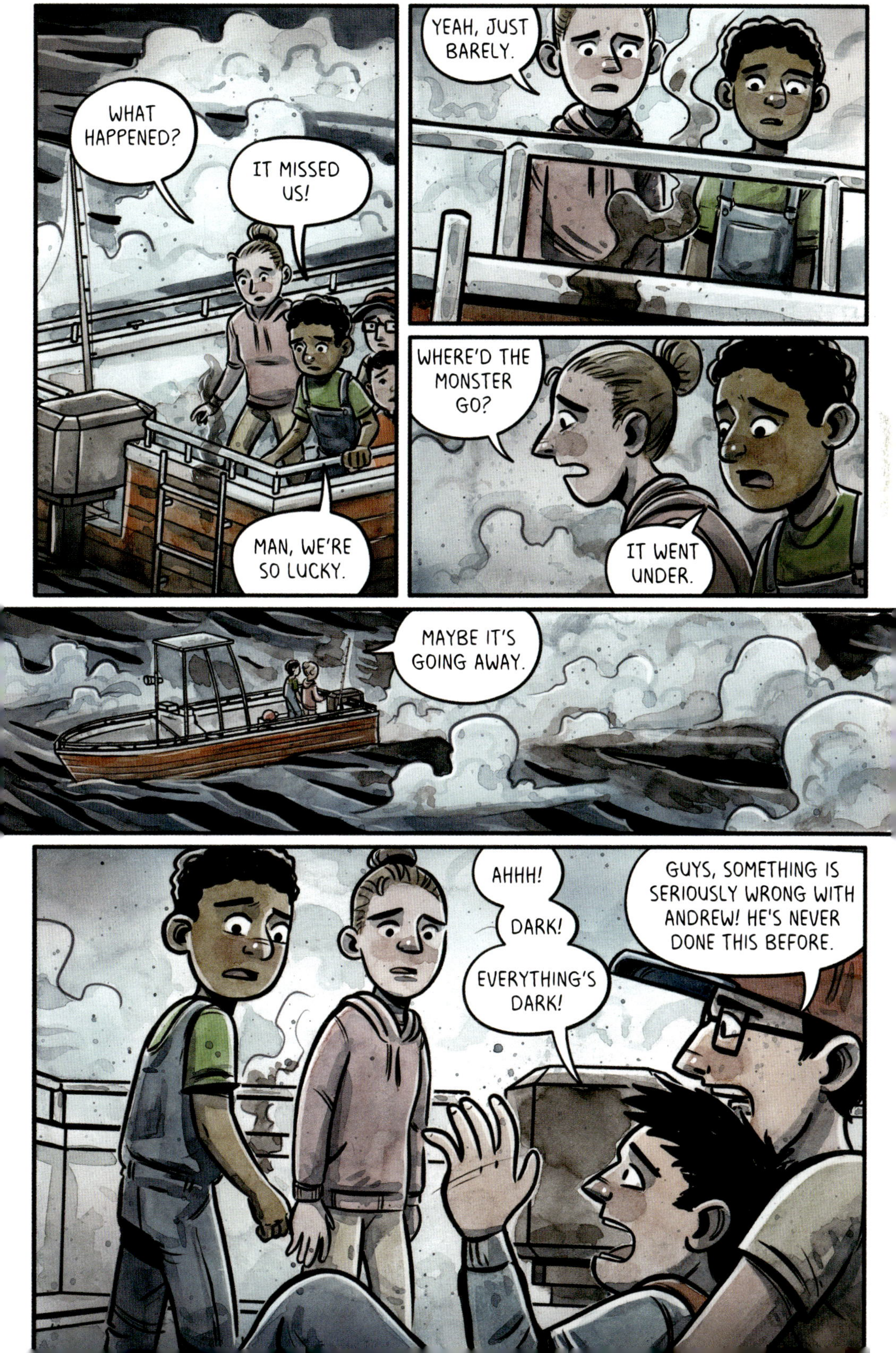
WHAT HAPPENED?
IT MISSED US!
MAN, WE'RE SO LUCKY.
YEAH, JUST BARELY.
WHERE'D THE MONSTER GO?
IT WENT UNDER.
MAYBE IT'S GOING AWAY.
AHHH!
DARK!
EVERYTHING'S DARK!
GUYS, SOMETHING IS SERIOUSLY WRONG WITH ANDREW! HE'S NEVER DONE THIS BEFORE.

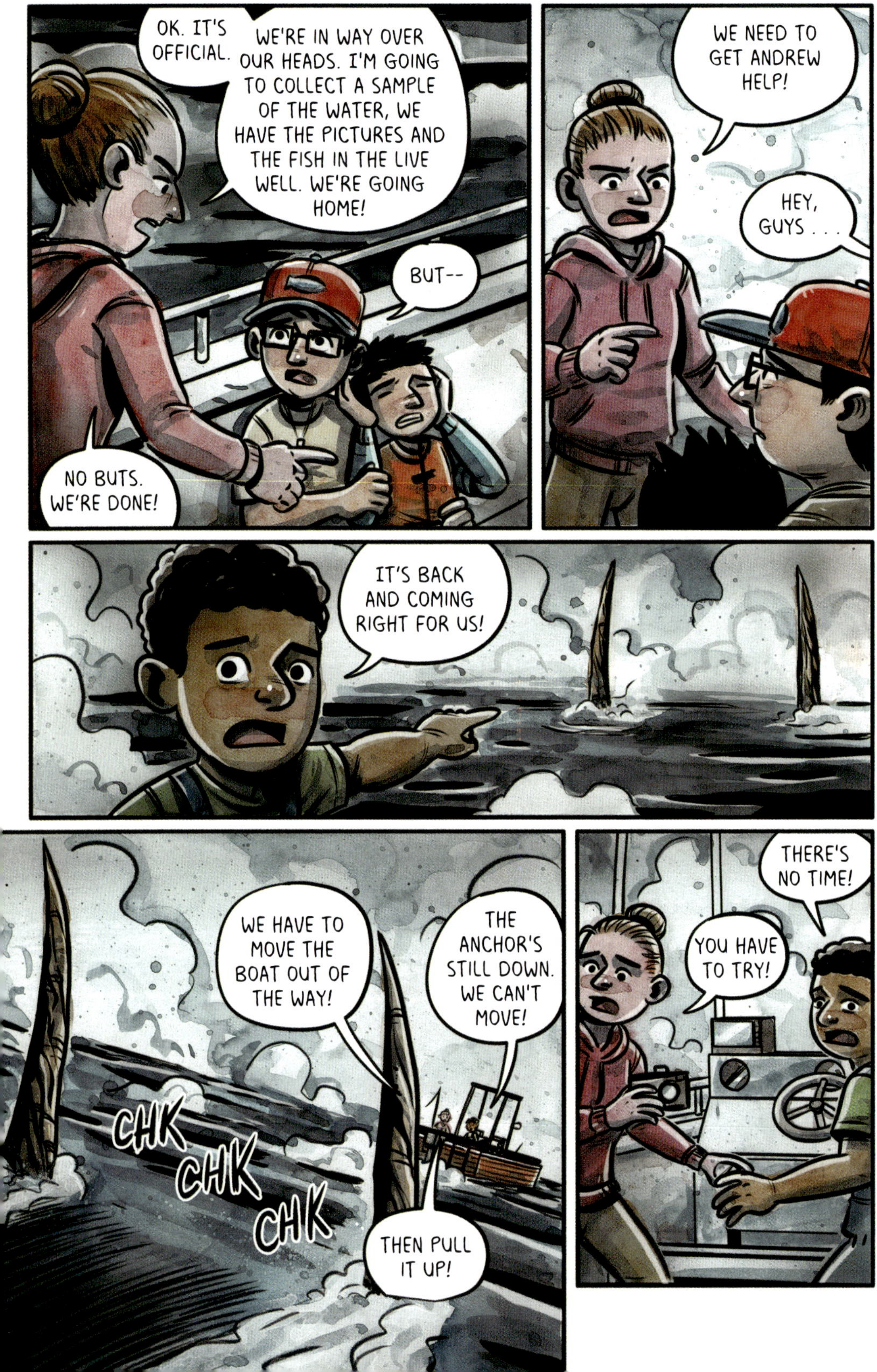
OK. IT'S OFFICIAL.
WE'RE IN WAY OVER OUR HEADS. I'M GOING TO COLLECT A SAMPLE OF THE WATER, WE HAVE THE PICTURES AND THE FISH IN THE LIVE WELL. WE'RE GOING HOME!
BUT--
NO BUTS. WE'RE DONE!
WE NEED TO GET ANDREW HELP!
HEY, GUYS . . .
IT'S BACK AND COMING RIGHT FOR US!
WE HAVE TO MOVE THE BOAT OUT OF THE WAY!
THE ANCHOR'S STILL DOWN. WE CAN'T MOVE!
CHK
CHK
CHK
THEN PULL IT UP!
THERE'S NO TIME!
YOU HAVE TO TRY!

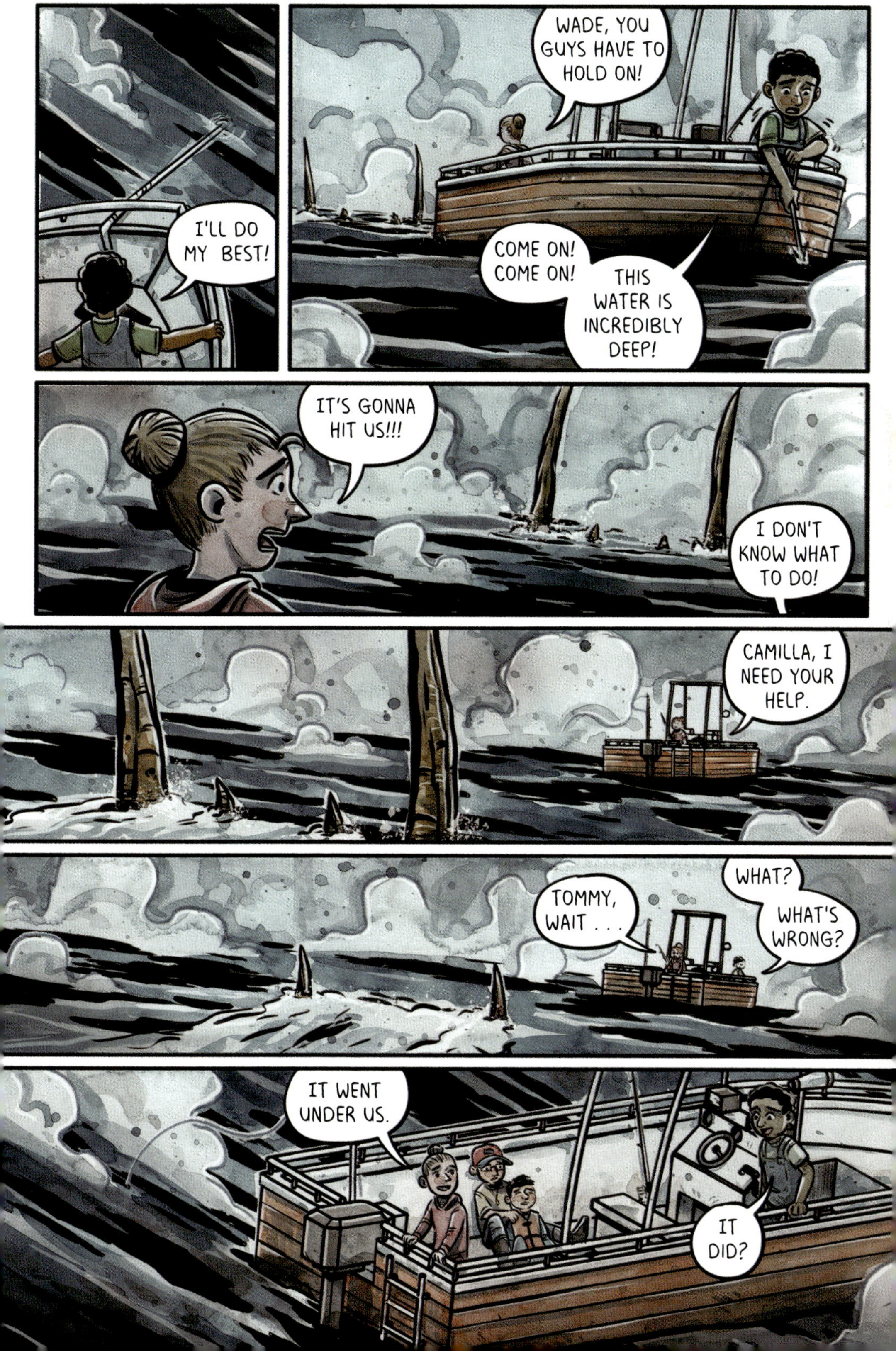
I'LL DO MY BEST!
WADE, YOU GUYS HAVE TO HOLD ON!
COME ON! COME ON!
THIS WATER IS INCREDIBLY DEEP!
IT'S GONNA HIT US!!!
I DON'T KNOW WHAT TO DO!
CAMILLA, I NEED YOUR HELP.
TOMMY, WAIT . . .
WHAT?
WHAT'S WRONG?
IT WENT UNDER US.
IT DID?

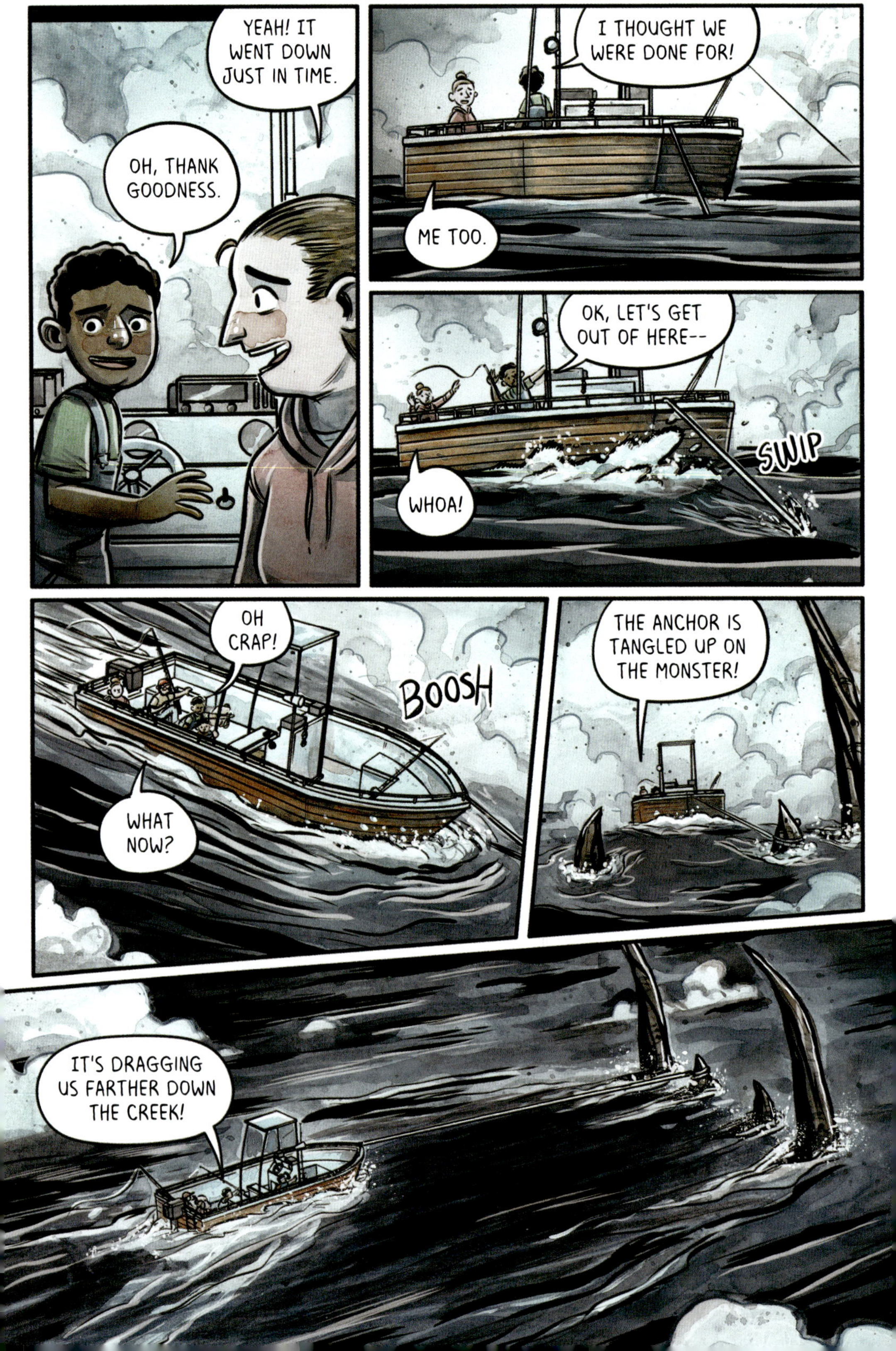
YEAH! IT WENT DOWN JUST IN TIME.
OH, THANK GOODNESS.
I THOUGHT WE WERE DONE FOR!
ME TOO.
OK, LET'S GET OUT OF HERE--
SWIP
WHOA!
OH CRAP!
BOOSH
WHAT NOW?
THE ANCHOR IS TANGLED UP ON THE MONSTER!
IT'S DRAGGING US FARTHER DOWN THE CREEK!

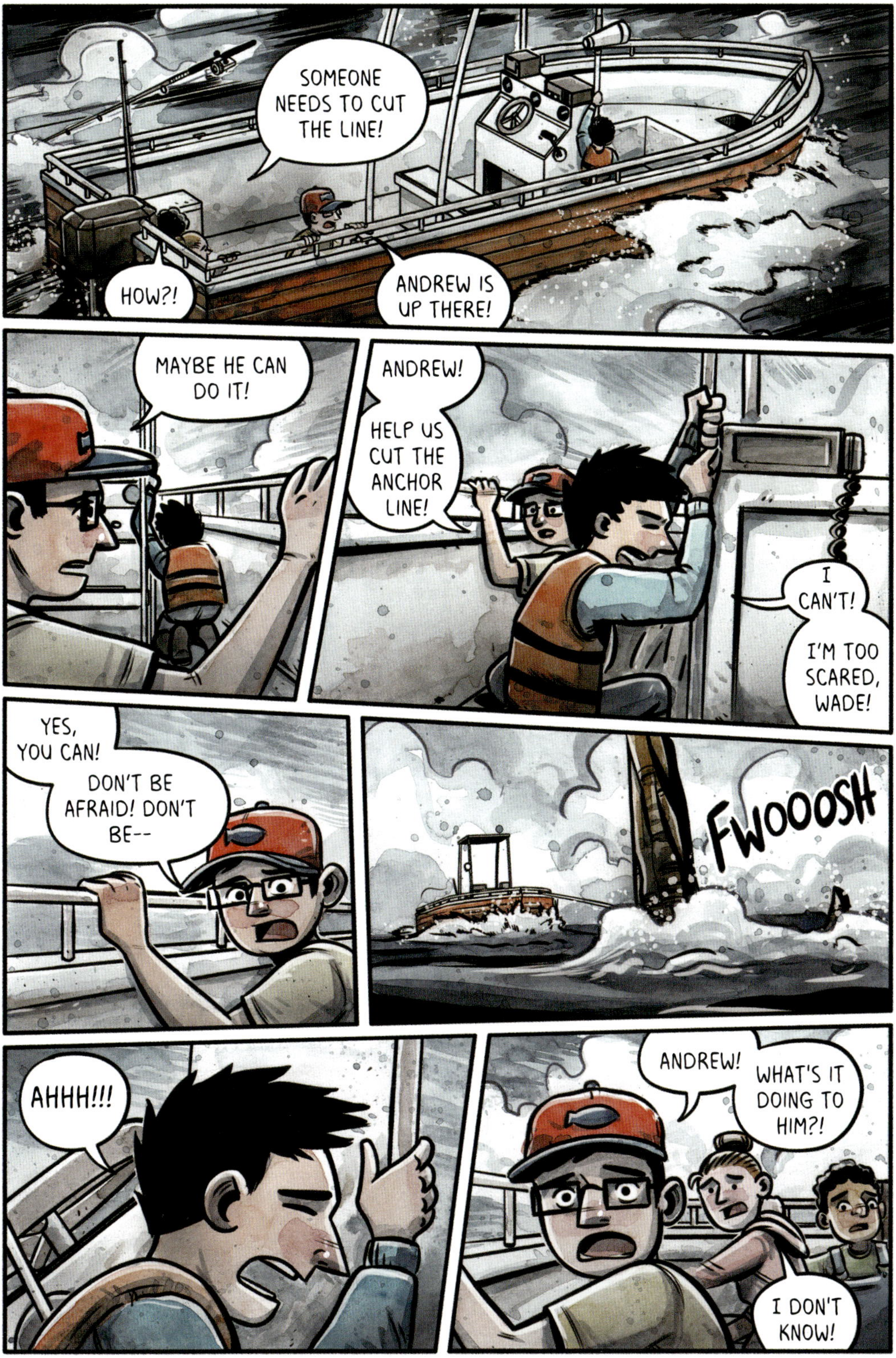
SOMEONE NEEDS TO CUT THE LINE!
HOW?!
ANDREW IS UP THERE!
MAYBE HE CAN DO IT!
ANDREW!
HELP US CUT THE ANCHOR LINE!
I CAN'T!
I'M TOO SCARED, WADE!
YES, YOU CAN!
DON'T BE AFRAID! DON'T BE--
FWOOOSH
AHHH!!!
ANDREW!
WHAT'S IT DOING TO HIM?!
I DON'T KNOW!

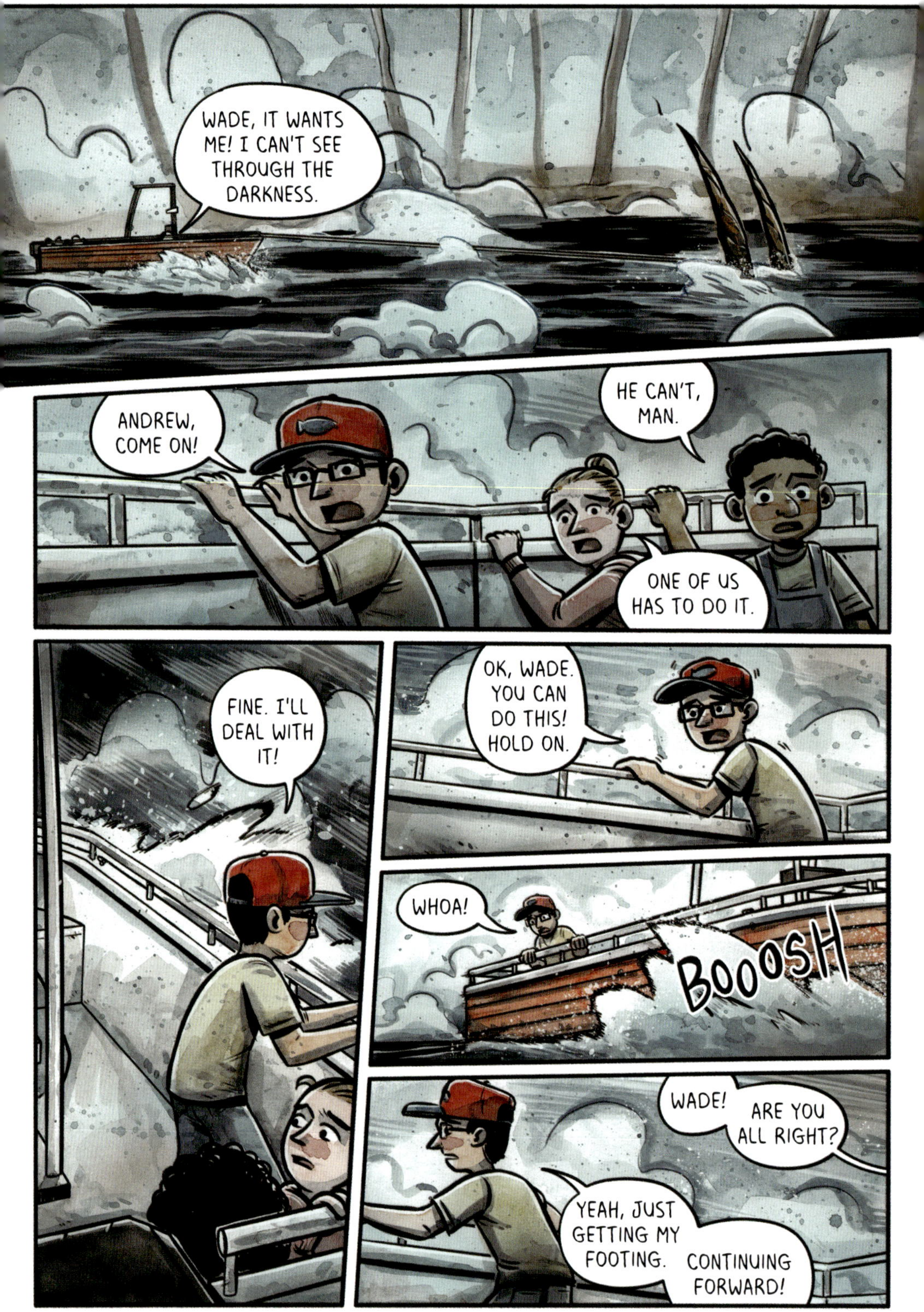

WADE, IT WANTS ME! I CAN'T SEE THROUGH THE DARKNESS.
ANDREW, COME ON!
HE CAN'T, MAN.
ONE OF US HAS TO DO IT.
FINE. I'LL DEAL WITH IT!
OK, WADE. YOU CAN DO THIS! HOLD ON.
WHOA!
BOOOSH
WADE!
ARE YOU ALL RIGHT?
YEAH, JUST GETTING MY FOOTING.
CONTINUING FORWARD!

ADAMSVILLE UNIV.
PLEASE, JUST GO AWAY.
MAKE IT GO AWAY.
WADE?
I'M SORRY!
JUST HOLD ON.
I'M GONNA TAKE CARE OF IT.
WHOA.

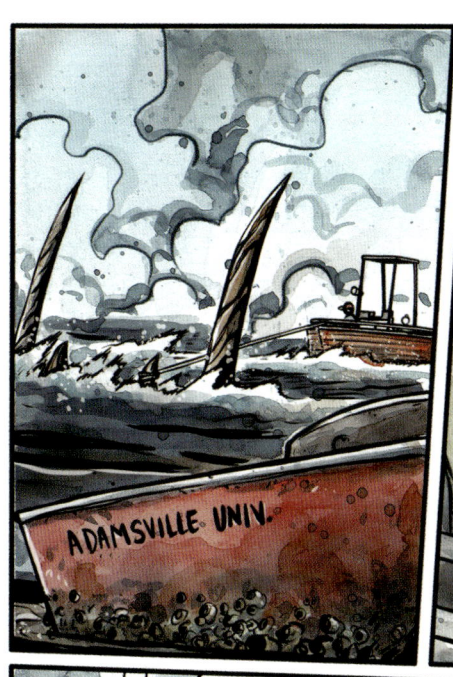

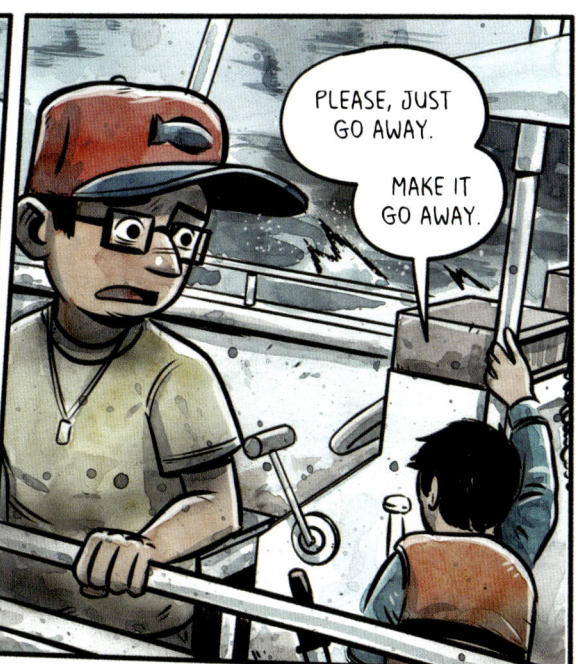

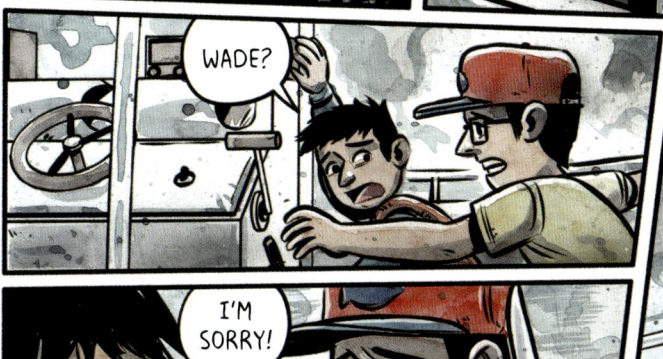

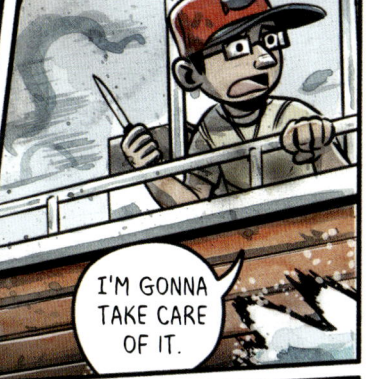

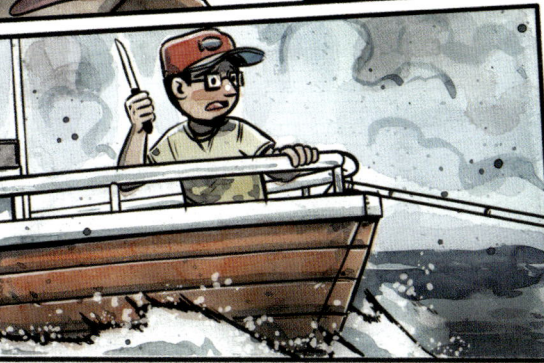

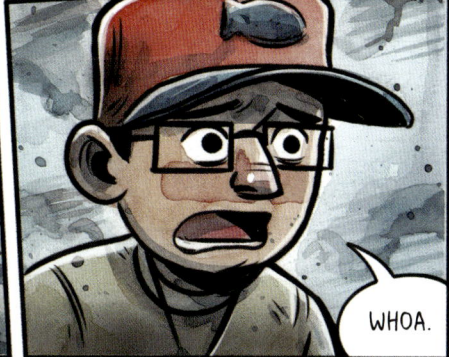

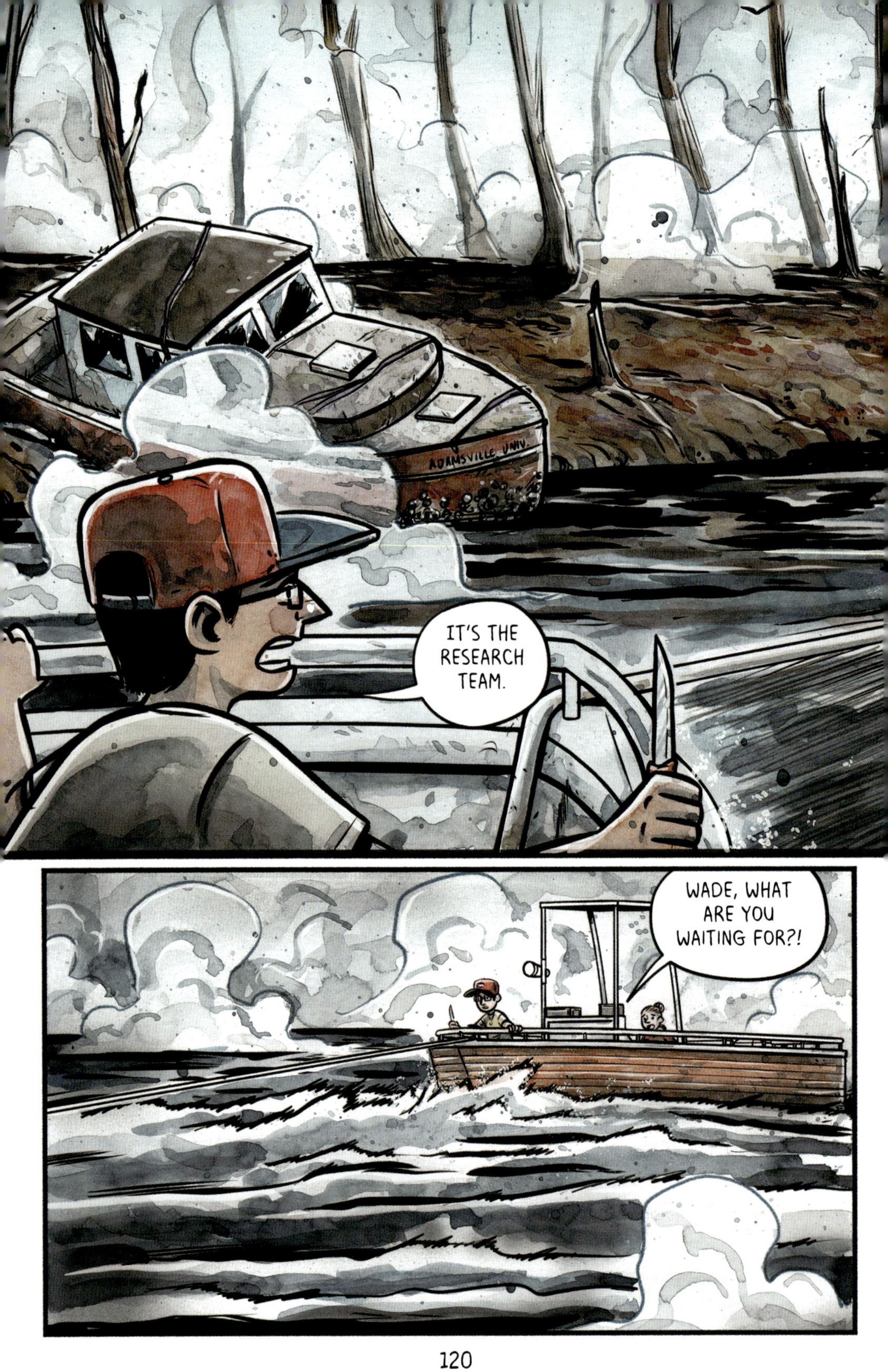
ADAMSVILLE UNIV.
IT'S THE RESEARCH TEAM.
WADE, WHAT ARE YOU WAITING FOR?!

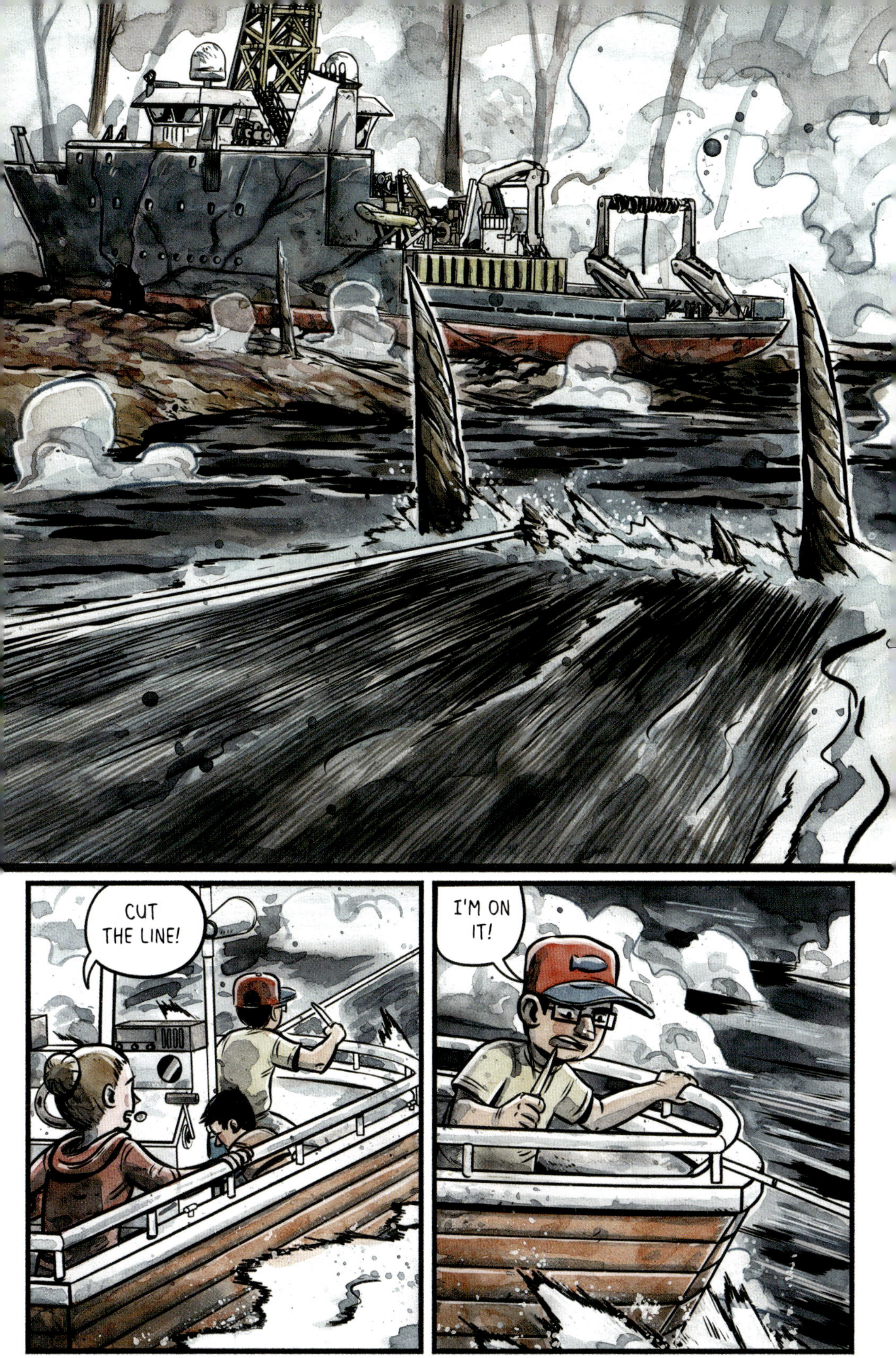
CUT THE LINE!
I'M ON IT!

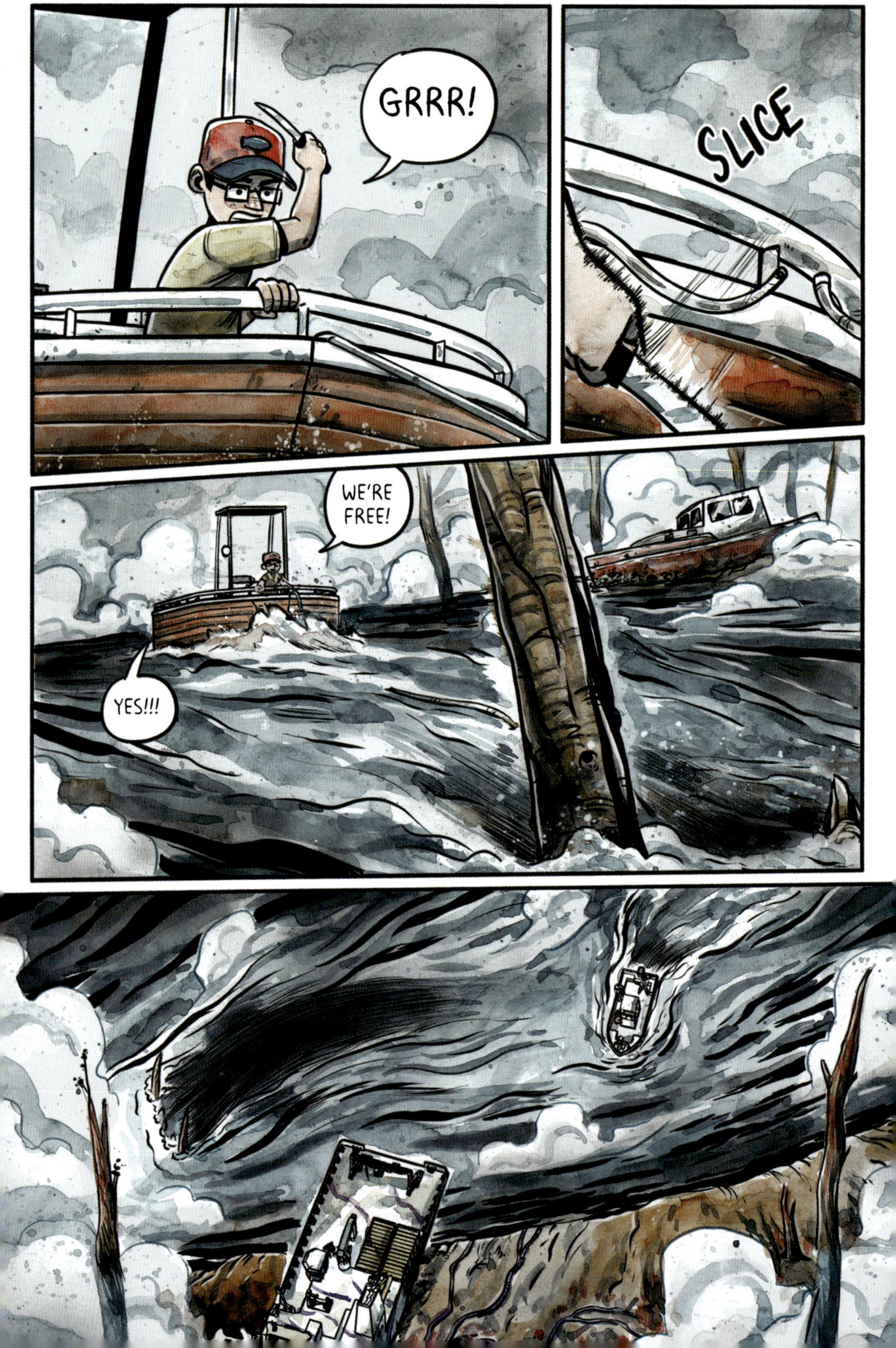
GRRR!
SLICE
WE'RE FREE!
YES!!!

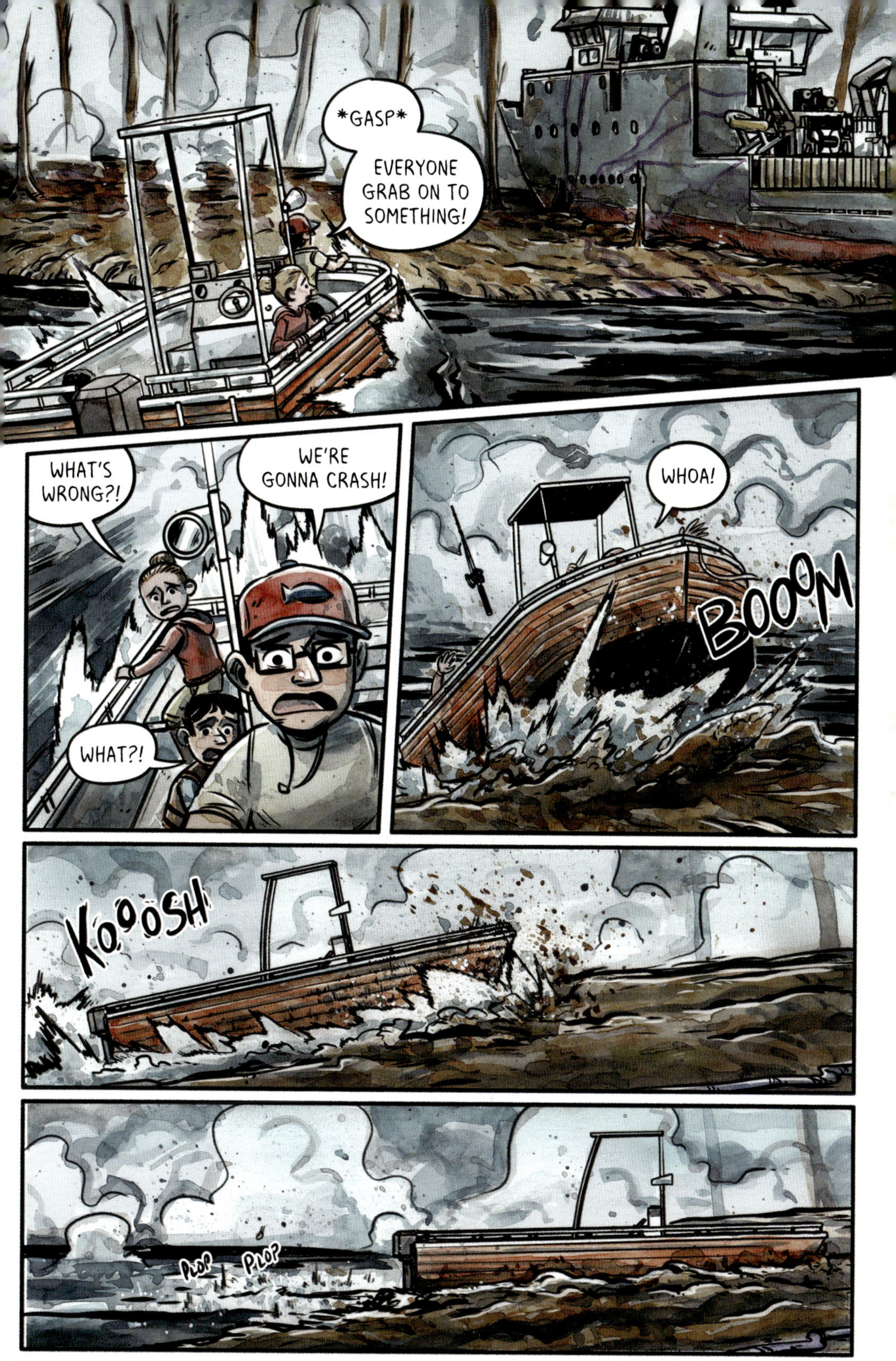
GASP
EVERYONE GRAB ON TO SOMETHING!
WHAT'S WRONG?!
WE'RE GONNA CRASH!
WHAT?!
WHOA!
BOOOM
KOOOSH
PLOP
PLOP

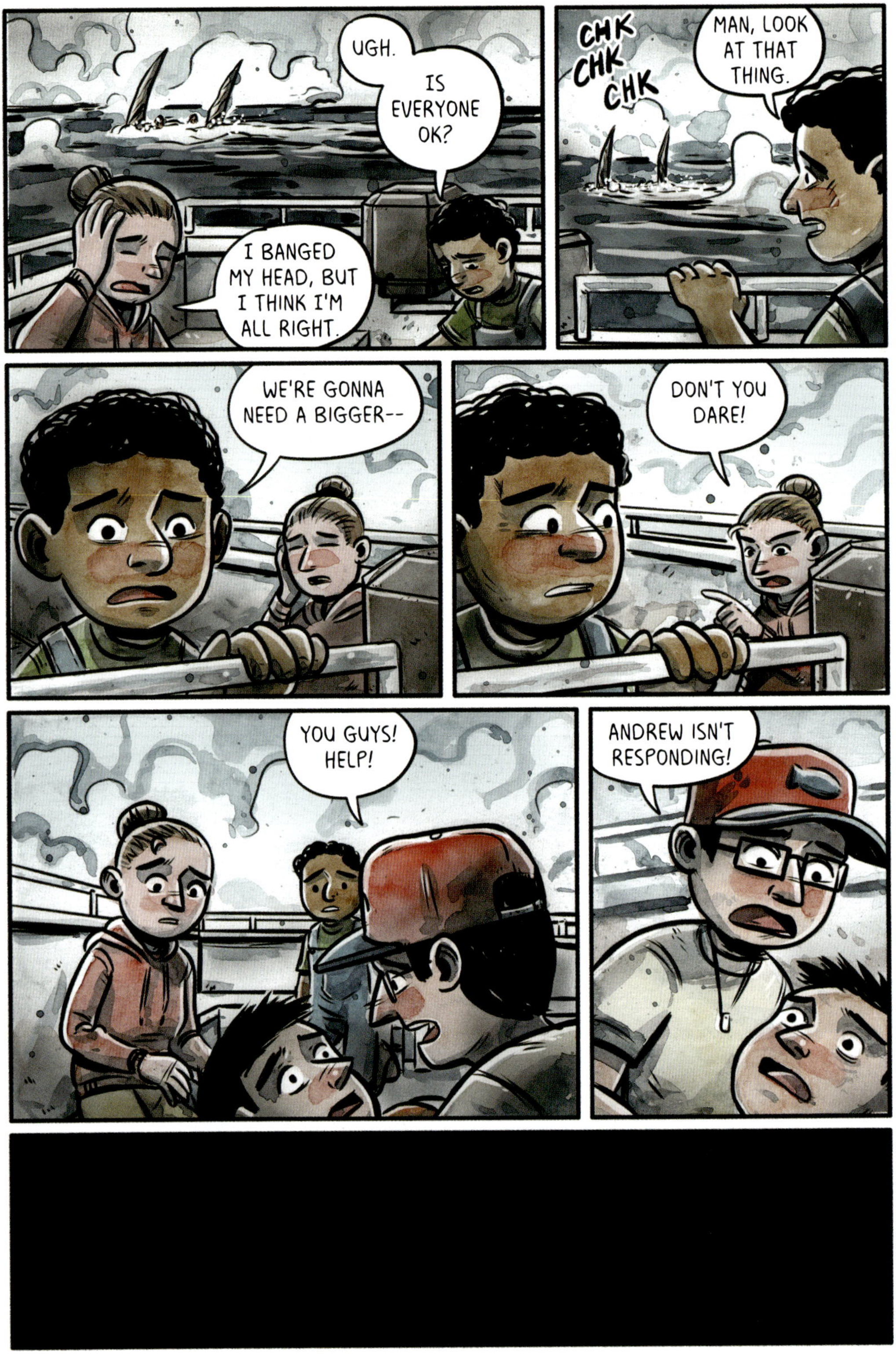
UGH.
IS EVERYONE OK?
I BANGED MY HEAD, BUT I THINK I'M ALL RIGHT.
CHK CHK CHK
MAN, LOOK AT THAT THING.
WE'RE GONNA NEED A BIGGER--
DON'T YOU DARE!
YOU GUYS! HELP!
ANDREW ISN'T RESPONDING!

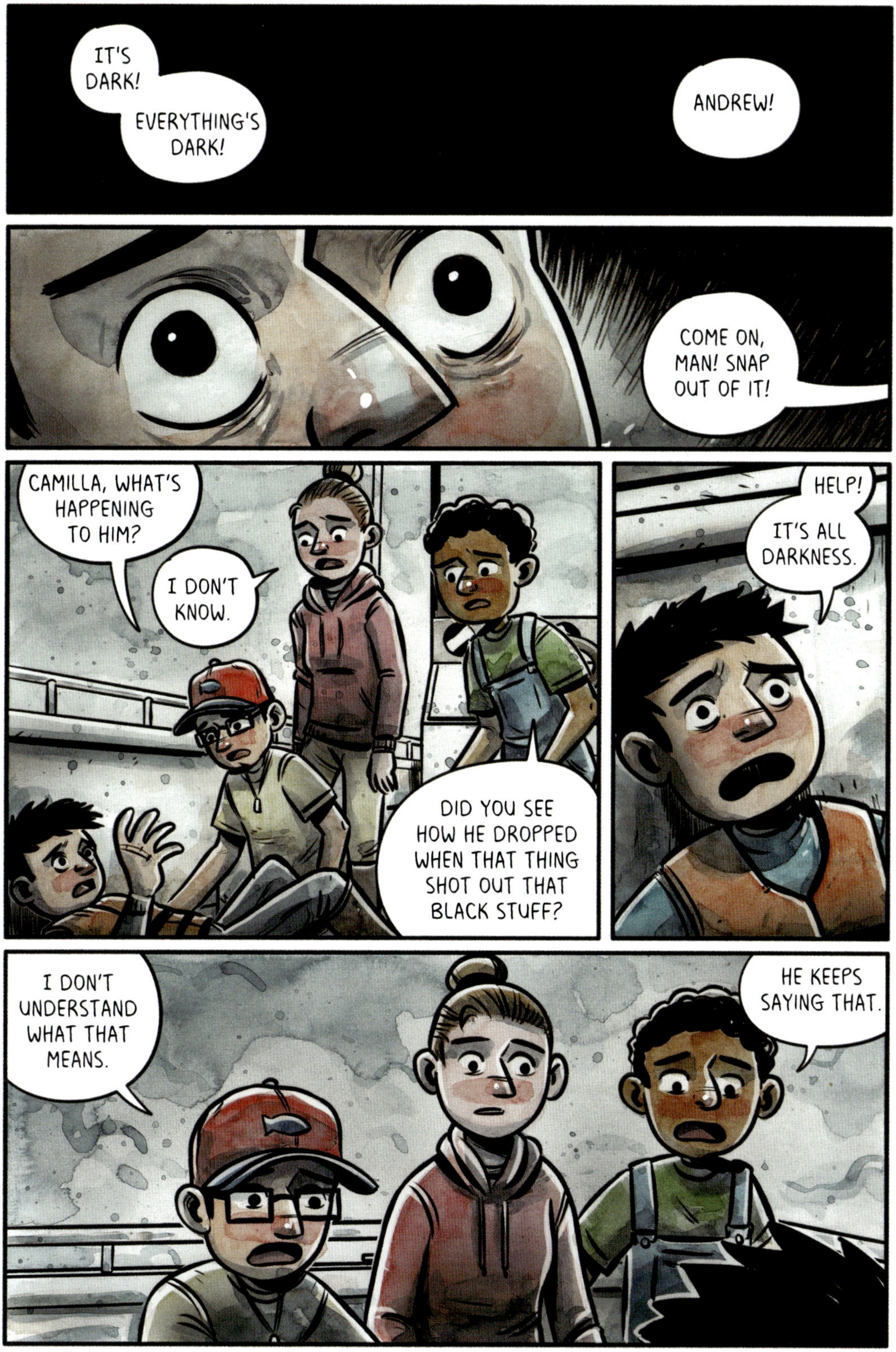
IT'S DARK!
EVERYTHING'S DARK!
ANDREW!
COME ON, MAN! SNAP OUT OF IT!
CAMILLA, WHAT'S HAPPENING TO HIM?
I DON'T KNOW.
DID YOU SEE HOW HE DROPPED WHEN THAT THING SHOT OUT THAT BLACK STUFF?
HELP!
IT'S ALL DARKNESS.
I DON'T UNDERSTAND WHAT THAT MEANS.
HE KEEPS SAYING THAT.

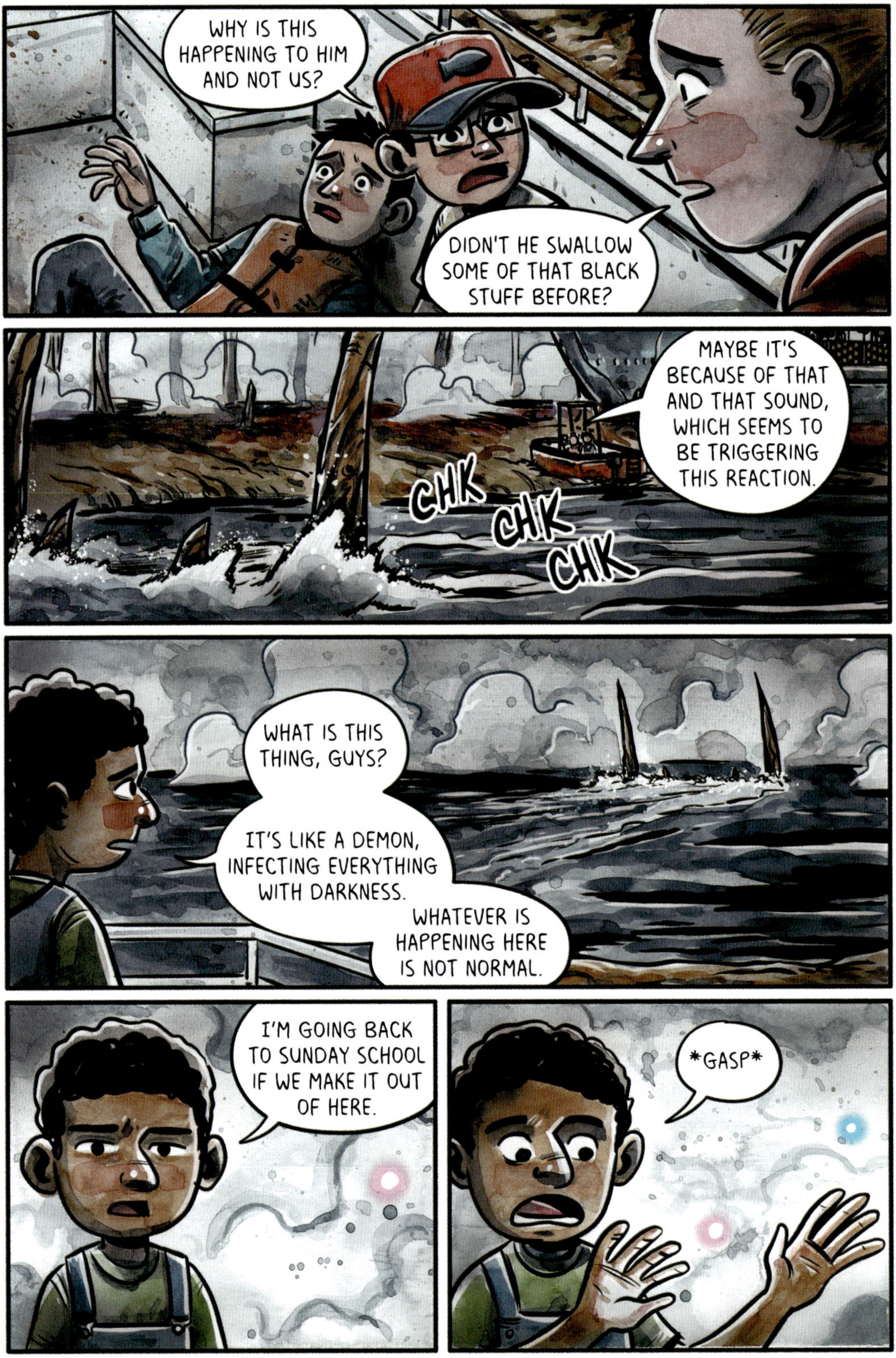
WHY IS THIS HAPPENING TO HIM AND NOT US?
DIDN'T HE SWALLOW SOME OF THAT BLACK STUFF BEFORE?
MAYBE IT'S BECAUSE OF THAT AND THAT SOUND, WHICH SEEMS TO BE TRIGGERING THIS REACTION.
CHK
CHK
CHK
WHAT IS THIS THING, GUYS?
IT'S LIKE A DEMON, INFECTING EVERYTHING WITH DARKNESS.
WHATEVER IS HAPPENING HERE IS NOT NORMAL.
I'M GOING BACK TO SUNDAY SCHOOL IF WE MAKE IT OUT OF HERE.
GASP

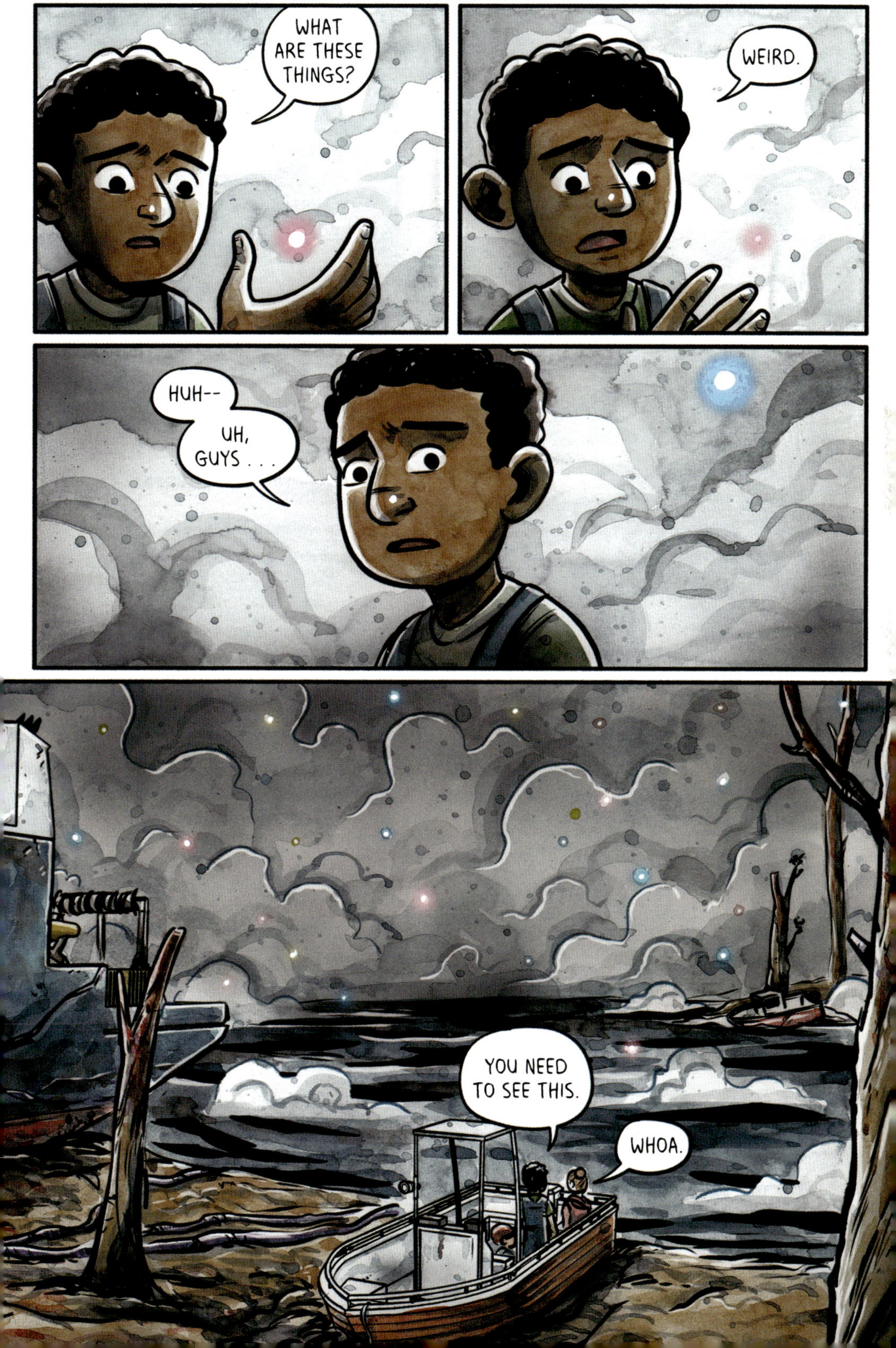
WHAT ARE THESE THINGS?
WEIRD.
HUH--
UH, GUYS . . .
YOU NEED TO SEE THIS.
WHOA.

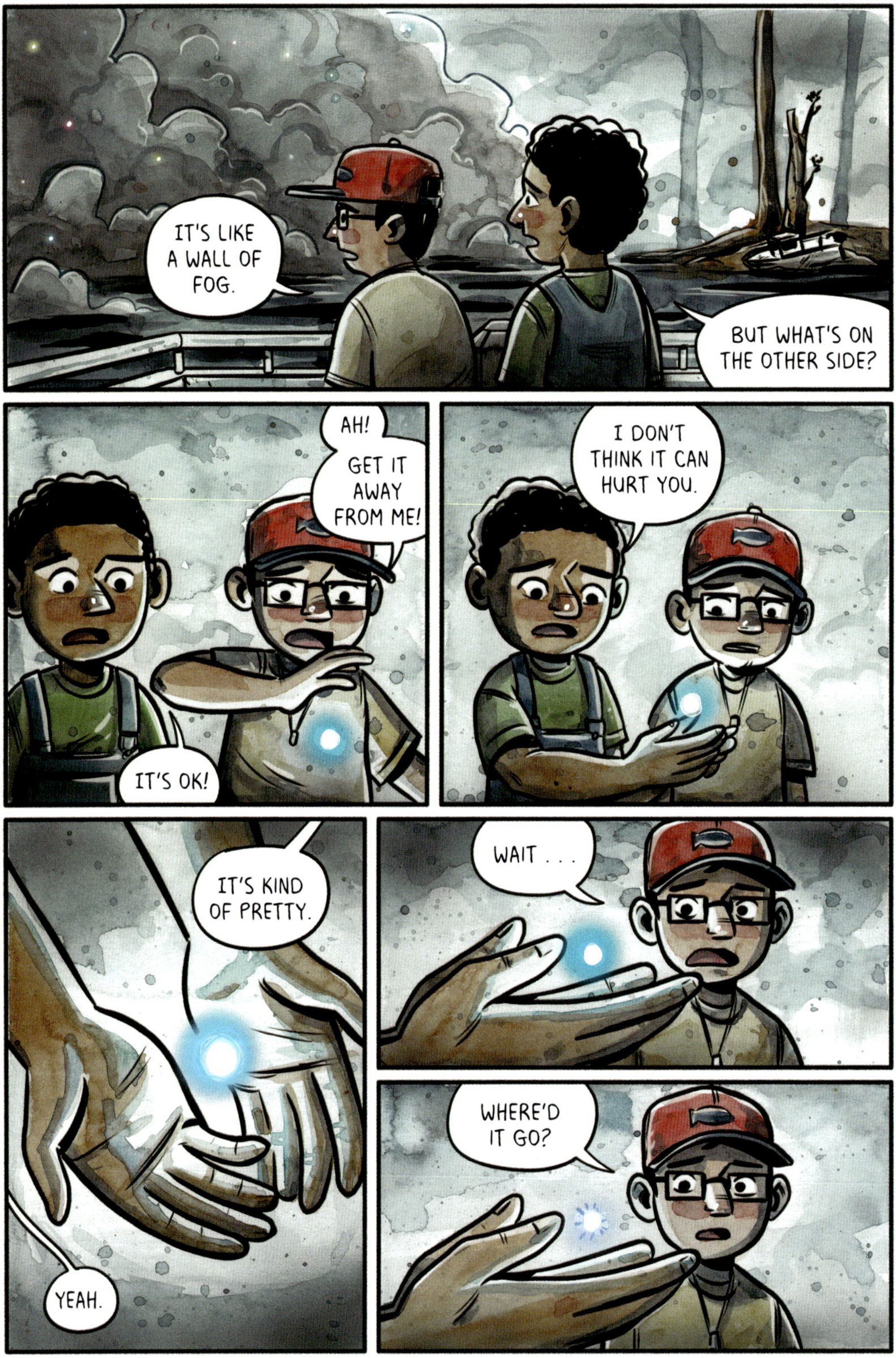
IT'S LIKE A WALL OF FOG.
BUT WHAT'S ON THE OTHER SIDE?
AH!
GET IT AWAY FROM ME!
IT'S OK!
I DON'T THINK IT CAN HURT YOU.
IT'S KIND OF PRETTY.
YEAH.
WAIT . . .
WHERE'D IT GO?

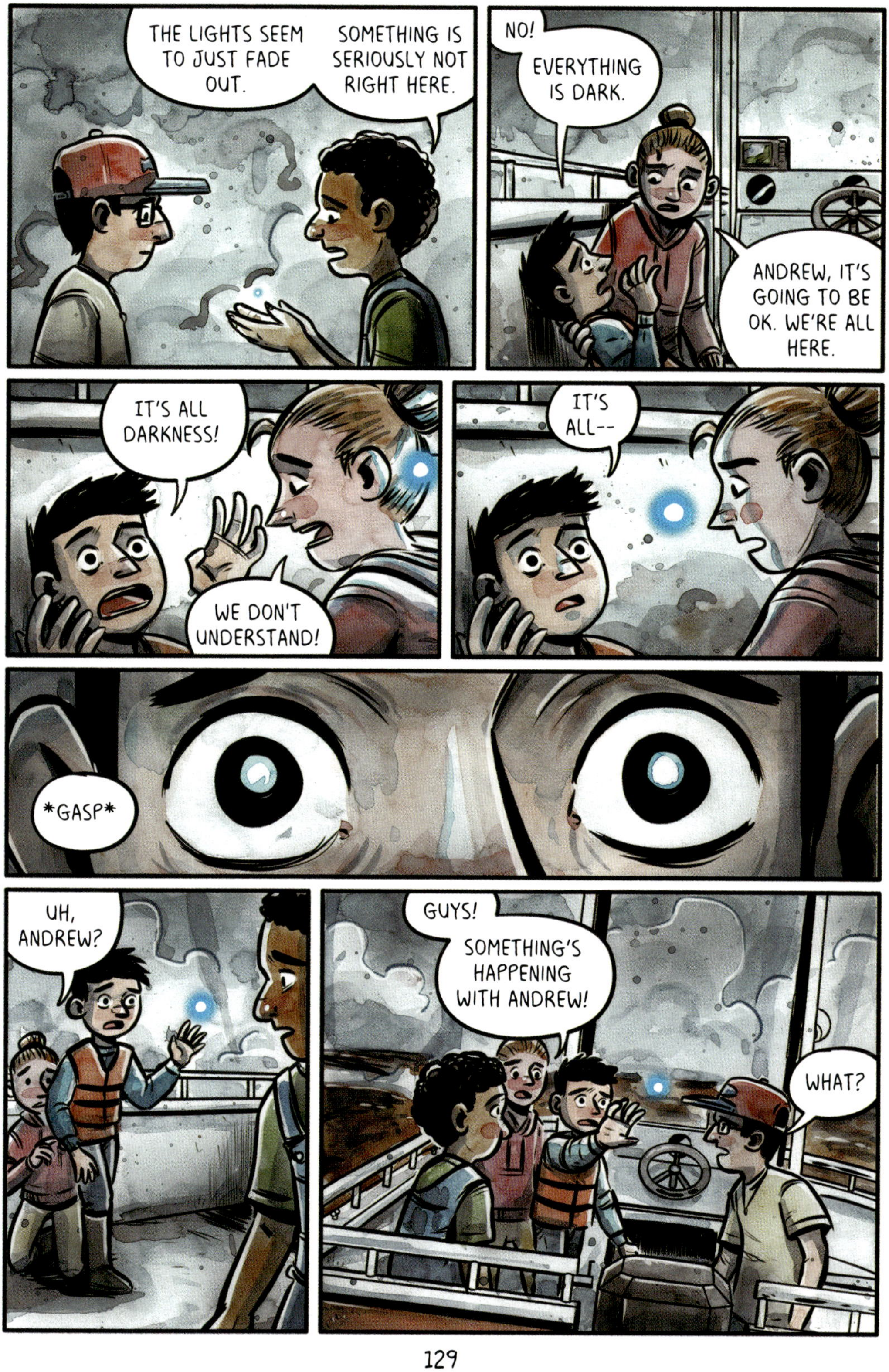
THE LIGHTS SEEM TO JUST FADE OUT.
SOMETHING IS SERIOUSLY NOT RIGHT HERE.
NO!
EVERYTHING IS DARK.
ANDREW, IT'S GOING TO BE OK. WE'RE ALL HERE.
IT'S ALL DARKNESS!
WE DON'T UNDERSTAND!
IT'S ALL--
GASP
UH, ANDREW?
GUYS!
SOMETHING'S HAPPENING WITH ANDREW!
WHAT?

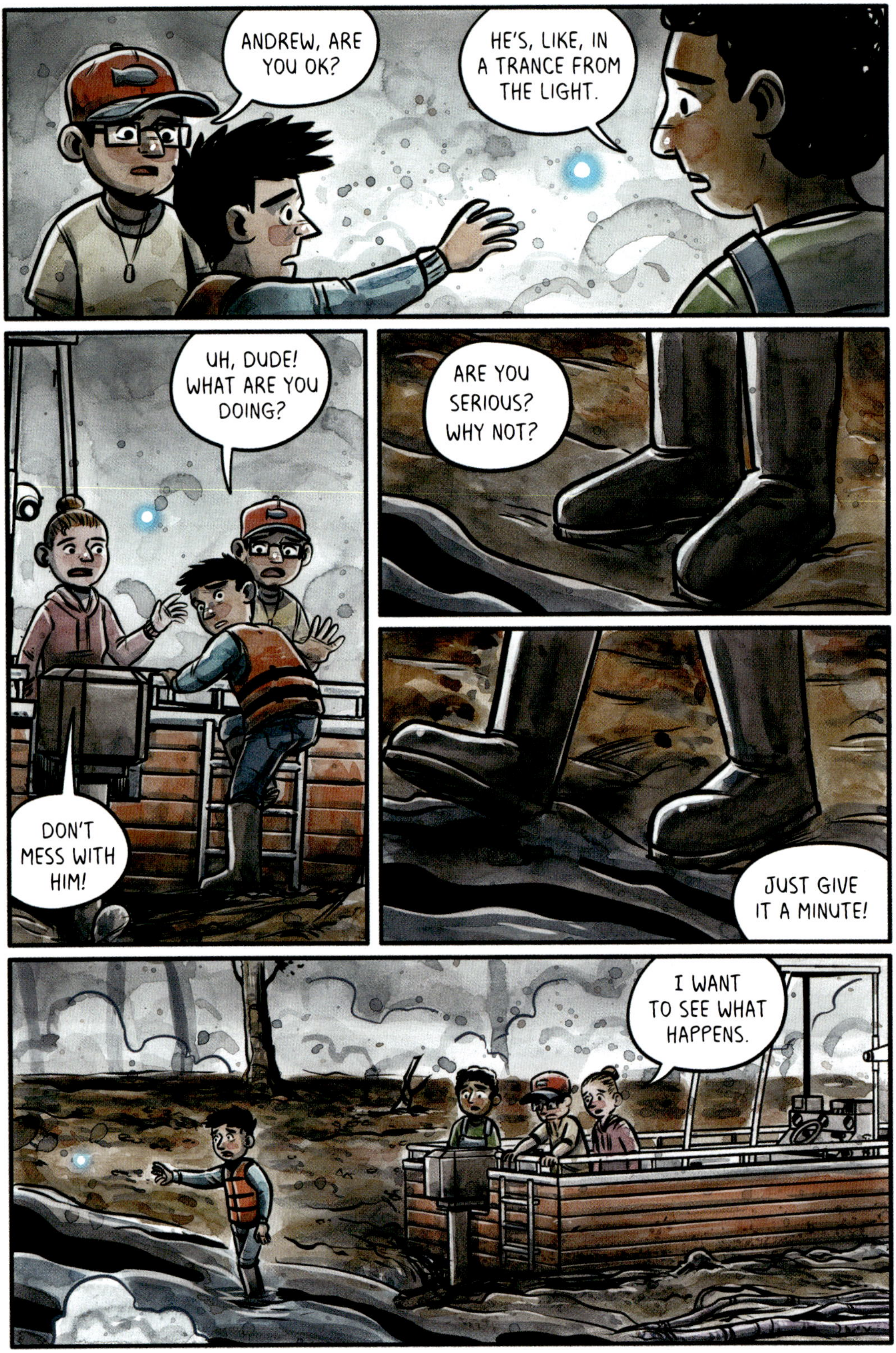
ANDREW, ARE YOU OK?
HE'S, LIKE, IN A TRANCE FROM THE LIGHT.
UH, DUDE! WHAT ARE YOU DOING?
DON'T MESS WITH HIM!
ARE YOU SERIOUS? WHY NOT?
JUST GIVE IT A MINUTE!
I WANT TO SEE WHAT HAPPENS.

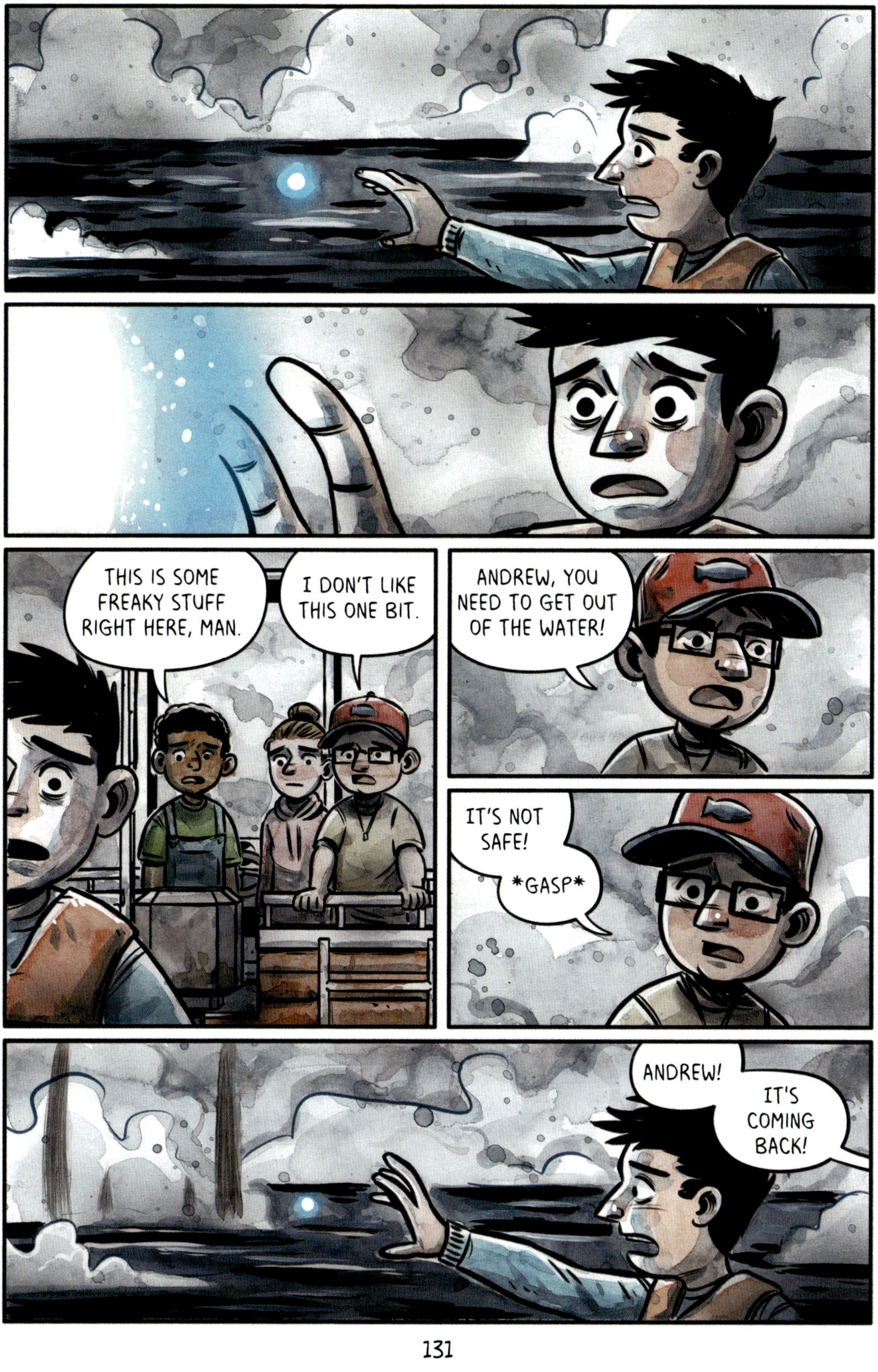
THIS IS SOME FREAKY STUFF RIGHT HERE, MAN.
I DON'T LIKE THIS ONE BIT.
ANDREW, YOU NEED TO GET OUT OF THE WATER!
IT'S NOT SAFE!
GASP
ANDREW!
IT'S COMING BACK!

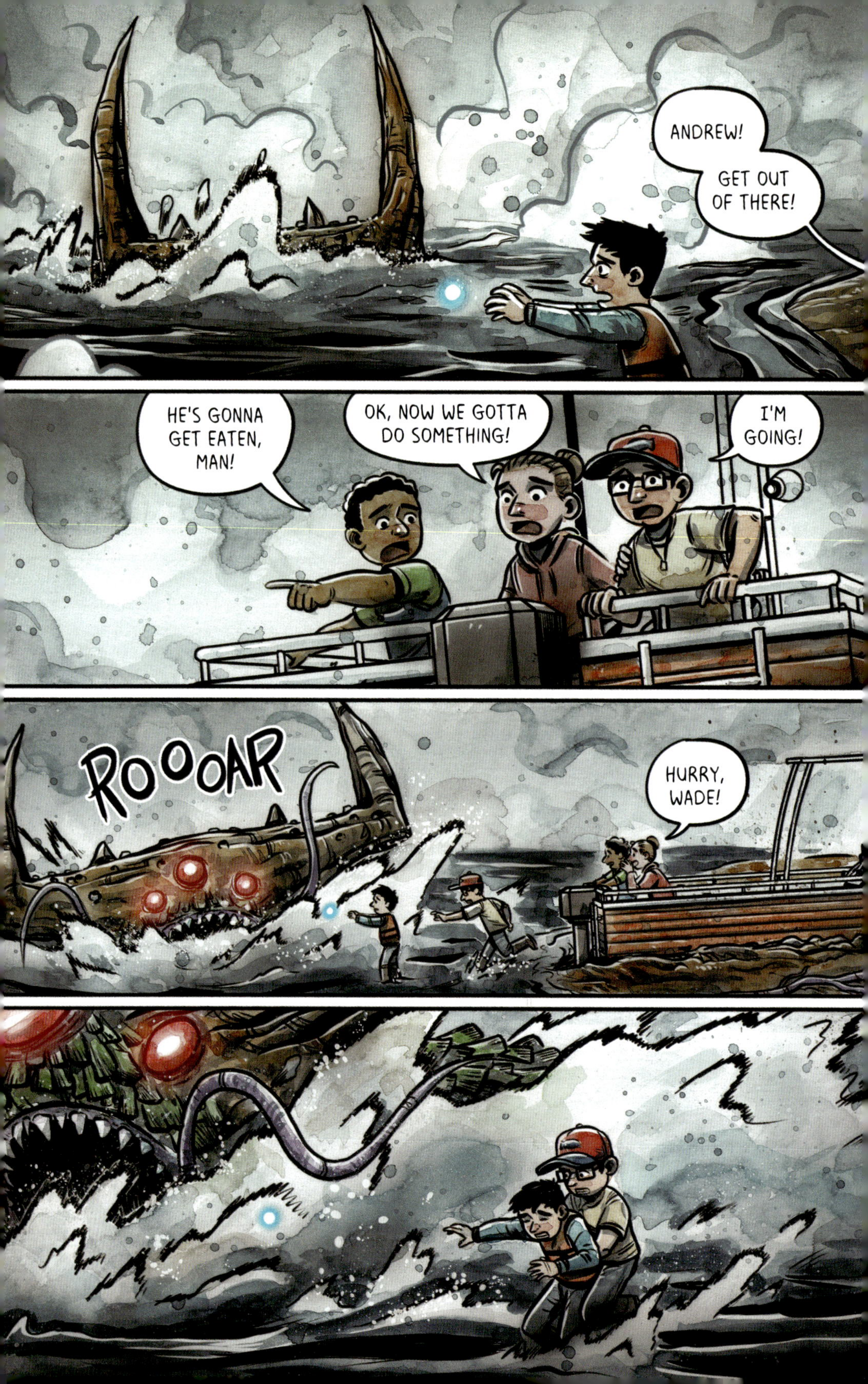
ANDREW!
GET OUT OF THERE!
HE'S GONNA GET EATEN, MAN!
OK, NOW WE GOTTA DO SOMETHING!
I'M GOING!
ROOOAR
HURRY, WADE!

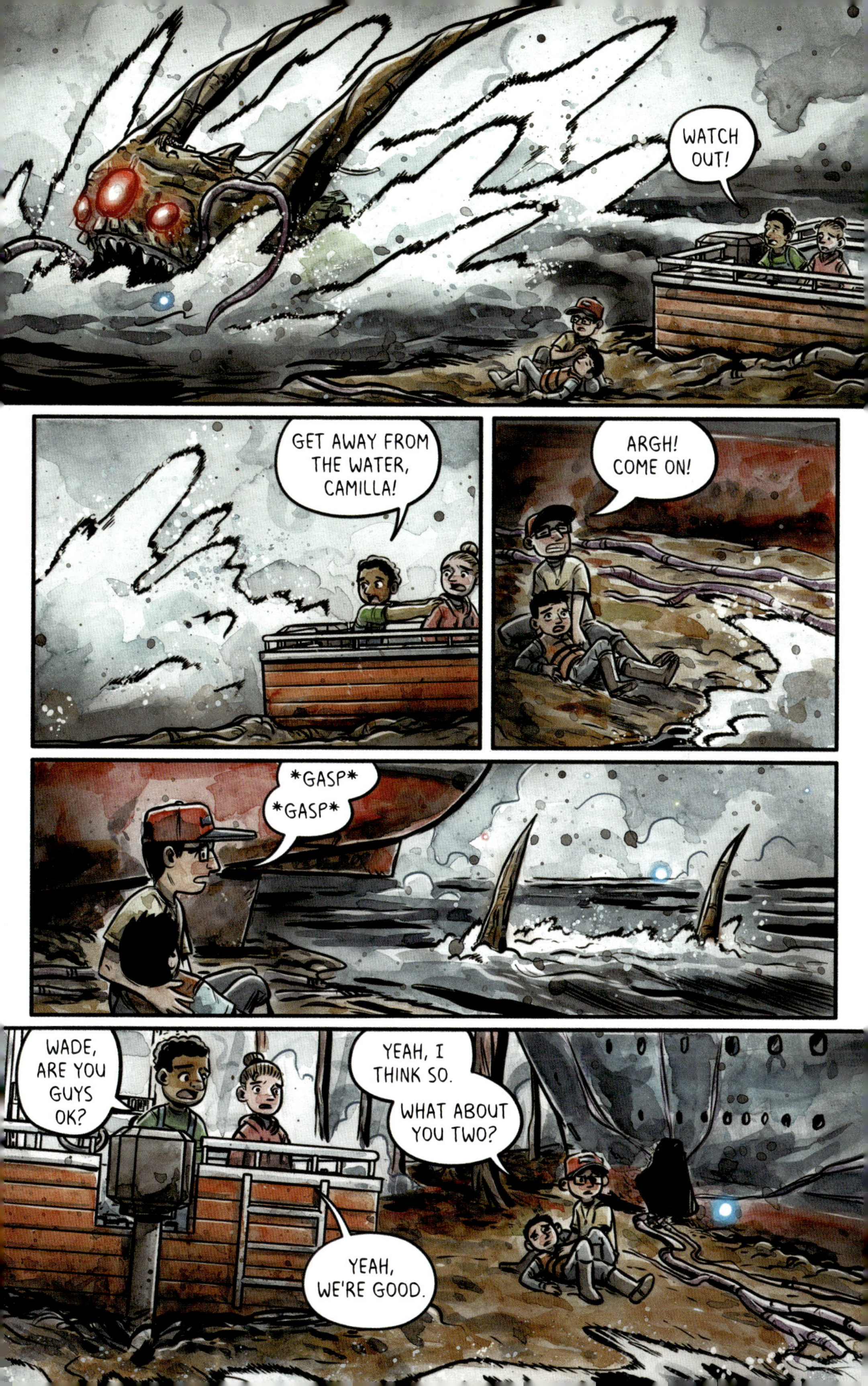

WATCH OUT!
GET AWAY FROM THE WATER, CAMILLA!
ARGH! COME ON!
GASP
GASP
WADE, ARE YOU GUYS OK?
YEAH, I THINK SO.
WHAT ABOUT YOU TWO?
YEAH, WE'RE GOOD.

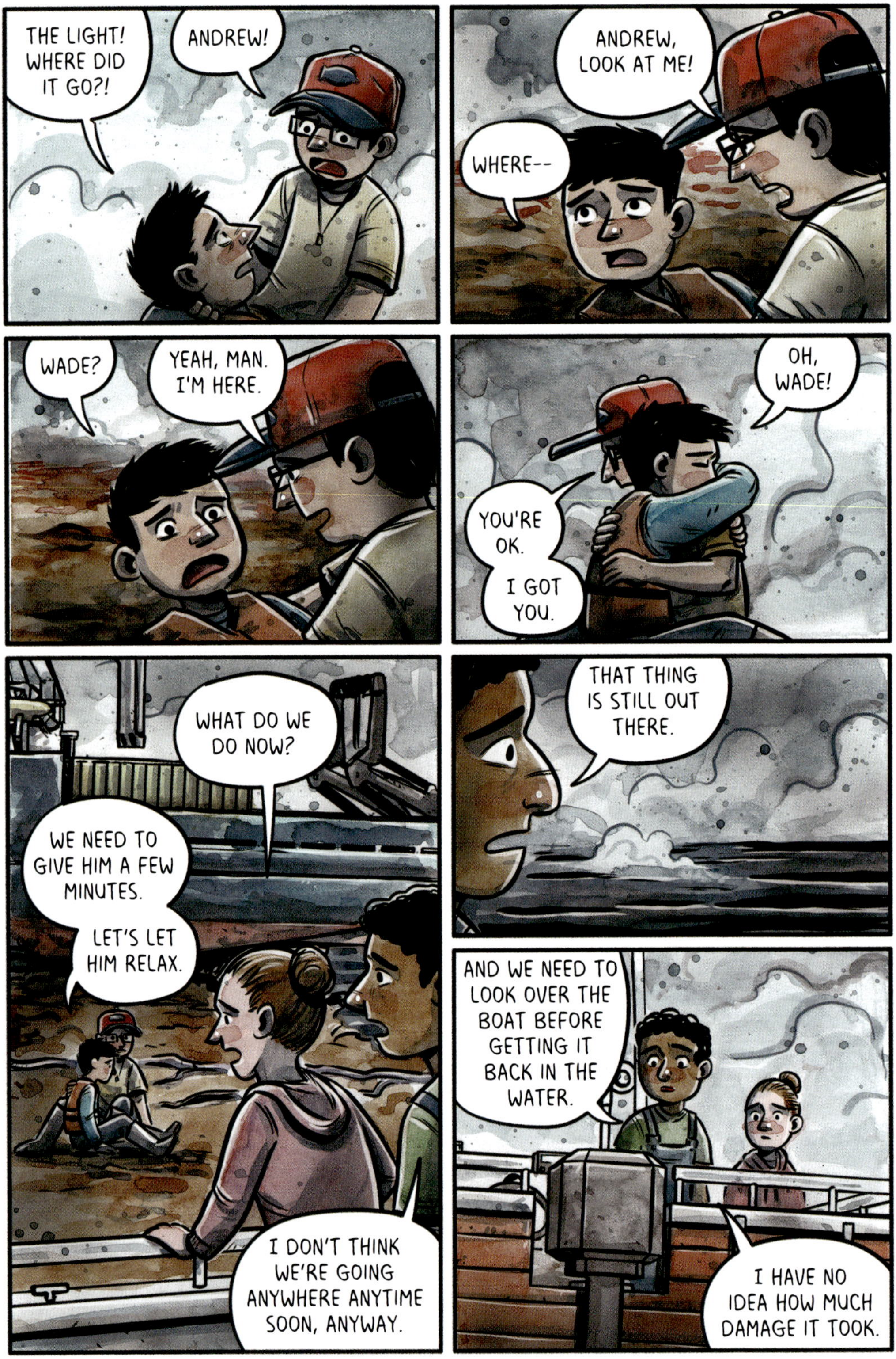
THE LIGHT! WHERE DID IT GO?!
ANDREW!
ANDREW, LOOK AT ME!
WHERE--
WADE?
YEAH, MAN. I'M HERE.
OH, WADE!
YOU'RE OK.
I GOT YOU.
WHAT DO WE DO NOW?
WE NEED TO GIVE HIM A FEW MINUTES.
LET'S LET HIM RELAX.
I DON'T THINK WE'RE GOING ANYWHERE ANYTIME SOON, ANYWAY.
THAT THING IS STILL OUT THERE.
AND WE NEED TO LOOK OVER THE BOAT BEFORE GETTING IT BACK IN THE WATER.
I HAVE NO IDEA HOW MUCH DAMAGE IT TOOK.

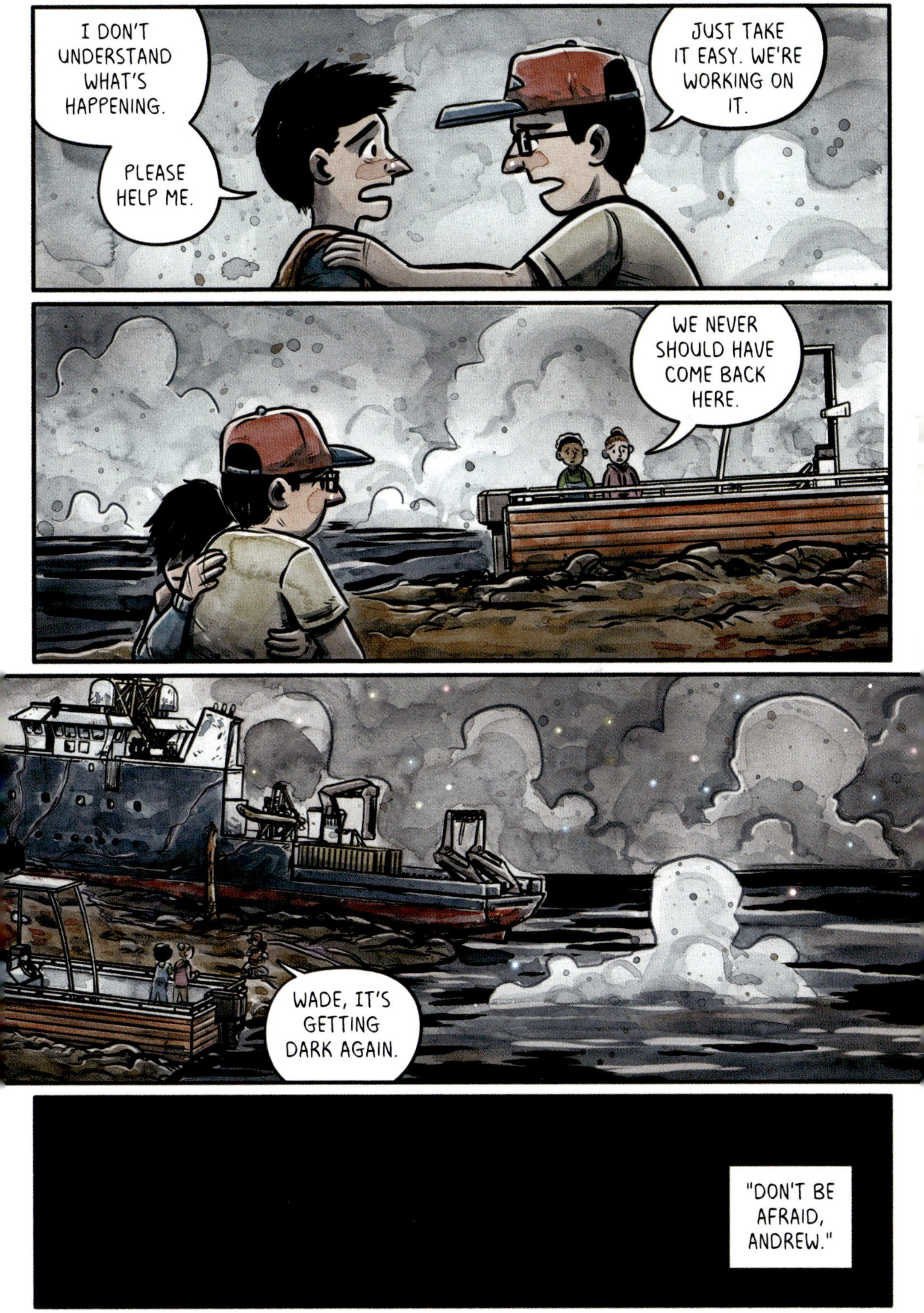
I DON'T UNDERSTAND WHAT'S HAPPENING.
PLEASE HELP ME.
JUST TAKE IT EASY. WE'RE WORKING ON IT.
WE NEVER SHOULD HAVE COME BACK HERE.
WADE, IT'S GETTING DARK AGAIN.
"DON'T BE AFRAID, ANDREW."

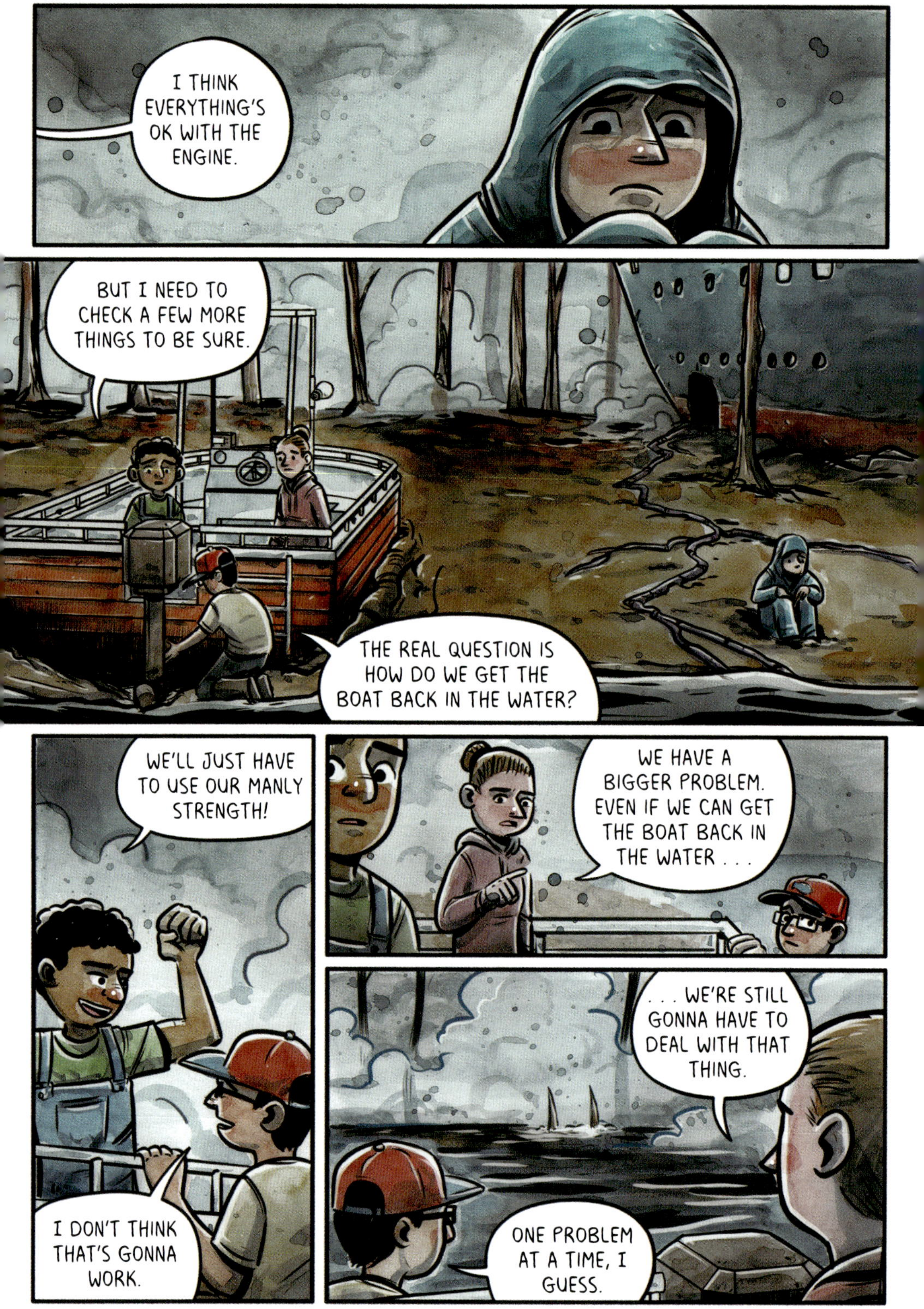
I THINK EVERYTHING'S OK WITH THE ENGINE.
BUT I NEED TO CHECK A FEW MORE THINGS TO BE SURE.
THE REAL QUESTION IS HOW DO WE GET THE BOAT BACK IN THE WATER?
WE'LL JUST HAVE TO USE OUR MANLY STRENGTH!
I DON'T THINK THAT'S GONNA WORK.
WE HAVE A BIGGER PROBLEM. EVEN IF WE CAN GET THE BOAT BACK IN THE WATER . . .
. . . WE'RE STILL GONNA HAVE TO DEAL WITH THAT THING.
ONE PROBLEM AT A TIME, I GUESS.

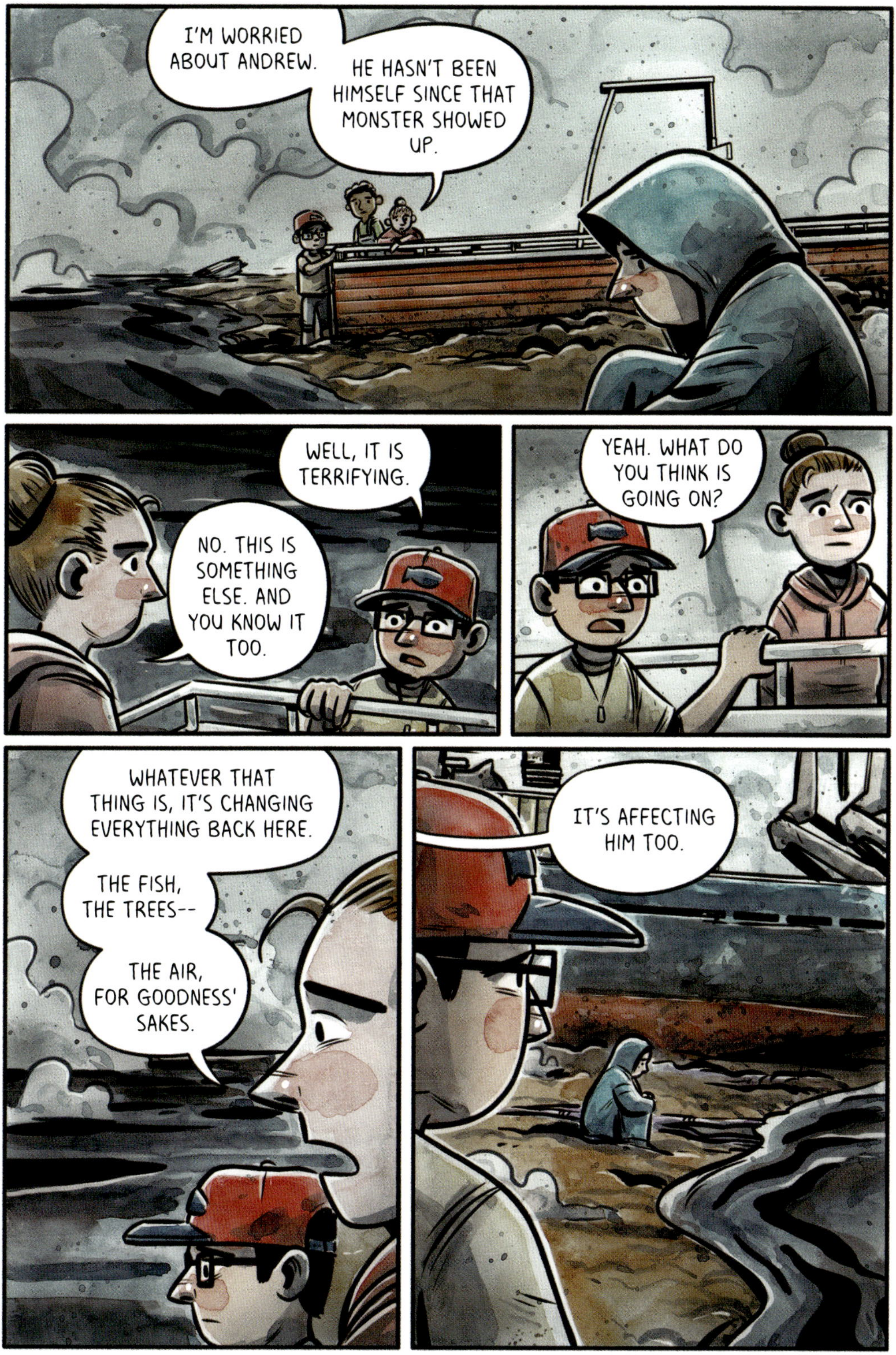

I'M WORRIED ABOUT ANDREW.
HE HASN'T BEEN HIMSELF SINCE THAT MONSTER SHOWED UP.
WELL, IT IS TERRIFYING.
NO. THIS IS SOMETHING ELSE. AND YOU KNOW IT TOO.
YEAH. WHAT DO YOU THINK IS GOING ON?
WHATEVER THAT THING IS, IT'S CHANGING EVERYTHING BACK HERE.
THE FISH, THE TREES--
THE AIR, FOR GOODNESS' SAKES.
IT'S AFFECTING HIM TOO.

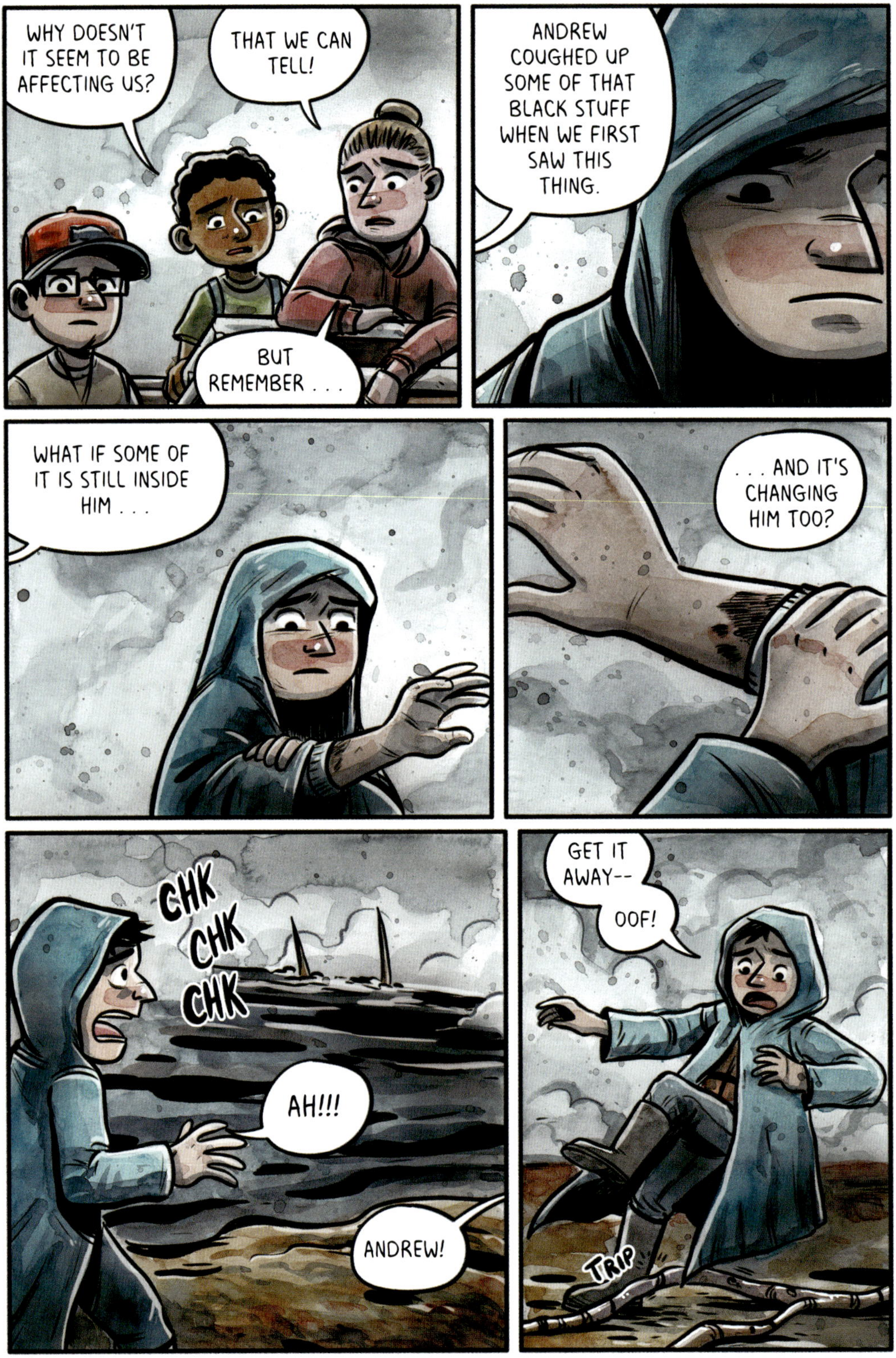
WHY DOESN'T IT SEEM TO BE AFFECTING US?
THAT WE CAN TELL!
BUT REMEMBER . . .
ANDREW COUGHED UP SOME OF THAT BLACK STUFF WHEN WE FIRST SAW THIS THING.
WHAT IF SOME OF IT IS STILL INSIDE HIM . . .
. . . AND IT'S CHANGING HIM TOO?
CHK
CHK
CHK
AH!!!
ANDREW!
GET IT AWAY--
OOF!
TRIP

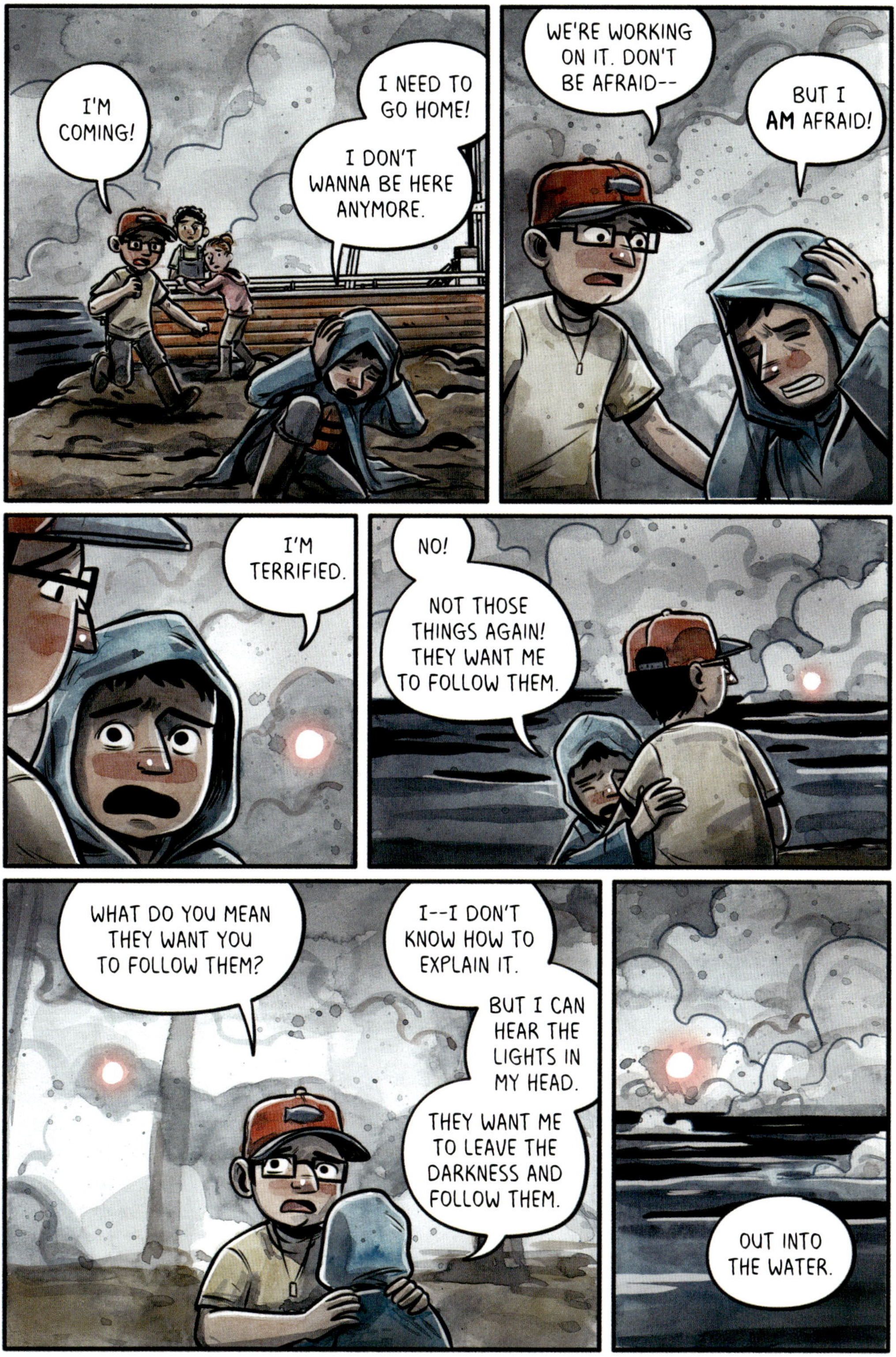
I'M COMING!
I NEED TO GO HOME!
I DON'T WANNA BE HERE ANYMORE.
WE'RE WORKING ON IT. DON'T BE AFRAID--
BUT I **AM** AFRAID!
I'M TERRIFIED.
NO!
NOT THOSE THINGS AGAIN! THEY WANT ME TO FOLLOW THEM.
WHAT DO YOU MEAN THEY WANT YOU TO FOLLOW THEM?
I--I DON'T KNOW HOW TO EXPLAIN IT.
BUT I CAN HEAR THE LIGHTS IN MY HEAD.
THEY WANT ME TO LEAVE THE DARKNESS AND FOLLOW THEM.
OUT INTO THE WATER.

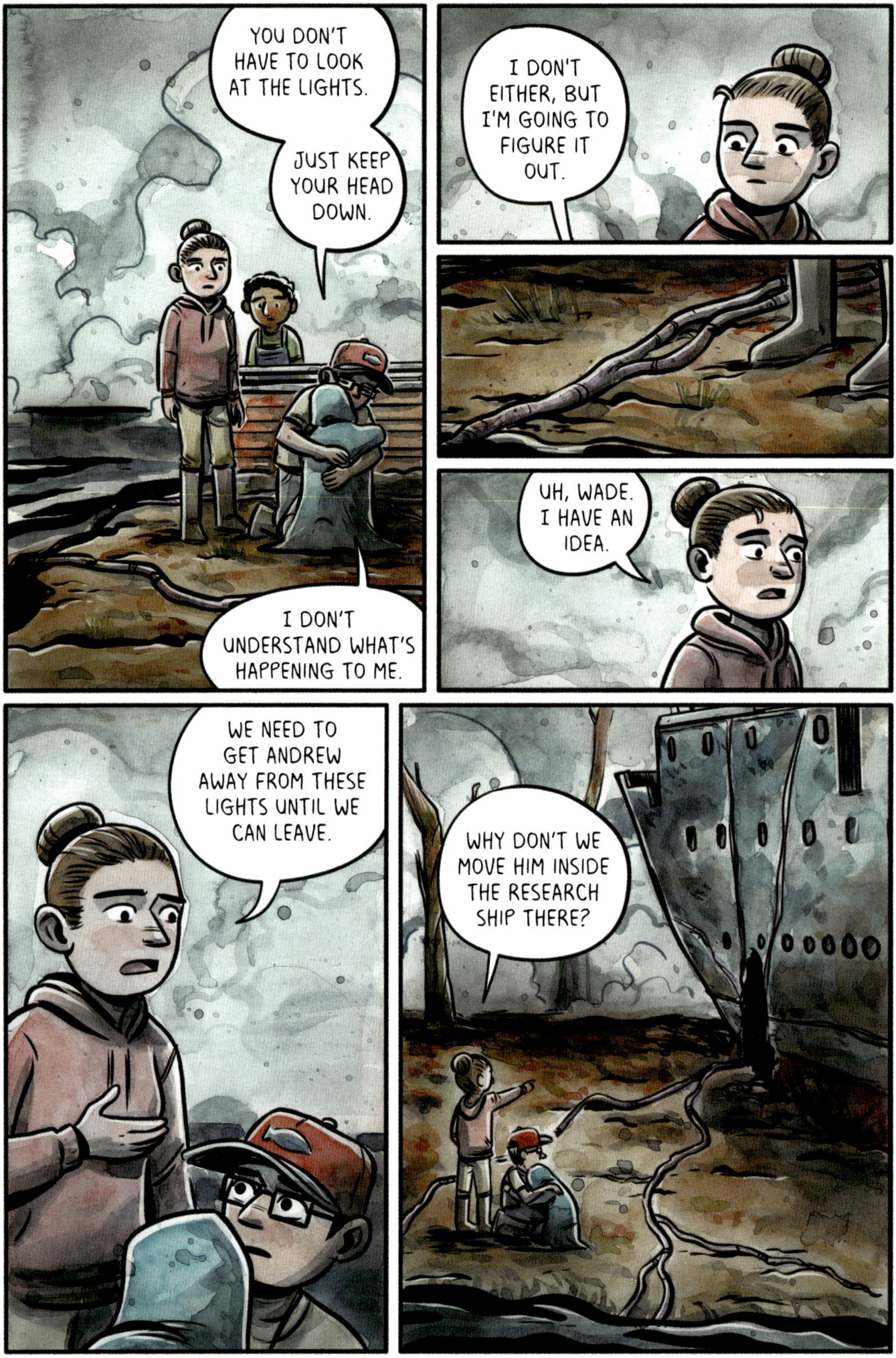
YOU DON'T HAVE TO LOOK AT THE LIGHTS.
JUST KEEP YOUR HEAD DOWN.
I DON'T UNDERSTAND WHAT'S HAPPENING TO ME.
I DON'T EITHER, BUT I'M GOING TO FIGURE IT OUT.
UH, WADE. I HAVE AN IDEA.
WE NEED TO GET ANDREW AWAY FROM THESE LIGHTS UNTIL WE CAN LEAVE.
WHY DON'T WE MOVE HIM INSIDE THE RESEARCH SHIP THERE?

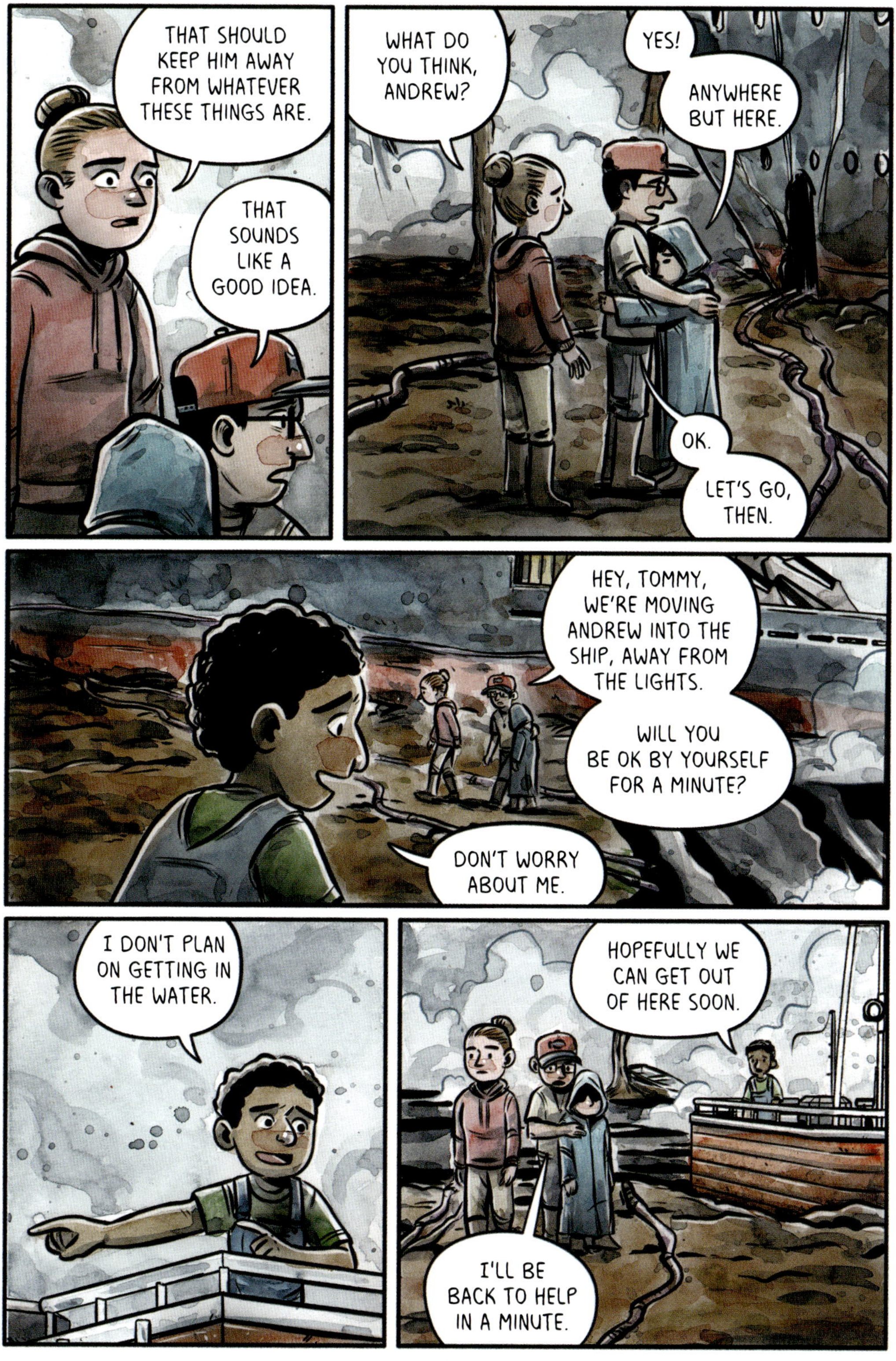
THAT SHOULD KEEP HIM AWAY FROM WHATEVER THESE THINGS ARE.
THAT SOUNDS LIKE A GOOD IDEA.
WHAT DO YOU THINK, ANDREW?
YES!
ANYWHERE BUT HERE.
OK.
LET'S GO, THEN.
HEY, TOMMY, WE'RE MOVING ANDREW INTO THE SHIP, AWAY FROM THE LIGHTS.
WILL YOU BE OK BY YOURSELF FOR A MINUTE?
DON'T WORRY ABOUT ME.
I DON'T PLAN ON GETTING IN THE WATER.
HOPEFULLY WE CAN GET OUT OF HERE SOON.
I'LL BE BACK TO HELP IN A MINUTE.

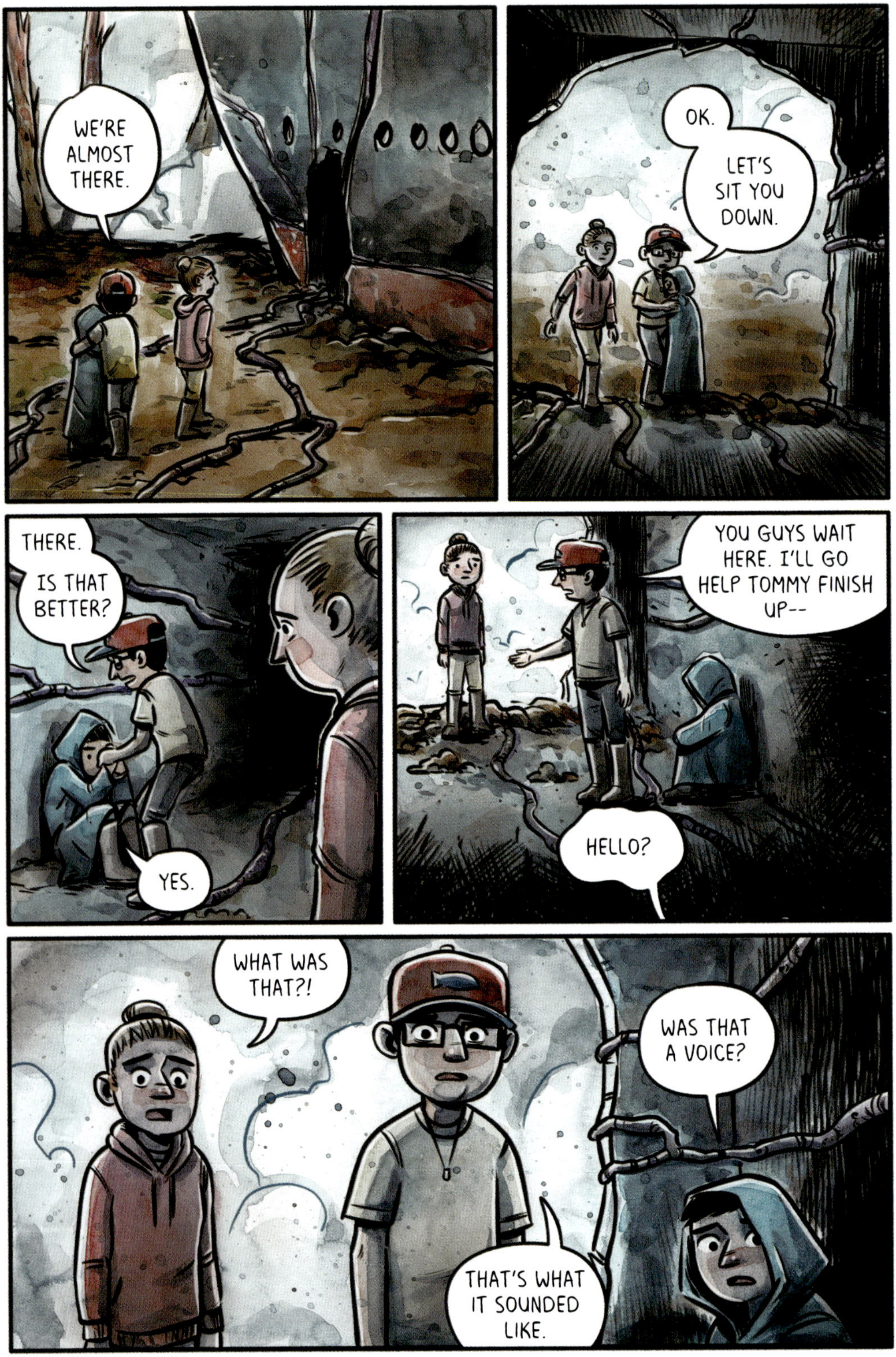
WE'RE ALMOST THERE.
OK.
LET'S SIT YOU DOWN.
THERE.
IS THAT BETTER?
YES.
YOU GUYS WAIT HERE. I'LL GO HELP TOMMY FINISH UP--
HELLO?
WHAT WAS THAT?!
WAS THAT A VOICE?
THAT'S WHAT IT SOUNDED LIKE.

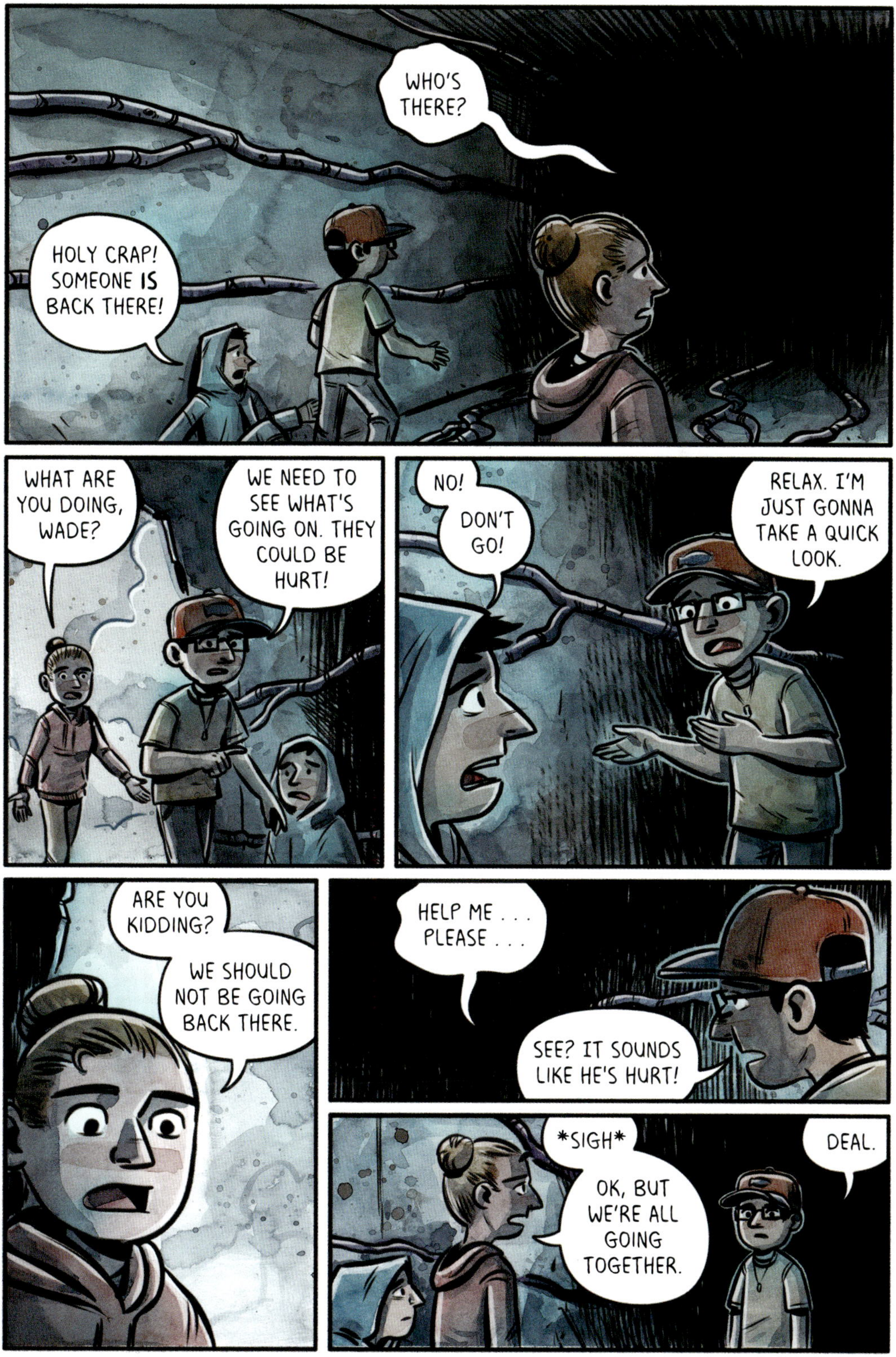
WHO'S THERE?
HOLY CRAP! SOMEONE **IS** BACK THERE!
WHAT ARE YOU DOING, WADE?
WE NEED TO SEE WHAT'S GOING ON. THEY COULD BE HURT!
NO!
DON'T GO!
RELAX. I'M JUST GONNA TAKE A QUICK LOOK.
ARE YOU KIDDING?
WE SHOULD NOT BE GOING BACK THERE.
HELP ME . . . PLEASE . . .
SEE? IT SOUNDS LIKE HE'S HURT!
SIGH
OK, BUT WE'RE ALL GOING TOGETHER.
DEAL.

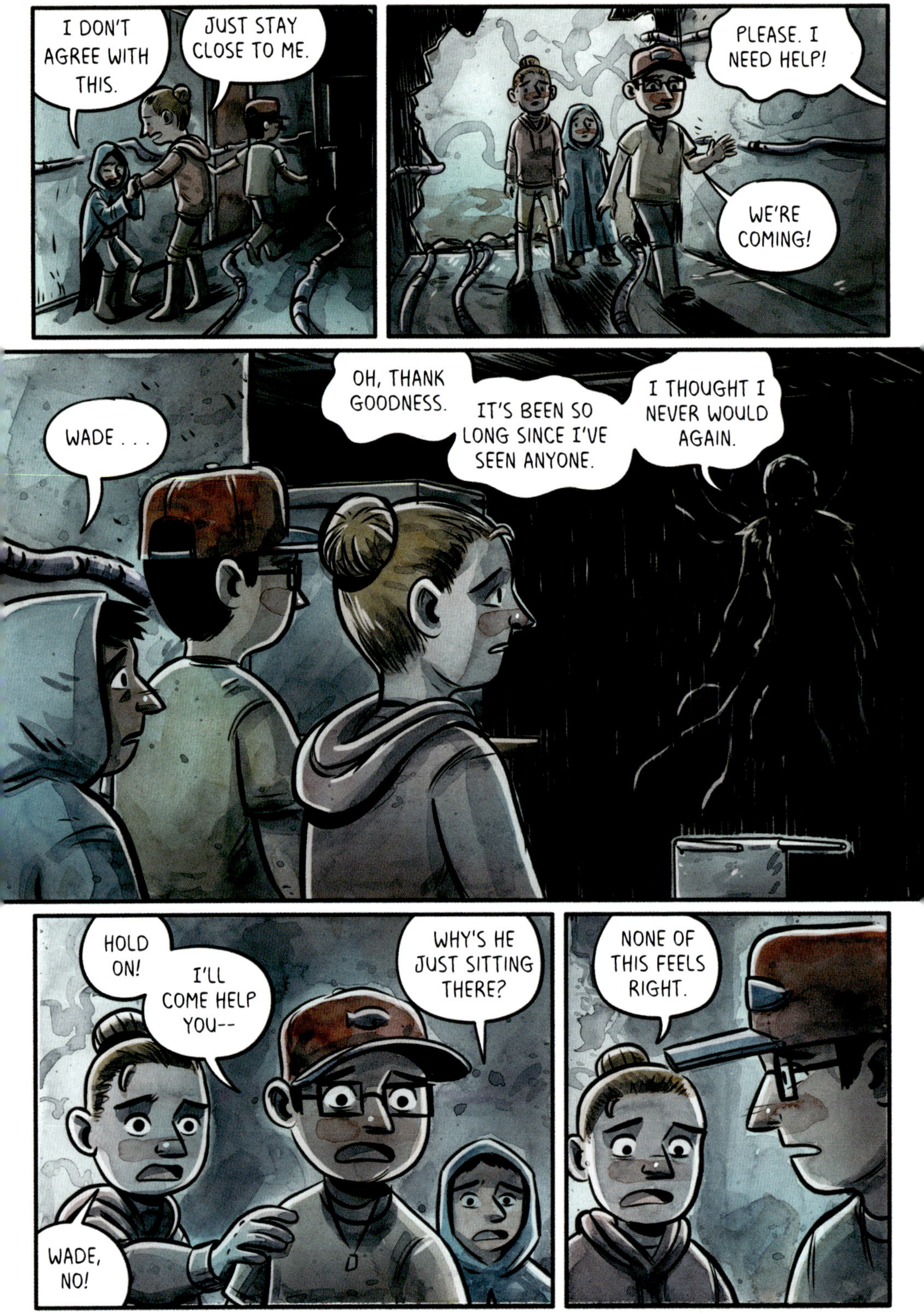
I DON'T AGREE WITH THIS.
JUST STAY CLOSE TO ME.
PLEASE. I NEED HELP!
WE'RE COMING!
WADE . . .
OH, THANK GOODNESS.
IT'S BEEN SO LONG SINCE I'VE SEEN ANYONE.
I THOUGHT I NEVER WOULD AGAIN.
HOLD ON!
I'LL COME HELP YOU--
WHY'S HE JUST SITTING THERE?
WADE, NO!
NONE OF THIS FEELS RIGHT.

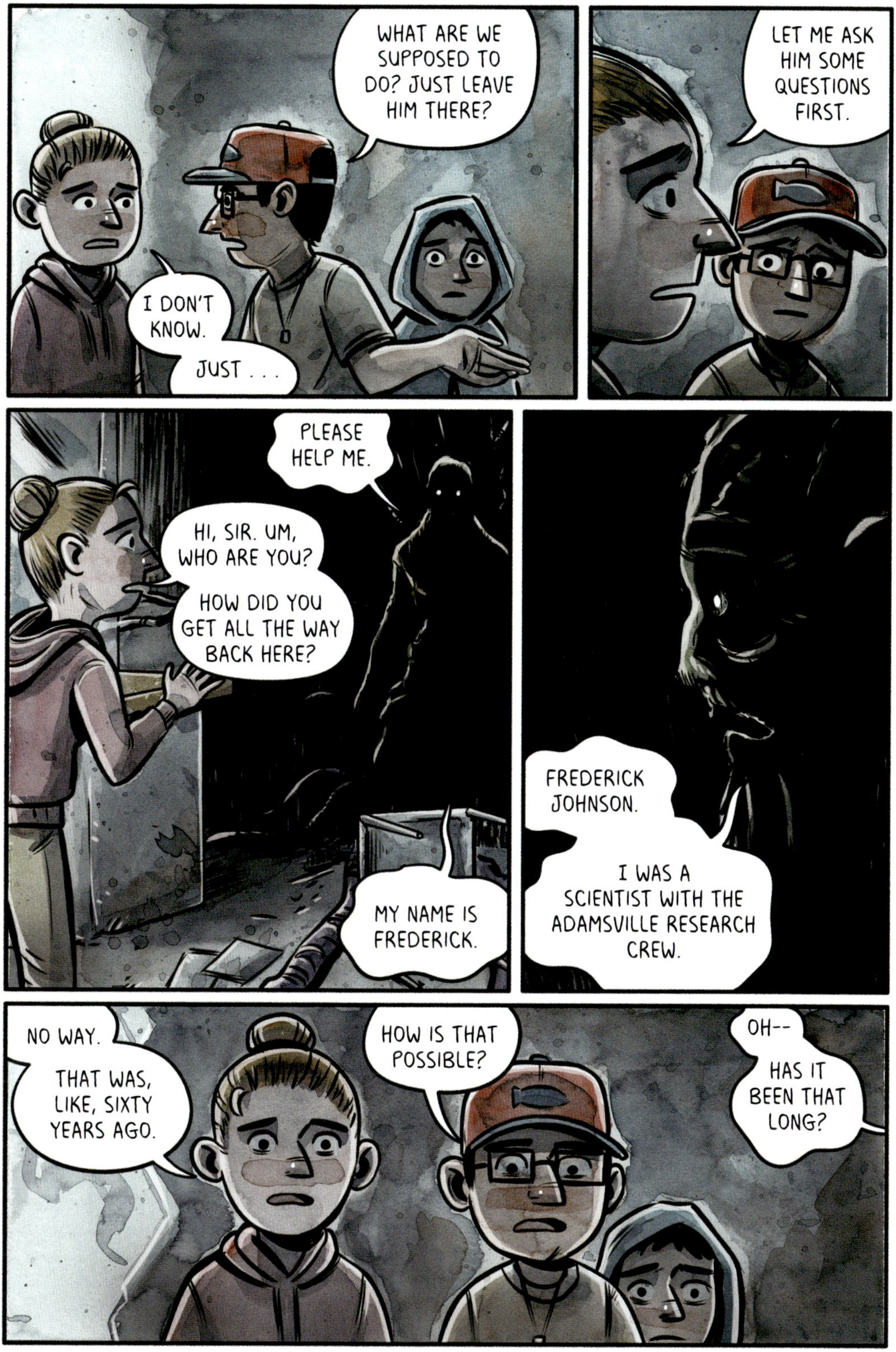
WHAT ARE WE SUPPOSED TO DO? JUST LEAVE HIM THERE?
I DON'T KNOW.
JUST . . .
LET ME ASK HIM SOME QUESTIONS FIRST.
PLEASE HELP ME.
HI, SIR. UM, WHO ARE YOU?
HOW DID YOU GET ALL THE WAY BACK HERE?
MY NAME IS FREDERICK.
FREDERICK JOHNSON.
I WAS A SCIENTIST WITH THE ADAMSVILLE RESEARCH CREW.
NO WAY.
THAT WAS, LIKE, SIXTY YEARS AGO.
HOW IS THAT POSSIBLE?
OH--
HAS IT BEEN THAT LONG?

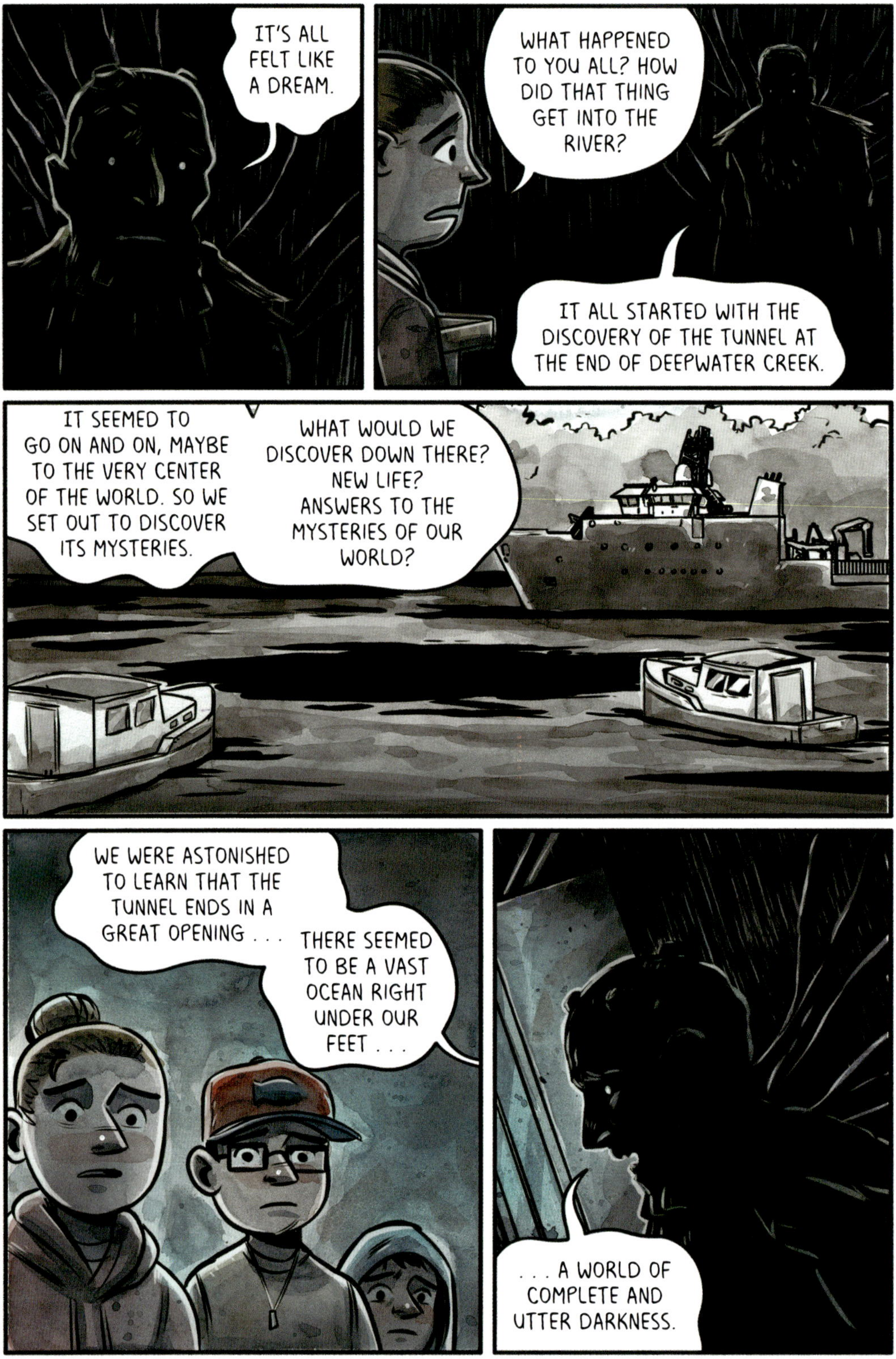
IT'S ALL FELT LIKE A DREAM.
WHAT HAPPENED TO YOU ALL? HOW DID THAT THING GET INTO THE RIVER?
IT ALL STARTED WITH THE DISCOVERY OF THE TUNNEL AT THE END OF DEEPWATER CREEK.
IT SEEMED TO GO ON AND ON, MAYBE TO THE VERY CENTER OF THE WORLD. SO WE SET OUT TO DISCOVER ITS MYSTERIES.
WHAT WOULD WE DISCOVER DOWN THERE? NEW LIFE? ANSWERS TO THE MYSTERIES OF OUR WORLD?
WE WERE ASTONISHED TO LEARN THAT THE TUNNEL ENDS IN A GREAT OPENING . . .
THERE SEEMED TO BE A VAST OCEAN RIGHT UNDER OUR FEET . . .
. . . A WORLD OF COMPLETE AND UTTER DARKNESS.

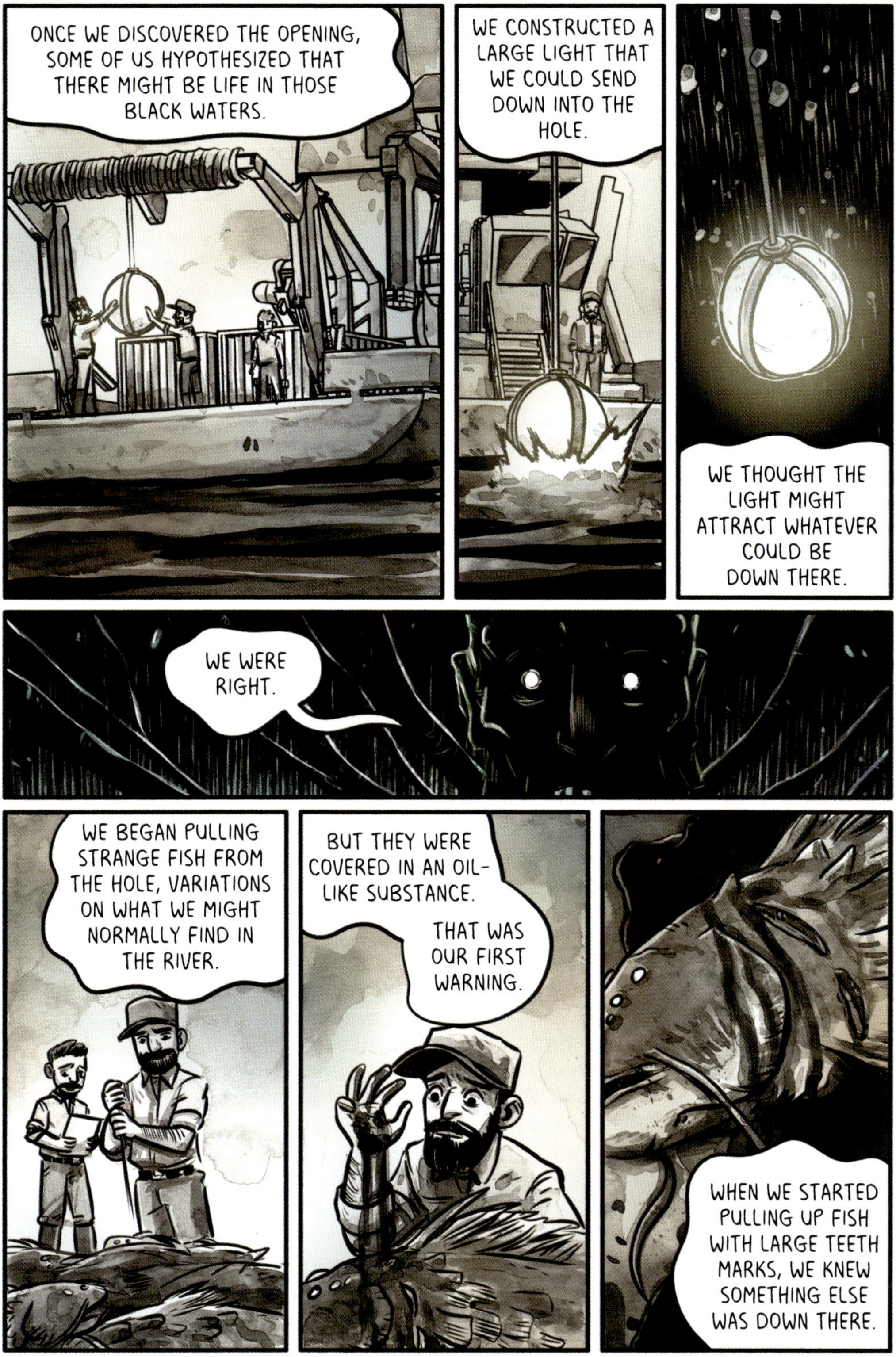
ONCE WE DISCOVERED THE OPENING, SOME OF US HYPOTHESIZED THAT THERE MIGHT BE LIFE IN THOSE BLACK WATERS.
WE CONSTRUCTED A LARGE LIGHT THAT WE COULD SEND DOWN INTO THE HOLE.
WE THOUGHT THE LIGHT MIGHT ATTRACT WHATEVER COULD BE DOWN THERE.
WE WERE RIGHT.
WE BEGAN PULLING STRANGE FISH FROM THE HOLE, VARIATIONS ON WHAT WE MIGHT NORMALLY FIND IN THE RIVER.
BUT THEY WERE COVERED IN AN OIL-LIKE SUBSTANCE.
THAT WAS OUR FIRST WARNING.
WHEN WE STARTED PULLING UP FISH WITH LARGE TEETH MARKS, WE KNEW SOMETHING ELSE WAS DOWN THERE.

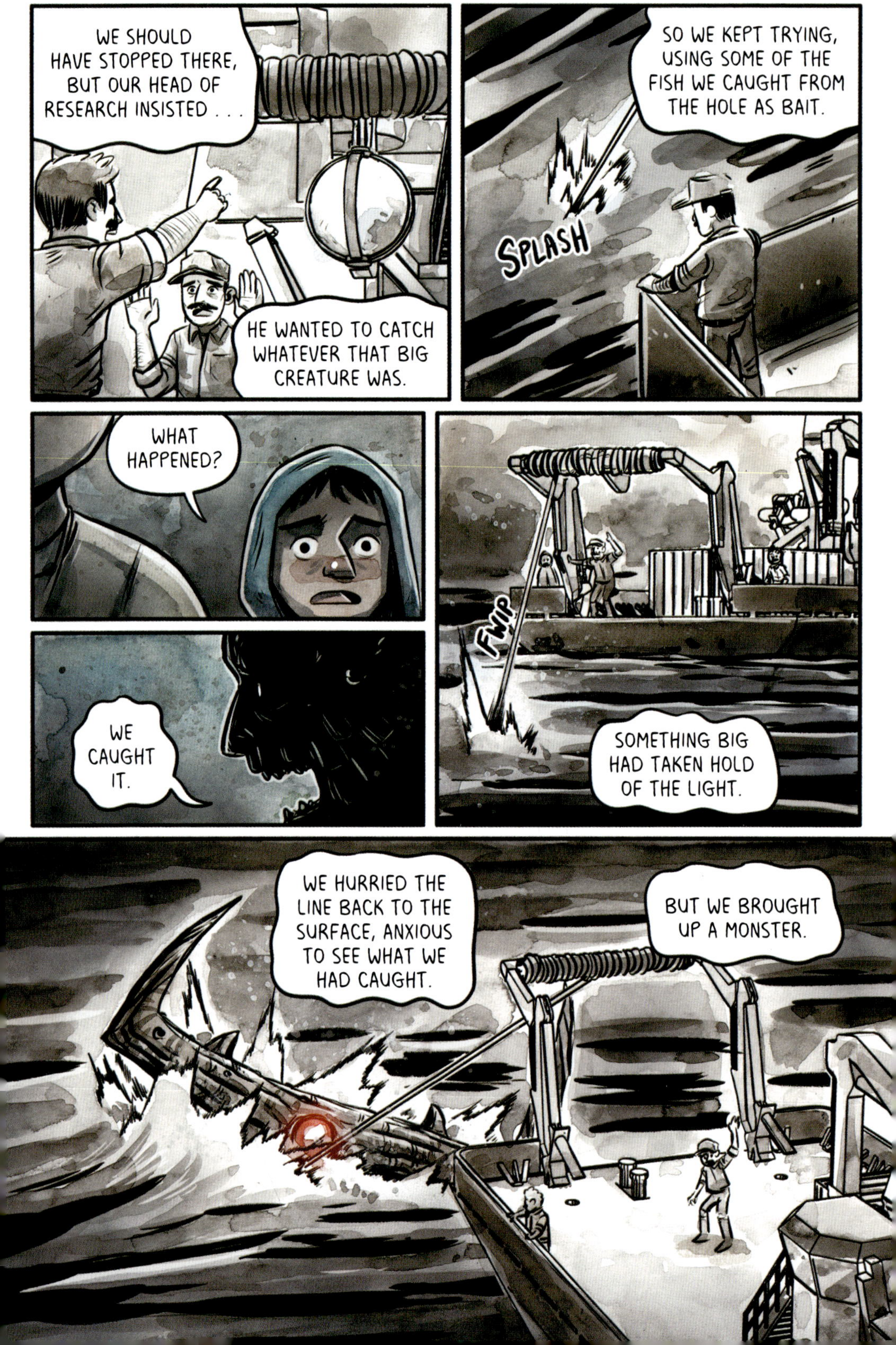
WE SHOULD HAVE STOPPED THERE, BUT OUR HEAD OF RESEARCH INSISTED . . .
HE WANTED TO CATCH WHATEVER THAT BIG CREATURE WAS.
SO WE KEPT TRYING, USING SOME OF THE FISH WE CAUGHT FROM THE HOLE AS BAIT.
SPLASH
WHAT HAPPENED?
WE CAUGHT IT.
FWIP
SOMETHING BIG HAD TAKEN HOLD OF THE LIGHT.
WE HURRIED THE LINE BACK TO THE SURFACE, ANXIOUS TO SEE WHAT WE HAD CAUGHT.
BUT WE BROUGHT UP A MONSTER.

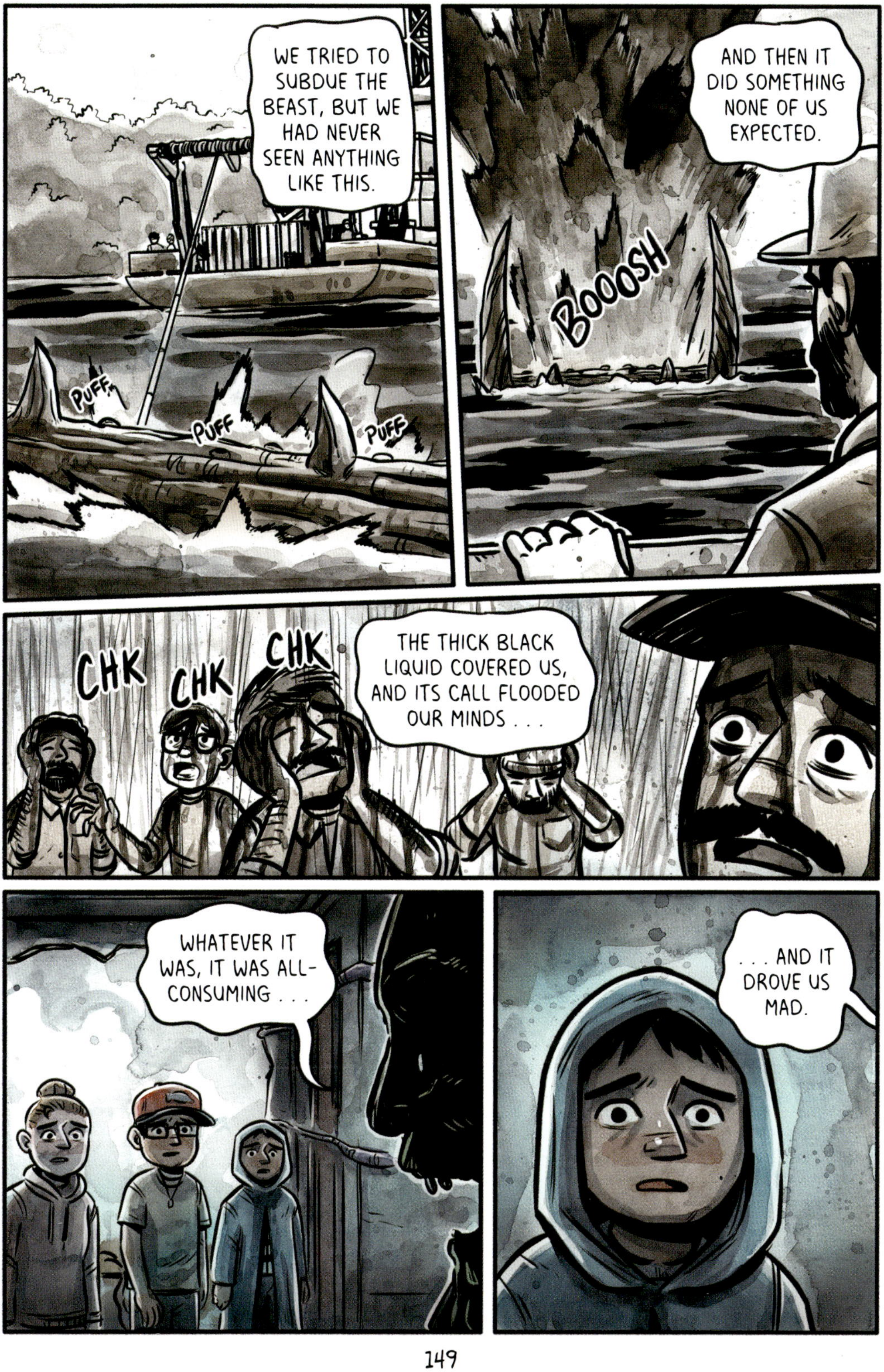
WE TRIED TO SUBDUE THE BEAST, BUT WE HAD NEVER SEEN ANYTHING LIKE THIS.
PUFF
PUFF
PUFF
AND THEN IT DID SOMETHING NONE OF US EXPECTED.
BOOOSH
CHK
CHK
CHK
THE THICK BLACK LIQUID COVERED US, AND ITS CALL FLOODED OUR MINDS . . .
WHATEVER IT WAS, IT WAS ALL-CONSUMING . . .
. . . AND IT DROVE US MAD.

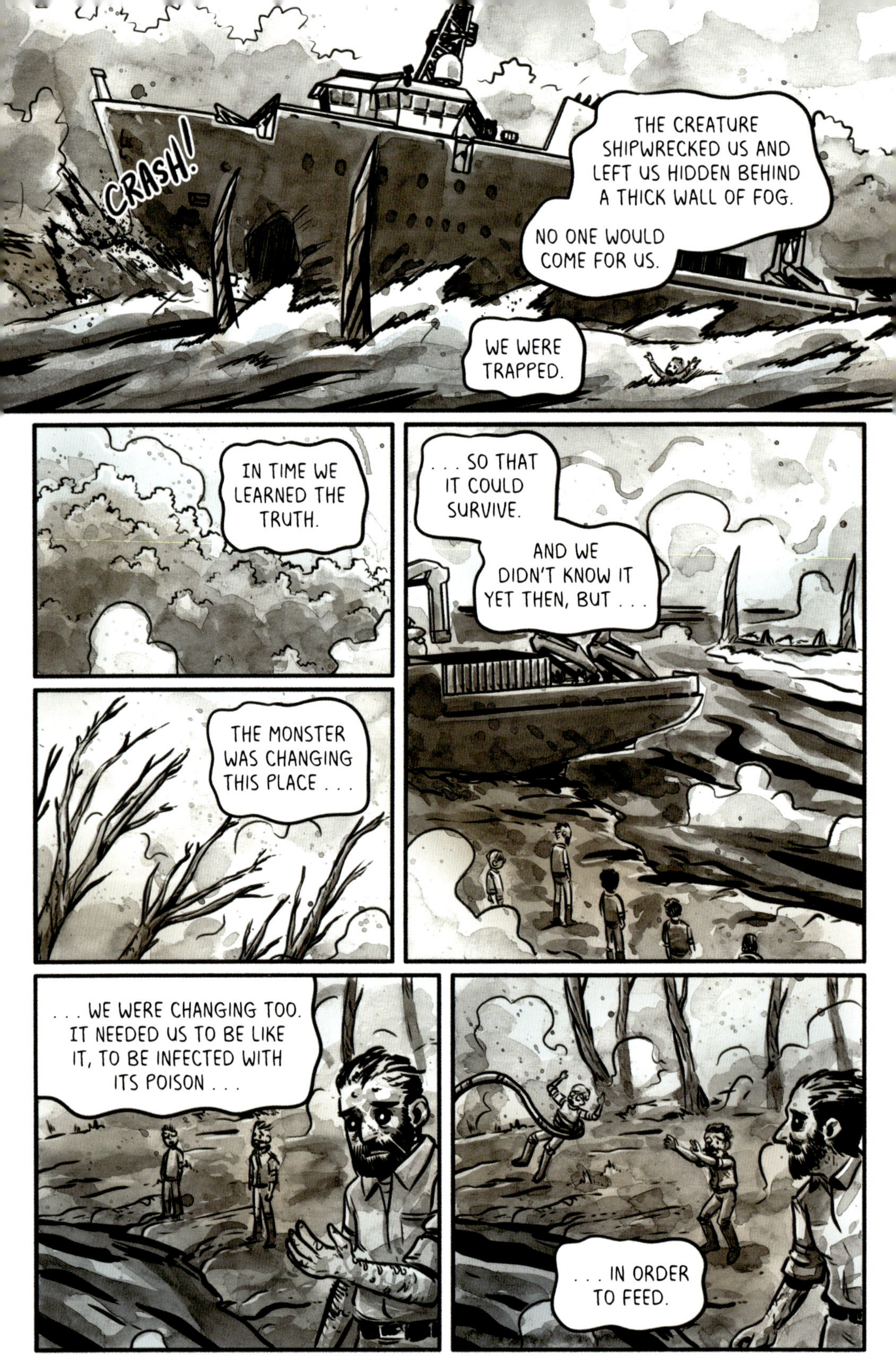
CRASH!
THE CREATURE SHIPWRECKED US AND LEFT US HIDDEN BEHIND A THICK WALL OF FOG.
NO ONE WOULD COME FOR US.
WE WERE TRAPPED.
IN TIME WE LEARNED THE TRUTH.
THE MONSTER WAS CHANGING THIS PLACE . . .
. . . SO THAT IT COULD SURVIVE.
AND WE DIDN'T KNOW IT YET THEN, BUT . . .
. . . WE WERE CHANGING TOO. IT NEEDED US TO BE LIKE IT, TO BE INFECTED WITH ITS POISON . . .
. . . IN ORDER TO FEED.

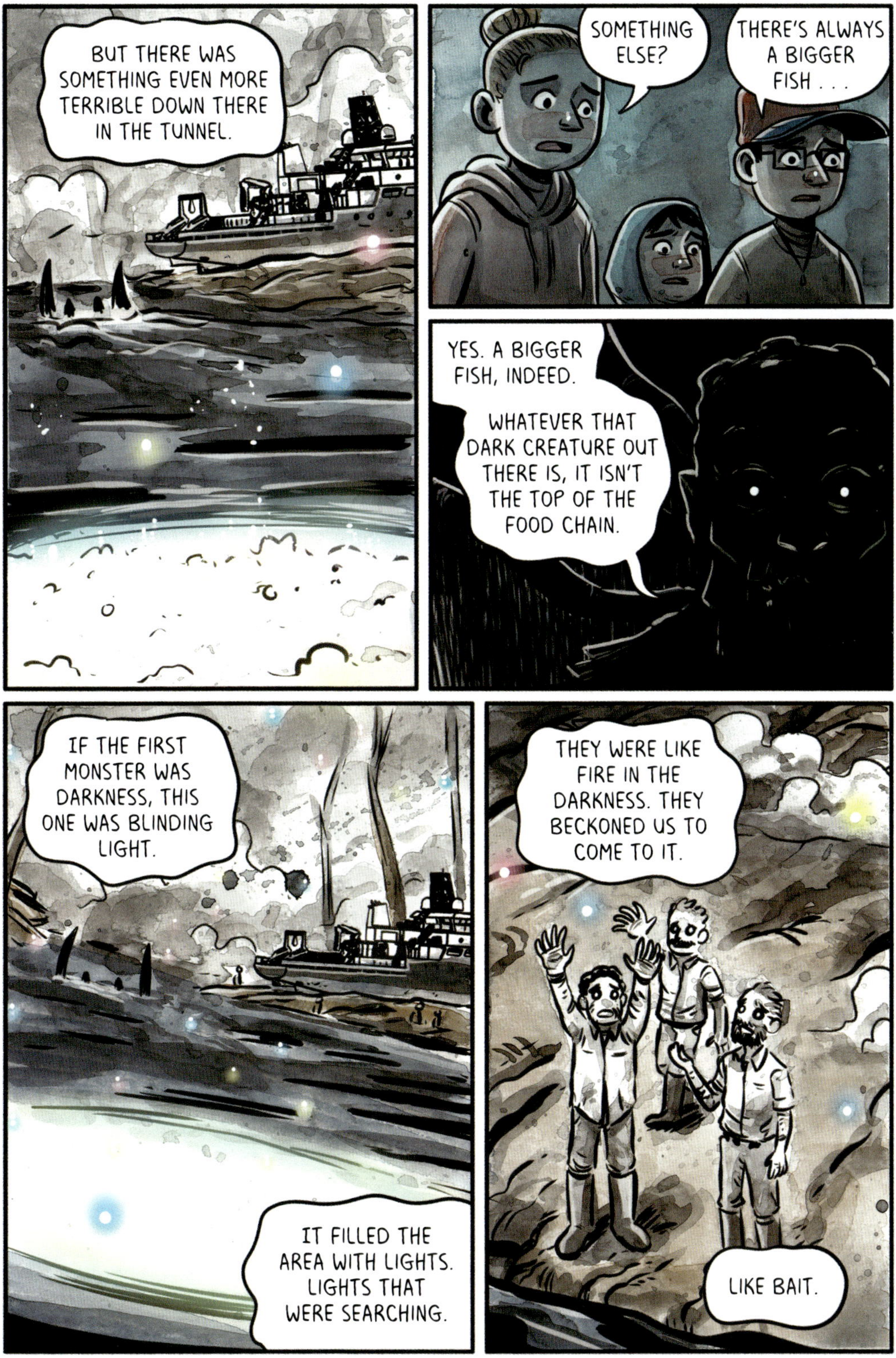
BUT THERE WAS SOMETHING EVEN MORE TERRIBLE DOWN THERE IN THE TUNNEL.
SOMETHING ELSE?
THERE'S ALWAYS A BIGGER FISH . . .
YES. A BIGGER FISH, INDEED.
WHATEVER THAT DARK CREATURE OUT THERE IS, IT ISN'T THE TOP OF THE FOOD CHAIN.
IF THE FIRST MONSTER WAS DARKNESS, THIS ONE WAS BLINDING LIGHT.
IT FILLED THE AREA WITH LIGHTS. LIGHTS THAT WERE SEARCHING.
THEY WERE LIKE FIRE IN THE DARKNESS. THEY BECKONED US TO COME TO IT.
LIKE BAIT.

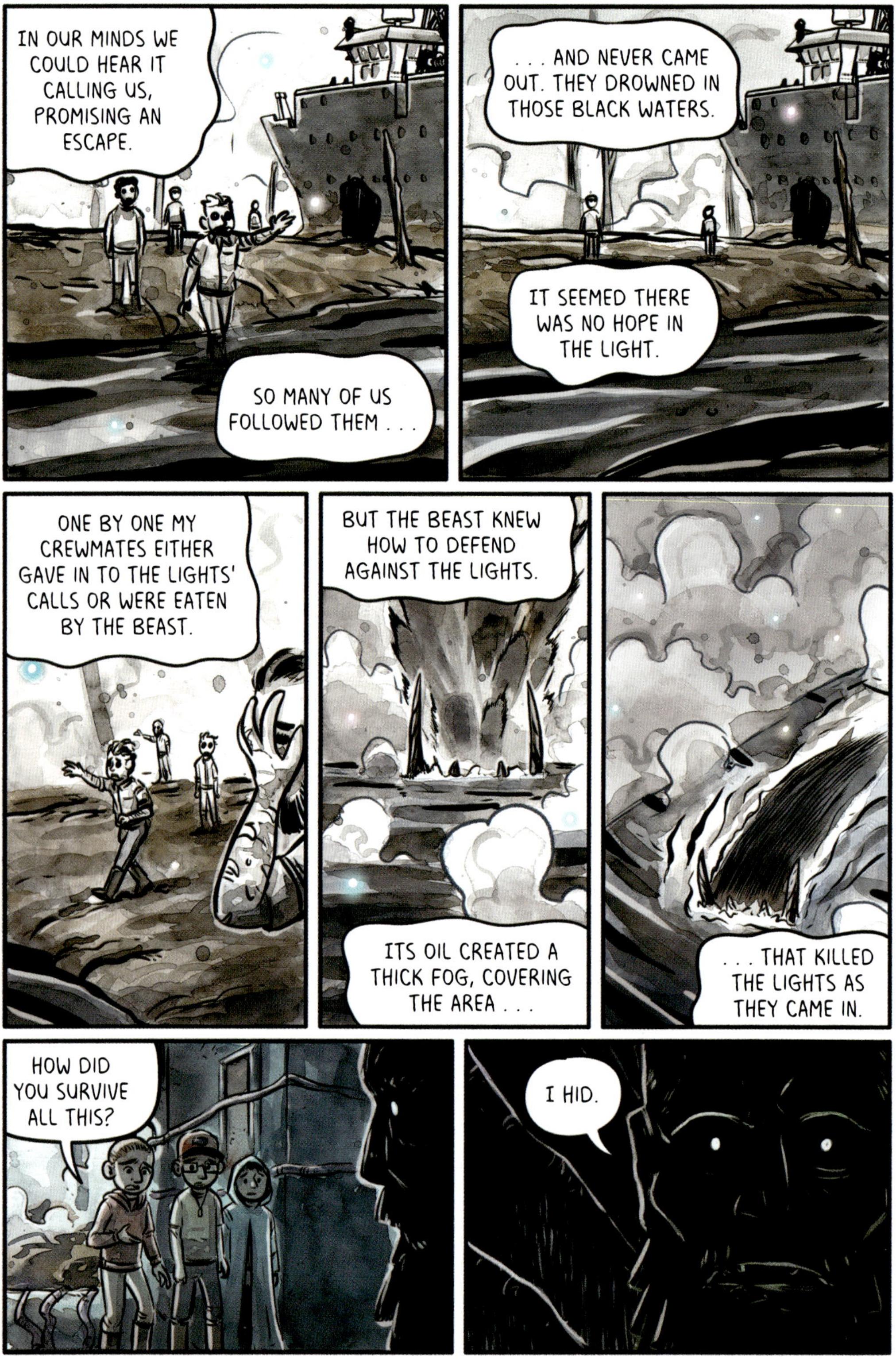
IN OUR MINDS WE COULD HEAR IT CALLING US, PROMISING AN ESCAPE.
SO MANY OF US FOLLOWED THEM . . .
. . . AND NEVER CAME OUT. THEY DROWNED IN THOSE BLACK WATERS.
IT SEEMED THERE WAS NO HOPE IN THE LIGHT.
ONE BY ONE MY CREWMATES EITHER GAVE IN TO THE LIGHTS' CALLS OR WERE EATEN BY THE BEAST.
BUT THE BEAST KNEW HOW TO DEFEND AGAINST THE LIGHTS.
ITS OIL CREATED A THICK FOG, COVERING THE AREA . . .
. . . THAT KILLED THE LIGHTS AS THEY CAME IN.
HOW DID YOU SURVIVE ALL THIS?
I HID.

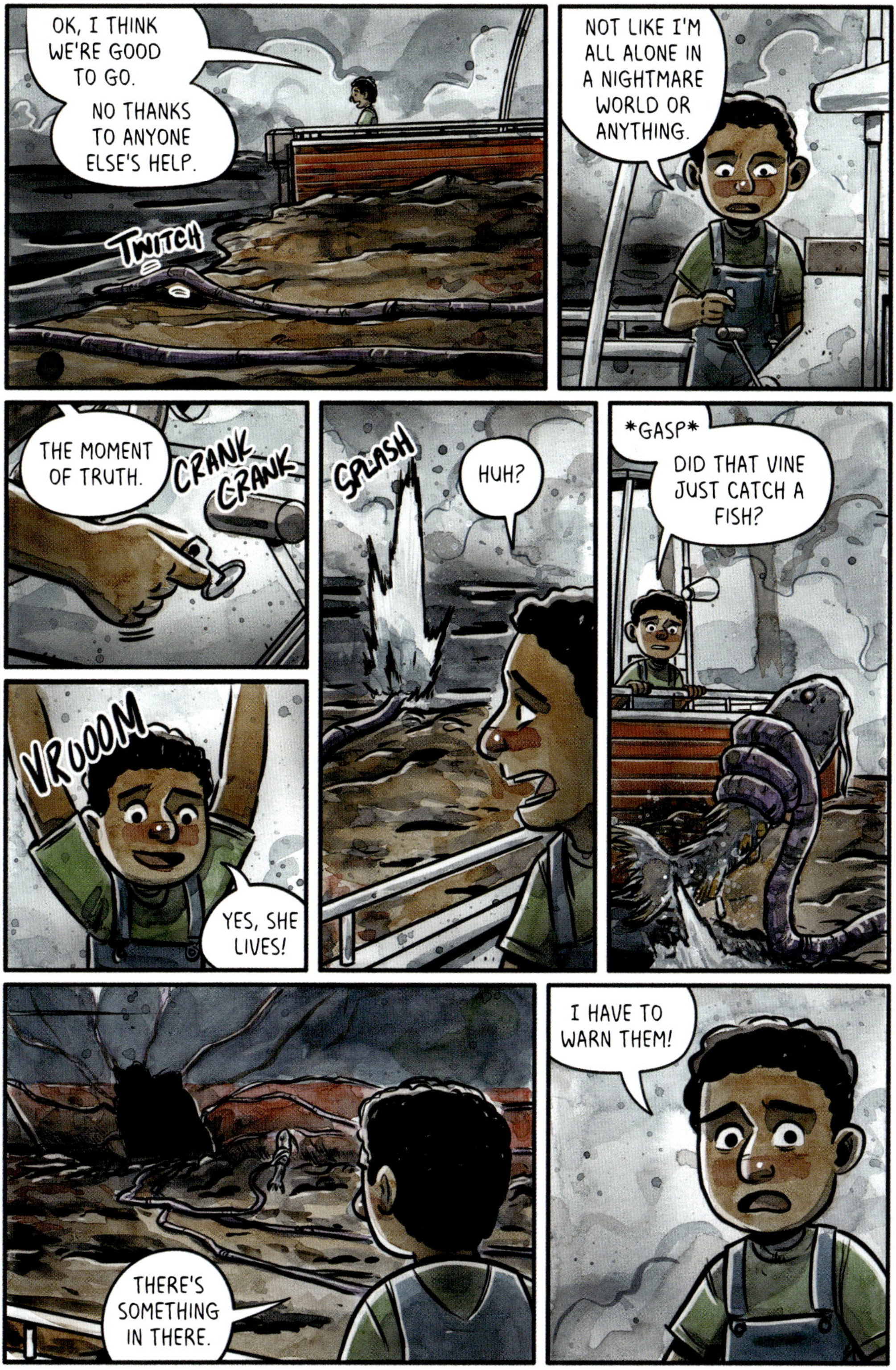

OK, I THINK WE'RE GOOD TO GO.
NO THANKS TO ANYONE ELSE'S HELP.
TWITCH
NOT LIKE I'M ALL ALONE IN A NIGHTMARE WORLD OR ANYTHING.
THE MOMENT OF TRUTH.
CRANK CRANK
VROOOM
YES, SHE LIVES!
SPLASH
HUH?
GASP
DID THAT VINE JUST CATCH A FISH?
THERE'S SOMETHING IN THERE.
I HAVE TO WARN THEM!

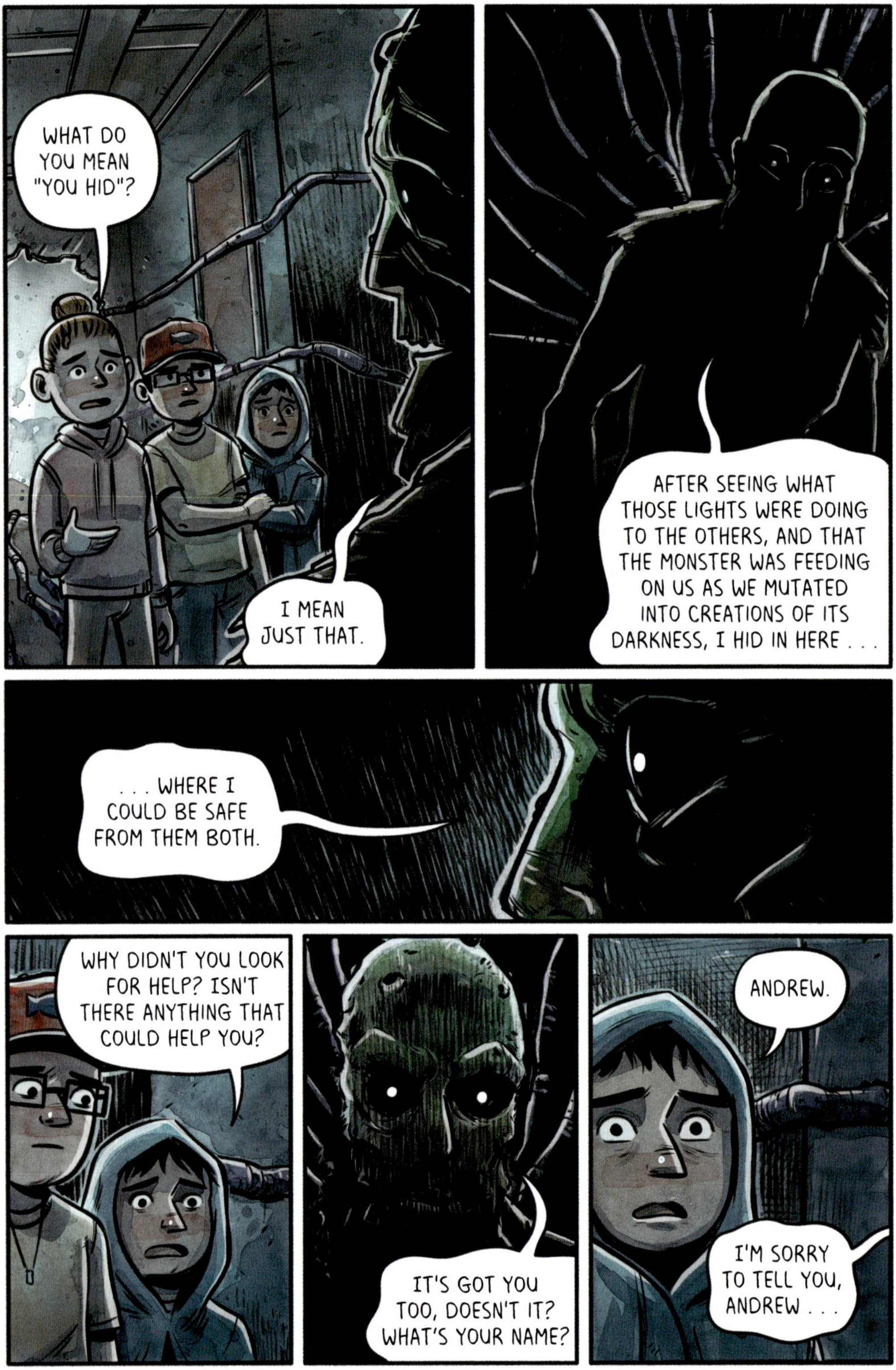
WHAT DO YOU MEAN "YOU HID"?
I MEAN JUST THAT.
AFTER SEEING WHAT THOSE LIGHTS WERE DOING TO THE OTHERS, AND THAT THE MONSTER WAS FEEDING ON US AS WE MUTATED INTO CREATIONS OF ITS DARKNESS, I HID IN HERE . . .
. . . WHERE I COULD BE SAFE FROM THEM BOTH.
WHY DIDN'T YOU LOOK FOR HELP? ISN'T THERE ANYTHING THAT COULD HELP YOU?
IT'S GOT YOU TOO, DOESN'T IT? WHAT'S YOUR NAME?
ANDREW.
I'M SORRY TO TELL YOU, ANDREW . . .

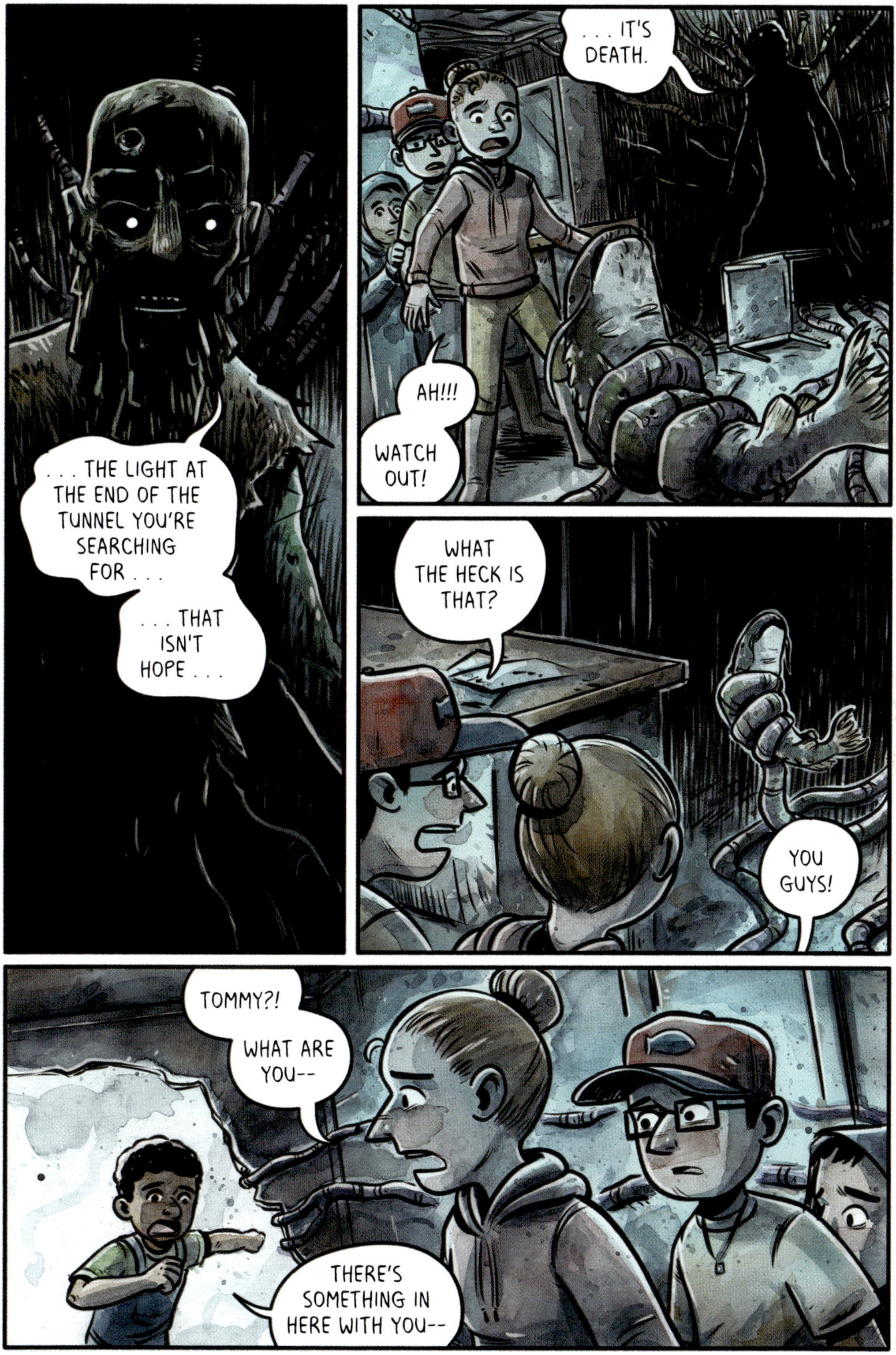
. . . THE LIGHT AT THE END OF THE TUNNEL YOU'RE SEARCHING FOR . . .
. . . THAT ISN'T HOPE . . .
. . . IT'S DEATH.
AH!!!
WATCH OUT!
WHAT THE HECK IS THAT?
YOU GUYS!
TOMMY?!
WHAT ARE YOU--
THERE'S SOMETHING IN HERE WITH YOU--

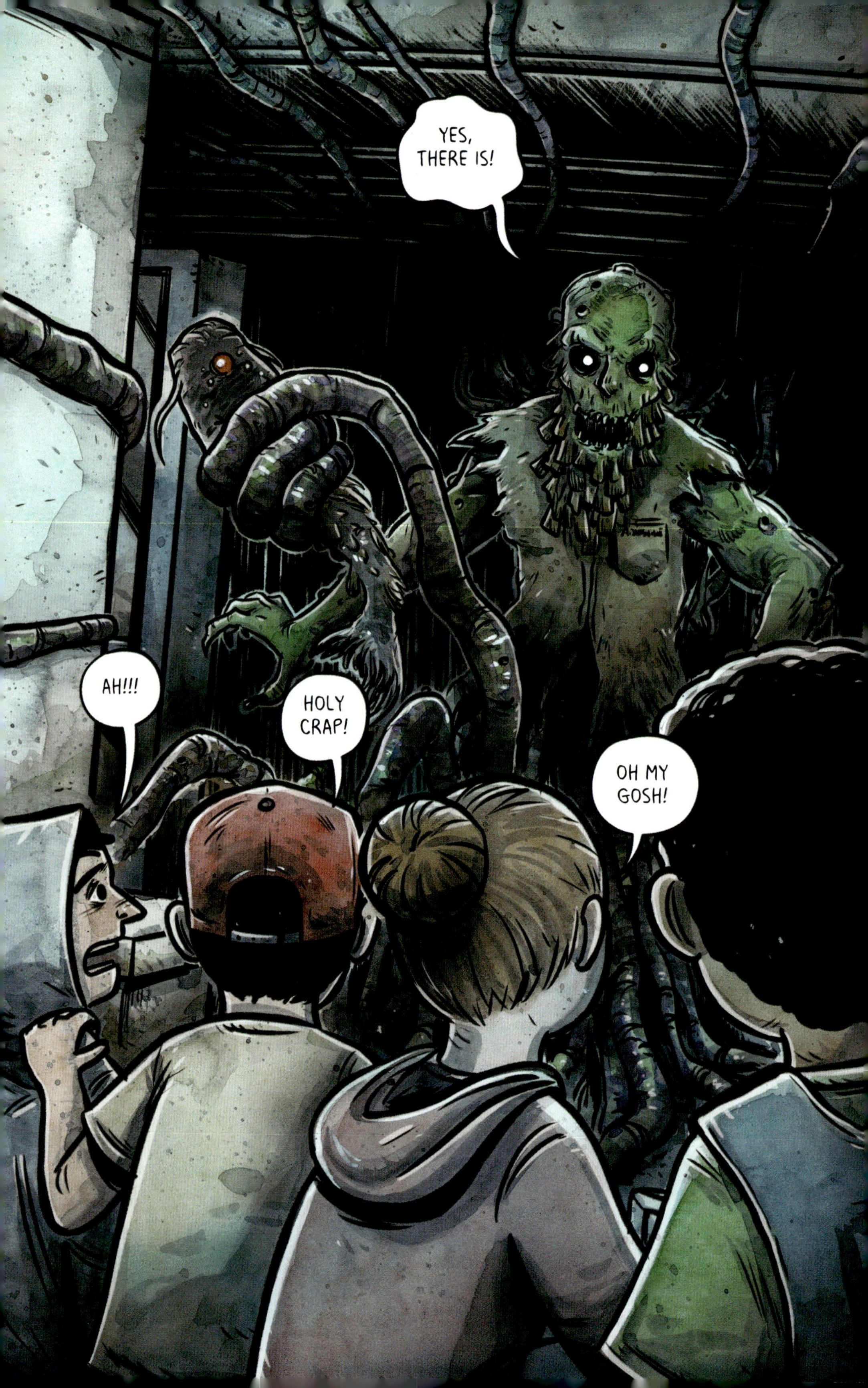
YES, THERE IS!
AH!!!
HOLY CRAP!
OH MY GOSH!

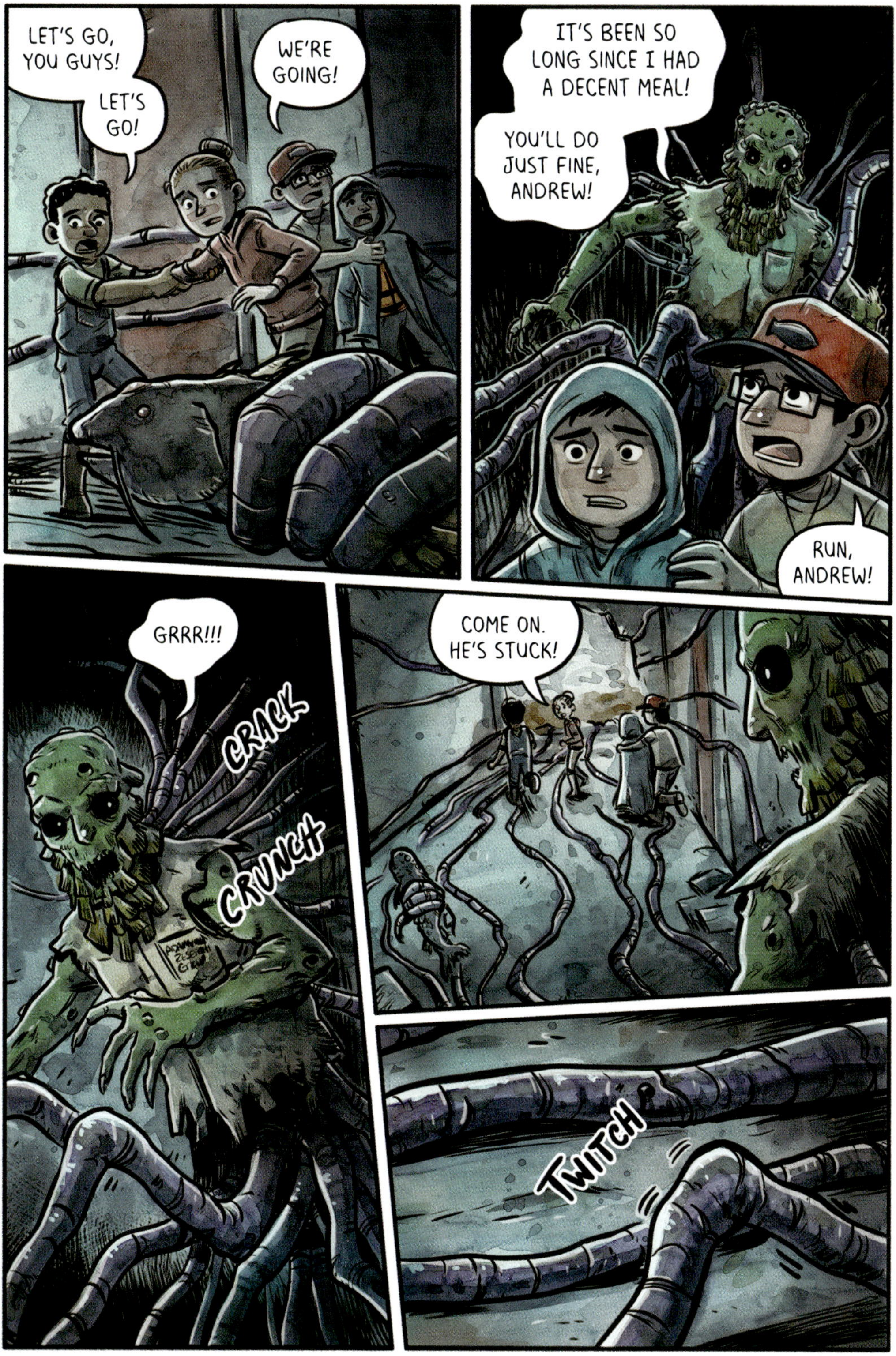
LET'S GO, YOU GUYS!
LET'S GO!
WE'RE GOING!
IT'S BEEN SO LONG SINCE I HAD A DECENT MEAL!
YOU'LL DO JUST FINE, ANDREW!
RUN, ANDREW!
GRRR!!!
CRACK
CRUNCH
COME ON. HE'S STUCK!
TWITCH

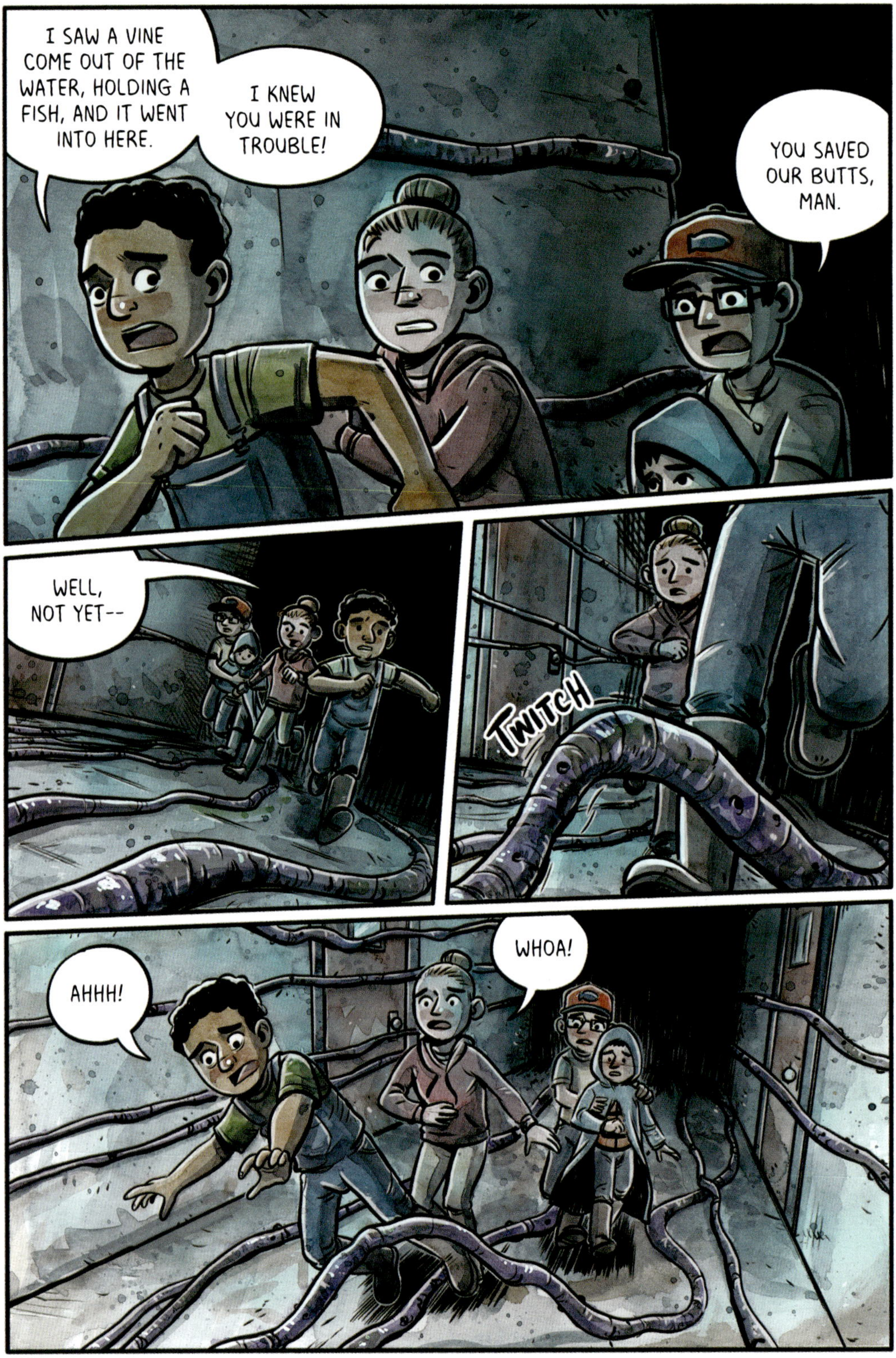
I SAW A VINE COME OUT OF THE WATER, HOLDING A FISH, AND IT WENT INTO HERE.
I KNEW YOU WERE IN TROUBLE!
YOU SAVED OUR BUTTS, MAN.
WELL, NOT YET--
TWITCH
AHHH!
WHOA!

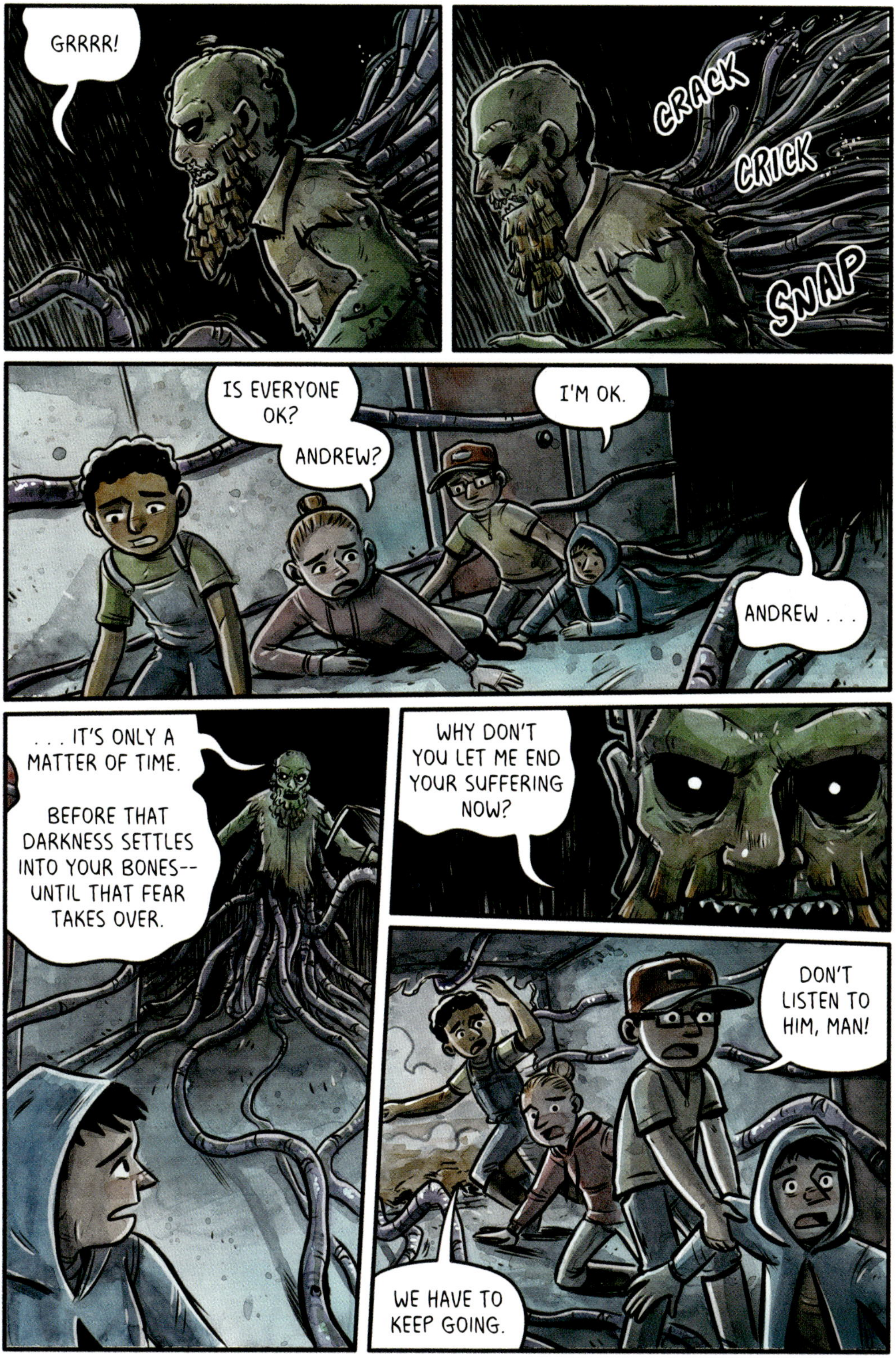
GRRRR!
CRACK
CRICK
SNAP
IS EVERYONE OK?
ANDREW?
I'M OK.
ANDREW . . .
. . . IT'S ONLY A MATTER OF TIME.
BEFORE THAT DARKNESS SETTLES INTO YOUR BONES-- UNTIL THAT FEAR TAKES OVER.
WHY DON'T YOU LET ME END YOUR SUFFERING NOW?
DON'T LISTEN TO HIM, MAN!
WE HAVE TO KEEP GOING.

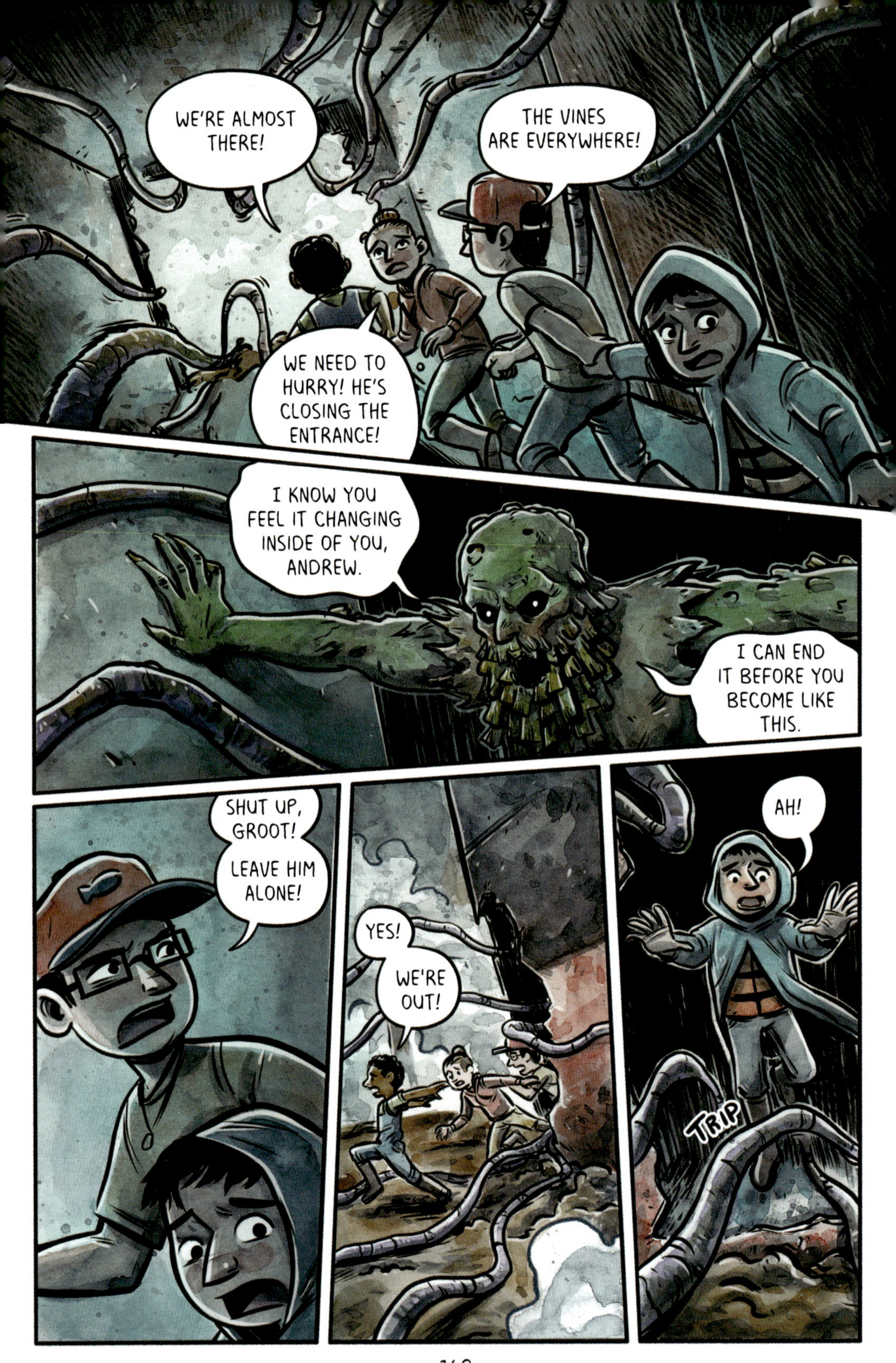
WE'RE ALMOST THERE!
THE VINES ARE EVERYWHERE!
WE NEED TO HURRY! HE'S CLOSING THE ENTRANCE!
I KNOW YOU FEEL IT CHANGING INSIDE OF YOU, ANDREW.
I CAN END IT BEFORE YOU BECOME LIKE THIS.
SHUT UP, GROOT!
LEAVE HIM ALONE!
YES!
WE'RE OUT!
AH!
TRIP

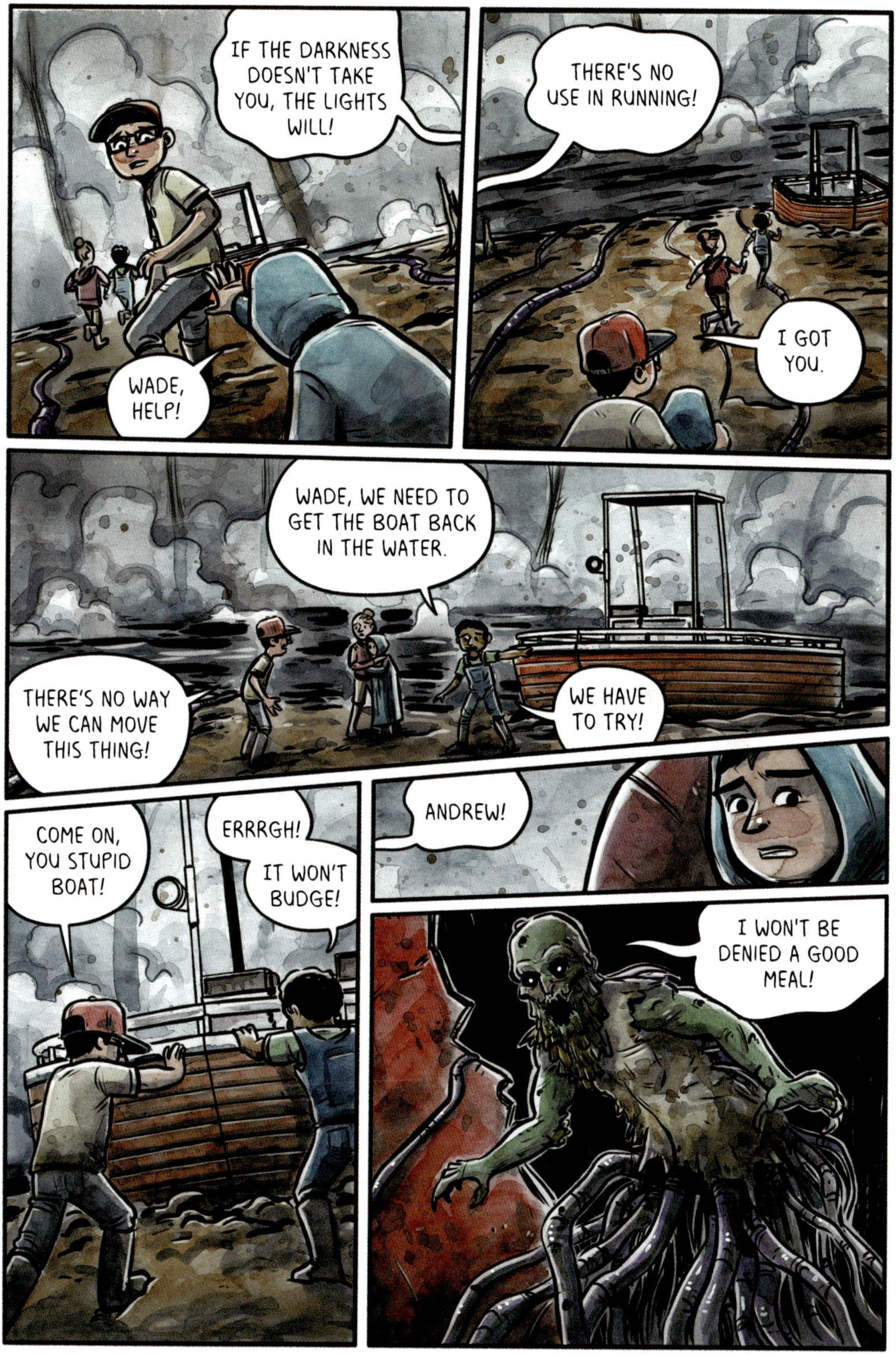
IF THE DARKNESS DOESN'T TAKE YOU, THE LIGHTS WILL!
WADE, HELP!
THERE'S NO USE IN RUNNING!
I GOT YOU.
WADE, WE NEED TO GET THE BOAT BACK IN THE WATER.
THERE'S NO WAY WE CAN MOVE THIS THING!
WE HAVE TO TRY!
COME ON, YOU STUPID BOAT!
ERRRGH!
IT WON'T BUDGE!
ANDREW!
I WON'T BE DENIED A GOOD MEAL!

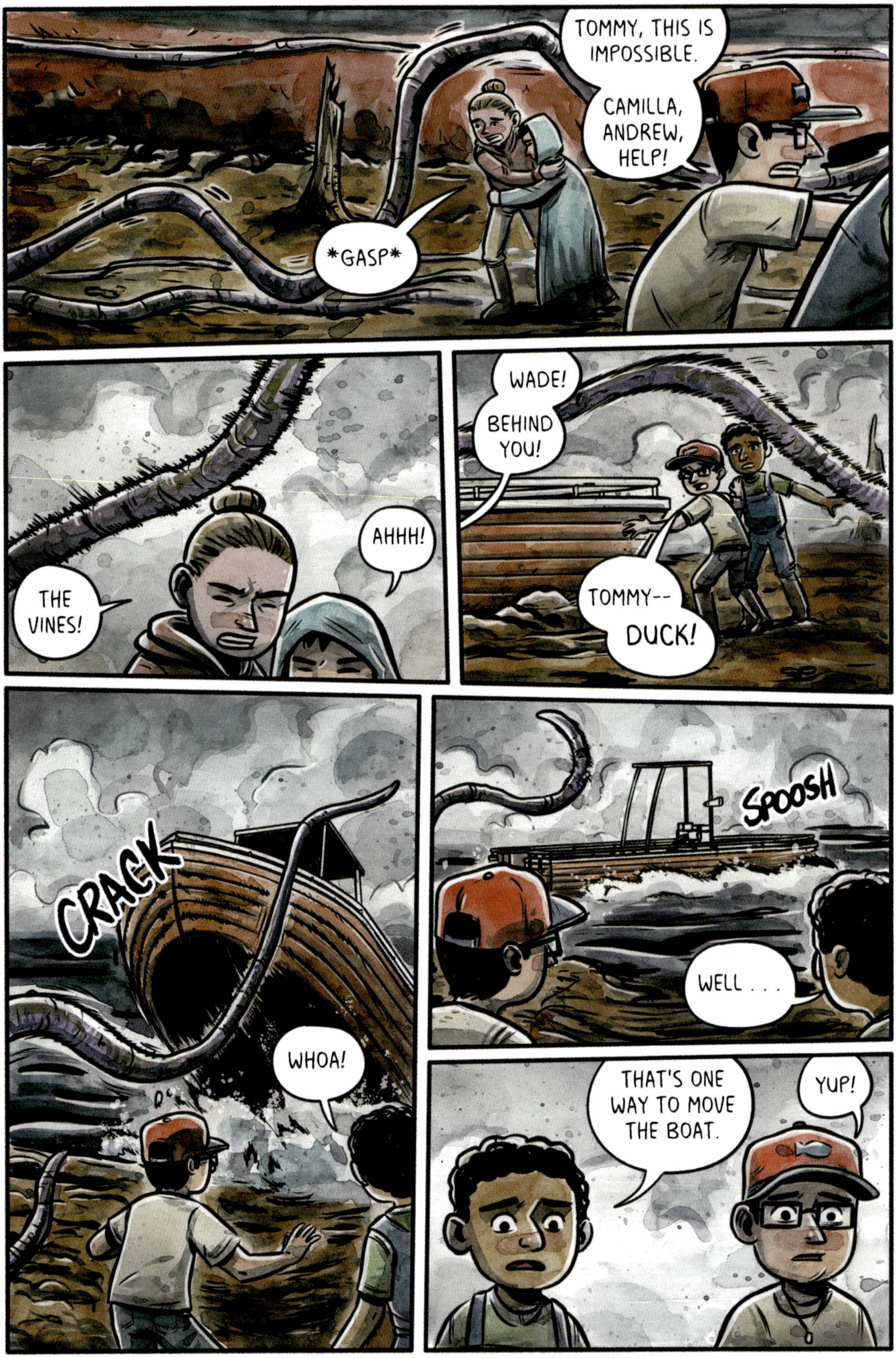
TOMMY, THIS IS IMPOSSIBLE.
CAMILLA, ANDREW, HELP!
GASP
THE VINES!
AHHH!
WADE!
BEHIND YOU!
TOMMY--
DUCK!
CRACK
WHOA!
SPOOSH
WELL . . .
THAT'S ONE WAY TO MOVE THE BOAT.
YUP!

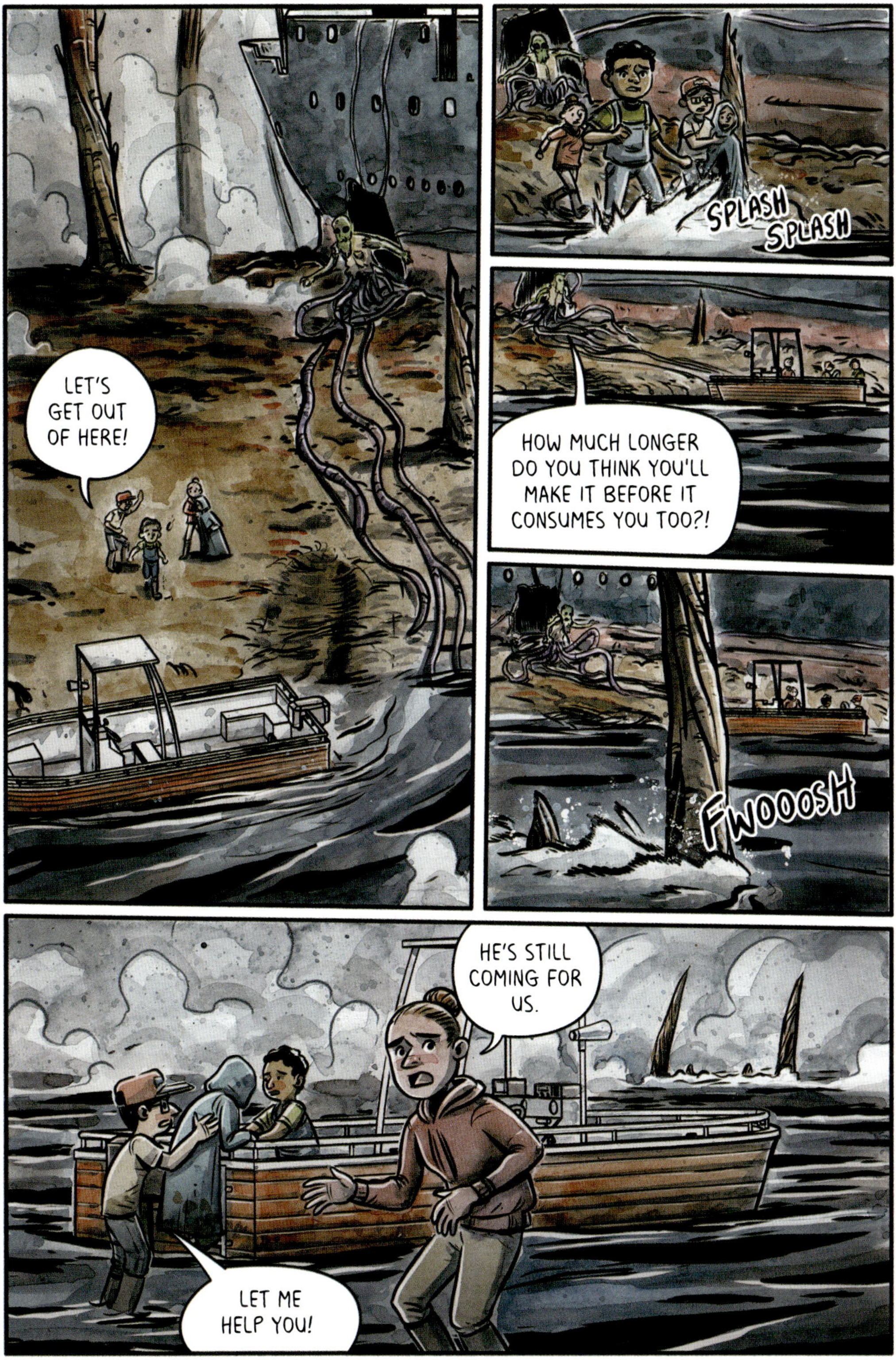
LET'S GET OUT OF HERE!
SPLASH SPLASH
HOW MUCH LONGER DO YOU THINK YOU'LL MAKE IT BEFORE IT CONSUMES YOU TOO?!
FWOOOSH
HE'S STILL COMING FOR US.
LET ME HELP YOU!

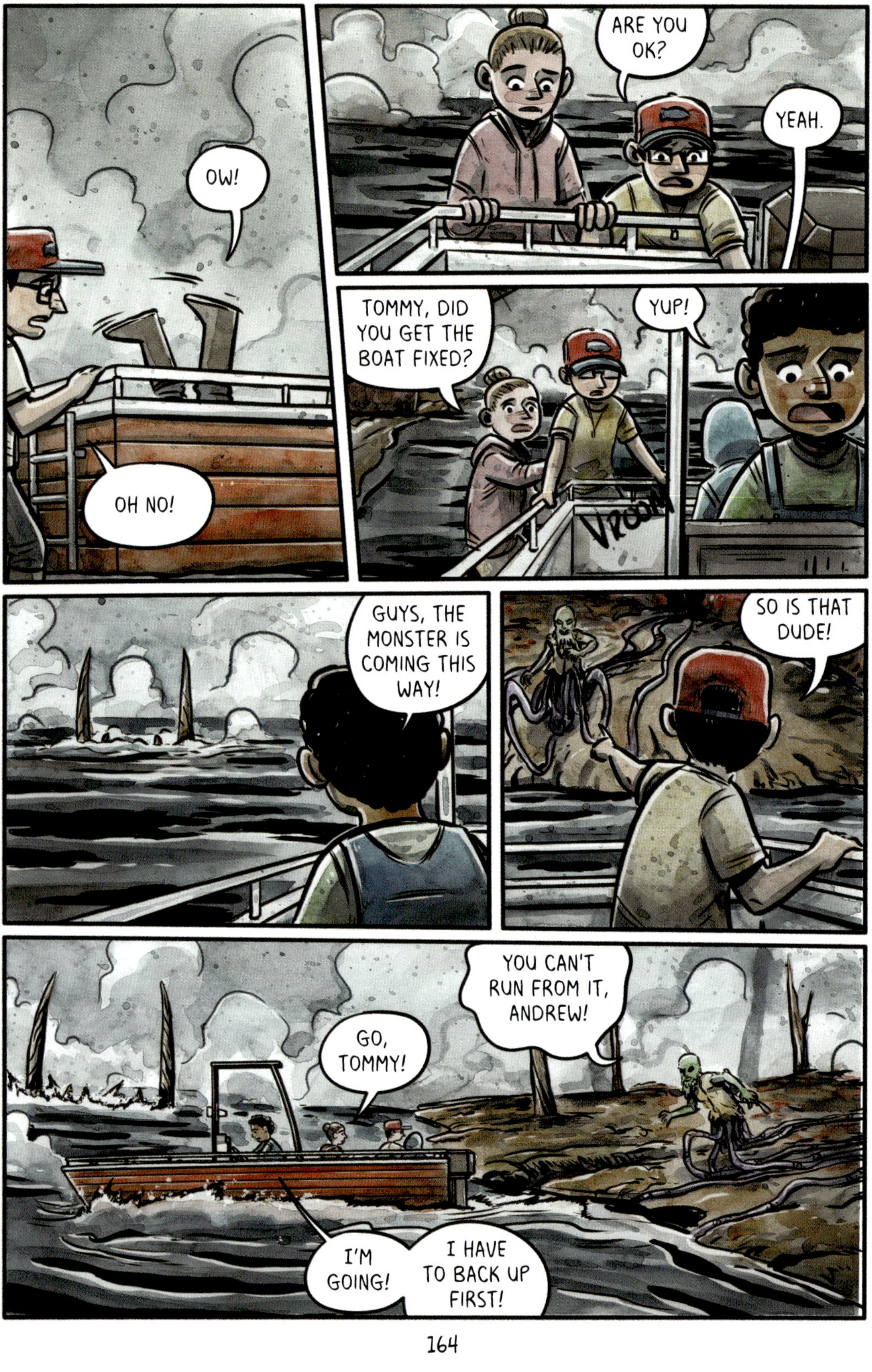
OW!
OH NO!
ARE YOU OK?
YEAH.
TOMMY, DID YOU GET THE BOAT FIXED?
YUP!
VROOM
GUYS, THE MONSTER IS COMING THIS WAY!
SO IS THAT DUDE!
GO, TOMMY!
YOU CAN'T RUN FROM IT, ANDREW!
I'M GOING!
I HAVE TO BACK UP FIRST!

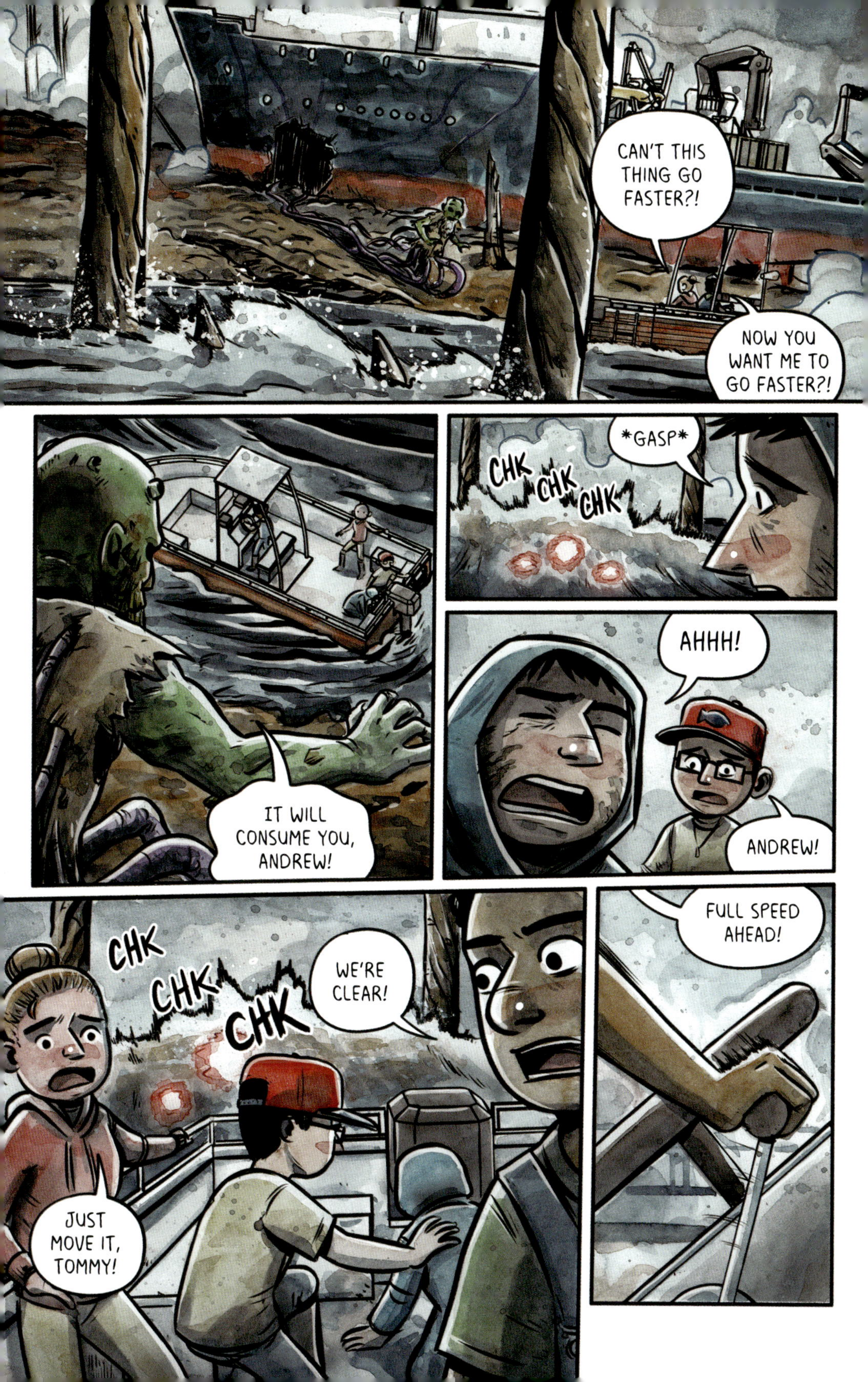
CAN'T THIS THING GO FASTER?!
NOW YOU WANT ME TO GO FASTER?!
IT WILL CONSUME YOU, ANDREW!
CHK CHK CHK
GASP
AHHH!
ANDREW!
CHK CHK CHK
WE'RE CLEAR!
JUST MOVE IT, TOMMY!
FULL SPEED AHEAD!

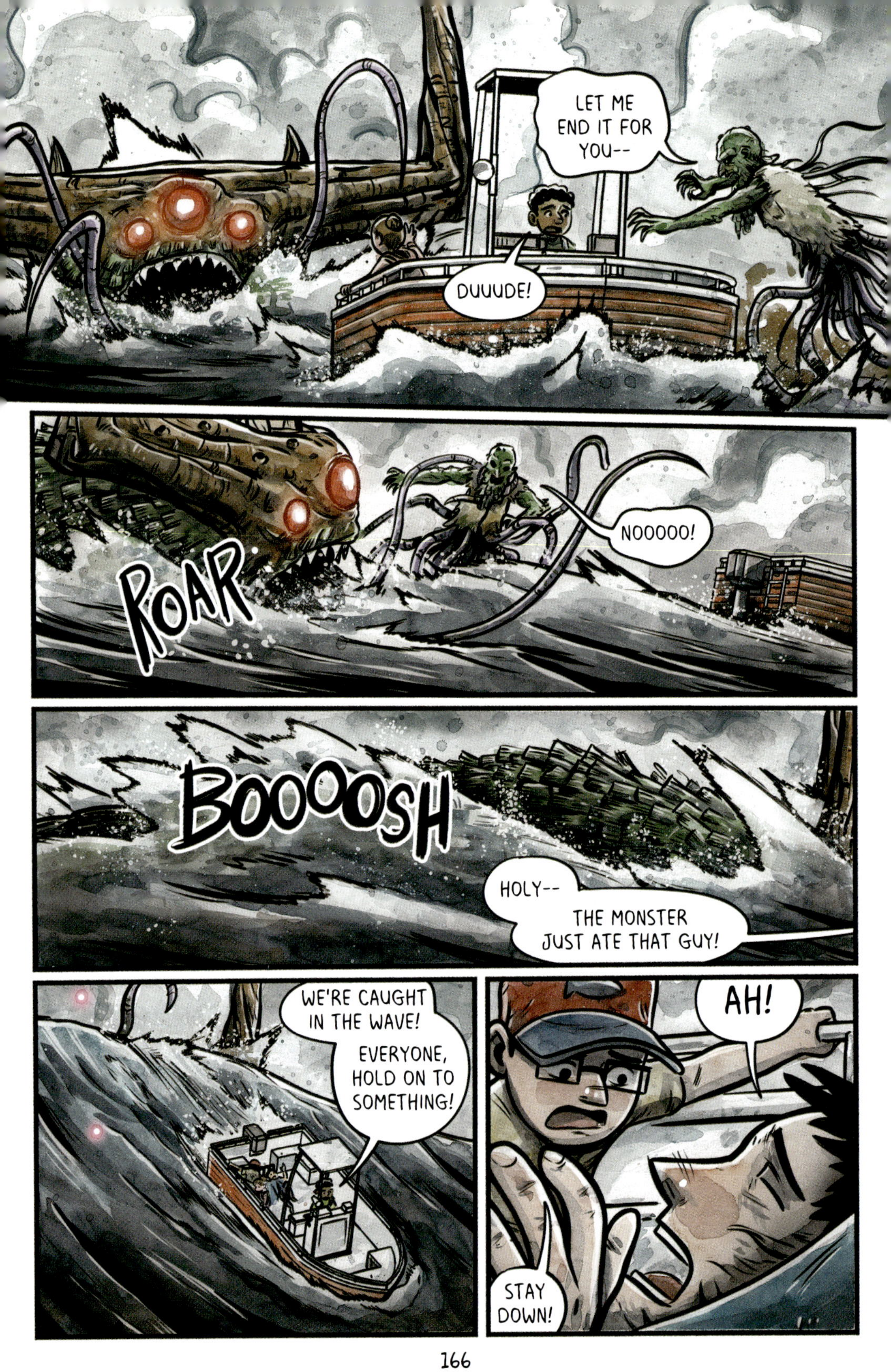
LET ME END IT FOR YOU--
DUUUDE!
ROAR
NOOOOO!
BOOOOSH
HOLY--
THE MONSTER JUST ATE THAT GUY!
WE'RE CAUGHT IN THE WAVE!
EVERYONE, HOLD ON TO SOMETHING!
AH!
STAY DOWN!

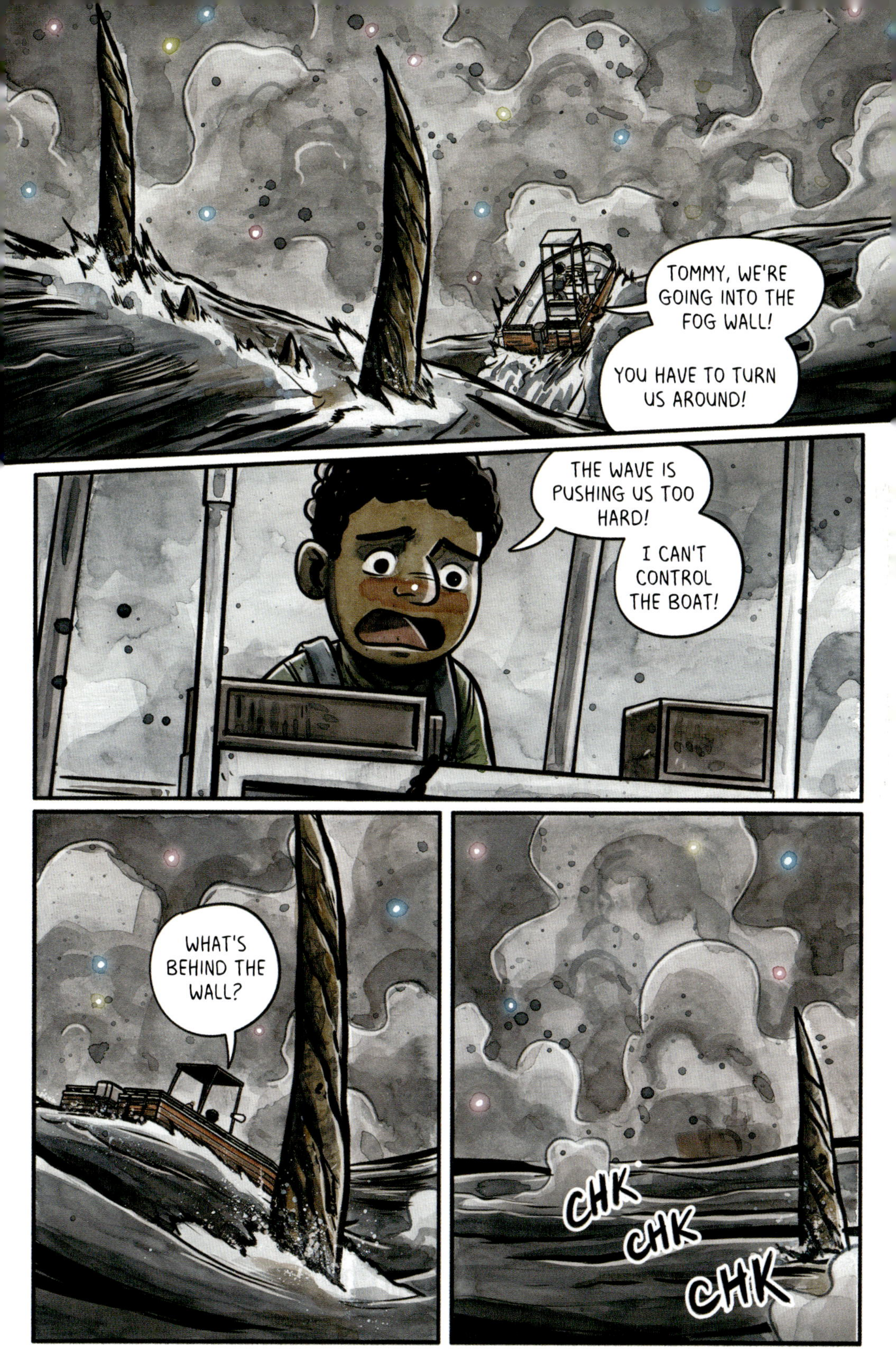
TOMMY, WE'RE GOING INTO THE FOG WALL!
YOU HAVE TO TURN US AROUND!
THE WAVE IS PUSHING US TOO HARD!
I CAN'T CONTROL THE BOAT!
WHAT'S BEHIND THE WALL?
CHK
CHK
CHK

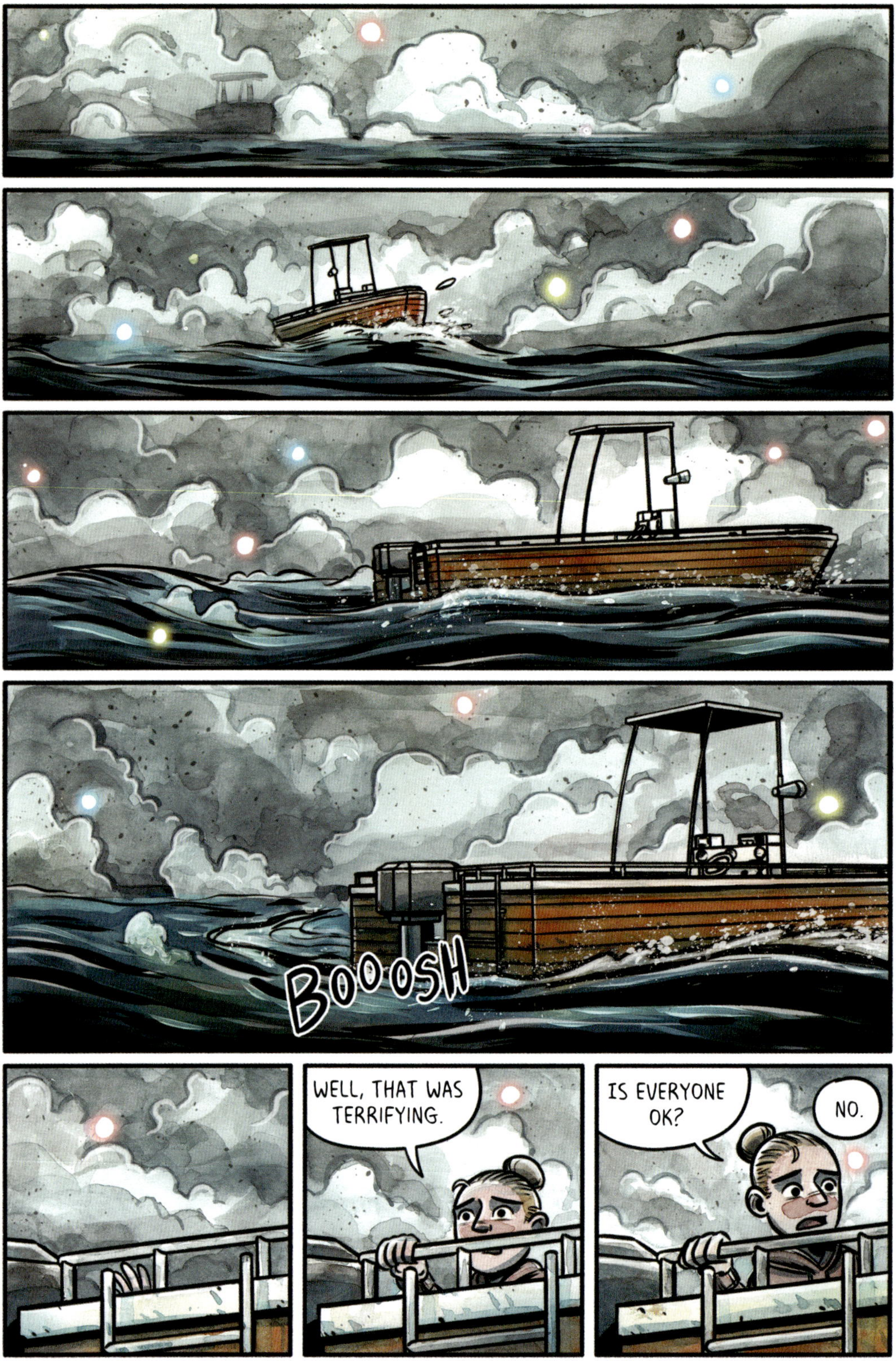
BOOOSH
WELL, THAT WAS TERRIFYING.
IS EVERYONE OK?
NO.

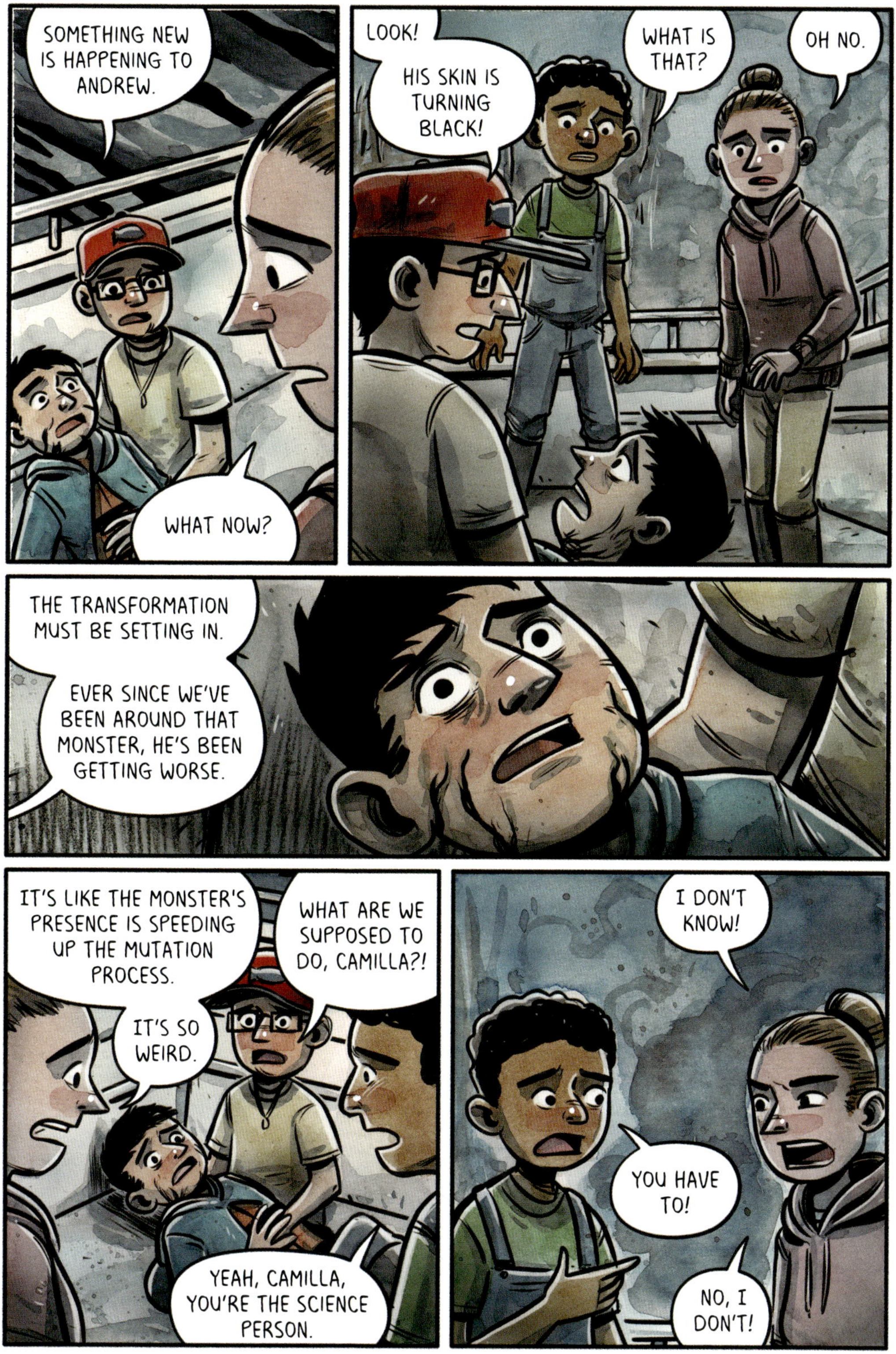
SOMETHING NEW IS HAPPENING TO ANDREW.
WHAT NOW?
LOOK!
HIS SKIN IS TURNING BLACK!
WHAT IS THAT?
OH NO.
THE TRANSFORMATION MUST BE SETTING IN.
EVER SINCE WE'VE BEEN AROUND THAT MONSTER, HE'S BEEN GETTING WORSE.
IT'S LIKE THE MONSTER'S PRESENCE IS SPEEDING UP THE MUTATION PROCESS.
IT'S SO WEIRD.
WHAT ARE WE SUPPOSED TO DO, CAMILLA?!
YEAH, CAMILLA, YOU'RE THE SCIENCE PERSON.
I DON'T KNOW!
YOU HAVE TO!
NO, I DON'T!

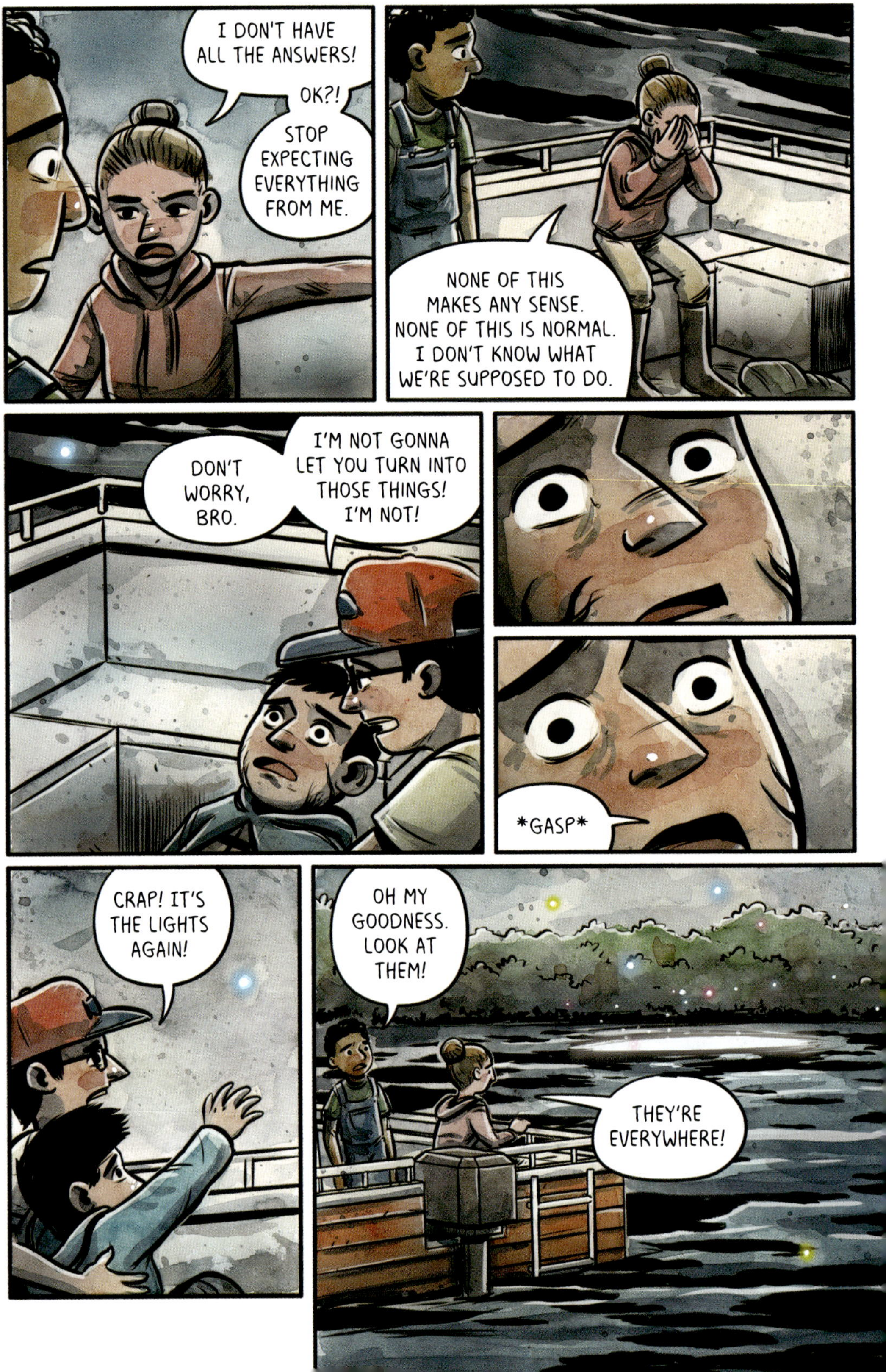
I DON'T HAVE ALL THE ANSWERS!
OK?!
STOP EXPECTING EVERYTHING FROM ME.
NONE OF THIS MAKES ANY SENSE. NONE OF THIS IS NORMAL. I DON'T KNOW WHAT WE'RE SUPPOSED TO DO.
DON'T WORRY, BRO.
I'M NOT GONNA LET YOU TURN INTO THOSE THINGS! I'M NOT!
GASP
CRAP! IT'S THE LIGHTS AGAIN!
OH MY GOODNESS. LOOK AT THEM!
THEY'RE EVERYWHERE!

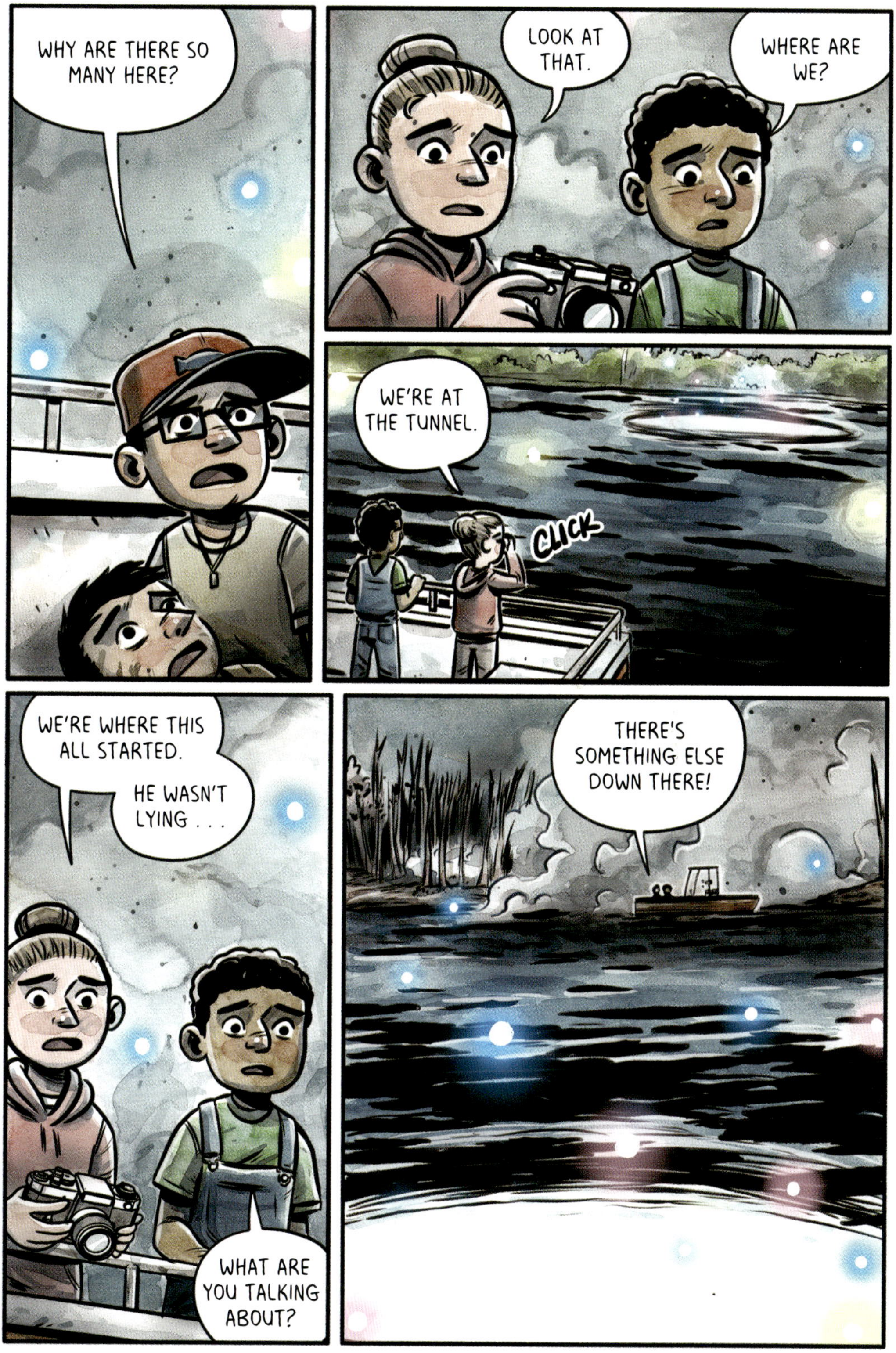
WHY ARE THERE SO MANY HERE?
LOOK AT THAT.
WHERE ARE WE?
WE'RE AT THE TUNNEL.
CLICK
WE'RE WHERE THIS ALL STARTED.
HE WASN'T LYING . . .
WHAT ARE YOU TALKING ABOUT?
THERE'S SOMETHING ELSE DOWN THERE!

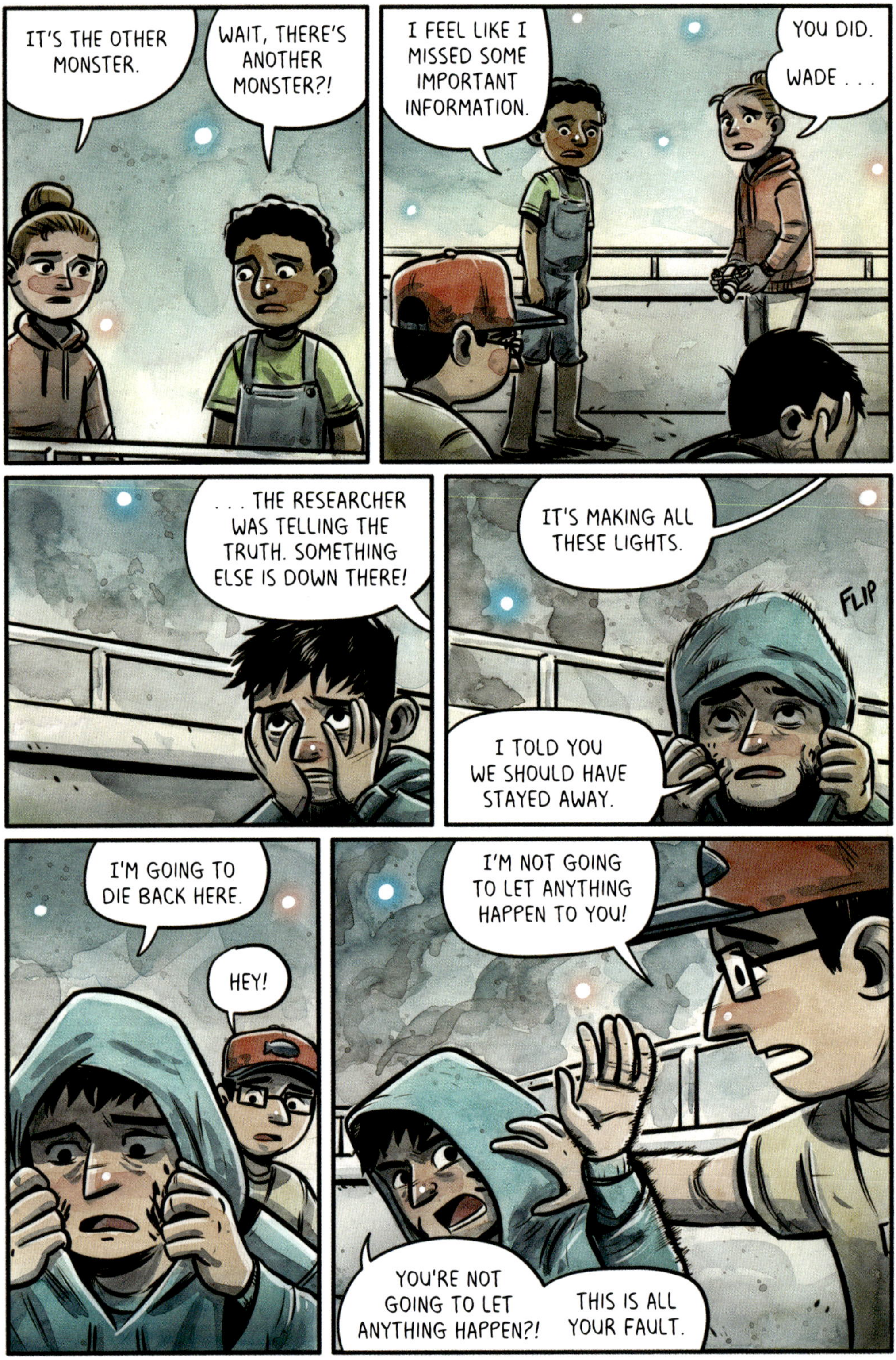
IT'S THE OTHER MONSTER.
WAIT, THERE'S ANOTHER MONSTER?!
I FEEL LIKE I MISSED SOME IMPORTANT INFORMATION.
YOU DID.
WADE . . .
. . . THE RESEARCHER WAS TELLING THE TRUTH. SOMETHING ELSE IS DOWN THERE!
IT'S MAKING ALL THESE LIGHTS.
FLIP
I TOLD YOU WE SHOULD HAVE STAYED AWAY.
I'M GOING TO DIE BACK HERE.
HEY!
I'M NOT GOING TO LET ANYTHING HAPPEN TO YOU!
YOU'RE NOT GOING TO LET ANYTHING HAPPEN?!
THIS IS ALL YOUR FAULT.

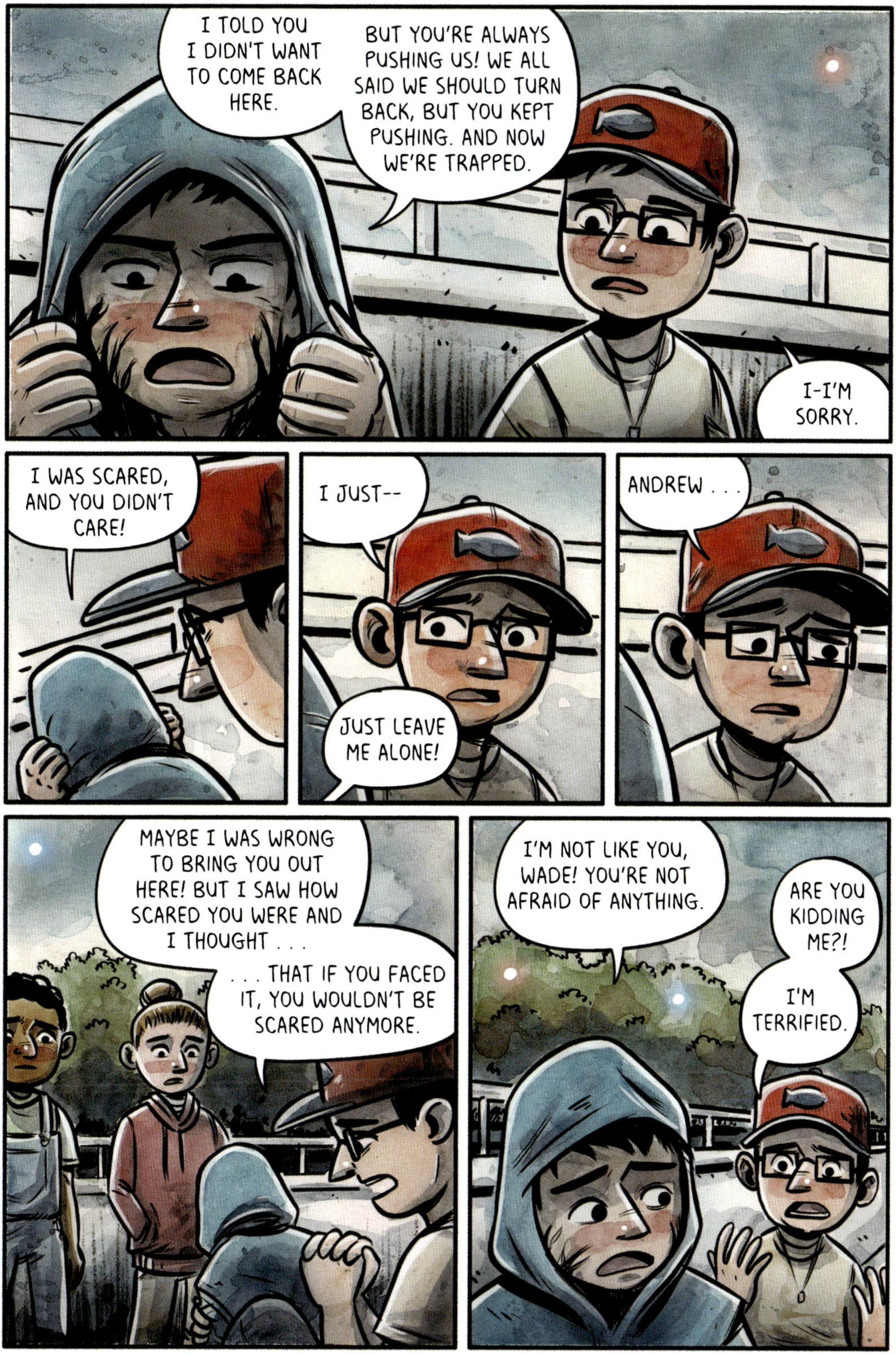
I TOLD YOU I DIDN'T WANT TO COME BACK HERE.
BUT YOU'RE ALWAYS PUSHING US! WE ALL SAID WE SHOULD TURN BACK, BUT YOU KEPT PUSHING. AND NOW WE'RE TRAPPED.
I-I'M SORRY.
I WAS SCARED, AND YOU DIDN'T CARE!
I JUST--
JUST LEAVE ME ALONE!
ANDREW . . .
MAYBE I WAS WRONG TO BRING YOU OUT HERE! BUT I SAW HOW SCARED YOU WERE AND I THOUGHT . . .
. . . THAT IF YOU FACED IT, YOU WOULDN'T BE SCARED ANYMORE.
I'M NOT LIKE YOU, WADE! YOU'RE NOT AFRAID OF ANYTHING.
ARE YOU KIDDING ME?!
I'M TERRIFIED.

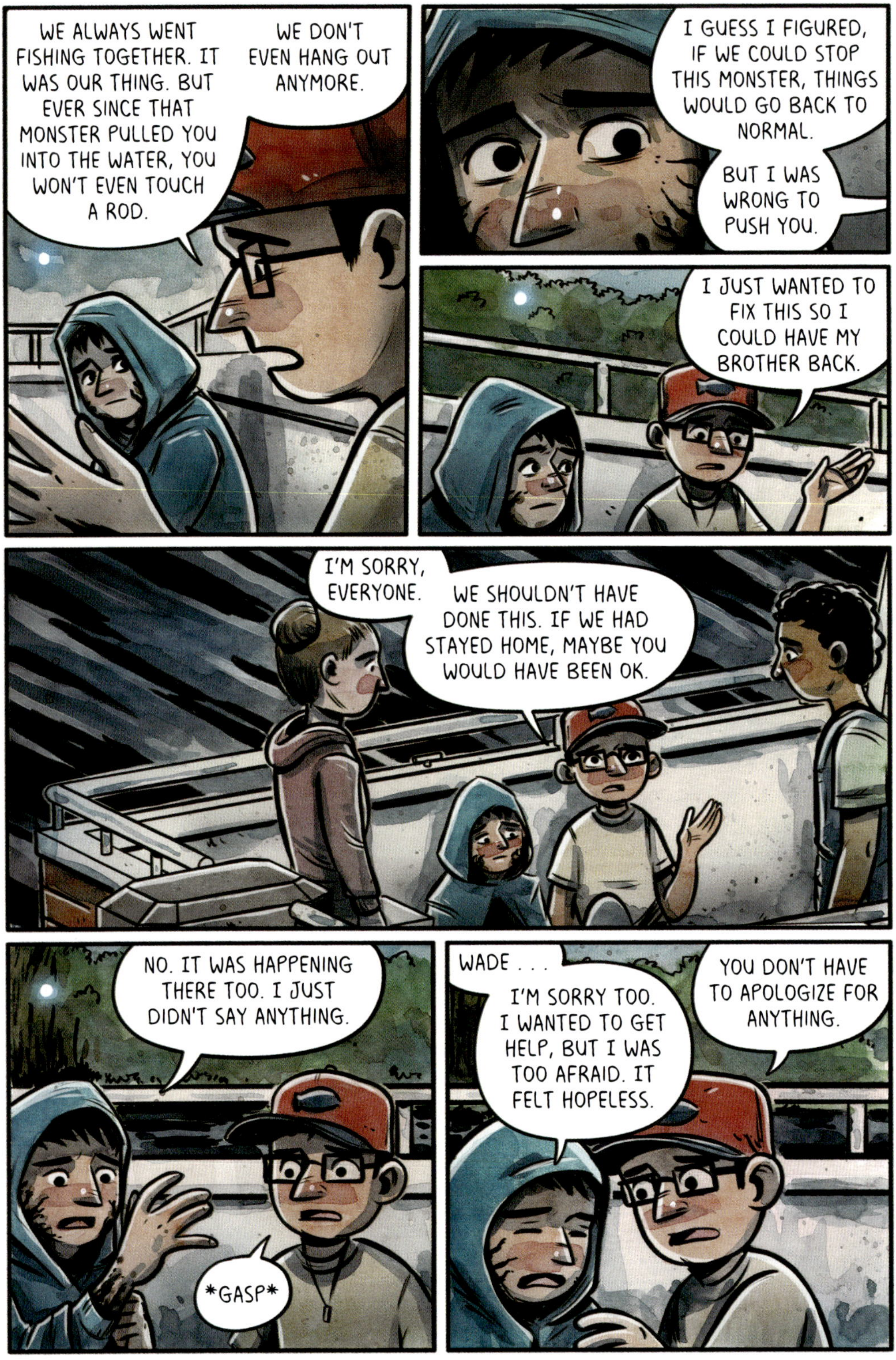
WE ALWAYS WENT FISHING TOGETHER. IT WAS OUR THING. BUT EVER SINCE THAT MONSTER PULLED YOU INTO THE WATER, YOU WON'T EVEN TOUCH A ROD.
WE DON'T EVEN HANG OUT ANYMORE.
I GUESS I FIGURED, IF WE COULD STOP THIS MONSTER, THINGS WOULD GO BACK TO NORMAL.
BUT I WAS WRONG TO PUSH YOU.
I JUST WANTED TO FIX THIS SO I COULD HAVE MY BROTHER BACK.
I'M SORRY, EVERYONE.
WE SHOULDN'T HAVE DONE THIS. IF WE HAD STAYED HOME, MAYBE YOU WOULD HAVE BEEN OK.
NO. IT WAS HAPPENING THERE TOO. I JUST DIDN'T SAY ANYTHING.
GASP
WADE . . .
I'M SORRY TOO. I WANTED TO GET HELP, BUT I WAS TOO AFRAID. IT FELT HOPELESS.
YOU DON'T HAVE TO APOLOGIZE FOR ANYTHING.

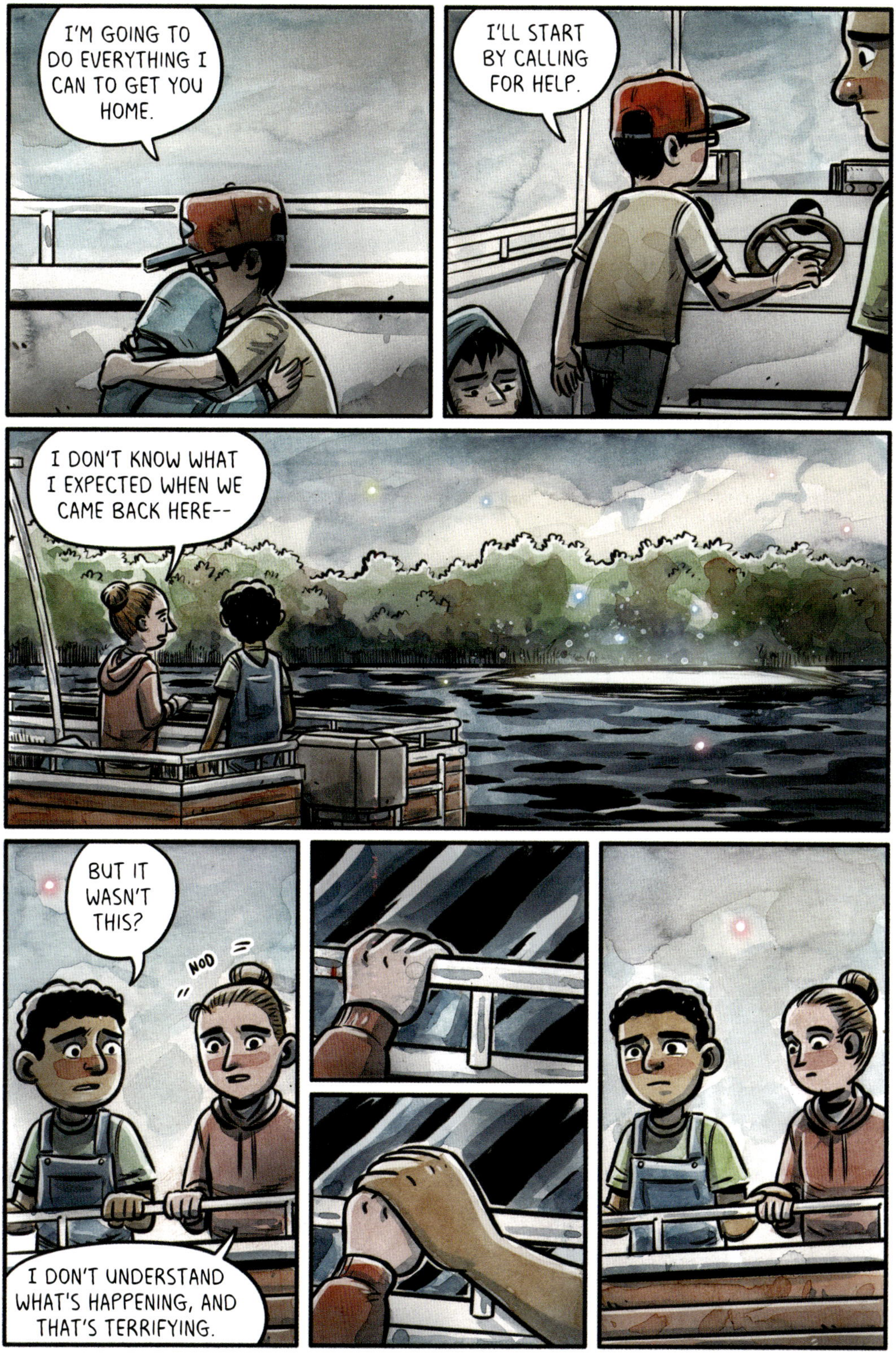
I'M GOING TO DO EVERYTHING I CAN TO GET YOU HOME.
I'LL START BY CALLING FOR HELP.
I DON'T KNOW WHAT I EXPECTED WHEN WE CAME BACK HERE--
BUT IT WASN'T THIS?
NOD
I DON'T UNDERSTAND WHAT'S HAPPENING, AND THAT'S TERRIFYING.

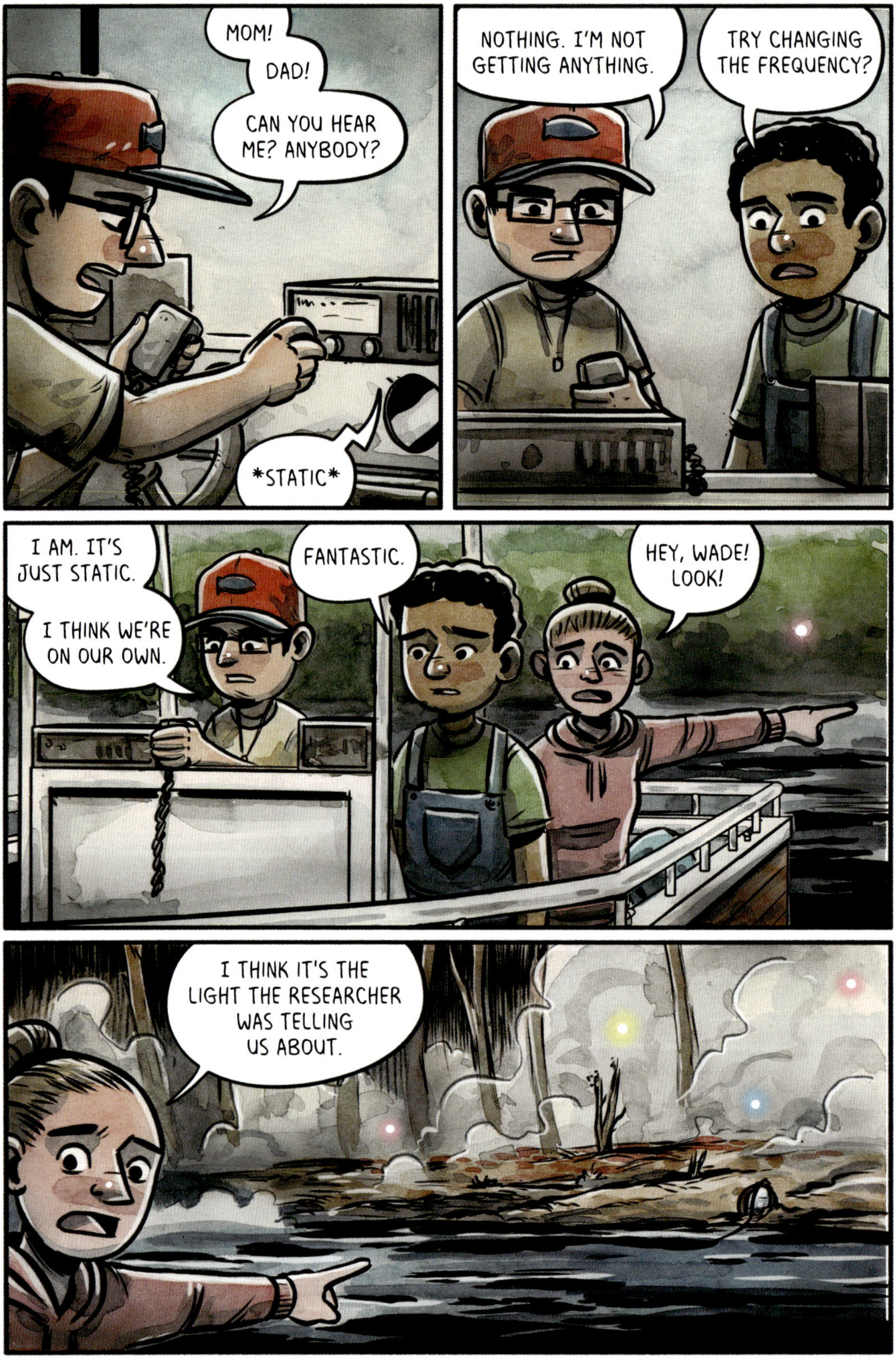
MOM!
DAD!
CAN YOU HEAR ME? ANYBODY?
STATIC
NOTHING. I'M NOT GETTING ANYTHING.
TRY CHANGING THE FREQUENCY?
I AM. IT'S JUST STATIC.
I THINK WE'RE ON OUR OWN.
FANTASTIC.
HEY, WADE! LOOK!
I THINK IT'S THE LIGHT THE RESEARCHER WAS TELLING US ABOUT.

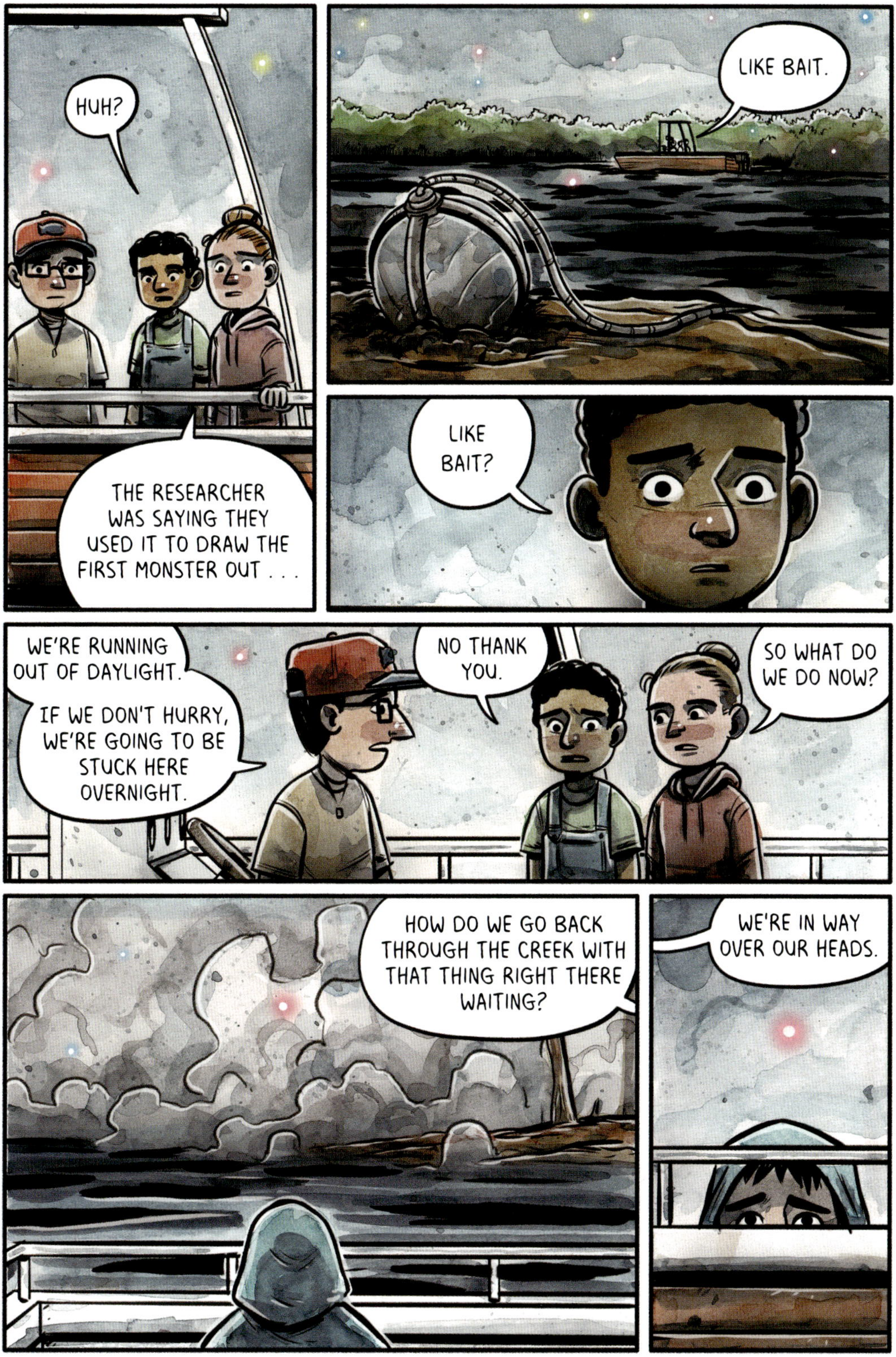
HUH?
THE RESEARCHER WAS SAYING THEY USED IT TO DRAW THE FIRST MONSTER OUT . . .
LIKE BAIT.
LIKE BAIT?
WE'RE RUNNING OUT OF DAYLIGHT.
IF WE DON'T HURRY, WE'RE GOING TO BE STUCK HERE OVERNIGHT.
NO THANK YOU.
SO WHAT DO WE DO NOW?
HOW DO WE GO BACK THROUGH THE CREEK WITH THAT THING RIGHT THERE WAITING?
WE'RE IN WAY OVER OUR HEADS.

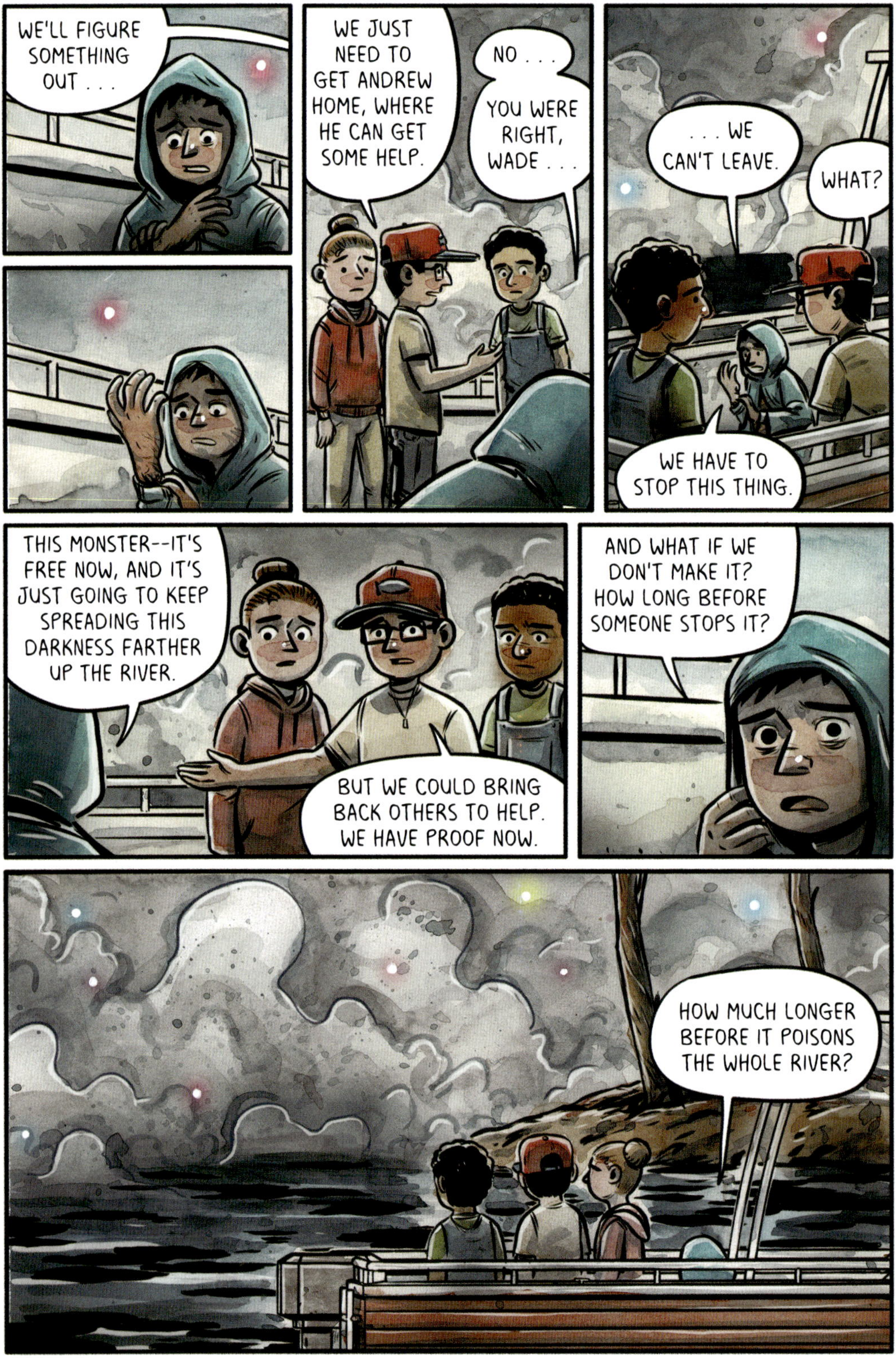
WE'LL FIGURE SOMETHING OUT . . .
WE JUST NEED TO GET ANDREW HOME, WHERE HE CAN GET SOME HELP.
NO . . .
YOU WERE RIGHT, WADE . . .
. . . WE CAN'T LEAVE.
WHAT?
WE HAVE TO STOP THIS THING.
THIS MONSTER--IT'S FREE NOW, AND IT'S JUST GOING TO KEEP SPREADING THIS DARKNESS FARTHER UP THE RIVER.
BUT WE COULD BRING BACK OTHERS TO HELP. WE HAVE PROOF NOW.
AND WHAT IF WE DON'T MAKE IT? HOW LONG BEFORE SOMEONE STOPS IT?
HOW MUCH LONGER BEFORE IT POISONS THE WHOLE RIVER?

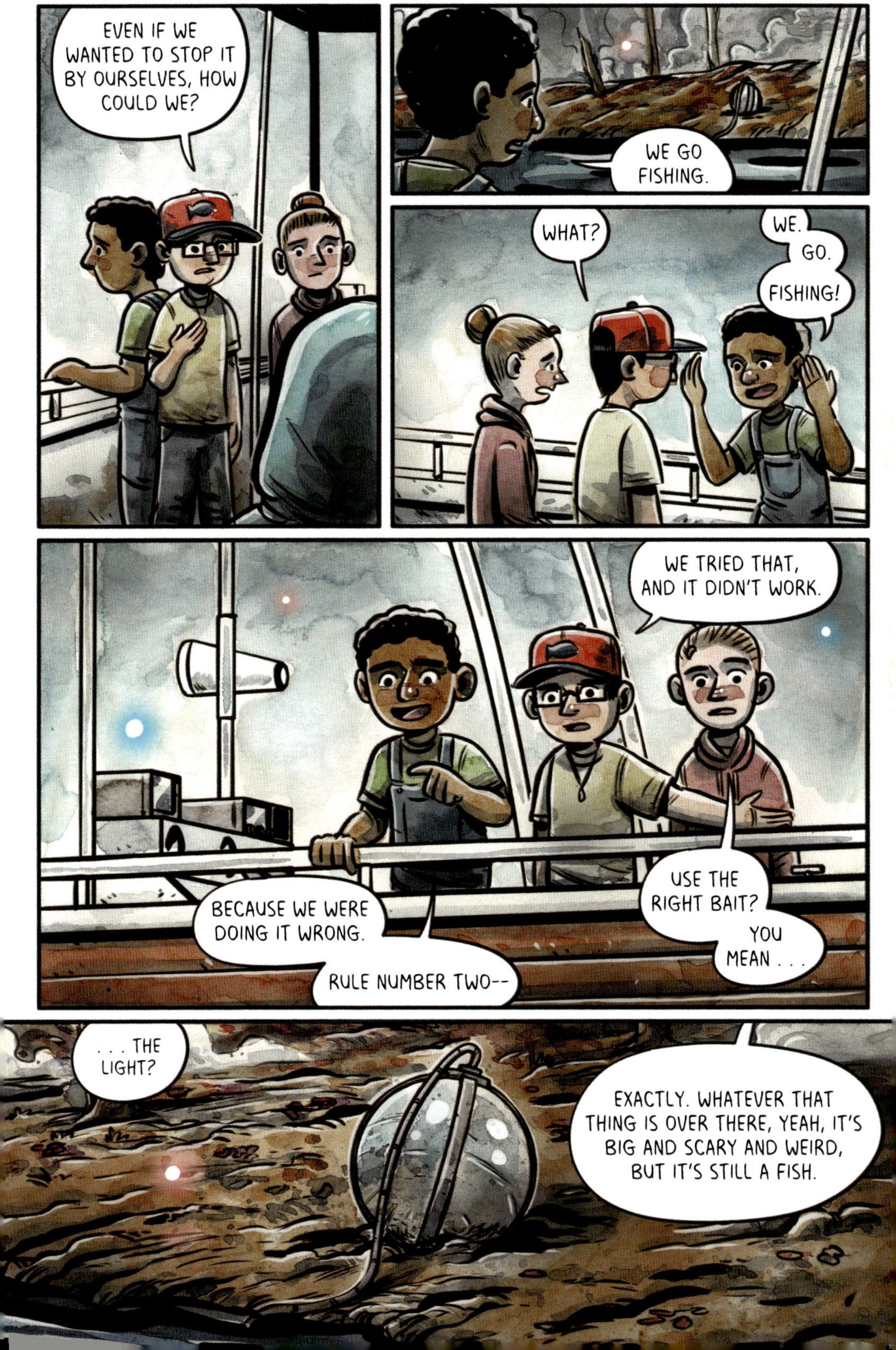
EVEN IF WE WANTED TO STOP IT BY OURSELVES, HOW COULD WE?
WE GO FISHING.
WHAT?
WE. GO. FISHING!
WE TRIED THAT, AND IT DIDN'T WORK.
BECAUSE WE WERE DOING IT WRONG.
RULE NUMBER TWO--
USE THE RIGHT BAIT?
YOU MEAN . . .
. . . THE LIGHT?
EXACTLY. WHATEVER THAT THING IS OVER THERE, YEAH, IT'S BIG AND SCARY AND WEIRD, BUT IT'S STILL A FISH.

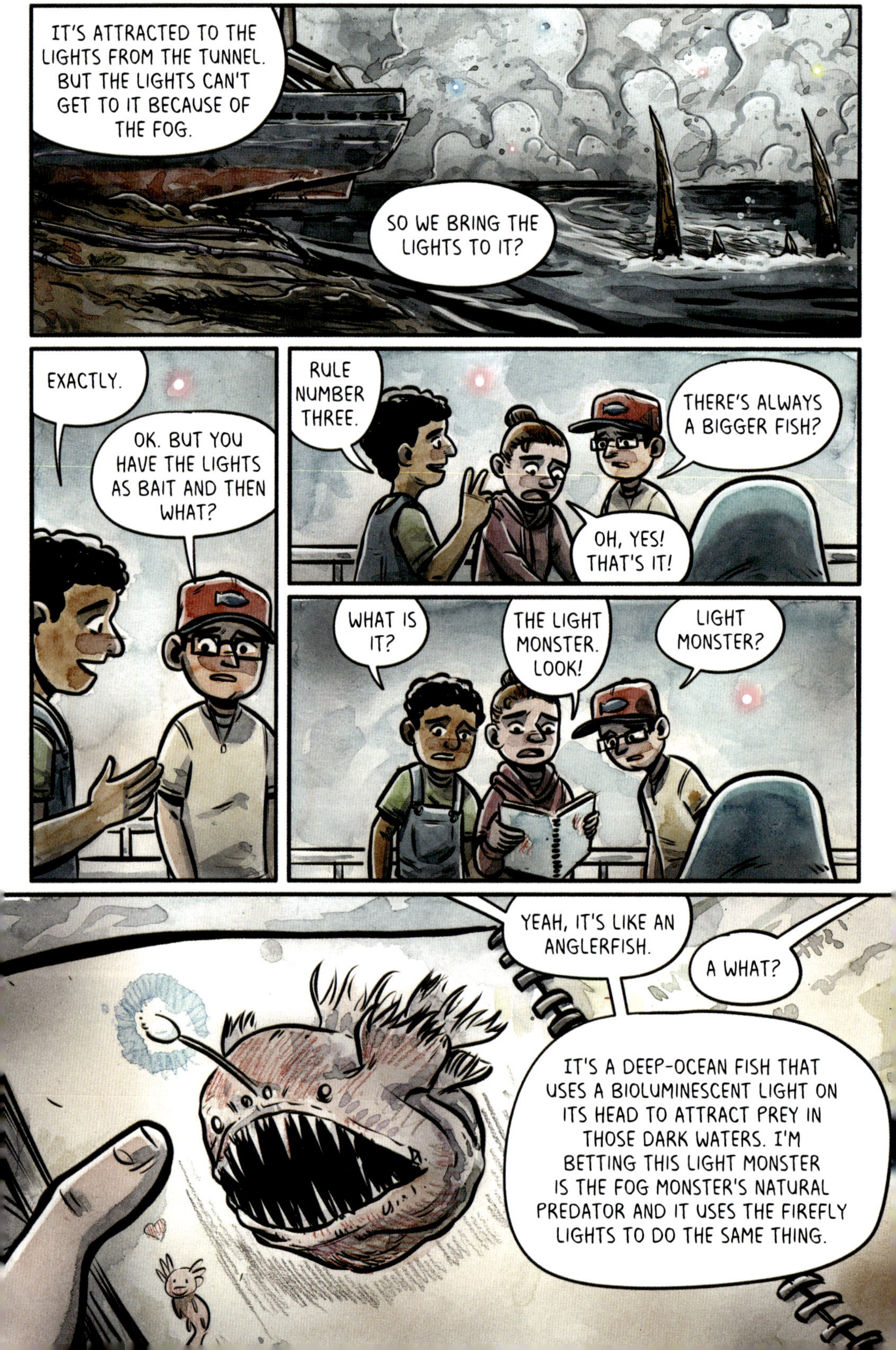
IT'S ATTRACTED TO THE LIGHTS FROM THE TUNNEL. BUT THE LIGHTS CAN'T GET TO IT BECAUSE OF THE FOG.
SO WE BRING THE LIGHTS TO IT?
EXACTLY.
OK. BUT YOU HAVE THE LIGHTS AS BAIT AND THEN WHAT?
RULE NUMBER THREE.
THERE'S ALWAYS A BIGGER FISH?
OH, YES! THAT'S IT!
WHAT IS IT?
THE LIGHT MONSTER. LOOK!
LIGHT MONSTER?
YEAH, IT'S LIKE AN ANGLERFISH.
A WHAT?
IT'S A DEEP-OCEAN FISH THAT USES A BIOLUMINESCENT LIGHT ON ITS HEAD TO ATTRACT PREY IN THOSE DARK WATERS. I'M BETTING THIS LIGHT MONSTER IS THE FOG MONSTER'S NATURAL PREDATOR AND IT USES THE FIREFLY LIGHTS TO DO THE SAME THING.

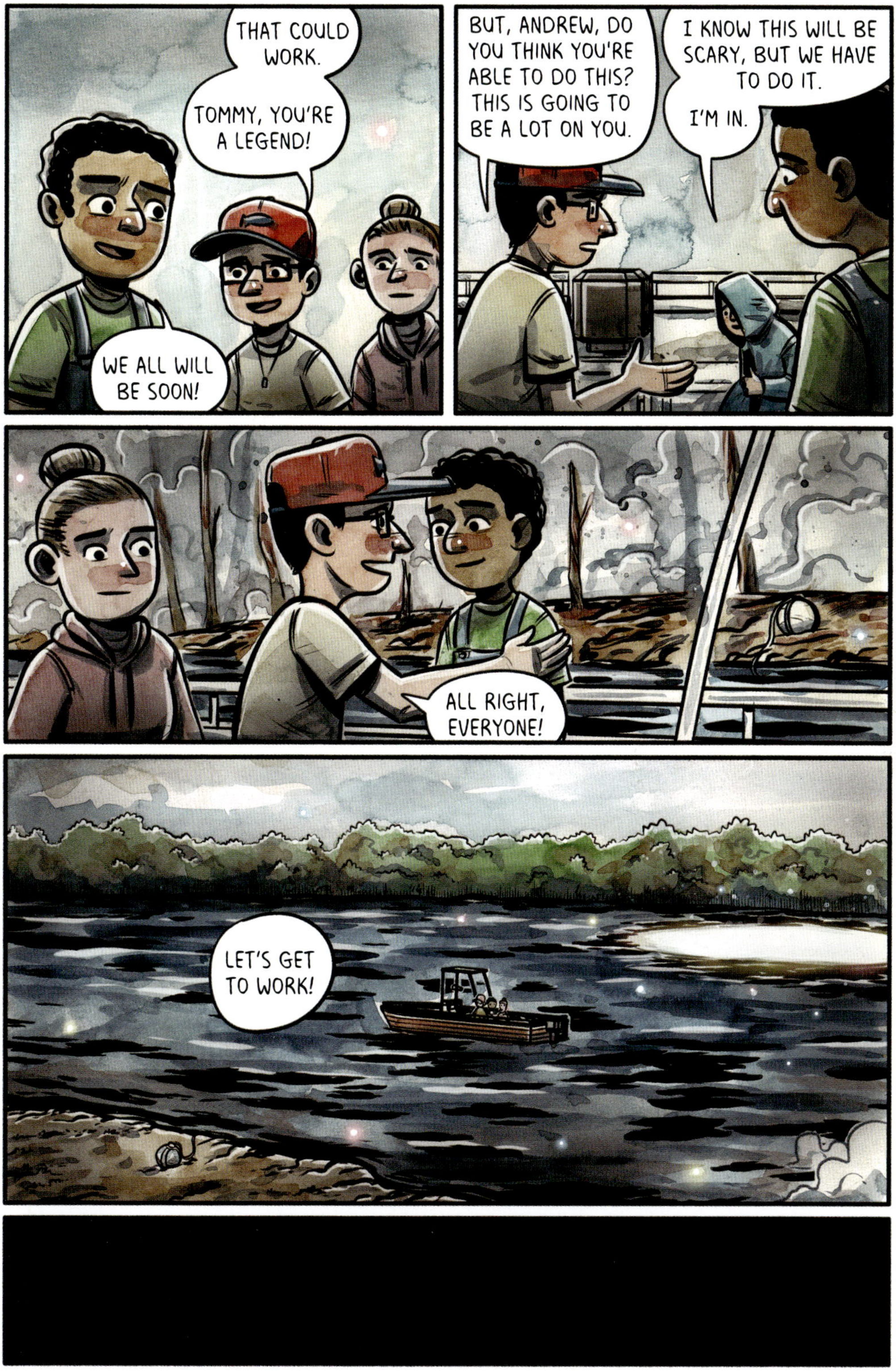
THAT COULD WORK.
TOMMY, YOU'RE A LEGEND!
WE ALL WILL BE SOON!
BUT, ANDREW, DO YOU THINK YOU'RE ABLE TO DO THIS? THIS IS GOING TO BE A LOT ON YOU.
I KNOW THIS WILL BE SCARY, BUT WE HAVE TO DO IT.
I'M IN.
ALL RIGHT, EVERYONE!
LET'S GET TO WORK!

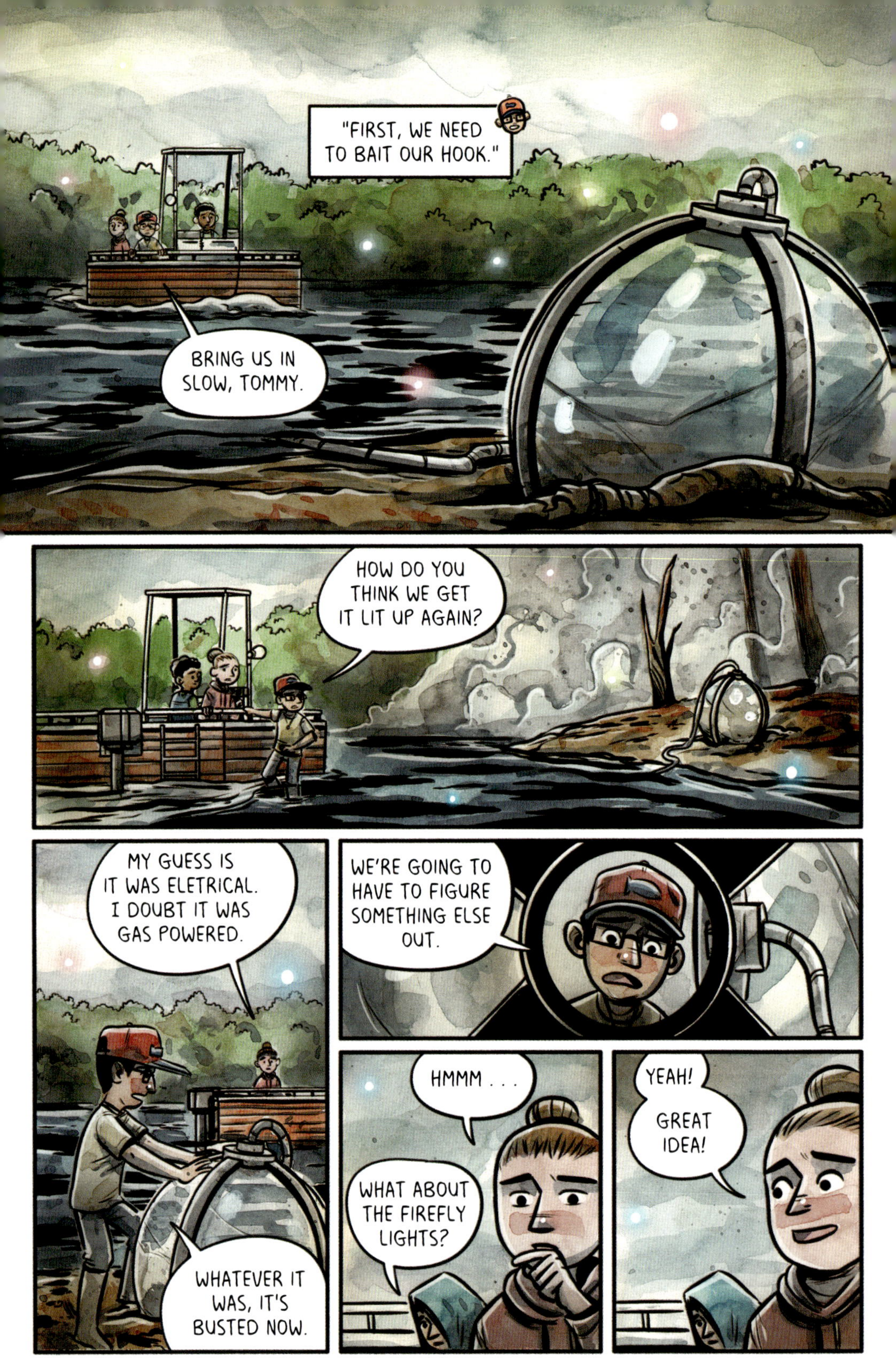
"FIRST, WE NEED TO BAIT OUR HOOK."
BRING US IN SLOW, TOMMY.
HOW DO YOU THINK WE GET IT LIT UP AGAIN?
MY GUESS IS IT WAS ELETRICAL. I DOUBT IT WAS GAS POWERED.
WHATEVER IT WAS, IT'S BUSTED NOW.
WE'RE GOING TO HAVE TO FIGURE SOMETHING ELSE OUT.
HMMM . . .
WHAT ABOUT THE FIREFLY LIGHTS?
YEAH!
GREAT IDEA!

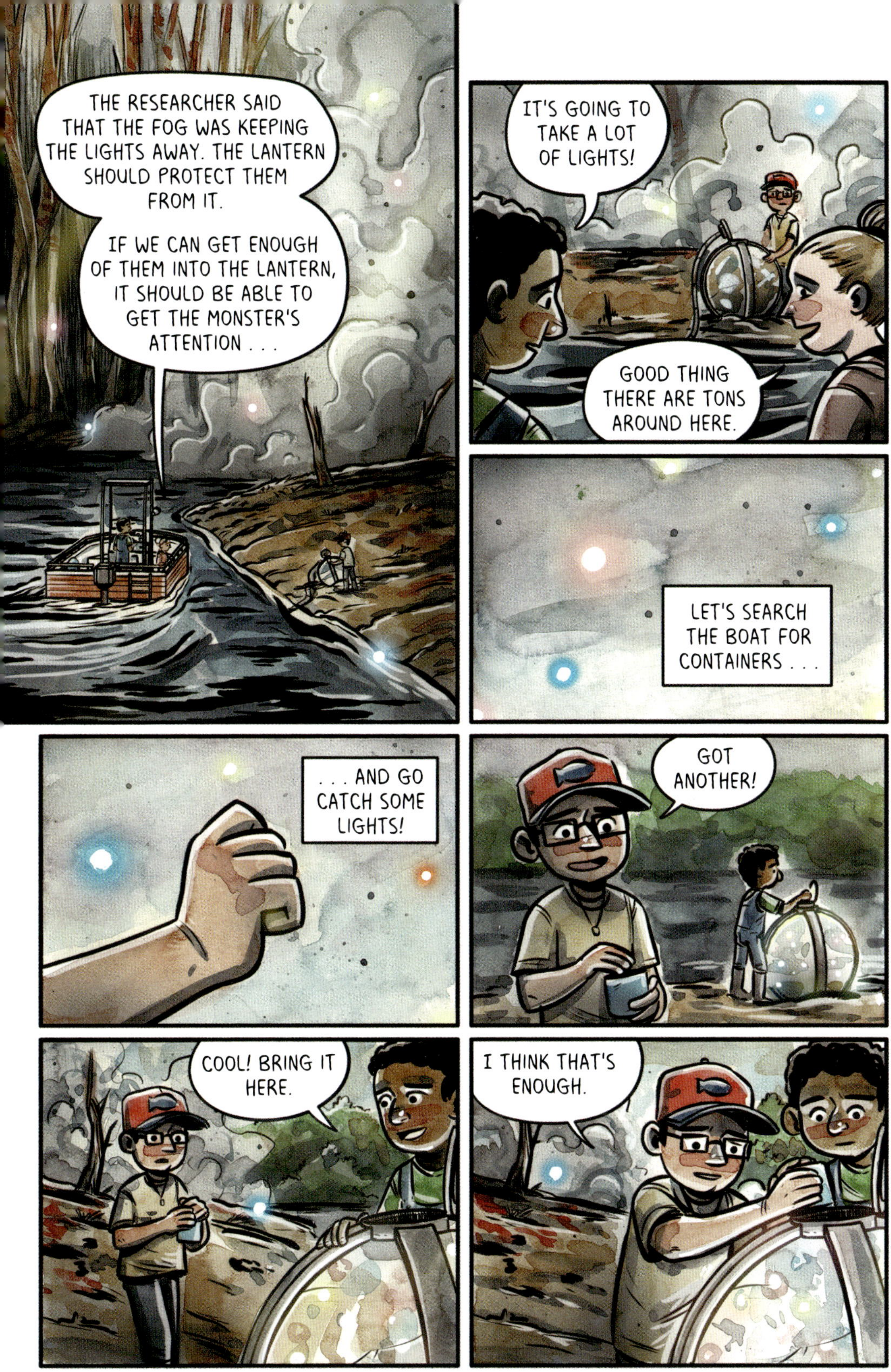
THE RESEARCHER SAID THAT THE FOG WAS KEEPING THE LIGHTS AWAY. THE LANTERN SHOULD PROTECT THEM FROM IT.
IF WE CAN GET ENOUGH OF THEM INTO THE LANTERN, IT SHOULD BE ABLE TO GET THE MONSTER'S ATTENTION . . .
IT'S GOING TO TAKE A LOT OF LIGHTS!
GOOD THING THERE ARE TONS AROUND HERE.
LET'S SEARCH THE BOAT FOR CONTAINERS . . .
. . . AND GO CATCH SOME LIGHTS!
GOT ANOTHER!
COOL! BRING IT HERE.
I THINK THAT'S ENOUGH.

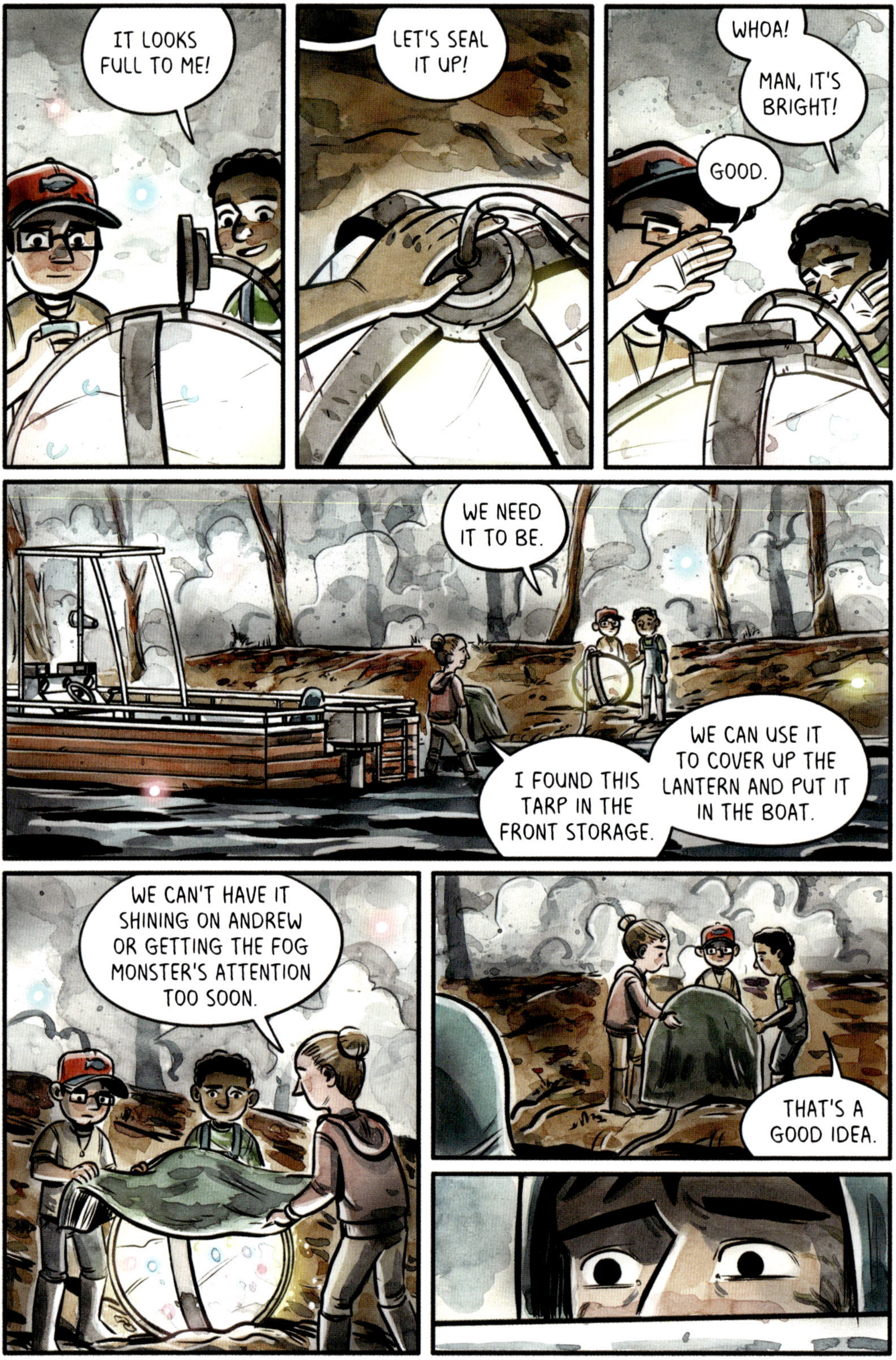
IT LOOKS FULL TO ME!
LET'S SEAL IT UP!
WHOA!
MAN, IT'S BRIGHT!
GOOD.
WE NEED IT TO BE.
I FOUND THIS TARP IN THE FRONT STORAGE.
WE CAN USE IT TO COVER UP THE LANTERN AND PUT IT IN THE BOAT.
WE CAN'T HAVE IT SHINING ON ANDREW OR GETTING THE FOG MONSTER'S ATTENTION TOO SOON.
THAT'S A GOOD IDEA.

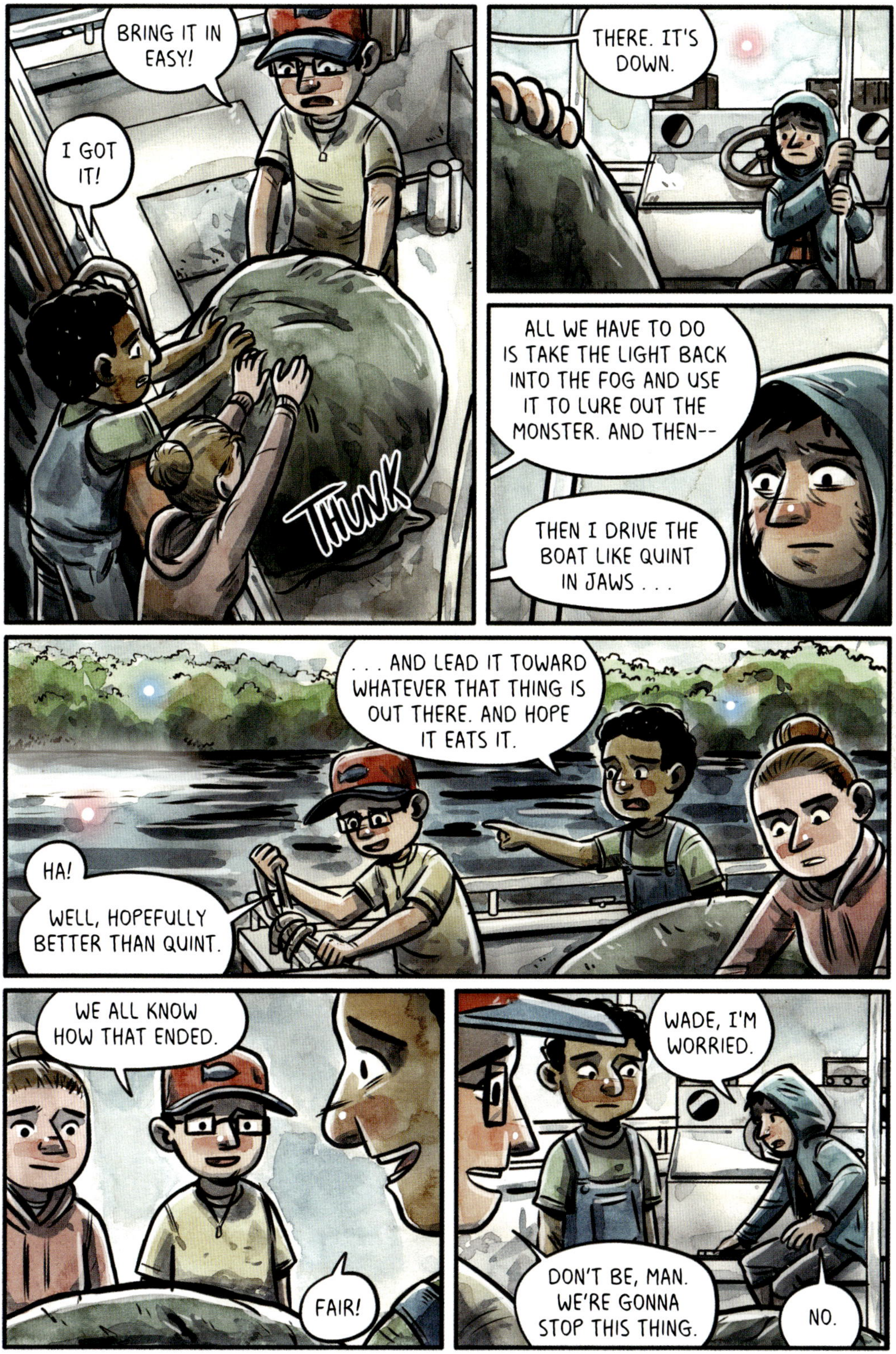

BRING IT IN EASY!
I GOT IT!
THUNK
THERE. IT'S DOWN.
ALL WE HAVE TO DO IS TAKE THE LIGHT BACK INTO THE FOG AND USE IT TO LURE OUT THE MONSTER. AND THEN--
THEN I DRIVE THE BOAT LIKE QUINT IN JAWS . . .
. . . AND LEAD IT TOWARD WHATEVER THAT THING IS OUT THERE. AND HOPE IT EATS IT.
HA!
WELL, HOPEFULLY BETTER THAN QUINT.
WE ALL KNOW HOW THAT ENDED.
FAIR!
WADE, I'M WORRIED.
DON'T BE, MAN. WE'RE GONNA STOP THIS THING.
NO.

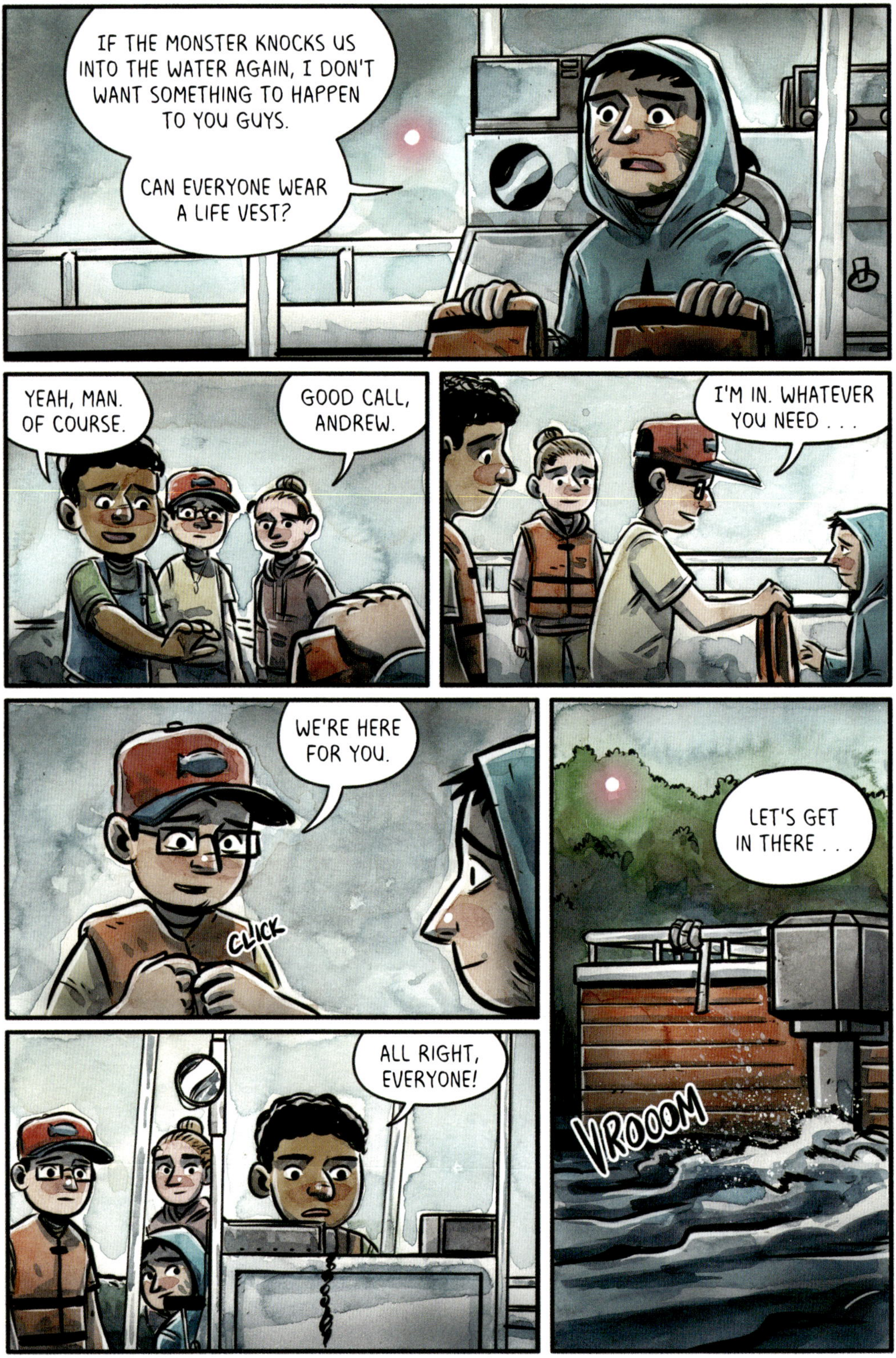
IF THE MONSTER KNOCKS US INTO THE WATER AGAIN, I DON'T WANT SOMETHING TO HAPPEN TO YOU GUYS.
CAN EVERYONE WEAR A LIFE VEST?
YEAH, MAN. OF COURSE.
GOOD CALL, ANDREW.
I'M IN. WHATEVER YOU NEED . . .
WE'RE HERE FOR YOU.
CLICK
ALL RIGHT, EVERYONE!
LET'S GET IN THERE . . .
VROOOM

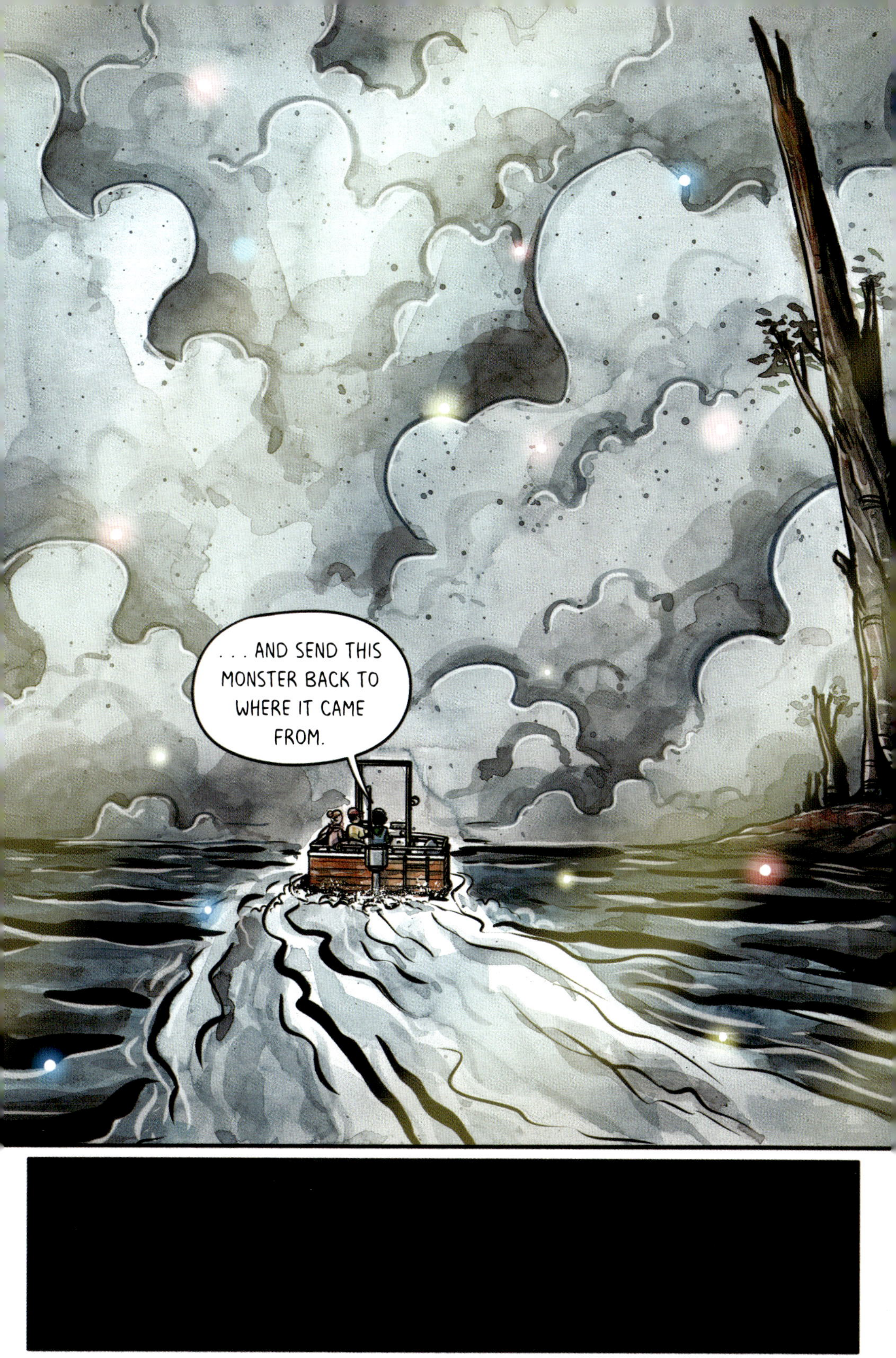
. . . AND SEND THIS MONSTER BACK TO WHERE IT CAME FROM.

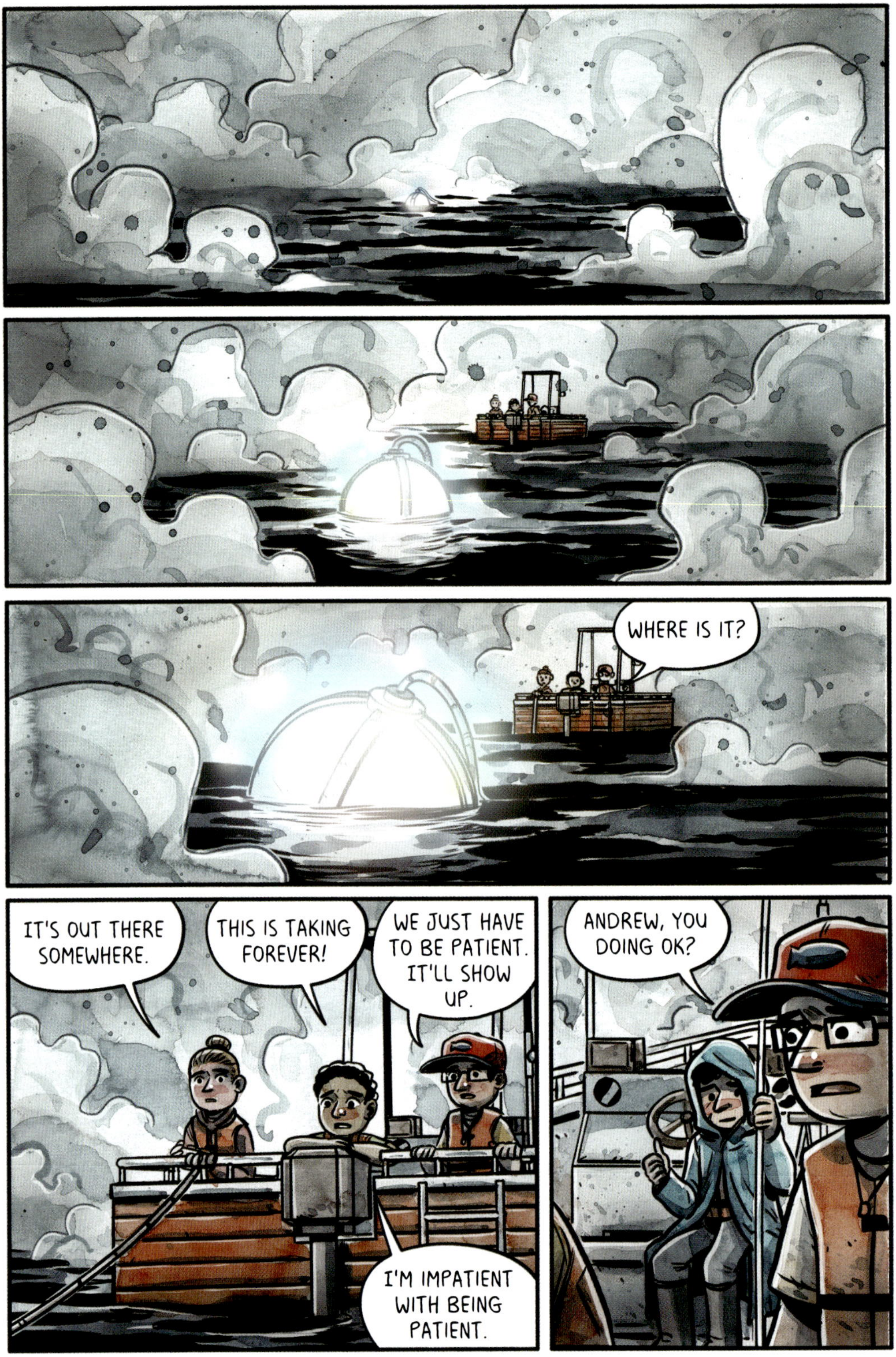
WHERE IS IT?
IT'S OUT THERE SOMEWHERE.
THIS IS TAKING FOREVER!
WE JUST HAVE TO BE PATIENT. IT'LL SHOW UP.
I'M IMPATIENT WITH BEING PATIENT.
ANDREW, YOU DOING OK?

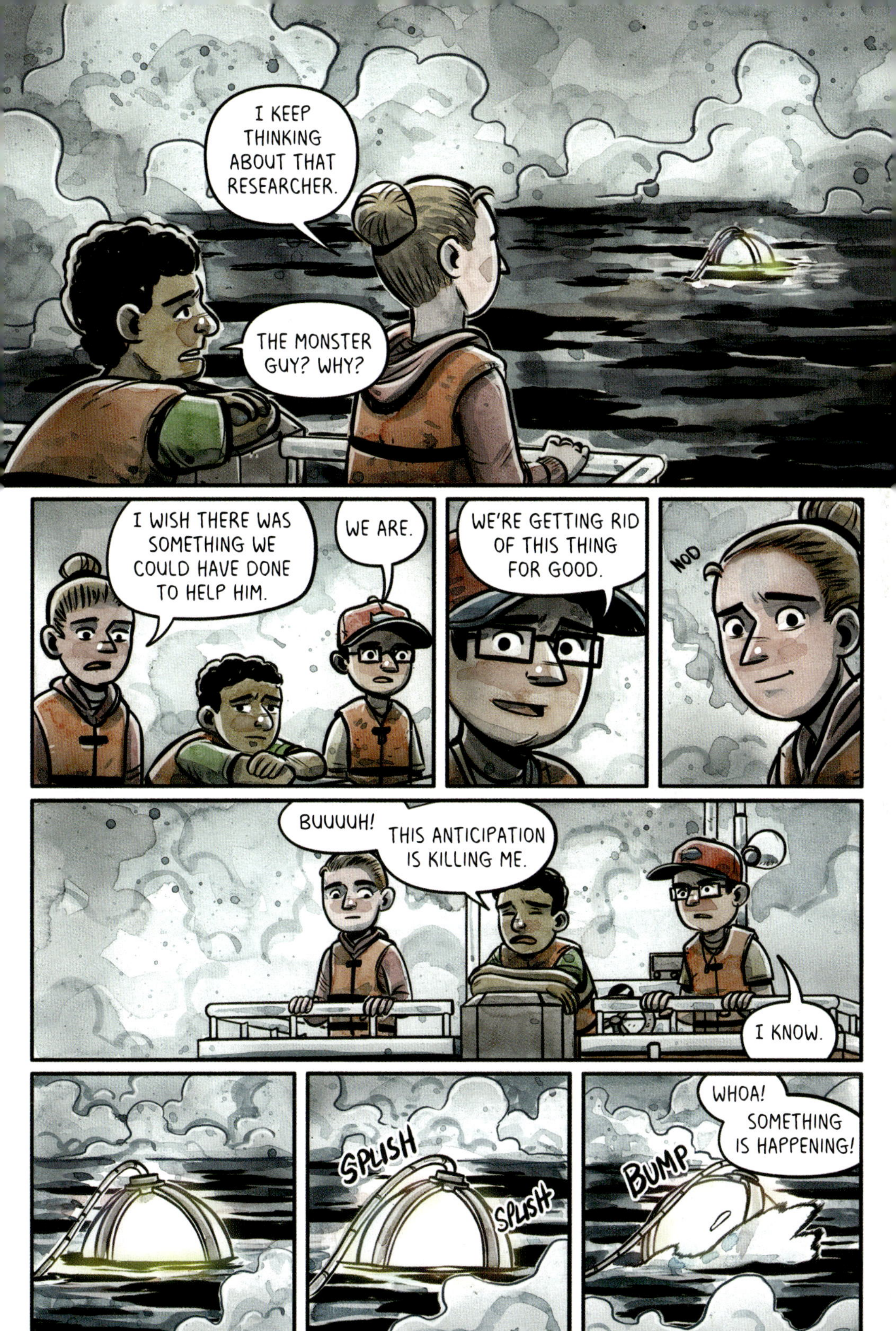
I KEEP THINKING ABOUT THAT RESEARCHER.
THE MONSTER GUY? WHY?
I WISH THERE WAS SOMETHING WE COULD HAVE DONE TO HELP HIM.
WE ARE.
WE'RE GETTING RID OF THIS THING FOR GOOD.
NOD
BUUUUH!
THIS ANTICIPATION IS KILLING ME.
I KNOW.
SPLISH
SPLISH
BUMP
WHOA!
SOMETHING IS HAPPENING!

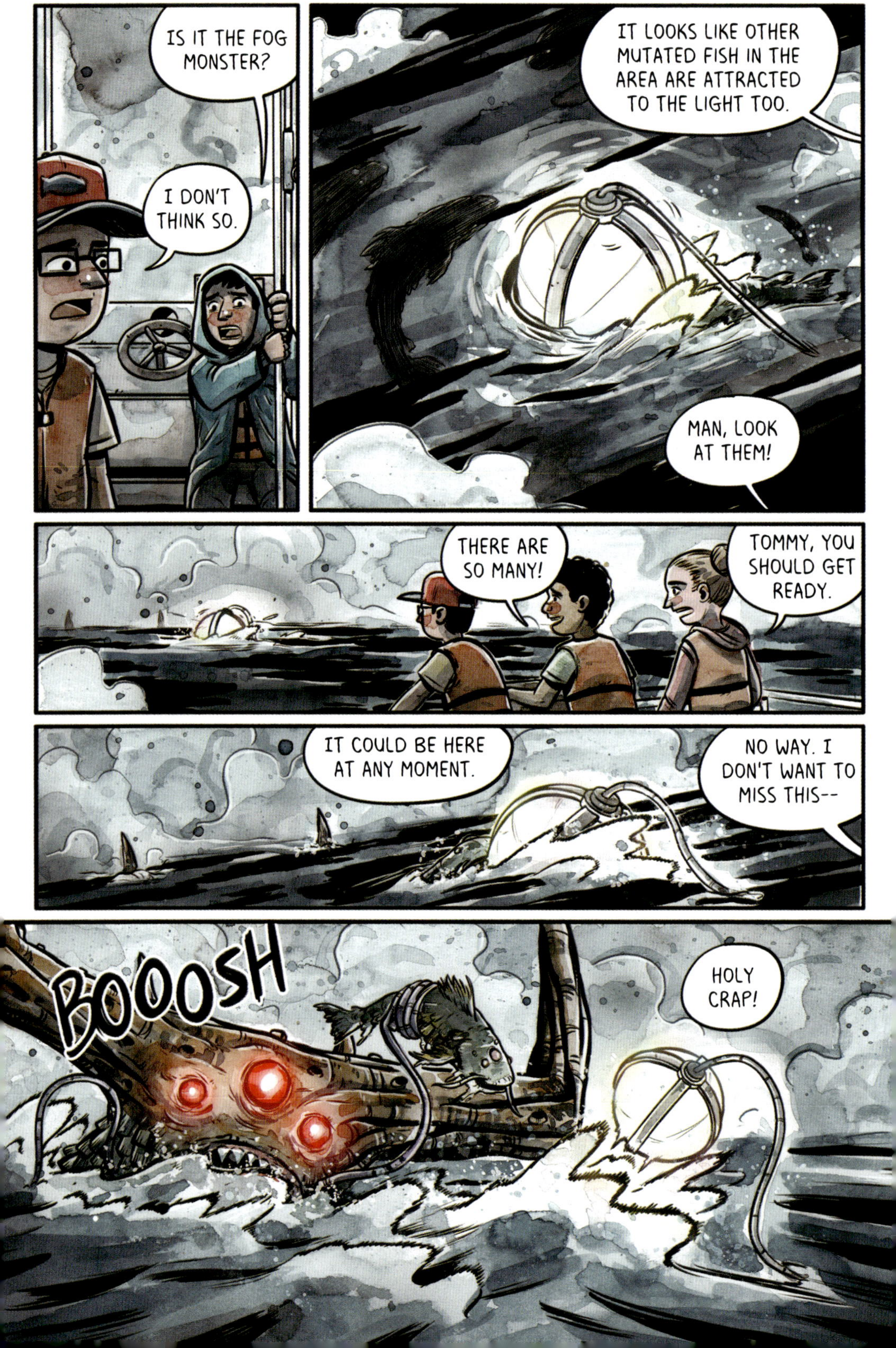
IS IT THE FOG MONSTER?
I DON'T THINK SO.
IT LOOKS LIKE OTHER MUTATED FISH IN THE AREA ARE ATTRACTED TO THE LIGHT TOO.
MAN, LOOK AT THEM!
THERE ARE SO MANY!
TOMMY, YOU SHOULD GET READY.
IT COULD BE HERE AT ANY MOMENT.
NO WAY. I DON'T WANT TO MISS THIS--
BOOOSH
HOLY CRAP!

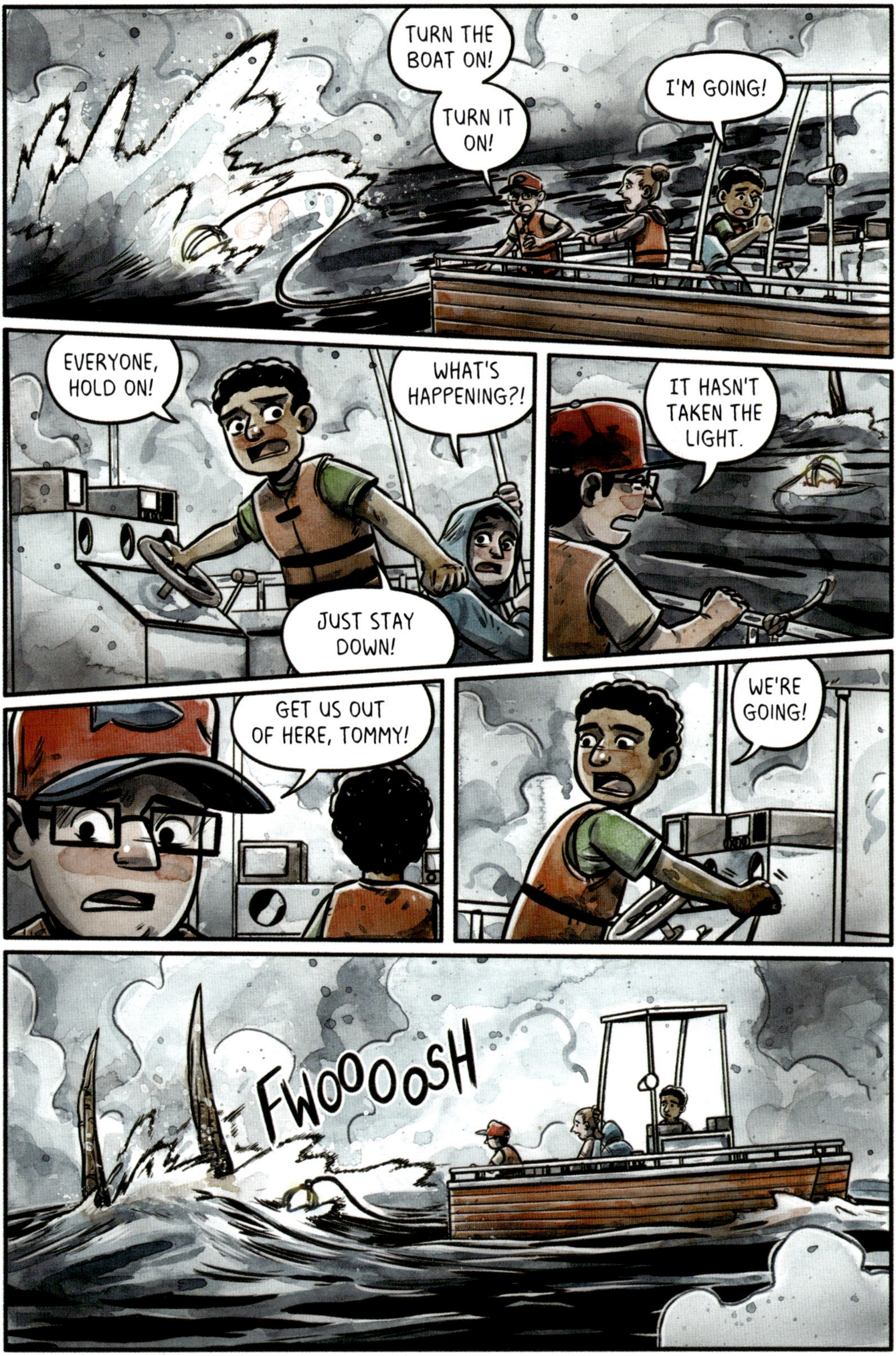
TURN THE BOAT ON!
TURN IT ON!
I'M GOING!
EVERYONE, HOLD ON!
WHAT'S HAPPENING?!
JUST STAY DOWN!
IT HASN'T TAKEN THE LIGHT.
GET US OUT OF HERE, TOMMY!
WE'RE GOING!
FWOOOOSH

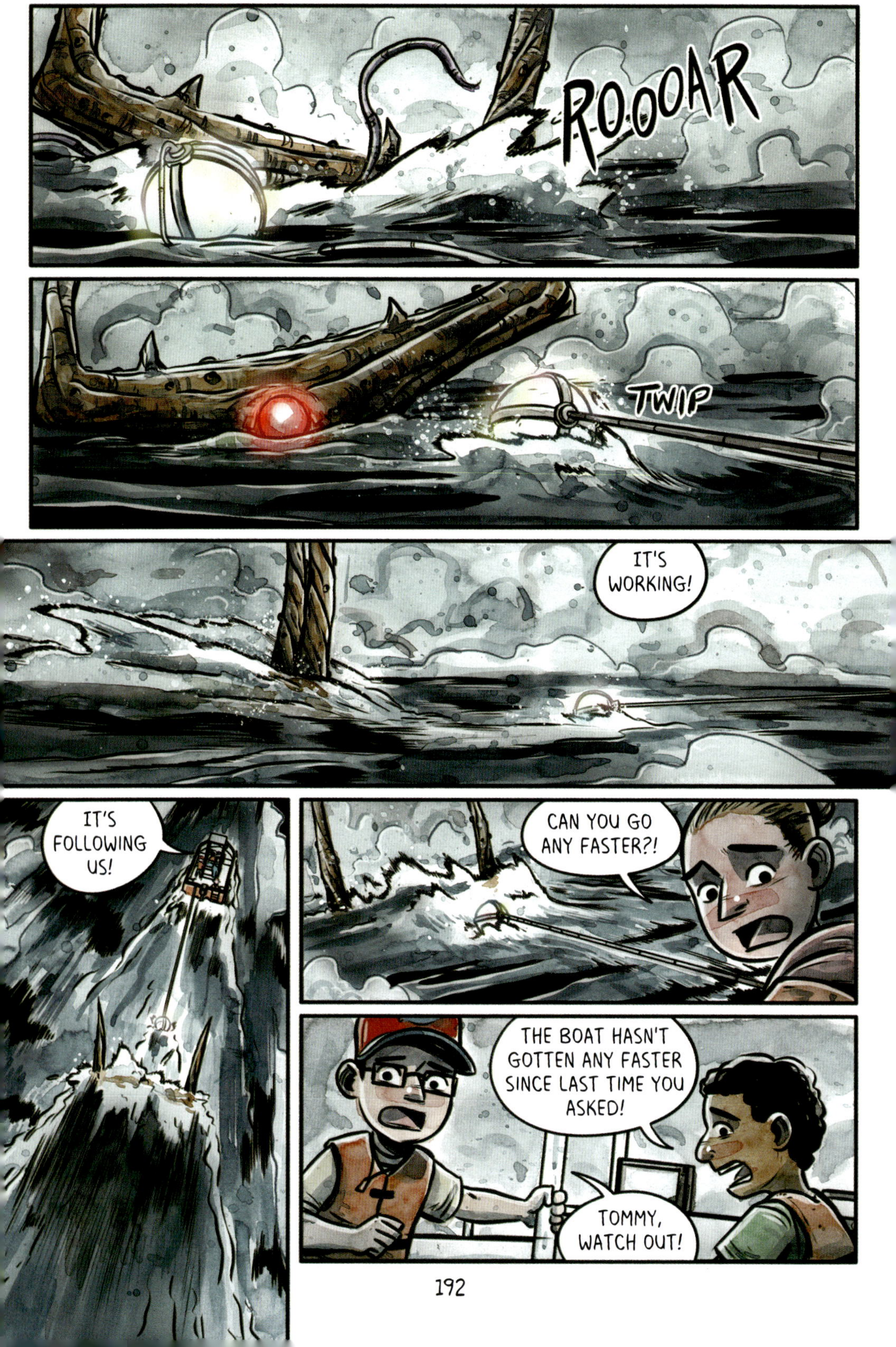
ROOOAR
TWIP
IT'S WORKING!
IT'S FOLLOWING US!
CAN YOU GO ANY FASTER?!
THE BOAT HASN'T GOTTEN ANY FASTER SINCE LAST TIME YOU ASKED!
TOMMY, WATCH OUT!

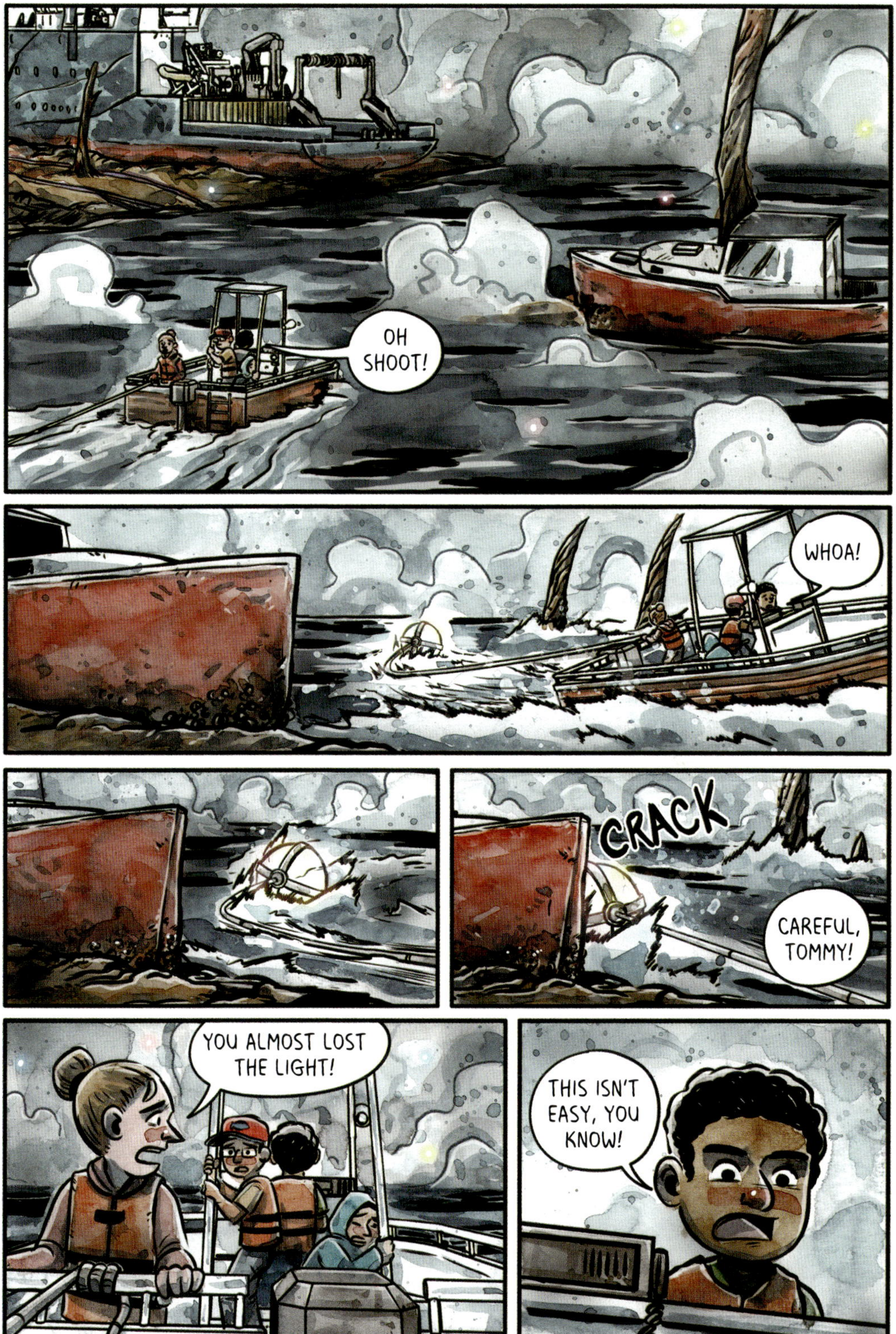
OH SHOOT!
WHOA!
CRACK
CAREFUL, TOMMY!
YOU ALMOST LOST THE LIGHT!
THIS ISN'T EASY, YOU KNOW!

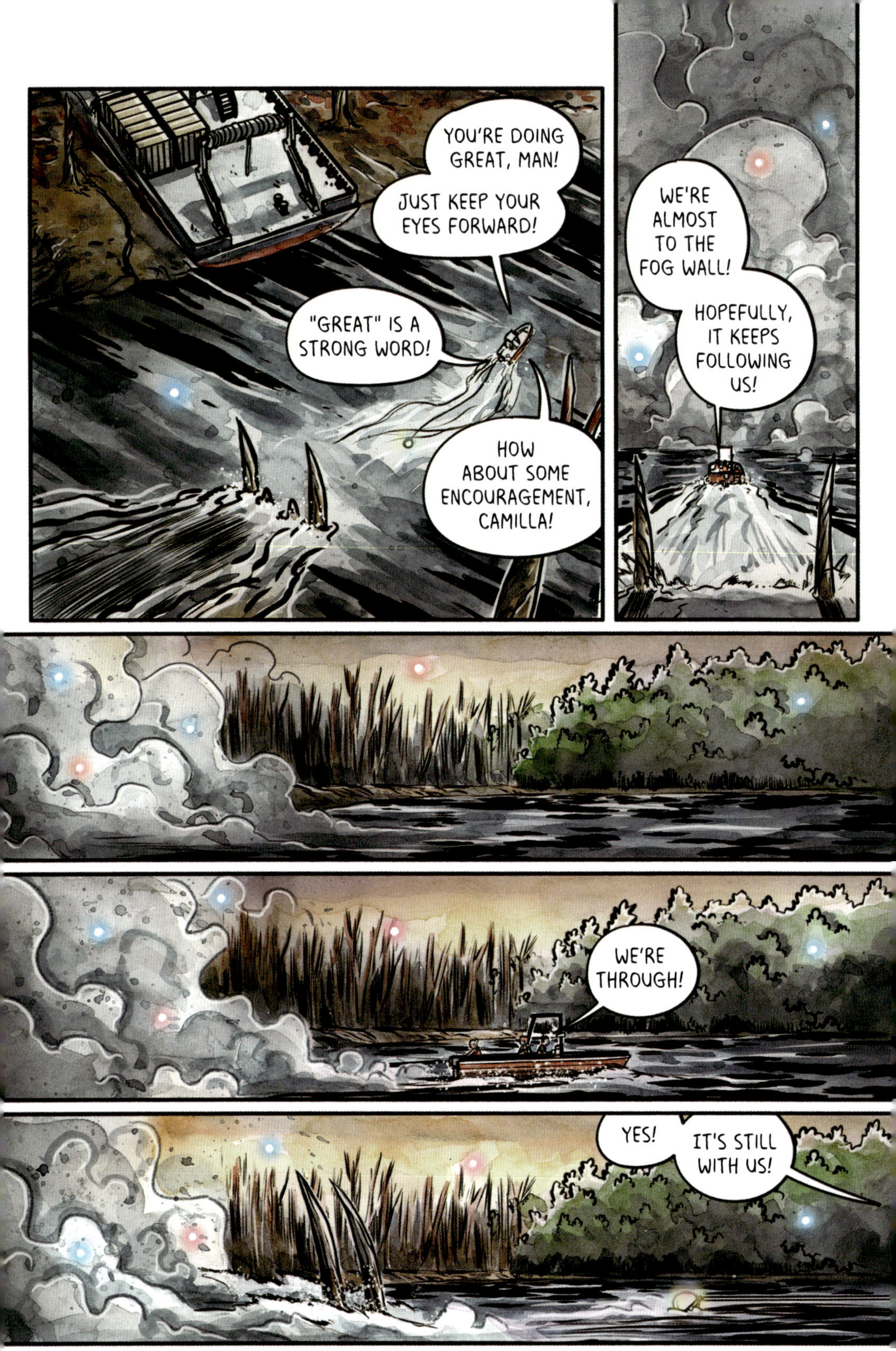
YOU'RE DOING GREAT, MAN!
JUST KEEP YOUR EYES FORWARD!
"GREAT" IS A STRONG WORD!
HOW ABOUT SOME ENCOURAGEMENT, CAMILLA!
WE'RE ALMOST TO THE FOG WALL!
HOPEFULLY, IT KEEPS FOLLOWING US!
WE'RE THROUGH!
YES!
IT'S STILL WITH US!

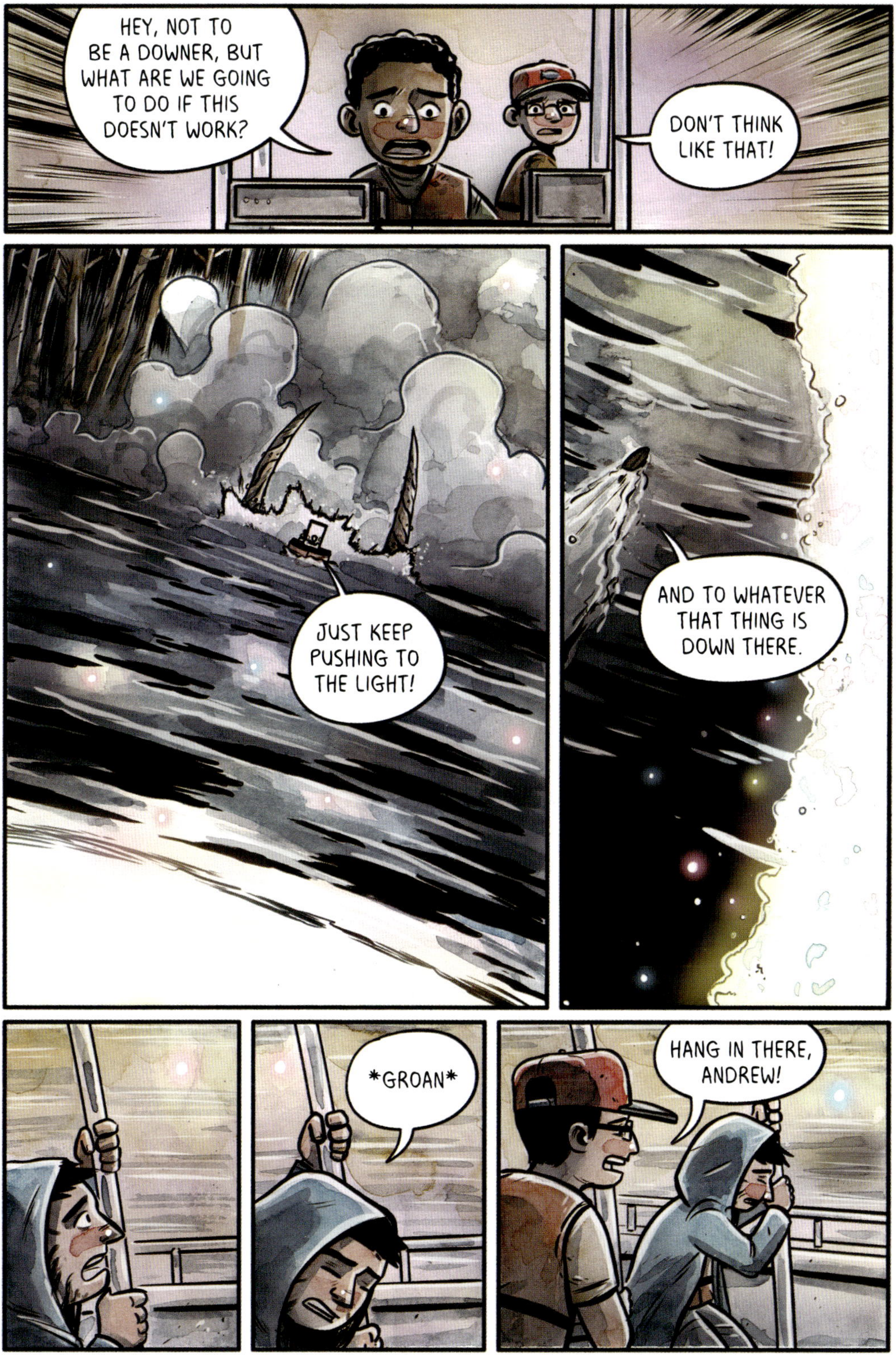
HEY, NOT TO BE A DOWNER, BUT WHAT ARE WE GOING TO DO IF THIS DOESN'T WORK?
DON'T THINK LIKE THAT!
JUST KEEP PUSHING TO THE LIGHT!
AND TO WHATEVER THAT THING IS DOWN THERE.
GROAN
HANG IN THERE, ANDREW!

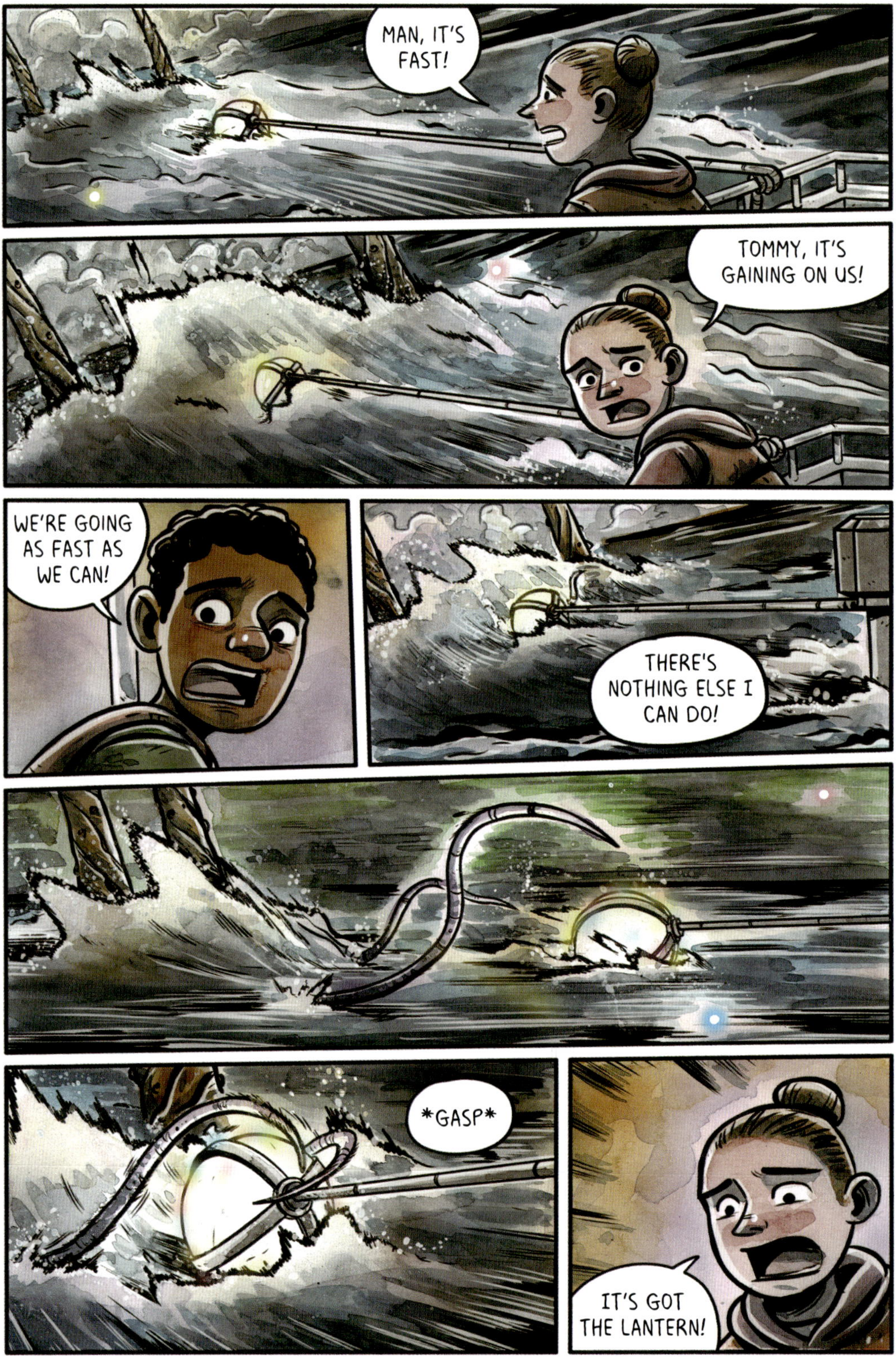
MAN, IT'S FAST!
TOMMY, IT'S GAINING ON US!
WE'RE GOING AS FAST AS WE CAN!
THERE'S NOTHING ELSE I CAN DO!
GASP
IT'S GOT THE LANTERN!

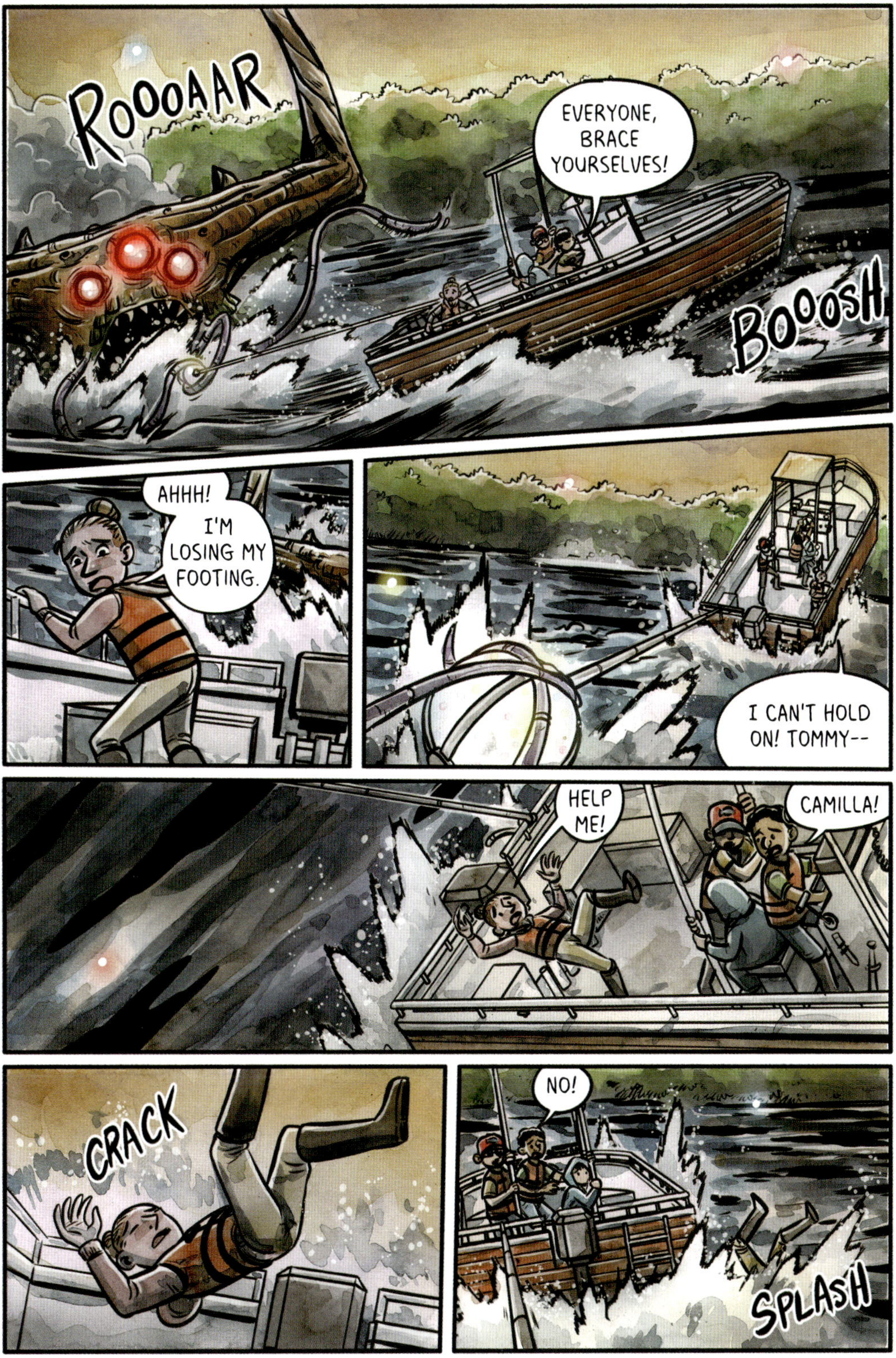
ROOOAAR
EVERYONE, BRACE YOURSELVES!
BOOOSH
AHHH!
I'M LOSING MY FOOTING.
I CAN'T HOLD ON! TOMMY--
HELP ME!
CAMILLA!
CRACK
NO!
SPLASH

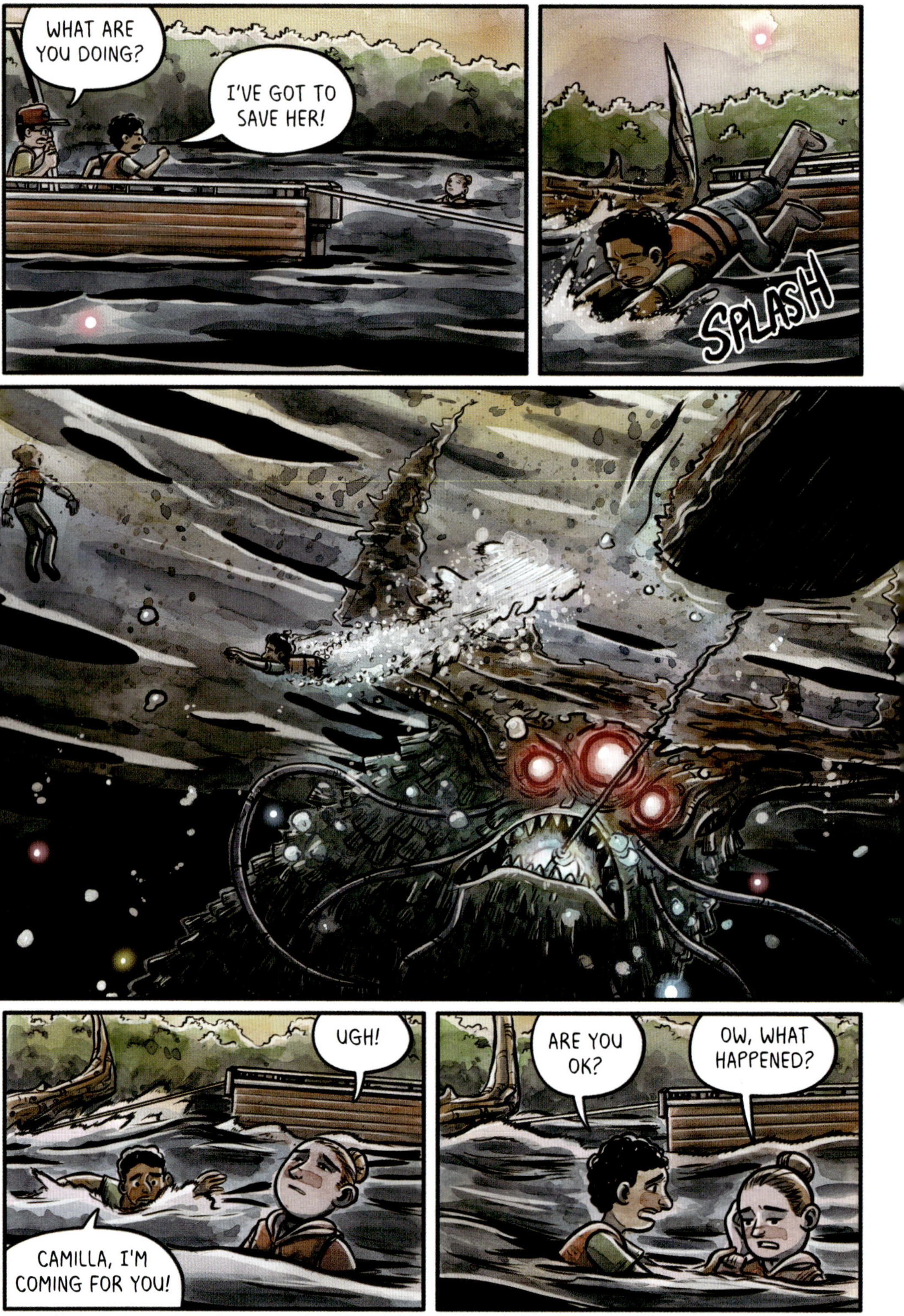
WHAT ARE YOU DOING?
I'VE GOT TO SAVE HER!
SPLASH
UGH!
CAMILLA, I'M COMING FOR YOU!
ARE YOU OK?
OW, WHAT HAPPENED?

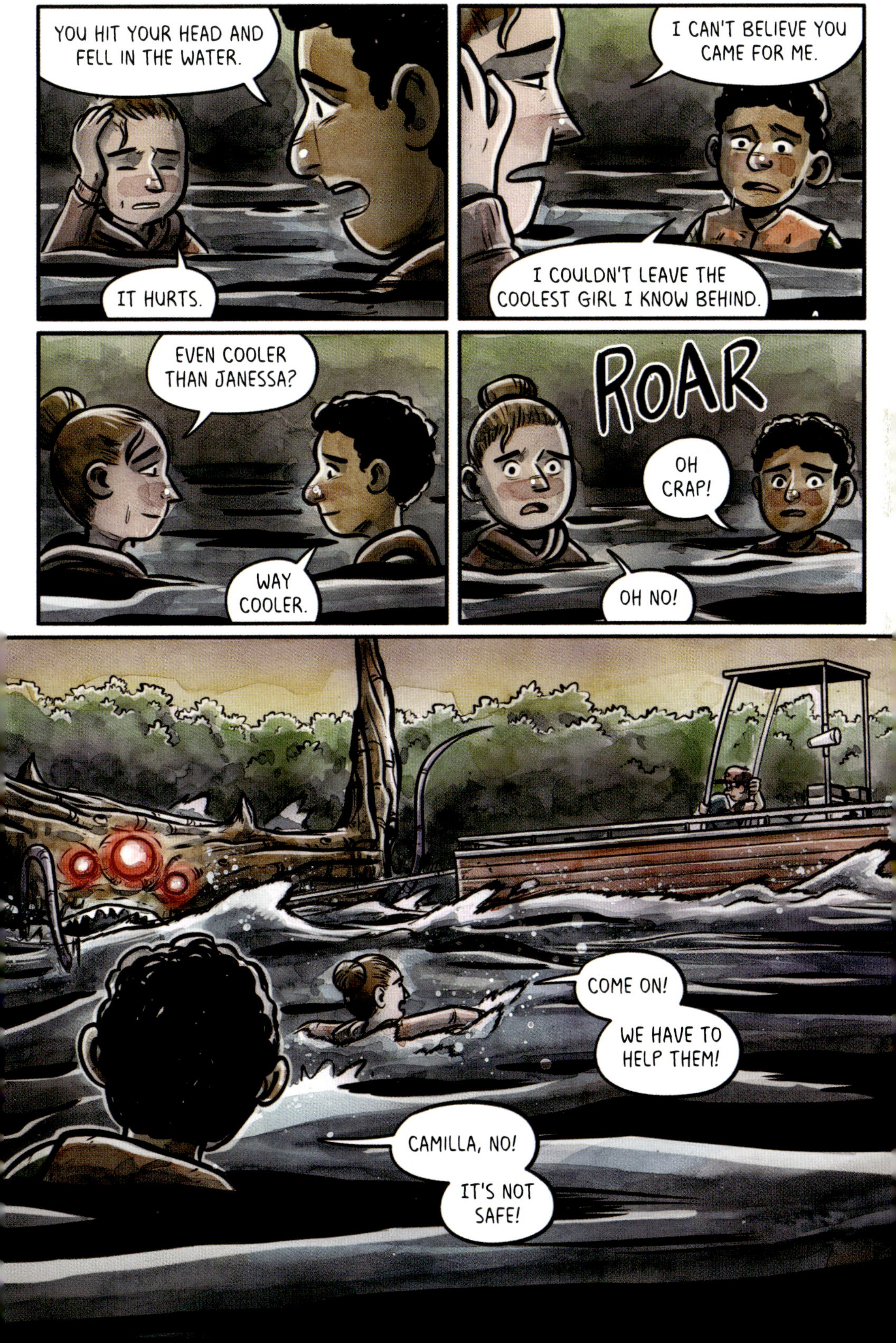
YOU HIT YOUR HEAD AND FELL IN THE WATER.
IT HURTS.
I CAN'T BELIEVE YOU CAME FOR ME.
I COULDN'T LEAVE THE COOLEST GIRL I KNOW BEHIND.
EVEN COOLER THAN JANESSA?
WAY COOLER.
ROAR
OH CRAP!
OH NO!
COME ON!
WE HAVE TO HELP THEM!
CAMILLA, NO!
IT'S NOT SAFE!

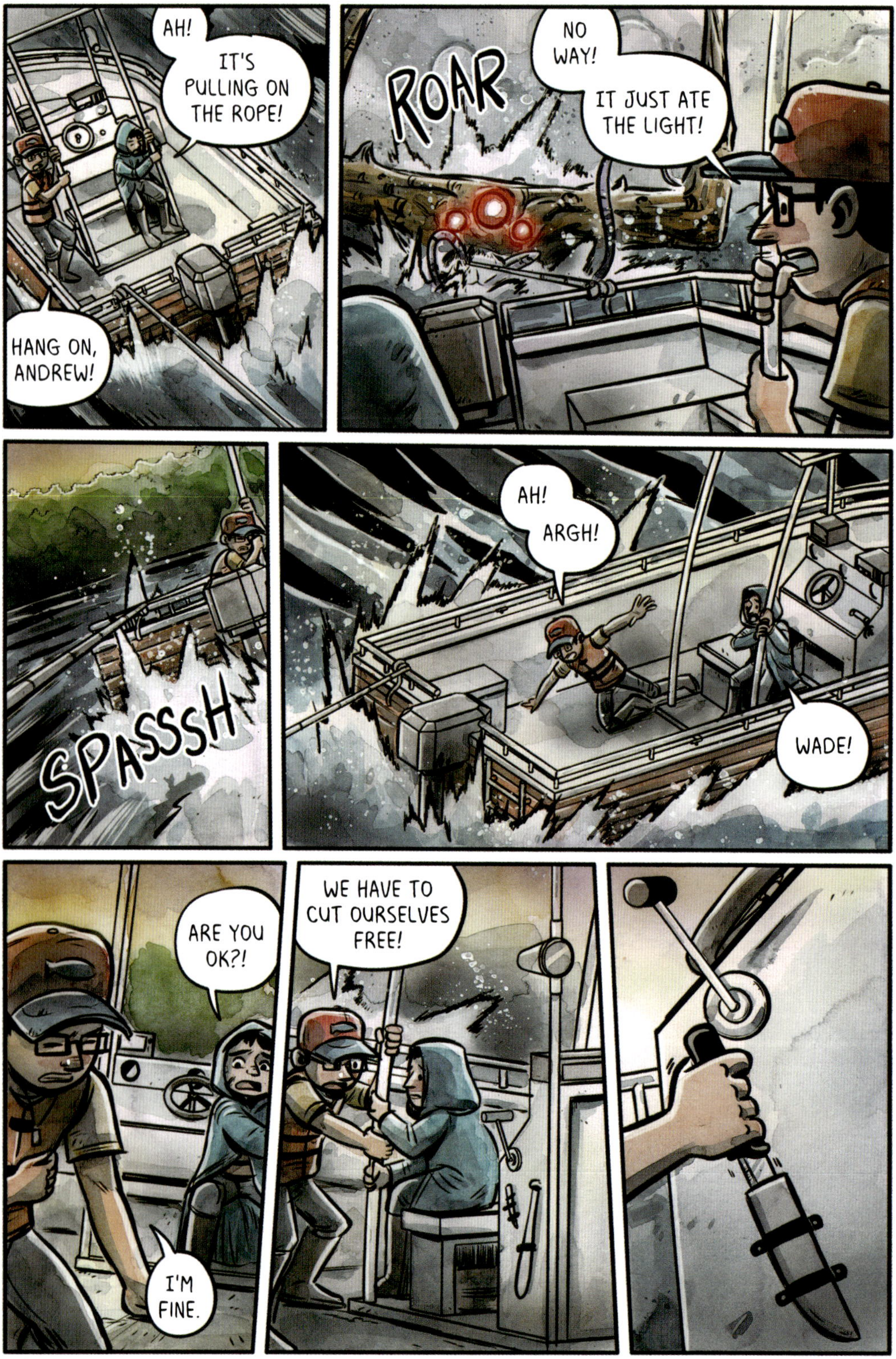
AH!
IT'S PULLING ON THE ROPE!
HANG ON, ANDREW!
ROAR
NO WAY!
IT JUST ATE THE LIGHT!
SPASSSH
AH!
ARGH!
WADE!
ARE YOU OK?!
I'M FINE.
WE HAVE TO CUT OURSELVES FREE!

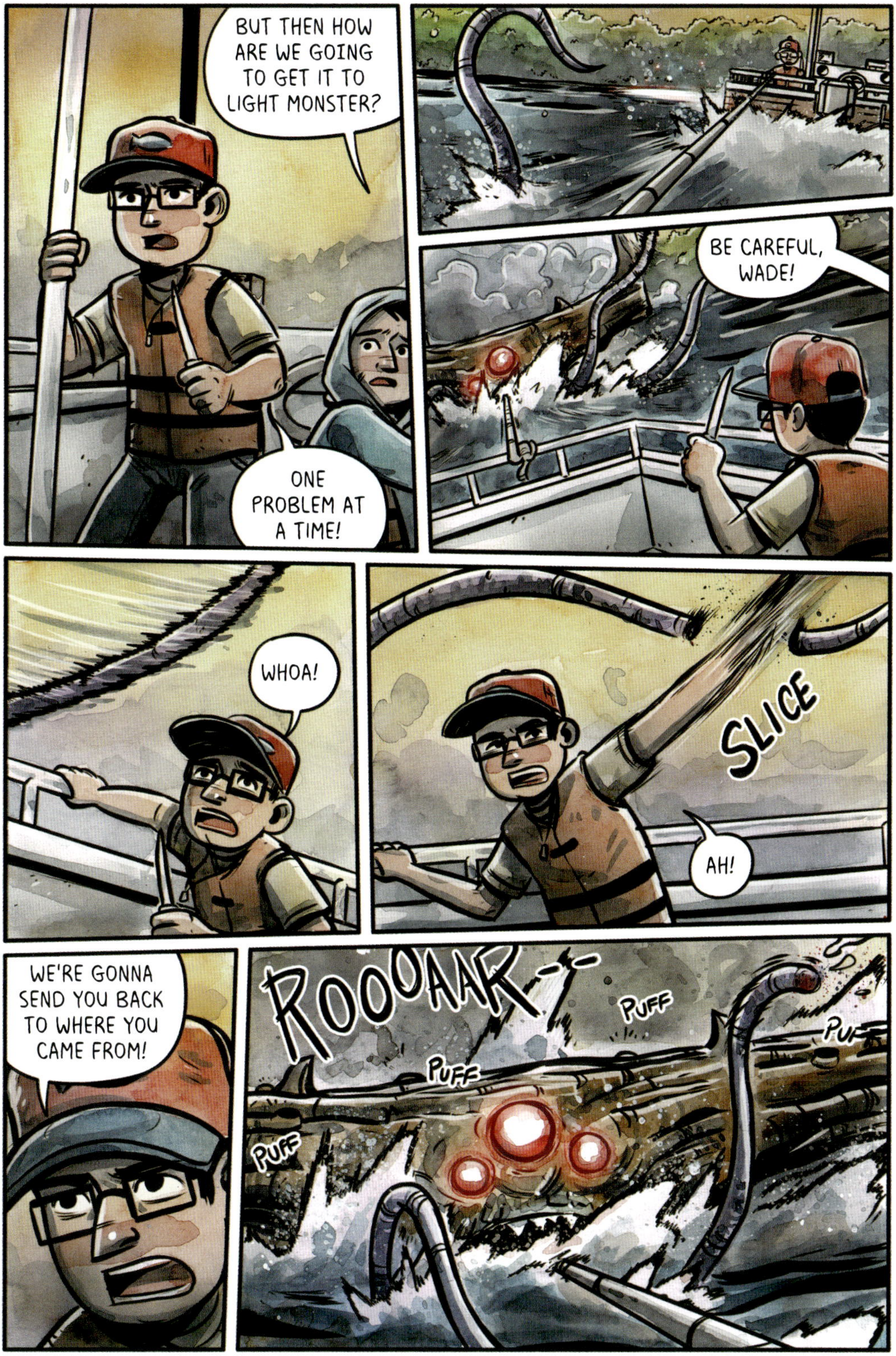
BUT THEN HOW ARE WE GOING TO GET IT TO LIGHT MONSTER?
ONE PROBLEM AT A TIME!
BE CAREFUL, WADE!
WHOA!
SLICE
AH!
WE'RE GONNA SEND YOU BACK TO WHERE YOU CAME FROM!
ROOOAAR
PUFF
PUFF
PUFF
PUFF

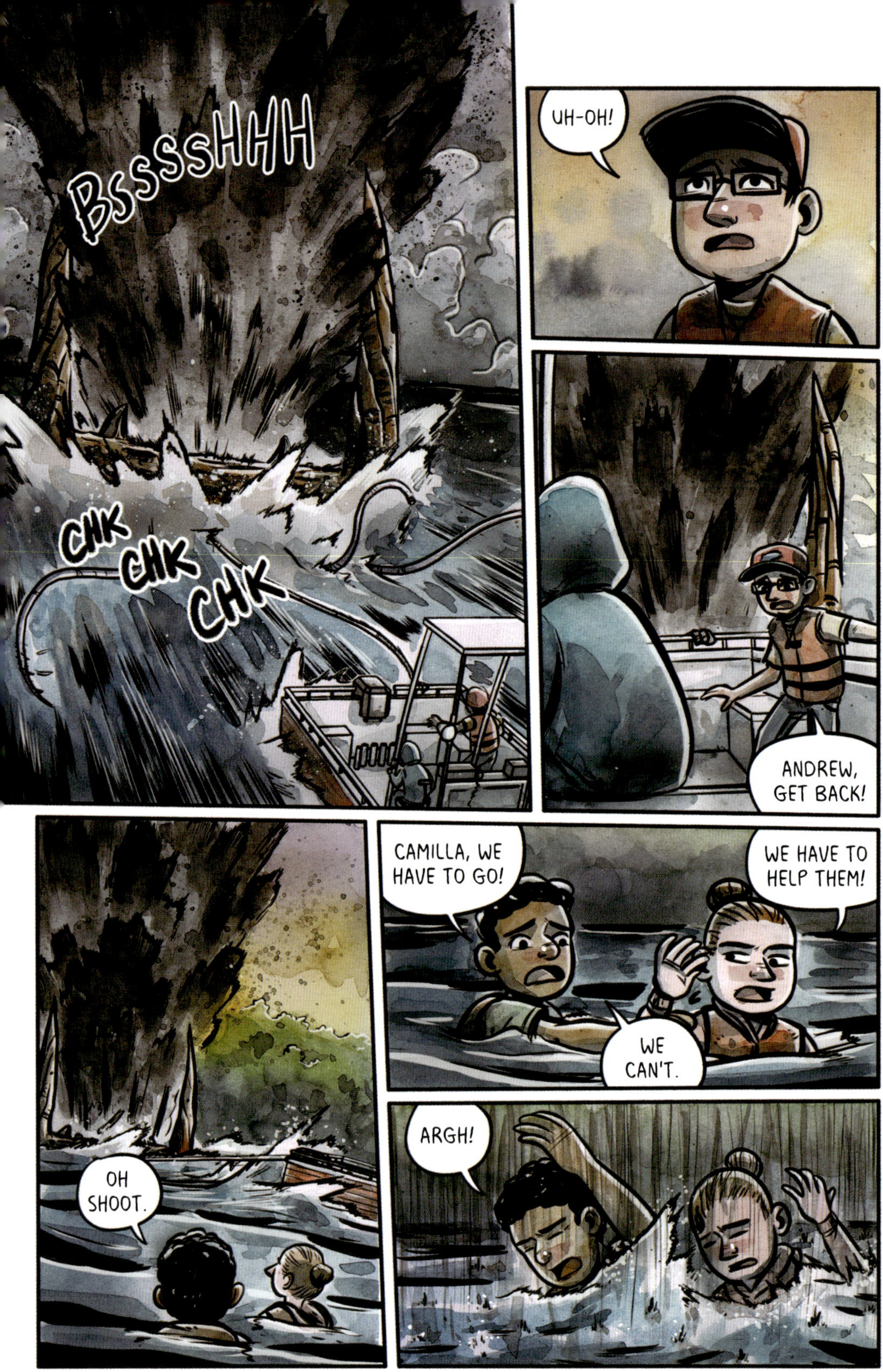
BSSSSHHH
CHK CHK CHK
UH-OH!
ANDREW, GET BACK!
OH SHOOT.
CAMILLA, WE HAVE TO GO!
WE HAVE TO HELP THEM!
WE CAN'T.
ARGH!

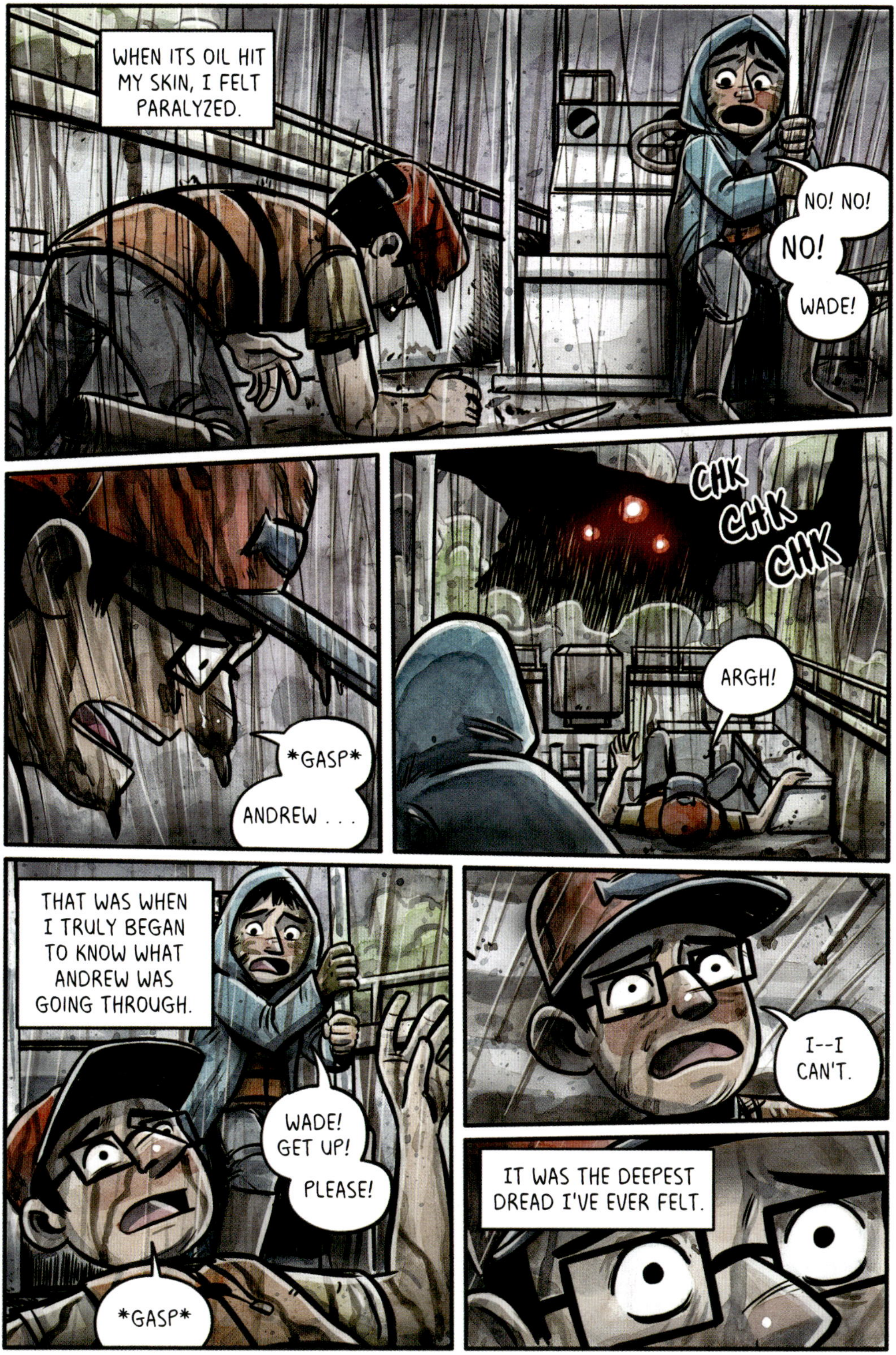
WHEN ITS OIL HIT MY SKIN, I FELT PARALYZED.
NO! NO!
NO!
WADE!
GASP
ANDREW . . .
CHK
CHK
CHK
ARGH!
THAT WAS WHEN I TRULY BEGAN TO KNOW WHAT ANDREW WAS GOING THROUGH.
WADE! GET UP!
PLEASE!
GASP
I--I CAN'T.
IT WAS THE DEEPEST DREAD I'VE EVER FELT.

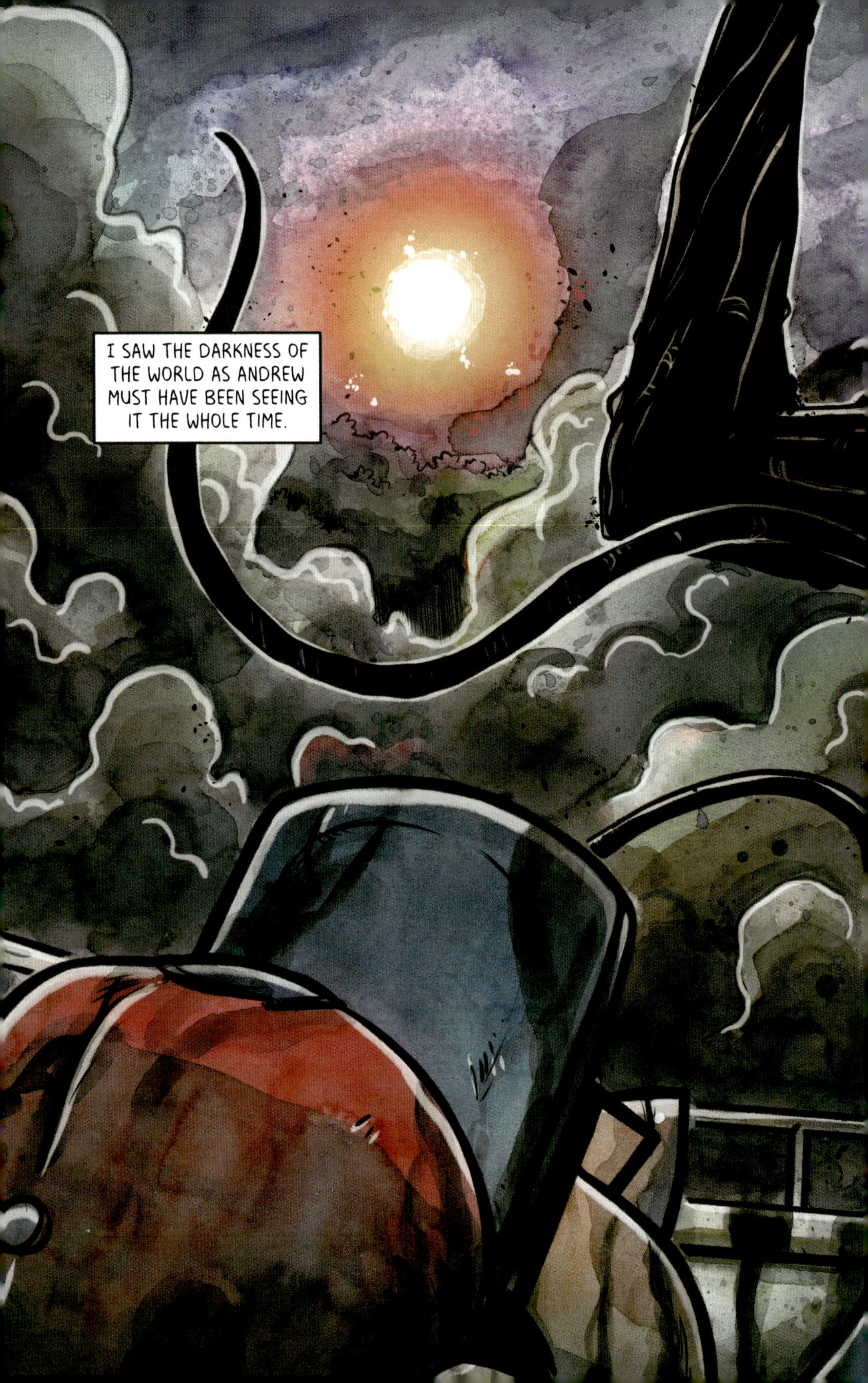
I SAW THE DARKNESS OF THE WORLD AS ANDREW MUST HAVE BEEN SEEING IT THE WHOLE TIME.

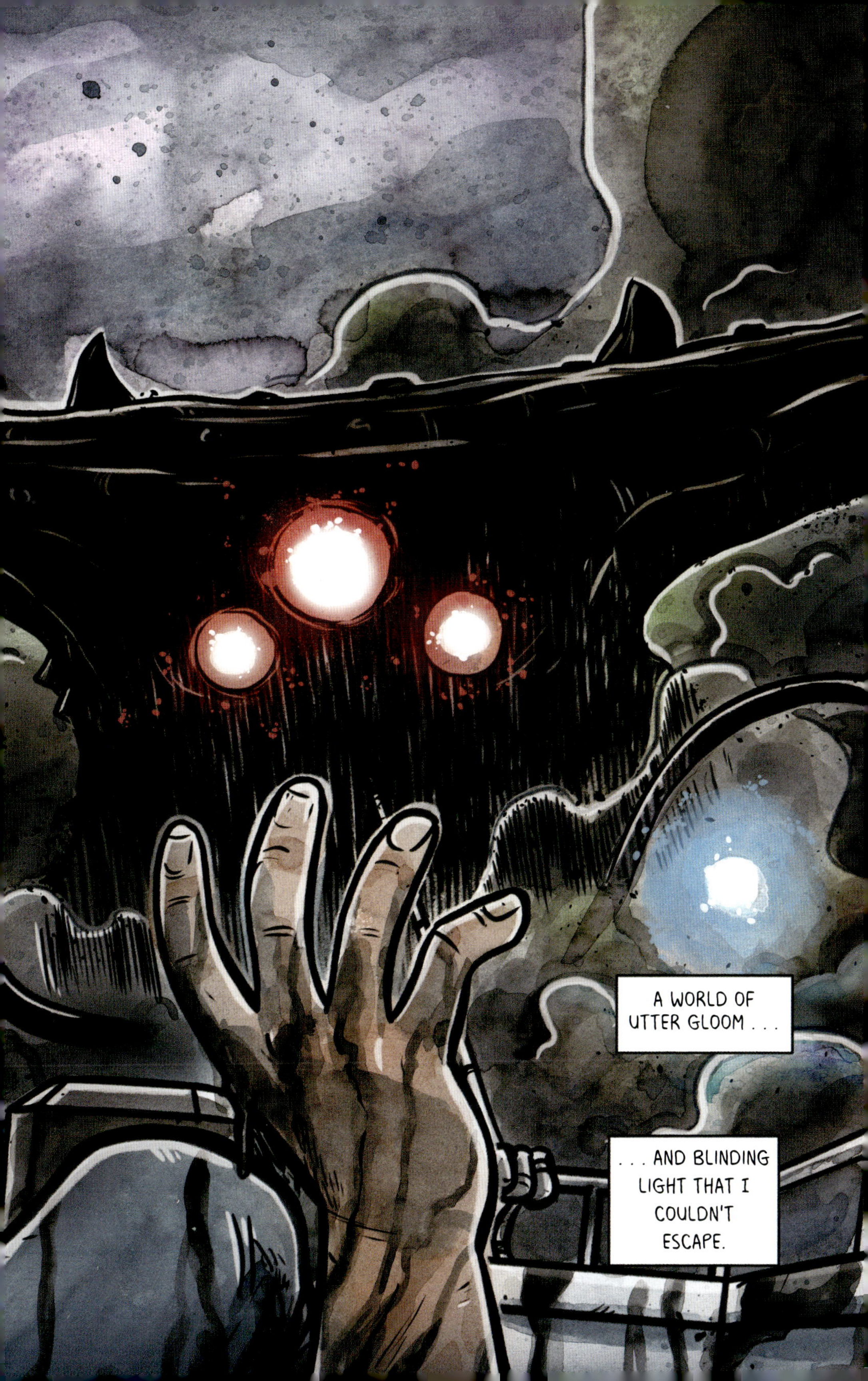
A WORLD OF UTTER GLOOM . . .
. . . AND BLINDING LIGHT THAT I COULDN'T ESCAPE.

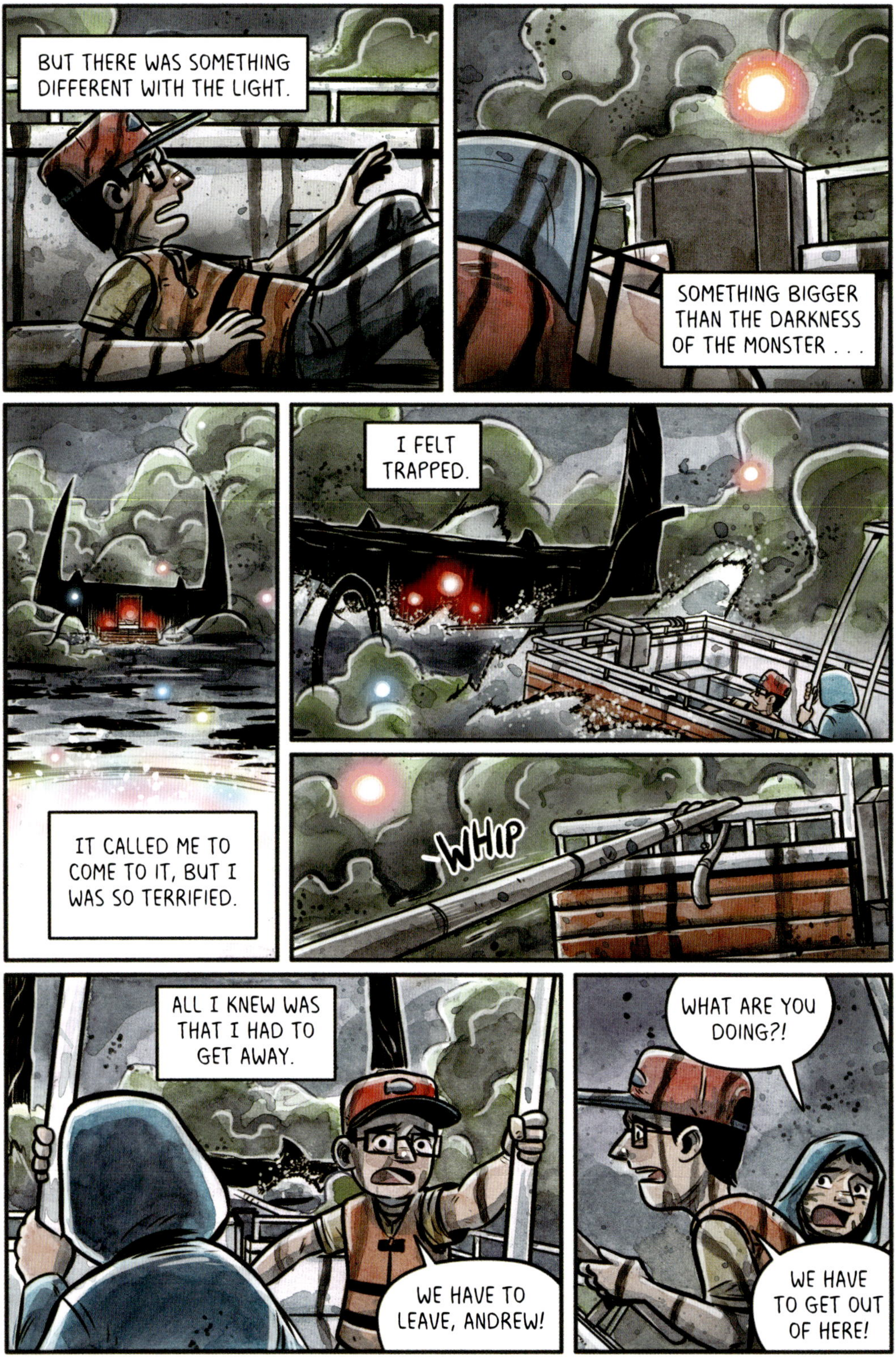
BUT THERE WAS SOMETHING DIFFERENT WITH THE LIGHT.
SOMETHING BIGGER THAN THE DARKNESS OF THE MONSTER . . .
IT CALLED ME TO COME TO IT, BUT I WAS SO TERRIFIED.
I FELT TRAPPED.
WHIP
ALL I KNEW WAS THAT I HAD TO GET AWAY.
WE HAVE TO LEAVE, ANDREW!
WHAT ARE YOU DOING?!
WE HAVE TO GET OUT OF HERE!

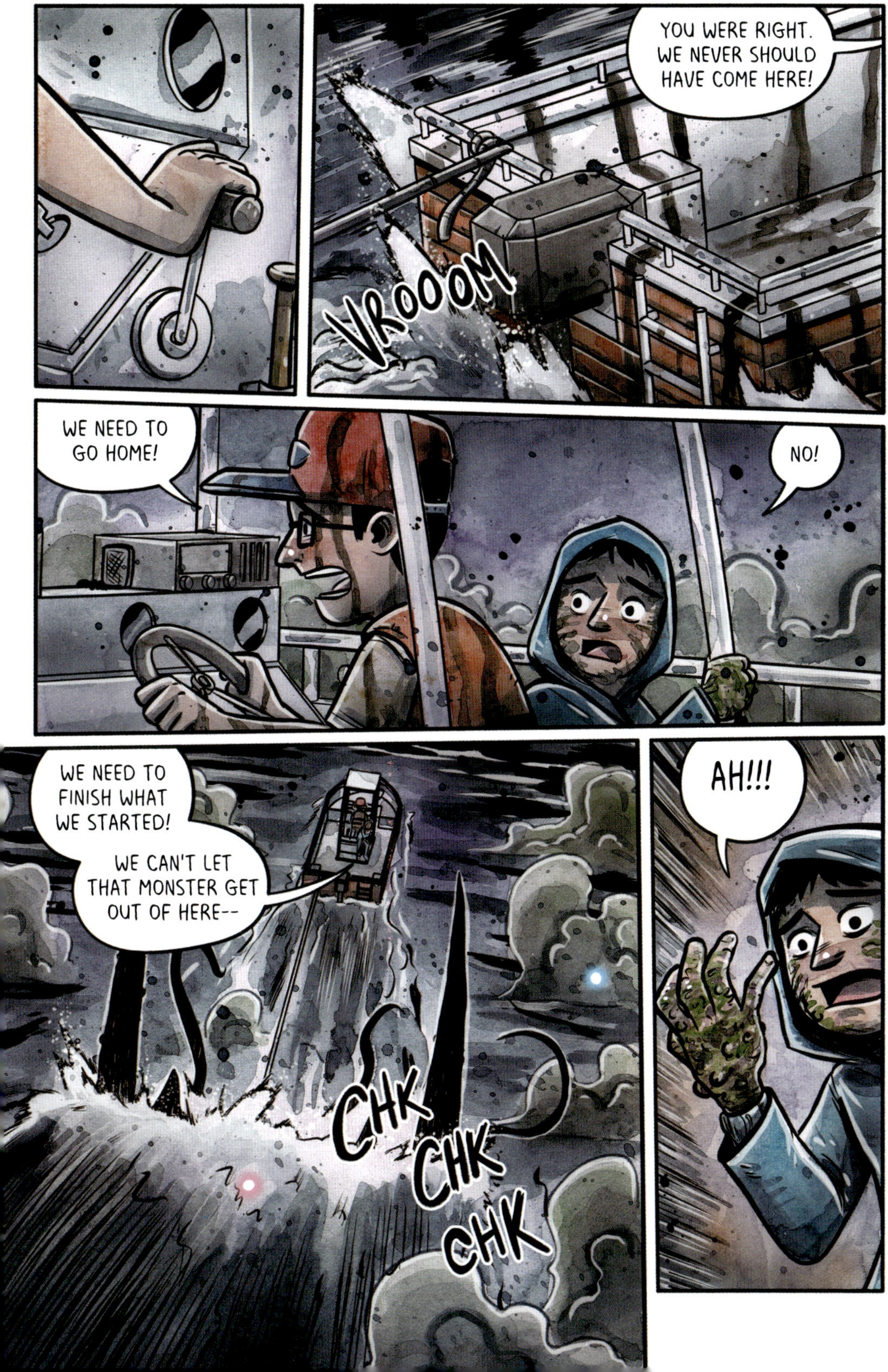
YOU WERE RIGHT. WE NEVER SHOULD HAVE COME HERE!
VROOOM
WE NEED TO GO HOME!
NO!
WE NEED TO FINISH WHAT WE STARTED!
WE CAN'T LET THAT MONSTER GET OUT OF HERE--
CHK
CHK
CHK
AH!!!

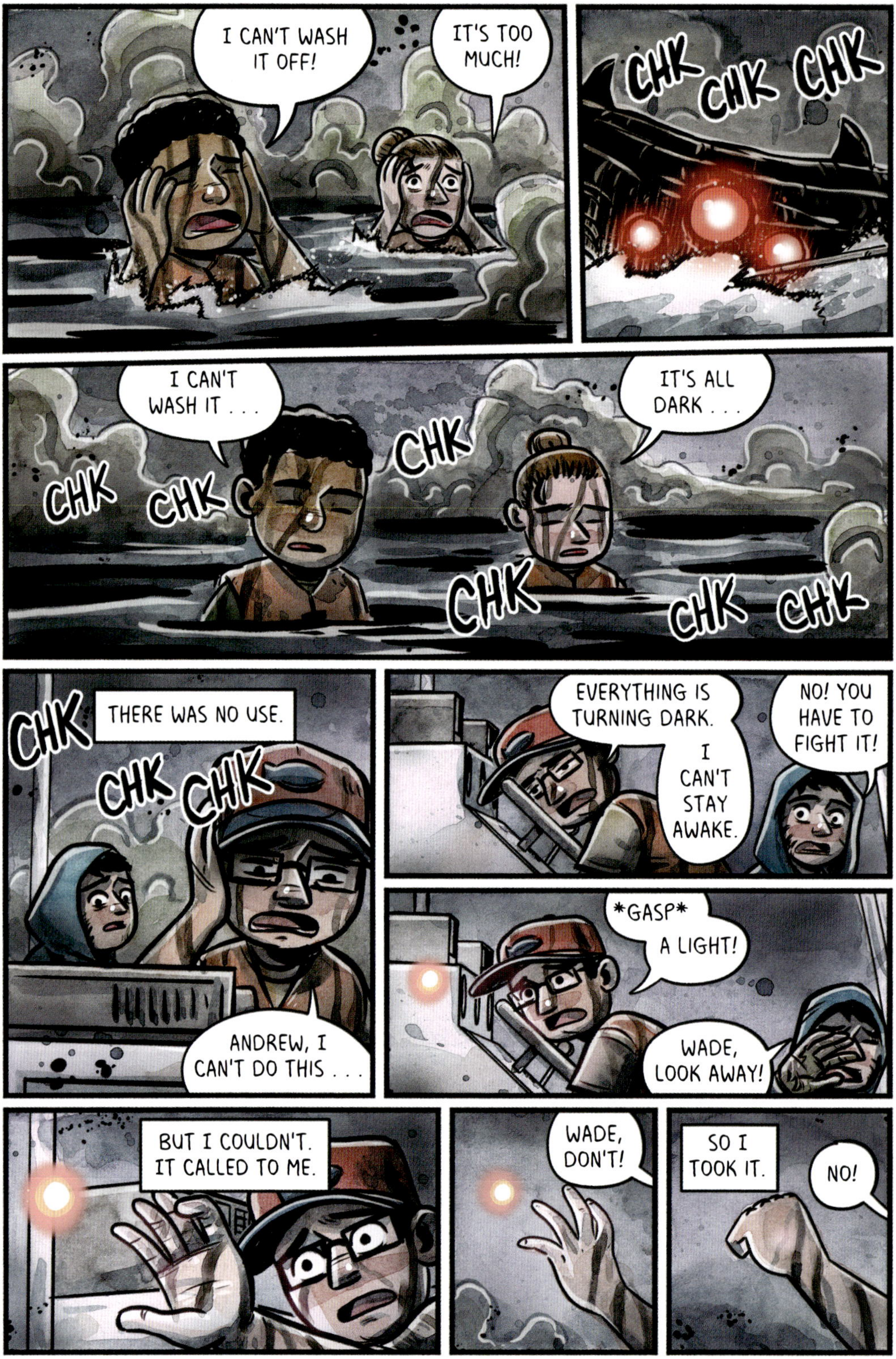
I CAN'T WASH IT OFF!
IT'S TOO MUCH!
CHK CHK CHK
I CAN'T WASH IT . . .
IT'S ALL DARK . . .
CHK CHK CHK CHK CHK CHK
CHK
THERE WAS NO USE.
CHK CHK
ANDREW, I CAN'T DO THIS . . .
EVERYTHING IS TURNING DARK.
I CAN'T STAY AWAKE.
NO! YOU HAVE TO FIGHT IT!
GASP
A LIGHT!
WADE, LOOK AWAY!
BUT I COULDN'T. IT CALLED TO ME.
WADE, DON'T!
SO I TOOK IT.
NO!

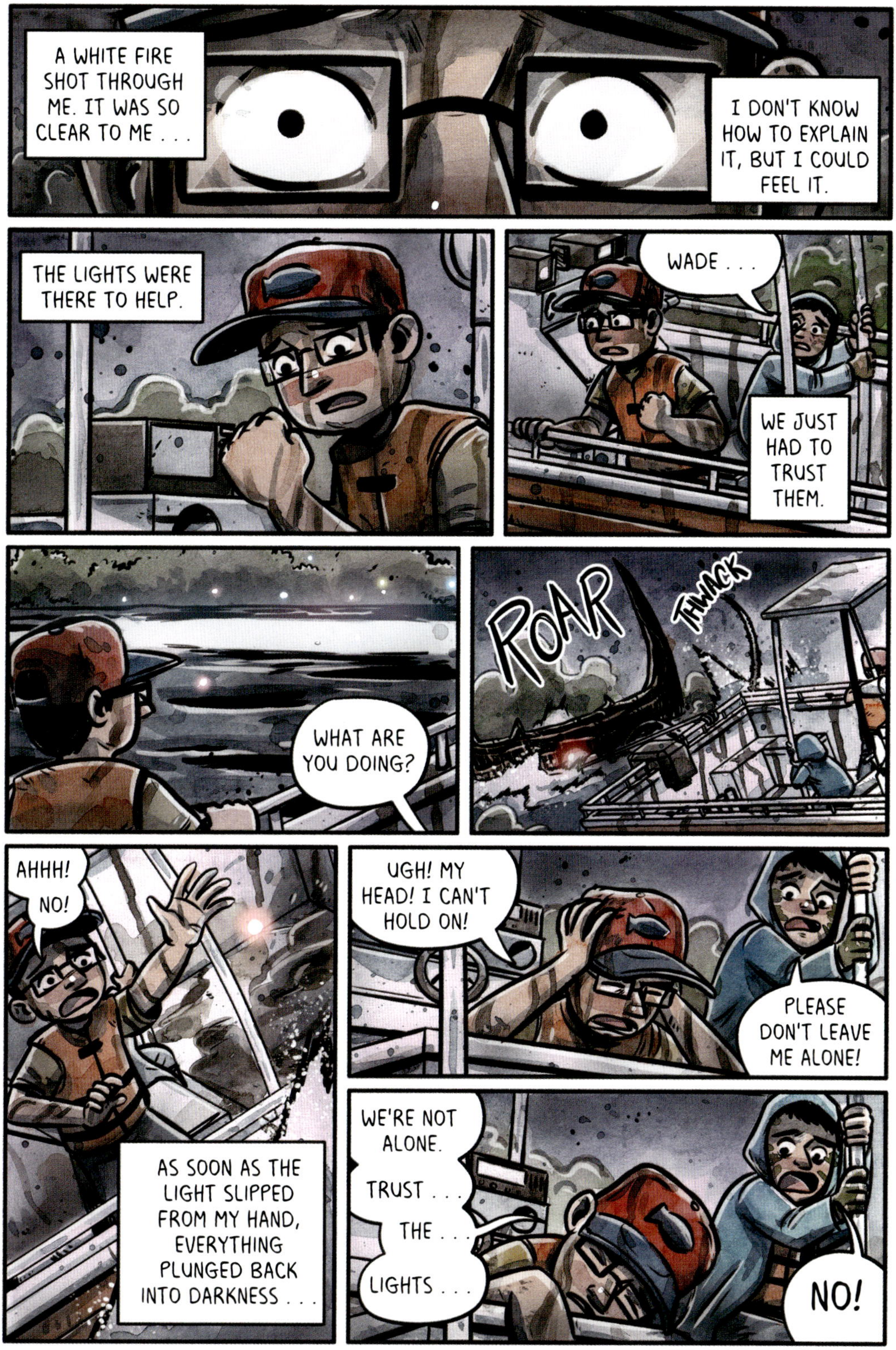

A WHITE FIRE SHOT THROUGH ME. IT WAS SO CLEAR TO ME . . .
I DON'T KNOW HOW TO EXPLAIN IT, BUT I COULD FEEL IT.
THE LIGHTS WERE THERE TO HELP.
WADE . . .
WE JUST HAD TO TRUST THEM.
WHAT ARE YOU DOING?
ROAR
THWACK
AHHH! NO!
AS SOON AS THE LIGHT SLIPPED FROM MY HAND, EVERYTHING PLUNGED BACK INTO DARKNESS . . .
UGH! MY HEAD! I CAN'T HOLD ON!
PLEASE DON'T LEAVE ME ALONE!
WE'RE NOT ALONE.
TRUST . . .
THE . . .
LIGHTS . . .
NO!

I CAN'T DO THIS! I NEED YOU!
CHK
CHK
CHK
CHK
CHK
CHK
ARGH!
MY HEAD!
OK, LIGHTS.
I DON'T KNOW IF YOU'RE GOOD.
BUT IF YOU ARE, PLEASE . . .
. . . HELP ME!
GASP

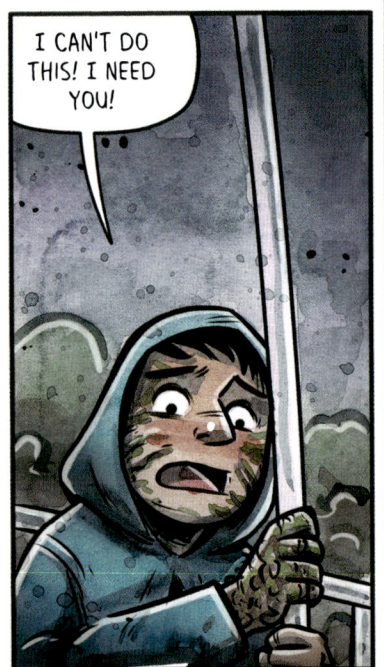

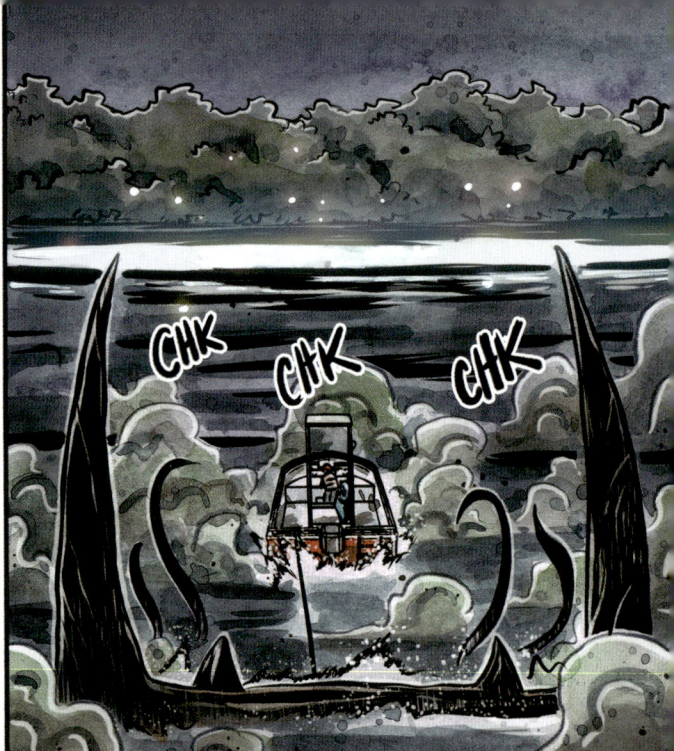

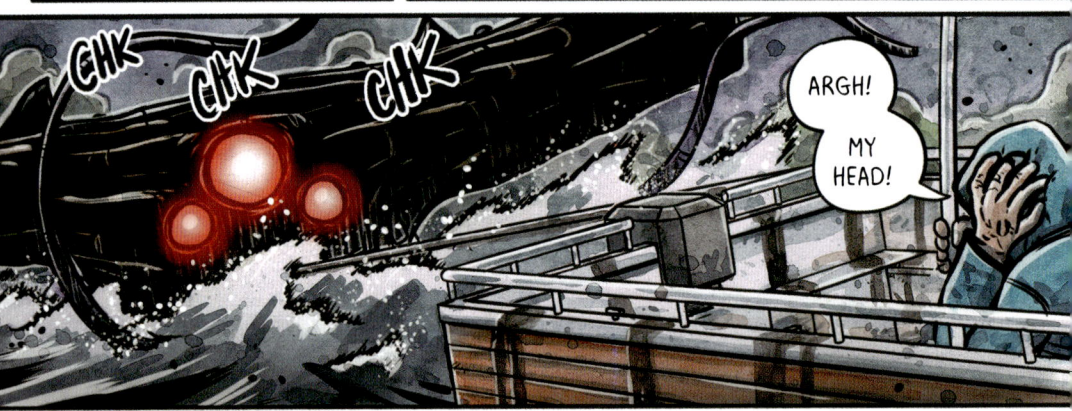

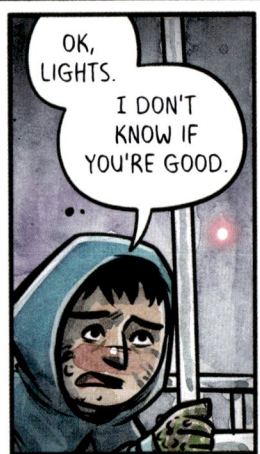

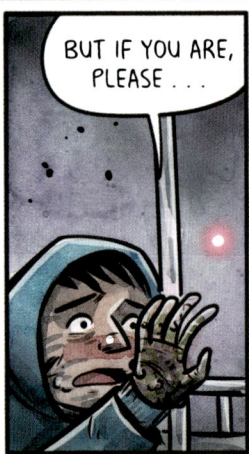

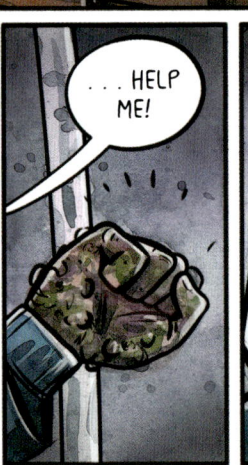

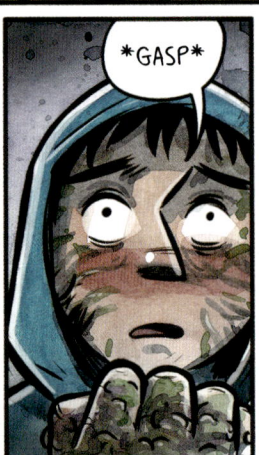

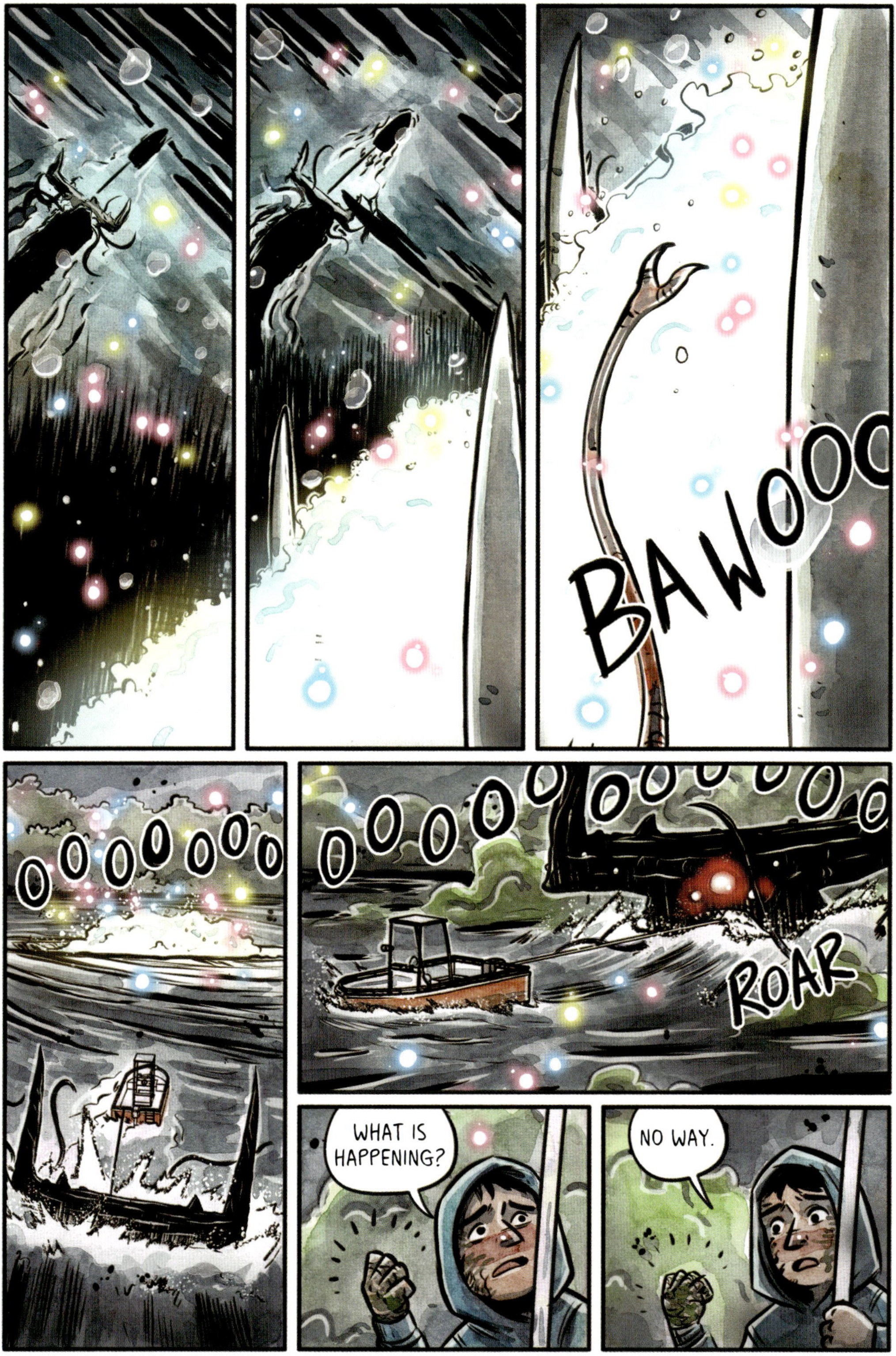
BAWOOO
OOOOOOO
OOOOOOOOOOO
ROAR
WHAT IS HAPPENING?
NO WAY.

GASP
NO!
I CAN'T COME TO YOU.
I'LL DROWN LIKE ALL THE OTHERS WHO'VE TRIED.
BAWOOOOOOOO
FWOOOSH

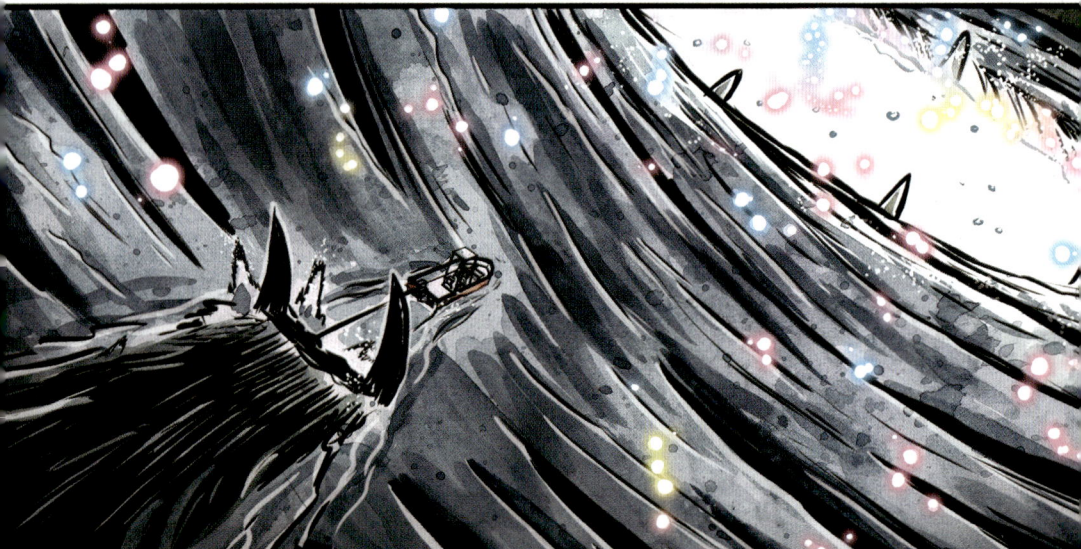

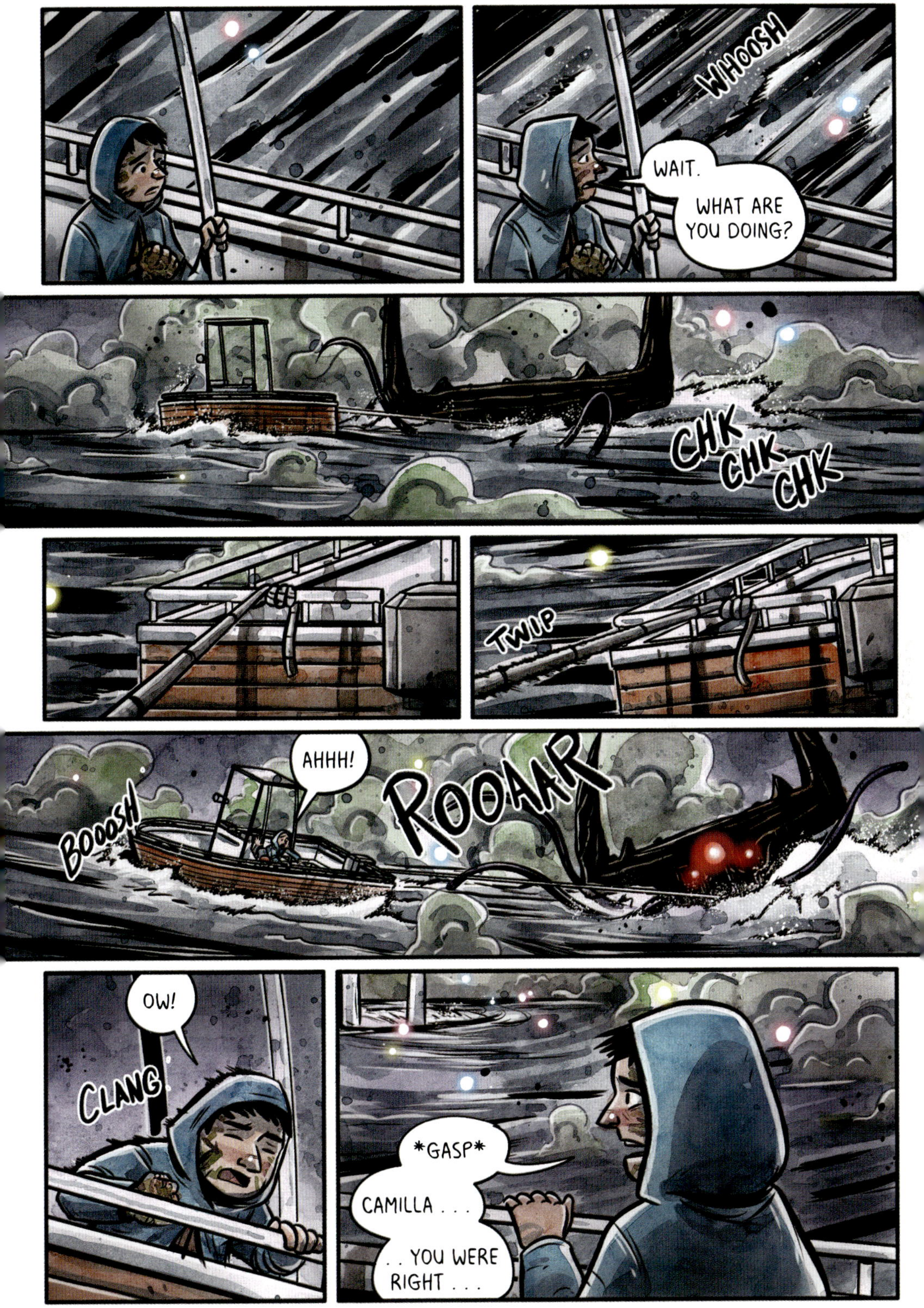
WHOOSH
WAIT.
WHAT ARE YOU DOING?
CHK CHK CHK
TWIP
AHHH!
BOOOSH
ROOAAR
OW!
CLANG
GASP
CAMILLA . . .
. . YOU WERE RIGHT . . .

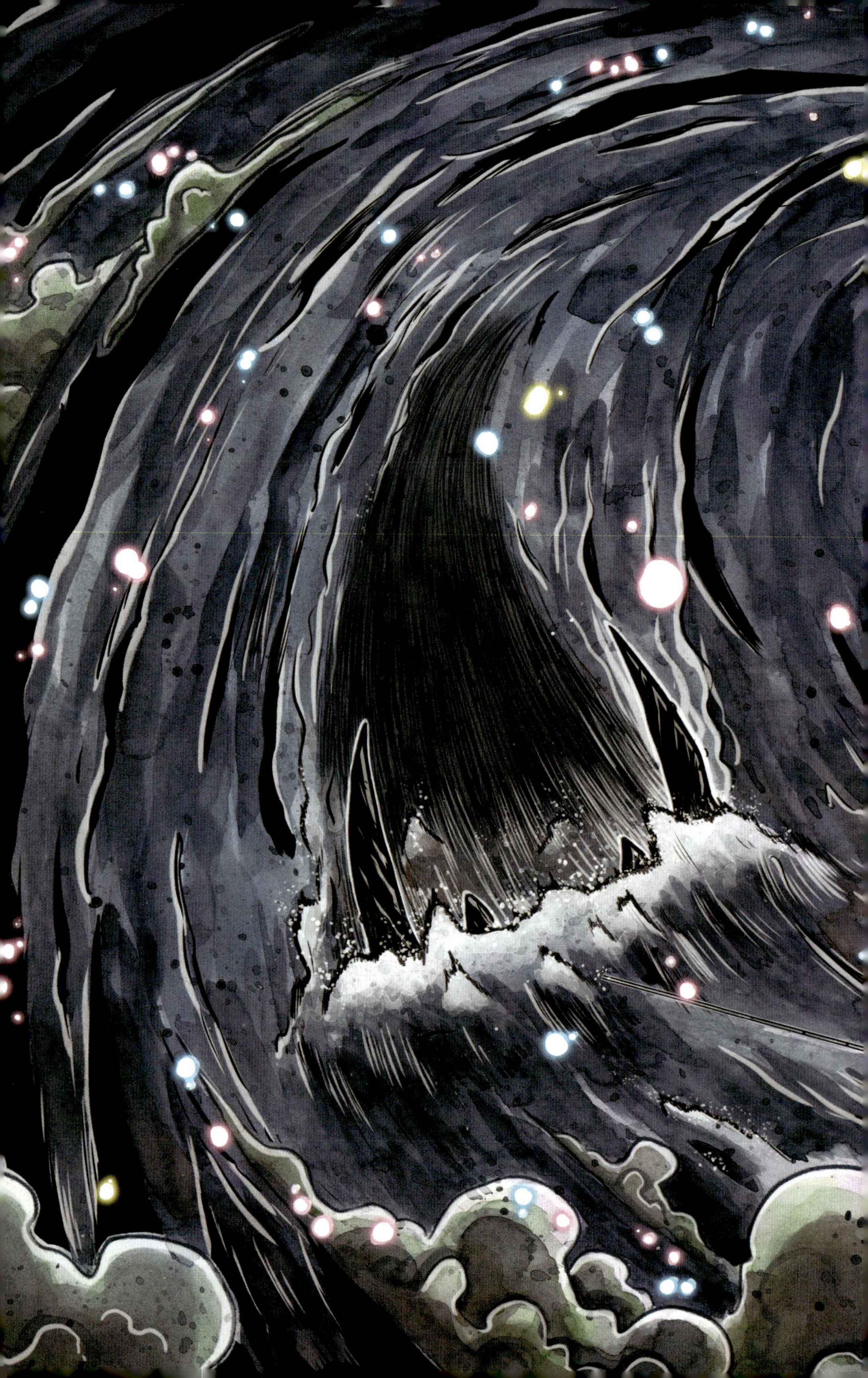

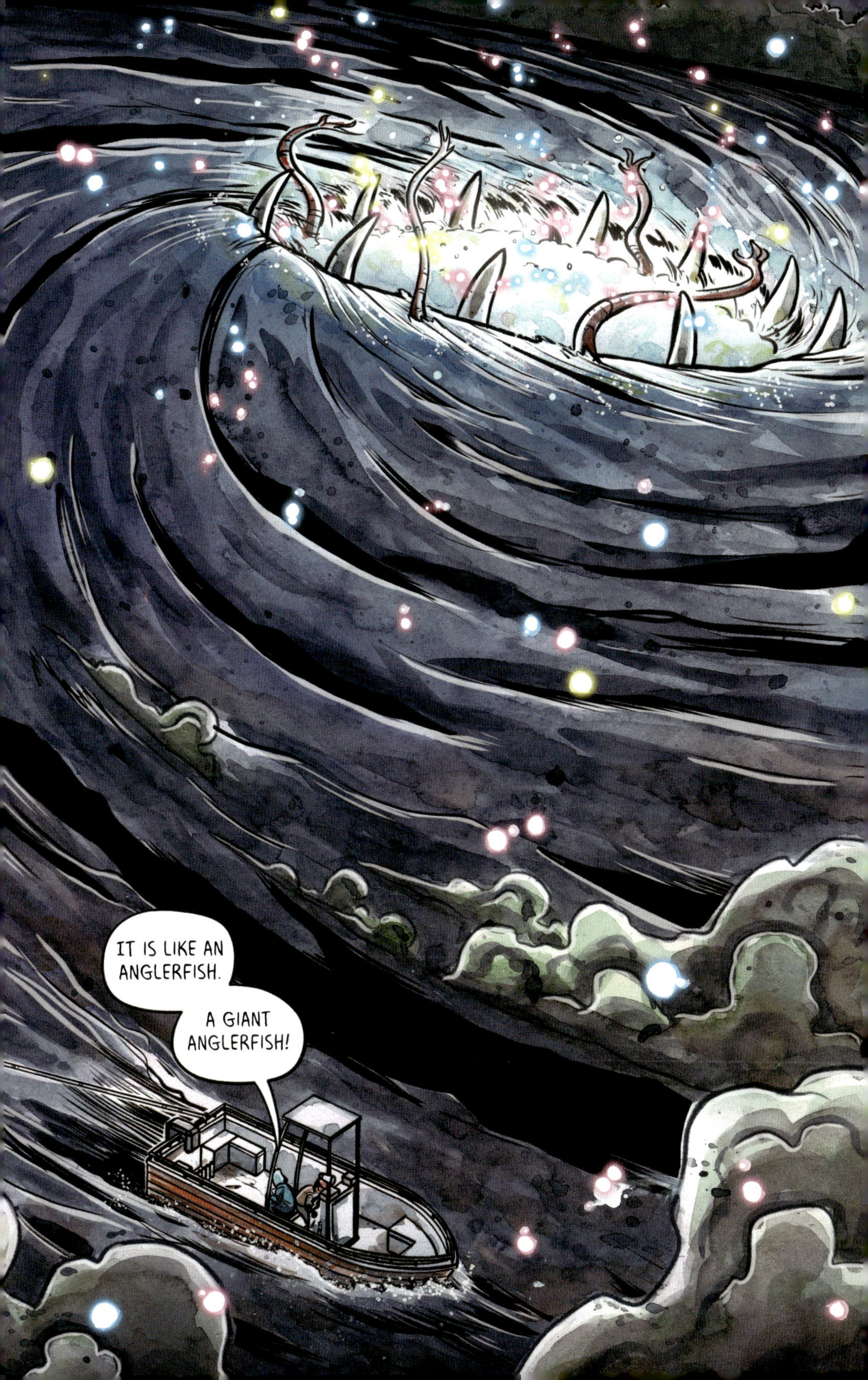
IT IS LIKE AN ANGLERFISH.
A GIANT ANGLERFISH!

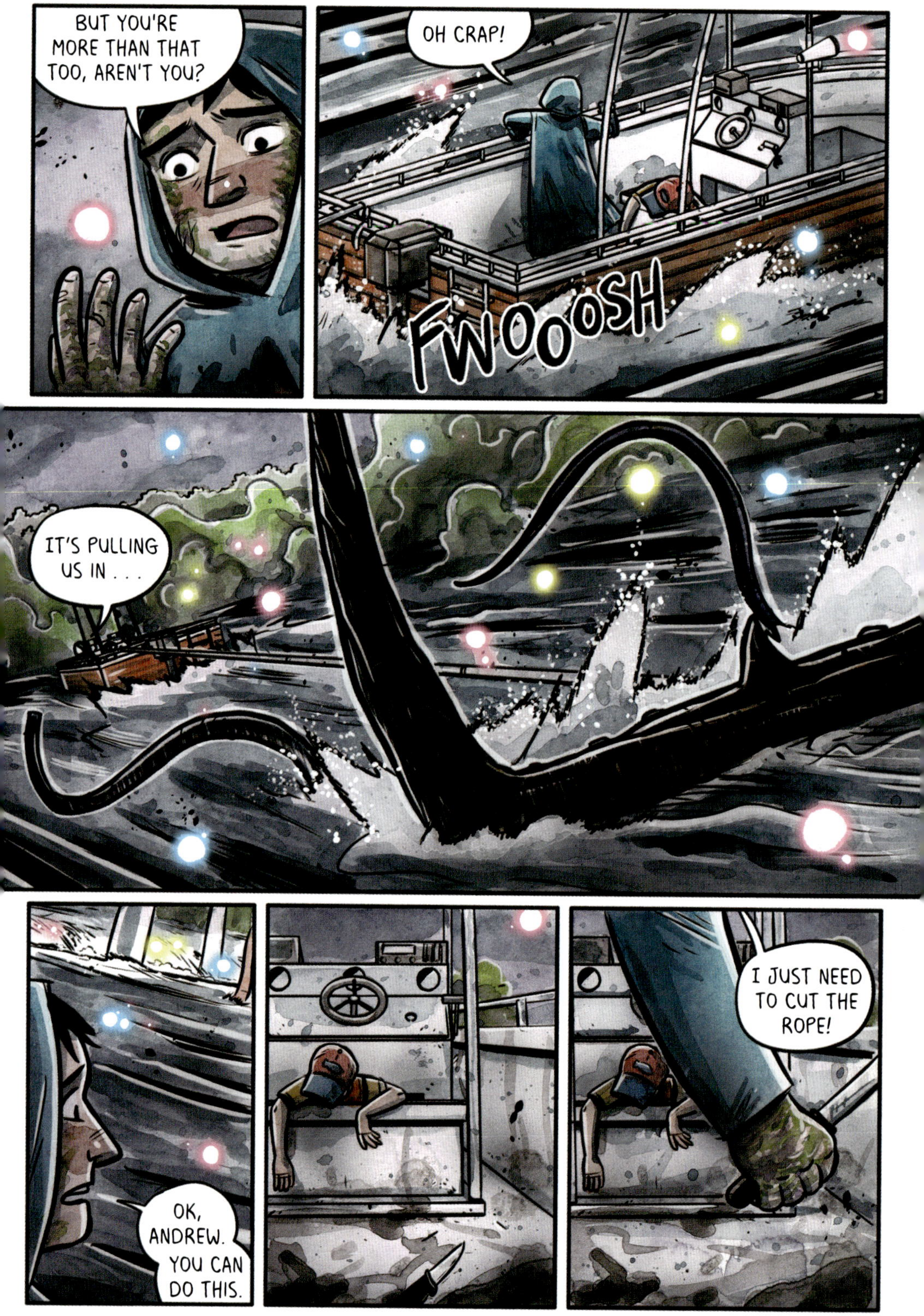
BUT YOU'RE MORE THAN THAT TOO, AREN'T YOU?
OH CRAP!
FWOOOSH
IT'S PULLING US IN . . .
OK, ANDREW. YOU CAN DO THIS.
I JUST NEED TO CUT THE ROPE!

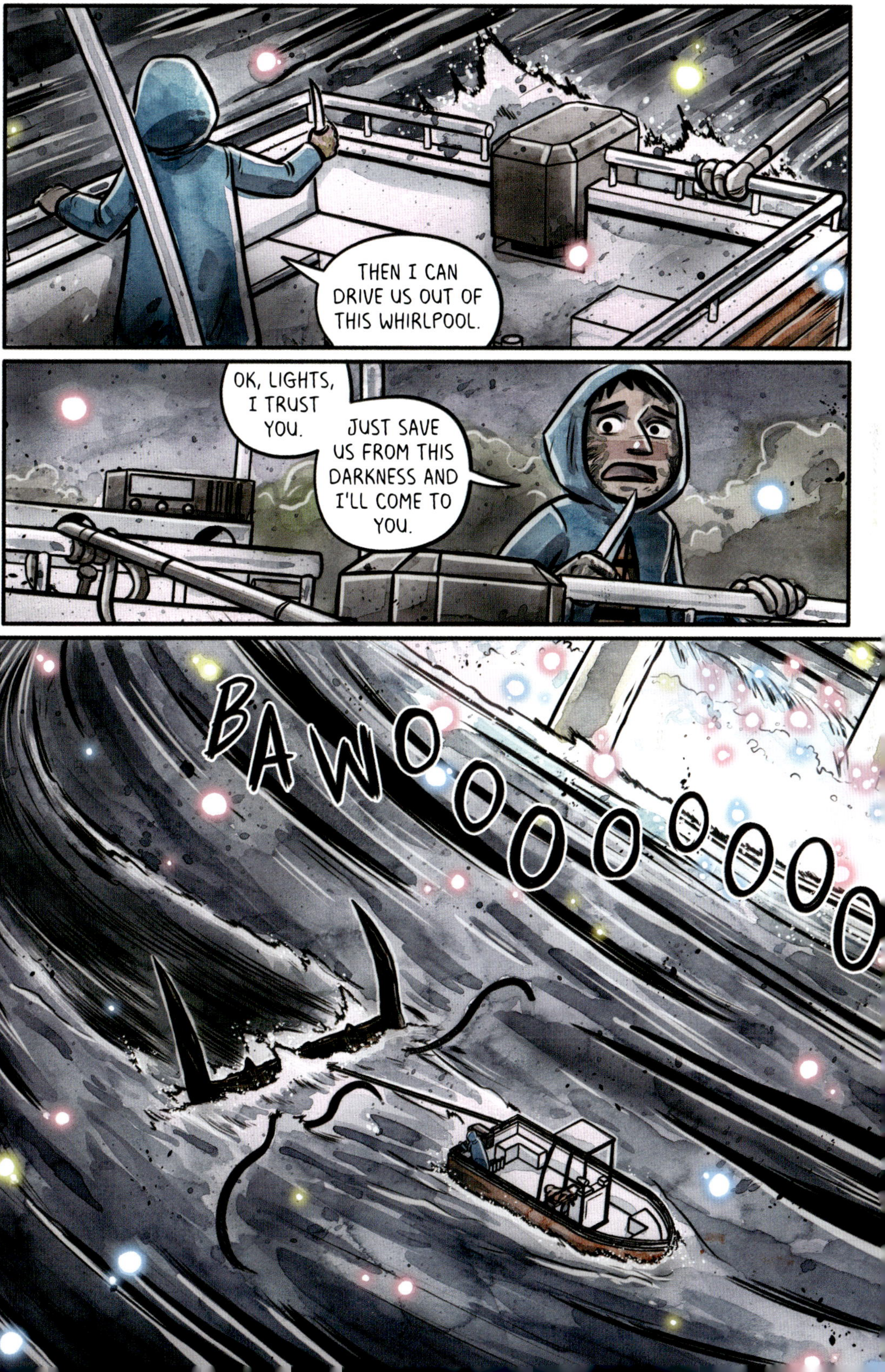
THEN I CAN DRIVE US OUT OF THIS WHIRLPOOL.
OK, LIGHTS, I TRUST YOU.
JUST SAVE US FROM THIS DARKNESS AND I'LL COME TO YOU.
BAWOOOOOOOO

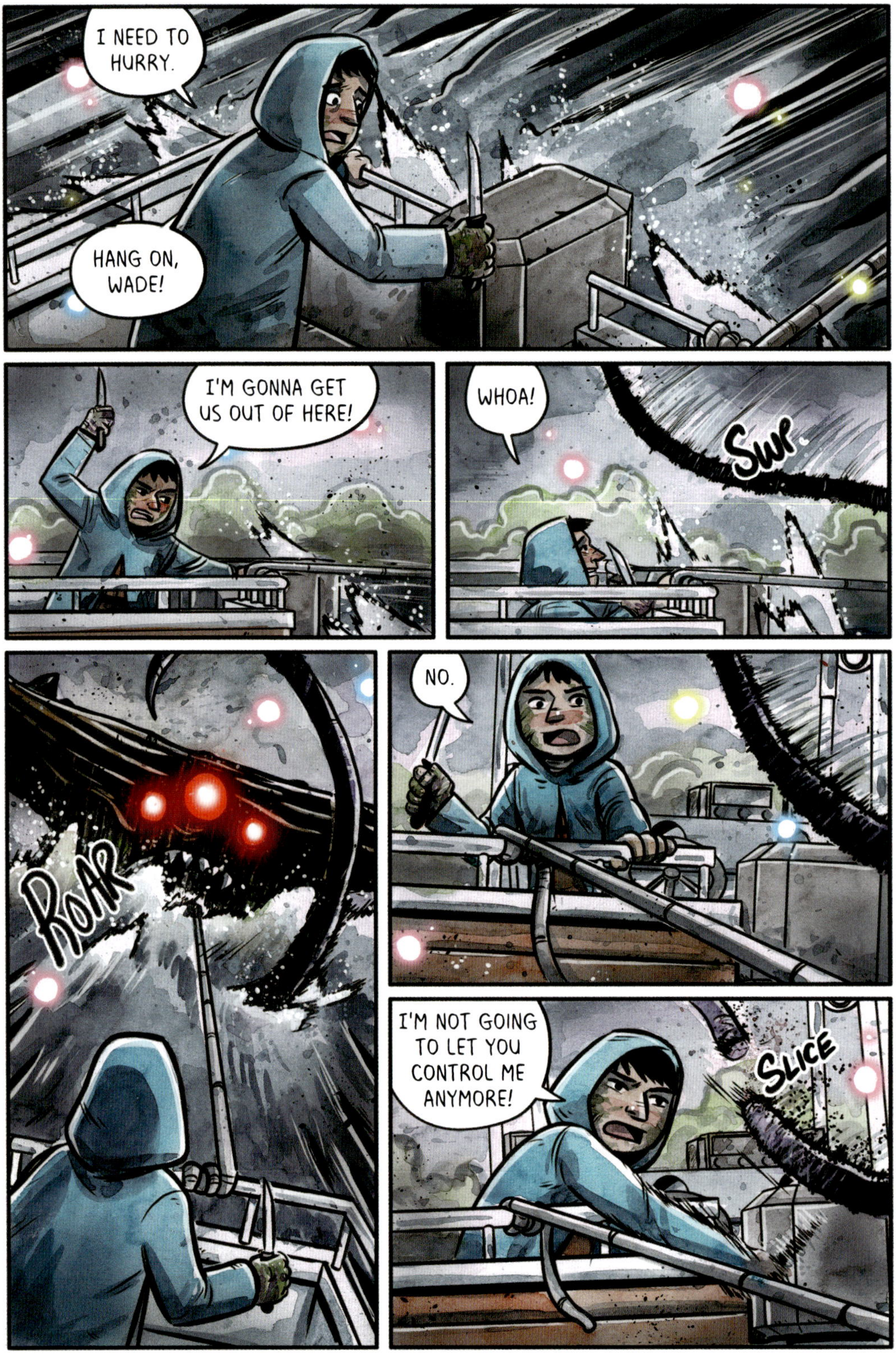
I NEED TO HURRY.
HANG ON, WADE!
I'M GONNA GET US OUT OF HERE!
WHOA!
SWP
ROAR
NO.
I'M NOT GOING TO LET YOU CONTROL ME ANYMORE!
SLICE

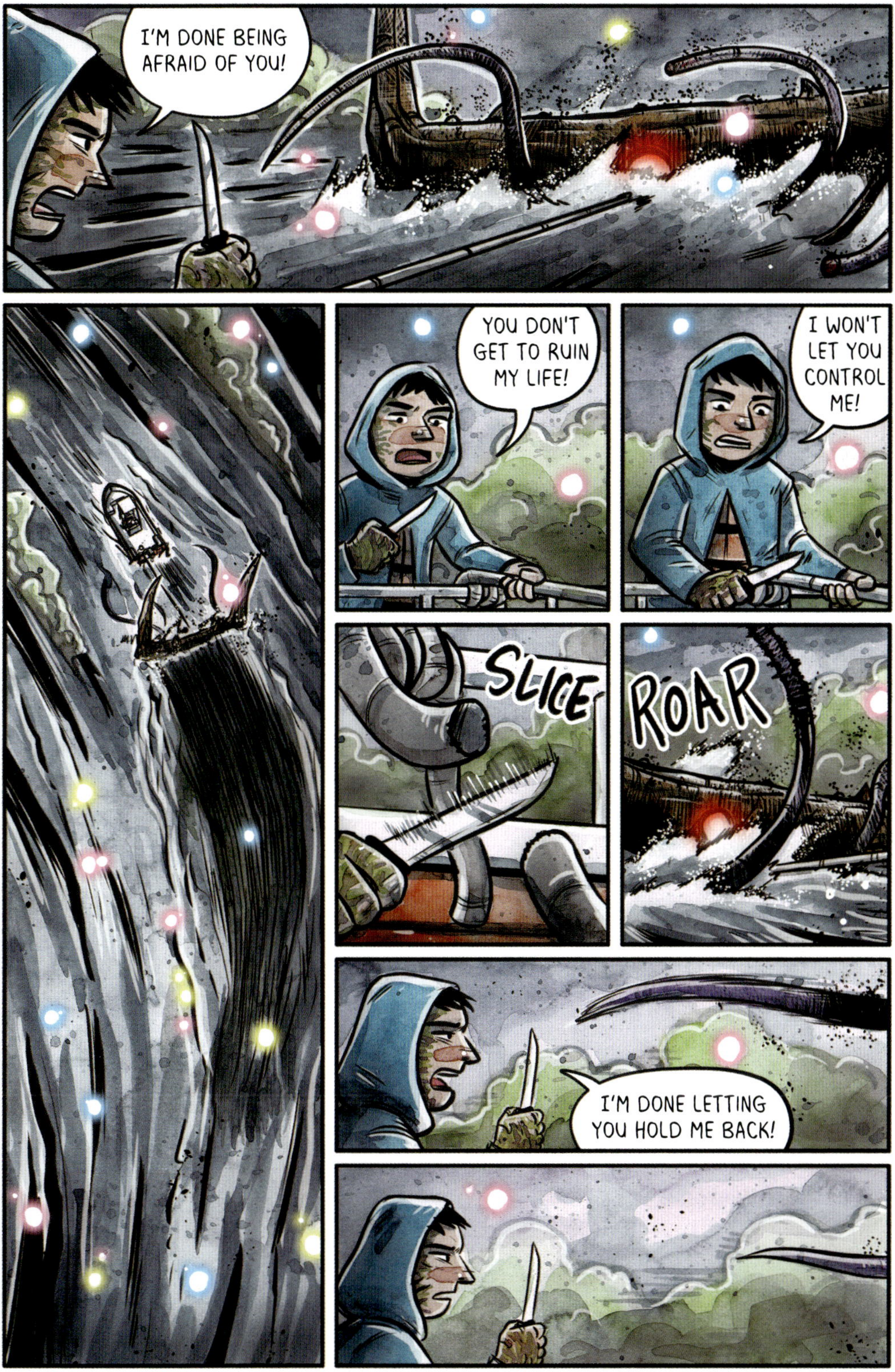

I'M DONE BEING AFRAID OF YOU!
YOU DON'T GET TO RUIN MY LIFE!
I WON'T LET YOU CONTROL ME!
SLICE
ROAR
I'M DONE LETTING YOU HOLD ME BACK!

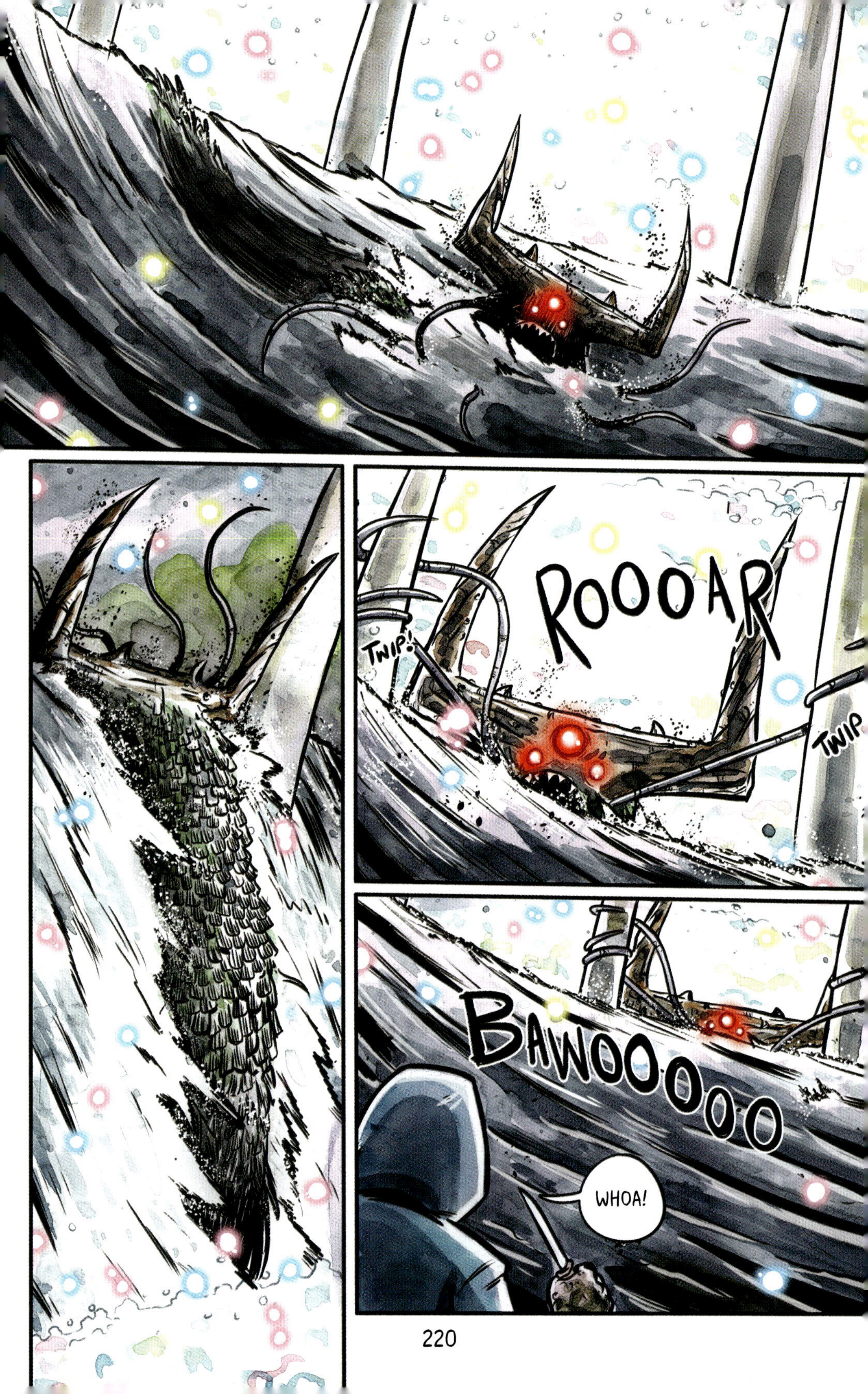
ROOOAR
TWIP!
TWIP
BAWOOOOOO
WHOA!

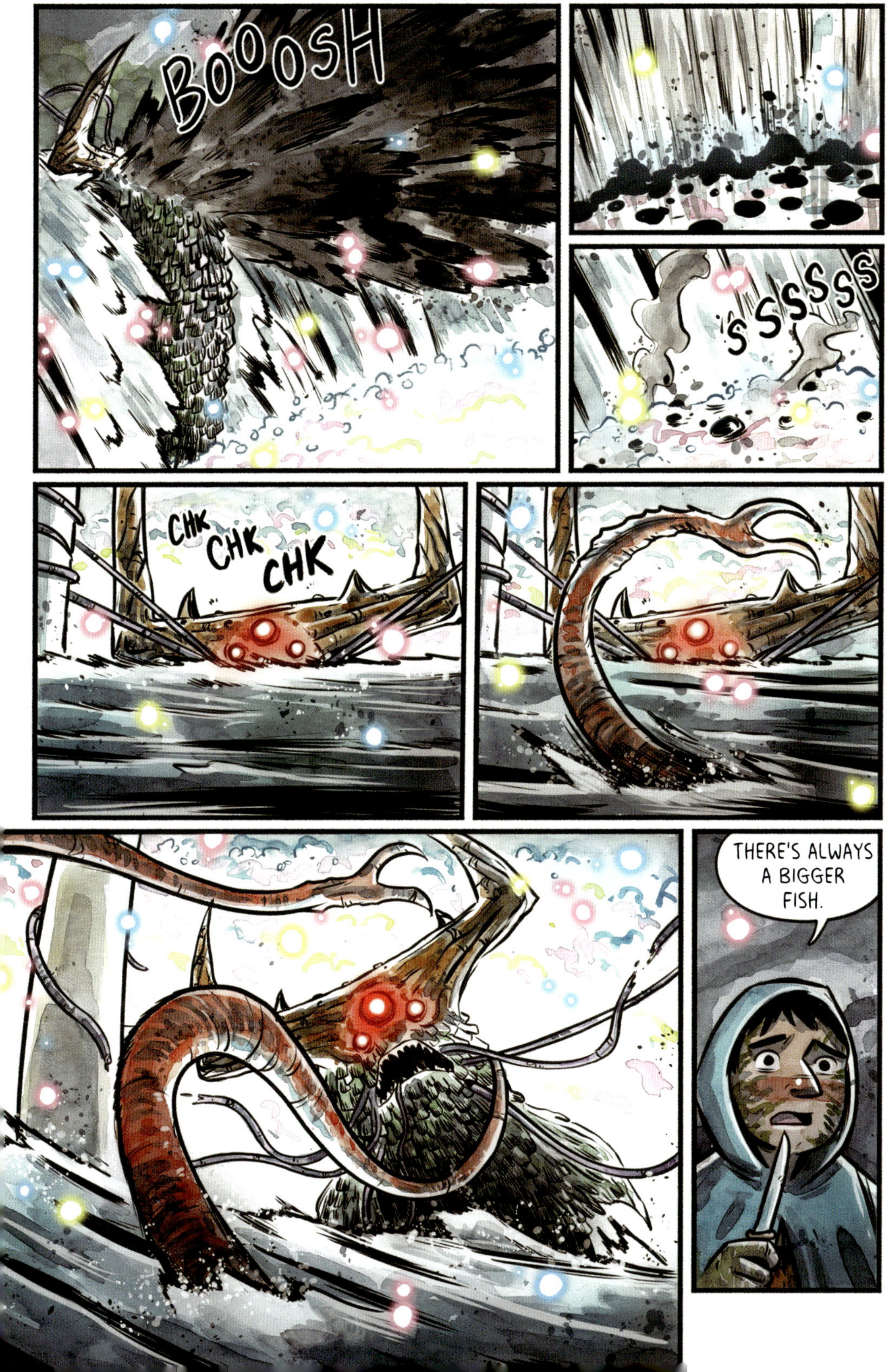
BOOOSH
SSSSSS
CHK CHK CHK
THERE'S ALWAYS A BIGGER FISH.

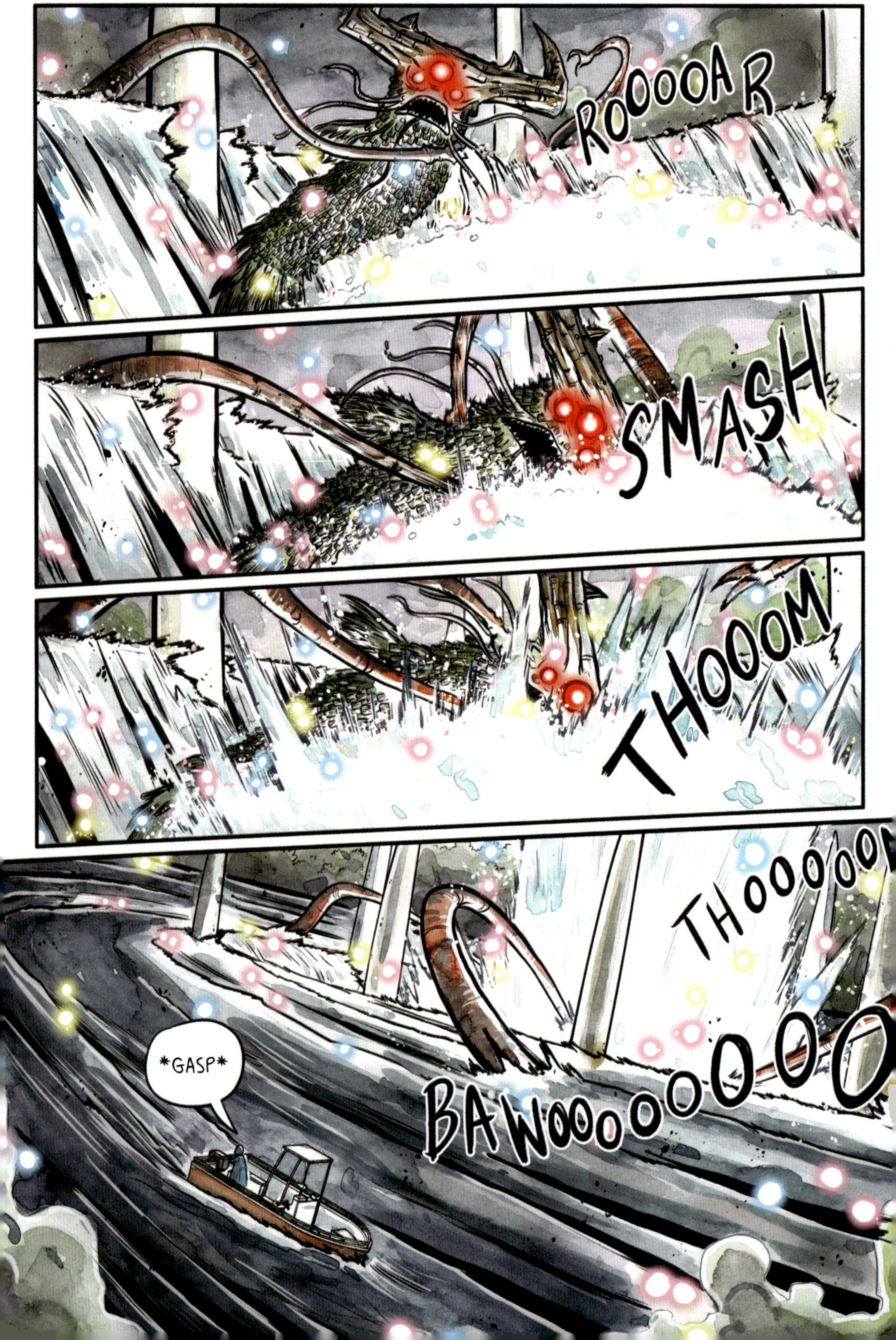
ROOOOAR
SMASH
THOOOM
THOOOOOO
BAWOOOOOOOOO
GASP

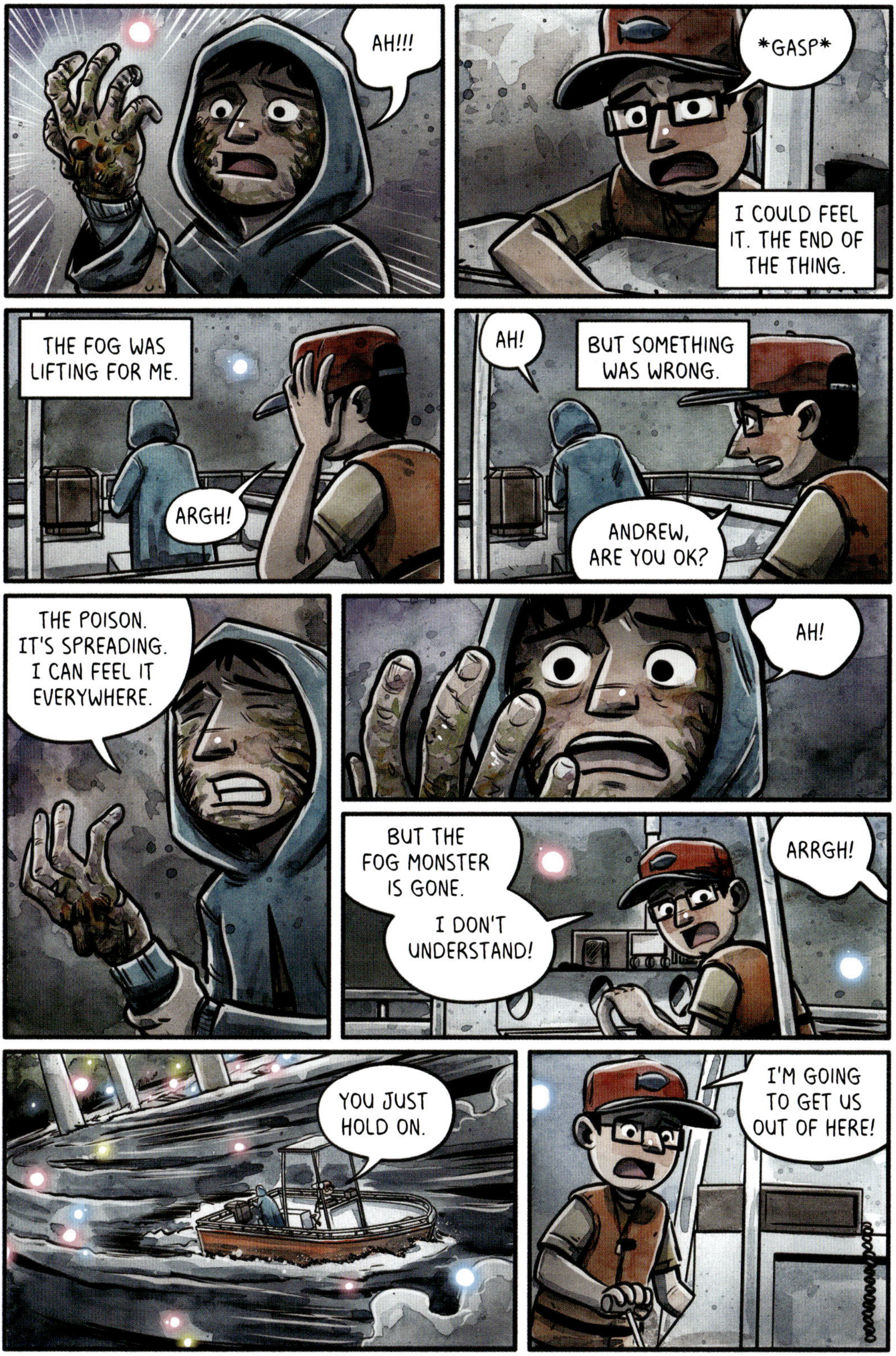
AH!!!
GASP
I COULD FEEL IT. THE END OF THE THING.
THE FOG WAS LIFTING FOR ME.
ARGH!
AH!
BUT SOMETHING WAS WRONG.
ANDREW, ARE YOU OK?
THE POISON. IT'S SPREADING. I CAN FEEL IT EVERYWHERE.
AH!
BUT THE FOG MONSTER IS GONE.
I DON'T UNDERSTAND!
ARRGH!
YOU JUST HOLD ON.
I'M GOING TO GET US OUT OF HERE!

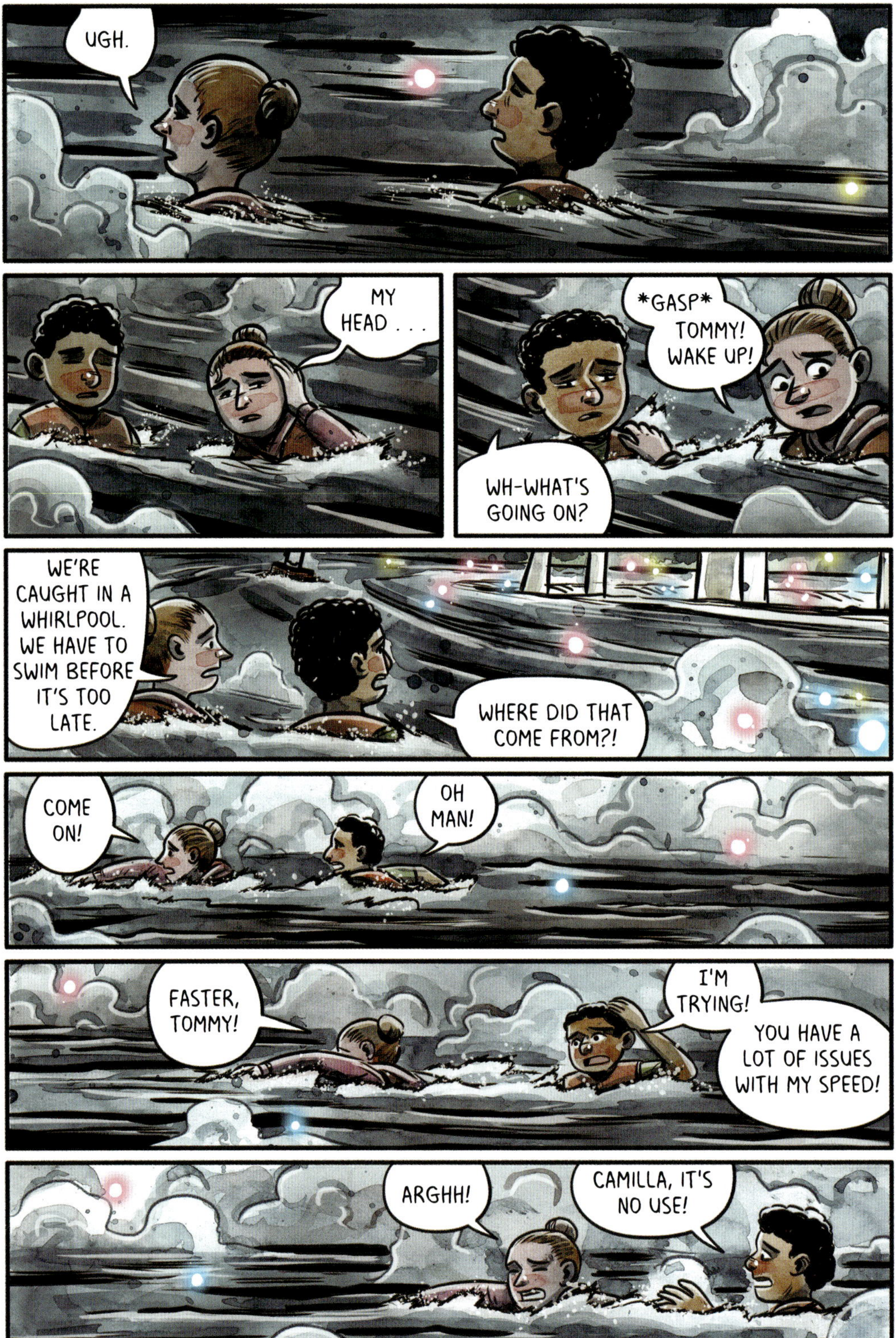
UGH.
MY HEAD . . .
GASP TOMMY! WAKE UP!
WH-WHAT'S GOING ON?
WE'RE CAUGHT IN A WHIRLPOOL. WE HAVE TO SWIM BEFORE IT'S TOO LATE.
WHERE DID THAT COME FROM?!
COME ON!
OH MAN!
FASTER, TOMMY!
I'M TRYING!
YOU HAVE A LOT OF ISSUES WITH MY SPEED!
ARGHH!
CAMILLA, IT'S NO USE!

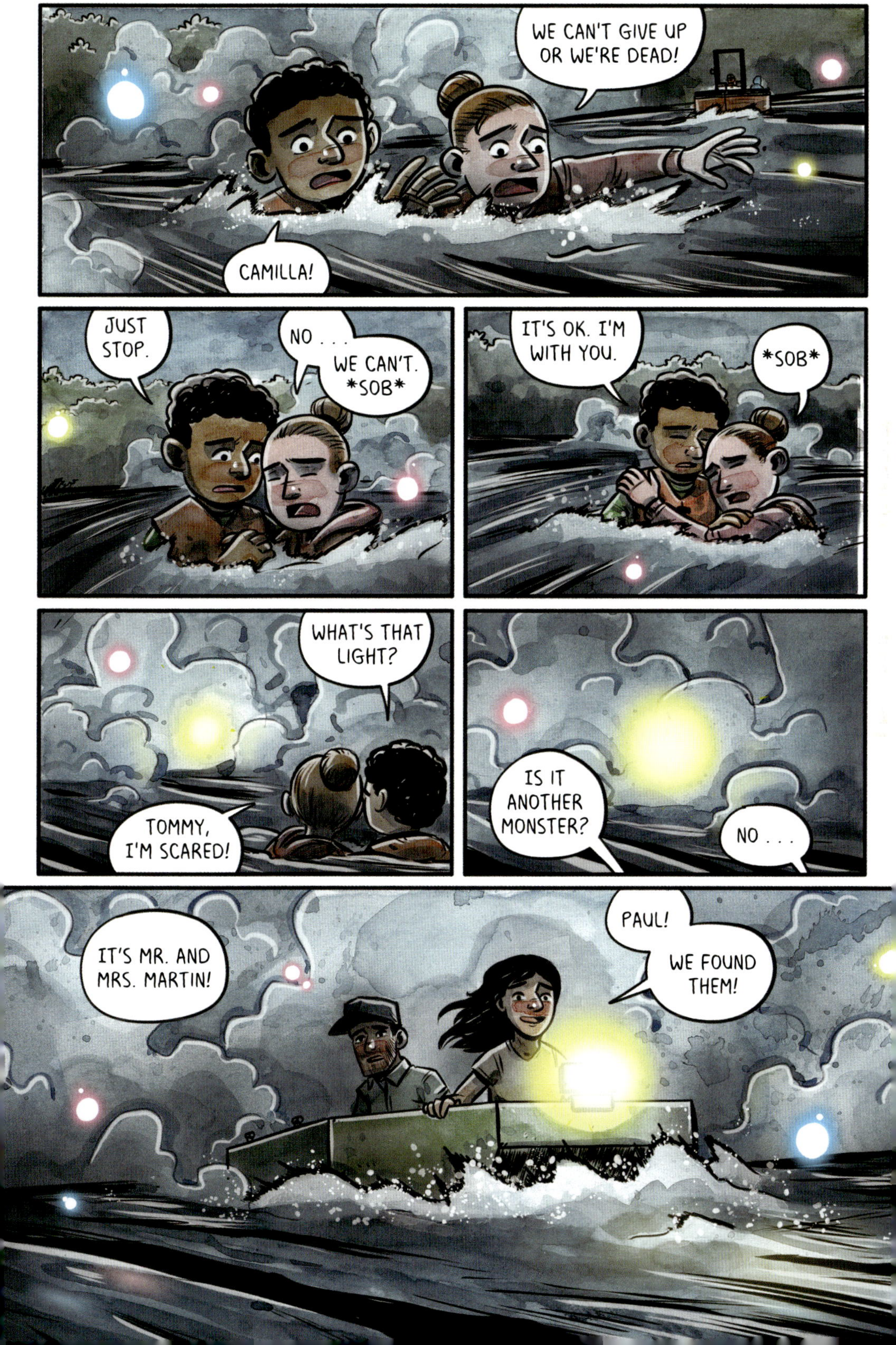
WE CAN'T GIVE UP OR WE'RE DEAD!
CAMILLA!
JUST STOP.
NO . . .
WE CAN'T. *SOB*
IT'S OK. I'M WITH YOU.
SOB
WHAT'S THAT LIGHT?
TOMMY, I'M SCARED!
IS IT ANOTHER MONSTER?
NO . . .
IT'S MR. AND MRS. MARTIN!
PAUL!
WE FOUND THEM!

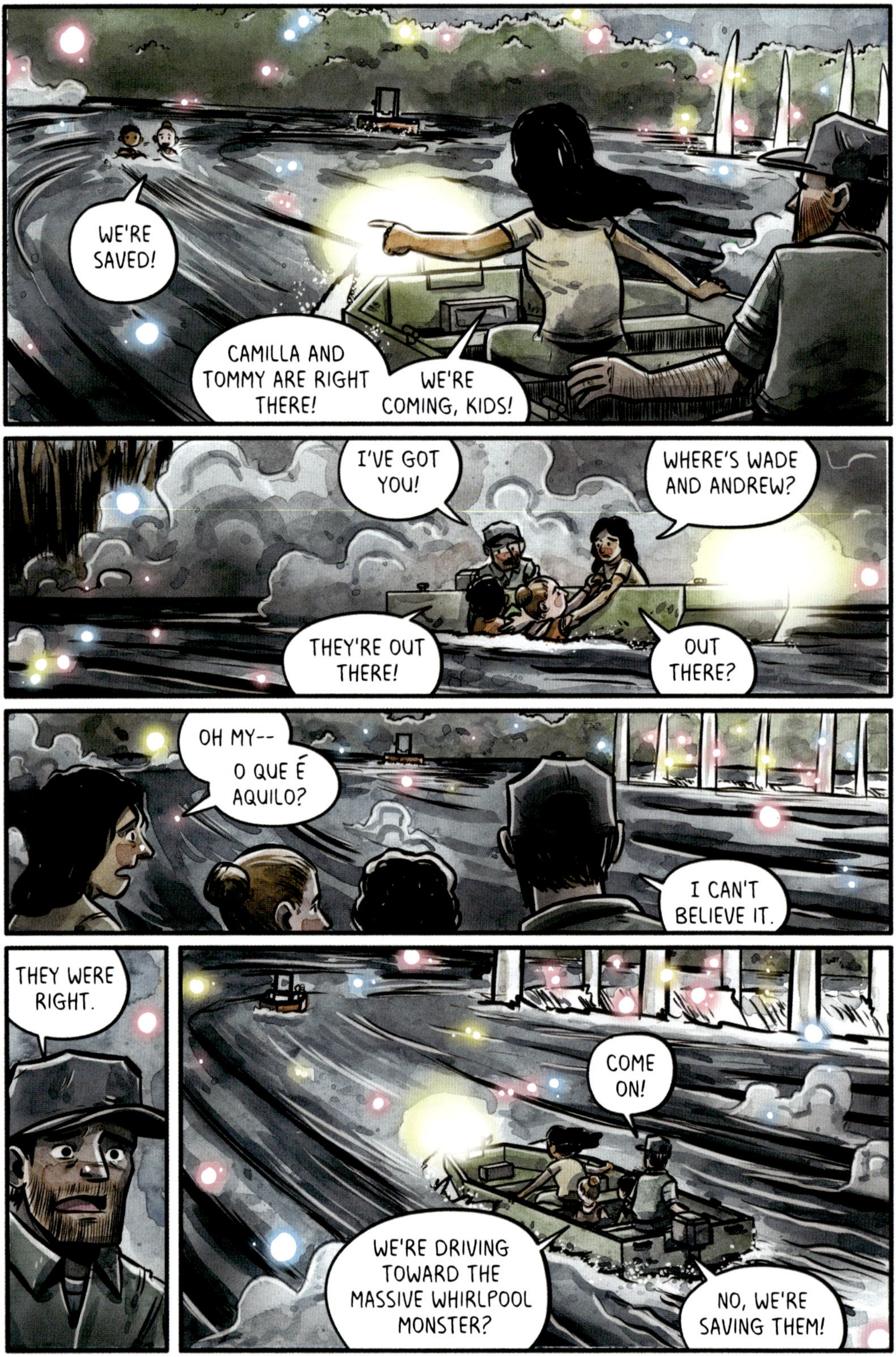
WE'RE SAVED!
CAMILLA AND TOMMY ARE RIGHT THERE!
WE'RE COMING, KIDS!
I'VE GOT YOU!
WHERE'S WADE AND ANDREW?
THEY'RE OUT THERE!
OUT THERE?
OH MY--
O QUE É AQUILO?
I CAN'T BELIEVE IT.
THEY WERE RIGHT.
COME ON!
WE'RE DRIVING TOWARD THE MASSIVE WHIRLPOOL MONSTER?
NO, WE'RE SAVING THEM!

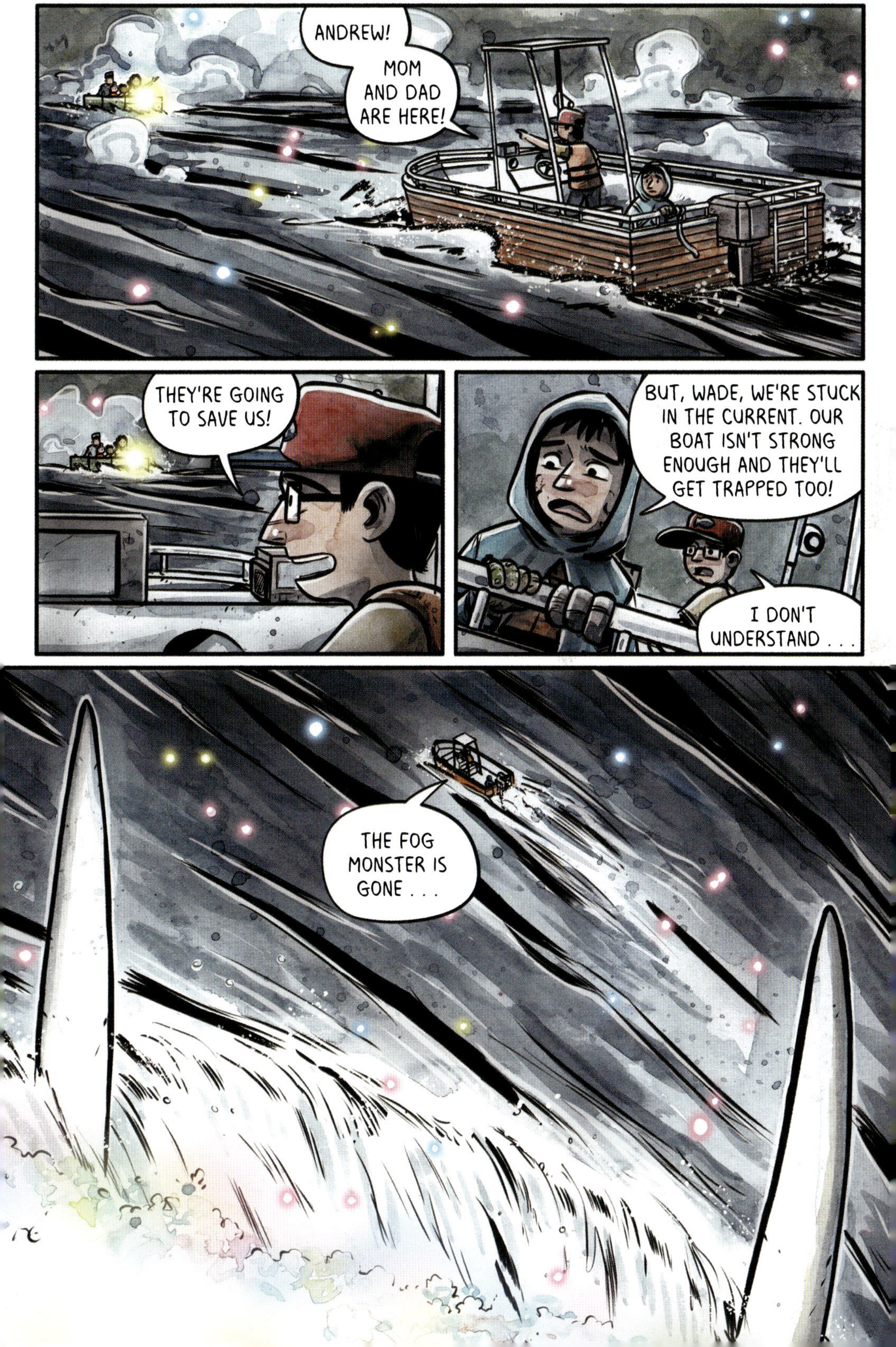
ANDREW!
MOM AND DAD ARE HERE!
THEY'RE GOING TO SAVE US!
BUT, WADE, WE'RE STUCK IN THE CURRENT. OUR BOAT ISN'T STRONG ENOUGH AND THEY'LL GET TRAPPED TOO!
I DON'T UNDERSTAND . . .
THE FOG MONSTER IS GONE . . .

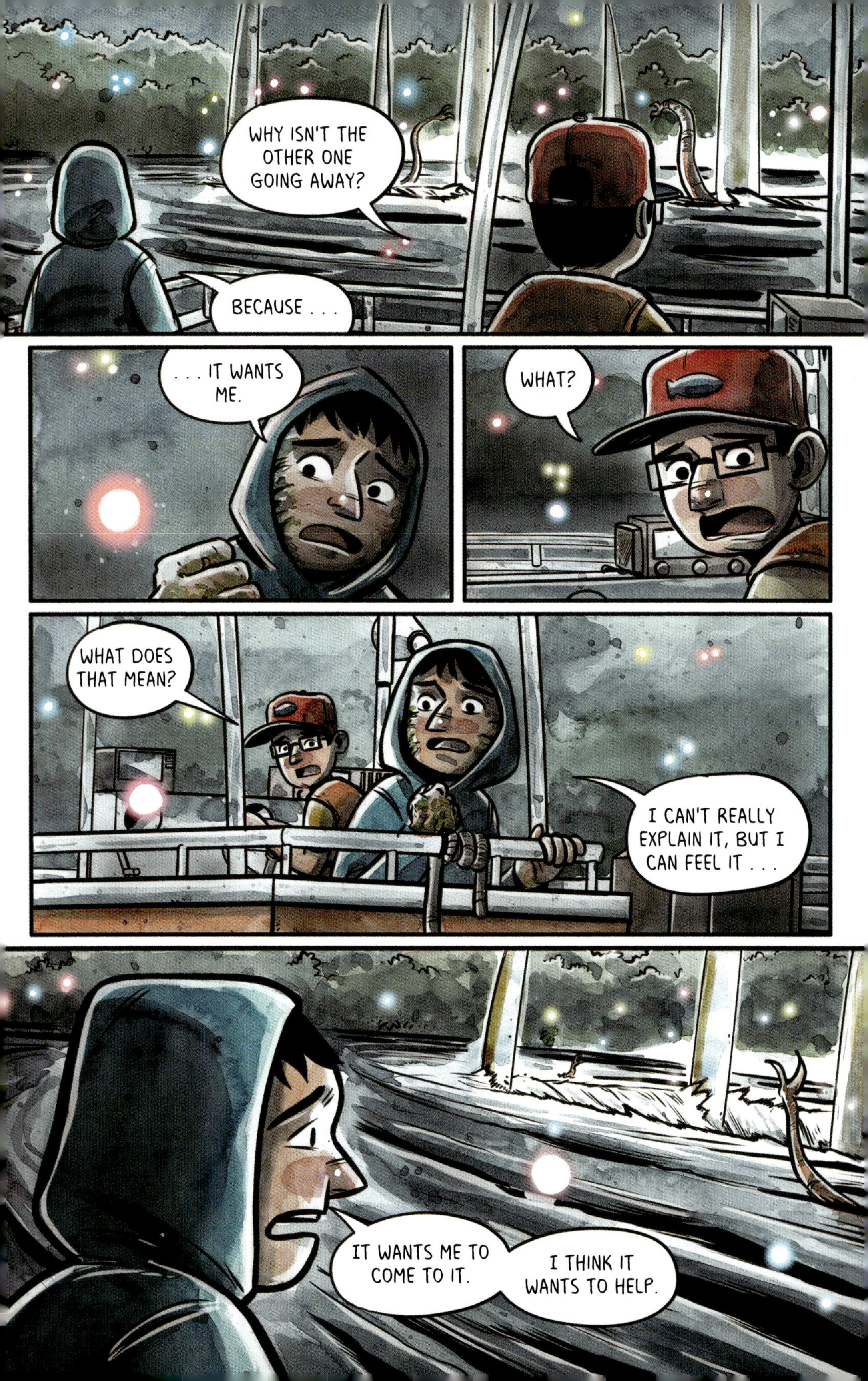
WHY ISN'T THE OTHER ONE GOING AWAY?
BECAUSE . . .
. . . IT WANTS ME.
WHAT?
WHAT DOES THAT MEAN?
I CAN'T REALLY EXPLAIN IT, BUT I CAN FEEL IT . . .
IT WANTS ME TO COME TO IT.
I THINK IT WANTS TO HELP.

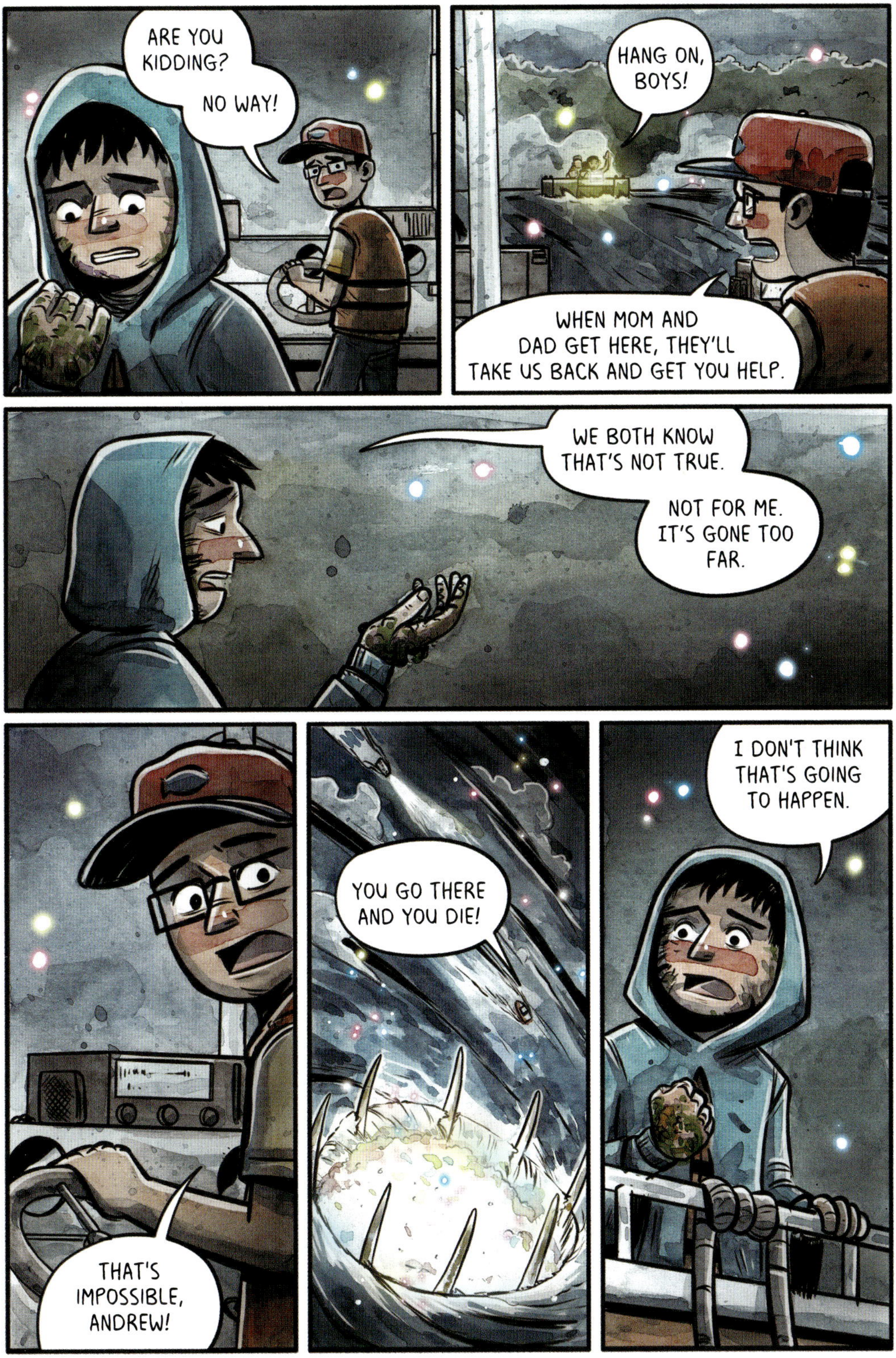
ARE YOU KIDDING?
NO WAY!
HANG ON, BOYS!
WHEN MOM AND DAD GET HERE, THEY'LL TAKE US BACK AND GET YOU HELP.
WE BOTH KNOW THAT'S NOT TRUE.
NOT FOR ME. IT'S GONE TOO FAR.
THAT'S IMPOSSIBLE, ANDREW!
YOU GO THERE AND YOU DIE!
I DON'T THINK THAT'S GOING TO HAPPEN.

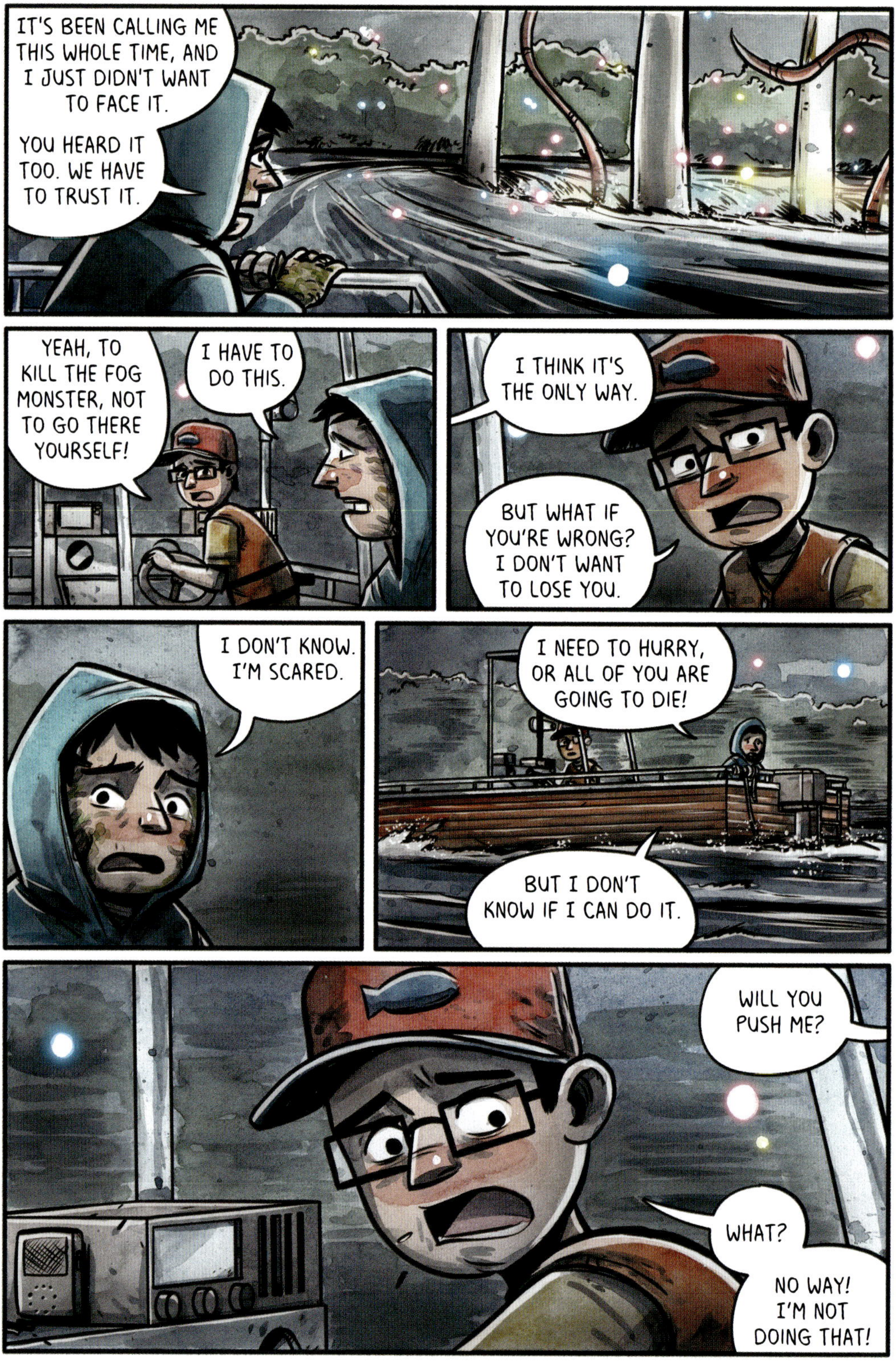

IT'S BEEN CALLING ME THIS WHOLE TIME, AND I JUST DIDN'T WANT TO FACE IT.
YOU HEARD IT TOO. WE HAVE TO TRUST IT.
YEAH, TO KILL THE FOG MONSTER, NOT TO GO THERE YOURSELF!
I HAVE TO DO THIS.
I THINK IT'S THE ONLY WAY.
BUT WHAT IF YOU'RE WRONG? I DON'T WANT TO LOSE YOU.
I DON'T KNOW. I'M SCARED.
I NEED TO HURRY, OR ALL OF YOU ARE GOING TO DIE!
BUT I DON'T KNOW IF I CAN DO IT.
WILL YOU PUSH ME?
WHAT?
NO WAY! I'M NOT DOING THAT!

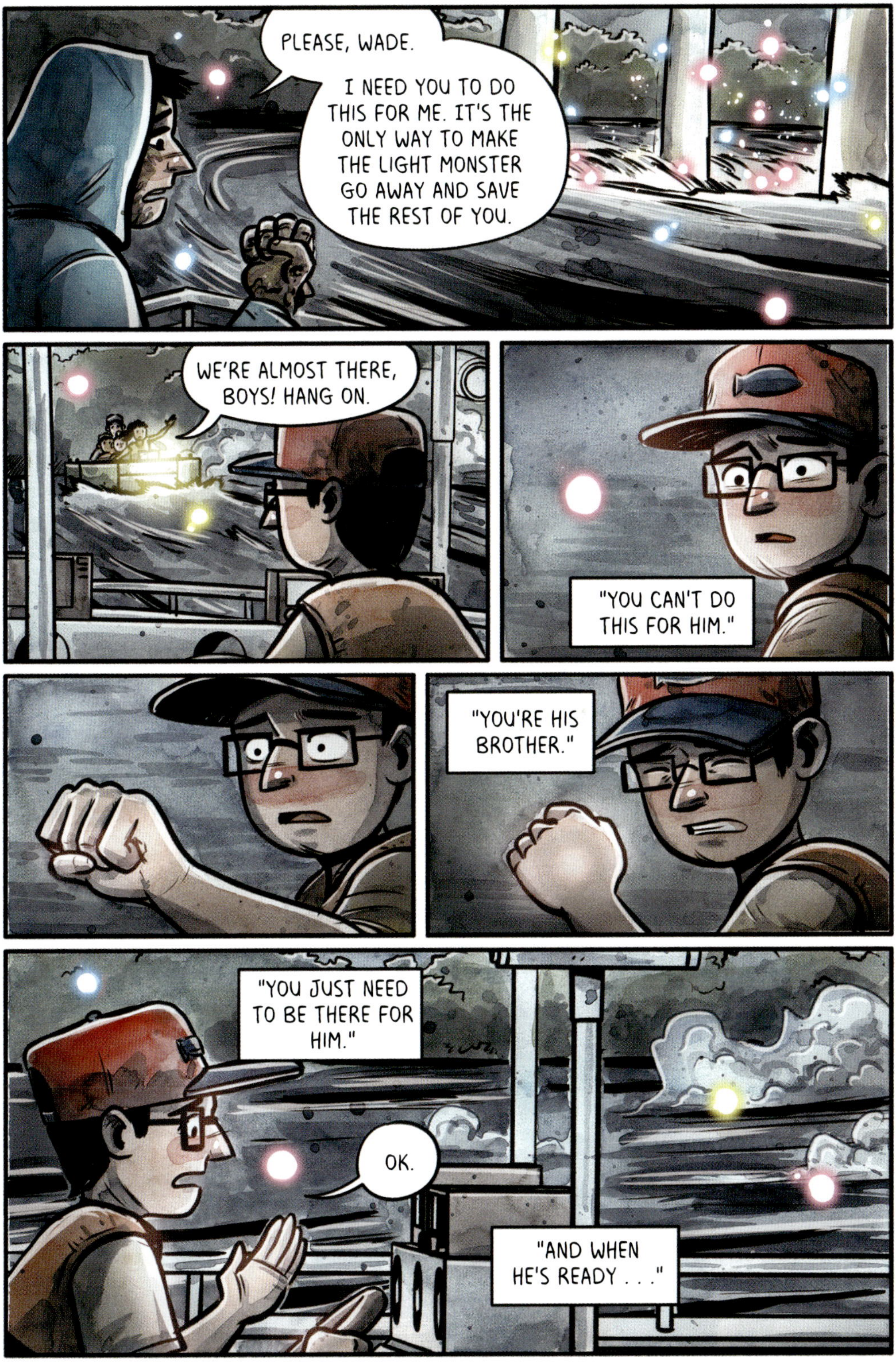
PLEASE, WADE.
I NEED YOU TO DO THIS FOR ME. IT'S THE ONLY WAY TO MAKE THE LIGHT MONSTER GO AWAY AND SAVE THE REST OF YOU.
WE'RE ALMOST THERE, BOYS! HANG ON.
"YOU CAN'T DO THIS FOR HIM."
"YOU'RE HIS BROTHER."
"YOU JUST NEED TO BE THERE FOR HIM."
OK.
"AND WHEN HE'S READY . . ."

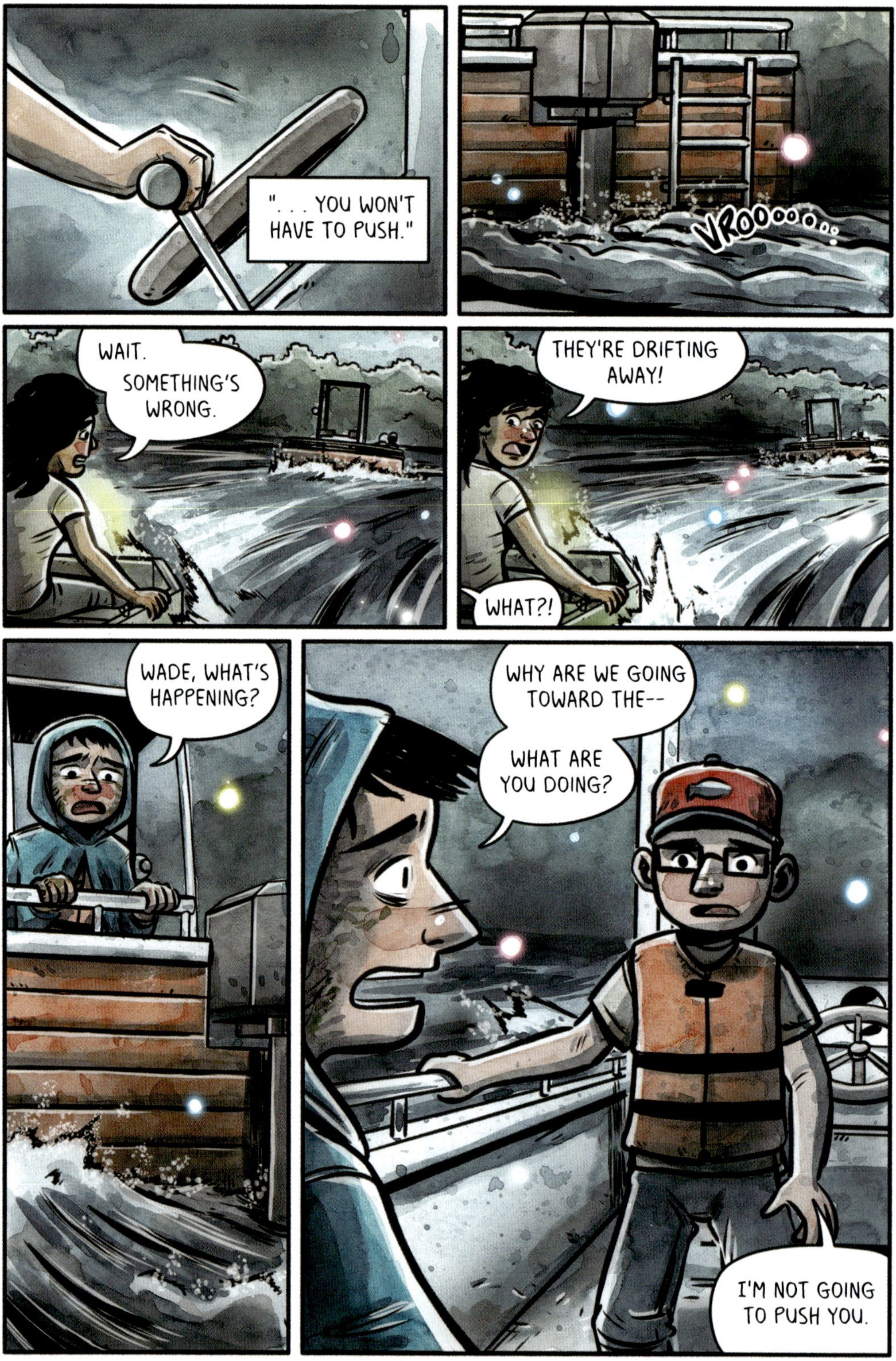
". . . YOU WON'T HAVE TO PUSH."
VROOooooo...
WAIT.
SOMETHING'S WRONG.
THEY'RE DRIFTING AWAY!
WHAT?!
WADE, WHAT'S HAPPENING?
WHY ARE WE GOING TOWARD THE--
WHAT ARE YOU DOING?
I'M NOT GOING TO PUSH YOU.

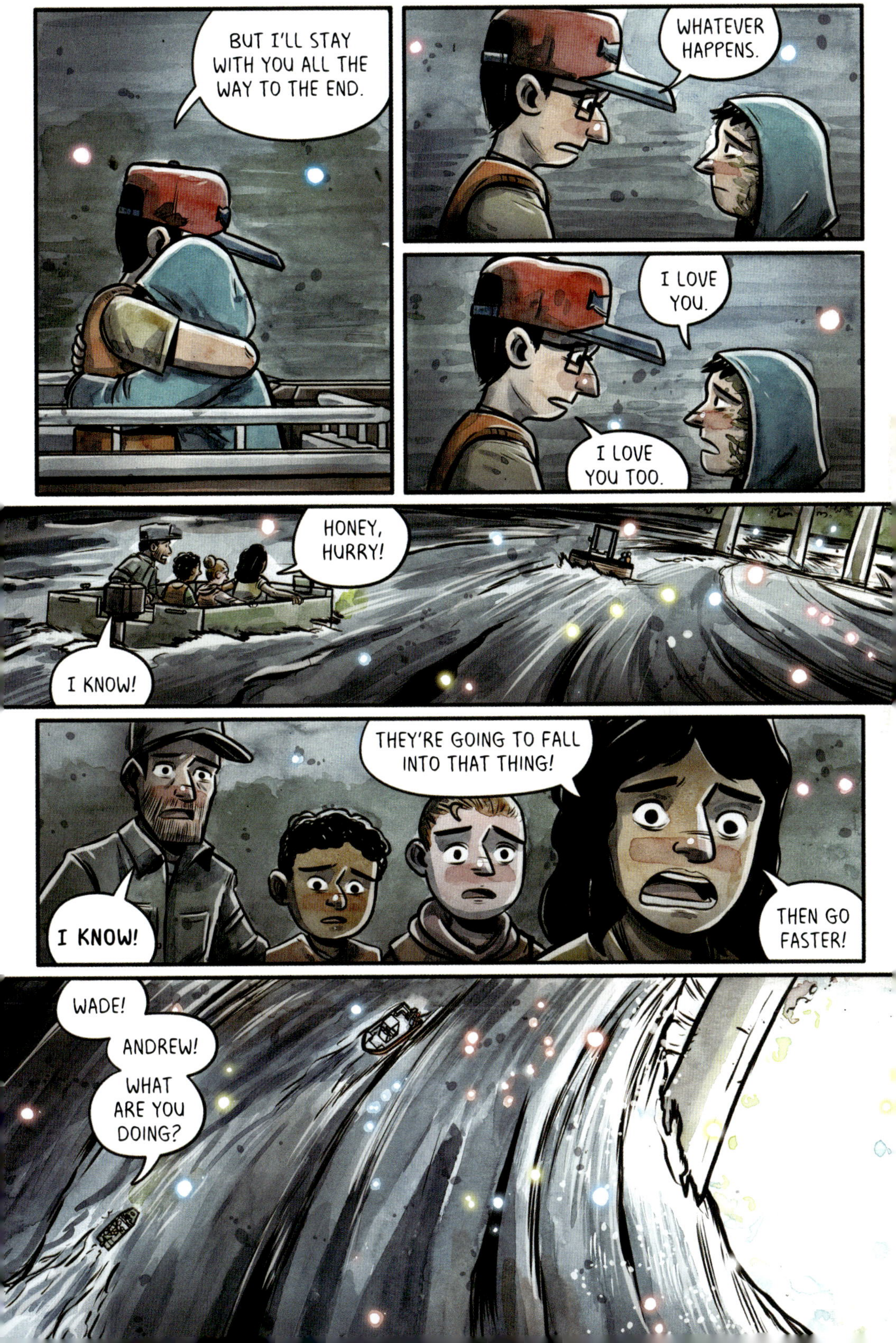
BUT I'LL STAY WITH YOU ALL THE WAY TO THE END.
WHATEVER HAPPENS.
I LOVE YOU.
I LOVE YOU TOO.
HONEY, HURRY!
I KNOW!
THEY'RE GOING TO FALL INTO THAT THING!
I KNOW!
THEN GO FASTER!
WADE!
ANDREW!
WHAT ARE YOU DOING?

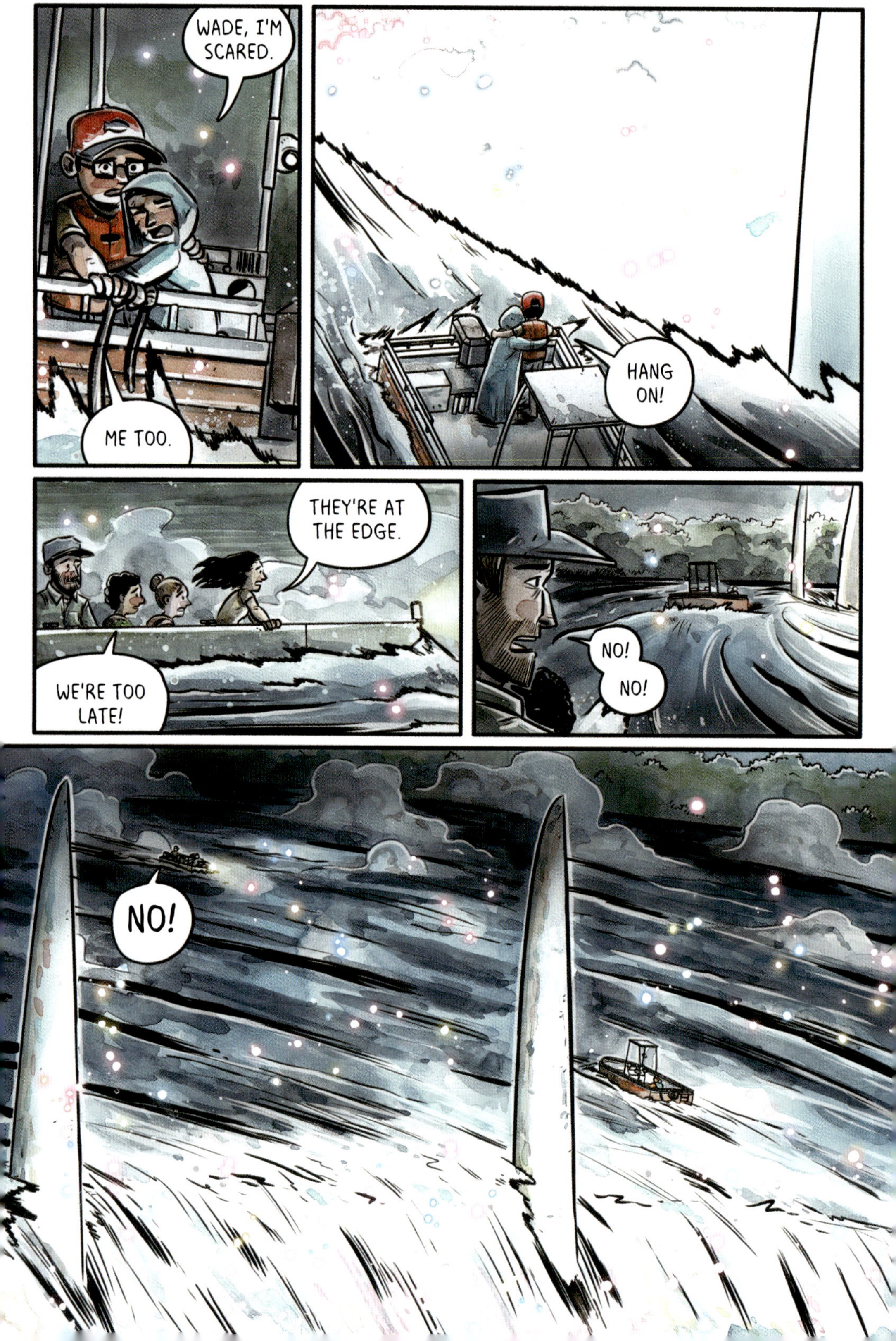
WADE, I'M SCARED.
ME TOO.
HANG ON!
THEY'RE AT THE EDGE.
WE'RE TOO LATE!
NO!
NO!
NO!

I'M SORRY!

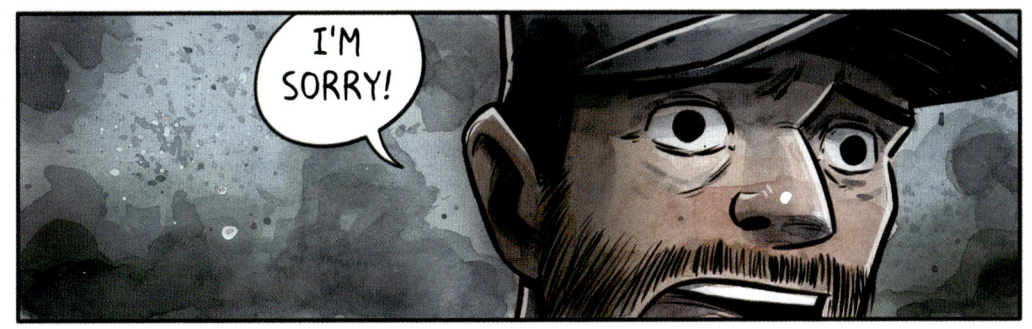

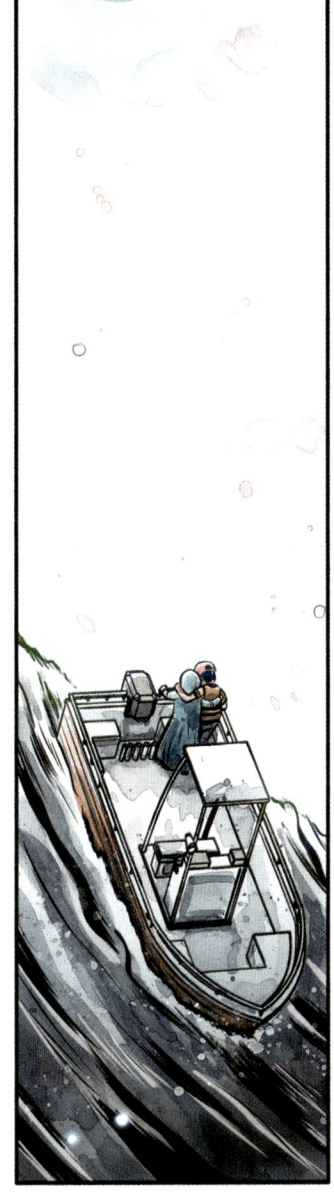

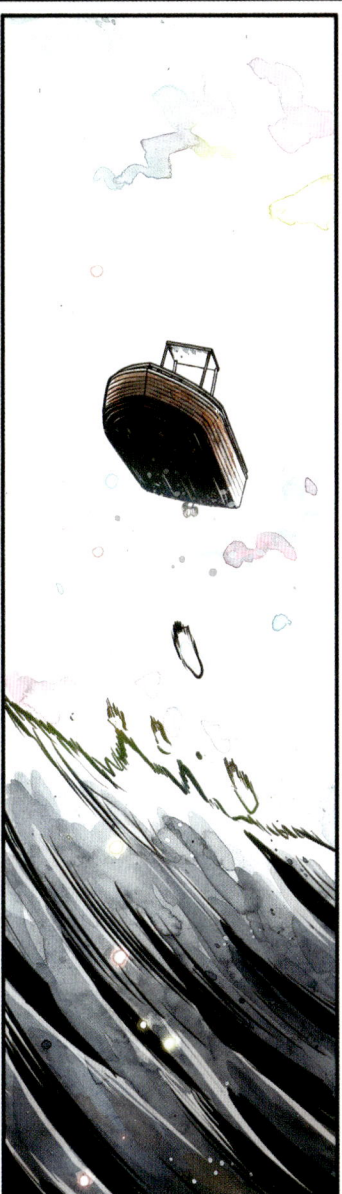

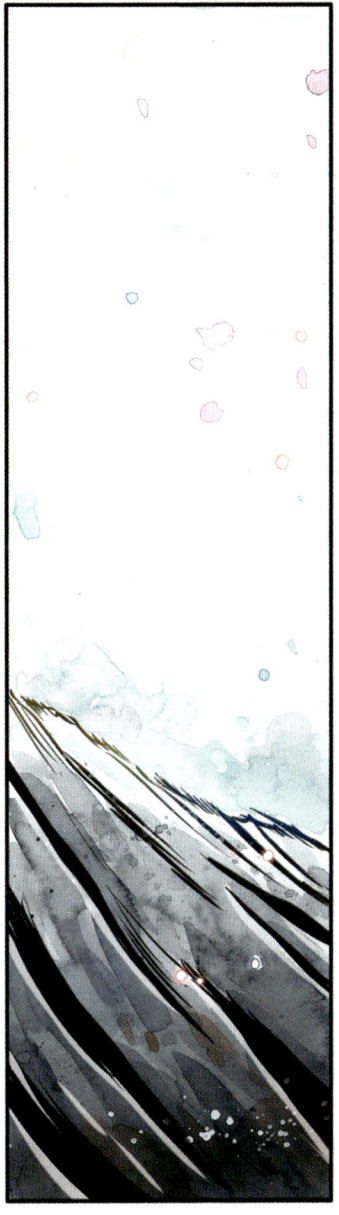

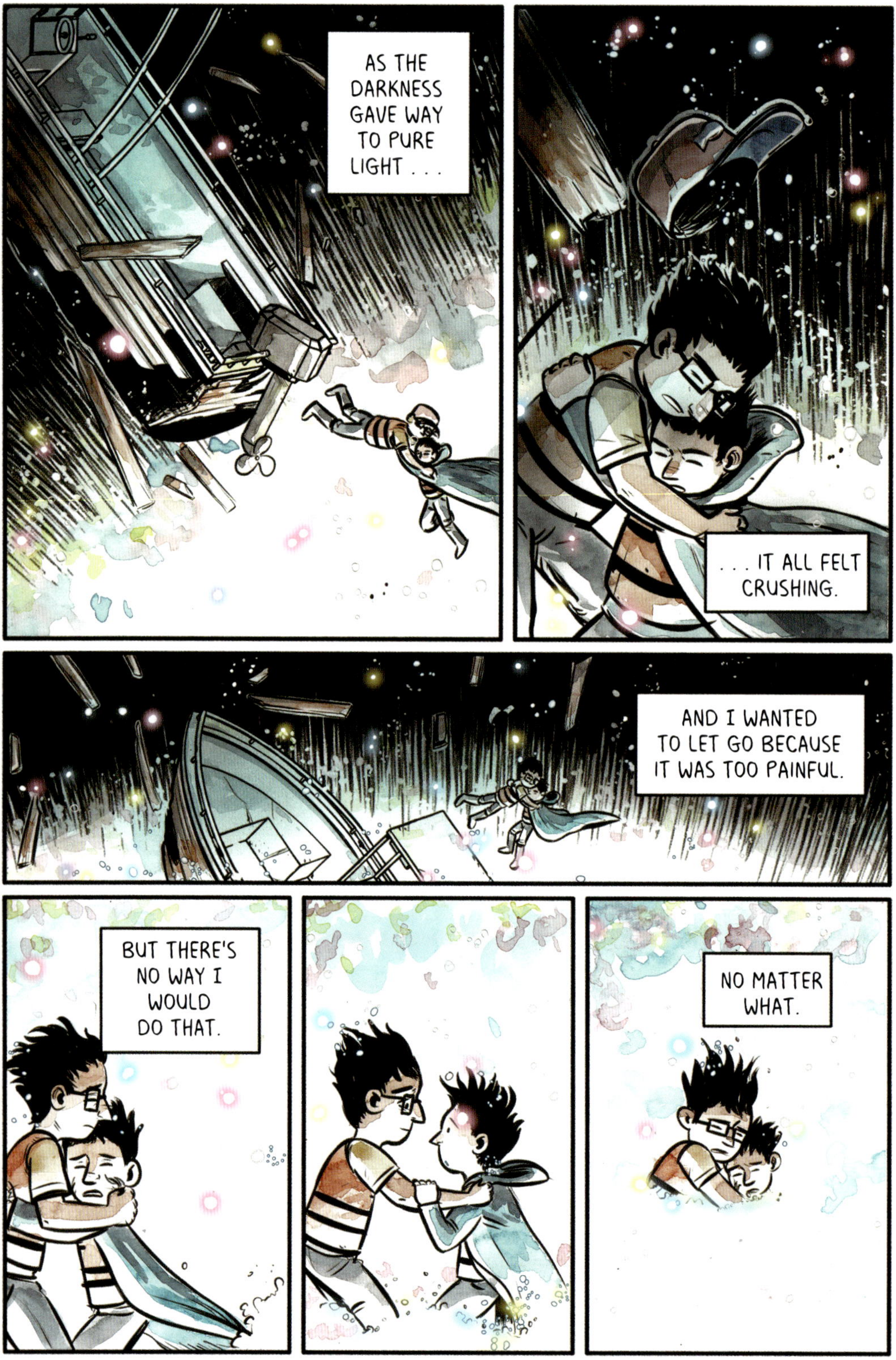
AS THE DARKNESS GAVE WAY TO PURE LIGHT . . .
. . . IT ALL FELT CRUSHING.
AND I WANTED TO LET GO BECAUSE IT WAS TOO PAINFUL.
BUT THERE'S NO WAY I WOULD DO THAT.
NO MATTER WHAT.

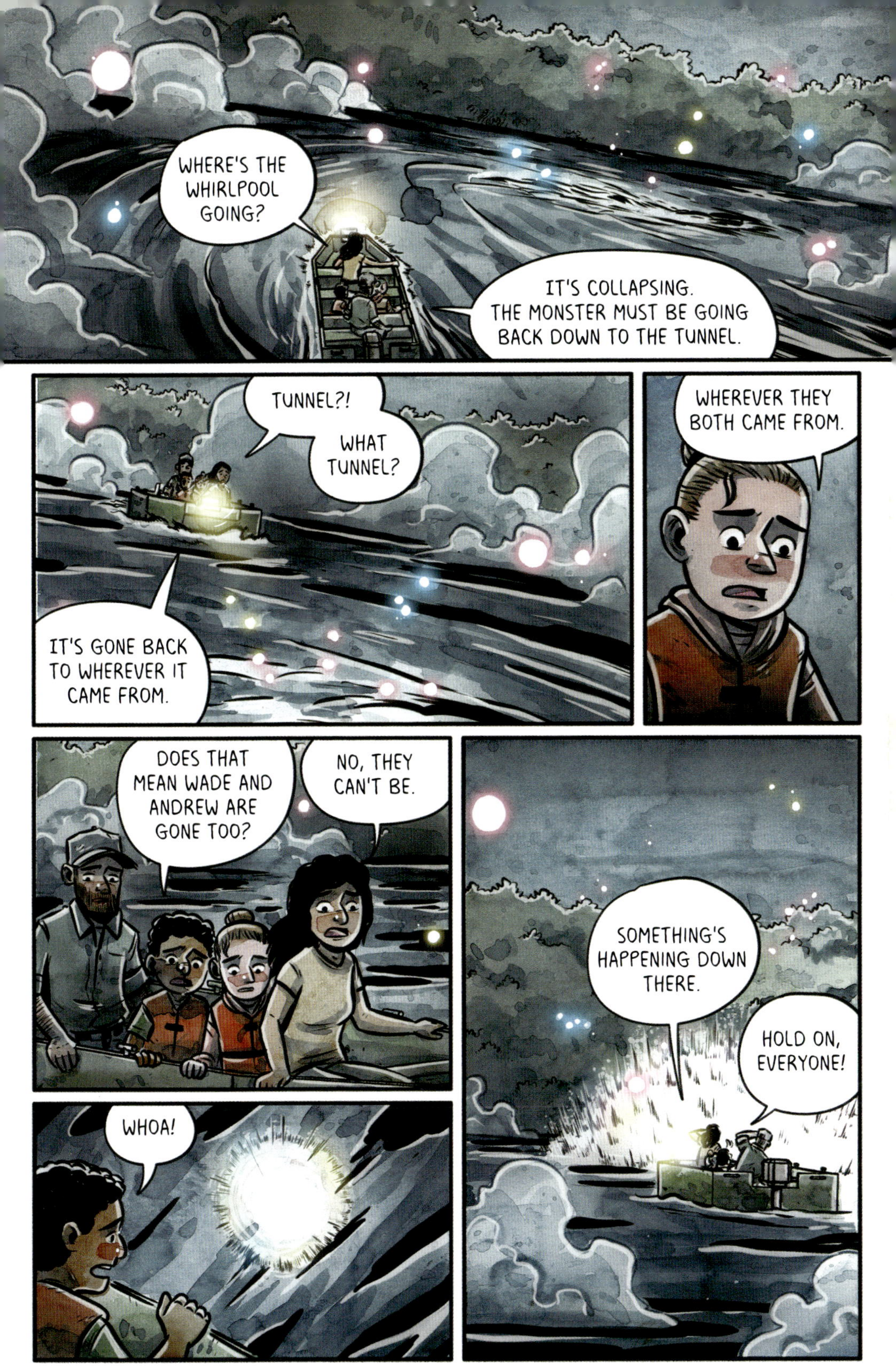
WHERE'S THE WHIRLPOOL GOING?
IT'S COLLAPSING. THE MONSTER MUST BE GOING BACK DOWN TO THE TUNNEL.
TUNNEL?!
WHAT TUNNEL?
IT'S GONE BACK TO WHEREVER IT CAME FROM.
WHEREVER THEY BOTH CAME FROM.
DOES THAT MEAN WADE AND ANDREW ARE GONE TOO?
NO, THEY CAN'T BE.
WHOA!
SOMETHING'S HAPPENING DOWN THERE.
HOLD ON, EVERYONE!

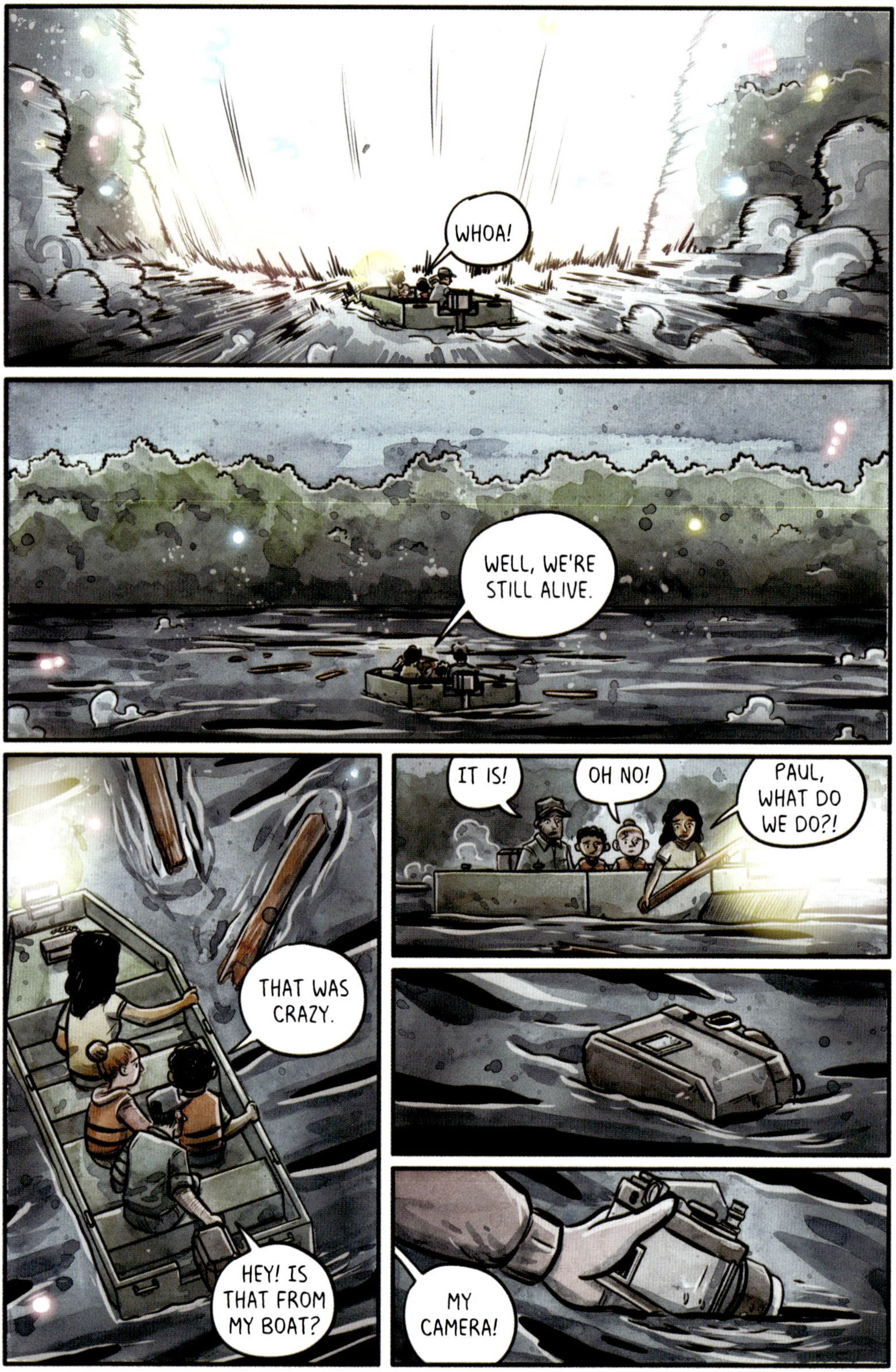
WHOA!
WELL, WE'RE STILL ALIVE.
THAT WAS CRAZY.
HEY! IS THAT FROM MY BOAT?
IT IS!
OH NO!
PAUL, WHAT DO WE DO?!
MY CAMERA!

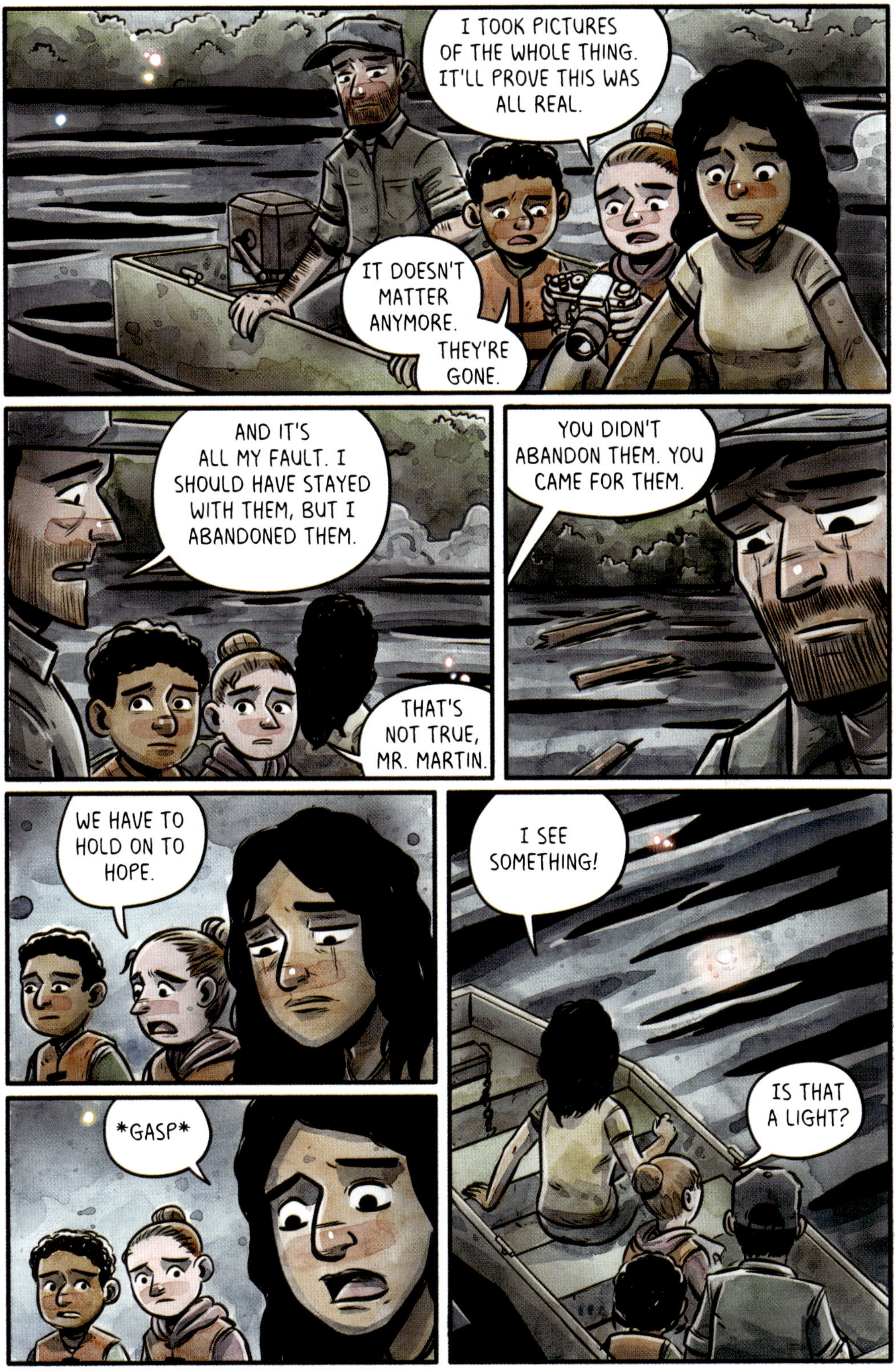
I TOOK PICTURES OF THE WHOLE THING. IT'LL PROVE THIS WAS ALL REAL.
IT DOESN'T MATTER ANYMORE.
THEY'RE GONE.
AND IT'S ALL MY FAULT. I SHOULD HAVE STAYED WITH THEM, BUT I ABANDONED THEM.
THAT'S NOT TRUE, MR. MARTIN.
YOU DIDN'T ABANDON THEM. YOU CAME FOR THEM.
WE HAVE TO HOLD ON TO HOPE.
GASP
I SEE SOMETHING!
IS THAT A LIGHT?

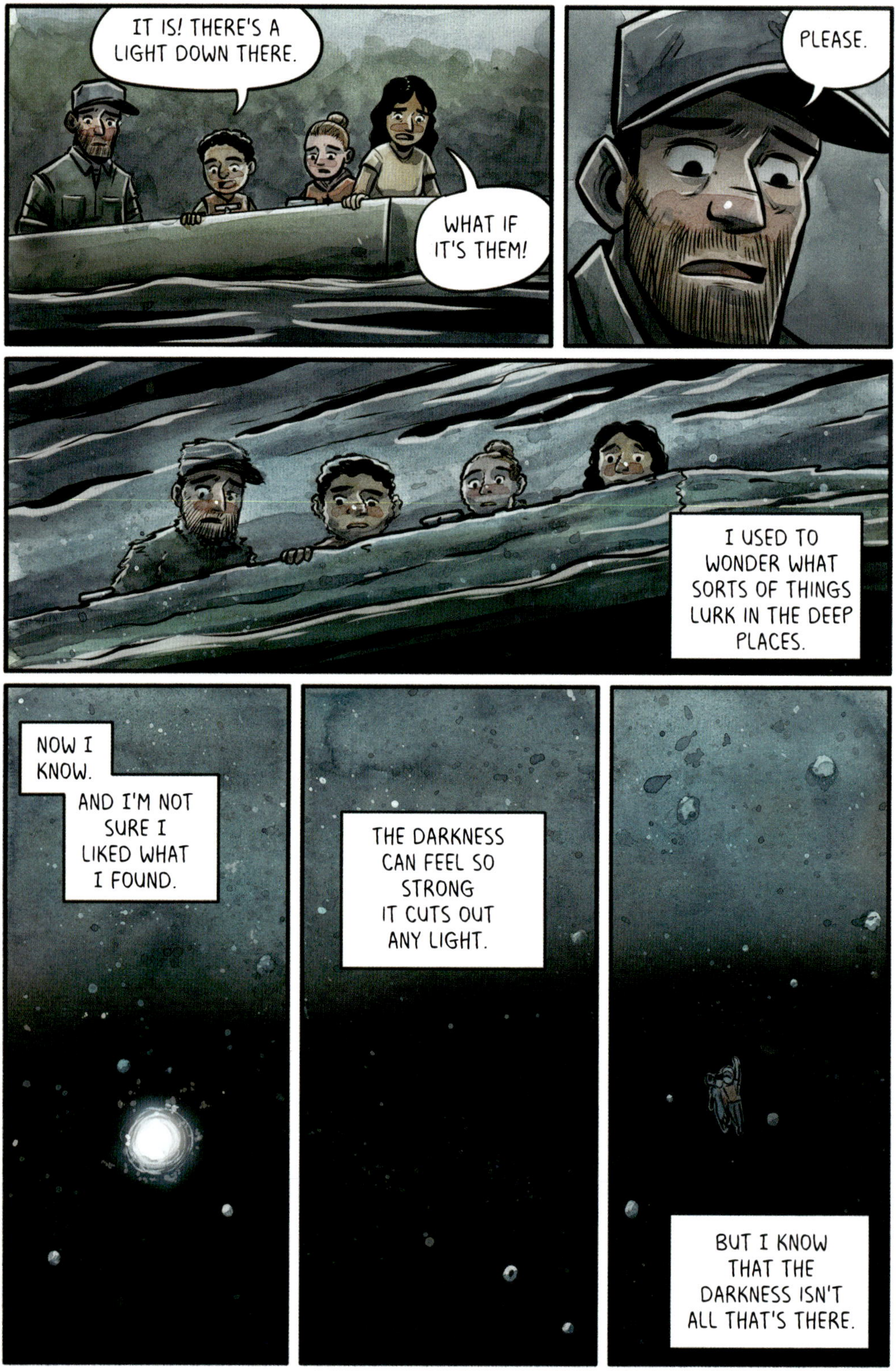
IT IS! THERE'S A LIGHT DOWN THERE.
WHAT IF IT'S THEM!
PLEASE.
I USED TO WONDER WHAT SORTS OF THINGS LURK IN THE DEEP PLACES.
NOW I KNOW.
AND I'M NOT SURE I LIKED WHAT I FOUND.
THE DARKNESS CAN FEEL SO STRONG IT CUTS OUT ANY LIGHT.
BUT I KNOW THAT THE DARKNESS ISN'T ALL THAT'S THERE.

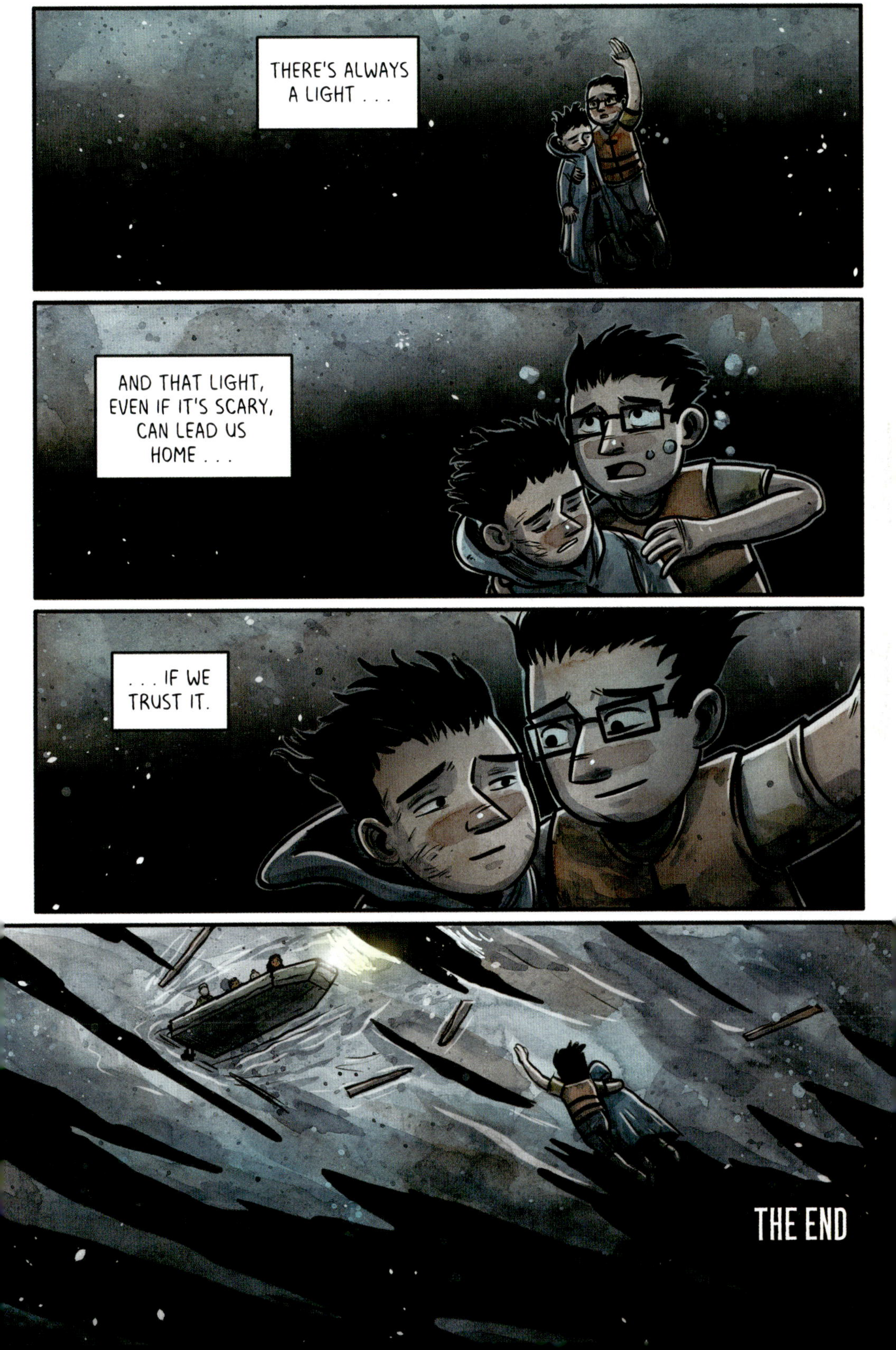
THERE'S ALWAYS A LIGHT . . .
AND THAT LIGHT, EVEN IF IT'S SCARY, CAN LEAD US HOME . . .
. . . IF WE TRUST IT.
THE END

BEHIND THE SCENES

While the core concepts of *Deepwater Creek*—a group of friends trying to find a monster fish and save Wade's brother, Andrew—have stayed much the same since the beginning, the execution of it has changed over time.

Initially, this was more of a nautical fantasy. The kids ventured into a world full of mermaids, ghosts, and other creatures while hunting for a mythical fish. Here's a look at some of the original concept art:

While this version was a lot of fun, the story never fully worked. That magical fish would eventually become the central threat of *Deepwater Creek*, and it would now be present throughout the story.

These were the very first drawings of what would become the monster. It started off as just strange doodles in my sketchbook that felt weird and creepy. But this visual language is what I have carried throughout.

As the story changed, so did the monster. It initially was less of a fish and more of a kaiju monstrosity!

Again, these ideas were fun. In the end, that was a very different book, and it never felt right. It became detached from the central idea that got me excited about a group of kids on a fishing adventure. The decision was made to reimagine the monster as a fish.

A lot of designs went into making it a fish. Ultimately, I went with something that felt like a cross between a Cthulhu-type creature and a Wells catfish—a giant fish that can grow up to fifteen feet long!

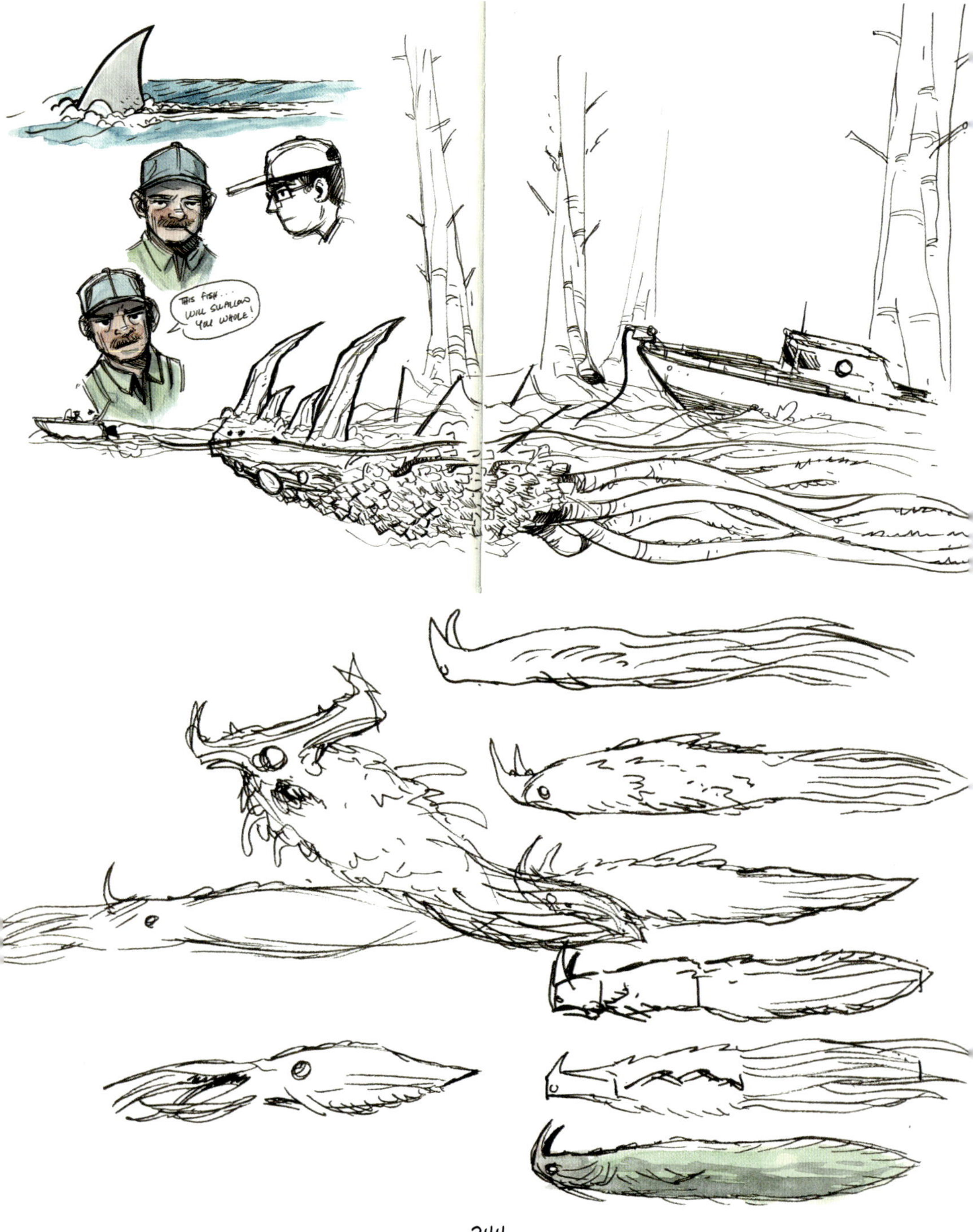
THIS FISH...
WILL SWALLOW
YOU WHOLE!

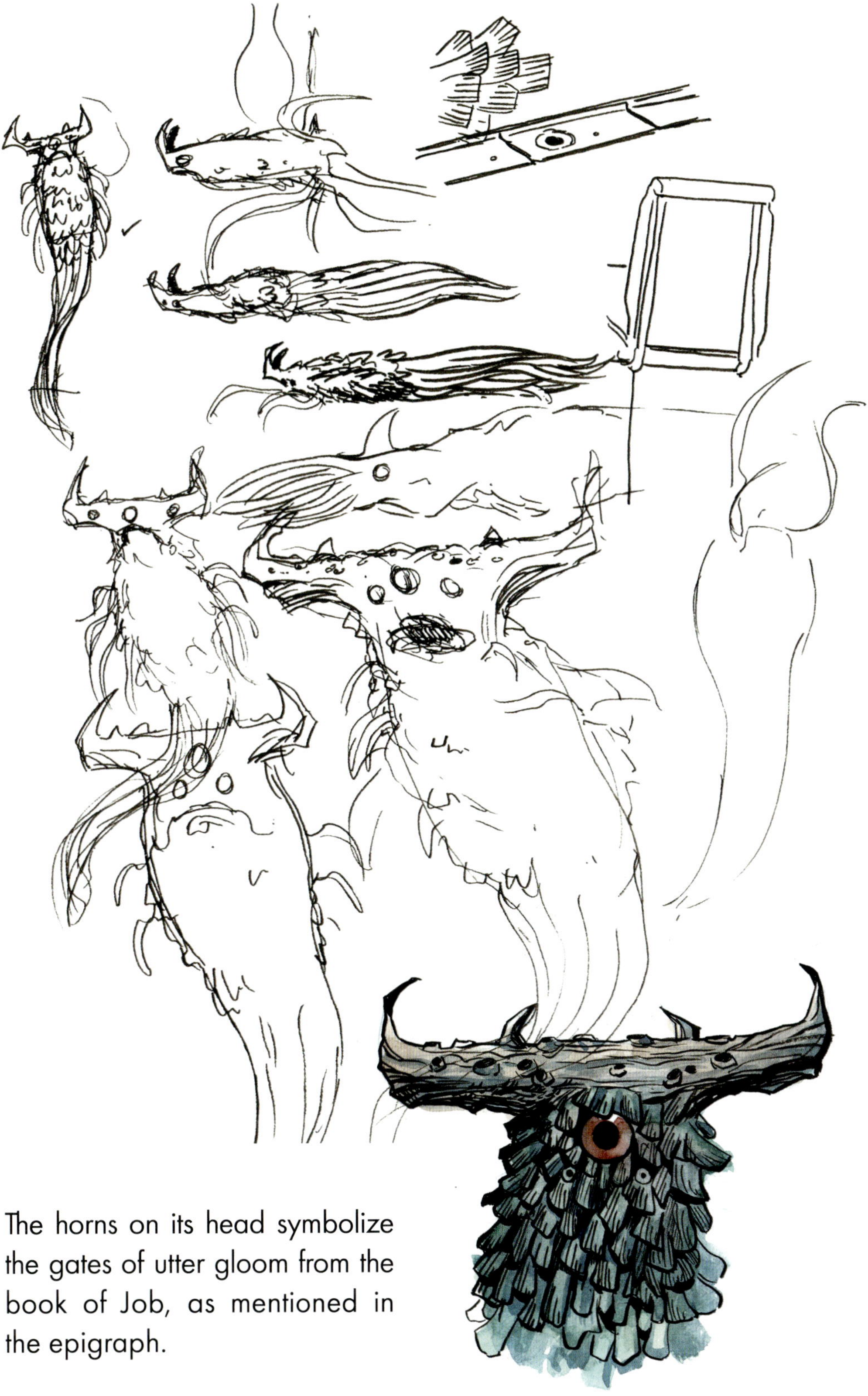

The horns on its head symbolize the gates of utter gloom from the book of Job, as mentioned in the epigraph.

Although the monster went through many iterations, the group of friends has stayed the same from start. These four characters came to me in a flash, and I loved them instantly. Here's an early image of them and their boat, before its design was finalized.

Here's a map of the creek I created to get a sense of the space the kids would be exploring.

Key landmarks show the destroyed dam at the midpoint, the wreckage of the research crew, and finally, the opening at the top with the wall of gloom and the unfathomably deep tunnel our monsters came from. I often wonder what other horrors are in the creek that we never saw.

I mulled over the decision to paint this book with watercolor instead of digitally for a long time, but these early sketches and the sample page below really resonated with me. I knew that this was the way to go, even if it meant a lot of extra steps in the process. This came from an earlier version of the story in which the kids landed one of the mutated fish on their first trip with Mr. Martin.

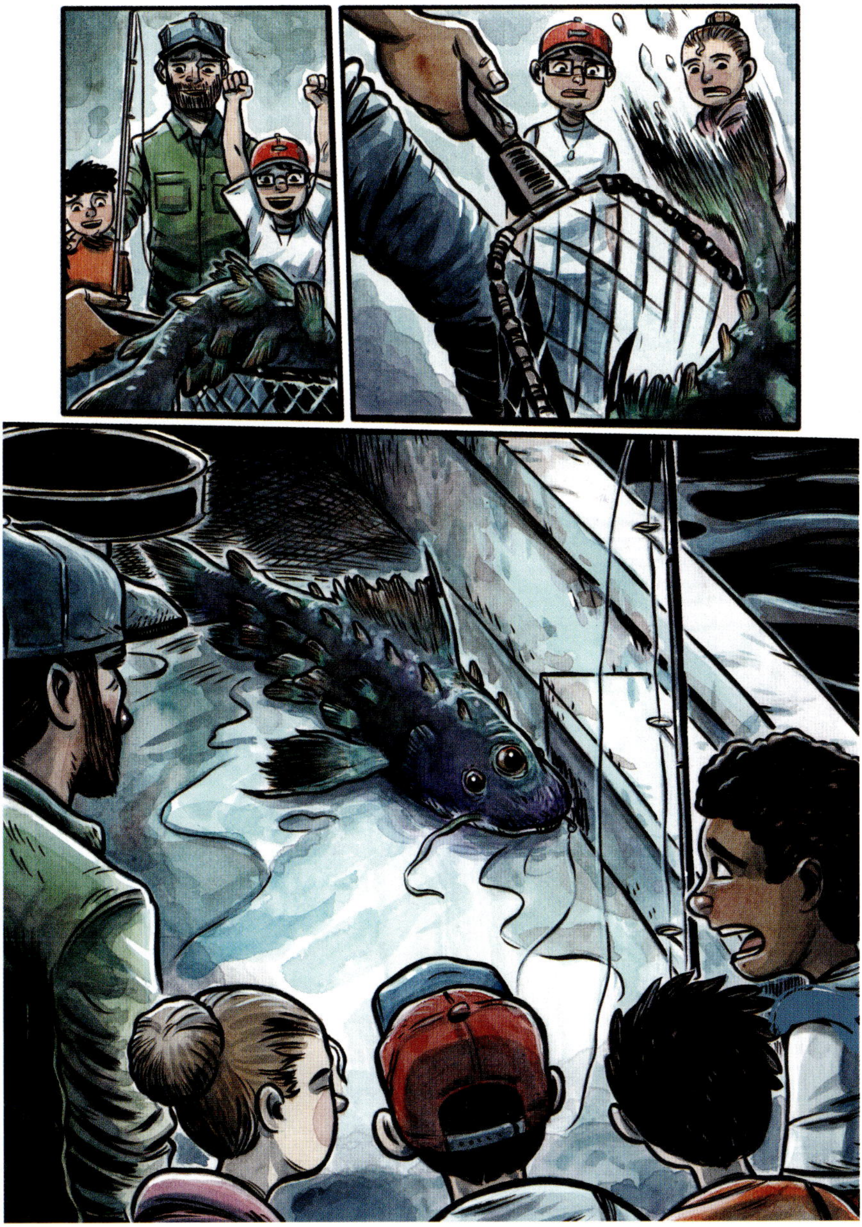

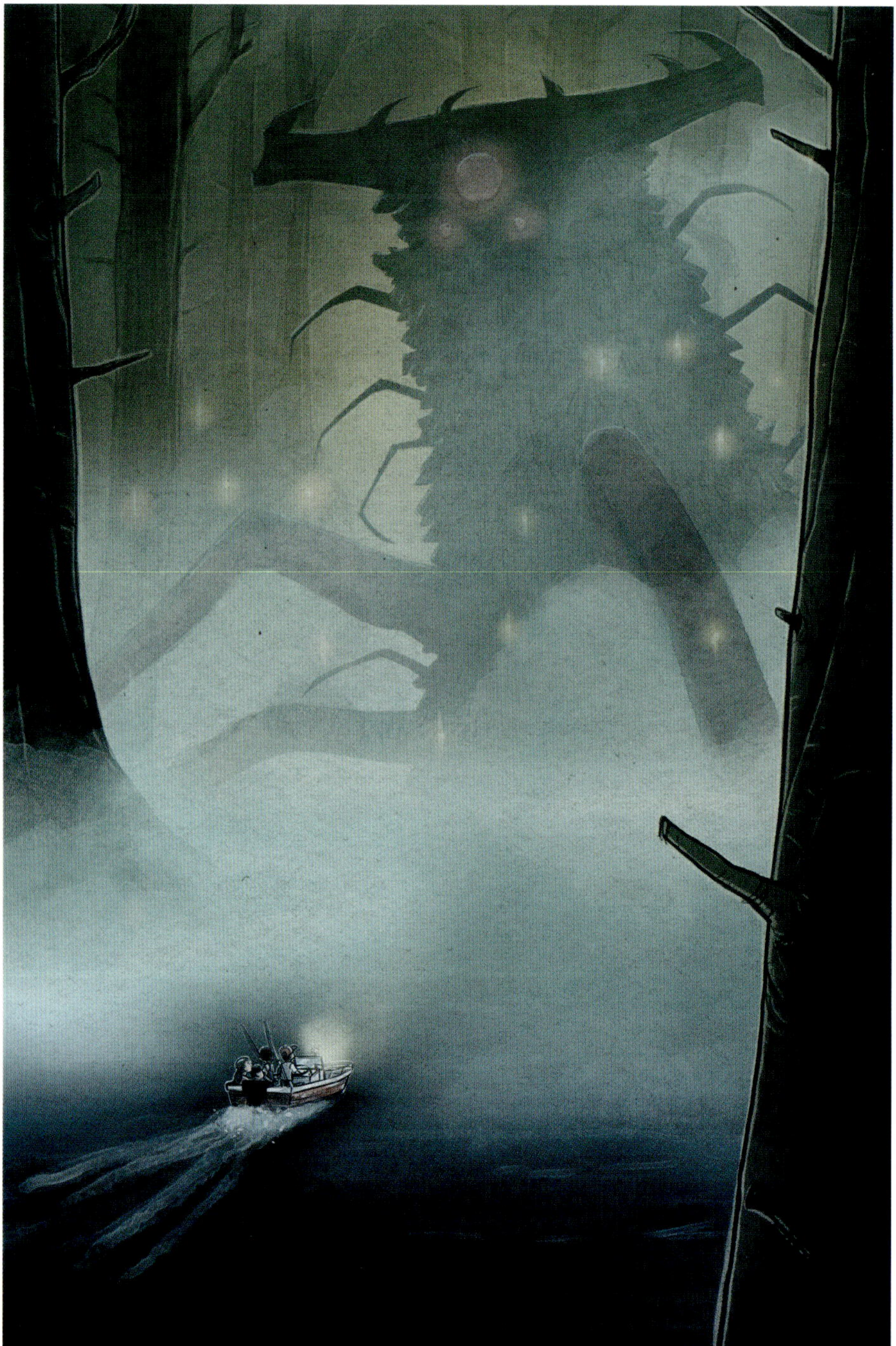

This was the original poster/teaser image I created for the book. While the story is very different from that idea, this image got me so excited about this story.

AUTHOR'S NOTE

This book was born out of one of the most challenging periods of my life. I'm not ashamed to say that the deaths and illnesses of several loved ones really took their toll on me. Life can come at you fast. It can be so difficult to find your way through the darkness. The lessons and themes in this book were hard learned in my life. I hope this book can give hope to those going through their own difficulties. I also hope it can encourage others who are supporting their loved ones. Remember, there's always a light, and there's always a bigger fish.

CREDITS

Written, illustrated, and watercolored by Michael Regina
Painting assistance by Story Regina
Additional production assistance by Viviane Regina, Journey Regina, and Shepherd Regina

ACKNOWLEDGMENTS

Writing acknowledgments can be tricky because I want to thank everyone who has encouraged me. I will surely miss some folks, but here it goes.

As seen in the credits, this book was a family affair. Things would have taken much longer and been more lonely if they hadn't jumped in to help me. To my wife, Viviane, and kids, Story, Journey, and Shepherd, thank you all so much for everything. I love you all, and I'm so thankful for you.

To my mom, who bought me the first comics that turned me on to this path. You've always encouraged me to chase my dreams. Thank you for everything.

To my dad, who gave me my love of fishing. Our times on the water are some of my favorite memories and inspired much of this book. I hope we get back out there to catch the big ones.

To the rest of my family, I love you all. Thank you for always standing by me.

To my fantastic agent, Elena Giovinazzo, who was always cheering me on with this crazy idea and believes in the stories I hope to tell. I'm so glad to have you in my corner. I can't wait to see what we do next.

To my editor, Chris Hernandez, for helping me form this book into what it is today. It was quite different initially, but your critiques helped me take this weird idea and turn it into something I am incredibly proud of. Thank you for trusting me with this story, believing in me, and being patient as I worked to get this right.

Thank you to the rest of the editorial staff and design team at Penguin Random House, Kyra Kruger, and Danielle Ceccolini. Your feedback and expertise have helped bring this book to a beautiful place.

To Josh Ulrich and Stephen McCranie, two of my best friends and brothers in comics from the beginning. You guys are always there to shoot it to me straight and push me to be better. I'm so thankful for both of you and our friendship all these years.

To Kazu Kibuishi, Wes Molebash, Brian Russell, Jason Brubaker, Mike Maihack, Jan Eldredge, Jonathan Stutzman, Trevor Henderson, Joshua Hauke, and every other creative friend I've made along the way. You all are awesome. Thank you for being my friends and inspiring me with your work. I'm rooting for all of you.

To my friends, church, TTRPG groups, booksellers, teachers, parents, librarians—literally anyone who has been there for me and supported my work—thank you. You all make my life fuller.

And lastly, to Christ, who is my light and strength even in the darkest of times. You've never let me down. I trust you, even when I don't understand.

THE NEW BABYSITTER IS A REAL NIGHTMARE...

"A suspenseful thrill ride for all ages!"
—**KAZU KIBUISHI, #1 *New York Times* bestselling creator of the Amulet series**

"Sharp dialog and beautiful, suspenseful storytelling."
—**MIKE MAIHACK, creator of the Cleopatra in Space series**

"A spine-chilling story with so much heart."
—**CHRIS GRINE, co-creator of the Animorphs graphic novel series**

"An excellent flashlight-under-the-blanket read."
—***KIRKUS REVIEWS***